Ill Met By Moonlight

BAEN BOOKS by Mercedes Lackey

Bardic Voices
The Lark and the Wren
The Robin and the Kestrel
The Eagle and the Nightingales
The Free Bards
Four & Twenty Blackbirds
Bardic Choices: A Cast of Corbies (with Josepha Sherman)

The Fire Rose

The Shadow of the Lion (with Eric Flint & Dave Freer)
This Rough Magic (with Eric Flint & Dave Freer)

The Wizard of Karres (with Eric Flint & Dave Freer)

Beyond World's End (with Rosemary Edghill)
Spirits White as Lightning (with Rosemary Edghill)
Mad Maudlin (with Rosemary Edghill)
Bedlam's Bard (with Ellen Guon)
Born to Run (with Larry Dixon)
Wheels of Fire (with Mark Shepherd)
Chrome Circle (with Larry Dixon)
The Chrome Borne (with Larry Dixon)
The Otherworld (with Holly Lisle & Mark Shepherd)
This Scepter'd Isle (with Roberta Gellis)
Ill Met by Moonlight (with Roberta Gellis)

Castle of Deception (with Josepha Sherman)
Fortress of Frost and Fire (with Ru Emerson)
Prison of Souls (with Mark Shepherd)
Lammas Night
Werehunter
Fiddler Fair

Brain Ships (with Anne McCaffrey & Margaret Ball)
The Sword of Knowledge (with C.J. Cherryh, Leslie Fish & Nancy Asire)

Ill Met By Moonlight

Mercedes Lackey
Roberta Gellis

ILL MET BY MOONLIGHT

A Baen Books Original

Baen Publishing Enterprises
P.O. Box 1403
Riverdale, NY 10471
www.baen.com

ISBN: 0-7434-9890-9

Cover art by Stephen Hickman

First printing, March 2005

Library of Congress Cataloging-in-Publication Data

Lackey, Mercedes.
 Ill met by moonlight / Mercedes Lackey, Roberta Gellis.
      p. cm.
 "A Baen Books original"--T.p. verso.
 ISBN 0-7434-9890-9
 1. Elizabeth I, Queen of England, 1533-1603--Fiction. 2. Great Britain--Kings and rulers--Succession--Fiction. 3. Great Britain--History--Tudors, 1485-1603--Fiction. 4. Mythology, Celtic--Fiction. 5. Princesses--Fiction. I. Gellis, Roberta. II. Title.

 PS3562.A246I45 2005
 813'.54--dc22

                                          2004026780

Distributed by Simon & Schuster
1230 Avenue of the Americas
New York, NY 10020

Production by Windhaven Press, Auburn, NH (www.windhaven.com)
Printed in the United States of America

10 9 8 7 6 5 4 3 2 1

Ill Met By Moonlight

Prologue

The great gold and black banners of King Oberon and Queen Titania flew over the Palace of Avalon proclaiming to those of the elfhame that the King and Queen were in residence. And none too soon; never mind that the elves and their Underhill kin lived long and slow lives, those lives still intersected with the mortals in the World Above, and in *that* world things were moving, and in directions that were—less than auspicious. Once again, there were choices to be made, and those choices would resonate Underhill for centuries to come.

Still, for this moment, Aleneil could only watch and wait, as her elders and superiors set the wheels of politics and progress in ponderously slow motion. Eirianell, who had been FarSeer in Avalon since Atlantis disappeared beneath the sea, summoned to her a young mortal servant and bid her go to the palace and ask Lord Ffrancon if an audience for the FarSeers could be arranged with the King and Queen. Then, once more, the four FarSeers raised the great lens and looked within.

They looked upon a mortal future far removed from the England of Great Harry's prime. The land of England in the World Above was dark, not black with horror, but gray with dullness and misery. No singing and dancing accompanied by hearty cheers bespoke the merriment of a masque. In ale-houses there was only silence or sullen exchanges where once raucous laughter

1

greeted bright-eyed poets with overlong hair who stood on tables declaiming verses of varying quality to the left eyebrow or shell-pink ear of their latest mistress. In a royal court that had once been almost blindingly brilliant with sparkling gems and garments of rich hues and cloth of silver and gold, there was only drabness. Suits of black, of gray, of flat, ugly brown bedecked the courtiers, and gowns of the same hues made plain the most lovely of women, who wore no adornment and kept their eyes always lowered. A young king ruled, fair enough of face but dour of expression—and of a mind and heart so closed that it permitted no new thoughts within.

What happened in the World Above was reflected Underhill; it might be slow in coming, but as life and liveliness drained from the World Above, it would drain from Underhill. Still, the reign of a single king, the lifetime of a mere mortal, was insignificant—so long as the damage to the World Above was limited to what was displayed here.

But the trouble was—it would not be limited to the vagaries of a humorless king in love with austerity.

The next vision was worse, but the FarSeers did not flinch, for they had seen this one over and over, ever since Great Harry had sired his first living daughter. Now black horror ruled the land except for the terrible red of fires which ate screaming victims—men and woman and occasionally (the FarSeers moaned in pain as the images crossed the lens, for they never grew accustomed to this) children. Books burned, too: English Bibles and any other text that raised any question about strict Catholic doctrine and abject obedience to the pope, no matter how corrupt and venal that leader might be. A dull-haired woman sat on the throne, her belly bloated, her once-sweet face twisted with misery and determination.

And then the prize—at the end of the storm and the tempest, came the rainbow. Color and life so vibrant it nearly burst out of the lens into reality. Theaters rose on the banks of the Thames with bright flapping banners to advise that a play was being given. Music and dancing gladdened the hearts of all. The presses clanged and rumbled as volumes of poetry and plays and books of theology and wondrous tales were imprinted for all to read. In the vision were some dark blots—poverty, cruelty, ignorance—but the FarSeers were aware that this was the human condition and simply accepted them. The mortals had been granted free will, and with that great gift came the privilege to abuse themselves and others; the point was to see to it that the bright and goodly things outnumbered the dark and dismal.

And reigning over all of this was the red-haired queen, whose golden eyes were alight with curiosity and intelligence, and who strove to mold her subjects into a unified nation without making all alike.

Even though the vision was unreal, an ephemeral thing, there came right through the lens a taste and smell of sweetness of new thoughts, new beauty, vibrant excitement. And in this Vision only, behind the queen, unmistakably, stood the Sidhe lord, Denoriel Siencyn Macreth Silverhair, and his twin sister, Aleneil Arwyddion Ysfael Silverhair.

Aleneil, the youngest of the FarSeers, sighed at seeing her image in the lens. "I thought, perhaps, the mortal world would proceed without our help. I do not know if Denoriel . . ." Her voice faltered, for her sibling had been sorely injured in protecting the red-haired babe who would be, if she lived, the queen of the joyous vision. She interlaced the long fingers of her supple hands together, to keep them from trembling. "It is possible that Denoriel will not be able. The channels through which his powers flow were burned and Mwynwen does not yet know whether they will heal or how they will heal."

"He *must* be able," Morwen, the next youngest of the FarSeers said, firmly, as if her own will could impose wellness upon Denoriel. "You saw what would come if you were not in the Vision. Dullness and misery we will survive. Other times like that have come and gone. But think what will follow if what is in the dark-haired queen's womb is born. Will Logres survive? Will Avalon?"

"Patience. Balance." The FarSeer with hair the color of old gold and a gown in the style of Periclean Athens held up a hand. "Eirianell has already requested an audience. Perhaps the High King has knowledge we do not." She lifted her hand, and the others rose with her, to fall in behind her. She led the way with head held high, and every sign of serenity as they bent their path to the High King's palace.

Aleneil wished that she had such serenity—then wondered if it really *was* composure on the part of their leader, or only a counterfeit. Aleneil was very young among the Sidhe, to them barely adult; the leader of the FarSeers was as ancient in mortal years as the style of gown she favored. She had thus had many years to cultivate a mask of calm repose.

There was no sign of what the FarSeers had read in their lens as they walked beneath the star-bespangled false-sky, between two rows of towering linden trees, covered with silver-green leaves and golden flowers. The path beneath them was of soft and springy moss, interrupted only by artistically placed stones and clumps of violets and bluebells. Ahead of them stood a palace of lacey marble and alabaster that had changed little over the passing of the years. Avalon looked as it had for countless centuries, dreaming in an endless, peace-filled blue twilight, as nightingales sang and crickets chirruped.

And unless the High King found some new wisdom, if Denoriel could not take up the task of guarding and guiding the young Princess Elizabeth Tudor, it all might end in fear and flame.

If Oberon had more knowledge than his FarSeers, he gave no sign of it. He greeted the ladies of the Visions not in his throne room where the entire Bright Court might listen to them, but in a private chamber. However, this was no intimate chamber where a king might shed his dignity and speak as an ordinary being with intimates, or even play for a time. They gathered in a room where gracefully arched openings in all four walls framed only blank alabaster panels. There were no places save the single door into it where this chamber was open to the palace or the grounds. This was where a king made arrangements and gave judgments he had no desire for his entire court to know.

The room looked cool and somehow as if it held apart from what happened within it. The walls were pale silver, slightly sparkling. There were no windows, which was somehow faintly oppressive, but light, the soft, silvery twilight of Underhill, suffused the chamber, coming from everywhere and nowhere. The ceiling was lapis-lazuli; the floor of blue-veined marble. At one end was a dais, and upon that were two thrones. They were not huge, nor encrusted with gems and ivory and precious almost-living shells as were the thrones in the Great Hall; these were made of a dark, shining wood twisted into strange seemings as if it had grown that way. The High King sat in one of these thrones, his Queen, Titania, in the other. Neither throne was larger than the other, mute testimony of their joint rulership, though Oberon had been High King longer than Titania had been Queen.

Having listened to the Visions of the FarSeers, High King Oberon leaned slightly forward toward them. Dark eyes—a black that somehow glowed—fixed on the four women who stood before the throne. They knew him of old, of course, but even so each stared in wonder at him. Power pulsed in him as if barely held in check, and he was beautiful . . . All Sidhe were beautiful, but Oberon was . . . different.

His hair grew from a deep peak on his forehead and swept back in gleaming black waves, the points of his ears showing through, enough to mark him as of elvenkind, if his beauty were not enough. His brows were equally black and high-arched over the fathomless eyes. In contrast his skin was white, not pallid and sickly, but with the hard, high gloss of polished marble.

He towered over all other Sidhe, and not by enchantment. Physical strength almost immeasurable was his, and formidable muscles in shoulders and thighs strained the black velvet tunic and black silk hose he wore. He was all in black, only lightened by silver piping on every seam and the silver bosses on his belt and on the baldric that usually supported the long sword which now leaned against his throne.

"You know I cannot do what you ask," he said. "I am High King of all the Sidhe—Seleighe and Unseleighe alike. If I favor the Seleighe over the Unseleighe, the Unseleighe could rightfully deny my right to rule. I do not say their rebellion would be successful—it would not. But *I* would know that I had been unfaithful to my trust, and my power would be lessened. And they, feeling restrained and persecuted Underhill, would meddle more and more in the mortal world so that in the end we might be exposed for what we are."

"But if the Inquisition comes to England, it will rip and tear until Underhill is exposed anyway. Remember El Dorado and Alhambra." Eirianell met the black eyes with calm. She had known those who wielded power enough to sink a continent and dared reason with King Oberon.

But he showed no anger, only smiled and then said, "If. There are three futures. When we know more, I will examine my constraints more closely."

"But I have no such constraints," Titania said, her green cat-pupilled eyes glowing with challenge.

Her voice was sweet and rich as warm honey and her presence

was the bright contrast to her husband's dark power. Titania was a wonder even to those she ruled. The Queen's lineage was pure High Court, Seleighe elven, except that she was even taller than most male Sidhe. Her body was, of course, perfectly perfect. Her hair was a rich gold, elaborately dressed in a high confection of tiny braids and curls, which showed off her ears; they were delicately shell pink, almost transparent—but the pointed tip of one ear was bent, which tiny imperfection made her somehow more perfect.

Oberon turned his head toward her, but he did not speak. Aleneil, who always watched the High King of the Sidhe as a doomed bird watches a snake, caught a fleeting glance from his dark eyes. She saw, or thought she saw, a kind of satisfaction in that glance. However, in the next instant there was nothing to be seen in Oberon's eyes but an avid sensual hunger, perhaps heightened by Titania's defiance.

The Queen's eyes glowed a bright, pure emerald, brilliant pools deep enough to fall into and drown. Her lips were pale rose, and through the ethereal light violet and white silk robes she wore, she looked . . . translucent, as if she were lit from within. The tip of Oberon's tongue flicked over his lower lip. Titania smiled.

"I desire greatly to see the red-haired child grow up to rule Logres," she said defiantly. "Do you forbid me, my lord?" The smile had not faded from her lips and her eyes, if anything, were brighter, almost casting visible sparks.

"No . . ." Oberon drew out the word and at last looked away from his queen toward the FarSeers. "I do not forbid, only caution. Do not act in your own person, my lady, and keep your favor for the red-haired queen secret." He shook his head before Titania could protest. "I say that more for her sake than for yours. She already attracts our Dark kin's regard; the attention of our Queen might well tempt them beyond caution."

Titania rose from her seat and Oberon rose too, more slowly. She gestured at the FarSeers. "I will see you ladies anon."

Chapter 1

The imp skittered sideways. Although it stood upright on its hind legs, it was no bigger than a mouse and looked much like one, with a round little body, and four thin legs and a long naked tail—except that it was bright red and quite naked. It had little beady black eyes, large round ears, and a pointed muzzle from which sharp little teeth peeked. Those sharp teeth and equally sharp, overlarge, claws on stick-thin front and rear limbs, from which a sick yellow-green slime oozed, curbed any desire to laugh in the one to whom the imp was squeaking. It might be small—but size was no measure of how deadly a thing was, especially Underhill. *Most* especially when the thing was Unseleighe.

Pasgen Peblig Rodrig Silverhair frowned and moved a finger just as the imp leapt toward him, and the creature squalled and made a convulsive movement to retreat. It was held suspended midair, its struggles quickly subdued as if a heavy, invisible blanket had been wrapped around it.

If anything, the creature looked more comical than before, hanging helpless as it was, squirming and writhing. However there was another, more pressing reason not to laugh than the imp's poisoned claws, which in any case had been neutralized for now. It carried a summons from Prince Vidal Dhu.

Pasgen did not frown, but he was—perturbed. Prince Vidal

7

Dhu. Vidal summoning him. For the past four years Vidal had been hanging between life and death, saved from perishing of iron poisoning only by his healers, who, themselves constrained by blood oaths, died draining the poison out of his blood. Now it seemed that Vidal had at last recovered enough to emerge from hiding. And he should not have been able to find Pasgen.

"So Prince Vidal wants me," Pasgen murmured. "How interesting." His frown grew blacker, and he raised his eyes to stare at the little monster. "How did you find me?"

The imp squeaked "Let me go. Let me go. Prince Vidal will punish you if you harm me."

The invisible blanket tightened around it. It tried to struggle, could not. The power that held it tightened more. A despairing squeal contained the word "Token."

"Give it to me," Pasgen said, the edge of command in his voice.

The creature's mouth opened and it disgorged a small, coiled object, wet with slime. An immaterial hand slid through the field that englobed the imp, seized what it had vomited and carried it toward Pasgen. As it approached, he could sense the drumming beat issuing from it, a drumming that perfectly matched the beating of his own heart.

Another gesture with one finger and the imp was dead, crushed to a formless lump of red, mottled and streaked with green-yellow gore. The force that held it then carried the mess outside to be consumed by the things that scavenged Pasgen's gardens. Its death had been quick, too quick for the creature even to squall. Pasgen could not allow anything that knew the location of his private domain to live, but all the years of Vidal's training had not been able to teach him to enjoy pain. He could be vicious when necessary, but he was never cruel just for amusement.

Cleaned and dried by other invisible forces, the brown scrap was clearly preserved skin attached to a thin layer of flesh. His own skin and flesh, Pasgen knew, from the vibration of congruence. He stared at it, appalled. He had always been careful about hair clippings and nail parings, making sure to burn them. And all the while Vidal Dhu had his skin and flesh. When and how had Vidal obtained so powerful a token? More important, was this the only one the Black Prince had? And now what was *he* supposed to do with it?

Pasgen held out his hand and the scrap of brown leather was

laid upon it. Pasgen closed his hand. He was immediately aware of a feeling of constriction. He opened his hand again; it was trembling. If he could not close his hand on the thing without feeling choked, what would happen to him if he tried to destroy it? Had Vidal known he would kill the imp? Had Vidal hoped he would kill himself too, unaware of the token?

Nonsense, he told himself. He had not been aware of any sense of confinement when the token was inside the imp. Most likely it was only because he knew he was closing his hand over it that he felt closed in. Nonetheless panic still rose in him at the thought the token might fall into anyone else's hands. Yet if he could not test its properties himself, who could he trust to touch it?

That question was answered before it was quite complete in Pasgen's mind, and the answer calmed and simultaneously raised a new wave of panic in him. His twin sister Rhoslyn could be trusted to know about the token and to test its effect on him, but if Vidal had a token from him, it was all too likely that the prince had one or more from Rhoslyn also. He had to warn her—not that he knew what good a warning would do . . . or would it be worse if she knew?

Pasgen rose from the stark white chair on which he had been sitting, his hand held carefully in front of him . . . and stood irresolute a condition that had not afflicted him for many, many years. Should he go to Rhoslyn at once or should he first go to Caer Mordwyn and discover what Vidal wanted?

What Vidal wanted. Pasgen brought his skittering thoughts to bear on that. The fact that Vidal was able to want anything was another shock. Pasgen cursed softly, his eyes on the token lest it fall to the floor. He had been inexcusably careless, assuming as the years passed that Vidal would die or remain a near-inanimate hulk.

Pasgen himself had recovered in two years from the wound he had received in the battle waged against his half-brother and half-sister and their Seleighe allies. But *he* had only been scraped by a passing elf-shot; not exactly harmless, but nowhere near as deadly as Cold Iron to one of the Sidhe. Vidal had been shot with a bullet from FitzRoy's mysterious gun.

Well, FitzRoy was dead. He would shoot no one again. Pasgen's lips twisted. And if someone had to be shot by a mortal, Vidal surely deserved it more than anyone else. Unfortunately it seemed that Vidal had survived with enough mind and will to demand his presence . . .

Or was it unfortunate?

The idea that had come to Pasgen seemed to lift an enormous weight from his heart, and it removed his indecision. He would go to Rhoslyn, warn her about the token, and leave his with her—obviously he could not carry it with him to Caer Mordwyn. It would be safe with Rhoslyn; more to the point, it would be safe being guarded by the creatures his sister had set about her to ensure her own safety. Pasgen shuddered gently as he thought of the big-eyed, childlike girl constructs with their wire-thin fingers that could be gentle as a butterfly or cut right through flesh and bone. They guarded Rhoslyn's domain every bit as efficiently as his own burly male guardians—better, perhaps, because invaders were prone to underestimate them.

He looked down at the scrap of skin and flesh in his hand and went to the black lacquer desk under the window. The top was glass-smooth, the surface clear except for the low gold-wire stand holding three thin gold pens. No design marred the perfect surface of the drawers on each side of the kneehole. Only absolutely plain pulls—octagonal bars of pure shining gold—were fastened to the face of each drawer.

Pasgen opened the middle drawer on the left-hand side of the desk with his free hand. It held a variety of boxes of different sizes and materials. He removed a small tortoise-shell square from the front of the drawer, struggled for a while to open it single-handed, and then, grimacing—because he was reluctant to have even his near-mindless and totally enslaved servants in the vicinity of that token—moved away and summoned an invisible servant to separate top and bottom.

He bade the servant clean the box and then dismissed it. After a moment, he drew a deep breath, deposited the token inside the box, and closed it. For a while he stood with his eyes closed, just breathing deeply and evenly. Finally he opened his eyes and looked around at the white leather chairs and settles, the black-framed chairs for visitors (not that he ever had any), the black lacquer side tables and low, central table, the black and white tiled floor.

All were clear and bright. No fog or dullness, as if he were peering out through some obstruction, obscured his view. It *had* been his too-active imagination, after all. He uttered a deep sigh, tucked the box into the bosom of his doublet, and left the house.

Usually Pasgen took his time when he crossed the garden and park in his domain. The beautiful, symmetrical order of the flower beds, the hedges, the trees with their ordered branches and precisely placed leaves always soothed him. There was so much disorder in his life, in his mind, in his heart, that the rigid and mathematical precision of the place was a balm to his spirit.

Today Pasgen merely hurried down the lavender graveled path that branched off the main way, which led to a stark but plainly marked Gate. That Gate had six exits, all equally unpleasant; two of those six *could* be fatal. It was a trap for the unwary, a clever way of disposing of any who thought to spy upon him or worse, and make a quick getaway. The side path took several turns and even crossed the kitchen garden before it petered out. A few steps beyond the little square that seemed the termination of the path, two slender white-barked saplings stood about two feet apart, exactly like similarly paired birch trees all along the path. Pasgen stepped between them, and was gone.

He emerged in a narrow alley that led to a quiet back street from which one could hear the sounds of a busy market. The alley was empty, as it had always been since Pasgen cast an aversion spell on it. The two doors that had once opened into the alley were boarded up. The street beyond the alley was not always empty; only a little of the aversion spell leaked into it, but people using it had a tendency not to linger and those whose houses backed on it tended to use their front doors. Today the street as well as the alley was empty, and Pasgen strode toward the sound of the market.

It was not large, an open area perhaps three or four streets square, but then the merchants were diminutive, the tallest coming only to Pasgen's elbow, so each booth did not take up much space. The customers, however, were of all sizes, many of them Sidhe, and a few even larger folk, which made the market seem very crowded. Pasgen did not mind at all. He slowed his pace to a shopping stroll and was soon indistinguishable from the many other Sidhe. Seleighe, or Unseleighe? There was no telling. Anyone who came here was careful to make his—or her—costume as neutral as possible.

He even stopped at a booth displaying a wide variety of amulets. Most were simply small carved figures of everything and anything, even of every religious symbol—the Christian cross, the Moslem crescent, the Hebrew six-pointed star, and the symbols of every pagan god Pasgen knew . . . and a number that he did not recognize. Curiously, he touched the cross.

"Fine work," the little brown merchant said. "Won't burst if you put a spell on it. Sold a lot of them. Seem to like love spells they do. Seen them glow a little with a love spell."

The little man had an inordinately long and pointed nose that drooped a bit toward his long and slightly upturned chin. His ears were too large, the lobes hanging a bit below his chin and his hair was thin and scraggly. Pasgen shook his head but smiled and took up four anonymous-looking ovals, a wooden rose, a ceramic coiled serpent with lifted head, a leaping horse of bone, and a glass Sidhe head, with open eyes and mouth, that clearly split apart just behind the pointed ears to hold something small.

"How much?" Pasgen asked, reaching for his purse. He spoke in the common trade-tongue used in every marketplace Underhill that was not large enough to have a universal translating spell.

"Gold I have, master," the gnome replied in the same language. "Bespell for me an amulet and you will have paid."

"Or overpaid," Pasgen said, still smiling, but with his voice turned hard. "What kind of spell?"

"Sleep. That should be easy enough for you, master."

It was easy. Pasgen looked down at the table, saw several more charming or frightening figures. "For what I have in my hand, one use," he said. "If you want an amulet that will always bring sleep . . ." Suddenly he realized that very few Sidhe were capable of creating such a spell. To do so would mark him in the gnome's memory. He shook his head. "I cannot do that," he said, "but for five uses . . ." He narrowed his eyes as if considering what he had offered. "Yes, for five uses, I will take these—" he marked the amulets with his finger "—as well as what I have in my hand."

The gnome protested and bargained. Pasgen allowed himself to be divested of three of the amulets he had marked because to fail to chaffer would also mark him as unusual; however, he was growing impatient and finally made as if to throw down the amulets he was holding and walk away. That brought the gnome to heel and he accepted Pasgen's last offer of the five-times spell for the handful of amulets.

"Which shall I bespell for you?" Pasgen asked, about to pick up any amulet the gnome indicated.

Instead the little brown creature pulled a box from under the counter and opened it. Inside was a very plain oval, lightly inscribed with a small tree entwined with a clinging vine. When Pasgen picked up the amulet, it was blood warm in his hand, but it was the material of which it was made, not magic that warmed it. He bent his head and began to murmur. He could see the gnome straining to listen but ignored him. He doubted the creature could make his harsh and scratchy voice sound the liquid vowels and sweet tones of the elven-mage-tongue.

"So." Now Pasgen was in a hurry, and he dropped the amulet back in its box. "You can give the amulet to the person you want to wear it all the time, or you can lay it on that person's forehead or breast at the time you want the person to sleep. Then, to invoke, you say '*Minnau ymbil*' and when you want the person to wake, you say '*Deffro deffroi.*'"

"And to whom do I complain if the spell doesn't work?" the gnome growled as Pasgen picked up the amulets for which he had bargained.

Pasgen started to turn away, but then hesitated and said, "Cry for justice to Vidal Dhu at Caer Mordwyn."

"Vidal Dhu is dead," the gnome protested. "You know we are between the Bright Court and the Dark and we had that news from both sides."

"Oh, no," Pasgen said, with a lifted eyebrow. "Then I give you a gift, along with the price of the amulets. I assure you he is alive and well and will be holding court at Caer Mordwyn ere long—but the spell will work. Never fear it."

And he slipped away, weaving skillfully among the booths and the customers. Actually he made two rounds of the market in random fits and starts until he began to move into less crowded areas and finally slipped behind a booth displaying very small gardening implements. There he waited rather patiently, considering his urge to continue to his goal, but he neither heard nor felt any magic. Finally he took out the amulet of the snake and sang to it the spell that opened a small, one-passage Gate.

Clutching the amulet in his hand, he walked away from the

market into the narrow streets of the town. The houses were hardly higher than his head and after some random turns and crossings, he could see that no one was following him. Then he walked directly out of town until the open ground that faced him blended into a formless mist. He invoked the Gate and stepped through, although if he had not known that he had passed through a Gate, he could easily have believed he was still in Gnome Hold.

Here, however, the mists were not formless. They swirled and twisted, retreating from him and then billowing toward him as if an erratic wind blew. Only there was no wind. Pasgen set out into the chaos with a steady step. As he went, he turned his head sharply to sniff in a wisp of mist that was passing his shoulder. A sharp scent, but not unpleasant.

A little later, he stuck out his tongue to taste a cloud that had formed directly in front of him—and that was sweet, decidedly sweet. Pasgen smiled and began to draw into himself some of the energy Rhoslyn might have used to create a construct. By the time he came to the Gate he had sensed at about the middle of this Unformed land, he had restored all the power he had used to create the gnome's amulet and build his Gate.

The Gate in the Unformed land took him to another busy hold, the next to a dead elfhame. Pasgen did not linger nor leave the Gate. He turned his back on the crumbling hall and averted his eyes from the encroaching "garden" of viciously snapping "plants" and putrescent flowers. Fortunately, this Gate had three unused settings. Quickly, he willed a new terminus in another Unformed domain where he built another Gate that, at long last, deposited him at the edge of Rhoslyn's holding.

As always he sighed, mingled exasperation and appreciation, because the scene before him was both untidy and, somehow satisfying. There were no long, perfect vistas; the view was broken by little ponds around which there were patches of trees, then meadows cropped smooth by dainty sheep. Sheep? What were sheep doing in an Unseleighe domain? When the Dark Court wanted mutton, they engaged in a riotous hunt on mortal flocks, left grazing injudiciously too near a Stone Circle, a Standing Stone, a Barrow, or some other passage into Underhill. Pasgen shook his head. Not that they often did such a thing, at least, not for the meat. Venison, boar, and pheasant were more like to grace the tables of elvenkind. Or peacock and antelope, had anyone a taste for the exotic.

Beyond was a patch of woodland from which emerged a babbling brook following a wavering course over stones of every size and shape. He sighed again as he invoked the minor spell that would in effect give him seven-league boots and take him in three steps to Rhoslyn's castle. A castle . . . Again he shook his head. It was a mortal child's dream, that place; a fairy-tale castle with pretty towers and turrets and bright flags snapping in the nonexistent breeze.

His last step took him to the drawbridge over the moat—the shining, clear moat in which one could see large, bright-colored fish swimming. That was new. The moat used to look like a moat in mortal lands, or one in Unseleighe Underhill—muddy, green with algae, and clogged with razor-sharp swamp grass. It had never held golden fish with trailing fins before. Those were Seleighe things. If Vidal saw . . . If Vidal had a token and found Rhoslyn's domain and saw what looked too much like a Bright Court palace, he would tear it apart and break Rhoslyn's heart.

Pasgen swallowed hard, clenched his jaw, and reminded himself that—*that was then, this is now*. Vidal would do no such thing. Pasgen knew he had been close to matching Vidal's power before the disaster, and he had spent his years in learning new magic and finding new sources of power, while Vidal had been lying insensate, unable to learn or do anything. Vidal could do nothing to harm Rhoslyn that he, himself, could not counter . . . unless Vidal had also spent the years in growing stronger. And how could he? Surely the time had passed in weakness and pain.

As Pasgen set his foot on the first step of the portico that enclosed the castle door, it opened and two of Rhoslyn's constructs barred the way, standing and watching him. He was surprised. All of Rhoslyn's constructs knew him and all had been instructed to let him pass without hindrance.

"Who are you?" one of the constructs asked. "What do you want here?"

"I am Pasgen Peblig Rodrig Silverhair," he replied. "I am Lady Rhoslyn's brother and I have free passage into the lady's home. Are you new-made that you do not know me?"

It was impossible to tell one of Rhoslyn's constructs from another, except by the ribbons around their necks. They all looked like starveling girl children with huge eyes and small mouths. But those pursed lips could open wide as a lion's maw and show teeth that were as long and pointed as any wolf's. And the long, thin fingers on their sticklike arms . . . Pasgen had seen those fingers slice up an ogre as if he were a cheese.

For a long moment the constructs stared at each other in silence and Pasgen began to debate in his mind whether he could destroy them before they wounded him . . . and what his sister might do to him if he destroyed her toys.

Then Rhoslyn was there, stepping out of a shadow as if she had been conjured.

"Pasgen," she said, and looked at her constructs. "What ails you? Do you not know my brother?"

"Yes, lady," the girl with the yellow ribbon whispered, flexing her hands, "but this one is not the same. He has two hearts."

As Denoriel passed through the door to Aleneil's house, he wondered whether Elfhame Avalon was not just a bit too open to passersby. Elfhame Logres was open too—the gardens, woods, and meadows, but the palace Llachar Lle had defenses. Even his own apartment inside the palace had a door that would exclude any who had not been sealed into its memory.

Of course with the Academicia in Avalon where most of the Magus Majors lived and worked, an inimical intruder would not last long. Not to mention what King Oberon and Queen Titania could do should anyone be foolish enough to invade the place . . .

Denoriel found himself smiling, and relaxed; he was being foolishly protective. Surely he did not need to be concerned for the safety of his precious sister and Avalon. He was still smiling when Aleneil stepped from the doorway of her solar. She smiled at him, and then laughed aloud.

"I guessed you would be coming here as soon as Mwynwen told you, but so quickly . . ." She frowned anxiously. "Oh, you didn't make a Gate, did you?"

"No, no. I will go strictly by the rules. I remember all too well what happened two years ago when I carelessly tried to light a candle. I have no desire at all to feel again as if every vein in my body is afire." He grinned at her. "Miralys brought me by his own sweet ways without regard to Gates or other Passages."

"Ah." Aleneil turned and led the way into her solar. "I suppose the elvensteeds use magic, but it is something completely unlike our own."

"I think," Denoriel replied, having had quite some time to actually think about such things *and* great need to actually do so, "that it is more that they are like otters that slice through the water of magic, and we are the poor ducks, paddling furiously across the top of it and doing as much splashing and churning as getting anywhere."

That made Aleneil laugh. "Oh, please. A *swan* at least! Well, thanks to Miralys, then. He must have felt your need."

He gave her a comical little bow.

She smiled at her brother as he sat in his favorite chair, fingering the mother-of-pearl design inset into the arm, but she still felt concerned. The blue-green pattern of the cushions no longer picked up gold highlights from his hair; that was pure silver now. And there were small lines graven by pain and tension around the emerald eyes with their catlike pupils, and around his well-shaped mouth.

"Are you sure you are well enough?" Aleneil asked. "I know Mwynwen must have said you were, and I suppose Treowth also approved, but—"

His lips thinned. "I hope they are right. As I said, I do not enjoy being afire. But four years, Aleneil . . . eight long seasons. I am beginning to think I would rather not exist than be imprisoned and powerless for much longer." He saw the distress on her face and reached forward toward the settle to pat her arm and smile. "I am sure Mwynwen erred on the side of caution rather than optimism."

"Unless your endless complaints wore down even Mwynwen's patience," Aleneil said, but she was smiling again.

"And you do not give Treowth proper credit," Denoriel said, grinning. "I know he is more concerned for his reputation and his skill in magic than for the welfare of any people, but it would reflect ill on him if his magic killed me."

Aleneil laughed aloud, making a gesture that waked a peculiar, invisible movement in the air. By the time she spoke again, a small table had appeared beside Denoriel's chair bearing a flagon of his favorite wine and a delicate glass.

"So, what is permitted you now?"

"Passive magic. I may go through a Gate and visit the mortal world, so I want to see Elizabeth—and Harry wants me to see her. He worries about her . . ." He hesitated and then continued.

"I don't think Mwynwen likes his concern with Elizabeth. I think she fears he will want to return to the World Above and she does not want to tell him that he cannot, not really. Oh, for a few hours, even a day or two, but not to live. The elf-shot still poisons him and she must drain it every few weeks. I hope if I see the child and can assure him of her health and safety he will be more content."

"You think he will believe you more readily than me? I have been visiting her regularly all this time and telling him that she is safe and happy. She has a most loving governess in Katherine Champernowne. Blanche Parry is now chief of the maids and a close companion."

Aleneil caught her brother's look of sudden concentration, and felt both alarmed and pleased. This was the first time in four mortal years that Denoriel had shown interest in the child they had all worked so hard to save.

"Does Elizabeth know what Blanche is?" Denoriel asked. "As a babe Elizabeth could see through illusion. Can she still do that?"

Aleneil sighed, for she had not been able to get as near to the child as she would have liked. "If she can, she does not speak of it. She is a strange, self-possessed, most unchildlike child and says very little ... but I think she does know what Blanche is and values her accordingly. She has other safeguards too. Dunstan is still groom of her chamber. Likely in a few years the office will be given to some high-born nonentity, but the whole household depends on Dunstan. He will retain his authority if not his title."

"Remind me to tell him that Lord Denno will assure him his salary if he be superceded."

Aleneil smiled. "I think that just, but not necessary. He is besotted of the child, and so are Ladbroke and Tolliver, who keep her stable. None would overlook any danger to her and all of them swear that there has been no intrusion from Underhill in all this time."

He nodded briskly. "Good enough. Still, I need to become reacquainted with her. She liked me well enough when she was a babe, but nothing compared with what she felt for Harry. If your FarSeeing is true—and I have never known it not to be—you and I will be with her when she is crowned, so she must get to know me."

"Crowned." Aleneil's smile turned to a frown. "My brother, you must never forget that is only one of the Seeings. There are two others. One is only dull and disgusting, but the other is of the dull-haired queen with the swollen belly. We all feel it. The Great Evil will grow inside her. If that comes to pass, I do not know if Underhill will survive. We must keep Elizabeth safe and in the line of succession. We must."

But now Denoriel straightened unconsciously in his chair, looking more like his old self—and a knight—than he had in many a season. And when he spoke, it was with all of the old certainty. "If we must, sister dear, then depend upon it. We will."

Chapter 2

It took Aleneil a week to convince Katherine Champernowne, Elizabeth's governess, that she should admit a foreign merchant to the little girl's presence. That he was noble, connected to Hungarian royalty helped . . . a little. That he had been the duke of Richmond's favorite—a fact attested to by several of King Henry's courtiers—also helped, at least enough that Mistress Champernowne agreed to introduce him to Elizabeth. From there on, she said, it was up to Lady Elizabeth herself. She was perfectly capable of exchanging a few icy politenesses and ending the interview.

On the day assigned, a bright but chilly Tuesday in late March, Denoriel passed through the old Gate Magus Major Treowth had established for him not far from Hatfield. The old palace was still a frequent residence for Lady Elizabeth, not princess now, but at least acknowledged as the illegitimate daughter of the king. For a time, some had hoped that Great Harry might claim otherwise, but he himself had stepped away from that abyss—he had recognized Elizabeth too openly and for too long to claim now that the girl was of another's get. Miralys emerged from a patch of woods alongside a farm road. Aleneil on Ystwyth followed almost on Miralys's heels.

Aleneil's frown of concern relaxed when Denoriel turned in his saddle to make a gesture of success. But he did not look at her long and had to struggle with his own expression before it gave her new cause for worry.

Not that the strong magic of the Gate had harmed him. He was no more aware of it—perhaps less aware—than he had ever been. It was Aleneil he found it hard to look at. He could not get accustomed to her appearance as Mistress Alana. Aleneil was beautiful—all Sidhe were beautiful—and Mistress Alana offended his eyes. She was . . . well, not ugly; plain was the best one could say. Her hair was a dull, muddy brown, her eyes small and pale fringed with scanty eyebrows and eyelashes paler than her hair. Her complexion was sallow, her nose an undistinguished button, her lips pale, her teeth yellowed and crooked.

It was true, however, Denoriel thought, as Ystwyth came alongside of Miralys at the place the farm track met the main road, that one did not dwell on Lady Alana's face. Her person faded into the background of her exquisite garments.

Just now, atop the muddy hair was a remarkable hat, perhaps a whisper ahead of the fashion but no more than a whisper. Lady Alana was never bold. Over her soft gold velvet coif—no woman went without a coif—was a round cap, a man's cap, of umber velvet with a rolled edge striped in gold. Ear flaps of brown velvet, so heavily embroidered in gold that it was hard to discern the original shade, depended from the sides of the cap going around to fit the back of the head to confine her hair. And just above the ear flap on the right side of the cap, was a jaunty, sleek, red pheasant feather.

Her riding dress was every bit as elegant as the cap. Over a high-necked chemise with a ruffled collar—the low, bare, square neckline most fashionable in women's gowns would not be suitable for riding—Lady Alana wore something very like a man's doublet in a warm brown and gold brocade. From under the doublet flowed a very rich umber velvet skirt embroidered in gold, split from waist to hem fore and aft for riding as were the several petticoats (Denoriel had not bothered to ask how many) that supported the skirt. The velvet was covered—to protect it from rain or mud splatters—with a heavily pleated brown canvas safeguard.

Denoriel's dress, although rich and elegant, could not compare in stylishness with hers. For comfort in riding, Denoriel wore a long-skirted doublet that came to midthigh of a deep rose velvet embroidered across the breast and around the neck in silver. The white shirt beneath it showed in small pleats at the neck and wrists where the full sleeves narrowed into a long, close cuff. Under the doublet were pale gray slops, also embroidered in silver, but they only showed when the wind blew back the skirt of the doublet. Long hose, gartered both above and below the knee were covered almost completely by tall boots, slit at the back and turned down to the knee.

The costume was not as sumptuous as those he had often worn when he visited FitzRoy in company with George Boleyn, but George was long dead, and Elizabeth was living—at least at present—in less exalted state than FitzRoy had been. At present the king had a living *legitimate* son as his heir, and Elizabeth's position was very uncertain.

They paused at the entrance to the main road to make sure no one was coming along who might wonder what so elegant a pair had been doing up the farm track. Denoriel looked down at Aleneil and frowned.

"You said Elizabeth rode. Not I hope on one of those lunatic sidesaddles that have become the fashion."

Aleneil shook her head. "Not for serious riding, no, and until now she has been kept too much in the background to ride in processions."

He raised an eyebrow. "Serious riding? What can you mean? She is no more than eight years old."

Aleneil pursed her lips, and for the first time, looked just a trifle annoyed with him. "Nonetheless, she rides very well and loves the exercise, although her father has not yet given permission for her to go hunting."

"Hunting? A girl-child?"

Denoriel couldn't help himself; he goggled at Aleneil. It was one thing for an elven maiden to decide to take to the hunt and even to arms—there were, in fact, female knights, and woe betide him who thought them any less in prowess than the males! But a mortal girl-child? Hunting? Even the ladies hardly did more than genteelly toss a falcon into the air and permit their falconers to retrieve bird and quarry!

But—what really worried Denoriel—to go hunting, in the half-wild woods, would give enemies more opportunities at the child than he cared to think about.

Aleneil gave him a reproving frown. "Yes, indeed, and do not you *dare* quarrel with her about it or she will take you in dislike, and that would be a disaster. She is very tenacious of her likes and dislikes."

"But if it puts her in danger—"

"Denor—I mean, Lord Denno," Aleneil said sharply, "this child is not another Harry FitzRoy. Do not expect the same goodness, the same sweetness, from her. She learned many bitter lessons while you were healing and she does not give her trust for a smile and a hug."

The road was empty, and they moved out onto it, now riding side by side. "You sound almost as if you do not like her," Denoriel said.

"I don't know that I do," Aleneil admitted. "But young as she is, I respect her. And . . . and I am a little afraid of what she will become. There is a way that she can look at you that is—disturbingly calculating. Even now, every single person who has ever seen her remarks that she has great dignity."

Denoriel was not convinced. "Harry could be dignified too, but it was all outside. Inside he was a little boy who wanted to be loved."

There was a rather longer silence than Denoriel expected and he looked down at Aleneil, who sighed and shook her head.

"I have no idea what is inside Elizabeth," she said at last. "She will not let me close enough. I do not know that she has ever confided in anyone. I hope you will be able to forge some bond with her quickly, but you will not have much time."

"Why not? Did you not tell me that her governess was of an obliging nature, very romantic, and not too wise?" He smiled, confident in his ability to win over any mortal woman. "Surely I should be able to make her welcoming to me, especially as I am willing to contribute lavishly to the household expenses."

Aleneil shook her head. "Oh, Kat Champernowne is not the problem. You will wind her about your finger in a quarter of an hour. The trouble is that the king is planning to have all his children live together as soon as it is judged that Edward is not likely to take any disease from the others."

"Will it matter?" Denoriel asked. "Norfolk's children lived with Harry. In a way it was convenient because it was not so obvious that I was guarding Harry."

Aleneil sniffed with gentle disdain. "If you think Harry was well guarded after the attempt on his life, you will find that *nothing* compared with the guards and attendants around Edward. No one gets to see the boy except by the king's own permission."

Denoriel shook his head. "But I don't want to see Edward—"

"Unfortunately, when the children are in the same household with the same tutors, Edward's guards will guard Elizabeth too, just as Harry's guards watched Norfolk's children. It will not be easy to reach her. I do not know whether Kat will even be allowed to receive *me* so casually after the households are joined. You, being male, might have greater difficulty."

"Hmmm. But you think that if she takes to me, she will be able to ... No, she is too young to have any influence."

"I do not know. She is ... exceptional. However, what I meant was that if you find favor with her, she will remember and welcome you more gladly when the households are separated, as they will be from time to time."

They had reached the gate to Hatfield Palace by then and Denoriel made no reply, only smiling at the guard, who seemed to know Lady Alana quite well and nodded acceptance when she said that Lord Denno was expected. However, they did not ride straight up the wide road to the central courtyard. About two-thirds of the way along, she turned right onto a side path that took them to the east wing of the palace. Here a lesser courtyard was guarded by a familiar figure.

"Gerrit!" Denoriel exclaimed. "How surprised I am to see you, and how glad. I am sorry I did not enquire about you, but after that crazy attempt to take the princess—"

Gerrit shook his head and looked anxious, his eyes warning. "Lady Elizabeth, yes. But I don't remember too much about that night. Only that after it ... His Grace of Richmond sickened and ... he died, m'lord. He ... he asked for you sometimes."

"I didn't know," Denoriel said, allowing his eyes to fill with tears. "Harry knew I was bound to leave the very next day on a trading venture I could not delay any longer. At first I received letters from him. He never said he was sick. When I heard ... I simply could not come back to England in time. I am sorry. I should have thought of Harry's dependents."

"Oh, no. No need to worry for that, m'lord. His Grace's will took care of all of us. But you know, we were so used to being together . . . it was like a family. And when Ladbroke came and told me that he and Dunstan had got taken into Lady Elizabeth's service, I . . . we all came and spoke to Dunstan." He uttered a low chuckle. "That Dunstan. It's lucky he don't want to be God, 'cause I think he might just wheedle his way up on the heavenly throne."

"Ladbroke and Dunstan are in service to the prin—to Lady Elizabeth too? I am delighted. And the boy, Tolliver, was it?"

There was nothing to surprise Gerrit in Lord Denno not seeming to know what might have become of Henry FitzRoy's servants even though he was in the company of Lady Alana. For all Gerrit would know, she had never noticed them in FitzRoy's service. Many of the nobility never "saw" servants and guards. And Gerrit, of course, did not know that she was not human.

Dunstan and Ladbroke did know who Lord Denno and Lady Alana really were because they had been mortal servants Underhill, but they could not speak their knowledge. Neither bribe nor torture could wring the information from them even though they were exceptions to the general rule that a human released from Underhill had his mind wiped of all memory of the place. Dunstan and Ladbroke had been allowed to keep their memories the better to assist Denoriel and Aleneil in protecting Henry FitzRoy. Instead, they had been deprived of the ability to speak of what they knew.

Gerrit grinned. "Oh, Tolliver's here. Not so much a starved boy anymore, m'lord. Real hafling, he is. Half in love with m'lady. Follows her like a puppy when she's out of the palace."

"Well, it cannot hurt to have a devoted and watchful eye on her," Denoriel said, frowning suddenly. "I know there is a true heir to the throne now, may he thrive and live long, but there *might* be those who wish her ill for . . . for reasons . . . best left unsaid."

"Yes, m'lord." Gerrit looked slightly startled and slightly concerned too. "Thank you, m'lord. I'll keep that in mind and warn the others."

"Good man." Denoriel nodded to him and rode through the gate into the courtyard where Aleneil was already dismounted and waiting for him.

Ladbroke was holding Ystwyth—carefully not touching the illusory rings of the bit. "Glad to see you home safe at last, m'lord," he said to Denoriel as he dismounted.

"And I am glad to see you here in Lady Elizabeth's service."

Ladbroke took hold of Miralys's halter, taking care not actually to put any pressure on it because he knew it would simply slip off the elvensteed's head. He bobbed a bow as he clucked to his charges and began to turn toward the stable. He stopped, uncertain of what Denoriel knew, and then decided to give him the basic information he might need.

"Lady Alana was good enough to recommend us to Lady Bryan, who was then governess, when several of the stablehands left because they didn't want to be in a disgraced household. And then the groom of the chamber was discovered to be lining his pockets in anticipation of being without a position so he was dismissed. Lady Elizabeth recognized Dunstan, too—"

Denoriel did his best not to goggle. "At three?"

"Lady Elizabeth is a . . . is unusual, m'lord."

At that moment Reeve Tolliver, who Denoriel remembered as a starved boy of twelve plucked from a workhouse, came to the door of the small stable and called that the stalls were ready. He was now a tall, broad-shouldered young man, still with an unruly shock of hair above a plain but pleasant face.

"I'll take these two in and settle them. You go take a look at the brown carriage horse's off fore. I was just about to do that when Lady Alana rode in."

"Not favoring it," Tolliver said, frowning slightly.

"No, but it looked swollen," Kip replied. "Maybe it was just the light, but it can't hurt to look."

And while he looked, Ladbroke would remove the bridles, which had no bits attached and were so loosely fastened that Miralys and Ystwyth could rid themselves of the head-furniture with a brisk shake. Denoriel smiled, lifted a hand, and followed Aleneil toward the entrance to the east wing of the palace where Dunstan was waiting, bowing correctly but grinning with obvious delight to see Denoriel.

A flick of the eyes showed that Dunstan had noticed the hair, now silver rather than blond, but all he said was, "If you will pardon me for saying so, m'lord, I am very glad indeed to see you here again, safe and sound after your long voyage."

Denoriel smiled. "You are certainly pardoned for saying you are glad to see me. I hope all is well with you, that you are satisfied with your new service."

"Very satisfied, m'lord." Dunstan's lip twitched. "It's a bit quieter than serving His Grace the duke of Richmond, but that's all to the good."

"Yes, indeed," Denoriel agreed, and then, lowering his voice, "but don't forget that it might get livelier at any time."

Concern showed in Dunstan's eyes, but he only bowed to Aleneil and gestured for them to follow, saying, "Mistress Champernowne is awaiting you in the presence chamber, so please you."

They passed through a large room, obviously serving as the great hall. There were trestle tables stacked along one wall, and a wide door led to a somewhat smaller but still large room, the general reception room. There two pages, a footman, and three young gentlemen (whom Denoriel did not recognize) lounged and made idle chatter. They all looked at Dunstan, but no one made any move to question his right to escort people through the Lady Elizabeth's apartment.

Then Denoriel realized that they all recognized Lady Alana. The footman bowed to her as did two of the gentlemen, but they all returned to their conversations only casting a curious glance or two at Denoriel. On his way out, Denoriel resolved, he would stop and talk to the gentlemen, and the pages too, if he could find a cause.

Past the large reception room, Dunstan gestured them into the presence chamber and closed the door behind them. He turned to Denoriel as if he were about to ask a question, but the door on the other side of the room opened and a young woman, likely in her early twenties, stepped through. She was smiling and holding out her hands, which Aleneil hurried forward to take.

"My dear Lady Alana—" Mistress Champernowne's voice was mild and sweet "—how delighted I was to receive your message two days ago. Your last letter had been so uncertain about when you would be able to come again that I was quite in despair."

"I am sorry for that, Mistress Champernowne, but you may blame my cousin . . . well, I call him cousin although it was by a long-ago marriage. A crusader uncle took . . . who was she to you, Lord Denno?"

"Great-grandmother, I think, although she might have been a great-great-grandmother. I am not certain and, as you know, I have no way of checking the church records any longer."

Aleneil put her hand on Denoriel's arm and patted it consolingly. "God's Grace, Denno, I am so sorry to have reminded you."

To insinuate himself into the ranks of the higher nobility of England wealth alone would not have been enough. Aleneil had tampered a little with the minds of two of King Henry's friends so that they "remembered" Lord Denno Siencyn Adjoran's story. He was now supposed to be a Hungarian nobleman, cousin to Hungary's king, and from a family grown very, very rich from trade. Lord Denno himself had been abroad on a trading mission when the Turks had overrun Hungary. In the disaster, his entire family had been killed. Their Hungarian lands had been confiscated, but there was no way for the Turks to lay hands upon the wide-spread trading empire his family had controlled. After some years of rootless wandering, Lord Denno Siencyn Adjoran had come to rest in England, a country he had found so much to his taste that he had made it his home.

Denoriel smiled and shook his head. "It is all very long ago now and not very painful, although sometimes I still grieve for my little brother Imre—he who gave me the iron cross. Or, perhaps the grief is really for my Harry—" he bowed to Katherine Champernowne "—beg pardon, I mean the late Duke of Richmond. But we were very close. I gave him the cross when—"

"An iron cross, plain black iron on an iron chain!" Mistress Champernowne asked eagerly.

"Yes, that is it." He nodded. "It is of no real material value though it meant a great deal to me. Because he was so like my little brother, I gave him the cross to protect him, and I suppose when Harry . . . when Harry was lost, the cross was lost also—"

"No, no, it wasn't." Mistress Champernowne smiled with genuine pleasure at being able to help someone. "Lady Elizabeth has it. She is absurdly attached to the thing and wears it constantly. But I am sure she would return it to you if you told her—"

He managed to look shocked, pleased, and embarrassed at the same time. "No! Grace of God, no! I am utterly delighted to learn that the cross was not lost, but I am very eager to have Lady Elizabeth keep it and continue to wear it. Harry was devoted to her. It will be—will be as if some part of him is still watching over her."

"It is very plain and not very suitable to a highborn lady's dress," Mistress Champernowne said, clearly somewhat disappointed at not having a reason to wrest Elizabeth's unsuitable adornment from her.

"I am sure the duke of Richmond gave it to her because he believed she might need it. That cross was said to have been made from the nails of the True Cross or part of the blade of the lance that pierced Christ's side—" He shrugged. "—but I do not know that any of that is true. It was also said to be invested with holy protective spells. Imre gave it to me to keep me safe on what he believed was a dangerous voyage. Holy Mother help me! Perhaps if I had not taken it—I did not believe in it, you see; I took it only to cheer him because he feared for me." He allowed his expression to cloud, and his eyes to darken with feigned pain. "But mayhap—if I had not taken it, I would have drowned on that stupid voyage and he would have lived!"

"Denno!" Aleneil said sharply. "You could not know. Do not begin again to distress yourself over what was beyond your control. Your father sent you on that voyage; you did not ask to go. In fact, if I remember aright, you argued bitterly to stay in Hungary."

"Yes, I did." Denoriel cast a quick glance in Mistress Champernowne's direction and was satisfied with what he saw. The lady was highly impressed, and highly intrigued too. He found a rueful smile. "There was this young lady of whom my father did not approve." He sighed.

"That is a very sad tale," Mistress Champernowne said, sighing too. "But you now believe that the cross is a powerful relic? That it has protective powers?"

"*I* believe it, yes, but you know the old saw that God helps those who first help themselves. I believe the cross has power—perhaps no more than that it is God's symbol, but that is power also. And I desire with all my heart that Lady Elizabeth continue to wear it. Nonetheless, I would not walk down a dark alley without my sword just because I was wearing a holy relic. And you should not relax your vigilance for Lady Elizabeth's safety because she wears the cross."

"No, of course not." Mistress Champernowne shook her head and laughed lightly. "But who would wish to harm her? So sweet a child. So clever. All who meet her love her. Still, I understand better why she always wears the cross . . . only why did *she* not tell me of its power?"

"Likely because she does not know herself why she keeps wearing it," Aleneil said in Lady Alana's soft voice and smiling. "Is it not possible that Richmond gave it to her and explained that she must *always* wear it, that it would keep her safe from danger. She was only three. Doubtless all she remembers is that she must wear the cross, not why."

Mistress Champernowne frowned. "It is just as well that she does not remember too much about the happenings of that year. I suppose she has forgotten." But her voice was uncertain and she sighed. "At least she has stopped asking for Richmond."

"You did not tell her he . . . he had passed on?" Denoriel asked.

"I was not here then and cannot say what I would have done, but Lady Bryan felt there had been too much death around the poor child. She told my lady that Richmond had been sent away on a diplomatic mission and later that he was to live in foreign lands until Prince Edward was grown and acknowledged as the true heir. But as soon as she learned to write, she wished to send him a letter." Mistress Champernowne sighed again. "The devices I was put to to prevent it."

"Why prevent it?" Denoriel asked, thinking of the joy a letter from Elizabeth would bring to poor Harry.

"Well, I did not understand it myself and let her write a note. Fortunately I asked Lady Bryan what to do about it, and she explained to me that for a child whose mother had been executed and who had been declared illegitimate and out of the succession to write to the 'deposed' heir begging him to come back to England and take care of her might be . . . ah . . . misunderstood . . . and that I must discourage her from ever writing to Richmond again."

"The king—" Aleneil put her hand on Denoriel's arm "—is grown more and more suspicious as he grows older. He has a . . . a love-hate feeling for the child. As his daughter—so clearly his daughter with her pale skin and red hair and those long-fingered hands—he loves her, but as her mother's daughter he is suspicious of her, too ready to believe she might wish him ill, and perhaps even hates her."

Katherine Champernowne, who would not have spoken so clearly herself, nodded. "So do not mention Richmond, I beg you, even though you were his especial friend. I *think* she has forgotten . . . but she is very tenacious . . ."

A tap on the door heralded Dunstan and a servant carrying a tray with wine and cakes for refreshment. Mistress Champernowne nodded approval, said she would fetch Lady Elizabeth, and went back through the door through which she had come. Denoriel poured wine for himself and Aleneil.

"That was very clever," Aleneil murmured. "I didn't know you remembered that I told you Kat didn't like the cross. But there's no doubt she believed you. She's not stupid, you know, but she is very credulous. She'll stop trying to get Blanche to get rid of it. And, at worst, if she decides she can't stand Elizabeth wearing it, I'm sure she'll give it back to you."

Denoriel shuddered slightly, but before he could reply, the door opened again. Through it came a little girl, seven or eight years of age, slight-boned and slender. Her skin was very fair, her hair brilliantly red; in the dull interior light her eyes appeared to be dark. She began to come forward, a hand graciously extended to greet Aleneil and then hesitated for just a moment when she saw Denoriel.

Behind her was Mistress Champernowne and just behind her but well to the side so she could see the whole room was Blanche Parry, one hand raised to clasp the necklace of crosses that Denoriel knew lay under her chemise. Blanche remained in the doorway, watching, as Mistress Champernowne came forward.

"Lady Elizabeth, may I present to you Lord Denno, distant kin to Lady Alana, whom you know." Aleneil dropped a low curtsy and Mistress Champernowne continued. "Lord Denno has been away on a long voyage, but he says he knew you when you were little more than a babe and he wished to pay his respects now that he is back in England."

Denoriel bowed, sweeping off his hat. He saw Elizabeth look at the side of his head toward his crown and he swallowed nervously, wondering whether he had forgotten to mask his long, pointed ears with illusion. Then she transferred her gaze to his eyes. Nothing showed in her face, but Denoriel knew that she saw the long, oval pupils of a Sidhe rather than the round ones of a human. As an infant and a young child she had been able to see through illusion. Apparently she still could, but she gave no other sign than the quick movement of her eyes.

"I am very glad to see you again, Lord Denno," she said, with the gravity of a woman of forty. "I hope your voyage was profitable enough to make up for your long absence from those you knew and loved in England."

Denoriel's lips parted, but words stuck in his throat. What she had said was the sharp-honed rapier-prick of an angry woman—but she was only eight years old. Doubtless it was an innocent platitude. But he was thrown off balance and before he could think of a suitable answer Elizabeth had turned to Aleneil with an impish smile.

At first he thought she would advance on poor Aleneil, whose lips were already tight with discomfort from the iron cross, just to see her retreat or suffer more pain in silence. But although Elizabeth held out her hand, she moved no closer to Aleneil, only smiling with real warmth. Denoriel was a little surprised at the evidence of Aleneil's reaction because the cold iron of the cross Elizabeth wore had awakened no more than a distant, dull ache in his bones and he was actually closer to her than Aleneil was.

"Greetings, Lady Alana." Elizabeth barely touched Aleneil's fingers and then stepped back, almost to Denoriel's side, although she did not seem to notice that. "What do you think of my dress?" she asked.

It was in the height of fashion, children and adults wearing the same style—a rich light green brocade overgown with a low, square bodice edged in elegant, dark green embroidery. Above the bodice her chemise, high-necked and tied to form a ruffle, filled in the low décolletage of the gown, which was tightly fitted to the waist. The sleeves fitted the upper arm closely, then widened greatly and were turned back to show a gold velvet lining.

The skirt was split in front, opening into a broad V to expose the kirtle beneath. This was of the same gold velvet as the lining of the sleeves and was enlivened by the girdle of richly embroidered dark green satin, loosely tied at the groin and flowing down over the underskirt. On her head Elizabeth wore a dark green French hood, also lavishly embroidered, set well back to show her bright hair. Since her skirts swept the floor, he could not see her shoes.

Aleneil laughed aloud. "If the dress is your own doing, my lady, I would say that you no longer need me here giving you advice."

"Oh, no, I never meant that," Elizabeth said, looking distressed.

"Of course you didn't, my poppet," Mistress Champernowne said, putting an arm around the little girl's shoulders. "And Lady Alana didn't mean she wouldn't come to visit anymore. She was just complimenting you on your excellent taste. It is true, too. I had suggested a red kirtle, but Lady Elizabeth complained that it was too glaring and she was quite right. The gold goes better with her hair also."

"Yes, it does. But I never thought Lady Elizabeth would suspect me of giving up my visits. Indeed, I take too much pleasure in her company, and in yours, Mistress Champernowne, to stop coming. Nonetheless, we must stop chattering about dress. Nothing could be duller for poor Denno, who looks respectable only because he allows his man to chose his clothing."

"I am not so bad as that," Denoriel protested, smiling. "But it is true enough that clothing does not hold much interest for me. Still, I can tell when a dress is becoming, and Lady Elizabeth's dress is very becoming indeed."

It was a proper response, but the smile that Denoriel produced to go with it was patently artificial. Kat Champernowne might not be the most perceptive person, but she had adequate skill to recognize a polite falsehood.

"And so it is," she said, "but I doubt we can find more meat in that subject. I understand from Lady Alana that you are devoted to gardens, Lord Denno. Since the day is so mild, perhaps you would be willing to accompany Lady Elizabeth into our garden. We are just about to begin spring planting, and Elizabeth and I do not agree on what should be done. You must have seen a great many gardens, some in distant lands. We would welcome your opinion."

Denoriel gave a prompt, relieved approval. Walking in the garden might provide an opportunity for him to talk in a less formal way with Elizabeth. There was a brief, less strained, period while Dunstan returned the cloaks he had taken when he led Denoriel and Aleneil into Elizabeth's quarters and instructed servants to bring cloaks for Mistress Champernowne and Elizabeth. When they passed into the great hall and thence through a side door into the rather barren garden, they had sorted themselves out into two couples, suitable to the rather narrow paths between the fallow beds.

As soon as there was a distance between them and Kat Champernowne beside whom Aleneil was deliberately walking with tiny, mincing steps, Elizabeth looked up and said, "Should I put my cross into its pouch so you could take my hand?"

"God's Grace, no!" Denoriel exclaimed. "No, you must never cover your cross or take it off. And if someone should ever ask that of you, run away. Run away quickly to Blanche Parry or if you cannot reach her to Dunstan or Ladbroke or your guardsmen."

"Ah." The stiffness in Elizabeth's shoulders relaxed and when she glanced up again, her eyes no longer looked dark. In the bright daylight they were like molten gold. She sniffed slightly in a pretense of hurt, and said, "You do not wish to hold my hand?" Then the eyes darkened to dull brown again. "You used to hold *his* hand."

His. The emphasis made certain it could only be Harry she meant, even though her governess had said she believed the child had forgotten her half-brother. She had been only three when Harry went Underhill and at that time he was almost a man and he and Denoriel no longer held hands. Could what she said refer to tales Harry had told her about his own childhood? How could she remember anything like that?

She was staring up at him . . . challenging? "I am one of those that cold iron touches only lightly," Denoriel said, wondering if he were mad to say so much to a girl-child of eight years. But surely the remark would be meaningless to anyone to whom she repeated it. "So, if you will do me the honor of permitting it, I will gladly hold your hand."

He held out his own and she grasped it and squeezed it, pulling on it so that Denoriel bent closer to her. But it was not affection she wanted.

"Where is my Da?" she hissed.

Denoriel blinked, swallowed. Elizabeth had always called Henry Fitzroy her Da. It had been explained to her more than once that he was not her father but her half-brother. Her father was King Henry VIII. Even at two she had had the ability to look down her nose at adults far taller than she was in a kind of exasperated contempt. "Of course," she had said all those years ago. "King Henry VIII is my father, but he" —pointing at Harry— "he's my Da."

Denoriel swallowed again, snapped back to the present by an impatient tug on his hand and the repeated, intense, if low-voiced "Where is my Da?"

"Far away," Denoriel said, keeping his voice so soft it would not carry even on a vagrant wind to those behind. "You know that. You know he was sent away after your father married Queen Jane and there was a hope of healthy male issue."

"Sent away." Elizabeth's tone was so flat that Denoriel squeezed the hand he held comfortingly.

"It was not cruelty on the king's part," he assured her. "To travel to strange places was always what Harry wanted. When he was a little boy he used to beg me to take him with me on my voyages. He wanted to be a merchant so he could travel."

She turned her head away and bit her lips. "He is dead," she whispered. "Why do you lie to me? I hate lies."

"Child," Denoriel murmured. "I do not lie. He is *not* dead. I swear it. But he is *very* far away."

"Then why does he not write to me? Why cannot I write to him?"

"That would be dangerous, Lady Elizabeth, and you know it. If your letter fell into the wrong hands it could be made to sound as if you preferred Richmond to Prince Edward, as if you might be conspiring to commit treason. Harry is over twenty now, a fine man. Your brother Edward is hardly more than a babe, still subject to many threats to his health. For you to urge Harry to return to England . . ."

"But if I just asked about his health, told him about my lessons and that I still remembered him and loved him. What could be wrong in that?"

Denoriel bit his lips. The wrong might be in wakening in Harry a longing for the mortal world to which he could never return. And yet Harry loved Underhill, loved Mwynwen; the one thing that made him discontented in Underhill was his concern for Elizabeth. Why should he not receive a letter from her?

"Let me think," Denoriel muttered.

It would not be a rapid correspondence. He could say it would take two to three months for the letter to go to Harry and the same time for his reply to return. There could not be much danger to Elizabeth in writing two letters a year.

"There is the problem of how to send such a letter," he continued. "You know your governess has been forbidden to allow you to write—"

"She will not know," Elizabeth interrupted sharply. "I write all the time, lessons, letters, copies of sermons and hymns and poems. Unless I ask her to look at my work, she allows me to practice in privacy."

"Excellent, only that was not what I meant. The letter cannot be sent as yours usually are, by the king's messengers and—"

"I may be a little girl but I am not an idiot," Elizabeth interrupted again. "If I knew how to send a letter or where to send it, do you think I would not have done so?"

Denoriel had to laugh. This was no sweet child who first desired to be good and obedient. This was a young devil who first desired to have her own way. She was looking up at him again, and her eyes were lion-yellow, almost glowing from within.

"I suppose you would have. That you had been forbidden would not have troubled you, would it? But, Lady Elizabeth, the prohibition was for your own protection, not a whim of your governess."

There was a silence in which her face froze into a pale mask. Denoriel felt a pang of remorse when he saw how stricken she was. She believed, alas, that the only danger that could threaten her came from her own father, and that King Henry should not trust her was almost more than she could bear. Still, Denoriel did not dare explain that there were others who wished her ill.

Finally she said, "Then why are we talking about this?"

Perhaps it was unwise to reawaken Harry's strong feelings for Elizabeth . . . no, that was silly; Harry felt just as strongly about the child as he had when he was with her. More important, Denoriel was reasonably certain there could be no earthly repercussions, since her letter would come directly to him. There was no chance anyone else would see it and he ached for the child's loneliness and longing.

"We are talking about this because I know where your 'Da' is," he said, "and I can send him a letter from you."

The eyes raised to his were wide and bright with hope. "And will you?" she breathed.

"Of course." Denoriel chuckled. "I am not an idiot either. Would I have said I knew where he was if I did not intend to serve as your messenger? But it will not be quick, my lady. Richmond really is far away and my trading ships do not sail direct from here to there as the king's ships do on his command. It will be some months before Richmond receives your letter, and more months before his reply can come back to you."

"And you hope I will forget." A slow smile curved her thin but well-shaped mouth. "I never forget anything."

He looked deeply into her eyes, and what he saw there brought the fervent ring of truth into his answer. "No, my lady, I do not believe that you will forget. I do not believe that you will ever forget anything that you have willed yourself to remember."

She held his eyes with that strange, too-wise gaze. "Good," she said.

Chapter 3

"Two hearts!" Rhoslyn exclaimed, taking a step backward and crying, "Avaunt!" coupled with a gesture designed to break illusion.

However the being standing on her step remained Pasgen, a Pasgen with a very irritated expression, who snarled at her, "I have not got two hearts! I have a finding token, and if those idiot constructs of yours will not try to tear me apart, I will show it to you."

Knowing that her "girls" would protect her against any attempt to harm her no matter what she said, Rhoslyn barely hesitated before she ordered, "Watch only," as Pasgen reached into the front of his doublet and removed a small, square, tortoise-shell box.

"Tell one of your girls to take it and open it, but not touch what is inside."

"Elyn." Rhoslyn gestured and the girl with the yellow ribbon around her neck stepped forward and took the box.

"It is this that is beating like his heart," the construct said, turning her enormous eyes up to her mistress's face. "He does not have two hearts now. Should we let him in?"

Rhoslyn laughed weakly. "Yes. Let's all go in. Sorry, Pasgen."

He made an irritated growl and then said, "No, the girls were right, and the more alert they are now the better. Vidal is up and around again."

"Vidal!" Consternation and disappointment surged within her, and since this was Pasgen, after all, she did not mind that it showed on her face. "But I thought we were rid of him. And the court has been . . . almost a pleasure to attend since you have ruled it." Then, belatedly, she realized that the shock must have been even greater for her brother. "Oh, Pasgen, I am so sorry. You must be disappointed too."

"On the contrary, I would be delighted . . . except for what Elyn holds." He looked more angry than afraid, but he was her twin; how could she not be aware that with Pasgen, anger was often a mask for fear? "I know Vidal is in Caer Mordwyn because an imp summoned me to 'attend' Vidal—and it came to my own domain, to my own withdrawing chamber."

Rhoslyn just stared at him, eyes wide. "How?" she whispered. "How did he find your domain?"

"With what Elyn holds." He shook his head like an angry stallion. "The accursed creature had swallowed it and just followed the beat of my heart. No more than elvensteeds or air spirits do the imps need Gates."

Before she spoke again, Rhoslyn gestured and the girl with the violet ribbon went through the door and stood waiting. Elyn followed, still carefully holding the tortoise-shell box in her spider-leg fingers. Roslyn crossed the huge hall, larger inside than it would seem possible from the external appearance of the castle.

In the middle of the hall was a raised central hearth on which a bright fire leapt and crackled—smokeless, of course; this was no mortal hall to be plagued by smoking fires. On the right, a magnificent staircase rose to an upper story; the balustrade of carved battle maidens, outstretched spears and arms making a banister. On the left a pair of doors stood open. Three others, closed, broke the gray stone wall. Between the doors hung marvelous tapestries, showing scenes of the wild hunt and embattled knights. At each door were suits of armor which looked like nothing more than inanimate decorations.

Pasgen, however, had no doubt that a word or gesture from Rhoslyn or any sign of danger would animate them. And that the battle maidens would also come to life and give a good account of themselves. Rhoslyn made for the open doors and Pasgen followed her into another unexpectedly large chamber. Tall arched windows admitted the silvery twilight of Underhill and between them a large stone hearth held another leaping fire.

To each side of the fireplace were high, carved chairs, cushioned in embroidered velvet. Two on each side of the hearth angled toward each other with a small but equally elaborately carved table between them. Pasgen could feel his nose wrinkle. They were so ornate that he could not help himself, and the footstools in front of them were all carved too. There was hardly a straight line or simple, unadorned curve in the room, except the large polished wood table in the center. Given free rein to indulge her taste for frills and frippery, Rhoslyn had let no decorative opportunity go unexplored. Unfortunately.

He sighed softly, his eyes caught by more tapestries, these with more homely scenes—of men and women seated for a banquet, others engaged in an elaborate dance, and a group listening to a handsome mortal playing a lute and singing. He looked away, only to note still more tapestries on the far wall with a row of elaborately carved chairs in front of them. The chairs for the table, of course. Pasgen sighed again.

Rhoslyn broke into his attempt to find a restful place for his eyes, urging him toward the tall, cushioned chairs. The fire lit the area with a warm, golden glow. Each took a chair angled so that conversation would be easy. Crinlys, the girl with the violet ribbon, went to stand beside Pasgen's chair. Elyn stood by Rhoslyn's.

"What will you do now that Vidal knows where your domain is?" Rhoslyn asked, anxiously. "Will you destroy it and begin anew? I will help. I will make whatever you desire—"

Pasgen smiled slightly; he knew how proud Rhoslyn was of her own domain, and he would not hurt her feelings by telling her what he thought of her creations. "Thank you, sister, but it will not be necessary. Vidal knows no more now than he knew when he sent the imp abroad. I retrieved the token and destroyed the imp. There was no tracking spell—I made sure of that."

"No tracking spell," Rhoslyn repeated slowly. "That . . . that seems very careless." She hesitated, then said again, "Very careless. Even more careless than Vidal used to be."

"I think so too."

Rhoslyn's eyes lit and the set of her mouth hardened. "Then drive him out . . . destroy him. Rule the Unseleighe as you were plainly meant to do. I will stand by you. My girls . . . I can make more, and more of your guards also to fight for us." And, as Pasgen shook his head, she cried, half in disappointment, "Why not? Surely you are not afraid of him?"

"Not at all," Pasgen assured her, smiling. "I think I am stronger now than Vidal was at his best, and I suspect he is far from his best now. Very simply, my dear Rhoslyn, I do not wish to rule an Unseleighe Court." A delicate shudder passed through him and he was no longer smiling. "Horrible beasts! Even the dark Sidhe are little more than beasts. They cannot let an hour pass without conspiring to overthrow whoever has charge over them—and if they cannot overthrow him, they spend their time in making his rule as difficult as possible. I cannot think of anything I desire more than to be free of the burden of ruling them."

"I see." Roslyn shook her head. "I thought you took some pleasure in bringing the court to order, in directing the depredations of the ogres and bane-sidhe." She sighed, and looked at him with undisguised admiration. "It was so clever to use them to clean out Beelzebub's domain and give it as a feasting hall to the dark Sidhe."

The faint smile returned to Pasgen's lips. "I did enjoy that, but I was not exactly overjoyed that the High King held me responsible for controlling their excursions into the mortal world. It is like herding cats! No, worse, for at least cats do not take a malicious pleasure in doing whatever will cause the most chaos in order to disgrace the herder! Let Vidal have his throne back. Let him be the one Oberon calls to answer for a whole herd of sheep slaughtered, or goblins playing tricks on miners, or boggles waylaying too many travelers."

Rhoslyn's brow wrinkled. "But Vidal will be even worse at controlling them than you are, especially if he is so much weaker now. No one can bind them completely."

"Actually Vidal will not be worse at controlling them," he felt himself forced to admit. "All I did was destroy the ones who disobeyed me and the others cared very little for that. They have no imaginations, and do not connect the disappearance of those who transgressed with what they themselves might do in the future. Vidal makes them tear each other apart right in the court and issues orders in the lulls in the screaming. That generally makes an impression, at least on those with enough mind to remember for more than a few minutes."

Rhoslyn shuddered. She remembered being forced to watch such events. "But will he not hate you and fear you more than ever now? And . . . and he had a token for finding you." Her voice rose with fear. "What if he has another? How can you be safe from him?" She drew a sharp breath. "If he had a token for you, has he one for me? How did he get them?"

"He got them from me." The voice was soft, a little hoarse, and broken with tears. "One from each of you."

Both Pasgen and Rhoslyn jumped to their feet and faced the door they had carelessly left open, believing they were alone in Rhoslyn's portion of the castle, except for her servants, who could not be subverted.

"Mother!" Rhoslyn breathed.

"Llanelli!" Pasgen exclaimed.

Both her children looked at Llanelli Ffridd Gwynneth Arian, Rhoslyn with tears of love and despair in her eyes and Pasgen with exasperated irritation. However, neither approached her. The Sidhe woman hardly seemed real, she was so fragile; less than translucent—almost transparent. Her skin was like white alabaster, untouched with any hint of pink, her hair was like a worn gilt mist, thin and a little tarnished, her eyes were so soft and faded a green that they were nearly colorless too. There were no such beings as elven ghosts, but if there had been, Llanelli would surely have been taken for one.

"She's got some of the drug again," Pasgen said, as if the fragile beauty before him was deaf and senseless. "That is the limit, Rhoslyn. You cannot control her. I will—"

"Pasgen, do not talk about me as if I were a block of wood, or a statue you no longer care for." Llanelli's voice was no longer broken. A thread of Pasgen's exasperation seemed to have caught in it and strengthened it. "I am your mother. And I am not drugged, nor have I been these four or five mortal years."

Pasgen's frown did not fade in the least. "Then how did Vidal get tokens of our flesh, if you did not sell them to him to feed your vice?"

"Pasgen!" Rhoslyn cried.

Llanelli put a pale hand on the table to steady herself. "I am sorry about the tokens, but I had no choice but to yield them to Vidal. They were taken when you were both infants. He was going to take you away from me, separate you, and have you brought up by Sidhe he trusted." She closed her eyes for a moment. "I do not know whether you would have survived at all. But I tell you this, if you *had* done so, you would not have survived with whole minds."

Pasgen and Rhoslyn looked at each other. Had she bargained to save their minds or to keep them for herself? Could they believe her about anything? She had told them how, desperate to have a child, she had forced three mages to work a terrible magic involving the death of several mortals to force enhanced virility onto Kefni Deulwyn Siarl Silverhair and fecundity upon herself, then laid an enchantment on him that drew him to her bed despite the fact that he had a life-mate.

On the one hand, they knew she could be selfish and weak, totally without loyalty or gratitude. She never for a moment regretted the deaths of the mortals although they had been faithful servants; she cared nothing for the ruination of the young mages, mad and dead after the blood magic they had done. She had obtained what she wanted, a child . . . better, two children. The only thing she regretted was that Kefni, breaking free of her ensorcellment, fled to his true love . . . and made her pregnant too. She had not forgiven him for that. She had wanted a child, but she had wanted Kefni nearly as much. She certainly had not wanted her rival to share in the results of *her* magic.

Then the Unseleighe had taken both sets of twins, and Llanelli blamed Kefni still for having rescued the children of his life-mate first and for having died instead of successfully rescuing *her* children.

Still, on the other hand, both knew that she was utterly, completely devoted to them, without doubt or reservation. She had given up the life she dearly loved in the Bright Court, had given up the light, the laughter, the poetry and art, the dancing and singing—everything that made a Seleighe life sweet—to follow her children into hatred and pain and ugliness. And she had worn away her substance protecting them from the hatred and pain and ugliness, showing them that there was light and laughter and beauty despite what they were surrounded by.

"How?" Pasgen asked, a little less harshly. "How did you find the power to bargain with Vidal?"

Llanelli smiled slightly. "It did not take much power. I laid a death spell on both of you so that you could not be separated from me for more than a stadia or for more than half a candle-mark. The spell wore off eventually, of course, but by then Vidal was taken up with other things."

"But if he had not believed you and took us away, we would have died," Rhoslyn cried, as if she could not believe what their mother had just revealed.

"Yes, but Vidal would not have had you nor the hope of what you might become." She looked proud of herself and her machinations.

"*You* would not have had us either," Pasgen remarked with raised brows.

Llanelli seemed to fade even more, and shrank a little. "I knew that," she whispered. "And in the end, though he did believe me, still he threatened to take you unless I offered him some other hold over you. That was why I agreed to take a token from each of you and give it into his keeping. He suspected me, you see, of trying to escape with you back to some Seleighe dominion, and the tokens would allow him to find you no matter where you were."

"And they still do," Pasgen growled.

His glance at his mother was cold. She wilted still more and Rhoslyn went and put an arm around her, murmuring that she was tired and should go with her maids and rest. At Rhoslyn's gesture, the door their mother had shut behind her when she entered opened. Two pretty maids, one brown-haired the other blond, both with round, rosy cheeks and large blue eyes, stood in the doorway. They were plump and soft-looking, nothing like Rhoslyn's starveling girls, but Pasgen was not deceived by their mortal appearances and did not doubt they were as strong and deadly as the other constructs.

Both maids rushed into the room as soon as the door opened, the blonde murmuring that it was very wrong to shut them out while the other, at Rhoslyn's gesture, lifted Llanelli as if she were a small child and carried her away.

Rhoslyn sighed and turned back toward Pasgen. "She still has power to bespell, and if I put strong enough protections on the constructs to resist her spells they would become no more than wooden automata." She shrugged. "She has been so compliant since you were ill, that I relaxed my vigilance."

"Do not make her unhappy," Pasgen muttered, then, as if he

were ashamed of the soft sentiment, he explained. "She knew we would be deeply worried about how Vidal got the tokens. She knew we would not like the answer to the puzzle, but she confessed anyway to give us peace of mind. Whatever she is, Rhoslyn, she will still sacrifice herself for us. And it *is* a relief to know how Vidal obtained that token and that only one was given."

"But could he have divided it?" Rhoslyn frowned and then coming back toward Pasgen, said, "If you will trust me enough to leave it with me, I will try to call to it everything of like nature."

Pasgen sighed. "I brought it to give to you. I . . . I do not know what power it has over me, if any. When I first took it from the imp, I closed my hand on it . . . and felt I was choking, that I was being closed in. But I had felt no constriction or other ill effect when it was inside the imp, so I wondered if it might have been because I *knew* what I was doing to the token. Will you test it for me, Rhoslyn?"

She did not answer immediately, instead coming to him and putting her arms around his neck in a rare embrace. Even when she spoke it was not to reply to his question. She said, "I love you, brother."

Pasgen raised a hand and drew it gently down her cheek. "And I, you," he murmured. "That we are two, together, against all outsiders . . . makes living possible."

They stood for a moment, and then Pasgen turned slightly away. Rhoslyn released him immediately and began to talk of the practical necessities for the testing. That Pasgen not know what or when the test would occur, but that she have some way of knowing if he reacted though he was nowhere near her. She fell silent, biting her lip, then sent Elyn to fetch two of the small creatures she used to keep watch on her mother.

When she returned, Elyn handed him a little creature like a furry, rainbow-colored snake that began to quiver as it nestled just under his collar. Curled on Rhoslyn's shoulder the small creature's twin also quivered. Pasgen's quieted under his hand, having faithfully registered his slight uneasiness when he contemplated facing Vidal Dhu, and Rhoslyn's also stilled.

Rhoslyn nodded; the creatures faithfully reflected one another, and Pasgen's reflected what *his* current state was. They agreed that she would do no testing while he was in Vidal's presence, but might before others, who would not matter much.

And Pasgen taught her the spell that he had used to catch and hold the imp. Once it was caught, Rhoslyn's girls would be able to extract her token from it and dispose of it.

"I'll go to Vidal now," Pasgen said.

"Save yourself all the Gating," Rhoslyn said and snorted. "You might as well go directly to Caer Mordwyn. Lord of Darkness, when I think of all the trouble you and I have taken to conceal our domains, and all the while he could have found us at any time, I am almost out of patience with Llanelli."

"No," Pasgen replied. "He still does not know where we abide. At least, not yet, and I hope to keep that secret from him still. I will not be quite so circuitous, but I will not give him any direct route to you either. I'll go out to the Unformed land and then Gate to the Goblin Fair. I doubt Vidal will trouble to follow every Gating to the market to try to find you when he already has a more direct way." He paused for a moment and then added. "I wonder why he only used the token now if he has held it since we were babies."

Rhoslyn laughed. "Would you lay odds that he had put it in safekeeping in his own secret place and forgot he had it? And when he was beginning to recover enough to need some occupation, he began to look through his treasures and found the tokens."

Pasgen stared and then laughed also. "You may be right. That sounds very much like what Vidal Dhu might have done." The little creature under his collar quivered again, reacting to his renewed anxiety, then stilled as Pasgen touched Rhoslyn softly on the shoulder.

"Be careful," she whispered, "the weakest-seeming snake has the most virulent poison." And Crinlys of the violet ribbon walked him to the outer door and shut it behind him.

At the edge of Rhoslyn's domain, Pasgen created a small Gate which deposited him near a Gate in an Unformed domain. Pasgen didn't know which domain; it felt as if he had never been in it before, but he resisted pulling in any of the moving mists and simply Gated to Goblin's Fair. He walked quickly through the market to yet another Gate, which he patterned to take him to Caer Mordwyn. Fortunately the terminus was close to the castle and Pasgen did not have to make his way through the half-finished surroundings.

He was a little surprised when he had mounted the black

marble steps and the great doors did not open for him. Was this a sign of Vidal's spite? He raised a hand to blast the doors open and then dropped it. He did not, after all, want to give Vidal any indication of the strength he now had, and if he wanted Vidal to rule the Unseleighe Court again, he must hide the fact that he was now probably stronger than the old prince, even from the old prince himself.

In fact, Pasgen thought, as he went meekly aside to the small door that was used by the mortal servants, if he did not want Oberon demanding that he continue supervision of the Dark Court, he had better make sure the Unseleighe would obey Vidal. So, if he, who had defeated and killed dozens of the strongest of them, seemed overawed by Vidal, bowed to him, obeyed him, the dark Sidhe and the Unseleighe creatures would assume he was afraid and they would be more afraid.

Pasgen walked slowly down the red and black corridor considering his thoughts. Could he swallow his pride and seem to cower before Vidal Dhu? Could he remember to endure the sneers of the dark Sidhe, the filthy tricks of the ogres, witches, and the other spiteful, evil creatures without losing his temper and blasting them into nothing or rendering them incapable of offense in other ways?

The doors of the throne room were also closed and it was quiet behind them. Pasgen listened for a little while, but no burst of shrieks and catcalls assaulted his ears. So, it seemed that Vidal was not holding court and had summoned him to a private meeting. So much the better. A smile curved Pasgen's lips and was immediately suppressed into an expression of (he hoped) acute anxiety. He could much better endure to crawl to Vidal without an audience.

Almost eagerly, Pasgen turned his back on the throne room doors. To the right and left of the entryway, great staircases curved gracefully upward. To the left was the way to the tower of the FarSeers. To the right were private apartments and guest suites. Pasgen was glad he had never been able to stomach Vidal's apartment; he had left it closed and unused and had adopted for himself the guest suite at the very end of the corridor. He did not go that way now, but went to the first, most elaborate door.

Once more the door did not open. Pasgen stood outside it, blinking with surprise. This could not be spite or a desire to

shame him before the others of the Unseleighe Court; this must
be either because Vidal did not know he was there or because
Vidal was not strong enough to open the door by magic. Pasgen took a deep breath. Was it possible that Vidal had not been
restored fully from the poisoning of the iron bolt Henry FitzRoy
had fired at him?

If that were true, if Vidal was so diminished, what should he do?
Must he drive the weakened ruler out and take his place? Pasgen's
teeth set hard. No. He had barely tasted the power that could be
sucked from the Unformed lands and the strange directions in
which that power could lead him. There were so many questions
he had not had time to find answers for because the ogres were
quarreling with the witches or the bane-sidhe were eating the
boggles or some other silly crisis demanded his attention.

He would leave those joys to Vidal. He would even help Vidal
if he seemed to be losing control. He would grovel, pretend
terror . . . No, not that. Thanks to the Powers That Be he would not
need to diminish himself. He had never groveled, never showed
fear, even when he was frozen with it within. He merely needed
to act with respect, perhaps a little more respect than he had
showed Vidal in the past, and accept and obey Vidal's orders.

That settled, he called out, "Prince Vidal, I have come in answer
to your summons."

Now the door jerked open and Vidal Dhu rose slowly from the
thronelike chair in which he had been sitting. Pasgen bowed his
head in greeting, but not before he took a quick look around.
Aurelia, Vidal's consort, was not present. Pasgen was not surprised.
He now understood that Vidal did not want an audience any
more than he did. Vidal wanted to be sure of his domination of
Pasgen before he let even his consort watch their meeting.

Then under his lashes, Pasgen took a good look at the ruler
of the Unseleighe Court. Almost, he lost control of his mouth
and sneered. Vidal's appearance was no more than a weak, flawed
imitation, an imperfect image, reflected in a dark mirror, of High
King Oberon.

Vidal's hair was also black, also slicked back from a deep point
on his forehead, but somehow the hair looked limp and greasy
rather than appearing as a vibrant mane. Vidal's eyes were also
black. Pasgen almost sighed to see the vitality that had been there
so utterly erased. They were just a pair of dull irises surrounded

by slightly bloodshot whites. The memory of Oberon's penetrating, too-keen eyes came back to Pasgen and he banished it quickly, unable to restrain a slight shiver.

That worked out to his advantage, however, because Vidal noticed and puffed himself up to roar, "Shiver you should! But don't think that that will save you. I know. I know what you did. Killing my boggles and ogres! Setting yourself up as prince of Caer Mordwyn! Sitting in my chair—"

Pasgen shook his head, irritated by Vidal's pettiness. "No. I never did that."

Vidal laughed. "Couldn't break the protections on it, could you?"

Pasgen prevented himself from showing any surprise, but he *was* surprised. He had not known there were protections on the chair—it seemed such a childish thing to do that it had never occurred to him. What did it matter who sat in the chair; it was not the black throne that bestowed authority over the creatures of the court. Only a great enough power of magic and will could do that. Pasgen had never sat in Vidal's chair because from the beginning he wanted no sense of permanency about his selection as ruler of Caer Mordwyn. And, truth to tell, he shunned the quasi-throne because the ostentatious bit of furniture had always struck him as pretentious and thus ridiculous. And furthermore, it was an inferior attempt to replicate something like the High King's throne. Pasgen flattered himself with the thought that he never copied anything of anyone's if he could help it.

"No, I could not," Pasgen agreed, willing to flatter Vidal about the chair. "But taking your place was no notion of mine. I was barely out of a sickbed myself. What happened was that King Oberon called me before him and bade me bring your Dark Court to order or he would destroy it."

"Destroy it?" Vidal looked contemptuous. Or tried, at least. "How could he destroy an entire Unseleighe Court?"

"I do not know, Prince Vidal, but I could not argue with High King Oberon." Pasgen shrugged. "He said that whole herds of sheep had been slaughtered and other mischiefs had been perpetrated, and that masses were being sung in several churches preparatory to following the perpetrators back to their homeplace. You can well imagine just how unlikely it is that your lesser creatures would be able to hide their trail from a tracking party of truly angry and determined mortals. That would have meant the discovery of Underhill, and once they knew where to come, hordes of mortals—all armed with steel weapons—would have descended upon us."

Vidal did not answer, only stared back at him, mouth thin with rage. Ogres—or whatever was large enough and numerous enough to slaughter a whole herd of sheep—did not Gate to the mortal world. They used a few natural portals that were part and parcel of Nodes that conducted power between Underhill and the World Above . . . and those could be penetrated as easily by mortals as by those of the Unseleighe Court.

Most of the portals were hidden by barrows and mounds, but anyone who knew where the secret opening was would be able to move right into Underhill—and cold iron did not cause the disruption in these portals that it did in Gates. The Sidhe had magic and fearsome allies, but the mortals were as numerous as ants, and they had iron. Entered into the domains of the Sidhe, they could do damage.

Pasgen shrugged. "King Oberon gave me no choice. He said I *must* prevent further incursions into the mortal world or he would banish me to it stripped of all power. He said also that he would render Caer Mordwyn back into its component mists and disperse those who lived in it so far and wide within Underhill that no two members would ever meet again."

"He takes too much upon himself," Vidal growled.

Pasgen made no direct answer to that since it was obvious that neither he nor any other Sidhe could prevent King Oberon from doing whatever he wanted to do. Instead he said, "I told him the court was no responsibility of mine, but he said he had just made it so and that if there were further incidents that raised talk of powers beyond human ken, or movements to discover from where the plagues came, he would make me suffer for it personally."

A flash of satisfaction passed over Vidal's face; Pasgen saw it although it was masked by a black scowl in another instant. Vidal would do his best, Pasgen knew, to bring Oberon's wrath on him. It was not something Pasgen wanted to dwell on.

He had always *respected* Oberon, whose Thought had once or twice brushed his mind, but having come into personal contact with the High King, he had been awed. No, in his own mind let him be honest. He had been terrified of Oberon. Though the High

King generally confined his attentions to the Seleighe Courts, he never forgot that he was High King over *all* the Sidhe, and still had power over Seleighe and Unseleighe alike.

"Power," Vidal said. "That is what is lacking. I need evil times in the mortal world. I need war and famine. I need grinding sorrow and pain and agonizing death. I need the Inquisition . . ." His eyes brightened with a clear idea and he asked, "Where is Elizabeth?"

"Who?"

"Elizabeth. Princess Elizabeth." Vidal looked at Pasgen with narrowed, suspicious eyes. "Elizabeth. The child we were taking into our keeping when I was struck down." His mouth worked for a moment and he snarled, "We will need to arrange a fitting punishment for Henry FitzRoy, but that can wait until I devise a suitably agonizing death."

Speechless, Pasgen stared blankly at Prince Vidal, absorbing the fact that the once dangerously powerful ruler of Caer Mordwyn had large holes in his memory. Clearly he did not remember what had happened in the then Princess Elizabeth's chamber; Pasgen wondered if Vidal even knew how much time had passed. How had that come about? Had Vidal's servants not enough free will to seek out news? Had those who did have free will, like the healers, been afraid to tell him the truth?

"I suppose your sister has her," Vidal continued. "Rhoslyn has a strong liking for mortal children. But this one is too valuable to leave in her hands. Elizabeth must be taught the beauties and joys of pain. She must be delivered to my care at once."

Carefully Pasgen raised his strongest shields. He was not happy about being the one to break the bad news to Vidal. The prince did have a tendency to execute the messenger.

"Rhoslyn does not have Elizabeth," Pasgen said, deciding that it would be better to be blunt and unambiguous. "The child was never taken. Your plan failed, and we were forced to flee in confusion."

"Not taken!" Vidal roared, taking a threatening step forward. "Liar! My plan worked perfectly. The guards I had bespelled or replaced let us through. We came into the child's chamber—"

"Where Denoriel and his servants were lying in wait for us!" Pasgen spat, bitterness sharpening his voice. "Your perfect plan was an utter disaster. The mortal and the changeling he carried died. The Sidhe who was wounded fighting the mortal guards is also dead. I was wounded both by iron and by elf-shot. You were so near death we all despaired of your survival. And Aurelia . . . I do not know what happened to her, but she was unconscious and could not be roused."

"I do not believe you," Vidal said, but he came no closer; his eyes were haunted, his face drawn.

"Then send someone you trust to the mortal world and have him ask about the Lady Elizabeth. You will learn soon enough that she is alive and well among her mortal kin." He fought to keep his lip from curling. "Or have your Seers scry into the past and show you the disaster so that you can see it with your own two eyes."

Vidal shook his head. "I cannot believe that after all that effort and loss no one had sense enough to snatch up the child. The dead changeling could have been left in its place. The maidservant would have been blamed . . ."

Pasgen shook his head sharply. "No one could touch Elizabeth. Denoriel had put a shield on her that Aurelia could not breach—she was trying to do that when the maid struck her from behind. And even if the shield on Elizabeth could have been broken, no one could touch her with that iron cross on her."

"Cowards! Cowards all." Vidal snarled, his face twisting. "The Gate was right there. I saw you open it. The pain the iron would give would not have lasted long. And we would have had her!"

Pasgen stared him down. "I was in no condition to be snatching a shielded child. I had been wounded twice and was barely conscious—I could scarcely drag myself through the Gate. In fact no one was unhurt except Rhoslyn and the other dark Sidhe, and FitzRoy was standing beside Elizabeth's bed with that device for throwing iron bolts. He was ready to kill us all. He said we had the choice of going through the Gate I had made or dying then. He meant it. And he could have done it, as easily as drawing breath."

"FitzRoy . . ." Vidal subsided, and licked his lips. "Surely there is a way to set a curse on him that—"

"FitzRoy is dead. Long dead." Pasgen seized on that fact with which to pacify Vidal and lead into the next piece of bad news. "FitzRoy died as slowly and as painfully as you could have desired. It was said that his body literally rotted away. They had to wrap him in a sheet of lead to bury him."

Vidal's eyes widened. "He was falling apart? Rotting away? Ahhh."

Vidal paced slowly away from Pasgen, licking his lips again as he contemplated FitzRoy's dissolution. He murmured to himself and nodded his head, walking away and then back and away again, pacing, deep in some pattern of thought.

Now Pasgen was grateful for the hours he had spent, somewhat unwillingly, listening to Rhoslyn talk about events in the mortal world. He himself had very little interest in what happened in the World Above, but to Rhoslyn the fecundity and activity of the mortal world was fascinating. Thus she had maintained her contact with Lady Mary—Princess Mary before Henry had declared her illegitimate—and brought Pasgen news. Pasgen listened because he was fond of Rhoslyn, but he remembered everything because that was how his mind worked.

In the past, the sour-bitter ooze of power that came from the misery of mortals had been as important to Pasgen as it was to all the Unseleighe. It was the power of pain and death that those of the Dark Court used, but in the weakness that Pasgen suffered after his wounding that power had become repugnant. Then, one day out of idleness and boredom he had accompanied Rhoslyn to one of the Unformed domains where she created constructs and had reached out to a curl of mist and breathed it in; it tasted almost too sweet, like overripe berries . . . but the warmth of power had blossomed in him.

He had pursued another wisp, but that had filled mouth and throat with pain. He had been unable to spew it out or take it in; it had been like trying to swallow a barbed chain. He would have choked to death if Rhoslyn had not rushed to him and said a special healing spell, one she had bought at considerable cost for just such a situation. Occasionally, deep in her work, she breathed in some mist and needed the protection.

Pasgen had asked how she told the difference between the sweet-tasting mist and that which could kill. But she knew nothing of the gentle mist and she warned him against experimentation. At first, head and chest still sore from his second experience, Pasgen had heeded her, but weakness and boredom had worked on him until he tried again, more cautiously but persistently.

In time he had discovered a fountain of power in the Unformed lands and he had discovered that spells were not necessarily fixed things. Sometimes they could be taken apart and rejoined in new ways. It was not the safest occupation; he had several times nearly been killed by a devouring mist or swallowed up in a spell gone wild, but he was never bored and never without a source of power. He did not need the diversion of mortal activities to ward off ennui, nor did he require the sour-bitter power that drained from their ills anymore.

For the third time Vidal approached Pasgen, but this time he stopped, still smiling. "So FitzRoy is dead, and painfully. Good. I am only sorry I was not well enough to attend his deathbed. And you said . . ." Doubt suddenly marred the pleasure. "You said, long dead. How long?"

Pasgen met the prince's dark eyes. "Over four mortal years."

"Four *years*!" Vidal staggered back and sank down into his elaborate chair.

"You were in great pain, Prince Vidal. I suppose your healers kept you in a trance. And it was a long healing. I was hurt less, but I was near two years abed."

"Four years," Vidal muttered, then sat up straighter. "Well, that is not all bad. It will be all the easier to seize Elizabeth."

Pasgen shook his head, slowly and deliberately. "Much has happened in the World Above. It is no longer worthwhile to seize Elizabeth. She is too old to be brought up in our way of thinking. If she is broken, she will be useless to us, just another mortal slave, and surely we can get plenty of those without bringing the High King's wrath down on us."

"No." Vidal leaned forward, and his eyes which had been unfocused were now sharp. "We must have her or she must die. If she becomes queen, we will starve for power in the Unseleighe Courts."

Pasgen shook his head again. "A mighty labor for no purpose. There is very little chance that Elizabeth will ever be queen. Anne Boleyn succumbed to our magics, and brought about her own disgrace and demise. After Elizabeth's mother was executed, Henry married again and Jane Seymour gave him a living, healthy son. Elizabeth has a legitimate brother now. Edward is the undoubted heir to the throne. And if Edward should fail, Mary is next in line. Once Mary is crowned, she will bring back the pope and the Inquisition. Elizabeth is of the reformed kind. She will doubtless be condemned by the Inquisition and removed without our ever being involved."

Vidal laughed at him. "Timid and lazy, little Pasgen. Again no. I have been to the FarSeers. Even without you and Rhoslyn—I was annoyed when I could not reach either of you for days on end . . ."

The prince paused suggestively, but Pasgen did not respond, only raising his brows inquiringly. Vidal shrugged and continued.

"The FarSeers make out three clear and distinct futures. One is with the boy king." Vidal twisted his mouth. "The future with him is endurable. Let him live or die as fate wills. To meddle with him would surely bring violent retribution from Oberon. And Mary's future is what we all desire. But Elizabeth's future is still in their Seeing. There is no sign that she will be taken by the Inquisition, even if Mary should come to the throne. I want her here in Caer Mordwyn . . . or dead."

"To bring her here would be a grave error, I believe," Pasgen said. "If, as you say, her future is still strong enough and probable enough to bring an image to the FarSeers, the Bright Court will be watching her." He paused, pursed his lips. "I have a feeling that Queen Titania has a special interest in Elizabeth, possibly through my half-brother."

What flashed in Vidal's eyes at the mention of the Queen made Pasgen swallow hard to kill a laugh. Should he encourage the flicker of lust in Vidal? Titania had a streak of wildness, and like many powerful females was attracted by males who were dangerous. If she had one of her temporary fallings-out with Oberon, she might take Vidal—but she would eat the prince whole. Pasgen had to clear his throat to disguise another laugh.

He dropped his eyes and continued hurriedly, "In any case, Prince Vidal, there is no hurry. Two lives stand between Elizabeth and the throne. Get your own news about the mortal world from those you trust. Then . . . we will see."

As soon as he said those last words, Pasgen realized he had made a mistake, but it was too late to recall them. He could only try to look as if he did not realize what he had said.

"*I* will decide. You will obey," Vidal snapped. "Remember you are no longer usurping my place as prince." Then he shrugged. "Well, I suppose after four years a few more weeks cannot matter, and it is true that I had better find a more reliable source than you for information. But I will hold court tomorrow. I expect you and Rhoslyn to be there . . ." He paused, frowned at Pasgen, and asked, "How did you know I wanted you?"

Pasgen raised his brows, seemingly in surprise at the question. "Your imp came and told me."

"Oh, did it? And where is my imp?"

"How should I know? It squeaked out your message and was gone. I thought you snatched it back."

Vidal stared at him but Pasgen just stared back and finally the prince waved dismissively at him. The door was now open again. Rebellion quivered under Pasgen's breastbone, but he stilled it. To teach Vidal his true place would mean that he himself would be trapped as ruler of the Dark Court, perhaps forever, and freedom from Vidal was not worth that particular price. Pasgen turned on his heel, and left.

Chapter 4

Once Denoriel had agreed to deliver a letter from Elizabeth to FitzRoy and bring back his reply, she had become the most amazing piece of mischief. It was hard to believe that he had thought her unapproachable, unemotional, and standoffish. She knew how to use charm with a skill worthy of a woman grown. Denoriel was soon aware that she could bend him this way and that like a willow withy in a high breeze.

And always with a purpose. Charmed, he might be; blinded he was not.

Sometimes Harry's too clear perceptions as a child had made Denoriel sad because he felt the boy had been robbed of the sweet trust that was one of the joys of childhood. On the other hand, Elizabeth's constant testing of him often turned his blood cold. Beneath her warmth and vivacity, there was a part of her that trusted nothing and calculated everything. Oh, he understood this intellectually; she really did not dare to trust anything or anyone, for even at her young age she had seen more falsehood and betrayal than many adults. It was hard to look into those eyes and see, instead of open trust, a closed calculation. And yet, he was drawn to her more and more irresistibly.

She believed in no one, and, perhaps, in nothing. She had begun testing that very first time they met, telling him of her plans for the garden, mixing quite clever suggestions with some that would have produced an ugly clash of colors or scents. Denoriel, who had perforce become quite an expert on gardens while Harry was a child, had approved heartily of the good notions, suggested changes in other plans, and told her outright that the bad ones were ridiculous.

Angrily, Elizabeth had supported her own ideas, saying that if he could not understand a plan just because it was unusual that he could not expect her to favor him. And when he said baldly that stupid was stupid, not unusual, she had burst into tears and claimed that if he loved her as he said he did, he would see that what she wanted was best.

He had almost yielded despite the thrill of horror that passed through him over those last words. She was so small and fragile, so pathetic and seemingly alone in her desire to try something new. Even her devoted governess disapproved of the changes in the garden. And what would be lost if he pleased her? Only a bed or two of inappropriate plantings that could be dug over without real loss.

Denoriel knew it was only the assumption that what she wanted was always best that saved him. He had tried to pacify her, using softer language and explaining carefully about the scents and the flower colors and the types of foliage, but he had continued to deny that what she wanted was best . . . just because she wanted it. And then, just as they were about to part at the door, she had stopped crying, turned her golden eyes up to him, and, with a brilliant smile, asked him to come again *soon*. He was fun to be with, she said. He gave her a good argument—right or wrong.

In fact, it was not until he and Aleneil were near the Gate that would bring them back Underhill that he realized she had been testing him, that she had probably not been interested in changing the garden in the first place. A kind of shiver ran up and down his spine and he suffered the strongest desire to put his long, strong hands around her long, graceful neck and strangle her . . . at the same time that he wanted to make her laugh and kiss her.

Those feelings became more and more familiar over the following year. There was never any trouble about access to Elizabeth, no need for secrecy as there had been when he went to see Harry. Mistress Champernowne invariably greeted him with delight and the servants took him for granted. He had begun cautiously. The second time he came, he came alone. Aleneil did not accompany him because he wanted to see whether he would be admitted on his own; however, as a special passport and an excuse, he brought as a gift a bolt of amber silk that just matched Elizabeth's eyes.

He and his silk were welcomed with joy. He made nothing of the gift. He was a merchant; a ship was in. The cloth reminded him of Lady Elizabeth, and so . . .

Elizabeth had not, as he almost hoped, forgotten what she considered the real purpose of his visit. She had ready a thin parchment, folded small, which she slipped to him while her governess was examining and exclaiming over the bolt of silk. Nonetheless, she quarreled with him again, this time over a contested translation of some French poetry. And she almost convinced him to agree with her again because her ploy was entirely different. Now she was a proud scholar, who might be crushed and lose her taste for learning if she were found at fault.

This time it was his knowledge that she must not be pandered to over languages that saved him; she would need to be fault-lessly fluent if she came to rule. So he appealed to her pride this time; what would others think of her, her learning, and her intelligence, if she presented a flawed translation to them? While she was still blinking from that, he added another argument: if her teachers were thought to have indulged her, they would be taken from her and replaced with others who were harsher. And a third, before she had entirely comprehended the second—she wished to perfectly understand what those around her were say-ing, and if he did not correct her, then she might find herself making flawed assumptions.

Her eyes flashed at that, and he thought that he had rendered her entirely speechless with rage, and wondered if he had over-stepped the bounds this time.

But again, when he thought she was so angry she would turn her back and leave, she suddenly smiled her brilliant smile and begged him to come again, come again soon.

He thought, as he traversed the Gate, that it had been the last argument that had convinced her. The appeal to her pride was one thing, but that she might miss some clue, some hint that could reveal further danger, or assure more safety—that was what had won her. And it was so sad to think that she, so young, so small, *knew* the awful truth that (in the mortal world at least) there was only one person she could absolutely rely on.

Herself.

Denoriel made a mistake in delivering Elizabeth's letter to Harry openly. Mwynwen did not take in good part the idea that Harry should maintain any close association with the mortal world.

"You idiots," she fumed. "Can you imagine what would happen if anyone should see a letter from the duke of Richmond, who has been dead and buried these four years? What clearer betrayal of the existence of Underhill could there be? Oberon would put us all in frozen sleep until the sun grew cold."

"Well, I wasn't going to sign the letter 'Richmond,'" Harry said, but the way his eyes slid away betrayed that without the reminder he might have done so.

"I doubt Princess—no, Lady Elizabeth—will be satisfied with a note signed 'Harry.' It isn't as if she could remember your handwriting. She was only three." Mwynwen rounded on Denoriel, pent-up fury flickering in her eyes. "And you are the ultimate fool Denoriel, to remind the child about her half-brother. Could you not leave her memories alone?"

"I?" Denoriel protested. "I did no such thing! The first thing that little devil said to me when we were private is 'Where is my Da?' Even then I tried to put her off, but she was having none of it. She accused me of lying and said Harry was dead . . ." Denoriel swallowed and said more softly, "But her voice, her face, it was as if the last hope to which she had clung was gone."

"And would that not have been better?" Mwynwen snapped. "To let her grieve and put away that hopeless hope?"

"No!" FitzRoy exclaimed. "No! I will not have my dearling Elizabeth grieving for me when I am hale and well."

"Yes, you are hale and well so long as I draw the elf-shot poison out of you. Harry, you *cannot* go back and live in the mortal world."

FitzRoy stepped closer and put his arm around her. "Go back to the mortal world? Mwynwen, my love, how did you ever get such a mad notion? I haven't the smallest desire to live Overhill. Without the hunts? Without Lady Aeron? Above all else, without you?" He kissed her mouth, softly, tenderly. "It is not because you keep me alive that I remain Underhill. I *love* you, Mwynwen."

Four years was long in mortal time. Fitzroy had entered Underhill as a callow boy. Now he was a man, with a man's emotions, which had grown far past his early dependence on the Healer. He did not lie. If anything, the simple words did not give near enough of truth. And she? She was elven, famed in tale and song for having no hearts. He sighed. "Do you even know what love means?"

She turned to him with distress, and a hint of tears in her voice. "I know that without you my life would be empty. Is that enough?"

"Ah! A time-filler. That's what I am." But FitzRoy laughed as he spoke, pulled her closer, and kissed her again. He was careful, too, to tuck the letter away into one of the wide sleeves of his gown without bothering to read it. Instead he began a conversation with Denoriel about a domain that had brought a new patient to Mwynwen—a Sidhe almost torn apart by tooth and claw.

Through the malfunction of a Gate, the patient had chanced upon a forest like those traders to Afrique had seen or heard of, so lush it was almost impenetrable. Unfortunately for the accidental arrival, the undergrowth was not at all impenetrable to the beasts that had attacked him, though he could not guess whether they had come at him by mischance or deliberate malice.

It made a fine way to deflect Mwynwen from Elizabeth's letter. Should they go look at it, Harry asked, eyes alight? Should they seek out the ruler of the domain and protest the danger to innocent passersby? Just the two of them, or should they form a party? Mwynwen now had something much more immediate to alarm her—the idea that Harry and Denoriel would hare off unaccompanied into a place of danger. Denoriel seemed to understand exactly what Harry was about, and soon alarmed Mwynwen even further by teasingly being enthusiastic about the idea.

Fortunately, before the subject ran dry, Mwynwen was called to attend a patient. FitzRoy and Denoriel left the house hurriedly; Miralys and Lady Aeron were waiting and they mounted and rode away. By silent mutual consent, they begged their elvensteeds to carry them to FitzRoy's favorite place, the tiny domain they called Shepherd's Paradise.

Both often speculated about the maker. They had left a message the second time they came, begging pardon for the intrusion, thanking the owner for devising a place so wondrously peaceful and pleasant and begging permission to come again. But there was no reply to the message and they never met anyone nor was there ever any sign that anyone had been there except them. The sky was always blue with puffy clouds; the grass was always green and lush; the sheep were always placid; the lambs frisked and frolicked and were always friendly.

Shepherd's Paradise had become a haven for them when they wanted to talk, particularly about the mortal world, because Mwynwen did not like to hear about it at all. She seemed to feel that FitzRoy's entire life should be forgotten—as if he had been raised by her as was the changeling Ritchie, who was now buried in FitzRoy's grave. But FitzRoy did not want to forget. He enjoyed many of the memories of his childhood and young manhood and he was very interested in the welfare of the friends he had left behind and in the nation he still loved.

He knew he could not return, and honestly, he did not want to. He was not a child; he knew very well that if anyone ever caught sight of him, and he was recognized, he would be taken at the best for a ghost, and at the worst, for a demon or evil seeming. He also remembered the restrictions under which he had lived, the guardsmen, the constant oversight of his every word and gesture. He knew, too, that if he were alive in England now, or if he could by some miracle reenter the World Above, he would be watched ever more closely, constantly suspected of treason toward his baby half-brother. No one would ever believe that FitzRoy did not want to be king.

And those who wanted power—or the throne—would never give up trying to use him as a pawn in their plots. There would be no peace for him, no freedom, ever.

They dismounted, and Miralys and Lady Aeron moved toward the flock of sheep and began to graze on the ever-lush grass. FitzRoy sank down on a convenient log with a great, curved branch to support a sitter's back and eagerly pulled the letter from his sleeve to read.

"What a child," he breathed, when he had read the letter for the second time. "How can she have remembered that?"

"What?" Denoriel asked, making himself comfortable on another natural-seeming seat.

FitzRoy elaborated. "The whirligig I gave her soon after Anne's . . . death. It would have been in July, I think, and she was no more than two years and ten months old. The toy had a central shaft that could have been taken for a figure and, oh, perhaps ten curved, upright bars that spun and rotated around the central shaft—"

Denoriel grinned suddenly. "I remember that whirligig now. It was worthy of dwarf making, so subtle and complex a toy. I confess I was considerably impressed."

"Well, yes, but you were a good deal older than *three* when you saw it!" Harry laughed. "And do you remember what she said when I gave it to her?"

Denoriel frowned and shook his head but felt no shame. The likelihood was that he had not been with FitzRoy when he gave the toy to Elizabeth.

"At the time she said that it was the perfect toy for her, to remind her of her father at the center of the world and everything and everyone going round and round him. I remember because it made me feel cold inside. As if she knew he had murdered her mother and she must never forget he was the most important and dangerous being in her world. My heart ached for her that day. In the letter she asks if I remember—as if I have forgotten anything about her. She was a light in my soul from the day she was born."

The young man's eyes were bright with remembered joy and Denoriel shook his head. "She and that world are gone from you."

FitzRoy smiled. "I do not regret the world for a moment. Only Elizabeth . . ."

"Do not say it where Mwynwen can hear you—do not even think it near her," Denoriel warned. "She has some power to know what is in another's mind. It is natural to a healer. And she does love you, Harry. She is jealous of Elizabeth."

"A woman cannot be jealous of a child! I love Elizabeth as a daughter or a baby sister." He flushed slightly. "I assure you that is not how I think of Mwynwen."

Denoriel laughed. "I should hope not, as she is old enough to be your great-grandmother ten times over. No, you need not be angry with me. I know you do not think of her that way either, only as a desirable woman. But she is aware of your youth, and that you are a mortal, drawn to mortal things. It would not be the first time that a woman of the Sidhe had lost a mortal lover to a mortal woman. Have you never heard the tale of Tam Lin?" Denoriel shook his head. "You would say her fears are ground-less, but a woman in love can be jealous of anything—specially a Sidhe who is denying her nature."

Harry pursed his lips, and frowned. "She wants me to be Ritchie, but I cannot. I am a man. I think. I reason."

Denoriel shook his head. "Never mind that, Harry. She loves you. You wish to please her. She will gradually come to accept you as you are. And once she believes that you can be a man, a mortal, and still love her and be contented Underhill, she will be satisfied. Meanwhile we can only hope not to make her uneasy by our talk of the mortal world."

Harry closed his eyes briefly, and nodded.

"In the meantime," Denoriel continued, "I have a problem you might be able to help with. Elizabeth's maid, Blanche Parry, ran down to the stable to tell me that a few days ago Elizabeth had wakened in the night crying that something was watching her."

FitzRoy jerked upright. "Something was watching her? The Unseleighe? More than watching? Threatening? You know she could always see the horrid things that evil black prince sent to harm her."

"Vidal?" Denoriel replied, with a lifted brow. "But you shot him with an iron bolt. Surely you told me that. He must be dead."

"Must he? He was armored." FitzRoy sighed. "I saw him fall, that was all. Surely they have healers in the Dark Court."

Denoriel replied skeptically, "Well, I will ask about his fate to be sure, although I know I heard that the Unseleighe Court was running wild and that Oberon had ordered Pasgen—you remem-ber, my half brother—to bring order, lest they lead angry mortals Underhill, seeking revenge. Hmmm. Would Pasgen . . ." He shook his head. "No, he would never hurt a child."

"Would he not?" FitzRoy snapped.

Denoriel thought for a moment and then shook his head. "No, because Rhoslyn would never forgive him."

"She tried to abduct me." FitzRoy's lips were thin.

"But she would not have *harmed* you," Denoriel insisted. "She would have raised you, as Mwynwen raised Richey—ah, perhaps with rather different principles. But once the changeling had died in the mortal world and they believed Richmond was dead . . . Well,

I am glad I stopped her. Life in the Unseleighe Court is not as pleasant as that in the Bright Court."

But that raised a new concern in FitzRoy's mind. "Will they try to seize Elizabeth?"

"I cannot think why Pasgen should want to do so," Denoriel replied. "Simply to take her would truly bring Oberon's wrath down upon him, and unlike you, she is two removes, maybe more, from the throne, especially if King Henry should marry and beget a child again. You might have been the heir. You were the firstborn *son*. Bastard sons have been put on the throne before this; baseborn daughters, never."

FitzRoy shook his head violently. "Not me. I would have fled to Ireland before anyone could put me on a throne. But—they could not know that, could they?"

"No, they could not." Denoriel narrowed his eyes in thought. "And Rhoslyn swore she would make no more changelings, not changelings like Richey, who could really have been mistaken for you. So they cannot hope to substitute a construct for Elizabeth."

"Then why are they watching Elizabeth?"

Denoriel shook his head. "I cannot be sure, but Aleneil says the FarSeeing is unchanged, that it is not settling on one ruler. All three futures manifest, and Elizabeth's is as bright as ever. It might be that there is a party, quiet now because King Henry is alive and well, that will push for Elizabeth to rule if Prince Edward should die. They would be those that profited most from the dissolution of the monasteries and fear a return to Catholic rule under Mary."

"And the Dark Court desires Mary to bring in the Inquisition." FitzRoy shook his head sadly. "I can hardly believe she would do that. She has a sweet nature and was always kind."

"I only know that Aleneil and her 'sisters' see the fires and hear the screams of the dying." Denoriel shivered, as if a shadow had touched him for a moment. "Nevertheless, it is not my part to meddle with Mary. My part is to protect Elizabeth. I will see that Blanche has an air spirit who can fetch me in case of need."

FitzRoy's head came up, like a hound scenting a hare. "If there is a fight, take me."

Denoriel laughed. "Oh, no. Whatever the result of the encounter, I doubt I would long survive it if Mwynwen learned I had taken you. Still, I do not think the purpose of the watcher is to do harm. But I need to be closer to the court than when I watched over you. I fear that Elizabeth will be in more danger from the parties around King Henry, and perhaps from Henry himself, than from Unseleighe enemies. I have been away and lost all my contacts. George Boleyn is dead."

"But most of his friends are still in favor—or are in favor again. Wyatt certainly." FitzRoy thought a moment, hmmming to himself, then nodded. "Go to Norfolk. He is not as powerful as he was because the Seymours are closer to the king than he is now, but he still knows everyone and if he is willing to talk to you . . ."

"Norfolk does not like foreigners," Denoriel objected, making a face.

"Perhaps, but I think that was mostly because he feared I would be king and bent awry by your influence. Now that he is your object, he may think your foreign knowledge is of value." FitzRoy chuckled. "And he will not fear your influence on himself. He will be sure he is far too clever to be trapped by any scheme of yours."

"Which will be perfectly true," Denoriel said, also chuckling, "since my only scheme will be to hear the news, and *that* he will give me to prove his knowledge and influence has not waned significantly."

Pasgen went home after his meeting with Prince Vidal and tried to put it out of his mind. He was not very successful, because a summons for him and for Rhoslyn to attend Vidal's court was deposited in the elegant and empty house in the small domain where he and his sister were supposed to live. He knew that there was no choice; they had to attend to lull Vidal into believing that they were still his shivering pawns.

The court session some days later made it no easier for Pasgen to reestablish his equanimity.

Vidal was at his worst, sneering and condescending, casting little nuisance spells at the dark Sidhe and at some of the Unseleighe beasts. There was a growing mutter of rebellion, snarls, even a few catcalls, and more than once Pasgen felt the glances of the dark Sidhe and the other creatures of the black ways sweep over him. He guessed that if he nodded his head or made a single gesture at Vidal that the would-be Unseleighe prince would soon be dead.

Alas, after that would come "Long live the new prince," and Pasgen had no intention of accepting that role, for the moment he took Vidal's place, the others would begin conspiring against *him*.

Thus he sat quiet, head bowed, although his stomach roiled and his bowels cramped. He even jumped and winced when one of Vidal's little ribbons flew at him. He did not allow it to touch him—that was too dangerous just for verisimilitude—but he made it seem that Vidal had only intended to force him to show fear. After that the rebellious mutters died away. The court knew Pasgen's strength; he had demonstrated it more than once. If he accepted Vidal's insults, they had to believe that Pasgen felt he would have no chance to defeat the Black Prince.

Nothing transpired at the court. Vidal set in motion several projects that Pasgen knew he had been contemplating before the attempt to take Elizabeth, but they had nothing to do with England's royal family. And aside from demonstrating that Pasgen would bow to his rule, Vidal seemed to have had no purpose in summoning him.

For several days after that event, Pasgen pretended it had not taken place. It had gone sorely against his grain not to reply in kind, not to show Vidal how little power he truly had. But after his first fury and frustration had abated, Pasgen realized that sooner or later Vidal would have to demand more of him than meek silence.

Pasgen had no intention of being involved in any of the disgusting amusements Vidal favored and had set in train at the court, but he dared not simply refuse to participate. Then he recalled Vidal's interest in Elizabeth and realized he could use the need to arrange her death or capture to avoid other activities. He had no personal interest in killing or abducting Elizabeth, but he would need to seem to be working toward those goals.

First he would need information with which to pacify Vidal and prove he was obeying him. Pasgen created a tiny Gate where he had built the large one through which they had escaped after the disaster in Hatfield, and sent through it a tiny, malicious atomy of an imp. He fixed Elizabeth's image into its mind and bade it find her. When it returned with the information that her private rooms were the same as those she had had as a child, Pasgen sent it out again with the order to watch and report all her activities and amusements.

The creature, accustomed to being invisible to mortal eyes, would have done her a mischief if it could. However, when it tried to approach to pinch Elizabeth or pull her hair, it encountered something that made it squall in pain and forced it to leap away to avoid further hurt.

The sound was small because the creature was so small, but Elizabeth woke, and seeing it hanging on a far corner of the bed curtains, cried out for Blanche.

Her nursemaid came at once, and within moments, Blanche's actions told Elizabeth that the creature was no nightmare. That Blanche knew it was there was obvious; that she could not see it nor pinpoint its location was equally obvious. Elizabeth, however, saw it clearly, and when Blanche unhooked one of the larger crosses from the necklace she wore, the child was able to point out where the imp was so that Blanche could beat at the bed curtain where it was trying to hide with the iron cross.

Squalling, the imp fled again, out of the bedchamber and into a private parlor, furnished not only with comfortable chairs but with a desk for writing. The remains of a good fire were banked in a substantial hearth, but the comfortable chairs were worn and the desk old and scarred with use. The imp had no understanding of what it saw, but when it fled back to Pasgen again, whimpering and cowed, he was able to take the images from it.

In one way the images came as something of a shock to him. Apparently Elizabeth could see through illusion and her maid could at least sense beings of the Unseleighe. That was a complication, but now that he knew, he believed he could work around it or even make it work to his benefit.

The images of the outer chamber, however, were all what he had wanted. They confirmed Pasgen in his opinion that Elizabeth was of little account in England's royal hierarchy. The room was too shabby to be that of one considered a royal heir. There were no pages, no servants waiting there, regardless of the hour, to run to satisfy royal whims, no esquires waiting to bear messages, no sign of the half-dozen tutors that a royal scion would require.

Nonetheless, since he had already been to the trouble of making the Gate and binding the imp to his service, he sent it back once more with new instructions. It was to avoid Elizabeth herself and her nursemaid. Instead it was to watch all the visitors and to note particularly those who were given personal access to the child.

It reported every day as soon as Elizabeth was in bed and no longer available to visitors, but some two weeks after Blanche had driven it out of Elizabeth's bedchamber it arrived in Pasgen's trap chamber much earlier. The elemental who watched the chamber signaled Pasgen, who Gated to the hidden entrance and released the imp. It was still chittering fearfully and told Pasgen of a Bright Court Sidhe that had very nearly caught it in a net of force. And it had very nearly let itself *be* caught because the Sidhe looked so much like its master.

"Denoriel," Pasgen muttered. "So I guessed rightly that he would be watching the child. Curse him. I thought he was burned out."

After a moment's thought, Pasgen shrugged and broke the binding that forced the imp to obedience. It spat at him and fled. Pasgen shrugged again. There was no point in continuing his surveillance. The "visitors" the imp had shown him over the past two weeks had been exclusively tradesmen, except one messenger from Henry or one of his ministers, who (from the lack of excitement Mistress Champernowne displayed) carried only entirely routine matters.

The only reason Pasgen had kept the imp watching was for some sign that the king was using or planning to use Elizabeth as a diplomatic pawn. If foreign dignitaries had come to look her over, for example, he might have had to consider acting at once. There was no such sign now, though there might be in the future; the child was young, and even a royal bastard could cement an alliance by marriage.

However, he could get political information in other ways less susceptible to detection by Denoriel. For now, it was not important enough to take the chance that Denoriel would again detect the presence of an agent of the Unseleighe Court. In the future he might need to bring Fagildo Otstargi back from his long sojourn in foreign parts.

It was unfortunate that Denoriel now knew the Dark Court's interest in Elizabeth persisted. He would have preferred that his half-brother, who was not nearly so powerless and stupid as Pasgen had believed, think that the girl had been forgotten.

No. Pasgen sighed as he Gated back to his home and workroom. He was falling into the old trap of discounting the cleverness and persistence of the Seleighe Sidhe, thinking them completely given over to dancing and singing and light-hearted love affairs. His mother was like that, or had been until she had followed her kidnapped children into Vidal Dhu's hands, but his father, Kefni Silverhair, might well have been of a different kind.

He closed the door of his workroom behind him, and spell-locked it against intrusion.

Kefni had successfully torn one set of his twins from Unseleighe keeping and would have had the other pair safe away also, had a mortal not been convinced by his priest to seal off Kefni's refuge. Perhaps Kefni could have survived bursting through the iron-guarded entrance to reach his Gate, but he feared the infant twins he carried could not. Pasgen sighed. Kefni was always said to have had more courage and strength than sense.

Well, that was not true of one set of his offspring, and it was wise not to assume it was true of those who still dwelled among the Seleighe. Also, Pasgen told himself, he must never forget that Aleneil was a FarSeer. Whatever the pallid Sidhe in Vidal's tower Saw, she Saw also. And what she Saw, Denoriel knew. Curse Denoriel! From where had he drawn that white lightning with which he struck down Vidal? There was nothing like it even in the most dangerous of the chaos lands.

Power . . . such a great power . . .

But then, Pasgen bit his lip and shook his head. That was too much power. He had sensed Denoriel's pain when he used it. What *he* had found in the chaos lands was better, safer, more easily controlled, less apt to burn the hand that wielded it.

His eyes fixed again on the little bubble of force that held a twisting red mist which curled, coiled, unwound into a thin wisp and then coiled and snapped at the force bubble. It was almost animate. The tiny bit Pasgen had drawn out burned him even before he tried to absorb it. As if it knew. As if it resisted domination or assimilation. Pasgen watched the mist as it knotted into a tight ball with one sharp spike extended. The dull mortal world with its petty strivings for power over the twitterings and scrabblings of other mortals slipped from his thoughts. *This* was real power, and the only power worth having.

Chapter 5

Pasgen never did tame the red mist, but his attempts diverted him so completely from mortal affairs that when, months later, Vidal summoned him (Pasgen was relieved that the summons came through the empty house) he did not associate the summons with affairs in the mortal world. He had already sent word to Vidal that the Lady Elizabeth was of no account, but that he was watching her nevertheless, and he had heard nothing.

Vidal did demand that he and Rhoslyn attend the court periodically, and his purpose was clear—to prove himself superior to the twins. This seemed like just another such summons.

In one way the summons were useful because they marked the progress of Vidal's and Aurelia's continued recovery, and gave Pasgen a useful way to gauge their abilities without actually testing them. At first the stinging insects and tangling ribbons that Vidal had cast at him and Rhoslyn could be brushed away with a thought.

Pasgen had to remember to wince—and to remind Rhoslyn to wince—as if they had been startled, so that the court, in particular the other Sidhe, would think that the spells had missed them apurpose. The idea was to leave the others with the impression that Vidal was strong enough that the mere threat of punishment was enough to bring Pasgen to heel.

At the last summoning, however, the thought had not been

enough to deflect the spell completely. Rhoslyn had been touched by a stinging spark, had hissed with rage, and lifted a hand to send it back three-fold. Pasgen had barely been in time to stop her because he had noticed that Aurelia was no longer sitting beside Vidal like a stuffed toy. She still did not move or speak, but there was now a gleam in her eyes that hinted some, at least, of the force of that spell had come from her.

Another matter to consider. If Vidal and Aurelia had learned how to blend their power as he and Rhoslyn could, that might be trouble. Such blended power could be too much to counter even for him if they both continued to gain strength, and it would surely be dangerous for Rhoslyn if she were alone.

Of course there was a little matter of personalities; neither Vidal nor Aurelia was of a sharing kind . . . but still, now that they were regaining their strength, it behooved him more than ever to attend the court and measure just how strong they had become.

He met Rhoslyn at the empty house—which was not really empty, just empty of them. It was quite an elegant place, modeled on a Roman domus of the classical period. The only break in its outer facade of pure white marble was a single door, guarded by a bronze gate and a burly construct. The door opened into a narrow hallway through which one could see a handsome atrium. The square area, open to the sky and centered on a pool where golden fish swam amid exquisite water lilies, was paved in marble veined with blue and green.

On the opposite side of the atrium, the door to the tablinium stood open. Unlike the tablinium of a true Roman domus, this one did not hold any bed. There were several low tables accompanied by large cushions and three-legged stools, and the opposite wall was a huge window containing a door that opened into the back garden.

Wings to either side of the tablinium held doors opening into rooms furnished as bedchambers. Occasionally those rooms had been occupied by guests, and the sitting rooms and libraries opposite—on the same side as the entrance—had been used as well, and bore the faint traces of the auras of those who had passed through the doors. Not enough to identify anyone, but enough to show that the house was not merely a show place. But the main purpose of the house was so that Vidal or anyone else who wished to communicate with Pasgen or Rhoslyn would have a place to send messages.

The almost mindless constructs that accepted such messages for Pasgen (male) and Rhoslyn (female) had no other function than to be bound mentally to far more intelligent servants in Pasgen's and Rhoslyn's private domains. The bonds were one-way and any touch on them shattered them immediately.

The other purpose of the empty house was that Torgen and Talog were stabled there, and beyond the stable was a park where the not-horses could graze if they chose (although they preferred to hunt and eat flesh, as if they were descended from the ancient dire-wolves) and where at least a dozen Gates were sited. Every Gate had termini at Caer Mordwyn and all three of the great markets. None could be used to reach Pasgen's or Rhoslyn's domains. The two empty places for patterning were sometimes spelled for a guest's convenience; otherwise they remained blank.

Rhoslyn sighed when she saw Pasgen coming toward her on the garden path. "If you hadn't insisted I come, I would have sent a message with an excuse," she said testily.

"I might need you," Pasgen replied, and then, in response to her wide-eyed expression of surprise, added, "It occurred to me, unpleasantly, that Vidal has grown stronger each time he called a court, and the last time his spell was strong enough that I could not divert it without counterspelling. And then I noticed that Aurelia was watching more keenly than she has watched anything since they reappeared."

"You think it was *her* spell?"

"Her spell?" Pasgen looked blank and then blinked. "I had not thought of that at all, but you could be right, of course. She has looked so much like an image rather than a creature with life and sense that I never thought of it. But she was strong before whatever happened at Hatfield. What I thought was that out of need they had learned to join."

"Join," Rhoslyn repeated, and shivered. "That would be bad."

"Yes, but good or bad we must know what to expect."

To that, Rhoslyn only nodded and looked ahead to where the servants, alerted by feeling the presence of their masters, were leading the not-horses. Rhoslyn mounted Talog without difficulty. Pasgen had more trouble. He had not ridden Torgen at all in the two years he had been ill, and he did not ride very often now because he spent so much time in his workrooms. Even when he was out hunting mists in the Unformed lands, he often did not take Torgen because he only needed to go a few feet from the Gate.

Once the not-horses were under control, Rhoslyn and Pasgen went to the nearest Gate—a fantastic structure designed to look like a gaping mouth with far too many fanged teeth—which was large enough for the two not-horses abreast. They thought of Caer Mordwyn, Pasgen set the Gate spell in motion, and they rode into the fanged mouth, and instantly out of a shadowy structure that might have been a bit of dead woodland with great trunks, stripped of bark, leaning against one another, or a very large and rather ruinous barn. It was not enough of one or the other to be readily identified, but the first thing that sprang to mind was that the work of creating it was second-rate and sloppy.

Pasgen snorted and even Rhoslyn looked dissatisfied. Despite their differences about what was beautiful, neither tolerated shabby or careless work. However, neither spoke. This was Vidal's domain and the careless, unfinished-looking surroundings might house prying eyes and listening ears. Certainly the Gate that at one time had terminated very near the castle, now had released them at what looked like the border of the domain.

"The horses will have a nice run," Pasgen said.

"That was what I hoped. I have been away and Talog needs exercise."

Rhoslyn grinned and picked up the pace so that they arrived at the black gate of the palace at a near gallop. Indeed, they were coming so fast that Pasgen had to circle Torgen before he could slow him enough to pass through. And that left the not-horse in such a fury that he savaged the first servant who came to take him, leaving the long, thin newtlike thing mewling, with its face torn open and its bowels oozing onto the cobblestones of the courtyard.

"Tsk," Rhoslyn said, gesturing first at the servant, who dissipated into mist, and then at Torgen, who ceased from plunging to the end of the rein that Pasgen had dropped and appeared fixed immovably to the ground. "That will be enough temper for one day, I think."

Both not-horses now allowed themselves to be led away and Pasgen and Rhoslyn joined the gathering throng of dark Sidhe, boggles, bane-sidhe, red-caps, trolls, ogres, phookas, and other creatures who were mounting the black marble stair to the entrance of Caer Mordwyn. Faintly a cry came from beyond the great open doors. The twins glanced at each other.

"Shields?" Rhoslyn murmured.

"Ready," Pasgen replied.

Inside, the unrelieved black of the external palace was brightened, if not much lightened, by red marble veined with gold. The floors, too, had golden lines snaking curvaceously across their width. Rhoslyn frowned, not recalling whether the floor had always been so enhanced, just as a rather small ogre tripped over one of those curving lines, fell to the ground and began to shriek as something in the floor rose up to pierce him.

Whatever it was did not hold him long, for a moment later the ogre jumped up, wailing. The experience had not been fatal—seemingly Vidal did not wish to diminish his court further, perhaps because he had finally realized that during his illness many had slipped out of his control and not returned. However, the little ogre seemed shrunken in size and could only stagger forward with a stain of dark blood trailing from his belly. Pasgen's and Rhoslyn's glance met; doubtless this was a new way for Vidal to suck power from his subjects.

Pasgen's hand closed on Rhoslyn's arm and she felt the tingle of a shield sliding over her. It was just as well, in being careful to avoid another trap on the floor they came too close to one of the pillars, which lashed out at them with red ribbons that had been invisible against the red marble. The ribbons shriveled on touching Pasgen's shield, but others were not so fortunate. The twins heard grunts and cries from those both before and behind.

As they took their places in the front row of the throne room, Pasgen sighed. Vidal *was* growing stronger. He looked alert and mildly dissatisfied over someone or something that had not yet arrived. Aurelia, beside him, was actually smiling. Pasgen pushed a little more power into the shield and tried to watch all around him for the next attack without seeming to do so.

Thus Pasgen was taken completely by surprise when Vidal said, "I visited the FarSeers' tower a few days ago. Tell me, Lord Pasgen, why my FarSeers are still having Visions of the reign of Elizabeth. Why has she not been removed, one way or another as I ordered?"

Pasgen almost asked "Who?" as he had asked the first time Vidal had mentioned Elizabeth, but recalled himself in time. He shrugged, gestured indifference.

"I have not forgotten nor intended to disobey your command, Prince Vidal. I have merely been trying to be rid of the girl in a way that cannot be traced to the Unseleighe. Although she has been declared illegitimate, she is still part of the royal family, and Oberon—"

"Oberon is not the ruler of this court!" Vidal roared.

Pasgen shrugged again. "No, but since there is no hurry about being rid of the child, why chance enraging the High King?"

"Oh?" Vidal glowered down at him dangerously. "And how do you know there is no hurry to be rid of Elizabeth? You have not been near the FarSeers' tower."

"The matter is clear without FarSeeing," Pasgen retorted. "Whatever the FarSeers envision for the future, the girl is of no importance *now*, and as the young prince grows and thrives she becomes steadily less important. At this time she still has guards and a household, but those have been reduced greatly over the years, and it is most likely that when the prince comes to the throne and is betrothed or even wedded, she will become more of a nuisance than an asset. I thought it well worthwhile to wait until she is left unattended most of the time. Then an 'accident' could be easily arranged at a time when no one is likely to question being rid of an inconvenient burden."

"Not unreasonable, my lord," Aurelia said, shocking Pasgen as she spoke. Her hand rose uncertainly toward her temple and then dropped. "I can see no reason to call Oberon's attention to us."

Pasgen hid his surprise as best he could, but he would have been less surprised, and certainly less dismayed, if one of Vidal's statues stood up and spoke the same words. So. Aurelia was back in her right mind. How long had she been feigning feeble-mindedness? What had she noticed?

Vidal snorted, but said to Pasgen, "Very well, but see that the accident is arranged in no long time." He then turned his eyes to Rhoslyn and asked, "And what have you to tell me of *your* charge?"

Rhoslyn sighed, her relief obvious. "Lady Mary goes on much as before. She worships by the old rite as much as she can in secret. She has asked the Imperial ambassador, Chapuys, to obtain a secret pardon from the pope for her for having accepted her father as supreme head of the English Church and for going to worship where his rites were used. There can be no doubt that if she comes to the throne, she will restore the pope, the old rites, the opportunity for abuses such as the indulgences, and everything as it was in her mother's lifetime, and all those who oppose this restoration of the old ways will pay for their obstinacy."

Aurelia frowned and asked, "And the people? Will they gladly set aside the reformed religion? If they are willing and eager for the restoration of Catholicism she will have no need to call in the Inquisition."

"She will," Rhoslyn said firmly. "The common folk are mostly just confused, and the older people, at least, are uneasy with this change in what they have always believed, but the younger folk have taken to the new reforms with zeal. And many are very glad to be free of paying what they call 'Peter's pence' and will resist its restoration. Even among the high families that may think with nostalgia of the days when the supreme head of the Church was far away rather than in their laps, most do not want to turn back again. They have profited by the dissolution of the monasteries and convents. They have all gladly taken lands that once belonged to the Church. If the old religion is restored and the monasteries and convents are reestablished, Mary might try to force those families to disgorge what they so greedily swallowed. And there are those who sincerely believe that the old religion was corrupt and that the path to salvation lies in faith rather than good works. True, there may be some who will welcome the return of the old ways, both high and low, but by no means all. No, no. There will be enough resistance."

Vidal nodded sharply, but Aurelia frowned. "We need the power that Mary's Inquisition will bring us. What of the boy who stands between her and the throne?"

Even Vidal shrank slightly away at those words. "No!" he exclaimed, before either Pasgen or Rhoslyn could say anything. "Beseech instead for Edward's health, because if aught befalls that child there will be such investigations into his fate as will uncover the intrusion of a mote of dust—both from King Henry and from King Oberon. Besides, it will be well for us if Edward comes to the throne."

"As well as if Mary rules?"

Vidal pursed his lips and his eyes slid sideways to Aurelia, but he only said, "Different, yet Edward's reign will provide us with power. There will be much misery and no few confiscations and executions. And Mary herself will be watched, which will further embitter her, and make her more apt to the hand of the Inquisition when she comes to power." He pointed at Rhoslyn. "You are specially commanded to take care that no harm comes to Mary. I will not interfere with the prince, since he will serve us well, but Mary is to be guarded carefully and kept in reserve."

"Yes, I agree." There was now a slightly rough timbre to Aurelia's voice; it was no longer as smooth and sweet and poisonous as poppy syrup. "But for how long, my lord? For how long? Mary is mortal, not Sidhe. She is already over twenty years of age and she is sickly—"

"True. True. Which is why–" Vidal turned and pinned Pasgen with his gaze "—I want Elizabeth gone."

"Elizabeth is not the first problem," Rhoslyn said quickly. "Nor even the second nor the third. Mary is very worried because her father is seeking a new bride, and he is seeking a bride among the nations that cleave to the reformed religion. If the king produces another son, Mary's chance of coming to the throne could almost vanish."

She was not certain why Pasgen was reluctant to deal with Elizabeth, but she had sensed her brother's tension. What she suspected was that he could not bear to harm a child, and she resolved immediately to do all she could to help him. A new wife for the king was a good distraction. But Vidal merely shrugged. It was Aurelia who leaned forward with interest.

"A new wife?" She smiled slowly and for a moment she was again almost the vital, glowing creature she had been before whatever had happened to her at Hatfield. "I can take care of that! Just be sure to let me know when the lady is due to arrive and bring me something that belongs to the king."

"You will not bespell the king," Vidal snarled, fear greasing his pallid skin with a sheen of sweat.

"No," Aurelia agreed. "I will cast a spell that repels the king, a spell that will make him hate whoever carries the spell, but the king himself will not be bespelled."

"Ah." Vidal sat back, satisfied. He waved at Rhoslyn and Pasgen.

"You are both to bring me news from the mortal world, and that is to be your prime business." He waved again, dismissal this time. "You may go, both of you. My further business does not concern you."

For a moment Pasgen was so paralyzed with rage he just froze in place. Then Rhoslyn took his arm and tugged at it. With a harsh, indrawn breath Pasgen erupted forward toward Vidal's throne. Vidal half raised a hand. The air tingled with leashed magic. Rhoslyn pulled urgently on her brother's arm, meanwhile casting a silencing spell on him. He almost pulled away. Rhoslyn hissed, "Shields," and dragged him into the aisle. By the time he had reinforced the shields and broken the silencing spell they had reached the outer door, and he no longer needed to be silenced.

He breathed out an angry puff of air and said, "I suppose that was very effective in making me seem afraid of Vidal so I should thank you."

"Yes, you should." Rhoslyn laughed. "You were going to destroy all our careful work for the last half year just because Vidal dismissed you publicly. And what is so funny is that you *don't* want to be involved in whatever business he has with the ogres, and hags, and boggles, and bane-sidhes, do you?"

Pasgen sighed, then also laughed. "No, you are right, I don't. But I don't favor being virtually banished to the mortal world as a news gatherer. Rhoslyn, I have no interest at all in the mortal world any longer. I have found such wonders here, Underhill."

"Yes, I know." Rhoslyn sent out a mental call to the servants to bring their not-horses. "But you would have even less time, much less, if you found yourself again ruler of the Unseleighe. Give Vidal what he wants and then pretend to go traveling or something."

Pasgen seized Torgen's reins from a trembling servant who showed bloody bite marks. He struck the not-horse a tremendous blow on the forehead and mounted, pulling back on the double reins to raise a barbed wheel from the bar across the mouth to stab the upper palate if the creature lunged.

"Now that," Pasgen said, easing the reins as Rhoslyn mounted, "is a *very* good idea."

He was somewhat surprised at Rhoslyn's easy agreement to "giving Vidal what he wants" which meant Elizabeth's death. Part of his reluctance to harm the child was his fear that Rhoslyn would be seriously angry, would cut him off. He rather resented his need for her approval but did recognize it. In the past they had competed more than cooperated, but the shared problem of their mother had brought them closer, and when Oberon had forced him to whip the Unseleighe Court into order, he had become completely estranged from the other dark Sidhe. Now—well, he was interested only in his researches into power and did not often seek companionship, but he needed *some* contact with fellow beings and only Rhoslyn and his mother would respond.

Had Rhoslyn known how Pasgen interpreted her remark, she would have been horrified. She had not been thinking about Elizabeth at all when she said Pasgen should satisfy Vidal. It seemed to her that it was Vidal's order to bring news from the mortal world that had infuriated Pasgen and on their way to the Gate, she pointed out that she could easily take over much of the information-gathering. Also he had already established a persona that would permit him to learn what was necessary with very little effort on his part.

To Pasgen it seemed as if she had simply dismissed Elizabeth from her mind and gone on to a subject she considered more important. He was aware, if not entirely approving, of Rhoslyn's fascination with the mortal world.

"You are quite right," he said. "I was thinking myself that it was time to bring Fagildo Otstargi back from his foreign sojourns and reinsinuate him into court life."

Unfortunately it was already past time. A treaty for the marriage of King Henry and Anne of Cleves was engineered by Thomas Cromwell in October, and the bride arrived in England on New Year's Day 1540.

Pasgen had delayed his "return" to avoid involvement in whatever Aurelia did, but Rhoslyn, who actually introduced Aurelia into Lady Mary's entourage told him that her act was so smooth and innocent no suspicion could possibly have attached to her.

Most of the crowd of ladies who greeted Anne presented her with some small gift of welcome. Aurelia's was a tiny, exquisite scent bottle to be worn on a belt or a bracelet or a necklace. Several of the other ladies handled it and admired it, and Anne attached it to her belt at once. Rhoslyn herself was only minimally aware of a faint aura of distaste, but the king's face changed drastically from willing expectation to dire disappointment as soon as he approached his bride. It could be seen by all that he hated her on sight.

Likely Aurelia's mischief was only the final catastrophe among Cromwell's failures, although once Pasgen began to study current politics in England he realized there were many causes for the minister's fall. All in all he was glad he had not "arrived" yet. Cromwell might have appealed to his old advisor for help, and there would have been nothing Pasgen could do to help him. Pasgen might have arranged for Henry's distaste for Anne to fade, but that would not have saved Cromwell and would have infuriated Aurelia.

Despite FitzRoy's suggestion, Denoriel made no attempt to approach the duke of Norfolk for several months. In that time he assured himself that there were no Unseleighe influences near Elizabeth. He managed to get into every room in Hatfield—using the Don't-see-me spell—to investigate the portions of the palace that were closed off, and he also made excuses and efforts to speak to every person of her household, even the lowest of the servants.

None had the taint of the Unseleighe and he found no lingering echoes of imps or other unsavory creatures either inside the palace or in the grounds; he had been particularly careful in the garden. Finally he had Aleneil bind one of the air spirits to remain near Elizabeth and watch for any shadow of the Dark Court. The one place where Denoriel detected a faint Unseleighe presence was his own house in London, where a strong whiff of imp hit him one day when he opened his clothes press.

He no longer wore any of the clothes. It was far easier for him to create the garments on his body Underhill than to go to the trouble of actually putting on small clothes, hose, slops, shirt, doublet, sleeves, gown, and all the other oddments required. While he had guarded Harry, he had had friends who came to visit him and it was often necessary for him to change his clothing in their presence if they were going to some dinner or other entertainment. At present he had no such visitors and only kept the garments in the wardrobe for verisimilitude.

Scenting imp, he summoned his servants—Low Court Sidhe

who were supposed to have come with him from Hungary and hardly spoke English—and bade them remove and examine every garment for malign spells or substances. Nothing was found. Puzzled, Denoriel cleansed the wardrobe and bade his servants destroy everything in it and order new clothing from his tailor, who had his measurements. He bid one dryad to choose colors and fabrics for three suits, a satyr to make three other choices, a nymph to select sleeves and adornments. :*Tell the tailor,*: he said to them, :*that the clothes I had left here were out of fashion because I had been gone so long.*:

He then Gated hastily to Hatfield, which he entered cloaked in the Don't-see-me spell, and rushed through the rooms and out into the garden. He could find no trace of any Unseleighe intrusion, and grew more puzzled by the moment. What could an imp want in his clothes press? Nothing occurred to him, and he could only assume that the imp had been foiled in whatever it intended by an intrusion by one of his servants.

Having satisfied himself that Elizabeth was safe, he knew he should simply go away. However, since he was already at Hatfield, he yielded to temptation, mounting Miralys just out of sight of Hatfield and riding in for a visit. He received the punishment he deserved in the tepid welcome proffered. Elizabeth and Blanche walked to the garden with him but hardly tried to mask their conviction that he was only finding an excuse when he asked if they had been disturbed by any uncanny presence, while the air spirit was offended by the idea it had been lax in its attention.

Even Kat Champernowne was somewhat less welcoming than usual, commenting that he was a rather more frequent visitor than she expected. Beside that, Elizabeth irritated him further, after he had said farewell, by stopping him from leaving to demand, in a low but angry voice, the response to her letter to Harry.

"I cannot make the ship sail faster," Denoriel snapped. "And if it founders, it will be some months before I know and can send Harry a message to write again."

"Liar," she breathed, so low he almost could not hear. "He is dead."

"What would it profit me to lie to you?" Denoriel grated between his teeth. "I could have said in the beginning that I did not know where he was."

"But that would have gained you less credit with me."

"Credit with you?" Denoriel almost howled, at the last moment bringing his voice down to an outraged whisper so it would not echo past the garden and into the audience chamber. "Why should I want to have credit with you, you noxious brat?"

She laughed aloud at his exasperation, but her eyes were sharp and so bright that Denoriel blinked. "No one else would *dare* call me a noxious brat," she said. "I am the king's daughter."

"And I called the Duke of Richmond 'Harry' even though he was the king's son, although I admit I never called him a noxious brat—but that was because he did not deserve it."

However, this time Elizabeth did not, as she so often did after driving him into a temper, smile and beg him to come again soon. Her eyes darkened and she looked down.

"True enough, my Da was too sweet-tempered to be a noxious brat . . . but *I* am not, and I do not want to see you again until you have his letter. You said months—months have passed. I have enquired how long a voyage to the Indies takes. Yours is overlong." Whereupon she turned on her heel and walked through the gate toward the door of the palace.

Denoriel fought down a strong desire to run after her, although whether to wring her neck or to take her in his arms and comfort her, he did not know. He told himself that if he did not return for several weeks, it would serve her right. She was safe enough with the air spirit and Blanche to watch for Unseleighe intrusion and her guardsmen (who Denoriel had determined had taken her to their hearts as they had taken Harry), to watch for human dangers.

He swore as he walked toward the stable where Miralys waited that he would not be coerced into giving her Harry's letter, which had been waiting in his London house for some weeks, but he sighed as he swore, fearing he would not keep the vow. Ridiculous as it was, because most of the time they were together they only quarreled, he missed her terribly if more than a few days passed between visits.

Elizabeth was so clever, so acute, that she was drawing him into a real interest in political events in England. She said the most outrageous things, betraying a political cynicism that should have been far beyond a child of eight. But few things were beyond her; she was frighteningly precocious. Then again, she had to be. If she were not, she would have been in far more danger.

Nor was Elizabeth only clever in English politics. She was making him into a student of classical times. There, of course, he had a strong advantage because he could learn from Aleneil's fellow FarSeer Rhonwen, who had lived in the glory of Greece and Rome, what had happened and how close they had come to living what they wrote. Thus, the discussions he and Elizabeth had about Greek philosophy and Roman virtue were quite exciting, as he tried to communicate Rhonwen's revelations without exposing how he obtained the information.

Perhaps, he thought, he should just yield, Gate back to Hatfield and give her the letter. He could tell Mistress Champernowne that he had forgotten his gloves and remembered before he was too far to return. Then he was quite annoyed with himself. If he gave her the letter at once, she would know he had been holding it.

He Gated to the London house where he came up from the cellar into the kitchen. The servants hardly glanced at him as he passed them, then he came out into the garden and to the small stable where Miralys, already divested of harness, snorted at him. But he knew he would have to give Elizabeth the letter soon, so he returned to the house, went to his little-used office, and extracted the letter from the locked letter press on his desk. There, biting his lip, he perused it once again. It was signed only "*Da*" and it mostly was a proof that Harry was who he claimed to be by reminiscing about incidents that only Henry FitzRoy could have known.

It was not a perfect device because neither Denoriel nor Harry was certain what a child of not-quite-three would have been able to remember. It was, however, the best they could do. At least, if the letter were discovered, it would not betray the existence of Underhill. It should be meaningless or at worst be assumed to be from one of Anne Boleyn's friends because it related to incidents that took place mostly before the queen was beheaded.

Denoriel had barely begun to reworry that subject when a tap on the door made him slide the letter into the letter press again and call "Come." He knew the tap. It was both polite and brisk and always heralded his mortal man of business, Joseph Clayborne.

"I am glad to catch you momentarily at home, my lord," Clayborne said dryly. "I have seen so little of you since you arrived back in England, that I can only hope you are aware that the king is likely to rid himself of his bride."

Denoriel sighed. He had been reprimanded ... again ... for neglecting his business. He and Joseph had had this mild confrontation before. He had explained—at some length—that he had hired Joseph just so that he would not need to worry about his business. Joseph invariably replied that this was a path to disaster by putting strong temptation into an underling's hands without adequate supervision. Lord Denno, Joseph insisted, should know about his business.

Smiling, Denoriel said, "In fact—good afternoon, Joseph—I am aware."

Master Clayborne frowned slightly, acknowledging the subtle rebuke, then sighed, equally slightly, and said, "Good afternoon, my lord. I am sorry if I offended by not greeting you, but I have this fear you are going to slip away from me before I say what I must."

Denoriel laughed and leaned back in his high-backed chair, gesturing Clayborne to take one of the stools on the other side of the table. "Justified, Joseph, justified." The temptation to return to Hatfield washed through him again like a warm wave, but he rose above it and continued blandly, "However, this afternoon I am at your disposal. I would have sought you out myself in a little while."

Clayborne's lips did not twitch, but his eyebrows did. Denoriel grinned.

"No, really," he said. "Tentatively, I have accomplished my first goals. I have, I believe, fixed my interest with Lady Elizabeth and reestablished certain friendships in the country. Now I hope soon to make friends at court."

Clayborne's eyes brightened and he sat up straighter, laying the papers he had carried into the room on the table. "Lady Elizabeth, not the prince?"

"At Prince Edward's present age, it would be a waste of my time and, I suspect, at any time in the future there will be so many seeking the prince's attention that a foreigner like me would receive scant welcome. Lady Elizabeth is easier of access, she remembers me kindly from when she was a babe—a very remarkable child is Lady Elizabeth—she trusts me, and I learn from her governess, Mistress Champernowne, that when the prince is past any danger of taking a childish illness from her, she will be sent to live with him."

"Ah!" Clayborne sounded satisfied and smiled, his tight-lipped accolade of approval. "Access through the back door, as it were. Will the prince like her?"

"I am sure he will be utterly enchanted—as I have been, I am afraid. I will have to arrange for you to meet Lady Elizabeth."

"I would like that, but unfortunately Lady Elizabeth has almost no intercourse with the court at present and there is bound to be some disruption of trade if King Henry sets Anne of Cleves aside." Clayborne shook his head sadly. "Cromwell is lost, I fear, and I can only hope that his fall does not damage the contracts we have made with the Flemish. France and the Empire seem to be at odds again, but it is always useful, my lord, to know how the wind is blowing before it is strong enough to blow us over. If it were possible for you to—ah—renew your friendship with the king's friends . . ."

Denoriel nodded. "That should not be too difficult. I have some books of Italian poetry that should serve as a good reintroduction to Wyatt. But he will only give me court gossip. I think I will need a patron among the older and higher nobility."

"Perfect, my lord, but I do not think you should try to approach the Seymours." Clayborne pursed his lips in thought. "The Earl of Hertford does not like foreigners and is of too serious a disposition—he would not be very sympathetic to a friend of Wyatt's, and his brother . . . I do not know what to tell you, my lord. Thomas Seymour would likely welcome you and your full purse warmly enough, but he is said to use 'friends' and then cast them aside. He is . . . ambitious, my lord."

"It is fortunate that I only seek to make a profit." Denoriel smiled without much mirth, then said, "My cousin, Lady Alana, thought I should try the Duke of Norfolk."

"Lady Alana, is a clever woman . . . wise, too, which attributes sometimes do not go together." After a moment, Clayborne nodded. "The duke of Norfolk, yes. He is not as powerful as he used to be, but he may well be again if the king's interest in Catherine Howard continues to grow."

"Then I had better move quickly. I am sure he will remember me and I recall he was greatly taken with some Turkey carpets I gave him." Denoriel laughed briefly. "He displayed them as a kind of 'payment' for the gift and if I remember correctly we sold quite a few. Hmmm. What do we have in the warehouse that might interest him?"

"I remember the Turkey carpets. Unfortunately we have no rugs at present. However, I do have some Flemish tapestries."

Denoriel would not much have cared if all the warehouse had was Irish wolfhounds or solid gold fool's-bells, so long as the objects served as a proper gift for the duke. "The tapestries will do. Even if Norfolk does not want them, they will be excuse enough for me to request an audience. And I can say I do not have carpets but could obtain them."

"Can you?"

The question was bland, but Denoriel cursed himself for stupidity. Joseph Clayborne had to be clever to manage what at first had seemed to be and now was indeed growing into a complex trading network. Yet Joseph had never seemed to see that Denoriel's servants were rather strange and that his master's arrivals and departures were very peculiar. Denoriel was careful that Miralys was in the stable when Lord Denno arrived, but it was rare that anyone ever saw the horse come down the street with Lord Denno on its back. And the excuse of being a wine fancier must be growing very thin. All too often Lord Denno came up from the cellar without ever having been seen going down into it.

Actually, Denoriel was certain that Joseph knew there was something uncanny about the household and he was certain that Joseph had watched and considered and probably decided there was nothing evil about it. Denoriel wished he could tell Joseph the truth; the business would be even more profitable if he could satisfy strange requests very quickly, without having to pretend that the goods had been shipped from a distant port.

Could he do that, Denoriel wondered, and trust to Joseph's loyalty never to speak of it? Of course, it was forbidden and Oberon would have his hide if Joseph spoke out of turn, but what proof would Joseph have? Surely anyone he told would think him mad. Was that enough protection? Or could Joseph be bespelled not to disclose his master's conversation? He would have to ask Aleneil.

"Yes, I can," Denoriel said in answer to Joseph's question about whether he could procure rugs for the Duke of Norfolk. He smiled.

"And someday I might tell you how I can manage such a thing, but for now we had better stick to the Flemish tapestries. I will write to Norfolk later. I see you have come armed with documents. Tell me about those for which you need my approval. And I pledge you that I will do my best to pay close attention."

Chapter 6

When the imp that had been sent to examine Denoriel's clothing returned, Pasgen was again wrestling with the red mist, which ate anything introduced into its space. Even small amounts of the mist, wisps swallowed by larger creatures, would slowly consume the host from within. Pasgen had twice needed to make an englobing shield large enough to contain a host rapidly disintegrating into red mist and remove the ravenous thing to the domain where he had first found the stuff.

Thus Pasgen did not immediately collect the information the imp had gathered. A few days or a few weeks would make no difference. There was no particular hurry, after all. Whenever he was ready to do it, the girl was dead. This needed no elaborate planning, no army, no changeling substitute. Pasgen had decided he would simply go to Hatfield disguised as Lord Denno, go into the garden with the child, stab her or strangle her, leave her there, and flee.

Lord Denno would be blamed and hunted not only through England but in all other places where England had influence or even simple contact. Even an enemy would not shelter a monster who murdered an innocent eight-year-old girl-child, much less the beast that had slain the king's daughter. So Pasgen would not only have fulfilled Vidal's order, he would also have destroyed any usefulness Denoriel would have in the mortal world. All his "friends" all his "connections" would be lost to the Bright Court.

But there was no hurry. Pasgen continued to work with the red mist as a week passed, wondered why it could not eat the globe of power in which he contained it, began to consider whether the boundaries between the domains were a kind of wall of pure power. He made notes of this information and considered how he could test it.

In the containment room far below, the imp squalled with hunger and diminished in size as it consumed its own substance to remain conscious and coherent. Although he did not wish to, Pasgen heard; he was attuned to the containment room where he held prisoners and subjects of experiments. First he calculated how long the imp could be ignored before it lost the information it had been sent to gather. Then he wondered why he did not simply collect the information and let the imp go. And then, at long last, he understood that he had been delaying because he did not wish to kill a child.

She was not important, he thought. Let her grow to maturity. When she was a woman . . . But the purpose of killing Elizabeth had nothing to do with Elizabeth herself. It had all to do with reestablishing Vidal as prince of Caer Mordwyn. Pasgen sighed, glanced once more at the red mist, and created a Gate that took him to the containment room and winked out of existence as soon as he arrived.

The imp fell silent when Pasgen appeared, quivered a bit as Pasgen extracted from it everything it had seen in Denoriel's clothes press, and disappeared as Pasgen released it from the spell that had bound it to observing Denoriel's clothing and simultaneously sent it out into his domain. There it would return to its usual task of gleaning anything, creature or plant, that faded or died. Thus it would keep Pasgen's property flawless and regain substance.

Rather disturbed by the revelation that killing Elizabeth would not be pleasant and that it was his own reluctance, not his concern for Rhoslyn's feelings, that was deterring his action, Pasgen determined to act and be finished as soon as possible. Reviewing the images of the garments the imp had discovered in Denoriel's clothes press, Pasgen chose what he believed was a sufficiently elegant suit for visiting a princess and created it on his body.

His next act was to create two packets of twenty golden half-crowns, which he dropped into his purse. Scowling at the way the purse now dragged at his belt, Pasgen removed the rolls of gold coins. After a moment's thought, he tucked the bribe into the front of his doublet. Before a mirror, he recreated Denoriel's silver hair, the round ears and round pupils of mortals, set his hat on his head. He shuddered slightly. He did, indeed, appear to be his half-brother.

Pasgen turned away from the mirror and considered his options for entering Hatfield. He could not take the not-horse. Nor could he use the Gate he had created to escape from Elizabeth's apartment when they had tried to abduct her. That Gate would open into her bedchamber if he tried to reawaken it and Denoriel never visited Elizabeth's bedchamber. Neither of those options seemed viable, and he dismissed them.

However, the imp he had sent to watch for visitors had passed along other images, one being the path that led to the main entrance of the palace, now closed, and the branch that led around to the entrance to Elizabeth's wing. He could create a temporary Gate just at the beginning of that side path and walk. His lips thinned a trifle at the thought of the energy he would need to expend to create a new Gate, but then he shrugged. He could renew his strength in almost any Unformed land.

The creation of the Gate went smoothly, although the echo of the energies involved sent the air spirit rushing through the palace and the garden. By the time it actually found the Gate, Pasgen was walking unhurriedly along the path toward the palace. A brief inner survey showed the air spirit a Sidhe; an even briefer outer survey showed a familiar face and figure. The air spirit had no capacity to wonder why a Gate had been created, when its master usually arrived on Miralys. It returned to the vicinity of Elizabeth.

The guards at the gate both smiled and wished Pasgen a good day, calling him Lord Denno. He only nodded in return to the greeting, not certain how Denoriel would respond, but he did not cross the courtyard, which would have taken him close to the stable. He slipped around the far edge of the open space taking any cover he could find, until he was able to reach the door to the great hall of Elizabeth's wing.

No one questioned him; many smiled and would have spoken but he quickly begged pardon and claimed a need for haste. In the audience chamber, real good fortune smiled on him. Mistress Champernowne was giving instructions to one of the grooms, but when she saw Pasgen, although she looked surprised, she came forward with an outstretched hand and a broad smile.

"I am so glad to see you," she cried. "Whatever did Elizabeth say to you to drive you away for so long? She has been weeping over it in secret, although she will not confess. Or was it my fault, saying you were coming too often? I am so sorry, Lord Denno, but we are warned not to allow Lady Elizabeth to become too attached to anyone not appointed by her father."

Pasgen took her hand and kissed it, although he shuddered inwardly at the need to touch a mortal. Still, it was a small price to pay her for supplying so much necessary information. He now knew exactly what to say.

"No, no. Really the fault is mine for taking some umbrage at your kind hint. I am aware that the king's children must be carefully guarded but I was . . . hurt. The fact is that I needed to be away for some time and I took a petty revenge by leaving without a word instead of warning you about my absence. I, too, am sorry and I have brought a little token of peace."

So saying he extracted the rolls of half-crowns from his doublet and pressed them into her hands. She stared, lips parted, as she felt the weight of the coins.

Too much, Pasgen thought. *It seems that Denoriel is not as generous in paying his way as I believed.* Then he realized he need only make this sound like a special bribe and she would accept it.

He leaned forward. "Since Lady Elizabeth still seems to remember our quarrel, perhaps you would send her into the garden where I could talk with her alone?"

"Yes, of course," Kat Champernowne said, looking at the rolls of coins in her hands. "I will make sure she goes to meet you too and doesn't suddenly conceive of a will to be stubborn." And she helped him again, by waving him toward a door he would not have noticed but Denno would surely have known.

Through the door was a well kept but narrow lawn and a short, stone-paved path to a gate. Pasgen went through the gate, closing it behind him, and along the gently curving path that led deeper into the garden. When he was just ahead of a curve that would hide him from the house, he stopped. Two or three steps would take him and the girl out of sight—at least from the garden gate and the windows of the lower floor. If someone was looking out of the windows above, they would be able to see what he was doing, but they would be too far away to help or even summon help before he was gone.

He did not have long to wait before the garden gate opened and a girl-child with bright red hair and an upright carriage came through. Behind her was a maid. Pasgen's lips thinned. He had told that stupid woman that he wanted to speak to Elizabeth alone. He tried to think of a spell that would prevent the maid from following Elizabeth and yet not alarm the child so that she would run away.

Just as the words formed on his lips, he swallowed them back. Was that not the maid that had struck and then damaged Aurelia? If it was, she might be protected, and if the spell failed to take hold, she would cry out and warn Elizabeth. Let the child come closer. He would deal with the maid when it was necessary.

In the event something better happened. The maid looked at Pasgen and then stopped near the gate as the child came forward. Pasgen moved back a few steps and then a few more, until he was sure that he and Elizabeth would be hidden from the house and the maid at the gate. He would have liked to go a bit farther, to where he now saw there was a side path even better concealed, but the child was frowning and she was still not in arm's reach.

"Why are you wearing those strange clothes?" she asked.

Strange clothes? But they had been in Denoriel's clothes press, so he must have worn them. Perhaps not recently, Pasgen realized. And then he noticed that Elizabeth was wearing a very plain gown. Possibly he was overdressed?

"We had quarreled," he said. "I wished to wear my very best to show I was sorry."

She dropped her head a little and did not move forward. Pasgen stopped backing away. Elizabeth looked around at the walk, at a row of bushes that divided the bed of flowers near the path from a bed that fronted another path. She seemed to understand that the bushes would hide them from sight and Pasgen was afraid she would insist on returning to where the maid could see them, but she did not.

Instead she asked sharply, but in a low voice that would not carry, "Where is the letter from my Da?" And she held out an imperious hand.

Taken completely by surprise, Pasgen opened his mouth, closed it. Was Denoriel acting as messenger for a secret correspondence between King Henry and his daughter? That was ridiculous, impossible to believe. Whatever could she mean? Ah. It was not impossible that the child, thinking Denoriel of more influence than he was, had asked him to carry a letter to her father.

"I have no letter from your father," he admitted, "but—"

"I told you—" she began angrily, taking another step toward him—and then blinked and murmured, "My father . . ."

She backed away a step. Pasgen reached out toward her—not too fast. He did not wish to startle her into full flight when he could see she was not ready to run. She was staring at him intently, and then he realized that alarm was growing in her eyes. Pasgen took two quick steps forward, now almost touching her, and an ache began deep in his bones.

"Elizabeth," he said softly but intensely. "Put your cross in its special pouch. You know I cannot bear it."

Somehow what he said had been horribly wrong. The child's eyes widened and just out of his grasp she turned to run, whispering, "You're not my Denno," over her shoulder.

Teeth gritted against a rising agony, Pasgen leapt forward. It would take almost no time for him to break that scrawny little neck. He need only withstand the pain for a moment, he told himself, as he threw an arm around her. But what lanced through his arm was no sharper ache; it was a torment he had never expected, as if his forearm above the wrist had been pierced with a red-hot poker and sparks from it flew up along the arm to his elbow.

He released the child, thrusting her away with his other hand so forcibly that she stumbled forward a step or two and then fell. He had somehow twisted her as he pushed so that she had fallen on her back, and he saw that the black iron cross lay bare on her breast. His arm throbbed in waves of agony and an ugly aura rose from the child, who was fumbling at her side, perhaps to bring out another cross.

"Blanche," she shrieked. "Blanche, come quickly!"

Pasgen hissed, "Silence!" as if it were not already too late—his keen ears could hear hurried footsteps beyond the curve of the path.

Her neck was thin and naked. He would not need to touch the

cross. One squeeze . . . Pasgen forced himself one step forward. Pain drummed in his bones and the injured arm felt as if it would burst open to allow lava to pour out. Another step.

"Blanche!" Elizabeth screamed, trying to slide herself backward.

Her heel was caught in her gown and would not grip the earth. Her hand scrabbling at her belt pulled up the chain of her tiny housewife with its needles and pins and spool of thread and tiny scissors. Scissors! The iron cross had made him let her go. The scissors were also iron.

"If you try to put your hand on me," she quavered, "I will stab you with my scissors. Iron scissors. I will stab you."

The pain—burning in the flesh and lances of agony down his bones—was so intense that Pasgen's vision was blurring. His right arm hung useless at his side, feeling stiff and bloated, the fingers too swollen to bend, and a flower of blue-white agony bloomed just above his wrist.

Scissors. If she stabbed him, if the iron came into contact with his naked flesh, it would be far worse than what the cross had done through the silk of his sleeve. For one moment, Pasgen hesitated. But that this puny mortal girl child should threaten him raised such a flood of fury in him that he took another step toward her, prepared to fling himself atop her and break her neck.

Only a flaming arrow pierced his cheek and suddenly the whole world was afire. And a woman's voice, strong and resonant, was chanting words he did not understand, but they were wrenching at his power, tearing him loose from the world. He heard "Be gone" and screamed, because the backlash from his collapsing Gate, also torn from its anchor, battered at him, bruising his flesh and cracking his bones. A void opened, impenetrable blackness, waking in him terrors he had not known since infancy, and he cried, "Mother!" and saw Llanelli's face, and saw no more.

As she ran toward Elizabeth, Blanche Parry managed to wrench off and throw one of her iron crosses at Pasgen. It struck him on the cheek, raising a red welt, and he staggered back, away from the child. Blanche then unhooked her necklace and waved it over Elizabeth, chanting the strongest spell of exorcism she knew.

Elizabeth was weeping in gasping sobs, struggling to sit up, her eyes almost black with shock. The creature in outdated court clothing no longer looked much like Lord Denno to her. His hair was now gold rather than silver, his eyes were a different color, more gray than clear green although they too were oval-pupilled like a cat's, and his ears were longer and more pointed than dear Denno's. Worse, his whole face was twisted with rage and pain.

"Be gone!" Elizabeth screamed as for one moment more he seemed to strive to throw himself at her, but then he screamed too, and ... vanished ... crying "Mother" as he disappeared.

Blanche threw herself down beside Elizabeth and gathered the child into one arm, still holding the necklace with its many iron crosses high between them and where Pasgen had been.

"My fault. My fault," she breathed, holding Elizabeth tight. "As soon as I saw those clothes—years out of date they were, and all wrong for coming to visit you—I should have known there was something wrong with Lord Denno. I should have taken you back to the house."

Elizabeth took a deep tremulous breath and her shivering began to diminish.

After a few minutes more, Blanche murmured, "I don't feel any bad thing anywhere near now, lovey. Do you think if I help you, you could walk back to the house?"

"Not yet," Elizabeth whispered. "If I go back now, everyone will see that I have been crying and believe that Lord Denno did something wrong. There's an arbor with a bench. Let's go there and sit."

Blanche frowned fiercely. "What do you mean they will believe Lord Denno did something wrong? I *saw* him threaten you!"

As she spoke, Blanche lifted Elizabeth to her feet. The bench was no great distance and, although Blanche was nearly carrying Elizabeth for the first few steps, the child grew stronger and steadier and sat without support when they reached the seat.

After a while, Blanche said, "I cannot believe that Lord Denno tried to hurt you, but I saw it with my own eyes. What could have driven him to do such a thing?"

"It wasn't Denno," Elizabeth whispered, taking Blanche's hand and clinging to it. "He looked like Denno, but his hair was yellow, not white, and somehow ... I don't know ... his face was wrong, not Denno's. And ... and he thought I meant my father when I said 'Da.' Denno would never make that mistake. And he ... he told me to put away my cross ..."

"Told you to put away your cross!" Blanche stared at her with round eyes, but they were eyes full of belief, not disbelief. "No. Lord Denno would never do that. You must be right, lovey. It was someone who wanted us to think he was Lord Denno, so Lord Denno would be blamed—" Blanche's voice stopped abruptly and she folded her lips over what she had been about to say.

"For—" Elizabeth shuddered. "For killing me?"

"More like for stealing you away," Blanche said firmly.

Denoriel had just bid good afternoon to Joseph and drawn from the letter press a particularly thick and creamy sheet of parchment—he thought paper would not be elegant enough for a note to the duke of Norfolk—when the air spirit erupted into the chamber, shrieking, *"Come! Come! Danger! Come! Danger!"*

The creature winked out and Denoriel jumped to his feet. "Miralys," he called silently, "go to the stable in Hatfield. I am coming."

He ran headlong toward the back of the house and into the kitchen. A dryad looked up from some tubers she was scraping, but she said nothing as he careened across the room, through the door, and down the stair that led to the wine cellar. About two-thirds of the way back, he squeezed between two tuns. A pointed finger changed a spot of deeper blackness into an arch of stone, within which was a shield-shaped glimmer. One spot brightened at his mental demand. Denoriel, slightly dizzy with the expenditure of power, stepped forward and was in Elizabeth's bedchamber.

Empty! No scent, no feel of Unseleighe presence. He did not call for Blanche. He could not sense her either so she must be with Elizabeth. That reduced the terror that had almost blanked his mind, and he hurriedly slid out of sight of the door beside a large wardrobe, grateful that no one had been in the room when he stepped through the Gate.

Catching a shuddering breath, Denoriel sent a summoning to the air spirit, which appeared before him, cheerfully bouncing up and down on nothing. Firmly Denoriel subdued a violent desire to catch the little glittering nothing and tear it glitter from glitter. However, to express haste or anger would only muddle the creature further.

Denoriel swallowed hard. "Where is the danger?" he asked quietly.

The air spirit hung quietly for a moment. "None now. You were danger. Try to hurt child. Lady throw cross. Child cry 'Be gone.' Pulled on link. Took me elsewhere. Found you. Came back. Danger gone."

"*I* was the danger? *I* threatened harm to Elizabeth?"

The air spirit did not respond. Denoriel probed gently in its mind, saw himself in clothes he had not worn since he and George Boleyn disported themselves among London's amusements. A chill pervaded him. Only Pasgen looked enough like him, possibly "felt" enough like him, that the air spirit would make a mistake. Blanche would only have seen "him" and thought no more about another visit. Elizabeth? Elizabeth could see through illusion, but Pasgen looked like him without any illusion.

Denoriel shivered. "Gone where? Where did the danger go?"

"Ask child."

"Elizabeth?"

The air spirit bounced acceptance of the name. Surprise, disbelief, anxiety flickered through Denoriel's mind. He knew that Elizabeth could see through illusion, but that she could spell-cast, he could not accept. She was not yet eight years old, for Dannae's sake. He doubted *Treowth* had been able to spell-cast at eight.

"Where is she now?"

"Garden. With lady. Crying."

Crying? Elizabeth? He could not remember seeing Elizabeth cry. She must have been terrified. "Go back to her," Denoriel said to the air spirit, collapsed the Gate behind him, and cast the Don't-see-me spell.

Under its protection, he went to the door and listened. Nothing. Carefully he cracked the door a hair. Nothing immediately visible through the crack. Slowly, slowly, he let the door open—as if it had not been fully closed and was drifting open of its own weight. The room was empty.

With similar precautions he made his way downstairs and through the audience chamber. Softly, carefully, he unlatched the garden door and then watched until the leaves stirred with a breeze. A little push sent the door open and Denoriel slipped out just as Nyle caught the door and began to wiggle the latch.

He left the guard frowning at the door and hurried along the path, finding Blanche and Elizabeth just as Blanche said, "What do you mean they will believe Lord Denno did something wrong? I saw him threaten you," as she helped the child to her feet.

Denoriel shrank back around the curve, hoping Blanche would not sense him or the spell. She could not see through it, but Elizabeth could. He followed carefully, behind the dividing bushes and crouched down when they reached the bench and sat. His lips thinned when he heard Blanche accuse him again, but a moment later he almost threw caution away and leapt out when he heard Elizabeth say "It wasn't Denno." She knew. He could go to her and comfort her. He drew a breath to call her name and clamped his teeth over the impulse.

Fool! He was a fool! Yes, Elizabeth had seen through Pasgen's disguise, had seen the small differences between him and his half-brother. But how would he explain how he just *happened* to appear in Hatfield moments after an attack by a person who looked very, very much like him when he was supposed to be in London waiting for a ship to bring him a letter from Harry.

He was relieved when Blanche accepted Elizabeth's reasoning and agreed that it was not Denno who had offered harm. He was glad that Blanche had fixed on abduction as the worst threat. There was no need for the child to be more frightened; however, Denoriel's own heart clenched with fear. He suspected that Vidal wanted a more permanent solution to the threat of Elizabeth coming to the throne, and from the tension in the maid's body, she, too, feared Elizabeth was meant to die.

Denoriel backed down along the hedge, afraid that either the maid or Elizabeth would sense the storm of rage and fear that was shaking him. How could he protect her? He did not believe he could cast a shield around her as he had done for Harry. Harry never sensed the magic, but Elizabeth might, and might feel confined or suffocated.

He bit his lips and strained to hear, but Elizabeth and Blanche were discussing what to tell Mistress Champernowne. Denoriel gritted his teeth. It had been much easier with Harry, who had known from the beginning that he was a "good fairy," an "elven knight," and was not surprised or frightened when Denoriel did inexplicable things or appeared suddenly in places he should not have been. And Elizabeth—he felt disloyal for the idea, but truth was truth—Elizabeth was far keener of mind than Harry had been.

He could not stay and guard her himself; Blanche would soon sense his presence if he were close indoors, and Elizabeth might see right through the Don't-see-me spell. And he suddenly realized he could not wear the Don't-see-me spell for very long; his knees already felt soft and there was a hollow inner trembling in his body that warned him he would soon need to go Underhill to restore himself.

Underhill. Aleneil. She was welcome in Elizabeth's inner chambers where he was not. Between them he and Aleneil could surely arrange something. Still, he was not displeased when he heard Elizabeth say uncertainly that she should perhaps tell her governess the truth about the attack. That would provide Elizabeth with human guards at least. But after a considerable hesitation Blanche warned her to think about it a little.

"If you tell Mistress Champernowne, she will blame me for allowing you to go off alone with Lord Denno." Blanche sighed. "That would be only just. I deserve to be blamed, but—but another maid would be even less use in feeling the presence of evil. I am better than nothing."

"No!" Elizabeth flung her arms around Blanche and hugged her tight. "No. I will not tell, ever. You are the only one who feels what I see. If not for you, sometimes I would think—" her voice dropped "—think I was mad."

"There is another thing," Blanche said thoughtfully. "You cannot really explain to Mistress Champernowne why you believe the man who attacked you was not Lord Denno. Therefore, she will exclude Lord Denno from those allowed to visit you or, if you insist on seeing him, will surround you with guards. She *must*, Lady Elizabeth. Whoever it was will not again make any of the mistakes that betrayed him this time."

"But—" Elizabeth began and then shook her head.

She had never told even Blanche that Lord Denno was not a man as other men, that he had huge emerald green eyes with the slit pupils of a cat, that his ears were long and pointed, the tips showing through his hair. Thus she could not tell Blanche that the person who attacked her had much thinner and sharper ears and different-colored eyes.

Blanche cocked her head at Elizabeth's expression, but Elizabeth only shook her head; she could not explain, and, after another moment, Blanche sighed and added, "And I . . . forgive me, my lady, but I am not able to guard you as I should. It seems I cannot see clearly enough. I thought that person *was* Lord Denno."

There was a silence while Elizabeth thought about how frightened she had been and how much safer she would be with Gerrit and Nyle or Shaylor and Dickson watching. But then she could never talk to Denno about her Da. The guards had been her half-brother's, and "knew" he was dead. They had never said so, but their expressions . . . She very nearly began to cry again, but she swallowed the ache in her throat and thought about letters.

No, it would not be safe for the guards to see or hear about such an exchange. They knew she was not supposed to receive or send FitzRoy letters . . . Not that she had got any letter yet. Would there ever be a letter? Could a letter just be bait to draw her near? But then why had not that . . . that person held out a letter to her? She would have come close to take it and he would have had her.

She swallowed hard, wondering if that could have been Denno disguised and then disguised again just to seize her? For a moment she clutched Blanche's hand tighter, then relaxed her grip. No, that was silly. Denno *would* have held out a letter to her. That . . . person knew nothing, not even that it was her half-brother she called "Da," not her father.

"I would not want to be surrounded by guards when I am with Lord Denno," Elizabeth said slowly. "Sometimes Denno and I have . . . private things to say to each other. But I do not think whoever that was could hide himself from me again—and you may be sure I will not let even the real Lord Denno come close enough to seize me."

"Clever Lady Elizabeth! That is very wise."

Blanche gently drew her hand from Elizabeth's and the child released it readily. Then the maid took a small cloth from the pouch at her belt and moistened it with rose water from a small flask, also from the pouch. She used it to wipe Elizabeth's face, replaced everything, and tucked a few wisps of Elizabeth's hair more firmly under her headdress.

"There, love," she said, "no one will know you were crying now."

Elizabeth nodded and sighed. "I will have to tell Kat that Denno and I have quarreled again, so she will not wonder why he did not accompany me back to the house and bid her farewell. Let us hope that the real Lord Denno does not come tomorrow with a big smile on his face."

Was that a warning, Denoriel wondered? Had Elizabeth felt his presence and tried to warn him away? No, surely she was just voicing a fear. But he had been thinking about coming the very next day. Aleneil could guard her this afternoon, but what about the night? If he could Gate into her bedchamber, Pasgen could do so also.

Behind the hedge, Denoriel's knees gave way and he knelt, fighting back waves of faintness. He must go Underhill, and soon. And he could not come here tomorrow. If "he" arrived two days in succession, it would wake doubts in Mistress Champernowne. He would talk with Aleneil; perhaps she would know what to do. His head was spinning.

Meanwhile, Blanche carefully brushed Elizabeth's gown and straightened her headdress so there should be no sign of her struggle on the path, and they set off for the palace. Denoriel watched them go, and then forced himself to his feet and made his way out of the garden to the stable, where he dismissed the Don't-see-me spell in a patch of shadow just inside the door.

He stood there, leaning on the wall and breathing hard. Slowly the effects of using too much magic became less acute. He stood up straight. As long as he did not need to cast another spell, he could manage. As soon as he stepped into the light, Ladbroke went to fetch Miralys, who was in the rearmost stall.

"No one saw you ride in, m'lord," he whispered, handing the rein to Denoriel. "And what happened? I felt . . . well, I'm not sure what I felt but it was like a thunderclap."

Denoriel could only hope that no other mortals had been aware of the magical disaster, but Ladbroke had lived Underhill; he might be sensitized to magical events. And it was just as well, Denoriel thought. He had to warn Ladbroke about Pasgen. That was safe enough; Ladbroke and Dunstan remembered living Underhill, but were bespelled never to be able to mention it or magic or spells.

"Blanche drove off an Unseleighe disguised as me," Denoriel said. "I think the thunderclap was the collapse of the Gate he came through."

He didn't dare say that *Elizabeth* had banished her attacker and he was not certain of it; the evidence of air spirits was not always perfectly reliable. As it was, Ladbroke's eyes widened in alarm.

He did not acknowledge in any way what Denoriel had said about the Gate, instead he said, "A person came disguised as you, Lord Denno? My lord . . . My lord, how are we to be able to tell . . ." Miralys shifted, and Ladbroke's eyes were drawn to the elvensteed's head gear, which he could see, but mostly wasn't there. "Miralys?" he whispered.

The elvensteed's mane suddenly turned bright red, lifted into the air as if whipped by a mighty wind, and turned to brown again as it drifted down exactly as it had been.

Ladbroke began to laugh, then breathed out a long sigh. "Yes, it's Miralys. No one could ever make a copy of a horse like this one. You're Lord Denno all right."

"Good man. So, if you see 'Lord Denno' and Miralys is not in the stable or somewhere near, throw a horseshoe at him or try to tap him elsewhere with iron."

"Will do, m'lord. I'll set Tolliver to watching too. He's pretty good friends with the gardeners and suchlike. The lady won't come out of the house but there'll be eyes on her."

"Good! And warn Dunstan too. Lady Elizabeth is not going to tell Mistress Champernowne what happened because she is afraid that will result in Blanche being dismissed and the removal of Lord Denno's name from the accepted visitor's list, so Dunstan must be told. Not the guards, though, or I'll find myself with a steel sword through me."

"You would, too," Ladbroke said, smiling. "It's like Lady Elizabeth is a precious heirloom handed down from the duke of Richmond. She's a lot tarter than His Grace, but they're all mad about her. They really would die for her, and kill for her . . . gladly."

Just as well, Denoriel thought. *Definitely just as well.*

Chapter 7

Very faintly, at an immense distance, Pasgen heard a woman screaming. He tried to remember whether he had trapped a woman in his sealed chamber and why he had done so, but his mind remained blank and the screaming was coming closer. No one had ever escaped from that chamber; thus the screaming woman must be loose in his house.

He tried to open his eyes, and when they seemed glued shut, he tried to raise his hand to wipe at them. It was at that moment that he realized he was in intense pain. He ached all over, as if he had been battered with clubs, and his right arm was exquisitely painful. But not as painful . . . ah . . . now he remembered. Not as painful as when he had tried to seize Elizabeth and her cross had burned him even through the silk sleeve.

Elizabeth? Had it been Elizabeth who destroyed his Gate and hurled him into emptiness? It was her voice that cried "Be gone," but the spell . . . that had been cast in a strong woman's voice. The maid. And the spell had shaken him, yes, but he could have withstood it, had withstood it, until the child had cried "Be gone," and a rush of burning power had torn him free and flung him away . . .

"Hush, Mother, hush. You can see he is breathing and the swelling of his hand is already going down."

That was Rhoslyn's voice. A cool cloth, damp and scented with lemon and verbena dabbed at his eyes, wiped his forehead and cheeks. The screaming had stopped.

Pasgen was beginning to put things together in his mind. That must have been Llanelli screaming. Pasgen felt irritated by his mother's senseless emotionalism—and then suddenly remembered the black void into which he had been falling and the vision of Llanelli's face to which he had clung. He made a tremendous effort, and at last, opened his eyes.

"Pasgen? Are you badly broken anywhere? Must I summon a healer?" Rhoslyn's voice was steady, but her eyes were enormous and her skin was shiny and pallid.

He had clung to the vision of Llanelli and been spewed out by whatever spell had reft him from the mortal world to wherever Llanelli was . . . that would be Rhoslyn's domain. Rhoslyn was caring for their mother. If a healer were summoned, the location of Rhoslyn's domain might be exposed.

"No," he whispered. "I do not need a healer."

"You are black and blue all over," Rhoslyn said, her voice now trembling slightly. "Are you sure nothing is broken? You have no injuries I cannot see? Can you feel pressure anywhere inside you?"

Pasgen closed his eyes again and considered his aches and pains. He hurt comprehensively, but the pain seemed to be on the surface, of flesh and bone. He felt no inner gnawing, no draining of strength as there must have been if he were bleeding inwardly. Actually, he thought, as he again opened his eyes, he felt somewhat stronger than he had when he first became aware.

Tentatively he tried to move one leg, the other. Both responded— not without complaint but without any sharp increase in agony. His left arm also lifted to his will; his right was less responsive, and a hot, red spark of pain lit just above his wrist. He inhaled sharply but realized that what he felt was much diminished from the white-hot agony that had seized on him in the garden at Hatfield Palace.

"I do not need a healer," Pasgen repeated.

"Then I will have one of my girls carry you to bed," Rhoslyn declared, her voice less uncertain. "No," she continued, when he started to lift a hand in protest, "You cannot continue to lie on the floor in the middle of mother's solar."

So it *was* his mother's image that had saved him from being lost in the void. He looked around for Llanelli, but she had disappeared. He sighed. Just as well. He dared not thank her for being his soul anchor because to do that he would have to tell her of the danger he had been in, which would frighten her and make her fuss over him, demanding that he never expose himself again. As if living itself was not in some way or another dangerous. As if living beneath Vidal Dhu's rule was not more dangerous than anything in the World Above!

Dark. Why was it so dark? A sharp pang of fear that he had been hurt worse than he believed ended when his eyes snapped open and he realized he had let his heavy lids fall. The first thing he saw was Crinlys, she of the violet neck ribbon, looking at him as if he were a slab of meat; her spider-leg fingers twitched.

"Bed will do me no good if I am tossed onto it like a sack of wheat," he said with irritation.

Rhoslyn smiled at him. "No, Crinlys will be gentle, I promise." She looked at the starveling construct. "Crinlys, lift my brother and carry him to the bed Lady Llanelli has made ready in the blue room. Gently! Very gently. As gently as if he was a baby bird. He is not to be jostled or bruised."

Crinlys knelt by Pasgen, stared at him for a moment, and just before he could protest her too-avid attention, slid her hands and arms under his body. He was twice or three times her weight, but she lifted him in a slow, smooth motion that caused him no discomfort, nestling his head against her shoulder so he would not need to support it himself.

Eurafal of the orange ribbon was waiting by the bed, Llanelli standing just behind her. Pasgen drew breath to speak, without having the slightest notion of what he would say, but Rhoslyn, who had followed them, took Llanelli's hand and led her out of the room. Before the door closed, he heard his mother demanding that a healer be sent for, but he assumed that Rhoslyn would win that argument.

Somehow the two constructs managed to remove his clothing without causing him much discomfort. Then he might have dozed for a while, although he was only aware of closing his eyes and opening them again. Rhoslyn was seated by the bed.

"What happened?" she asked when she saw he was awake. "You appeared in Mother's parlor and she screamed."

Pasgen blinked twice, aware that he was mostly free of pain.

Cautiously, he stretched. His right arm was still sore and his body felt tender, but did not ache nor threaten to explode in more agony if he moved it. He asked in some surprise if Rhoslyn had taken up healing. She answered composedly that she had not, but that Llanelli knew some healing. Pasgen sighed and looked around, but Llanelli was not in the room.

"We have agreed that Mother will take the night watch," Rhoslyn said. "You will be asleep then and she will not wake you or trouble you with questions. Now, what happened?"

"Lady Elizabeth happened," he said, with weary resignation.

Rhoslyn shrank back into the chair, her eyes wide with horror. "What did you do?" she whispered.

"Nothing," he replied, more than a little irritated at the bald truth of the statement. "I never touched her. No, that's not true. When she turned to run away, I caught at her." He lifted his right arm from the bedclothes; it was still slightly swollen and where he had touched the cross, red blisters stood out on his white skin. "You need not waste any sympathy on Lady Elizabeth. I did her no harm. Rather, it was entirely the opposite."

"She was wearing FitzRoy's cross." Rhoslyn shuddered slightly. "I remember I could come no nearer than an arm's length to him when he was wearing it. And you touched it! But the cross could not have beaten you black and blue."

"No, that happened when they collapsed my Gate. The backlash . . ."

"They? What they?"

"The maid. I don't know her name but she was the one who damaged Aurelia. And . . . somehow Elizabeth helped her."

"Elizabeth?" Rhoslyn stared at him as if she suspected his mind had been damaged as well as his body. "Nonsense. Elizabeth is not quite eight years old, and a mere mortal child."

"Well, the maid was casting a spell. I felt it trying to shake me loose from my grip on the mortal world but I was holding against it until the child cried 'Be gone.' There was a . . . I'm not sure what. An explosion of power, I suppose. And I was flung away, flung into the void . . ." He stopped speaking, his voice not quite steady.

"Into the void?" Rhoslyn's voice had sunk to a whisper. "Such cruelty. Such viciousness. And she only a child."

Pasgen knew he should allow Rhoslyn to go on believing that Elizabeth had deliberately meant to consign him to the horror of fading slowly from life in the void. If Rhoslyn believed that, she would even help him dispose of the girl. But he could not. Something . . . something about the child . . . and Rhoslyn's pain, too, forced him to honesty.

"She did not consign me to the void," he said. "She had named no destination. I do not think she had any intention at all, save to fling me as far away from herself as possible." Having subdued the horrifying memory of that falling into nothingness, Pasgen managed a smile. "Likely she didn't know enough to say 'from whence you came.' But I admit I was as frightened as I have ever been. Like a babe, I called for mother, and the spell caught it and sent me to Llanelli."

Rhoslyn shook her head. "Are you sure it was Elizabeth who tore loose your Gate? It seems . . . She is so very young that I find it hard to believe."

Pasgen was silent, reconsidering what had happened in the garden at Hatfield. He remembered the pain that had made him release Elizabeth, remembered pushing her so she fell, remembered her threatening to stab him with her scissors, remembered his rage, his determination to break her neck. Then some flaming object had struck his cheek. He had heard the woman's voice chanting, had prepared to resist, to speak a counterspell, and a thin, high voice had cried "Be gone," and white lightning seemed to burst from the ground or from Elizabeth herself, and fling him away.

"I do not think," he said slowly, "that what the child did was part of the woman's spell. That had weakened my hold on my Gate and, yes, the command to 'be gone' became part of the spell, but the burst of power that collapsed the Gate and tore me loose from the mortal world . . . I think that was just a burst of panic, which fueled a tremendous release of power. The child is Talented, like her mother . . . ah, and untrained, too, like her mother. Like her mother. Hmm. I wonder . . ."

Rhoslyn narrowed her eyes. "What are you thinking, Pasgen? No one is going to execute an eight-year-old child for adultery or treason."

"Certainly not." Pasgen grinned suddenly. "But such a child might easily be removed from the succession, which would be sufficient for our purposes."

Rhoslyn sighed. "If the FarSeers then See only two futures for England, it will be enough. But as long as the vision of Elizabeth as queen persists . . ." She shook her head. "And I don't see how you will manage it. What could a child say or do that would be serious enough to get her disinherited?"

"About that I am not certain, but it will be easy enough for me to find out." He bit his lower lip in thought. "I said to you some time ago that Fagildo Otstargi should return to England and begin to tell fortunes and give advice again. As soon as my bruises are healed enough not to start gossip about who beat me, I will open Fagildo's house and send my card out to my old clients."

"Will they return after you left them with so little warning many years ago?" Rhoslyn raised a skeptical eyebrow, and Pasgen did not fault her for being skeptical.

He shrugged, slightly, and still felt an ache when he did so. "There is only one I really care about—Sir Thomas Wriothesley, who is now the king's secretary—and he will return both because my advice was very valuable to him and because I put a compulsion on him to favor Otstargi." He nodded. "I will have to forgo—for a while, at least—my hopes of breaking Denoriel's connection with the court." But at least such a move would satisfy Vidal Dhu's command to gather information about the World Above.

"Denoriel? What has he to do with this?"

Pasgen chuckled; even though it had gone wrong, the plan, at least, had been a good one. "I had disguised myself as Lord Denno—the persona he always used when he attached himself to Henry FitzRoy and has resumed to watch Elizabeth. I thought if I abducted her that Denno would be blamed and lose all his usefulness in the mortal world. And if the High King came to hear of it, Denoriel would have much to answer for."

"That was clever," Rhoslyn said almost purring approval. "I am so sorry you did not succeed. It would do our so noble half-brother good to be misspoken and banished."

She had never forgiven Denoriel for, as she believed, murdering the changeling she had created to replace Henry FitzRoy. Sometimes she would still dream of the sweet, loving child and wake up in tears. She remembered that horrible day too well and the unexpected power Denoriel had displayed. Her eyes narrowed.

"Wait, Pasgen. Are you sure that what collapsed your Gate came from within Elizabeth? Could that have been some latent spell that Denoriel attached to her or to some amulet that responded to the maid's spell?"

Pasgen stared at her for a moment, not really seeing her but trying to recall what had happened in those seconds before he had been battered and bruised and flung away. He could not pinpoint the cause of that burst of energy. It had seemed to come from the child, but that would also be true if there had been an amulet concealed about her.

Could an amulet survive such close contact with the iron cross? Pasgen could not answer that question, but he guessed now from Elizabeth's reaction to his suggestion that she cover the cross with the bespelled pouch that Denoriel did not do so. And that meant that Denoriel spent considerable time close to the child and the naked cross. And *that* meant that Denoriel could withstand the effect of cold iron . . . so perhaps he could devise an amulet that could also withstand the effect.

"It is possible," Pasgen said slowly. "It is more reasonable than that an eight-year-old child has such power. And if it is true, it will make dealing with her easier."

"Pasgen! You are not going to attempt to seize her again." Rhoslyn spoke in tones of an order, not a question, and a touch of resentment rose in him. "Do you never learn?"

But she was right, and he knew it, and every aching muscle reinforced it. "No. No. I will not go near the child. I must examine my resources. If Wriothesley has continued his climb in the court, I will have the perfect instrument for being rid of Elizabeth—one way or another."

Denoriel managed to mount without displaying any weakness and to hold himself steady in the saddle as Miralys took him past the palace gate and out into the road. He felt some concern about the effect of Gating when his power was at so low an ebb, but in fact Miralys must have managed the Gate because he was not even aware of the transition, only realizing he had arrived at Elfhame Avalon when the Gate appeared around him.

No one could mistake the glory that was Avalon's Gate. Overhead were the interwoven boughs of eight trees wrought of solid silver, and beneath Miralys's hooves, not marble, but a pavement-mosaic of an eight-pointed star, formed of thousands of pearly seashells, each smaller than the nail of a newborn baby's finger, and each so strong that thousands of years of contact with silver hooves and imperishable boot soles had not dimmed their luster or cracked even one.

The blind masks of all the guards turned toward him. Four featureless polished silver faces regarded him and then turned away; Denoriel knew he had been Seen and accepted and that he was free to go anywhere in Avalon. Just as well, too. Denoriel was a superior swordsman and he kept up his practice, but he knew that any of the guards could have taken him down in a few minutes. They were not automata, however. They were Sidhe who volunteered for this duty, serving for a hundred mortal years while training their replacements.

They were well rewarded, Denoriel knew, and had the intermittent pleasure of fighting periodic incursions of Unseleighe monsters. They had been particularly busy while Vidal was stricken with wounds from the mortal world; the Dark Court had been without governance and many thought if they could find the Gateway that the maidens and effete males of the Bright Court would be at their mercy. They would have learned better . . . except that none of those who passed the Gate had got farther than the Gate itself and its guardians.

If they had tried to come through in an organized force, it might have been different. Four guards, even guards such as these, could be overwhelmed by sheer numbers. But the one thing that the Unseleighe had always been short of was cooperation. It was easier to herd crickets than organize the quarrelsome Unseleighe Sidhe, their minions, and underlings. Only fear of a greater power could force them into a whole, and with Vidal Dhu gone, there had been no one hand to rule them all.

Once out into the silvery light of Avalon, Denoriel began to feel restored. Power . . . Avalon was replete with power and Denoriel's spell sucked it in and filled his channels more quickly than a Sidhe's natural slow absorption. Nonetheless he stayed mounted, allowing Miralys to carry him swiftly across the wide, flower-starred lawn. Often Denoriel would leave Miralys on the lawn to graze for the pleasure of walking among the sweet scents and gentle breezes. Today he only wished to reach Aleneil quickly.

Miralys sensed his hurry. Three huge strides brought them from the Gate to the white wall that was the back of the Academicia. As they approached, part of the wall shimmered open into a dark passage. Miralys approached without hesitation. Denoriel felt the chill tingle of some recognition spell, which also acknowledged them with a breath of welcome and allowed them to pass.

Another wide lawn, this broken here and there by formal beds of flowers. In the distance was a gentle forest of slender birches with silver-white trunks, quivering aspens, and delicate-leaved red maples. Before the wood were white cottages, the farthest to the left Aleneil's home.

Miralys took him right to the door, which opened as he dismounted to show Aleneil, dressed exquisitely as Lady Alana but wearing—Denoriel was grateful to see—her own sweet and comely face.

"What is wrong?" she asked, hurrying out to take his hand. "I felt your exhaustion and anxiety as soon as you passed the Academicia boundaries."

He slid from Miralys's back, and was glad when his knees held steady beneath him. "Pasgen attacked Elizabeth. I believe he tried to kill her."

"No!" Her hand flew to her mouth in horror. "Oh, no. He would not. Pasgen is not a monster. He is Sidhe. He would not harm a child."

Remembering Ladbroke's thunderclap and the air spirit's description of "gone," Denoriel grinned. "Well, he did not harm her. Between Elizabeth and Blanche, they collapsed his Gate and cast him right out of the mortal world."

"Elizabeth? I know Blanche can spell-cast, but she is not strong enough to drive off Pasgen . . ." She blinked, and seemed to realize that he was fairly on his last legs. "Oh, come in and rest, Denno, dear."

She led him through the small entrance with its graceful sword rack and a closed door to the right, a small table flanked by two straight chairs and bearing a crystal dish for tokens and a fluted vase with a few flowers opposite, and an arched opening into the main sitting room to the left. Placing him in his favorite chair, she took a seat at right angles at the end of the settle.

The gentle blues and greens soothed him and the iridescent mother-of-pearl insets were smooth and cool under his fingers. Most of his strength was slowly returning, as if the very air of Underhill could restore him, but he was still quivering with tension, the smile long gone from his face.

And he still thought that Pasgen's intention had been deadly.

"Can you think of a reason why Pasgen should disguise himself as Lord Denno and meet Elizabeth alone in the garden? He brought no changeling to take her place. What could he mean but murder?"

Aleneil shook her head. "I still cannot believe that. There are other things he could have intended. To attempt to abduct her while disguised as you would surely make trouble for you with Oberon as well as in the World Above. The abduction would not even need to succeed. Likely you could clear yourself with the High King, but it would ruin you in the mortal world. And—because we were foolish enough to call ourselves cousins for convenience—might well ruin me also. It would make us persona non grata among the English Court. Think, Denoriel. In every FarSeeing of Elizabeth as queen, you and I stand behind her. What if we were not there?"

The sharp knot of terror Denoriel had been carrying around inside him loosened. Surely Aleneil was right. Abducted was not dead. Elizabeth might be frightened, but she could be rescued. To abduct the daughter of the king would certainly be forbidden by Oberon and Denoriel knew he would easily receive permission to harrow all the Dark domains until she could be found. He almost smiled again, thinking how much he would enjoy a series of raids into Vidal's territory.

Aleneil sensed the easing of his anxiety. "Ah, you never thought of that, did you? But Vidal's FarSeers must get the same images we do. I do not think that Vidal wants to bring Oberon's wrath down on his head by arranging the death of a royal child, but attacks on you and me would certainly not be forbidden."

"No, and I do not care, if they prevent the Dark Court from aiming at Elizabeth, but still . . . No, someone more powerful than Blanche must watch over her, especially for the next week or so. Pasgen is going to be beside himself with rage at being thwarted by a maidservant and a child less than eight years old."

"Which brings me to ask how he was thwarted?" She tilted her head to the side, all curiosity now that her own fears were eased.

"I am not exactly certain," he replied slowly, "but I believe he was overconfident. From what the maid said, he must have copied some of the clothing from my clothes chest in Bucklersbury Street. Blanche said she should have prevented Elizabeth from going with him when she saw the clothes he was wearing. That might have alerted Elizabeth—she is *very* clever—so that she asked him some key questions."

"Key questions?" Aleneil asked sharply.

Denoriel shrugged. "She could have said, for instance, 'Have you seen my Da?' which I am certain Pasgen would have taken to mean her father. No matter what he said—yes or no—would have been wrong because 'Da' has never meant 'father' to Elizabeth. And perhaps if he approached her and her cross hurt him he would have told her to cover it. Then she would have known that the person was not me. Every time I see her I warn her never to put the cross away and not to trust anyone who urges her to do so."

"Even yourself?" Aleneil smiled.

"Most especially myself! I have told her that I have a brother who is mischievous and might lead her into trouble. But Pasgen and I are not identical. I think Elizabeth might see the differences between us if she were warned to look."

"How could a child see the differences if he were disguised as you?" she asked—but then blinked. "Oh, yes, I do remember that as a babe she could see through illusion. Do you think she still can?"

He nodded. "I think so. And I hope so, because she is clever enough never to give away what she sees. Except the time she saw that imp in her bedchamber."

"Yes, that was when you asked me to bespell an air spirit to watch over her." Aleneil frowned. "Why then is it that the air spirit did not give the alarm sooner?"

That, at least, he thought he had worked out. "Because Pasgen is enough like me that it just thought *I* was there. It had no reason to be alarmed until Pasgen began to threaten Elizabeth—which he must have done because then the spirit 'pulled the line to me' and, of course, arrived in London screaming of danger and that I must come at once. By the time I arrived, although I Gated direct into Elizabeth's bedchamber . . ."

His voice faded and he stared past Aleneil's shoulder. "Gated direct," he muttered. "Why was it so easy for me to open a Gate into Elizabeth's bedchamber?"

"Because Pasgen had made a Gate there the night of the battle," Aleneil said, her voice suddenly hard. "That is not a good thing. Having opened a Gate there once, he could do so again . . . Ah!

That was how the imp got into her room. Well. Something must be done about that. The chamber must be watched."

Denoriel had left off smoothing the mother-of-pearl insets in the arms of the chair and was wringing his hands. "What am I to do?" he breathed. "No matter what I said I would not be welcome in Elizabeth's bedchamber and I cannot wear the Don't-see-me spell day and night forever. I—"

She shook her head. "No, of course you cannot wear a spell for any length of time; however, *I* can make myself welcome in Elizabeth's bedchamber without any spells. Do you not remember that I have had an appointment as a maid of honor since Elizabeth was three? I seldom present myself for duty—it is agreed between Kat Champernowne and me that she can call on me if she needs me for some special purpose, but that I will not otherwise burden her household. Nevertheless, I *always* have a good reason for my presence there."

Denoriel nodded. "She is always short of money and most of the other maids of honor need their stipends."

"Exactly. However, if my cousin chooses to redecorate his house in London and I am sensitive to the smell of paint and polish, I believe Kat would allow me to stay at Hatfield until my cousin's house was again endurable." She smiled. "And if my cousin *then* has an incursion of relatives from the country—relatives with a large and noisy family—I will have further reason to stay. Should Kat begin to look askance at the drains on the household purse, my dear, considerate cousin will surely offer compensatory gifts for taking me off his hands."

Denoriel sagged bonelessly into his chair with relief. "Thank you, Aleneil. If you can watch over her, I will try to connect again with the duke of Norfolk. Perhaps he can explain why Elizabeth suddenly seems important to the Dark Court and we will better be able to judge how close a watch must be kept."

"And for how long." Aleneil was silent for a moment and then added, "I will Gate to Hatfield to arrive almost as soon as you left. I want to know *exactly* what happened in the garden . . . Blanche will tell me. We will have to take especial care if Elizabeth is like her mother. Untrained Talent is dangerous."

"It killed Anne," Denoriel muttered. "We must see to it that it proves a boon and not a bane to her daughter."

Chapter 8

Denoriel found it much easier to obtain an interview with the duke of Norfolk than he had expected. His formal note—on the thick, creamy parchment—received a prompt and courteous reply. It was in a secretary's hand, to be sure, but setting a date only a week later, on Tuesday, 25 May as an appointment for a meeting. The reply was no doubt composed by the secretary also, because Denoriel could detect no hint of why the response was so prompt and agreeable.

On the day, Denoriel examined himself carefully in the cheval glass to be sure that the pupils in his eyes were round, that their green was not so brilliant as to arouse unease, that his ears were rounded and low on his skull. His clothing was not sumptuous, the brocade of his doublet, soft violet on gray, subdued under a dark-gray velvet gown, his codpiece very modest, his slops and hose also gray, but lighter, so that the embroidery and clocking in silver barely glittered when he moved. It was also *very* rich, the cloth all silk, and heavy Oriental silk, not French.

Denoriel considered whether he should add jewelry, but in the end, aside from two rings, both on his left hand (where they would not interfere with his grip on the hilt of his silver-alloy sword), added only a single brooch, brilliant with diamonds. He wished Norfolk to know him prosperous, not to believe he was so rich as to be dangerous or ripe for plucking.

He then presented himself to his man of business. Joseph Clayborne examined him carefully and then nodded. "Just enough, I think," he said, "although the brooch might be on the ostentatious side."

Denoriel shrugged. "I can change it, but sometimes His Grace is so wrapped up in his own thoughts that he is a bit slow to notice things."

Joseph pursed his lips and then nodded. "And you're a foreigner, of course, so some bad taste is almost mandatory." He smiled as Denoriel laughed aloud and pointed to a fair-sized package at the end of the table. "There's the tapestry."

Having picked it up, Denoriel frowned. "I think I should not be carrying this myself. You'd better soon hire a footman, Joseph. It is too inconvenient not to have any servant who speaks English."

Clayborne looked at him for a moment then looked away and asked, "Too clever or too stupid?"

"Hmmm." Denoriel was in no doubt that Joseph was asking whether he wanted a man so clever that he would never ask about the peculiarities of his master's and the other servants' behavior or too stupid to notice. "Thank you for making the point. I must give the matter some thought. We had better discuss it when I get back. I wouldn't want to be late."

He was not. Miralys whisked him through the streets and left him just out of sight of Norfolk's house. It was too chancy for Denoriel to leave the elvensteed with Norfolk's ostlers; they would be sure to detect that the bit was missing and the halter loose enough to be thrown off with a toss of Miralys's head. And he could not, as he used to do at Windsor, insist on stabling his horse himself.

Most people walked in London, where the streets were so narrow and clogged that riding was slow and other modes of transport mostly forbidden. So the steward who came to the door to greet Denoriel was not at all surprised to see him afoot. He was a little surprised to see the duke's guest carrying a package, but merely summoned a footman to take it when Denoriel requested that service. And he led Denoriel directly to a well-appointed reception chamber, where considerably to Denoriel's surprise, the duke was already waiting.

He was seated in a handsome carved chair, perhaps just a trifle reminiscent of a throne; however, on the opposite side of the hearth, where a low fire warmed away the lingering coolness of morning, was a second chair. Denoriel did not allow the internal smile he felt to show. The duke wished to awe, but he kept in mind that many of his guests would not take lightly his sitting on a throne while they were offered stools.

Denoriel bowed. The duke gestured him toward the chair. *I have come up in the world*, Denoriel thought, *when I was coming to Harry I doubt he would have offered me so much as a stool. I wonder what he wants.* Denoriel bowed again, murmured something about being honored, and sat down. The footman holding the package waited beside and slightly behind the chair.

Norfolk came directly to the point. "I must admit that I was surprised to receive your application for an audience, Lord Denno. I thought that with your opportunity to influence the throne gone, you would not return."

"Opportunity to influence the throne?" Denoriel repeated trying to look astonished. "But I do not believe I ever spoke a word to King Henry . . . Oh, no, I did that one time when Ormond asked me to play the Lord of Misrule at a Christmas feast."

Norfolk's impatient gesture cut him off. "I meant through Richmond, if he had come to rule."

Denoriel took a sharp breath as if something had hurt him and looked away as if to hide the fact that tears had come to his eyes. Then he shook his head.

"You must believe what you will, Your Grace, but the truth is that I never thought of it." He allowed the corners of his mouth to droop a little, and widened his eyes in melancholy. "Perhaps if my business were failing or I in need, I might have become desperate enough to resort to such a use; one cannot always say 'Oh, but I would never do *that*' until one comes to the extreme, can one?" He shrugged. "But I was successful, rich, and growing richer by the day. My lord, what brought me here was Harry . . . I loved Harry. He was God's consolation for the brother the Turks had murdered."

"Yet you did not return to England when he was dying." Norfolk narrowed his eyes speculatively.

"I did not know!" All he had to do to make the words into a howl of pain was to remember his anguish when he knew Harry had been hit with elf-shot. "I received two letters from His Grace and both were . . . ordinary, giving me news of the kingdom and hoping I was well and that my business was prospering. He never said he was sick. And no one ever told me! Perhaps they thought I knew already; perhaps they simply did not think to tell me."

"Ah."

Denoriel heard a touch of satisfaction in the duke's wordless comment and again had to restrain a smile. So the duke had been angry at him because he had believed Denoriel truly loved Harry and he had been distressed by his lack of concern or judgment when Denoriel did not rush back to Harry's side when the boy began to fail. Actually, that made *him* feel a bit better about Norfolk.

"I do not know whether I would have reached England in time to be with him," Denoriel continued in a more moderate tone, "but I was sailing farther east and my messages were lagging behind me. The letter that told me he was dead did not reach me until I was on my way home. And after that, you are quite correct, Your Grace, I did not want to return to an England that seemed empty to me so I lingered in Spain and Italy and southern France."

Norfolk raised an eyebrow. "But you did return."

"I mourn him still," Denoriel said, gesturing at his subdued clothing, "but I discovered that I missed England itself. In the other lands, somehow I could not put down roots. I kept thinking of my house here in London and my memories of Harry. And when I returned, my roots *were* here. I was at home, in a way I had not been since my own land was lost to me."

"And there was another child in whom you were interested. Not so?" the duke asked shrewdly. "I have heard that you are a frequent visitor to Lady Elizabeth."

Denoriel allowed his face to light and produced a broad smile. "Indeed it is so!" he exclaimed. "If you remember, Harry was besotted with her, and half the time he dragged me with him so that I came to love her too. I cannot say she reminds me of my little brother nor of any of my sisters either, but she is so clever and pretty that I find myself besotted." He nodded at Norfolk. "And by the grace of God, the Lady Elizabeth is so far from the throne that no one could believe I seek that kind of influence through her."

"True enough, and the king is still young enough to breed more sons." Norfolk cleared his throat as if he had said more than

he intended, and added hastily. "You do not need my influence
or permission to continue your attentions to Lady Elizabeth, so
perhaps it is time to come to the business that made you ask for
an audience. What do you seek, Lord Denno?"

"A profit, Your Grace." Denoriel smiled again. "What else does
a merchant seek? I have no great estates, nor concessions from
any crown, and noble blood still requires sustenance and shelter,
so I continue to do as I must. Do you remember years ago when
Harry was, oh, seven years of age perhaps, that I had a shipment
of Turkey carpets? I gifted you with two, I think, and in thanks
you laid those carpets where they would be seen and told any
who asked who had provided them."

Norfolk actually smiled. "Yes, of course I remember. I still
have the carpets and they have worn so well that they scarcely
seem used."

Denoriel bowed slightly from the waist. "I sold several tens
of those carpets, Your Grace, because of your recommendation.
Different patterns and colors, but of the same make. I made a
very good profit. So now I would like to gift you with a fine
Flemish tapestry."

Denoriel gestured the footman forward and bade him unwrap
the package and hold up the tapestry. It was not overly large, a
long rectangle, showing a scantily clad female figure advancing
down a beflowered path toward what seemed to be a glint of
water. The colors were rich, the maiden luscious. Denoriel caught
the glint of acquisitiveness in the duke's eyes before Norfolk burst
out laughing.

"So, you want me to hang that work on my walls and tell
anyone who asks that you gave it to me?"

"Please, Your Grace," he protested, putting a twinkle of humor
in his eyes. "Do *not* say that I *gave* it to you."

Norfolk laughed. "Ah. And what am I to say that it cost
me?"

Denoriel grinned at him. "Whatever you think they might be
willing to pay. There are three other panels that are companions to
this. They would fit excellently well around the windows here—one
on each end and two between. Shall I send them, Your Grace?"

"Why not?" Norfolk tried to sound indifferent, but when
Denoriel began to rise from his chair, he added quickly, "Will
you have some wine?"

He eased back into his seat. "With great pleasure, Your Grace."

The footman had refolded the tapestry and set it on a small table. At Norfolk's signal, he went to fetch the wine.

The moment he was out of the room, Norfolk said, "Did you know that Lady Elizabeth wrote a letter to Queen Anne?"

"No, I did not," Denoriel replied, "but I am not surprised. Lady Elizabeth loves to write letters, and she is very pleased to have a stepmother. She hopes, I think, to be invited to court. Should she not have written?"

"Not to Anne of Cleves."

"But you said the king was young enough still to breed another son . . ." Denoriel covered his lips with his hand. "Ah. I see. I had heard the merest uneasy whisper." He pondered what to say that was politic. "How sad that the greatest king on earth has so little fortune in matters of the heart." There. Proper support for Henry without placing an iota of blame upon the man for what was, after all, largely his own fault for his roving eye.

Denoriel had heard that the king could not abide Anne of Cleves from the first time he laid eyes on her. Now he understood why Norfolk had tried so quickly to change the subject to business after his slip of the tongue about the king being young enough to breed another son. Clearly King Henry had found a new lady more to his taste. So Anne of Cleves would have to be removed.

There was not much Denoriel could do for the poor lady, except for one thing. He raised his brows until they almost touched the fringe of silver hair that crossed his brow. "I hope, Your Grace," he continued, "that no harm will come to Queen Anne. You know there are bonds between the German principalities from where Queen Anne comes and the Low Countries. Should Anne be ill-treated, there might be serious repercussions in trade."

"Is that so, Lord Denno?" Not sarcasm; Norfolk's expression was serious and intent.

"Yes, and the Hanse traders would also not be pleased." He nodded. "Recall where England's wool goes."

Norfolk licked his lips, thoughtfully. "I did not know you were connected with the Hanse. I thought your trade was with the East and southern Europe."

Denoriel laughed gently. "And you think I would have no use for furs or amber? And that the Hanse would have no use for silks and fine wool? I am not partnered with any Hanse merchant, but we trade . . . and we talk."

Norfolk stared at him hard for a long moment, then nodded. "No harm is meant to Queen Anne, I assure you. If she will be agreeable . . . ah . . . every arrangement will be made for her comfort and honor."

Denoriel pursed his lips. "Yet I think I once heard that the king swore he would not again have two living wives?"

"The situation is completely different." A flush rose in Norfolk's usually sallow cheeks and for a moment he would not meet Denoriel's eyes. Then he did meet them, challengingly. "The king now has a son whose legitimacy cannot be questioned. If . . . if another son should be conceived and born . . . if Queen Anne should accept a divorce, no one would dare raise any question."

It was no wonder that Norfolk was a trifle uneasy. He himself had sat as a judge on his niece Anne Boleyn's trial and condemned her to death for a series of adulterous affairs no one believed in—except possibly the king himself because he wanted to believe. Of course there had been no possibility of a clean annulment for Anne Boleyn; clearly the marriage had been consummated. A daughter the image of her father had been born. Besides that, Anne Boleyn would never have meekly accepted that her daughter be named a bastard. And by the time she had been willing to accept a divorce, it had been far, far too late. At that point, Henry would never have offered one.

There had been worse complications with regard to Anne Boleyn. For the king to be able to claim his marriage to Anne Boleyn was illegitimate would imply that his marriage to Catherine *was* legitimate. And the whole structure by which Henry had made himself head of the Church of England would collapse. He could not claim consanguinity, he could not claim infertility, he could only claim adultery, and the adultery of a queen was punishable only by death, not divorce.

The king's pride had been at stake, the king's power had been at stake, and the king's will was being thwarted. No, against those forces, Anne Boleyn had not had a hope; she had to die. Denoriel thrust the memory aside. He could only hope that Anne of Cleves was more amenable to reason. All she had to claim was that the marriage had not been consummated, and it would be annulled. The king would have his divorce.

"No, I am sure no one would have any doubts of the legitimacy of a second son if the king should marry again," Denoriel said softly. "And I will be sure to warn Mistress Champernowne to discourage Lady Elizabeth from any further attempt to correspond with the—present queen."

"That would be wise." Norfolk smiled thinly and added, "Specially as Lady Elizabeth's chances for an invitation to court may be much better soon. There is no need to speak of that just yet, but I hope you will not make yourself a stranger to my house, Lord Denno. You carry interesting news, and perhaps I can give you a hint about this or that which would be of use to Lady Elizabeth's governess."

He rose, and Denoriel rose too, and bowed. "You may be sure I will say nothing until you give me leave, Your Grace. I will see that you have the other three tapestry panels later today or tomorrow. And I thank you most sincerely for your permission to call on you again, and even more gratefully for any advice or information you can offer concerning Lady Elizabeth."

At almost the same moment, Pasgen in the swarthy disguise of Fagildo Otstargi, was also bowing, but in greeting. It had taken him somewhat longer to receive an appointment to meet Sir Thomas Wriothesley than Norfolk had taken to reply to Denoriel. In fact, it had taken the dispatch of an imp with a golden sovereign carrying a renewal of the compulsion spell. The sovereign, left where Wriothesley would be sure to find it, did gain Pasgen an invitation, but only to Sir Thomas's office, not his home. Sir Thomas Wriothesley had gained advancement without his former tame magician's advice, and had grown far more self-confident.

Thus, despite the spell, Sir Thomas did not look particularly welcoming and was, indeed, wondering why he had agreed to see the charlatan. Pasgen realized his subject was further annoyed, when he simply pulled a chair close to the table where Wriothesley sat and sank into it. Sir Thomas opened his mouth, likely, to tell Master Otstargi that he had changed his mind and had no time to give him after all, but Pasgen reinforced his compulsion.

What came out of Wriothesley's mouth then was, "You do not look at all well, Master Otstargi."

"I do not feel at all well, Sir Thomas," Pasgen snapped. "I have been traveling since the eighteenth of last month."

"You have been gone a long time. I suppose you must have come a long way." Curiosity barely tinged the otherwise cold and toneless remark.

"Very long—longer than you could know or understand." Pasgen hardened his voice as well. "But that is irrelevant. I have had things revealed to me which you should be aware of. On the eighteenth of April Thomas Cromwell was made Earl of Essex and on the nineteenth he became lord chamberlain. On each day there was a red flare, followed by a black pall in my glass."

Wriothesley stirred uncomfortably in his seat, but then said, "Whatever you think that means, Master Otstargi, it has nothing to do with me."

Pasgen gave a thin smile. "Yet it was only a few weeks after you and Sir Ralph Sadlier were appointed joint secretaries to the king."

Wriothesley snorted. "You can't have been so very far away if you got news of all of that in time to be here now. And really Master Otstargi, I have no time—"

"I told you I saw these things in my glass, not by any—mundane means." Pasgen's voice had become low and threatening. "Now I see that I am a fool for maintaining this connection with you. But when I saw disaster looming . . ." He shook his head sadly, as if Wriothesley was a fool hardly worth humoring. "Never mind. At least satisfy my curiosity. Not all Seeings are true and I want to know whether this one was correct, and if it is, whether it is also true that you and Sadlier executed several writs of confiscation and reassignment for the lord chamberlain with no other authority than his order."

Now Wriothesley looked startled. Those transactions were a private matter about which none other than those involved should have had information. Pasgen congratulated himself on setting Rhoslyn, in her persona as Rosamund Scot, a friend of Lady Mary, to investigating via the Imperial ambassador's spy network anything about Cromwell's financial transactions.

Rhoslyn had also told Pasgen of the increasing pressure on King Henry to rid himself of Cromwell, who was greatly hated for his harshness in dissolving the monasteries. Cromwell had profited from the dissolutions, yes, but so had many others and the king most of all. Yet it was Cromwell who was associated with the expulsion of the monks and nuns, and Henry, alert to the fact that the confiscation of monastic property was nearly complete, was seeking a way to leave that blame where it was. Most particularly the king wished to be sure the opprobrium did not flood over and stain him.

Cromwell was also connected with the most radical changes in religious practice. Henry had welcomed the impetus Cromwell's reforms had given to his claim to be supreme head of the Church of England. He had made no move to protect Bishop Samson of Chichester when he was imprisoned as a papist nor seemed to object when Cromwell threatened other bishops, but Rhoslyn said that the king must by now be aware of the rising anger against his minister. And Henry was not truly in favor of the Reformed religion; he wanted all the parties in a balance to which he held the key.

Rhoslyn was the source of far more useful information than Pasgen would ever had thought possible. For all that the Lady Mary had been relegated to a position of no overt power or importance, she was the center of an invisible web of those who had power now, and saw her as the way to much, much more of it.

Mary had told Rhoslyn that in spite of the favors recently shown the chamberlain, he was on the brink of disaster. She knew that Chapuys, the Imperial ambassador, was telling the king that Emperor Charles had a strong distaste for Cromwell, and Henry was looking to make alliance with the Empire against France.

In addition, Bishop Gardiner, a conservative Catholic, had told Mary that he believed the king's marriage to Anne of Cleves, distasteful to Henry from the beginning, was about to be dissolved. Henry had a new amour, the niece of the duke of Norfolk. All these things Mary discussed in whispers with her maids of honor, and all these things came straight to Pasgen.

Now Pasgen placed his hand on the edge of the table as if he were about to rise and said, "For the sake of our late connection, I will offer a piece of advice. You should go to the king at once, and declare the confiscations and reassignments to him, so that he knows what Cromwell is doing. It is very possible that the king will approve of Cromwell's action; if he does not, he will at least know that you acted only to oblige his minister."

Sir Thomas stood when Pasgen did, a deep frown marking his brow. "But to bring the matter to the king's notice when he might otherwise not have been aware might make trouble for Cromwell. And then would he not blame me in the future?"

"Cromwell has no future," Pasgen said harshly, half turning toward the door. In fact, he had used his FarSeeing talent to look at the English Court in the near future—alone, he could not look much further than that—and Cromwell had not appeared. Still, he decided to cover all possibilities. "Believe or disbelieve as you choose, I told you what my glass showed," he added. "Except . . . there is one chance he might save himself. If he immediately arranges a divorce from Anne of Cleves, the king might be so wrapped up in his new marriage, that Cromwell might slip away unharmed."

He left then, with no more than a brusque farewell, aware of Wriothesley's anger but pretending indifference. In a little over two weeks, however, he had won his gamble. On 10 June Pasgen received a note from Sir Thomas in a slightly shaky hand, requesting an appointment, and on 12 June, the man was escorted into Pasgen's parlor by one of his new bespelled English servants.

"You were right," Sir Thomas said grimly, attempting to conceal the fact that his hands were trembling. "I should have paid heed to your warnings. Cromwell has no future! He was arrested on the tenth at the very council table by the captain of the guard. Norfolk took the George from his neck and ordered me to take his garter. I—"

"Please, Sir Thomas, seat yourself," Pasgen said smoothly, gesturing toward a chair opposite his own. Well, the shoe was on the other foot, now! "Will you take some wine?"

"Yes, thank you, Master Otstargi. A glass would perhaps calm me." Wriothesley took the offered seat, looking very much in need of calming. "I have been uneasy since we spoke, most uneasy."

Wriothesley, Pasgen thought, hiding a smile by turning away to gesture to the servant, was much more polite than he had been at their first meeting. The servant went off, closing the door behind him, and now Wriothesley frowned as if he realized he had said more than he should with the servant listening.

Pasgen allowed his smile to show. "You need not be concerned about what my servants hear," he said. "I assure you that they *cannot* repeat anything. I am glad that you came to me, for you are in strong need of my advice. But you must not allow yourself to be shaken by untoward events, Sir Thomas. You will need to remain calm and steady, even in the face of accusations. There will be a time of upheaval—"

The pupils of Wriothesley's eyes contracted with alarm. "But not doom, I hope? No red flares or black curtains over my future?"

Time to twist the knife a little, to punish the man for his arrogance. He pursed his lips. "I have not specifically consulted your future, Sir Thomas. You did not seem eager for me to do so—"

"A mistake!" the fellow bleated, now truly in a panic. As well he should be. When the master fell into disgrace, he often took his underlings with him, and *they* had no one to protect them. "Forgive me!"

Pasgen nodded judiciously, sighed, then said, "A seeking out of one man's future takes time and effort, but I have been watching the general progress of affairs in England. You are not my only client, Sir Thomas, but most of the others are merchants, bankers, and suchlike. They only need to know the state of the kingdom to guide their businesses. They are of too little importance to impose their images on events. However, perhaps if you tell me exactly what has been happening in the court, I will be able to apply what I know in general to you."

Wriothesley had gone a little pale. "Ah, yes, that would give me a direction at least," he stammered. "Well, the king did not seem very angry about the confiscations, which was just as you implied—"

He stopped speaking abruptly as the door opened and the servant reentered carrying a tray upon which were two precious glass goblets held in twisted silver frames. At Pasgen's nod, the servant poured a rich, ruby-red wine into each glass. He offered a glass to Pasgen, who gestured toward Wriothesley. Sir Thomas then took his choice of the two glasses and Pasgen quietly accepted the other. A last gesture sent the servant from the room, shutting the door behind him, but Sir Thomas said nothing, seeming to be fascinated by the exquisite goblets.

"Go on, Sir Thomas," Pasgen urged.

"Yes. Oh, yes. The king was not angry, but he did remark that Cromwell took more for granted than he should and mentioned his persuasions toward a German alliance, which had brought no advantage at all at the cost of an unendurable wife. I remembered then what you said about the chance that Cromwell had to save himself and I went to him on the first of June, and again on the fifth and urged him to speak to Queen Anne, to get her agreement to a divorce and take that information to the king."

Pasgen cocked his head. "And did he take your advice?"

Wriothesley shook his head slightly. "No. All he said was that he could not think what to offer her or how to go about it."

"So I supposed it would be." Pasgen sighed theatrically. "The glass showed no escape, but my common sense told me there was a way out."

"And for me, Master Otstargi? What does common sense suggest for me?" Common sense, occult vision, Wriothesley would take any straw of hope, it seemed.

Pasgen smiled. His purpose had been accomplished. Sir Thomas Wriothesley was his creature again and would grow more dependent when accusations were leveled against him—as Pasgen would see that they were. Yes, Wriothesley would do as he was bid, and through his hands would flow Elizabeth's doom. It would be easy to arrange. Sooner or later the secretary of the king was likely to visit the king's daughter. It would be normal for Sir Thomas to bring a gift to Lady Elizabeth—a book, perhaps, in an elaborate binding with inset semiprecious stones. Something no young woman could resist touching, handling.

"Common sense suggests that you take the advice you gave to Cromwell. While others bend their efforts to exposing and destroying Cromwell, do you visit and carefully sound out Queen Anne." This, of course, was so logical that it was doubtful anyone would think of it. "Learn what will satisfy her, remembering that the king will not be willing for her to return to her brother where she might be free to say too much or make another marriage."

Wriothesley nodded eagerly. "I am very willing to take your advice, but I am not sure that Queen Anne will speak openly to me."

"If you need a woman's touch, let me recommend to you a friend of the Lady Mary, a Mistress Rosamund Scot." If Rhoslyn could not persuade the woman with sense, she could do so by magic, and it would scarcely violate the High King's admonitions. "I am sure, being partial to the Catholic way, that Mistress Scot will present your arguments convincingly."

Although Wriothesley did have a meeting with Mistress Scot and she, through a note from Lady Mary, gained an audience and spoke to Queen Anne, she hardly needed to have bothered. Raised in the strict and penurious court of her brother of Cleves, Anne had blossomed—at least in matters of dress and enjoyment of luxury—at the lavish court of Henry VIII. Rhoslyn found that Aleneil, as Lady Alana, a consummate authority on dress, was before her and already had Anne's close confidence. And what the Lady Alana had advised was precisely what Pasgen wanted.

Lady Alana had laid a good groundwork, confiding to Anne the king's interest in Catherine Howard. Restraining her shudders, Anne said, in her broken English, what amounted to "better she than I." But Lady Alana had passed a warning on along with the information—a warning that Anne had not needed, as it turned out, for the moment she heard about the king's new paramour, her hands had flown to her neck in an unconscious gesture of fear. The fear, of course, that it would be *her* neck that would next feel the edge of a blade.

Thus, when the duke of Norfolk presented King Henry's case to her, Anne hardly resisted at all; indeed, she did little more than to chaffer for the best possible bargain she could extract from the king. She was no fool, and understood when Cromwell fell that whatever political use she had had was over. As soon as Anne was certain that it was a divorce Henry wanted, not her head—and the king assured her of that himself—she became very cooperative.

She made no defense against Cromwell's assertion—in a paper written from his prison—that she had a previous contract to marry. On those grounds, the lords and commons of parliament addressed the king on the subject of his marriage on 6 July. Henry agreed to issue a commission to convocation to try the matter. On 9 July the convocation pronounced the marriage invalid, on the grounds of a possible precontract and on a lack of inward consent for the bridegroom.

Pasgen was hardly surprised. What the king wanted these days, the king got. And the Lady Anne was not doing badly out of the situation, either. She was shrewd, that German, from a long line of shrewd bargainers, and Pasgen had the odd feeling that of the two of them, it was Anne who would be the happiest with what she got.

Rhoslyn reported to Pasgen that though Anne went meekly off to Richmond, feigning distress over her husband's repudiation, among her own household she was radiant with smiles. A dutiful sister, she had obeyed her brother and would have endured the attentions of the gross and ageing monarch to whom she had been married. However, she was delighted with the bargain she had been offered. She would have a house and lands, four thousand pounds a year to spend as she pleased, and precedence at court over every lady except the wife and daughters of the king. And she did *not* have to return to her brother's Spartan and cheese-paring court. She had enough and more than enough to be supported in all of the luxury and pleasure that she had become accustomed to.

Henry was equally delighted with his former wife's cheerful complaisance, Rhoslyn told Pasgen, who was not terribly interested, but listened because he felt he had to be aware of what was going on in Henry's court. Anne's quick acceptance of the divorce, her quiet removal to a comfortable retirement, permitted Henry to marry Catherine Howard—eighteen to his forty-nine—on 28 July 1540, the same day that Cromwell was executed.

Pasgen made a disgusted noise and Rhoslyn nodded. It was not the first time Henry had celebrated someone's death with a new wedding. Then she giggled and commented that although Henry seemed to be in seventh heaven with his "rose without a thorn" the thorns would be pricking him soon enough. The girl was as light-minded as an air spirit, Rhoslyn said, and as promiscuous as a nymph. Rhoslyn had apparently taken no thought to what that might mean later.

At that comment, Pasgen sat up straighter, for the first thing that sprang into his mind was the fate of Anne Boleyn. If Catherine Howard was that promiscuous—if charges of adultery were real this time . . .

"Keep Mary away from her," he said. "We don't want Lady Mary smeared with Catherine's dirt when Henry is made aware of it, which I will make sure will not take long. Those favorable to the Reform religion will want to be rid of a wife who favors the Catholic rite."

"Simple enough." Rhoslyn shrugged. "Mary is already unhappy. She is hardly pleased at having a stepmother six years younger than she. Rosamund Scot will only need to mention this and that impertinence on Catherine's part—and there will be plenty of them because the girl is as heedless as a baby bird. Mary has great dignity and will withdraw herself from the court before long."

Pasgen nodded his approval. "And is there any way that you can encourage Catherine to favor Elizabeth?"

Rhoslyn pursed her lips and looked past her brother's shoulder at a handsome tapestry on the wall. "I am not as certain of that, as I am of keeping Mary clear, but I think . . . hmmm. Yes, perhaps. I can warn Mary that her father will be displeased if she is on bad terms with Catherine and suggest that she show herself willing to be friends. Then I can approach Elizabeth's governess, who is a good-natured fool, and ask whether Elizabeth would be willing to try to reconcile Queen Catherine and Lady Mary."

"Didn't you tell me that Elizabeth can see past your illusions?" he asked, sharply, remembering his own dangerous encounter with the child. "Didn't she ask why you had eyes like a cat and long pointed ears?"

"That was years ago. Mostly children grow out of that kind of awareness." Rhoslyn frowned a little. "But to be absolutely sure, I won't speak to Elizabeth herself. I'll bring Lady Mary's gift and note to Mistress Champernowne."

Pasgen nodded approval. "That should work very well. I've heard that Elizabeth has a real craving to go to court. Champernowne will jump on Mary's note and gift as an excuse to present Elizabeth, and Elizabeth is Catherine's cousin of some kind, isn't she?"

"Yes." Unlike Pasgen, Rhoslyn was interested in mortals and their relationships, and could chatter about them until he was ready to fall asleep with boredom. "Anne Boleyn's mother was a Howard, and so was Catherine's father. One was sister, the other brother to the duke of Norfolk; thus they are both Norfolk's nieces." She giggled again. "I doubt he will be able to squirm out of it this time when Catherine is exposed."

"Not until Elizabeth is established as Catherine's favorite," Pasgen warned. "We have come too far this time. There may be no better opportunity."

Chapter 9

"I don't like it," Denoriel said to Aleneil, who was curled up in a corner of his settle.

She was looking out of the huge window into a garden bordered by a lawn that ended in a tangled forest. She knew there was no garden and certainly no lawn, that likely beyond the window was one of the walls of the palace of Llachar Lle, but she was fascinated by the illusion, which was just a trifle different each time she saw it. She was not certain whether Denoriel simply changed the illusion almost every day or whether he had discovered a way to make the illusion alter itself. His studies with Treowth and Gilfaethwy were truly bearing fruit.

"Something smells of Unseleighe," Denoriel said when his sister did not respond to his first remark.

Aleneil shifted her gaze from the illusion to her brother. "I know you cannot keep the air spirit near Elizabeth when she is at court, but she has pretty well proven she has Sight. Has she complained about an Unseleighe intrusion? Has Blanche? And you get reports from Dunstan and Ladbroke and both tell you the child is happy. Has anything suspicious or dangerous happened?"

"No," Denoriel admitted. "But I feel . . . Am I to dismiss what I feel?"

"Usually I would say no. In this case . . ." Aleneil shook her head. "Denoriel, you are jealous of her joy in company other than yours."

"No!" Denoriel protested. "She is only eight years old. You talk as if we were lovers."

Aleneil sighed. "I don't mean you are jealous of her in that way. She may be but a child, but in many, many ways she has the intellect of an adult, and you do crave her company and resent being deprived of it."

"That is true." Denoriel also sighed but then grinned. "I really do miss being thrown into a rage every other time we speak. It is so stimulating." Then the grin faded into grimness and he shook his head. "Trust me, Aleneil—this is true danger that I sense. And there is something else, nothing to do with the Unseleighe. Norfolk is not as happy or confident about his niece's success as he should be. He is uneasy, like a man waiting for a blow to fall, and I fear that somewhat is amiss in that direction."

His sister's brows knit. "Are you sure? Is it not possible that the king's mood is sufficient reason for his disquiet? Henry has grown more and more . . ." she shrugged " . . . absolute. He hardly looks to his ministers for advice."

"True, but I am sure that Norfolk's anxiety has to do with Catherine." He frowned; he did not like the new queen, for she seemed to him as heedless as a flower sprite. "The girl is very shallow and very greedy, and I wonder how long she can be content with her lot."

Aleneil laughed. "Well, the king did not marry her for the power of her mind."

Denoriel laughed too, but uncertainly. "No. Anne Boleyn seems to have cured him of that." He sighed. "There is not a thing on which I can put a finger, except the knowledge that Elizabeth is so much in the queen's company puts me on edge. Why? Why would a light-headed and light-hearted young woman seek out the company of a child of eight?"

"They are cousins, and there are mortals, particularly female mortals, who simply love children and take the greatest pleasure in their company," his sister ventured.

Denoriel snorted gently. "But I do not believe Catherine Howard is one of those. In fact, she has not petitioned the king to bring Edward to court, and I think she could win more of the king's favor by coddling the heir. No, it sits like a lump in my breast that she wants Elizabeth for some purpose."

Aleneil just stared at him for a moment, but then she nodded her head slowly. "That has the ring of truth, but the purpose— ah—has no weight to it. It is as if she wanted the child to hold a skein of thread while she wound it." Her brows knitted while she thought. "Do you not think it is out of pure boredom? You know that the king intended to go on progress to Dover as soon as the worst of the winter was over, but then he fell ill and the royal party was confined to Hampton Court."

"Yes, and from what Dunstan told me, Henry's temper is so awful that anyone who could fled the court." Denoriel sighed. "Perhaps you are right, love. Since company is so thin and it is by *her* word that Elizabeth goes or stays, it is indeed possible that Catherine has kept the child by her for amusement. Elizabeth is a right minx and can make her company laugh, and it is true enough that when Henry is in a temper, laughter is hard to come by."

But even as he said the words, he knew they were nothing but a thin illusion over the truth—a truth he could not yet see.

The conversation between Denoriel and Aleneil took place in February, and still the king and queen lingered at Hampton Court. However, in March Elizabeth had returned safely enough to Hunsdon Palace some weeks before Henry and his queen were to begin an extended tour through his kingdom. At last, Denoriel was able to see Elizabeth and speak with her—and perhaps, probe at the truth for himself.

"And has being virtually a prisoner at Hampton Court for months finally cured you of your craving for the court and courtiers?" Denoriel asked as he and Elizabeth, warmly wrapped in heavy cloaks, walked in the formal garden, still mostly leafless in early March of 1541.

"Not at all," Elizabeth said. "My father was ill and we had to be quiet—no leaping about and singing loudly, so there were no masques or plays or even much music—but we were merry enough in the queen's chambers. One of the king's gentlemen, Thomas Culpepper, was often with us and he knew all sorts of games, with cards and with marked bones. How we all laughed when he lost most of the forfeits."

"Forfeits?" Denoriel said sharply. "You were gambling?"

Elizabeth looked at him sidelong, her thin, sensitive lips drawn back as if she were either displeased . . . or hiding laughter. "Only for comfits, or occasionally kisses."

A slight chill ran up Denoriel's back. "And who was winning these kisses?" he asked.

"Mostly me," Elizabeth said, giggling.

The cold sensation along Denoriel's spine increased. Elizabeth was clever and precocious, but whatever the game, what were the chances that an eight-year-old would often win against two adults? Unless they wanted her to win, or unless their minds were so busy with other matters that they played very badly indeed.

Unaware of his anxiety, Elizabeth continued blithely, "Culpepper said he had no money and the queen said she was afraid to be accused of corrupting the king's daughter if she gave me too many sweets. But I like being kissed. The queen gives gentle, tickley kisses, and Master Culpepper kneels down and formally kisses my hand—like an ambassador."

At least the man had sense enough not to taste the lips of the king's daughter, Denoriel thought, feeling somewhat better. He had swallowed a violent flash of rage at the notion that the queen might be trying to fix Elizabeth's affection on her favorite. Apparently that was not true. Even Catherine was not fool enough to believe her influence with the king would be enough to give Culpepper a royal wife. But Denoriel was still very uneasy. Something unhealthy had been going on. Were the queen and a gentleman alone with no better chaperone than an eight-year-old child?

And just who thought that an eight-year-old was a sufficient chaperone?

"Did no one else join the play?" he asked.

"Oh, yes, most times. Lady Rochefort and an old friend of the queen's, Francis Dereham. Lady Rochefort was mostly the one who walked with me to my apartment when the queen decided it was time for me to go to bed, but she never seemed to be much interested in the games, except the few times they played for money, and then I was sent away earlier."

They walked in silence for a few minutes, and then Elizabeth said, "What, no lecture on the sins and dangers of gambling? I do enjoy play, you know."

Denoriel laughed to cover his unease. "Not from me. Especially not if you win. The important thing to remember when gambling is to stop at once when you begin to lose. Who has been lecturing you about gambling?"

She made a face. "Kat. A brother or nephew or some such came to grief over gambling debts. And Dunstan . . . well, he doesn't lecture me, of course, but he was not happy about my being so much in the queen's company without any servants of my own." She hesitated and then looked up, meeting Denoriel's eyes fully with a too-knowing glance—which was not usual for her. "But there was nothing and no one there that should not be. And I have my cross."

She knew. She was all but saying in words that she knew he was no ordinary man, and that sometimes other strange beings and creatures appeared near her. That she did not say it in words said even more. Her self-possession was remarkable, even unnatural in so young a child. But Harry, not as clever as Elizabeth, had also been very self-possessed.

Also her life must have taught her to hold her tongue. It is not every child whose mother is murdered by her father and whose father is as powerful as a god in her little world—far too powerful to be questioned or criticized. Even a child might learn to think before she spoke and how not to speak at all of many things.

Denoriel took her hand and squeezed it gently, although dull pain ran up his arm. "Good. See that you wear it always, even when you sleep."

She smiled at him, and Denoriel was both relieved and annoyed. She was still testing him every time they met. In a way that was good, but it left a kind of sore place in him that her heart did not leap with recognition of his true identity as his did when he saw her. Aleneil said she did "recognize" him, but that the caution bred in her by her mother's fate and that of others, made her distrust her own instincts and demanded that she make sure.

When he had come to visit after Pasgen's attack on her, she had at first refused to go into the garden with him, even though he had brought her Harry's letter. She had not even allowed him to hand her the letter, but made him give it to Blanche, who carried it to her. And she had dismissed him immediately, although she did ask him to return the next day, promising she would provide Mistress Champernowne a reason for his second swift departure and early return.

The letter had not had all the effect Denoriel had hoped either. She had agreed to walk in the garden with him that day, but Nyle and Ladbroke followed not far behind, each armed with a steel-tipped crossbow. And she had said, eyes dark and averted, that the letter sounded as if it had been written by her Da, but . . . but . . . But Denoriel himself knew most of the incidents mentioned. He could have told someone and had the letter written. Why, she had asked, was it so important to him that she believe Richmond was still alive?

It was not important to him, he had told her. He knew his Harry was alive and well . . . and very happy, too. He was at peace with *his* knowledge. *She* needed to believe it so she could again be sure that there was someone alive who loved her with a perfectly pure affection, untouched by employment or hope of favor or even expectation of future good for others. And she needed to know it so that she would believe that Denoriel had not lied to her.

"But you do lie to me," she had said softly.

"No!" Denoriel had protested. "I never lie to you. I . . . I do not tell you all the truth because . . . because it is forbidden to me to tell you." And he raised a hand and ran a finger up to the peak of his ear. Elizabeth's eyes followed his finger as if they saw what it rested on. "But I do not lie," he continued, "and I swear, not on your God but on mine, that Henry FitzRoy, Duke of Richmond, Duke of Somerset, Earl of Nottingham, is alive and well."

She had walked in silence for a time, then reached into her deep-belled sleeve and brought out a much-folded sheet, solidly sealed. "Here is my reply to Da's letter." When she looked up at him this time, her eyes had brightened with hopeful gleams of gold. "But I need to see him. I *really* need to see him—"

"He *cannot* come," Denoriel interrupted. "Please, Lady Elizabeth, not only is he far away, but he would be in danger if he returned to England . . . and his return might place you in danger also."

The bright eyes misted over for a moment and then her thin lips firmed to a hard line. "A picture then. Ask Da to have a picture painted of him so that I will have something. Surely it is possible, no matter how far away he is, to find a painter who will do a portrait."

"Oh, it will be easy enough to find a painter who could do a portrait, but how will you explain a portrait of a ... such a portrait?"

"A portrait of a dead man?" she whispered.

"No, a live man, but most carefully hidden."

"Ah." Her eyes brightened again and then for a moment followed the edge of his ear to its point at the crown of his head—an ear that should be invisible to mortal eyes. "Why then, instead of a portrait let the picture be of a fanciful place with people in it so that the face might be pure imagination, a picture of a land of myth and fancy, wherein dreams may walk."

As if his memory of that meeting in the past summer, before Elizabeth had been called to court by the queen, had somehow been transferred to Elizabeth, who in the present was walking beside him without any guards, she wiggled a hand out of her snugly wrapped cloak and took his hand—starting a wave of pain up his arm—and asked, "When will you bring me the picture that you promised?"

"Now, do not begin that," he said. "When the ship comes, it will come. It could not turn around the day it arrived and start back. Harry has to find an artist and the picture has to be painted. And if the ship has gone to other ports, the picture must wait until it returns ... I will bring it to you as soon as it comes—unless you are at court again—and I beg you will not plague out my life until I have it."

She blinked at him owlishly. "Nonsense. If I suffer, why should you not suffer too?"

"Elizabeth!" he exclaimed. "What sort of Christian charity is that?"

"What do you care? You aren't a Christian." A moment later she burst out into giggles. "Oh, your face, Lord Denno. I wish I had a glass to show you your face. But it is the fate of those who court royalty to be the butt of their moods."

He frowned at her ferociously. And here was another attribute, not so pleasant, that she had learned from her father. "And you are not royalty! Do not put on dangerous airs. Nor do I court you for my profit."

"Then why do you court me?"

"Because I adore you, you noxious little brat!"

"Do you?"

She stopped in the path and swung around to take his other hand. Her eyes were bright gold, and the joy and tenderness in her expression rewarded him for much frustration and the pain that was creeping up both arms and beginning to permeate his whole body. She saw his struggle not to stiffen or lean away, let go of his hands, and stepped back.

She looked down at the ground. "I wish you could hug me," she murmured. "You used to hug Da. I know you did."

"I wish I could too, Lady Elizabeth, but it is not the cold iron that stops me. I could bear it long enough for a hug. It is because you are a girl, and Harry was a boy."

She sniffed. "What harm can a hug do? I have seen men hug women. My father hugs me sometimes."

"Yes, your father may, and perhaps your brother will hug you when you and he combine your households. As for other men and women . . . ah . . . I will explain that when you are somewhat older."

"Surely every hug is not a prelude to coupling."

Denoriel felt color rise in his face. Eight years old. What could she know about coupling? Well, perhaps she had seen cows or horses or the dogs on the estate.

"No, of course not," he said, starting along the path again. "However . . . never mind. I will explain some other day. But I spoke of your brother and that reminded me. Have you heard when you are supposed join him and do you know whether it will be at Hertford Palace or at Enfield?"

Her gaze intensified as she thought. "I think at Hertford because it is larger than Enfield. I think Mary is supposed to be with us there, and perhaps my father and Catherine will stop on their way north. Why do you want to know?"

"Because, as I said, I am enamored of you, you noxious brat, and I need to find a convenient small house to buy or rent nearby to where you live." They had begun walking again, and he looked down at her soberly. "You know that I will not be able to visit you so freely once you and Edward are lodged together. He is the heir, and is closely guarded and every stranger will be closely scrutinized. I am not likely to be an acceptable visitor to the prince—a foreigner and although I was a prince in my own country, I am now a merchant and have no claim to nobility in

England. I will need a special appointment each time I come, and Kat might be blamed for encouraging our friendship."

Elizabeth pulled her cloak more tightly around her, shivering slightly, perhaps from the chill breeze. "Does that mean I will not see you again until Edward and I are parted—which will happen a few times a year, I think?"

Denoriel chuckled a bit self-consciously. "That is what should happen. You will be doubly and triply guarded and Blanche and Mistress Champernowne will be with you, so you will be safe—"

"Even from—" Elizabeth made the gesture of a long, pointed ear alongside her own head.

"I believe so. I hope so. Things happened in Hatfield when you were a babe that made that place perhaps a bit vulnerable. But Hertford . . . Harry was never in Hertford Palace." He nodded decisively. "You have your cross and Blanche has her own weapons, and I think you should start to carry a steel knife—ask Dunstan or Ladbroke for one. Ask them for a bodkin; many ladies carry them, I believe. However, I will be near enough for Dunstan or Ladbroke or Tolliver to fetch me."

She looked up at him directly again. "Would you fight for me as I heard you fought for Da?"

"To the death, my lady." He stopped and bowed, face grim, then grinned and added, "And to make doubly sure you are safe and also to be sure that my blood is properly boiled at intervals, I will arrange to meet you and ride with you, whenever the prince does not accompany you, if you ride out."

She smiled and reached for his hand again, but walked nearly at arm's length so the iron cross hardly caused him a twinge. "I love to ride," she said, "and Edward is not much more than a baby, so I think I can beg for more vigorous exercise than he could take once or twice a week. If my own people accompany me—my guards think you almost one of the family—no one will know or care. We will make do."

A good plan, Denoriel thought. What she said was likely true. Since no one but Blanche knew of Pasgen's attack on her, no one feared for her safety.

However, in actuality they had plenty of time for more elaborate planning. By the end of April it was certain Elizabeth would join Edward in Hertford, and in the first week in May

Denoriel delivered to her—as an aid, he said, to furnishing her new apartment—a portrait of a young man with a look of her father.

Elizabeth stared at the image in silence for some time. The young man was dressed in clothing a good three hundred years out of date, a short, close fitting tunic with narrow sleeves over long hose, cross gartered to the knee. The tunic was open over a white shirt tied in a bow at the neck, and his hair was long, sweeping his shoulders and held back by a narrow golden band set just above a brilliant blue star emblazoned on his forehead. At his feet was a small creature that might have been a cat, except for the furry wings on its back, and behind him was a unicorn, silver-blue, with black eyes and a silver mane, a tail like a lion's, the beard of a goat, and cloven hooves.

"Oh," Elizabeth sighed, "I did remember. But he is much thinner and, and, he looks older."

Denoriel laughed. "He *is* older, nearly five years older and that makes a big difference. You would find he is taller too; a halfling has grown into a man. And he is thinner because . . . because he was very ill. That long trip he took saved his life, but he *was* very ill when he left England, which is why so many think he is dead. But he is not."

She nodded absently, still gazing into the picture, as if trying to communicate with its subject. "I am glad the picture is not too large. I can keep it with me, perhaps have a stand made for it for my bedchamber. Thank you, Lord Denno."

Her eyes searched his face, but he could tell her no more and she sighed and went away. On his next visit he told her he had rented a hunting lodge in the forest less than a mile from the main road into Hertford Castle, and Elizabeth surreptitiously, when Kat and Lady Alana were busy discussing necessary additions to Lady Elizabeth's wardrobe if she was to dine with Edward, kissed his cheek.

The king, however, was not yet ready to leave on his progress. He claimed to be still recovering, but Denoriel learned that negotiations were taking place to arrange a meeting between Henry and King James of Scotland. Henry hoped to wean Scotland away from its long alliance with France. Considerable private negotiation was also taking place between Mistress Champernowne and Sir William Sidney, Edward's chamberlain, about how the two households would arrange for and pay their private dependents.

Sir William bade Mistress Champernowne dismiss the guards; the prince's men, he said, could take over securing Lady Elizabeth's safety. Thereby he could save the cost of four men's stipend and food and drink allowance and yearly suits and shoes. They were combining to save the king money.

Elizabeth was horrified; she flew into a most unchildlike rage, absolutely forbidding the dismissal of men who had carried her about, told her tales, and allowed her—with discretion—to play with their weapons. Mistress Champernowne wrung her hands and wept.

The next thing, Elizabeth said furiously to Denoriel, who arrived later in the day, was that Sir William would want Kat to dismiss Ladbroke and Tolliver and have the prince's grooms care for her horses.

"On no account should you allow the guards or grooms to be dismissed," Denoriel said to Mistress Champernowne, who was sitting in the audience chamber with them because it was raining. "What does that fool think you will do when the households separate, as they are bound to do from time to time? Are you to hire new people? People you do not know whether you can trust?"

"I do not know what I can do," Kat quavered. "I fear the exchequer will send our allowances to Sir William. How am I to pay—"

"If the money is all that is troubling you," Denoriel said, smiling with relief that the difficulty was so easy to solve, "Let it trouble you no longer. Tell Sir William that you will not dismiss old, trusted servants and you will make shift to support them. I will provide any funds you need."

"I cannot accept so much, Lord Denno," Mistress Champernowne said. "That one time when you gave me fifty sovereigns I was so shocked . . . and I . . . Elizabeth needed new gowns. She grows, you know. But to accept more, and for I do not know how long . . . would that not be wrong?"

Denoriel blinked. He had never given Kat any money, fearing it would make her even more improvident than she already was. It must have been Pasgen, thinking that Kat would need a bribe to allow him to walk alone with Elizabeth.

"Would it be wrong, Lord Denno?" Elizabeth asked, looking from Kat to Denoriel. "I really, really do not want to part with Gerrit, Nyle, Shaylor, and Dickson, and I would almost give up my new gowns to keep Ladbroke and Tolliver. If Kat took the money, would it obligate me to you? Would you expect favor in return?"

"And what favor do you think you can extend to me, you repellent child? *Almost* would give up your new gowns!" Denoriel was not teasing her this time; she had gotten some appalling manners, and it was time someone delivered a set-down to her. "What a selfish brat you are! And just what would your men do if they were dismissed? How would they support themselves while they tried to find other positions? They have served you well and faithfully, never complaining when your household was stinted and their wages came late! I swear, I should turn you over my knee and lesson you. Do you think it would be too much favor granted me if you said 'Thank you'?"

Mistress Champernowne drew a sharp breath. Elizabeth did not generally take kindly to harsh criticism. She could be corrected, but it was needful to do it tactfully.

However, Elizabeth only shook her head, her eyes dark and her thin lips in a straight line. "It is not selfishness, Lord Denno. At least, not only selfishness. I admit, I would like some new gowns, for I love handsome dress, but I must make a show in my brother's household. He is very young and if his people see me shabby, they will not value me as I may need to be valued." She put out a hand and barely touched Denoriel's arm. "I do thank you."

Denoriel laid his hand over hers and sighed, deflated. "You are quite right, my lady. I am saddened that, young as you are, you need to think of such matters."

"It is sad," Mistress Champernowne said, "but I have explained to her that there will be much more coming and going of court officers in the prince's household than there has ever been in hers. Yet those who come to see the prince may well ask to see Lady Elizabeth, who *is* the king's daughter. And, indeed, she must consider that some day Edward will be king and must think well of her. She *must* have the gowns, but perhaps there is somewhere else I can save. I am appalled at needing to take so much from you."

He waved her objections aside. "Do not give it a thought. You need feel no guilt. I am rich. I am alone. I have no one else, since Harry does not need my help any longer. And these were my Harry's sworn men, before they were Elizabeth's."

"Harry?" Kat asked, looking confused.

"A friend. He has other sources of income now," Denoriel said with a glance at Elizabeth and then quickly, to divert Kat's mind from the fact that he had not really answered her question, he added, "Oh, and be sure that the prince's people do not try to sell off Elizabeth's horses—or appropriate them for themselves—and have her share the prince's. Her horses were specially chosen by Ladbroke. They are the best."

"We must make some concessions or Sir William will become suspicious. He might suggest that if we can manage on so much less, our separate stipend should be reduced." Kat looked worried, for the king's clerks were always seeking ways of diminishing the drains on his purse.

"Fine," Elizabeth said. "Agree to share servants, like cooks and cleaners. You can even offer to give up that fool groom of the chamber and the footmen. Only Dunstan must be kept, and he will not mind if you give him a lesser title."

"True enough," Kat sighed. "I do not know what I would do without Dunstan."

So the agreements were made with Sir William, but May passed and June also without any order to Elizabeth to move. Finally on July first Henry and Catherine left for the north. To save time they no longer planned a stop at Hertford. Nonetheless Elizabeth and Edward joined households shortly thereafter. Edward was thrilled to have a sister who gave him all of her attention and treated him with great respect.

Elizabeth was as happy as she could be. She now had a living doll—and a very clever one, too—that she could hug, fuss over, and encourage. She did not mother him the way that Mary had tried to mother her; perhaps because a great deal of Mary's "mothering" consisted of "no" to this and "no" to that, and "oh, my dear sister, you must not!" She happily oversaw his earliest lessons in recognizing letters and helped his baby hand steady his first pen to form the great *E*, the first letter of his name. She adored court formalities and behaved with a gravitas fitting a dame of forty when court officers or ambassadors came to meet her. And she rode out with her own four guardsmen and two grooms for exercise, returning with glowing eyes and rosy cheeks, at least twice a week.

Through Sir Thomas Wriothesley, Pasgen had almost daily news of the king's progress. Henry and Catherine made their way to York, where they were supposed to meet with King James of Scotland. That hope was doomed to disappointment, but otherwise the progress was very successful for Henry. As he passed through Ampthill into Lincolnshire and rode through that part of the country where the Pilgrimage of Grace had taken fastest hold, repentant subjects rushed to demonstrate their loyalty and made their submission on their knees. The clergy, too, came with professions of fervent loyalty and rich presents.

Other pleasant news buoyed the king's spirits. The fortifications at Hull were satisfactory, and at Pomfret at the end of August, he heard from his emissary to Edinburgh that King James was agreeable to meet him. Safe-conducts were prepared for those who would attend the Scottish king and Henry proceeded to York, arriving about mid-September.

In York, however, the king met with disappointment. James had not yet arrived nor sent any message giving a date for his arrival. After waiting until the end of the month, Henry learned that Cardinal Beaton had discovered the scheme for the kings to meet and prevented James, who was under his thumb, from going to York.

The return journey was considerably faster than the progress north, but the king and queen arrived at Hampton Court at the end of October in good spirits. In fact, Wriothesley reported with satisfaction, Henry intended to offer special prayers on All Saints Day "for the good life he led and trusted to lead" with his jewel of a wife.

"The bubble is about to burst," Pasgen said to Rhoslyn as they stood near the entry of a new Unformed land and contemplated a patch of mist that was behaving in a most peculiar manner.

Rhoslyn watched the self-adherent thing coil around itself and directed a gentle shaft of will at it, urging an opening out, a flattening.

"What bubble?" she asked.

"King Henry's bubble of happy marriage. He is about to discover that Queen Catherine was a whore before her marriage and managed to be faithful to him for perhaps a month before she went back to being a whore." Pasgen's voice was not full of the satisfaction that Rhoslyn would have expected.

The mist, rather than respond to Rhoslyn's will, had coiled up tighter and then lashed out at her. Pasgen pulled her back, raised a hand, and was about to direct a violent spell of dissolution at it.

"No, don't," she said, and cast a containment around it, whereupon it seemed to go wild, battering at the invisible force that restrained it. Smiling slightly in a "there, serves you right" way, she turned back to Pasgen. "I thought you intended that the king learn what Catherine is, but you don't seem very happy about it."

"Yes, it is what I intended, but it is happening too soon. I wanted Elizabeth to be summoned back to court when the king and queen returned so that she would actually be involved in the queen's disgrace. Unfortunately, my tool is a bit like your mist there, sidling up to me to get my advice but then acting on his own." Pasgen frowned. "One would think that after giving him ample proof of my power, he would pay more heed to it."

Rhoslyn began to move farther into the Unformed land, gesturing at the containment spell so that it would follow her, bringing along its prisoner. Pasgen continued at her side, occasionally reaching out to swipe at a thicker patch of mist with a wide-mouthed bottle he could seal.

"But he does want your advice?" she asked.

"On *everything*. I swear he asks how often he should breathe in and out. However, he is not quite as busy as Woolsey and Cromwell were, so he often takes time to think over what I have told him and suggested to him, and about half the time he finds variations he prefers."

Rhoslyn turned to her brother with a frown of her own. "You should lesson him sharply or do away with him and find a more malleable tool."

Pasgen sighed. "Not so easy. He is co-secretary to the king, a position in which he knows everything that is taking place, and I have worked on his mind so that I can extract anything from it and know whatever he knows. It would take me half a year to create the same kind of facility with another man's mind. Also—" Pasgen uttered a somewhat embarrassed laugh. "About half the time the variations on my suggestions that he uses produce better results than my own suggestions would have. He knows a great deal more about the politics of the court than I do."

"But in this case?" Rhoslyn prompted, still frowning.

Pasgen shrugged one shoulder. "Soon after the king and queen set out on the progress, I arranged for a man called Lascelles to confess to Wriothesley that his sister had been in the household of the duchess of Norfolk, where the girl Catherine Howard had been raised. That sister, being urged to ask for a position as maid of honor since she knew the queen, replied that she knew the queen all too well and had no intention of serving her and perhaps being ruined, if she had not changed her ways."

"Changed what ways?"

"Whoring," Pasgen replied flatly. "The girl is as promiscuous as a maenad. It was not hard to find someone willing and ready to tell the truth. Lascelles not only named two gentleman who had been intimate with young Catherine—her music teacher and her cousin, Francis Dereham—but described in some detail exactly what had taken place. Naturally Wriothesley came rushing to me, crying that he would resign his position, that it was impossible for him to go to the king with such a tale."

"Well, I wouldn't either." Rhoslyn laughed. "The king really *is* likely to behead the messenger who brings him that piece of news. Mary is so disgusted with his fulsome praise of that 'empty-headed little nothing' that she has refused flatly to make any further overtures to her. I did not press the point since Catherine only sent a rather cold note the last time Elizabeth carried a letter and a gift."

Pasgen smiled, finally. "*That* use worked perfectly, since it drew Elizabeth to the queen's attention and she called her to court and made a pet of her. I had hoped the same would happen when the queen returned from the progress and that Elizabeth would be implicated in the queen's adultery."

Rhoslyn breathed in sharply and Pasgen raised a hand to stem her angry remark.

"Elizabeth would not be punished with the queen or like the queen. Elizabeth is barely eight years old; however, she might well be considered soiled, considering that her mother was executed for adultery. It is a pity there are no convents now, for she might have been sent to one. But certainly she would have been banished to some remote manor and written out of the succession. That would solve my problem with Vidal. I think poor Elizabeth might actually lead a happier and fuller life if the weight of being third in the succession was removed."

"Possibly." Rhoslyn smiled at him but shrugged. "However, according to Mary the child already sees herself as queen. Certainly she bears herself most imperiously! She is like Henry, writ small!"

Pasgen turned his attentions to the pale-colored mists all about them. "That may mean stronger measures will need to be taken, but for now I am willing to wait and see. When I saw that Wriothesley was too terrified to go to the king himself, I pointed out that the queen's behavior was certainly a sin against God and suggested that he send the man Lascelles to Archbishop Cranmer."

"Now that was clever," Rhoslyn said, admiringly. "If I remember right, you told me that Wriothesley is of a conservative persuasion and favors the old rite. I know that Mary sends to him if she needs information or help. If so, Wriothesley will be delighted to get Cranmer, who is definitely of the reformed religion, into trouble with the king."

"And Cranmer, who really believes in the reformed faith, has been afraid that the queen's orthodox opinions would lead the king back to Catholicism."

Pasgen actually smiled; if there was one thing that made getting involved with the mortals worthwhile, it was being able to sow mischief among them. Had it not been for *his* ferreting out of information, his bribes, and his well-placed hints, Catherine Howard's amours might have gone on for years undiscovered. And it would not only be Catherine's neck that would feel the edge of a blade when everything had shaken out.

"So," Pasgen continued, "although Cranmer was also afraid, he brought the news to those members of the council that were in London. They launched an investigation and found so much evidence of the queen's promiscuity that they did not dare try to bury the evidence. Wriothesley believes that Cranmer will somehow make sure the king learns of his wife's adultery very soon."

Rhoslyn stood up a little straighter, and briefly lost interest in her captive mist. "When? I would like to be with Mary when the news breaks."

"Within the week."

Rhoslyn nodded and temporarily dismissed the mortal world from her mind as she gathered together the roiling mist of the Unformed land to create from it two more servants for Pasgen. One of his constructs had simply disintegrated; that happened from time to time when too much demand had been made on the contained power. The other had been eaten by the red mist he insisted on playing with—the thought made Roslyn look back at her spell of containment and the oddly behaving patch of stuff she had imprisoned. Pasgen was looking at it too.

She would give it to him, she thought. He had been ready to destroy it for threatening her, but once she had contained it, he had become curious. She smiled faintly as two large billows of the swirling mist first separated from the generalized fog and then began to thicken and swirl together as fingers of her power worked them like a woman spinning thread. Two at once was not easy, but she was very familiar with the pattern Pasgen desired and they were forming well. As soon as she had sealed the new servants to Pasgen's will, she would send a mortal servant to request permission to pay her respects to Lady Mary. There was this about the mortal world that was very exciting: things happened quickly there.

Lady Mary was delighted to grant permission to her dear Rosamund Scot to attend her, especially as Mistress Rosamund not only supported herself but often gave her lady welcome presents. Like Elizabeth's, Mary's household was often caught short. She told Mistress Rosamund to make her curtsey at Hampton Court because she intended to be there to welcome her father home. Rhoslyn hastened to agree and she with Mary and the ladies who attended her were present when the king gave thanks for the good life he led with his wife.

Mary sighed that at least Catherine was a good Catholic, but the very next day she told Rosamund Scot that the king was in a terrible rage. Accusations had been made against his wife that he could not believe.

Rosamund Scot proceeded to tell Lady Mary what the accusations were, and to give her enough details to make her sure that the accusations were true. Horrified, Mary retreated to one of her own castles. Wisely, she put as much distance between herself and scandal as possible.

The next installment came to Pasgen from Wriothesley. To clear the queen's name of such dreadful calumny, Henry had ordered his ministers to investigate in the deepest secrecy. Pasgen warned Wriothesley not to allow himself to hope she was innocent or he would be lost himself.

One minister rushed off to London to examine Cranmer's informant, but Lascelles did not falter and said that there were more people than only his sister who would testify to Catherine's ill behavior while she was a ward of the duchess of Norfolk.

Mannock, Catherine's music master, and Dereham were arrested and privately examined by Wriothesley. His trust and dependence on Master Otstargi was only confirmed. Wriothesley himself would have preferred if the gentlemen claimed Lascelles to be a liar and denied their guilt, but knowing how indiscreet they had been, they confessed readily. They pointed out that their association with Catherine had been long before she became queen and was thus not treason. To hope for escape was foolish; when the king learned the truth, he would take his revenge upon every possible target.

Wriothesley felt that Dereham, who was Catherine's cousin, was hiding something, but he did not press the man. Remembering Otstargi's advice, he did not release him from prison either.

Henry was overwhelmed by the evidence presented and dispatched several ministers together with Archbishop Cranmer to question the queen. Wriothesley, wiping sweat from his brow although Otstargi's parlor was not particularly warm, thanked God that he had not been required to accompany them. The queen had had hysterics, but when quieted by Cranmer's promise of forgiveness, confessed to her premarital guilt. Likely the king would divorce her, Wriothesley said.

Pasgen shook his head. "You must not hope for so easy a solution. The queen is guilty of worse, and she has involved others in her crime."

"Others?"

"Certainly Lady Rochefort, very possibly the Lady Elizabeth."

"That is not possible! Lady Elizabeth is a child, only just turned eight years old."

Pasgen shrugged. "My glass shows her as witness of the queen's friendship with certain gentlemen. The queen may well have thought that having the king's daughter with her would be a protection—as proof that she would not misbehave before a child. You know there will be conflicting testimony from the queen's women. Yet things may have passed that a child would see and speak of without understanding, things you and the examiners of the queen's ladies can use."

Wriothesley looked uncomfortable, but Pasgen knew that when his own hide was at stake, he would not hesitate to implicate, much less question, a child. "You say you know Queen Catherine guilty and that there is no hope her guilt will not be proven?"

Pasgen nodded gravely. "That is what I read when I look at her future."

Wriothesley sighed deeply. "I would have saved her if I could. The king's mood—except for that time when he was sick—has been so mild since they married. And this queen was no wild-eyed reformer pressing him to strip more and more from the Church. But it would not do for me to close my eyes to what is plain to all others."

"No, it would not." Pasgen leaned forward to underscore his words, gazing at Wriothesley intently. "And if, for example, during those 'innocent' games played with the Lady Elizabeth in attendance, the queen sent the child away *before* the gentlemen left, and no one thought to ask *that* question . . . It is my advice that you mention to the king the fact that the Lady Elizabeth may have been used by the queen before someone else speaks of it. Offer to question the child gently so that she will not suspect the reason or suspect what use may be made of her tales."

Wriothesley was silent, biting his lips gently for a moment. Then he said, "I have had occasion to speak with Lady Elizabeth in the past. She may be only eight, but she is *very* clever. I am not at all sure she will not guess my purpose and be silent or even lie. She loves the queen."

"Oh, I can assure you she will tell you the truth and all the truth." Pasgen smiled.

"You can?" Wriothesley looked skeptical.

Interesting, Pasgen thought. The child must be remarkable indeed, if a grown man did not think he could have the truth out of her. "You will ask her to swear on the Bible, will you not?" Pasgen asked.

Wriothesley nodded. "Yes, of course. But—"

Pasgen interrupted. "You will bring with you a Bible with a

tooled and bejeweled binding. One of those jewels will be an amulet that will force the truth from the child."

"I had no idea you could prepare such a device!" Wriothesley's eyes gleamed with interest.

Pasgen shook his head. "With good reason," he said giving his lips a wry twist. "Because I cannot. I was not idle in the years I traveled. Some new things I learned, but I was also able to purchase artifacts from magicians with skills other than mine. This amulet was one of the things I found, but its use is limited. The truth spell can be used only once. Then its force will be expended, so keep it covered until you ask Elizabeth to swear to tell the truth."

"I will be careful," Wriothesley said fervently, his expression a mix of disappointment that the amulet had only one use, and relief that there *was* such a thing that could have the truth out of someone. "But how can the amulet be set into the cover of the Bible if it cannot be touched by anyone?"

Pasgen shrugged. "There are many ways. The wearing of gloves when setting it into the cover is the simplest. But I will deal with that. When you are ready to leave London to question the Lady Elizabeth, I will give you the book and cover all prepared."

"The book must be a Bible," Wriothesley warned. "Lady Elizabeth is very likely to open it and look through for some verse she thinks will help."

"Oh, yes," Pasgen assured him. "Should it be in Latin or English?"

"Latin!" Wriothesley snapped, rising from his chair. "A Bible in English is an abomination."

On those words, to which Pasgen replied only with a low laugh, he rang for a servant who came and saw Wriothesley out. When he was sure he was alone, Pasgen opened a drawer in the table and withdrew a large book in a beautiful binding. The leather was intricately tooled into a lacelike design as a border. The face of the binding was worked into a large cross decorated with Celtic knots, which was gilded. At the ends of each of the arms was a small gold plaque bearing the symbols of the evangelists. And set into the center of the cross was what might have been a large bloodstone, almost black until it caught a gleam of light, which lit in the stone thin, crawling veins of red.

Pasgen did not touch the stone. He had tested it on a mortal servant, who had died by his own hand a week later. The spell was designed not to work immediately—that would have raised suspicions against Wriothesley, and Pasgen still found him useful.

It did not hold a truth spell, but it did not matter much whether Elizabeth told the truth or not, since she would not live long enough for her testimony to be used.

Chapter 10

Mistress Champernowne was even more grateful to Lord Denno than usual—and her normal state was complete reliance on him—when at the end of the first week in November she received a peremptory order to remove Lady Elizabeth from Hunsdon and return to Hatfield. If not for Lord Denno's precaution and generosity they would have arrived at Hatfield virtually bereft of servants and with no way to find well-trained help.

Instructed and funded by Lord Denno, Dunstan had been able to pay a retainer to most of the staff. Many had returned to their families and so found the small monthly fee sufficient to support them; others had found work but were willing to leave those positions for the more prestigious places in the household of the king's daughter. A few had to be replaced, but Dunstan seemed to have no difficulty in finding an experienced laundry maid and cleaner for Lady Elizabeth's bedchamber.

In any event, when Secretary Wriothesley arrived late in November, the household was comfortably settled and running smoothly. Mistress Champernowne could greet Sir Thomas with composure and show him into Elizabeth's private reception chamber, where refreshments swiftly arrived.

Her composure was only slightly disturbed when Wriothesley began to ask questions about the time they had spent at court at the queen's invitation. The investigation into Catherine's promiscuity had been kept so secret that no rumor of it had reached Hatfield. Mistress Champernowne could only conclude that the queen was asking for Elizabeth to come to her again and the king's secretary had been dispatched to be sure Elizabeth was willing and whether her time had been properly employed.

Thus Mistress Champernowne enthusiastically reported that Elizabeth, who loved her books, had continued her studies while at court. They had been slowed, of course, by the small entertainments designed to amuse the queen and divert her from worry about her ailing husband; however Elizabeth had made progress, since her time was most occupied by the queen in the evenings when the child would not have been studying in any case.

"And did you accompany Lady Elizabeth to the queen's apartment in the evening?"

Kat colored faintly. "I was not invited, Sir Thomas, but you must not think that Lady Elizabeth was not properly attended. Lady Rochefort always came to fetch her and always brought her back." She sighed. "I could have wished that the child was sent away earlier so that she could have had a longer night's sleep—but then, nights are very long in February, so Lady Elizabeth was not deprived of her rest."

Wriothesley tilted his head to the side. "Then you are not aware of the entertainment that took place within the queen's apartment?"

Kat considered this. Was he seeking to learn if Elizabeth had betrayed some information of a privy sort? "I was not there, but to some extent I do know, since Lady Elizabeth usually told me what they did."

"And that was?" Wriothesley leaned forward as if to catch every word.

Kat could not imagine why. Queen Catherine was hardly the sort to bother her pretty head about anything that was of a serious nature. "Well, the queen is very young," she said indulgently. "Sometimes they had musicians or a poet to read to them, but mostly I fear they played silly games with cards and marked bones. And for silly forfeits too, not money," she added, lest Wriothesley think that the pocket money given to Elizabeth's household had been gambled away.

Wriothesley continued his intent regard. Kat felt uneasy. "And do you know who the 'they' involved were?"

Did he think that Elizabeth had been exposed to some mean person of no rank? "The queen, of course, and Lady Rochefort and Lady Elizabeth. Francis Dereham, a cousin of the queen's, was often with them and a young gentleman of the king's Privy Chamber . . . ah . . . yes, Thomas Culpepper."

He continued to stare at her. She wished he would have done. "None of the queen's other ladies?"

Kat shook her head. How was she to know all this? "Very likely they came and went but did not join the games, which is why Lady Elizabeth did not mention them, but Lady Elizabeth and the others played in the queen's inner rooms, right next to her bedchamber because they did not wish any noise they made to disturb the king."

"They did not wish to disturb the king?" Wriothesley's tone was a trifle strange, and Kat looked at him questioningly, but he only cleared his throat.

"The king had been ill and was recovering only slowly," Kat said. "He needed his rest. I think the queen feared that hearing them laugh and cry out over the cards might make him restless and sad—feeling left out because of his weakness, you know."

"Ah," Wriothesley said and then, "If you please, would you ask Lady Elizabeth if she would join me here . . . and in private."

The request for privacy made Kat more uneasy, but Lord Thomas Wriothesley was the king's own secretary and surely would do the king's daughter no harm. Kat sighed a little as she went to fetch the girl, for Elizabeth was almost too clever. Thus all she said was that Sir Thomas wished to know whether Elizabeth had enjoyed her stay at court and the company of the queen.

While Elizabeth made small adjustments to her clothing and examined her hair and headdress to be sure she was neat, Wriothesley removed the Bible from the saddlebag in which he had carried it and laid it on the small table that stood between two chairs facing the hearth in which a generous fire burned.

Kat's explanation, coming so soon after Henry and Catherine had returned to Hampton Court, aroused in Elizabeth the same misapprehension as that of her governess. She came into the reception room smiling demurely. Sir Thomas rose at once and bowed; Elizabeth made a small curtsey to Sir Thomas, came forward to the chairs, and prepared to seat herself.

"One moment, please, my lady," Sir Thomas said. "I know this will seem silly to you and likely it is silly, but as the secretary to the king, I must be able to write a report in which I attest that what is said is true. Thus, if you would just swear on this Holy Book to tell the truth . . . ?"

He stepped back so that Elizabeth could see the gilded and bejeweled book on the table. A wave of revulsion made her hesitate, but the firelight was awakening strands and bursts of gleaming red in the black stone at the center of the cross and Elizabeth found herself fascinated. She took another step forward.

"It is only a formality, my lady," Wriothesley urged.

Revulsion still made an uneasy quiver in Elizabeth's middle, but she told herself that such a peculiar feeling was ridiculous. The book was beautiful. There was nothing about it to turn her stomach. She took another step closer. The red threads in the stone seemed to dance, to beckon her.

"It *is* a Bible, is it not?" Elizabeth asked.

"Indeed it is, my lady. Please feel free to examine the book any way you want." Sir Thomas laughed lightly. "It would not do me much good to have you swear on a collection of verse, now would it?"

Feeling very foolish, Elizabeth flipped open the volume. The familiar words leapt out at her, and she was immediately more at ease. She read a phrase, a sentence, turned more pages. It was indeed a beautiful book, carefully printed and with colored capitals and some key words overdone by hand in gold. Just the Bible, from beginning to end, because driven by caution she did look at the last few pages as well as riffling through to make sure nothing was concealed.

She smiled up apologetically at Sir Thomas. "It is so very beautiful," she said, "I could not resist looking through it," and closed the book.

The breath caught in her throat and she stepped back, only to tread on Sir Thomas's foot. He was right behind her.

"Just put your hand on the cross and swear to tell the truth," he said sharply. "You do not want to have me need to say to your father that you were unwilling to swear on the Bible to tell the truth."

"Of course I will tell the truth," Elizabeth said, so outraged that she laid her hand on the book at once. A sharp tingle ran from her palm, which had touched the strange stone, down to her fingers, and unconsciously she arched her hand upward. "Indeed, Sir Thomas, I cannot imagine what you think I have to lie about."

Sir Thomas laughed loudly and shook his head. "Nothing, my lady. I know from your governess that you are a good girl and did not even allow your stay in court to seriously interrupt your studies." He bowed again. "Do be seated, my lady, if you please."

She boosted herself up into the closest chair. The tingling was gone from her fingers but she still held her hand out toward the fire as if the heat would cleanse it.

"Oh, well," she said, "it was the middle of the winter, you know, and too cold to do much out of doors. And I had little to do most of the day, so it was no great burden to go on with my lessons. Anyway, I like reading Caesar. His memoir of the wars in France is quite exciting."

"I found them so myself, my lady. But Mistress Champernowne says that you were quite gay in the evenings. Not that there is anything amiss in that. A pleasant relief after working hard all day is surely a reward for virtue."

"I did enjoy being with the queen, Sir Thomas," she said, politely, wondering why he was staring at her so. "And I was greatly honored by her attention. I know she was worried about my father, the king's majesty, and we did what we could to relieve her anxiety."

"All her ladies, you mean?" Wriothesley asked sharply, hoping Elizabeth would say yes. Her evidence could not save Catherine, but it might not blacken her further.

"No," Elizabeth amended, "The queen thought that if we were a large crowd we would make too much noise. And she is not too fond of needlework, so she set the ladies at that and withdrew with me and Lady Rochefort and Thomas Culpepper."

"And Francis Dereham?" He watched her so closely that Elizabeth began to feel concerned.

"Oh, yes," she said carefully, "He was there most of the time, but he was very quiet. It was Master Culpepper who made the queen laugh the most."

"And did he make you laugh also?" The look had not changed, so whatever he was waiting to hear, she had not yet said it.

"Sometimes," Elizabeth said with a little hesitation, "but I was attending closely to my cards, which was why I won so many forfeits."

"Do you remember what made the queen laugh the most?"

What could possibly be wrong about making the queen laugh? Did he expect her to have heard something treasonous? "Not really," she told him, pretending indifference. "Something I remember about balls and bowls but I admit I did not see anything specially funny about it. Perhaps I did not understand."

"Did they ever speak of the king's majesty?"

Ah. Elizabeth was on firmer ground now and she was sure of what to say. "Oh, often." She smiled brightly. "The queen heartily wished him well again and deplored his continued weakness. She . . . she was looking forward to the progress they would make."

Wriothesley detected the hesitation and frowned. "You promised to tell all the truth," he urged.

Elizabeth sighed. "She was bored, Sir Thomas. She wished there was more diversion."

Elizabeth knew it was the queen's duty to be satisfied and happy just to be in the king's presence. She felt guilty about admitting that Catherine did not find Henry alone enough, that she longed for the feasts and the masques and the music and dancing that had enlivened the court when she and Henry were first married. To be confined to Hampton Court when most of the nobles had fled was trying Catherine's patience.

Noting the child's unwillingness to admit any fault in the queen, and finding the fault she admitted so innocent made Wriothesley much happier. Otstargi's amulet was certainly working, since Lady Elizabeth had given evidence she did not want to give, and the evidence would do the queen no harm.

"Queen Catherine is very young," Wriothesley said. "It is not surprising that she should find Hampton Court dull during the dreary winter."

This tacit pardon of Catherine's imperfection gave Elizabeth so much relief that she babbled happily about the games and the forfeits and, eventually, about Lady Rochefort taking her off to bed while the gentlemen—sometimes both sometimes only one, Culpepper—remained in the queen's chamber.

Sir Thomas questioned her more particularly about leaving the queen with the gentlemen, and she did her best to satisfy him, but, as she pointed out somewhat impatiently, she was gone from the chamber by then. How could she tell anything about what more was done and said within? No, she did not think they continued to play at cards as more than two hands were needed for the game. Possibly Francis Dereham who was musical played for them or read poetry.

All the while the strange stone, sometimes sparking with red lights as the fire leapt, attracted her at the same time that she wished to cover it up and push it away. Several times she reached toward it and twice actually touched it with the tip of a finger. Sir Thomas smiled at her each time, and certainly did not forbid her. Nonetheless, each time she found the touch vaguely unpleasant, and yet the stone was smooth and dry; how could there be anything unpleasant about a pretty stone?

Eventually Sir Thomas could find no more questions to ask. He thanked Elizabeth for her time and patience and took his leave, wrapping up and taking the Bible with him. Just before he covered it, Elizabeth, watching the crawling streaks and bursts of red in the dark stone, almost asked him to leave the book with her. When he covered it, however, she heaved a big sigh of relief and barely returned his bow with a nod of her head.

Later when Kat wondered why Sir Thomas had needed to question her so minutely but spoke hopefully of their being summoned to court by the queen, Elizabeth felt briefly uneasy. The anxiety passed, however, and she went about her daily life with a pleasant feeling of anticipation. Neither she nor Kat told Denoriel about Wriothesley's visit or what they believed to be its purpose. Both knew that Lord Denno was not happy about their sojourns at court and wished to put off as long as possible any mention of the approach of what he called his misery of loneliness.

Denoriel, who was well aware of the accusations against the queen from worried and frightened conversations he was never meant to overhear between Norfolk and his relatives, did not speak of the court nor the accusations to Elizabeth and Kat. However, once Dereham and Culpepper were brought to trial on December first, there was no keeping the secret any longer.

Since he knew of Elizabeth's fondness for Queen Catherine, Denoriel was not surprised that she reacted violently, but he had not expected the degree of fear and fury that overcame her. Her first impulse was to "slay the messenger" by flying into a near-hysterical rage. He should have warned her, she cried. See what came of not warning her, of trying to keep her ignorant. Because of that she had told Wriothesley things that not only could be used against the queen but might end in her own trial and execution.

"Ridiculous!" Denoriel exclaimed and Kat echoed him. "You cannot have told Wriothesley anything incriminating, either about the queen or about yourself." He turned to Kat. "When was he here? What did he say? Could you not have stopped him from frightening Lady Elizabeth?"

"He insisted on a private interview," Kat faltered. "He is the king's secretary. I could not refuse."

Denoriel's lips parted and then closed. He reached out and took Elizabeth's hand and stroked it. "My lady," he murmured, "you must not allow yourself to be so overset. From what you told me about your time with the queen, neither you nor she did anything or said anything that could be faulted. The games, the forfeits, these were all innocent. Unless—was there something you did not tell me or Mistress Champernowne?"

"No! But what I told you was enough! Master Culpepper kissed her hand and her wrist and forearm too! And I left them alone together more than once."

"But, Lady Elizabeth, you could do nothing else when the queen dismissed you," Kat cried. "You are only a little girl. You are not expected to understand such things. It was Lady Rochefort who was to blame, if anything done was wrong. But even she could not gainsay a dismissal from the queen. No blame will fall upon *you*."

"Yes it will! I should have told someone. I should have . . ." Her voice dropped to nothing and then rose hysterically. "They will try me and chop off my head!"

"Love," Denoriel murmured, taking her hands in his, "I swear to you that no harm will come to you. You are innocent, but even if you were not, no harm would come to you. If worse comes to worst, I will take you to your Da and he will protect you."

Elizabeth clutched Denoriel's hands. Hers were cold and shaking but she drew warmth out of his and the terror that had increasingly knotted her throat and roiled her belly diminished. To be safe in her half-brother's arms. Yes, she would be safe. There would be no need to kill herself, to jump from the wall or one of the towers and thus end her life quickly and without shame.

Kat looked puzzled when Denoriel called King Henry 'Da' but she saw the expression of relief smooth Elizabeth's pinched features; she assumed it was just a reminder of a relationship that was not totally formal, where personal affection could overrule strict justice.

"Of course you will be safe and protected, you silly child," Kat said. "Now, I know you grieve for the queen, but she should not have lied to the king. Likely if she had told him the truth when he first

courted her, she would have been sent away with a handsome present. You have never lied to the king, and you will be protected."

Not by the king, Elizabeth thought, restraining a shudder, but
her Da would protect her—and Denno knew where he was and
would take her there . . . and the warmth from her Denno's hands
flowed into her, pushing out the black cold that had been rising
daily to drown her in grief and misery.

Only, feeling a little more confident with Denno's warm hands to
comfort her, Elizabeth hoped she would not need to flee to the safe
place where her half-brother lived. She wanted to stay in England.
This was her place. She had a purpose here. Edward already loved her
well and they would be together again, she was sure. When he was
king she could be at court with him and he would listen to her.

Elizabeth saw then that Denno's face was pale and strained and
she thought the iron cross was hurting him. With a smile and a
murmur of apology she released his hands.

It had not been the pain from cold iron that had caused
Denoriel's discomfort. Elizabeth had been leaching power from
him at a dangerous rate. He had been shocked because it had
never happened before. Of course, they seldom touched more
than a glancing contact and she had never been in such a state
of terror before. Poor child. Would Catherine's execution, if it
came to that, remind her of her mother's trial and execution?
And Catherine was a Howard, just as Anne had been.

Elizabeth never spoke of Anne, and Denoriel hoped she did
not remember what had happened. Yet she remembered Harry
very clearly indeed. Was there some way he could soften the
blow for her?

After Elizabeth seemed calm and almost able to smile, Denoriel
took his leave and rode sedately away from Hatfield to the little wood
beyond the farm lane. From there he Gated back to London, arriving
still a-horseback in Miralys's stable. The horse-boy, a faun cloaked
in illusion, smiled at him, but made no move to do anything. Aside
from smiling back, Denoriel ignored him. The faun could and did
care for the horses of the occasional visitor to Lord Denno's house,
but he recognized an elvensteed and did not presume.

From the stable, Denoriel strolled into the office of his man
of business. Joseph Clayborne pushed aside the papers he was
studying and started to rise. Denoriel signed for him to remain
seated and hitched a hip over the corner of Clayborne's desk.

"What can you tell me about Sir Thomas Wriothesley?"

"Sir Thomas Wriothesley." Clayborne pursed his lips. "No particular family. Served Cromwell when he was Cardinal Woolsey's man. Rose with Cromwell—he was knighted when Cromwell was created Earl of Essex." Clayborne wrinkled his nose. "It appears he escaped being tarred with Cromwell's brush, by giving evidence against his master. I am not sure whether it was that or that he had already caught the king's attention, but he was appointed co-secretary to King Henry with Sir Ralph Sadlier."

Denoriel sat staring at the cabinets against the wall of Clayborne's office. There did not seem to be anything at all uncanny about Wriothesley; however he could have said something to Elizabeth, threatened her in some way, that—considering her background—induced panic. A terror so strong that she needed to draw energy from him?

"Have we any business with Secretary Wriothesley?" Denoriel asked. "I would like to meet him if I could."

"Had the situation in the royal household been other than it is, I would have said that Norfolk could have provided an introduction."

Denoriel laughed. "Two nieces caught in adultery is at least one more than Norfolk could expect to survive without a blemish. After presiding with his peers over the trial of Dereham and Culpepper, he left for his country estate at Kenninghall where he will watch over and question Lady Rochefort. He hopes, I suppose, to make her the instigator and reduce his niece's guilt."

"It will not serve, m'lord." Joseph seemed certain of that. Denoriel agreed with him.

"No, it cannot. It was the queen who committed the crime, no matter who persuaded her to it." Denoriel shook his head. "But if Lady Rochefort did urge Catherine to commit adultery . . . I wonder if I could find out . . ." Denoriel let his voice drift away, remembering that he *could* find out.

Clayborne shrugged. "That is far beyond my purview, m'lord, but I will look through our accounts and see if I can find a connection to Secretary Wriothesley or, perhaps, a trading venture in which he might be interested. He likes money."

Denoriel was satisfied to leave his meeting with Wriothesley in Clayborne's hands, and he was not disappointed—at least not in the fact of their meeting two weeks later. He was disappointed in a sense because there was nothing to connect Wriothesley with the Unseleighe—and Elizabeth now seemed to have taken a turn for the worse. First she had accused him again of lying to her. On another visit she had thrust the picture of Harry back at him, and when he came again she had refused to see him at all. Aleneil had been just as forcefully rejected.

Denoriel wanted to suspect Unseleighe tampering because a spell, once it was recognized, could be countered by another spell or broken, whereas a violent disruption of the mortal mind or spirit was much more difficult to cure. But Wriothesley had no magic, no Unseleighe taint, and no other strangers had had access to Elizabeth. Moreover, Elizabeth's own Talent made it impossible—at least for him—to detect a well-shielded spell laid on her.

In addition there *were* natural reasons for her anxiety. Culpepper and Dereham were executed on the twelfth of December and over the rest of the month and the beginning of January, the Howard family was severely questioned about Catherine's behavior as a girl. Parliament was summoned in December, and just before it convened on the sixteenth of January, many of the Duke of Norfolk's relatives were found guilty of misprision of treason for concealing Catherine's lack of chastity. They were sentenced to forfeiture of all their possessions and to perpetual imprisonment.

Although Kat assured Denoriel, on one last visit to Hatfield, that she had done her best to keep this information from the child, it was impossible to prevent the servants from gossiping about so lush a scandal. No doubt they gossiped only when and where they thought Elizabeth could not hear, but her hearing was keen and she was not sleeping well.

The punishment of the Howards induced a terrible panic in Elizabeth. No matter what Kat said, no matter that they had not again been troubled by questions about Elizabeth's stay in court, Elizabeth was convinced that she was soon to join her cousins and aunts and uncles and be thrust into prison. And then Catherine was executed on February 13.

At her wits' end, because Elizabeth was now refusing to eat as well as waking screaming three and four times a night, Kat wrote to Lord Denno and sent Tolliver racing to London to summon him. She had done everything she knew how to do; the physicians could find nothing wrong with Elizabeth except her hysteria. Kat had even written an appeal to the king to reassure his daughter. No reply came directly from Henry, who perhaps had been reminded of Elizabeth's mother, also executed for adultery, but Secretary Wriothesley had written that Elizabeth should be calm; no evil was imputed to her.

The letter had no effect. Lord Denno, Kat wrote, was her last hope, even though Elizabeth swore she would never see him again. Denoriel told Tolliver to rest his exhausted horse a day before returning to Hatfield, mounted Miralys, and presented himself to Kat just as dusk was falling. Kat was astonished, but went to rouse Elizabeth, who was now refusing to get out of bed. However, when Kat begged Elizabeth to talk to Lord Denno, the child began to scream with rage and fear.

"Denno is a liar," Elizabeth shrieked. "He will not save me. He cannot save me. No one can save me. Denno has given me false comfort in public while in secret he is trying to destroy me."

Without waiting for permission, Denoriel walked through the door into Elizabeth's bedchamber. Elizabeth grabbed a bowl full of soup she had not eaten from the table beside her and threw it at him.

"Lady Elizabeth!" Kat protested, retreating as the soup sprayed over her and the bedclothes.

Denoriel caught the bowl and then gasped with shock. He had not seen Elizabeth for nearly a month and the change in her was terrifying. She had never been round and rosy-cheeked, even as an infant. Her skin had always been pale, but there had been a sort of glow, a look of resilience, of health, to her face. Now the skin looked dull and her cheeks seemed to have fallen in so that she looked wizened, more like a shrunken old woman than a child.

"What is wrong?" Denoriel cried, covering the room in three bounds and going down on his knees on the little step stool Elizabeth used to climb into bed. "How am I trying to destroy you?"

She began to recoil, but he seized her hands . . . and felt his power being sucked away into a bottomless pit of black cold. Elizabeth no longer resisted, but burst into racking sobs and sank back on the pillows behind her. She made one feeble attempt to pull her hands from his, but desisted when he just tightened his grip.

"Blanche!" he roared, turning on Kat. "Where is Blanche?"

"No, no, don't call Blanche," Elizabeth sobbed. "I've nearly killed her."

"Don't be silly, Lady Elizabeth," Kat protested. "One doesn't say she is killing someone because that person is tired from nursing her." She looked at Denoriel. "Blanche is abed." Her voice quavered a little and she hastily added, "She has been sitting up most nights with Lady Elizabeth and is naturally worn out."

"Unnaturally worn out," Elizabeth sobbed. "She stops the dreams, but . . . but it is as if she catches them, and they hurt her."

"What dreams?" Denoriel asked.

He was grateful that he was kneeling on the stool. At the rate she was draining him, he was not sure his legs would support him for long. Soon he would have to withdraw from her or be useless to her. Almost unaware of what he was doing, he sought and found a glittering white line of power. Could he drink it and pass it through himself to Elizabeth or would it sear his power lines beyond repair?

"Of you!" Elizabeth's voice was so shrill and loud that it pierced through Denoriel's conflict about drawing power from the violent mortal source. "Of you telling me you love me and you cannot bear to see me shamed and hurt, so I should climb up the wall or to the tower and throw myself off. It would be only a moment's pain, you said, and then I would be safe forever from the shame of being daughter and cousin to queenly whores. Safe from being myself beheaded."

"No!" Denoriel cried. "I told you I could keep you safe and I can. That was not me in your dream! Did you not sense that it was not me?"

He felt Elizabeth's start of surprise and then a kind of softening in the tight tension with which she had gripped his hands. However, before she could speak, Kat came closer.

"Well, it was a dream, so of course it was not you," Kat said. "But I cannot think why Lady Elizabeth would mix your image into such a dreadful dream. What a terrible, horrible, unchristian idea to put into a child's head." She came and patted Elizabeth's shoulder. "I am sure Lord Denno would never give such advice in a true dream, but there are false dreams, Lady Elizabeth. Now get out of bed like a good girl and I will call a maid to change this wet coverlet."

Denoriel backed away as Elizabeth complied, walking slowly to a chair and seating herself. His blood beat in his throat and his mouth was dry. False dream! And the sucking out of his power. It *was* a spell! A spell of dissolution! Because she had Talent, she was especially vulnerable—like her mother. But Elizabeth had far more power than Anne. Her inner strength had kept her alive. Without her power, she would have been dead long ago. She had been resisting the spell—and drawing on Blanche for more power, which was why the maid was drained out.

Poor child. Denoriel swallowed. Pasgen. The spell must be Pasgen's. He had no proof, but if he could lay hands on Pasgen, he would wring his neck. Only it was more important to free Elizabeth than to hunt Pasgen. Denoriel was furious with himself for having missed the signs the first time Elizabeth's touch had drained him. He could have saved her months of agony. Now even an hour more seemed too long. He went down on his knee beside her chair and took her hands, then raised them to his lips and kissed them. Last, he folded them together and set them in her lap.

Softly, despairingly, Elizabeth began to cry.

"No, don't cry love," he said. "I think I know why you are having these bad dreams. And they are *just* dreams, sent to frighten you and torment you."

"Sent?" Kat cried, coming back into the room. "Sent by whom? And who would want to frighten and torment Lady Elizabeth?"

Elizabeth met Denoriel's eyes, and she looked even more frightened. She knew who might want to frighten and torment her, but she had no idea why the being who looked so much like her dear Denno hated her so much. And she could not get comfort from Kat because she and Blanche had never told Mistress Champernowne about the attack on her. She said nothing, her hands tightening in her lap until the knuckles showed white. Denoriel's jaws clamped shut for a moment; then he shook his head at Kat.

"I don't know," he lied, "but I will do my best to find out. And even if I cannot find out, I think I know how to make the dreams stop." He took Elizabeth's hands again, kissed the white knuckles. "You may have another dream tonight, but it will be a different kind of dream and the bad ones will go away." His voice shook a little, not with weakness but with his anger. "Of that you may be certain."

Chapter 11

Denoriel flung himself off Miralys and rushed into Mwynwen's house with a gross lack of ceremony. The soft, sweet music, the palest green, gently glowing walls, the silky carpet underfoot did not soothe him. He was shaking with need and anxiety and jumped a foot when Harry rushed through the door just behind him.

"Denno, what's wrong?" he cried. "I was riding and suddenly Lady Aeron just turned around and carried me home. I could feel her shaking under me. What's happened?"

"Elizabeth," Denoriel replied through tight lips. "Somehow my loathsome half-brother—"

"Elizabeth is dead?" Harry's voice scaled up to a shriek, ringing through the quiet house; his face was as pallid as it had been when he was first brought Underhill, a few days from death.

"No!" Denoriel grasped his friend's arm. "No. And she will recover well as soon as the spell is broken. Where is Mwynwen?"

"Here." Her voice was cold, her expression harder than Denoriel had ever seen it. "How dare you come rushing into the private part of my house without leave? What have you done to Harry?"

Denoriel swallowed. "Sorry. I gave him a shock. Pasgen has somehow managed to set a spell of dissolution onto Elizabeth—"

"Set a spell of dissolution on a child?" Mwynwen's horror

overcame both her jealous dislike of Elizabeth and her anger. Now she was as pale as Harry, but it was with anger, not fear.

"Please, Mwynwen," Denoriel pleaded, "come with me to the mortal world and break the spell on her. I know you do not like the mortal world, but Elizabeth has fought the spell for almost two months and I do not think she can resist much longer. I promised her . . . I will pay whatever you ask in service or in goods from the mortal world. I—"

"I want nothing from the mortal world," Mwynwen snapped. Then her eyes flicked toward Harry and her expression softened into a smile. "I have everything I need from there. Of course I will come and cure the child."

"Just let me get my gun," Harry said, "and I will be with you. And this time, I will make sure that the bolt goes home into that devil of a brother of yours if he shows his face."

"No," Denoriel said quickly. "Don't be a fool, Harry. You can't come to Hatfield. Half the servants will know you. Blanche certainly will and it's possible that Mistress Champernowne will have seen you on one of her visits to court. With Elizabeth so ill, there are people in and out of her bedchamber constantly. You've only been gone for four years. Nobody will have forgotten."

Mwynwen was obviously relieved when Denoriel told Harry he could not come with them, but Denoriel could see that Harry was going to argue.

"The likelihood of Pasgen turning up in Elizabeth's bedchamber is vanishingly small," he pointed out. "He set the spell and left it to work. I don't think he even cast it on her himself. He won't go near her for fear that Oberon will hear of it, so I am certain he placed it on an object and sent some poor unsuspecting fool to place it for him. If she . . . If the spell succeeds in its purpose there's no real way to connect him to it. Harry, the best thing you can do for Elizabeth is to write her another letter."

Harry rushed off and Mwynwen asked whether they would need to ride to the Logres Gate.

"It would be best. I think Lady Aeron would take you. Well, I'm sure she would if Harry asked her." Denoriel heaved a long, tired sigh. "Elizabeth was . . . was very near empty. She drained me. I don't think I could build a Gate right now."

"Why should you? Take as long as you like. You can Gate back to just after you left; it will take more magic, but you know that

you can reenter the World Above at any time after you left it."
She uttered a delicate, impatient snort. "Oh, come and sit down.
I was angry because I could feel Harry's fear, but you know you
are welcome here without special invitation."

Denoriel sank into the deliciously soft chair to which Mwynwen
led him and closed his eyes. "A few hours," he said, his voice
shaking. "I can chance that. But no more; you know that time
moves differently here and there, and I will not make her wait
out the night. I promised her a different dream, one that will
stop the evil. I will not make her wait longer than an hour or
two. Longer will be another broken promise. It is me she sees
urging her to death."

"She will not wait long," Mwynwen said, her voice firm. "And
that is *my* promise. We will come to her before she has had time
to miss you, but you must rest and recover your strength, or you
will do her and yourself no good."

"So why is she not dead?" Vidal roared.

A chorus of voices answered him. "Kill her!" "Be rid of her!"
"Yes! She must die!" "We hunger and if she comes to the throne,
no matter when, we will starve."

The low, angry growl came from the rows of dark Sidhe ranked
before Vidal's throne. Pasgen sat in the first seat among those, the
foremost on what would be the left side of the aisle from Vidal's
throne. Rhoslyn sat beside him. Years before Vidal had tried to
separate them, to set Rhoslyn on the other side of the aisle. He
had spoken of the honor of that place, first on his right hand as
Pasgen was first on his left.

Pasgen smiled slightly, remembering Rhoslyn's reply—loud and
clear ringing throughout the throne room—that she would rather
have less honor and more safety. That she would far rather sit next
to Pasgen than on Vidal's own throne. The smile did not linger on
Pasgen's lips. He raised his eyes calmly to meet Vidal's, noting that
the dark orbs were taking on luster. Vidal was still recovering.

"How clear do you wish to make it to King Oberon that the
Unseleighe had a hand in the death of the king's daughter?" Pasgen asked, smiling again. "What I have done cannot be followed
to any source other than a mortal who employs another mortal
as a foreteller and advisor. Did you not yourself forbid me to go
near the girl, Prince Vidal?"

"But we hunger!"

The undifferentiated growl came from the mass of dark Sidhe. Pasgen restrained a shudder. One sign of weakness and they would all be on him . . . and take Rhoslyn, who would try to save him, too. One at a time, he could defeat them. All together—not a chance in the world. But he had to make a show of strength against them, or they would be on him like wolves.

"You fools!" he said, standing and turning to look over them. "Elizabeth's death will not change that. Prince Vidal desires it as a safeguard for the future, but all that matters is that she not come to the throne as queen. Whether the child dies now or some years hence will make no difference to the power coming to us from the mortal world. If you hunger, go snatch a mortal or two and play with them. Take out the Wild Hunt and trouble your lord no more!"

"Only one mortal or two!" Vidal said sharply. "No more! And be sure the hunt takes them in places far from each other."

Pasgen dropped back into his seat, surprised at finding himself glad of Vidal's continued recovery, of the prince's ability to issue a confident command. Let Vidal continue to gain strength and agility of mind and he would no longer need to appear to support Vidal with respect and obedience. Pasgen found himself very tired of the Unseleighe of Vidal Dhu's court. He wanted to be free to follow his own studies and experiments. If Vidal again truly ruled the Unseleighe, Pasgen could withdraw himself and simply ignore Vidal's summons; he no longer feared the prince and he could protect Rhoslyn too.

"A little patience," Vidal was saying. "Soon will come the season for the Scots to raid. I have seen to it that King James did not meet with King Henry to make peace. I have also arranged for an English leader who is no longer willing simply to drive the Scots away. He will follow to punish, but the Scots will be warned of his coming and his men will be slain, he himself taken prisoner. The English will retaliate, and then the Scots will perforce make their answer in arms. There will be war—rapine, looting—and for us . . . power."

"Ah . . ."

Again that bestial, crude response, but this time of satisfaction. Pasgen thought of the chaos lands, of the wisps of sweetness here and there with longing. So much better than the bitter power coming from the misery of mortals. Somehow he must learn to breed that kind of mist. The red monster would grow if fed, though Pasgen was still trying to discover a way to destroy it. Surely he could find a way to feed the sweet mists. And the self-contained wisp of mist that Rhoslyn had given him was equally an enigma; it had a vigor that the sweet mists lacked. So much to learn. So much to do.

Rhoslyn pinched his arm, drawing him from his thoughts to the realization that the court was dispersing and that Vidal was beckoning him toward the throne. Rhoslyn let him pass and was about to follow him, but Vidal shook his head at her, smiling scornfully.

"He will not need your protection, mistress."

Some of the dark Sidhe had stopped and were looking avidly from the twins to Vidal. Annoyed, Pasgen raised a shield around them as if he were afraid; he wasn't. He could destroy any spell Vidal cast without a shield, but he was not ready for Vidal to know that or the other members of the court either.

"Go," Pasgen said to Rhoslyn, lifting his hand to touch the small furry creature under his collar.

Rhoslyn nodded and said softly, "Keep shielded for a half hour. The lindys will tell me after that if all is not well with you."

"It will be."

Pasgen turned away and came to the foot of the dais on which Vidal's throne sat. Although the purpose for which Rhoslyn had created the pretty snakelike creatures was finished—for two weeks Rhoslyn had done everything she could think of to Pasgen's token: burned it, thrown spells at it, locked it in an airless dark place, frozen it, all without Pasgen ever becoming aware of the mistreatment—the creatures had proven themselves useful in other ways.

Pasgen had forgotten to return the little thing. It was silent, noiseless, odorless and unobtrusive; it moved by itself whenever he changed his clothing. If anyone caught a glimpse of it, it could be taken for fur trim. And then Rhoslyn had been briefly trapped by a malfunctioning Gate. Pasgen's lindys had begun to vibrate so violently that he Gated with dizzying speed to her domain to find her missing. Fortunately before he had begun to wreak havoc to find her, the lindys had gone quiet and a few moments later, Rhoslyn herself arrived, a bit shaken but unhurt, and explained what had happened to her.

Obviously just knowing that the other was in trouble was not enough. Pasgen had spent a delightful few weeks working out a spell by which he, and he alone, could home in on Rhoslyn's lindys and Rhoslyn could equally find him. Now either of them knew if the opposite twin was in trouble—and where to find that twin. Rhoslyn was not as strong in magic as he, except for her ability to create, but if he needed her, she would arrive with a dozen of her "girls," who were mostly impervious to spells. Pasgen smiled up at Vidal Dhu. He would feel sorry for anyone Rhoslyn's "girls" took in hand.

However, Vidal did nothing more threatening than rise and walk through the door behind the throne. Having gestured the door to his private apartment open, he walked in and nodded to Aurelia, who was lying back on a black-velvet-covered couch of the old Roman fashion, her golden hair a brilliant halo around her pale face.

"Is your headache any better?" Vidal asked.

"Oh, yes. Golbuleum drew it out of me, but I had to speak to him most sharply and he collapsed once he had drawn out the pain. He says the pain is almost impossible to disperse, that it is nothing like any pain he has ever treated before."

A remnant of the damage done Aurelia by the maid with the necklace of cold iron crosses? Pasgen wondered. If so the recurring pain must be connected with cold iron. No wonder it was hurting the healer to draw it out.

Vidal's eyes narrowed and he confirmed Pasgen's guess by saying, "Those headaches are what remains of the harm done you in the World Above. What we need is a mortal who is Talented in healing. I know they do not live long, but probably it will live long enough to rid you of this problem." His eyes shifted to Pasgen. "So, since you have failed at your primary task, do you think you could at least find a healer?"

"Failed at his task?" Aurelia repeated. "You mean that Elizabeth is not dead? Why are you so inept, Pasgen? I did my part. Lady Rochefort was delighted with the necklace sent by her mother by marriage and wore it often. So she was often reminded of her losses—her position as sister to the queen and the terrible shame when her husband was executed for incest with his sister, and the fact that it was all lies, only because the king wanted a new wife."

"Yes, Aurelia," Vidal said, with oily satisfaction. "Your amulet did work perfectly. Lady Rochefort aided and abetted Catherine in committing adultery and she and Catherine lost their heads and half of Norfolk's family is in prison, but Pasgen's spells are not so effective. Elizabeth is alive and well."

"Lady Rochefort was not protected by my half-brother," Pasgen said flatly, swallowing rage. "And the High King has not forbidden us to meddle with *her*. I thought I had wakened enough distrust of Denoriel in Elizabeth and the governess, but unfortunately the child did not admit to the governess that Denno had attacked her, and the governess is more completely dependent on him than I knew."

"Governess! Pah! Your spell was too weak!" Vidal flung himself into his thronelike chair.

Stung, Pasgen snapped back, "I know that my second attempt was perfectly successful. Servants and idle equerries talk in ale-houses, and I have servants who listen. The dreams did work. Elizabeth did reject Denoriel and she was within days of dying of her own fear or flinging herself from the battlements for relief." Pasgen took a breath, grateful that Vidal had excluded Rhoslyn. She would have been furious over the pain he had inflicted on a child. A black scowl drew his brows together. He did not like to think about what he had done himself. It was one thing to make war on Denoriel, but another to strive for the death of a child.

"If she was all but dead, what happened?" Aurelia asked wasp-ishly.

"The governess panicked and sent for Denoriel even though Elizabeth swore she would not see him," Pasgen said sullenly. "In fact, she *did* refuse to see him, but he forced himself upon her and he recognized that she was bespelled. How he could tell in the mess of her own Talent and the miasma of that iron cross she wears..." He shrugged. "He fetched that pet healer of his, of the Seleighe Court, who found the spell and broke it."

Aurelia sat up on the couch and stared at him. "How? How did the healer work on her while she wore the cross? And did not you tell us that she would not take it off, that she ran from you when you told her to take it off?"

"How can I know?" Pasgen snapped. "I was not there, and Elizabeth can see any creature we send to spy on her or the nurse can sense it. But what I guess is that the healer cast a sleep spell on her and Denoriel removed the cross."

Aurelia shuddered, despite her pique, distracted by the very idea of handling something made of the death metal. "He can touch it?"

"He was always less sensitive to cold iron than most," Pasgen admitted with a shrug. "I know Koronos would send him to the fore when the hunt took down a mortal with steel weapons. I have heard from my mother that my father was the same."

"Too bad the talent did not come to you." Vidal sneered.

"True enough," Aurelia spat. "You do not seem to be good for anything! Is all my hard work to go for nothing?"

"For all of me, it can!" Pasgen snarled. "I will be more than happy to leave Elizabeth to your tender mercies in the future. But—" he started to repeat his warnings about Oberon, then shrugged. Enough. If Vidal wished to cross swords with the High King, on his head be it.

"Very well," Vidal said with a thin smile. "Busy yourself with finding a mortal healer for us."

Pasgen mistrusted both the smile and the easy agreement. He suspected that some open attack would be made on Elizabeth in such a way that the blame for it would fall upon him. He thought of Oberon's response to so blatant a violation of his command that neither the king nor anyone in his family should be the subject of Unseleighe attack, and grew cold within; now he regretted suggesting that Vidal do his own dirty work.

He thought of giving Vidal a warning, but instead bowed and withdrew. He had time to think before he acted. He knew that Denoriel had drained himself out putting wards on the walls of Elizabeth's chambers. If Vidal tried to build a Gate there, his spell would backlash on him. And Pasgen was very sure that Elizabeth would not emerge from those chambers for some time. He had learned that Elizabeth was using the effects of the spell as an excuse and had taken to her bed. No visitors—except of course his accursed half-brother and half-sister—were being allowed.

Nonetheless, he would need to keep an eye on Vidal. It would be impossible to keep Elizabeth abed for very long, and when she emerged from her bedchamber she would become vulnerable. Pasgen sighed as he walked down the corridor to the black marble steps. Something else to keep him from his own work, but he would have to make sure that Vidal did not make *him* the sacrificial goat for Oberon's wrath. Better by far that Oberon's anger should find the appropriate target.

Pacing the floor of his sitting room before the hearth in which Mwynwen's salamander danced merrily over the rainbow-colored flames leaping around some crystal logs, Denoriel was saying much the same thing as Pasgen had been thinking.

"We cannot keep her abed much longer." He looked at Mwynwen, who sat holding Harry's hand on the sofa while Aleneil fidgeted in one of the graceful armchairs. "Can you do nothing to protect her?"

"Mwynwen, please?" Harry pleaded.

"Do you think me a monster?" the healer exploded, and the salamander gyrated and hissed and leapt half out of the hearth. "I would protect the child if I could, but I cannot. Her Talent is totally unstable. Most of the time it is too tenuous for me to train, but there is a huge . . . reservoir, or well . . . full of power within her. And that, from what you told me, can burst out of her if she is threatened or frightened. Perhaps she could be taught to draw on that, but it is sorcerers who can store and use power in that way, not a healer. So Elizabeth needs to be trained by a sorcerer. If she knew the proper spells, I think she would be able to use them when she felt herself to be in danger."

"Trained by a sorcerer," Denoriel repeated. "But that would mean bringing her Underhill. Even if we could find a human sorcerer who was not a charlatan in all of England, we would not dare bring him to Elizabeth, much less take her to him. But bring the king's daughter here? Underhill? Oberon would fry us in our own skins."

"You brought me," Harry said.

"That was to escape the Wild Hunt of the Unseleighe and we were loose Underhill only because the Gate failed." He shook his head. "To bring a royal child to be trained by an elven or otherwise otherworldly sorcerer . . . Oberon would not countenance it."

Aleneil stood up. "But Titania is absolutely determined that Elizabeth should come to the throne, and Elizabeth cannot be crowned queen if she is dead. Moreover, what she knows Oberon would forbid is very tempting to Titania. Ordinarily I would not encourage her rebelliousness, but truly Elizabeth's life is worth a quarrel between the King and Queen. I will appeal to Titania."

"Ah . . ." Denoriel drew out the sound and looked down at his fingers uneasily. "Do I have to come with you? I know I am responsible for Elizabeth's safety, but the way Titania looks at me . . ."

Both Mwynwen and Aleneil laughed, and Mwynwen said, "No, I will go with Aleneil. I wish to make a point of just how horrible a spell was cast on Elizabeth. Titania is very fond of mortal children. When I describe the pain inflicted on this poor little child, she will be outraged."

The Queen was indeed outraged when they found her, but it took considerable effort to track her to her current location. Mwynwen and Aleneil first Gated from Logres to Avalon; but the Queen was not in the palace. On the advice of those maids and servitors left behind they then tried several meadows and woodland sites Titania favored. These too were empty of the Queen and her court, but they came upon one of the wee folk, a tiny flashing figure with butterfly wings, sucking nectar with its long tongue from some brilliant red lilies.

From a cascade of high tinkling, Aleneil made out the faery's words: "She has a new mortal child, taken away to save it from starvation and an early grave. To save them grieving for lost parents and siblings, she lets the mortal children she steals believe they have died and gone to heaven."

Then, perhaps because it was (by their luck) more pleasant and cooperative than its kind usually were, or, more likely, because it was curious to see Aleneil's and Mwynwen's reaction, it showed them how to Gate to the domain called Heaven. Likely it got its satisfaction because when the clouds that concealed the terminus Gate parted, Aleneil just stood there gaping around her.

"It really is heaven," Aleneil exclaimed.

"Well, I hope so," Mwynwen said doubtfully, looking around for the tiny, flashing creature, which was now gone. "The wee folk can be very mischievous and could easily misdirect us for amusement."

"No, no," Aleneil said. "I am sure this *is* the domain called Heaven. Mortals believe in a place called heaven to which they can go after they die if they have been sufficiently virtuous or religious or both."

Mwynwen looked at her blankly for a moment and then shrugged.

"I suppose because they live such short lives they must find some way to believe they will exist longer. And it is rather pretty."

From the Gate a luminous golden path led through a dense but brilliantly lit mass of clouds. Here and there reclining amid the clouds were golden-haired, round-eared creatures—which must be constructs—with huge white-feathered wings. When Mwynwen and Aleneil stepped forward onto the path, the constructs burst into song.

"Sweet Dannae," Aleneil muttered, torn between annoyance and amusement, "it's a hymn. Those wretched creatures are singing a hymn from the mortal church service. They are meant to be angels . . . mortal men's angels . . ." Amusement won. She burst into giggles. "I wonder if I could get permission to bring a few particularly obnoxious 'saints' to visit and introduce them to Titania."

Mwynwen did not answer. Her attention was fixed on a pair of huge gates, seemingly attached to nothing at all, that blocked the golden path. The gates were elaborately wrought of pearls, and before them stood a large male figure clad in a loose white gown. He had long white hair and a white beard that flowed down his chest.

"Is there some purpose for this nonsense?" Mwynwen asked. Obviously, in her case, irritation had won over amusement.

"Oh, yes." Aleneil laughed. "This is just how heaven is most often described in the mortal world. And look at the gatekeeper. One would swear he was St. Peter."

"I don't know who St. Peter is," Mwynwen admitted, "but I hope the construct has enough brains to be able to answer a simple question."

It did not have any brains at all. When Aleneil and Mwynwen approached it, and asked for Titania, it smiled and said, "Ah, a child of good heart. You are welcome here in Heaven." And it swung open the pearly gate and gestured for them to enter.

Fortunately there was no problem in finding Queen Titania. On the other side of the gate, the golden path narrowed into a little lane that passed between borders of bright, low-growing flowers over which could be seen an immaculate green lawn. In the distance there appeared to be gentle hills and possibly pretty woods. However, immediately ahead was a dais, covered with a thick Turkey carpet. On that was a low chair and in the chair a lady dressed in a soft blue robe.

Mwynwen breathed a sigh of relief. They had found the Queen. Aleneil bit her lips at the notion of Titania playing the Mother of God, but that was clearly what she was doing. On her lap was an extraordinarily pretty, if bruised, terribly thin, and dirty, little boy. The child looked somewhat stunned, but not at all unhappy or frightened.

Aleneil bowed; Mwynwen lowered her head. Titania barely glanced at them. She bent her head over that of the child and said, "Will you go now and play with these other children? I promise you they will be glad to have you with them."

"Yes, please come," a little girl with a wreath of flowers in her hair, chubby, bare feet, and a spotless white smock begged, holding out her hand.

"I have a toy horse that moves of itself," a boy of about the same age as the child in Titania's lap said. "You can play with it if you like. The lady will give me another if you wish to keep it—or she will give *you* another if you want a new one."

Aleneil watched as several other children extended invitations . . . all appeared to be human, but some were real mortal children, and some were constructs. The mortal children were extraordinarily well behaved, and the constructs were more intelligent than the gate-keeper. The child looked at the others doubtfully, as if he were not accustomed to acceptance, but Titania urged him to go, promising he could return to her later, and eventually he slid off her lap and took the hand of the little girl.

"I'm a bastard," he said to her loudly.

"Is that so?" she replied, smiling. "It doesn't matter in Heaven what you were before you came here. Would you like to look at Efan's horse, or would you like to have some milk and biscuits and play with my puzzle-box?"

Suddenly, although they could still see the children, Mwynwen and Aleneil could no longer hear them. Titania lost the softness of her pose, sat rigidly erect, and bent her gleaming green eyes on them.

"FarSeer and Healer. What do you want here? If you have come from Oberon, go back and tell him I said no. And do not come again."

"We have not come from Oberon," Mwynwen said. "In fact, we would prefer greatly if you did not mention to him that we were here . . . or what we asked of you."

"Is this concerning something you have Seen?" the Queen asked Aleneil, sounding puzzled, almost anxious.

Aleneil bowed her head. "It is no new Seeing, but is to do with what I have Seen in the past, a Seeing you know of and wish to see fulfilled. Elizabeth is being threatened."

"Denoriel is supposed to be guarding her." Titania cocked her head. "Where is Denoriel? There is something about him that I cannot fathom and I would like to know him better."

"Denoriel is in the mortal world guarding his charge," Mwynwen replied, and swiftly, to distract Titania, then added, "I have just come from the mortal world myself. Denoriel was forced to bring me where I ordinarily choose not to go to find and break a spelling cast on Elizabeth."

Titania sat straight up. "A spelling? Cast by whom?" she asked, sharply.

"We do not know, Queen Titania," Aleneil offered.

"However," Mwynwen added, "I think it must have been delivered by way of an amulet or a talisman carried by a mortal who himself or herself has no power. The spell had no . . . ah . . . signature by which I might recognize the caster."

Titania frowned, but it was in thought, not anger. "And Denoriel cannot discover who carried the spell?"

"He is almost certain who that was," Aleneil said, "but equally certain that the man had no idea what he had done."

Titania raised a delicate eyebrow. "But why do you come to me? This is something fully in the king's province. Let Denoriel speak to Oberon who will likely enough give him permission to remove any person that threatens King Henry's daughter."

Aleneil shook her head. "But, madam, the man does not threaten Elizabeth . . . not by his own will, at least. And he is apparently unaware that he ever threatened her by another's will. It would be useless to give him to the Wild Hunt. We, Mwynwen and I, believe that some faction of the Unseleighe Court is behind the danger to Elizabeth. It would not help for Denoriel to stop *this* guilty person because Vidal Dhu would simply send another to plot against the child's life."

Titania's eyes flashed, but she remained outwardly calm. "Vidal Dhu . . . I see. Do you want me to ask Oberon to give the dark prince a warning?"

Aleneil shook her head. "We fear it would not solve the problem, because there are mortal magicians too, and Elizabeth has mortal enemies. It would be easy for the Unseleighe to work through them so that nothing could be proved."

"Are you telling me that our dreams for a golden age of letters, music, and art are doomed?" Titania's full lips thinned to a hard line.

"Thankfully, no, madam," Mwynwen said. "Fortunately the child has Talent."

Mwynwen told Titania of the manifestations of that Talent, of Elizabeth's ability to see through illusion and see and sense Underhill creatures, of the burst of power that thrust an Unseleighe Sidhe back Underhill and destroyed his Gate, of the reservoir of power that had enabled her to fight the spell of dissolution until Denoriel could fetch a healer to her.

It was those final words that brought something more than curiosity and annoyance out of the High Queen. "Spell of dissolution? So much fear and horror laid upon a *child*?" Titania drew herself up and seemed to swell with anger so that Heaven shrank into a pale miniature around her. Her eyes were so terrible that Mwynwen, although she knew the rage was not directed against her, drew back. As FarSeer, Aleneil had experience of Titania in a rage because she gave much more free reign to her emotions than Oberon. No one stood firm before Oberon's rage; Titania's Aleneil could endure.

So she took up the tale, while Mwynwen recovered herself, and explained that they could not guess from where enemies would rise against Elizabeth. There were those who feared that if her brother's life should fail the people would prefer Elizabeth to her elder sister, Mary. And there were those who knew how much Edward had enjoyed her company and admired her and feared that she would influence the coming king too much.

"I could unleash such a plague . . ." Titania's eyes flashed emerald sparks.

"Madam, even Elizabeth could not bring a golden age out of the ruins of a plague." Aleneil spoke, not to soothe, but to direct. "Mwynwen gave the answer already. Elizabeth has Talent."

Titania did not immediately answer. "So did her mother, if I remember aright, and it was the Talent that left her wide open to evil influence and destroyed her."

"Because it was untrained," Mwynwen said firmly. "Because

Anne was terrified of it and would not learn how to control it. But if Elizabeth were properly trained, she could protect herself, and she has been exposed to those who use magic all her young life. It does not frighten her. On the contrary; she is fascinated by it."

"Ah." The Queen smiled and a moment later frowned. "So see that the child is trained. Why do you need to come to me?" Another pause. "And ask that I not mention to Oberon for what you asked me. What are you asking me?"

Mwynwen drew a deep breath. "I cannot train Elizabeth. Her Talent is uncertain at the moment, and comes and goes, but within her—I do not understand where or how stored—is a great well of power. I cannot reach it. I do not know how to tell her to reach it. I only know, from what I have heard *them* say, that this is what sorcerers have. Elizabeth needs to be trained by a sorcerer."

"And not a human sorcerer," Aleneil put in. "What mortal sorcerer would be able to resist boasting that he was training the king's daughter? He would whisper to a friend and that friend to another. Did you know, my queen that the mortals have passed laws in all lands forbidding the practice of magic? One hint of the child's Talent and the king and parliament would have her barred from the succession, perhaps even executed, burned, as they have burned too many already. We must bring Elizabeth Underhill for her training."

There was a long, deep silence. The Queen glanced over her shoulder to where the construct children now surrounded the mortal child. The expression on his face was heartwarming, bemused but full of joy. It was clear enough that he believed he was dead and in Heaven and he would know nothing but joy for eternity.

"It is easy enough to bring a child Underhill," Titania said, returning her gaze to Mwynwen and Aleneil. "But to return that child to the mortal world . . . that is nigh impossible. And to create what we desire, Elizabeth must remain in the mortal world."

"But she must remain alive and in her right mind," Aleneil pointed out.

Slowly, regretfully, Titania shook her head. "To release her to the mortal world after bringing her here we would need to wipe her memory of Underhill. I have done that now and again to a specially favored minstrel for the sake of having him sing to us." She shrugged. "Sometimes . . . the person is not the same afterward. In any case, for Elizabeth, what good would that be? It would wipe away all she learned here."

"I know of three mortals whose memory of Underhill has not been touched," Aleneil pointed out, "only the ability to speak of it, even in allusion, was blocked. Oberon did that to the child FitzRoy after Denoriel fled with him Underhill from the Unseleighe Wild Hunt, and there were the two mortals who are now servants to Elizabeth and who once served that same FitzRoy."

Titania gestured indifference. "The servants do not matter. If they cannot speak of Underhill no one else can learn of it from them, and they have no power. FitzRoy . . . yes. I remember. But I think that Oberon was willing to mark FitzRoy because he knew the boy would never be king. Elizabeth is different. She *will* be queen. To have a mortal queen who knows Underhill . . . That is *very* dangerous. She could decide she needed our wealth and gather a mortal army armed with steel weapons to overwhelm us."

Both Mwynwen and Aleneil looked appalled, but after a moment Aleneil said, "But can you not also plant in her the idea that all she sees Underhill is 'faery gold' that will melt away or turn to dross when brought into the light of the sun?"

"Ah." Titania cocked her head. "Now that is a thought that had not occurred to me." She nodded. "Yes, that is possible. I will even provide for her a gorgeous set of jewels that will become clods of earth wrapped in withered leaves if she carries them into the World Above." Her expression lightened into one of mischief. "Indeed, that is a good notion altogether. We must make a point of giving a handful of mortals such things, now and again, so that the tale may spread!"

"Then Denoriel may bring her?" Aleneil asked.

"Denoriel." Titania cast another glance over her shoulder at the now-laughing child but then smiled. "Yes, tell Denoriel to bring Elizabeth to his chambers in Llachar Lle." She paused and frowned. "He is to take care not to traipse all over Underhill with her first. I will come to the palace and see her there. I wish to see this prodigy for myself."

Chapter 12

Having delivered appropriate thanks to Titania, Aleneil and Mwynwen hastened away from Heaven. The glitter-winged wee folk had led them a complex path of Gating to find the domain, but the Gate at the end of the golden path had only one terminus: Avalon. They did not even step off the great eight-pointed star of tiny, glowing seashells but merely willed the Gate to move them again, to Logres.

There they found Ystwyth and Lady Aeron waiting and were whisked across the lawns and gardens to the entrance to Llachar Lle. Denoriel and Harry FitzRoy were still in the sitting room, although small tables holding the remains of a meal and flagons and glasses gave evidence that they had not neglected themselves. Harry jumped to his feet and turned toward the door when the salamander appeared suddenly among the crystal logs.

"Harry," Denoriel warned against too eager a question.

But it was Denoriel who protested when Aleneil said, "Elizabeth is to come Underhill. You are to bring her directly to Titania, Denoriel."

"For sweet Mother Dannae's sake," Denoriel groaned, "did you need to say *I* would bring Elizabeth to Titania? The child would have gone with you as Lady Alana."

"I am not so sure of that," Aleneil said. "Elizabeth has all the prejudices of her sex and upbringing. When she goes into danger, it is a man she wants beside her, not a weak female who knows only how to dress well."

"Besides, Elizabeth is not the point," Mwynwen said.

"Elizabeth is the main point!" Harry snapped.

Denoriel frowned at him. He had warned Harry more than once not to display his affection for Elizabeth so openly before Mwynwen, but Harry, who adored them both, loved them in such different ways that he could not conceive of jealousy between them. And Denoriel could not say to him that, except for the sexual relationship, Mwynwen's feeling for him was more like his feeling for Elizabeth than his feeling for her.

In the hearth, Mwynwen's salamander hissed and coiled furiously, dove into the heart of the flames that played over the crystal logs, and then began to dance more quietly.

"What can be done for Elizabeth is the main point, yes," Mwynwen said. "But what I meant was that Titania will likely provide more protection in more elegant ways at Denoriel's request than she would for me or Aleneil."

"Mwynwen is quite right," Aleneil agreed. "The Queen was only giving us half her attention. If we brought Elizabeth, she would get a simple suppression of speech to keep her from discussing the World Below—and the Queen might be a trifle careless so that more than mention of Underhill might be suppressed. If Elizabeth's speech or quickness of mind were damaged, it would be a disaster. Whereas you, my brother, are someone she wishes to impress. Her spell-casting will be exact and elegant in your presence."

Denoriel, wordlessly acknowledging these truths, nonetheless groaned again. He looked from one to the other, obviously distressed. "I do not want to be Titania's plaything. What will be left of me when she is done?"

Mwynwen giggled. "I will gather you together, my pet, and make all well." She laughed again at his expression of horror, and added, "But I am virtually sure you will escape more than curious notice. Just now, Titania will be much distracted. She has only this day obtained a new mortal child and I think Oberon may have heard rumors of it. She said, when Mwynwen and I came before her, that if we came from Oberon her answer was no and that we should not come again."

"That was why we took the chance of involving you," Aleneil added. "Elizabeth is not nearly so attractive as this darling little boy. He *is* darling and much hurt by unkindness and neglect. He will respond to Titania with adoration, whereas Elizabeth—if I guess aright and she is properly overawed—with court formality. It is the only way Elizabeth knows how to react to what she both fears and admires, like her father. Titania will be bored and wish to get back to her new plaything. But she *is* curious about you, Denoriel, and she will want to interest and impress you, so she will treat Elizabeth with care."

"I am impressed enough already," Denoriel replied ruefully.

Aleneil smiled. "However, I think she intends to keep Elizabeth's visit Underhill secret from Oberon. She gave strict order that you bring the child directly here to Llachar Lle and that she would come here. She said you were not to allow Elizabeth to wander all over Underhill as you did with Harry."

"That was not my intention at all," Denoriel protested. "Harry and I jumped through the Gate a finger-width ahead of the Wild Hunt and Harry's cross disrupted the Gate, which had been weakened by Pasgen's meddling. I hope we will have no such catastrophes with Elizabeth."

"Will you bring her soon?" Harry asked eagerly.

In the hearth, the salamander hissed violently and circled the gentle flames, making them leap high. Denoriel looked anxiously at Mwynwen, but her face showed nothing. That provided little comfort. A healer learns to present a pleasant countenance no matter what the turmoil within.

"As soon as I can," Denoriel said to Harry, "but it may take me some time to convince her. Remember, she has had two narrow escapes from death delivered by a creature that looked very like me. And once she was saved only by remembering that *I* had told her I would never ask her to remove or cover her cross. But to get her safely through a Gate, I must do just that."

They talked for a while about the problem, Aleneil offering to try to convince Elizabeth. Denoriel would have accepted, but Mwynwen pointed out that if Aleneil failed, Elizabeth would become even more suspicious. Eventually Denoriel decided he must just do the best he could; if he failed, he would try to enlist other Sidhe guardians to watch over her. Aleneil would wait at Llachar Lle for him.

He Gated to the farm near Hatfield and was greeted with anxious questions at the palace stable. Assured that Elizabeth was now recovering, Ladbroke led Miralys away. Denoriel passed on into the palace. He received sour looks from the two gentlemen in waiting, who regarded him with some jealousy, but was warmly welcomed by Mistress Champernowne, who showed him directly into Elizabeth's bedchamber.

The room was brightly lit by the sun, which poured light and perhaps some thin warmth through the glass of two south-facing windows. Opposite the bed in a fireplace that shared a chimney with the private reception room beyond, a lively fire snapped and crackled over freshly added logs. The leaping flames added light and warmth to the room, waking golden tones in the paneled walls, and made it nearly cozy.

Elizabeth was sitting up in bed. The terrible haunted look was gone from her eyes, and she held out her hand to him at once, but he recognized a tense anxiety in her and the hand she proffered trembled just a little. Denoriel sat down on the edge of her bed, ignoring Mistress Champernowne's slight frown, and took Elizabeth's hand.

"Did you sleep well?" he asked. "No evil dreams?"

Elizabeth smiled at him but she turned her head to look at her governess, and what she said was, "I am so thirsty, Kat, and I am sure Lord Denno would enjoy a bit of that treacle tart with some wine. Could you get it for me?"

Kat gave Denoriel—and the hand Elizabeth had not taken from his grasp—another worried glance, but she rose, nodded, and went out.

When she was gone, Elizabeth said, "Good dreams, but very strange. Who was the very beautiful dark lady?"

Denoriel did not ask how he could know who appeared in Elizabeth's dream or even say Mwynwen was a dream. It seemed that even Mwynwen's sleep spell could not completely close Elizabeth's mind, but that might be helpful now.

He said, "A very dear friend who came to draw out and banish the evil dreams. But you slept after she left, did you not? And had no dreams at all?"

"None that I remember, and I woke rested, so I suppose I slept well. The bad dreams, they were not because of . . . of what happened to . . . to Queen Catherine and the Howards, were they? They were to do with that . . . that evil person who looks like you? But he did not come again."

Denoriel nodded. "Likely not, but I fear he sent you something that carried those evil dreams. Do you know anything about magic, Elizabeth?"

She clutched his hand tighter. "I know the parliament passed a law making magic forbidden. I know that the Bible itself says 'thou shalt not suffer a witch to live.'"

"But he who looks like me—by the by, his name is Pasgen, so we may speak of him more easily. Pasgen does not live in England. He does not care about English law, nor for the Word of God, and he has ways to escape any consequences for his actions." He noted how Elizabeth's eyes widened. "He did use magic, to make himself look more like me than he already does, and I fear he used magic again to fix that bad dream into your mind."

Elizabeth's eyes were very wide now and dark with fear. "But he was not here, I swear it. I did not see him. Oh, I am sure it was truly you each time . . ."

She pulled her hand free of Denoriel's and shrank back in the bed so that Kat Champernowne, entering a moment later with a tray, saw her charge and Lord Denno decorously apart. Both took time to sample what Kat had carried, Lord Denno praising the refreshments and Elizabeth sighing with relief as the sweetened barley water soothed her tight throat.

Lord Denno then made several remarks about his horse, Miralys, and the house not too far away where he had lodging. Elizabeth asked if he would accompany her the next time she went hunting. Kat smiled because Elizabeth was taking interest in the world outside again, but when they began to speak of the hunt, Kat, who did not hunt, became bored. She fidgeted restlessly for a few minutes and then said she would go and write some necessary letters. Elizabeth smiled and agreed happily that she must go about her duties, because Lord Denno could keep her company.

As soon as the governess was gone, Denoriel murmured, "Only you and Lady Alana and Harry know the name of my horse, love. I am me!" But he did not reach for her hand again and said reassuringly, "I am quite sure Pasgen was not here. He knows you can see through whatever mask he wears. However, I fear he sent that bad dream attached to—to an innocent thing. Have you received any gifts lately?"

"My brother sent a letter." Her voice was thin and low, and her eyes suddenly glistened with unshed tears.

"Will you show it to me?" he asked, gently.

She hesitated, casting an uneasy glance sidelong at him, but finally got out of bed, went to her writing desk, and brought him a letter. It was written in a beautiful hand, all except a few large, shaky words at the very bottom. Denoriel touched it with one finger, sighed, and smiled.

"There is no harm in this. I do not know who wrote most of the letter—a man of middle years, I think—but the words at the bottom, those are by a little boy." He chuckled. "I can feel the struggle, the will, he used; he was determined to write in his own hand to his dear sister who had helped him learn to hold a pen."

Elizabeth almost smiled and she kissed the letter before she replaced it in her writing desk. Then she got back into bed, frowning thoughtfully. "I am sure we had some gifts of food, comfits and such, but you know those are all tasted by others before they come to me. I have not heard of anyone else having such terrible dreams and I think I would have heard. The servants talk."

"Indeed they do. And have you had any messengers from court? Any who spoke to you?"

She shook her head. "No one who came to my presence. Not since Sir Thomas."

So it must have been Wriothesley who had carried the spell, Denoriel thought. "Elizabeth," he said, "when Sir Thomas came to question you about your stay at court, do you remember anything strange? Did he give you something to look at, a comfit to eat, a toy?"

"The only thing he brought was a Bible. And it was truly a Bible because I looked through it. Surely there could not be anything evil hidden in a Bible." Her voice was uncertain, though, and she reached for his hand again. "That bad person, Pasgen, could not bear my cross."

Denoriel took the small hand in both of his and pressed it gently. "Magic is not inherently evil, love. It is not like a vampyre or a bane-sidhe or a black witch; they fear symbols of good. It is not the cross that drove off Pasgen; it is the cold iron of which it is made."

"Not the cross? It is not the cross that wards off evil? Ah, I remember. The cover was bound in gilded brass, not iron."

"Cover of what?" He leaned forward eagerly.

"The Bible. And that stone that I did not like . . . but I told myself it could not be harmful for it was set at the very center of the cross."

"There was a stone you did not like?" How clever, and how terrible, to have made the amulet into something the child would inherently trust!

Elizabeth nodded. "But it was so interesting, all black but with bright red sparkles and lines . . . It tingled when I touched it, though, and I took my hand away."

"Thank God for that! It was an amulet, carrying a sp—that evil dream." Denoriel sighed in relief. At least he knew the vessel that carried the spell and it was not in food or drink, which would have been a nightmare to try to divert from her. But Elizabeth looked more frightened and horrified than ever, and tears ran down her still-too-thin cheeks.

"Sir Thomas?" she whispered. "My father's own trusted secretary carried to me—"

"No!" Denoriel exclaimed, seeing that her mind had leapt to the conclusion that her father wished to be rid of her. "Do not blame Sir Thomas or his master. I am convinced that Sir Thomas had not the faintest idea what he was carrying and equally sure that your father loves you well and does not wish you any harm. Sir Thomas likes you and always speaks well of you, Lady Alana says, and that is surely why your father chose him to question you."

She looked up at him, eyes still filled with tears. "But then how came he to carry that Bible with that evil stone in it?"

"I am not sure of that," Denoriel said, "but I will try to find out. Most likely he took that Bible from one of the monasteries that had fallen on evil ways or it was given to him as a gift. You say it was very beautiful. I am sure he carried with him his very best Bible to do you honor."

"Then why did I see *you* begging me to save myself worse than death by dying?" she wailed softly.

"Because the sp—the dream had a sort of blank image that each person filled in with his or her own trusted friend," he told her soothingly. "You chose my image. That was all."

Denoriel did not think that was all. He was quite certain that the spell was no part of an artifact from a monastery that had fallen on evil ways. That spell had been crafted by Pasgen specifically to kill Elizabeth, and Wriothesley was Pasgen's tool, but he did not want Elizabeth to hate and fear any of her father's ministers. He wanted her to have protections that would foil any plot against her.

Besides, though Wriothesley might be Pasgen's tool, he surely had no idea what Pasgen was, or that Pasgen wished Elizabeth's death.

Elizabeth had not been comforted by Denoriel's explanation. "But what if he comes again with that Bible and wants me to swear to something?"

"Ah." Denoriel slightly tightened his hold on her hand. "Now we come to the real problem. And that is how to protect you even from those who wish you well and unwittingly bring harm."

"Can you?" she asked, hopefully.

He shook his head. "Unfortunately, not I. I have not the knowledge or the skill. I would have to bring you to those stronger and wiser than I, but the place is very far away."

Elizabeth started to shake her head, started to say that her father would never permit her to travel far from England, but she realized Denno knew that. She looked at the pointed ears, under the misty image of ordinary round ears; she looked into the brilliant green eyes with their long, oval pupils, like those of a cat. She looked carefully, very carefully at the white hair, but it stayed white and showed no glint of gold. Surely this was her Denno, not the Pasgen who wished her ill.

Very far away; that was what Denno said when he spoke of Da. And he was talking about magic. And that beautiful dark lady . . . surely she had come through the wall and Blanche had never wakened. But that was a dream. Was it a dream? Could the two "far aways" be the same far away?

Elizabeth looked down at her hand, clasped between those of Lord Denno and what she said instead of protesting that her father would not let her go, was, "As far away as my Da?"

Denno hesitated, then sighed and said, "Yes, that far."

Denoriel saw that she understood, probably too well. Her eyes lit suddenly and a faint pink rose into her pale cheeks. "Will I be able to see him?" she asked.

He began to assure Elizabeth easily that he would arrange a meeting and then remembered Mwynwen's jealousy. "I hope so," he said, "but I cannot promise. For one thing, it is possible that the person who will provide your protections will wish to see us immediately. She is too important and too powerful; it would be a bad mistake to do anything but obey her."

"Like my father?"

"Very like," Denoriel agreed. "She is—" he hesitated, then committed to the truth. "She is a queen in her own land. And then she may send us elsewhere after she sees you. So I may not have time to get a message to Harry. Also, Harry is not always easy to reach. I swear he is well. He is also young and very busy with various amusements. If I am permitted by the great lady who has agreed to help you, I will send a message to where Harry lives. If he gets it, he will come."

Elizabeth looked down at their hands and sighed. She was sure this was Denno, not the evil Pasgen, but he was still hiding something about Da from her. She gently removed her hand from his. She could see Denno's lips part, likely to assure her again that her Da was well, but he did not speak and she was glad of it. When he kept insisting, she believed him less and less.

Denoriel, watching carefully, guessed what she was thinking. He knew that sooner or later he would have to arrange a meeting for her and Harry. Meanwhile he had a greater problem: to convince Elizabeth that if he bade her cover her cross he was not Pasgen. He looked down at his own hands, now lying loosely clasped in his lap.

"I have kept my promise about stopping the bad dream, have I not?" he said instead. "And you are sure I am really me?"

Elizabeth did not reply, only watched him out of wary eyes. Denoriel sighed and asked her to ring her little bell for Blanche. She protested that the maid was sick with weakness, but then summoned her. Pale, with black rings under her eyes, Blanche rushed in a moment later with a long knife in hand. Denoriel jumped up. Elizabeth said, "No. It's really Denno." Blanche stared at him fixedly.

"I don't know," she whispered, tears coming to her eyes. "It's one of the Fair Folk, surely, but which one?"

"Come closer," Denoriel said, drawing a hard breath. He was now between Blanche's iron necklace and Elizabeth's iron cross and pain was growing in him. "I want you to take off your necklace and hold it in your hand so that you can hit me with it if necessary. I am going to do what I swore I would never do. I am going to ask Lady Elizabeth to cover her cross."

"Why?" Blanche's breath rasped in her throat.

"So that I can take Elizabeth to a great lady of the Fair Folk who will arrange for her to learn how to protect herself from anyone or anything that will give her bad dreams or do any other harm to her. I cannot take her over the path we must travel with the cross uncovered."

Suddenly Elizabeth said, "Can the dark lady who took away the bad dream come near my cross?"

"No," Denoriel replied. "She ... ah ... gave me an amulet to put you and Blanche to sleep. I moved Blanche away from your bed and I covered your cross. Then Mwy— the dark lady took away the bad dream."

"How did you get into my bedchamber?"

"Ah ..." Denoriel gave a quick glance toward the wall between the windows, then said, "By the path I wish you to walk. I cannot say more than that."

Elizabeth cocked her head. "So why are you spending so much time trying to convince me to cover my cross and come with you? You could have got another sleep amulet, I suppose. Are you not strong enough to carry me, Denno?"

He laughed uneasily. "Of course I am strong enough to carry you."

"Then why not just put me to sleep and carry me away?"

"Because you need to be wide awake and not frightened out of your wits to learn what you must learn," he said. "Because I wish you to know how these paths and doors are opened. And because Blanche must pretend to be keeping you abed when you are gone from this place so that no one will ever know you were gone."

Elizabeth reached into the neck of her nightdress and withdrew the black iron cross. Denoriel gritted his teeth as pain reverberated in his bones now that the iron was no longer somewhat shielded by the silk gown. Then she pushed the cross up along one side of the chain that held it, opened the flap of the small pouch that protected her soft skin from the sharp edges of the cross, and slipped the cross into the pouch. Denoriel let out his held breath in a long sigh.

"Then you will come with me?" he asked.

"Will you take me to see my Da?"

Denoriel stared at her. She was trying again to have her way, but to break a promise to bring her to Harry or Harry to her would be worse than not to give it.

"I cannot promise that," he said. "And I will not lie to you. I swore I would not lie to you, and to make a promise like that would be a lie. I can only promise to try to let him know you wish to see him."

"He knows that already," she said crossly, but before he could answer she turned to the maid and said, "Blanche?"

Tears coursed down the maid's face and her fingers were white where they clutched the iron necklace. "I don't know!" she wept. "I don't know. He 'feels' like Lord Denno to me, but I did not know the other was *not* Lord Denno."

"Were you as close to the other as you are to me?"

"No, but what proof is that?" She tottered across the room and put her arms around Elizabeth. "I don't know what to tell you, m'lady. I think, though, if he wished you harm, he would do that harm here. To take you away and let me see him taking you away . . . No, the king, your father, would not countenance an abduction—for his own sake as well as yours. Abducted, you could be used as a weapon. King Henry would overturn the whole earth having you sought—and that other one, he tried to kill you in the garden, not carry you away with him."

Elizabeth remembered that they had told her just the opposite—that Pasgen had been trying to abduct her—but she realized now that had been to try to ease her fear. Then she thought of that strange black stone with its crawling lines and spots of red and the despair that had filled her, as deep and black, with a stabbing red terror of self-slaughter.

"Will I really be able to stop people from giving me bad dreams if I go with you?" she asked Denoriel.

He looked at her sternly, and yet, with kindness. "If you are quick enough and clever enough, yes."

Elizabeth swallowed, then drew a tremulous breath. "Then I will need full court dress," she said to Blanche. "We are going to see a lady, who in her own land is as great as my father."

She slipped out of bed with Blanche's help, but the maid did not at once go to the clothing press. She turned to look at Denoriel.

"What am I to tell Mistress Champernowne?" she asked. "I can keep others out, saying that Lady Elizabeth is asleep, but I cannot stave off Mistress Champernowne. And what am I to say about where you have disappeared to if you do not leave by the door, Lord Denno?"

"If you can keep her out for half an hour, Lady Alana will come to visit and keep Mistress Champernowne busy. I hope to bring Lady Elizabeth back to you before the evening meal. But you need not bother to dress, Lady Elizabeth. I will be able to arrange suitable dress for you . . . ah . . . at the end of the path." He put out his hand.

"Are we going to the same country as my Da?" she asked. "And you will tell him I am there?"

"Yes."

She took another deep, tremulous breath. "May God's Grace keep me safe," she whispered, and put her hand in his.

Blanche sank down into the chair near Elizabeth's bed and put both hands over her mouth as if to hold in a scream.

A black spot appeared between the windows, just opposite where Elizabeth's cradle had stood when she was a babe. Her fingers tightened on Denoriel's as the blackness grew and grew, swallowing the wall and then the windows. Elizabeth began to tremble. Denoriel eased his hand from hers and drew her to his side, holding her firmly around the shoulders. Elizabeth could hear Blanche crying.

In the center of the blackness, but far, far away a bright point of silver light appeared. As the circle of blackness grew, so did that of the silvery light increase, reaching the size of a full moon in winter. It faded in brightness as it grew larger but took on lines and splotches, some darker, some brighter, shadows that shifted and formed evanescent pictures.

Despite the fear that was bringing a cold sweat out on her body, chilling her even in her heavy silk nightdress, Elizabeth leaned forward. Was that a silver tree? the graceful pointed tower of a castle in a picture? a gate? Insensibly she took a step forward, straining to see better. In reflex her hand clutched her cross in its pouch, but her fingers made no move to flip open the flap and pull the cross free. She was drawn to that place—drawn as she had never been before. It called to her. She took another step and another . . .

And then, her foot touched the edge of the blackness, and she fell!

Chapter 13

Elizabeth screamed, but there was no sound—
Somehow, that made things even more terrifying.

But before she could draw breath to scream again, she was standing quite solidly in the most gorgeous place she had ever seen.

Terror turned to wonder in a single instant. Above her head arched a dome of opal lace, iridescent, coruscating with light, yet plainly thick and solid as stone. The dome was supported on eight fluted pillars of . . . could it be? Could it really be? She had seen the stone in prized rings, small oval pieces of a rich orange flecked and streaked with less-desirable brown, and here there were pillars of pure orange as thick around as a ten-year-old tree . . .

If she was any judge of stones, those entire pillars *were* carved of chalcedony. At least the floor beneath her feet, although beautiful, was not an outrage to common sense; it was a simply a platform of the whitest, blue-veined marble.

There was no sun. Although it had been almost noon and sunny when she rose from her bed, the sky above her now, which she could see through the dome, was midnight blue and speckled liberally with stars. But there was no lack of light. She could see with perfect clarity, the platform itself and all around the platform on which she and Lord Denno stood, an even sward, starred with small, slightly glowing white flowers. She bent, Lord Denno's arm loosening enough to allow her freedom of movement, and peered around, looking for the large and brilliant moon which could give such a bright, silvery light. There was no moon.

Elizabeth turned her eyes up to Lord Denno, who was looking down, looking somewhat anxious. Before asking any of the other questions that filled her mind, Elizabeth became aware of an oddity. It was the depths of winter, the middle of February, and they were out-of-doors and she was barefoot and wearing only a nightdress. Admittedly, the dress was a heavy silk—another of Denno's gifts—and it was delightfully warm, but not warm enough for out-of-doors in February.

"Why am I not freezing?" she asked.

The anxious frown on Denno's forehead smoothed out and he broke into a delighted laugh. "Because you are now Underhill, where the weather suits the clothing, not the other way around."

"Underhill?" she replied, unable to understand what he meant. "The realm of the faeries, more like. Tell me true, am I asleep in my bed at Hatfield, dreaming?"

"No. You are here in the flesh. You must not think of yourself as dreaming," Denoriel warned. "It is beautiful here, Underhill—not Fae-land; the faery . . . they do not rule Underhill, thank God—but Underhill can be dangerous. Stay close to me where I can protect you. Do not wander away or let yourself be tempted away. Even here in Logres there are creatures, not evil, but mischievous, and with no understanding that someone might be hurt by their actions—the faery, the wee folk, for example, who are very beautiful but have not the sense of a puling babe. Creatures such as these for pure amusement might take you elsewhere and leave you there with no way to return or to call to me."

Feeling just a touch of chill, Elizabeth stepped closer and took Denoriel's hand. "Where does—" she began, intending to ask from where the light came without sun or moon, but in that moment a most magnificent horse appeared by the platform and she changed her question to "Where did that horse come from?"

Denno laughed again. "Hatfield, I suppose, but he may have made some stops along the way. It is Miralys, Elizabeth, come to carry us to Llachar Lle, the Summer Palace—although why it should be called the Summer Palace when the weather never changes, I do not know."

Elizabeth felt affronted. Denno teased her sometimes, but this time he was actually trying to make a fool of her. "I have seen Miralys when we went hunting. He was a black horse, very handsome, but nothing like *this* vision."

The creature was a brilliant silver with a blue-black mane and tail and eyes as green as Denno's own. The horse snorted and on his back appeared the most wonderful saddle of bright red leather with a high, golden pommel, and a second, pillion-seat (shaped much like a saddle rather than the simple pad she was used to seeing) behind the rider's seat that was clearly designed to carry a child. Elizabeth gasped.

"All the horses you have seen me ride were Miralys," Denno said, chuckling. "I have only one horse, but you know it would never do to allow anyone of rank or wealth to know I have only one horse, so Miralys changes his color and his shape just a little so everyone thinks I have a whole stableful."

Elizabeth opened her mouth, then closed it again while Denno lifted her up into the saddle. She closed her hands tight over the cantle of the rider's saddle, feeling nervous at being mounted with no reins in her hand. There was no way for her to control the horse, and she had not ridden pillion behind anyone since the moment she had first learned to control a pony on her own. Blanche did not ride at all, of course, but Kat only rode pillion—being able to ride out for pleasure or to hunt, without Kat, and being in full control of her own horse or pony had given Elizabeth some of the few moments of complete freedom she had ever felt.

Miralys did not need control, however. He stood like a rock until Denno was mounted. It was only then, when Denno rested one hand on his knee and adjusted the fall of his gown with the other, that Elizabeth realized there were no reins. She flung her arms around Denno's waist to hold on in case the horse should bolt.

They started off as the thought came to her, not in an uncontrolled gallop but at an easy canter. "Denno, where are we going?" she cried.

"To Llachar Lle, as I said." His voice was assured, perhaps held a note of surprise. "I have an apartment there where we can wait in comfort until we are summoned by Queen Titania. If you are hungry, we could have a nuncheon."

"But you have no reins," she wailed. "How can the horse know where you want to go? How can you control him?"

"Ah." Denno reached back and patted her shoulder. "Miralys always knows where I want to go. *How* he knows, I am not prepared to say . . . No, I don't mean I won't tell you, I just have no idea. When I was a boy, oh, four or five years old, a pony appeared, as it often happens for those of our kind. As I grew, he grew, and we have been together ever since. Miralys is not a . . . a horse. He is an elvensteed, who chooses to look like a horse most of the time. He can look like anything, I suppose, but since the elvensteeds' purpose in life seems to be to serve us as our friends and means of transportation, a horse is the best form to wear."

Protest against a place where anything could look like anything else, where the park was flooded with light without sun or moon, where the weather suited the clothes worn by each person—who was not a person but something else—rose to Elizabeth's lips. She did not voice that protest, however. Just ahead was a . . . no, it did not matter what Denno said; what she was seeing was a castle out of some mad artist's dream. Exquisite, yes, but utterly impossible.

"That cannot be real," she said. "It is just like a painting on the scene of a masque, an illumination, or a design for a tapestry. No one could build a spire like that. It would fall down. Denno, I *am* dreaming. That palace cannot be real."

The palace was far in the distance, yet by the time she finished speaking, Miralys had stopped by the wide marble stairs that led up to a portico which stretched all along the front of the building. Denno dismounted and lifted her down. The steps and portico were of the same brilliantly white, blue-veined marble as the platform on which they had arrived. The platform, although large, had not used enough marble to be out-of-sight costly, but this portico . . .

She remembered hearing a discussion of the cost of repairing a plain stone landing at Hertford Palace. She could not even guess the price of a marble porch of this size. Worse, before her were the most immense brazen doors she had ever seen. Surely doors of that size were either far too heavy to move or be supported by hinges or were so thin that the metal would crumple like paper. They were ten times man height, brilliantly polished, and elaborately worked in scenes she had no time really to see.

Elizabeth's disbelief startled Denoriel as did her expression of rejection, almost anger. Remembering what Titania had said to Aleneil about a reigning queen deciding the wealth of Underhill would solve her financial problems and bringing a horde of steel-armed mortals to raid, Denoriel felt he had better use that rejection.

"It is real Underhill," he said, "but if you take anything made by magic from Underhill into your world, it either vanishes away or turns to dross. Just as in the tales of King Arthur's sister, Morgana, and the palaces she would build in the wilderness which would vanish when morning came."

"Ah!" Elizabeth breathed out a satisfied sigh.

She had been growing more and more frightened by the idea of the wealth and skill that could build such a palace, such a landing place, out of such materials. Why should such people not rise up and overwhelm all England, take all of the people as slaves?

"You mean it is all held together by magic, and would not last where there is no magic?" she asked, seeking confirmation of her hope.

"Your world—we call it the World Above, or Overhill, or the mortal world—*has* magic. All people have magic, and I have brought you here to see if you could learn to use your magic to protect yourself." He looked down at her with no sign that he was humoring her, which was a comfort. "But Overhill magic is of a different kind than that of Underhill, a kind my people cannot use, and it does not lend itself to *making* things, or at least, not large things like a house. In your world, we are quickly depleted of our inner magic and become weak." He chuckled. "That is why my folk do not much care to live in the World Above."

"Ah," Elizabeth said again, no longer feeling like a poor relation allowed to live only on the sufferance of some infinitely more powerful being—a feeling with which she was too familiar. Now she began looking around her with bright interest.

They had climbed the steps to the portico. Elizabeth was just wondering how Denno would knock on the great doors when he led her aside to a human-sized portal. There he put his arm tight around her and drew her through what seemed like a short open passage. An icy chill ran down her from head to toe, but Denno marched her through it without allowing her to hesitate.

On the other side of the portal was a short corridor as high and wide as the great doors. It was, Elizabeth thought, larger even

than the great hall of the Tower, and at the end was a pair of
silver doors, also closed. Again she had no time to make sense
of the scenes worked into the doors; Denno led her into a side
corridor of normal size where the walls glowed softly in opalescent mother-of-pearl colors.

Elizabeth looked at them without envy. It was all very pretty,
but so were the masques that players presented to her. From where
she sat a masque looked so wonderful, so perfect, but when she
had called a player close, it was plain that the brilliant gown he
wore (for it was a boy playing the role of a woman) was made
of cheap, painted cloth, and when she had been taken to look
at the scenery, the impressive mountains became just purple and
blue daubs on canvas. So although this might look beautiful, it
was not real in the sense that it could exist in her world. And if
it could not exist in her world, it did not matter. Already in her
short life, Elizabeth had learned to dismiss from her mind those
things that could not affect her, for there was far too much to
worry about already.

A little way down the corridor, Denno stopped before an open
door leading to a meadow with a manor house, backed by a
dense wood, in the distance. Again Denno put his arm around
her and pulled her close. She heard him say a few words in a
strange language, and they stepped through the doorway into a
small, square hallway with open arches right and left.

"Where is the meadow and the manor house?" she asked,
amazed.

"That is only an illusion—" Denno began, then hesitated and
said, "You saw the illusion?"

"Yes, but did you not say that Underhill illusion is real?" she
asked, now thoroughly puzzled. "I saw a wide meadow with a
manor house and a wood in the distance. Is the palace we entered
also an illusion?"

"No. Llachar Lle is real. But what you might see through the
windows here is often an illusion," he replied, absently. "Hmmm.
So—in the World Above you can see through illusion, but not
here." He grimaced, so quickly she almost missed it. "Well. Since
you cannot see through illusion Underhill, you must be extra
careful not to trust too easily or quickly. Do not believe what you
see, unless I tell you it is as it seems, or you have confirmation
some other way."

That warning was frightening, but before Elizabeth could ask for reassurance, a shadow fell across the archway to the left.

"Is that you, Denno?"

The voice was familiar and Lady Alana stepped out of the arch leading to what was plainly a reception room. The back wall was a huge glass window, the glass smooth and clear as air, nothing like the small, uneven, faintly greenish panes in the windows at home. Through the window, Elizabeth could again see the wide meadow and the forest-backed manor house. She blinked, concentrated on looking through the house and field, but they did not grow shadowy and show what was underneath.

"Ah, my lady," Alana said, dropping a curtsey. "I am so glad that you agreed to come and arrived safely."

"Are *you* the great lady we have come to see?" Elizabeth asked, somewhat offended.

Alana laughed. "Oh, no, no indeed. The great lady is Queen Titania. I am of very little importance here, only Lady Alana. However, the Queen has not sent a message yet."

"Good," Elizabeth said, greatly relieved that she was not to meet a queen in her nightdress. "Then we will have time for Denno to provide court clothing for me as he promised."

"I will do that." Alana chuckled softly. "You don't want to present yourself in Denno's notion of what is the proper gown for someone of your slenderness and coloring. Come with me, love."

She held out her hand, but Elizabeth, warnings in mind, glanced up at Denno. He nodded and smiled approvingly. "Go with Aleneil. This apartment is well warded and there is nothing here that will hurt you, although you may see some strange things." Then he said to Lady Alana, "Don't take too long, Aleneil. I promised Blanche that you would divert Mistress Champernowne so she does not notice that Elizabeth is missing. And on your way, would you leave a message at Mwynwen's house that Elizabeth is Underhill?"

Some other message passed between them, Elizabeth guessed, but Lady Alana? Aleneil? only nodded so Elizabeth could not guess what it was. She could only follow Alana out of a door at the back of the chamber to a cross corridor from which a branching stairway rose to an upper floor.

That was impossible, Elizabeth thought, distracted from the slight fear the silent message had awakened in her. There was no room for an upper floor, but she said nothing. It was like the painted ocean of a masque in which you believed, even though you knew that the masque was being played in a palace hall very far from any water . . . except that here you could walk up the stair to the second floor.

At the top of the stair were three doors. Alana opened the first to the right, and there was a bedchamber looking a bit like her own in Hatfield. When the door was closed again Alana said, "Take off your nightdress, Lady Elizabeth," and Elizabeth did so. "Now, take your cross in its pouch, and put it in this bag—"

Alana held out a small bag made of much thicker stuff than the thin silk of its usual pouch. For a moment Elizabeth hesitated, then with a shrug, obeyed, and hung the whole around her neck. If she could not trust Denno and Alana, she was without hope anyway. She drew the drawstring tight around the encased cross. Then Alana said, "There."

Elizabeth looked down at herself and a squeak of protest forced itself through her lips. In spite of all the wonders she had seen since she walked through the black space in the wall, she could not believe this. Yet she *was* fully and most exquisitely dressed.

She could feel underclothes, linen drawers, silken chemise, a farthingale with its stiffened hoops. How had they found their way over her body? There was her nightdress at the edge of the bed still sliding down to the floor. Lady Alana put out a casual hand and caught the heavy silken garment; with the other hand, she turned Elizabeth so that she could see herself in a handsome cheval mirror.

The gown was breathtaking, in the most glorious colors of silver and scarlet, with a wide, square neck above which the snowy white chemise barely peeked. Around her neck was a thick gold chain set with brilliant rubies supporting an oval brooch, also of gold with four oval rubies in the center and huge teardrop pearls hanging from the base. The upper sleeves of the silver gown were tight to about the middle of her upper arm, and folded back over the upper sleeve, from just below the elbow, were huge fur cuffs of a silver fur Elizabeth could not identify.

From those cuffs protruded a very full lower sleeve of red silk brocade, slashed to show dazzlingly white silk puffs of the chemise. The outer gown was of silver silk, brocaded with darker silver in a pattern of giant leaves, the skirt divided in front to show the second skirt of the undergown beneath. The undergown matched the lower sleeve, a dull red silk brocaded in an elaborate diamond pattern in gold.

Elizabeth gaped at herself. She had never seen so rich a dress. Not even Catherine Howard, who had adored fine dress before she sinned and was executed, had anything as grand as what Elizabeth was now wearing.

"Ohhh, it is *so* beautiful. Can I take it home?" she breathed.

Lady Alana laughed. "Only if you wish to step through the Gate and find yourself naked, my heart. No, love, you will have to wear your nightdress when you go back, but if you like this gown, Denoriel will save it for you and you can wear it when you come Underhill again."

"But I will have outgrown it by then," Elizabeth said, tears of disappointment rising to her eyes.

"No, love." Alana patted her cheek. "Whenever you put it on it will be the right size. But I doubt you will wish to wear it often. I think you will find it too restrictive if you wish to see the sights of Underhill. Never mind." She waved at a closed wardrobe. "You will find what you need in there, if you should come again, and I pledge you, the gowns you find there will please you just as much. Now, I must run away to keep Blanche out of trouble."

Having seen Elizabeth safely back into Denno's care, Lady Alana stepped out of the door. Denoriel did not watch his sister go but stared at Elizabeth. "God's Grace," he said, "can you walk in that?"

"Yes, certainly," Elizabeth said, making sure her back was very straight and upright, her head high. "It is really very light, because the skirt is supported by a farthingale instead of layers of petticoats. The fur . . ." she lifted her arms. "No, the fur is very light too. Denno, why does Lady Alana call you Denoriel, and I heard you call her Aleneil?" Anxiety tightened her mouth. "Are you really my Denno?"

"Yes, I am," he said, and took her hand and squeezed it gently. "Aleneil and Denoriel are our names Underhill. Denno and Alana are what we called each other when we were too little to say our full names."

"Oh." Elizabeth was relieved. "The way Edward called me Bess when I first came to Hertford. He could say Elizabeth but only very slowly, so I let him call me Bess."

"Exactly. We are the same people. But you had better still call us Denno and Alana in your world." She began to think that she liked this Denno better than the one in her world, even though his eyes and ears were so odd, and there was no illusion of humanity to concentrate on—he smiled a great deal more. "Are you hungry? Can you eat with those sleeves on your arms?"

Elizabeth laughed. "Yes to both."

"Then come into the other room," Denno said, snapping his fingers at the empty air.

They entered the dining room in time to see plates settle themselves noiselessly on the polished surface of the table. Elizabeth drew in a sharp breath as soup was ladled from a serving bowl hanging midair into eating bowls at each place and a breadbasket seemed to float through the air and set itself between the places.

"Sorry, my lady," Denno said, smiling reassurance. "I never bothered to make my servants visible."

Elizabeth's eyes widened, but she sat down—carefully arranging her elaborate skirts—in the seat Denoriel indicated and reached for her spoon. "Then how do you know when they are finished serving?" she asked.

Denoriel grinned. "I just start to eat and they get out of the way or avoid me."

Elizabeth did not smile in response. "That cannot make for the growth of loyalty," she said. "And you cannot even see the expressions on their faces or how they hold their bodies. How can you trust them?"

He raised an eyebrow at her. "And who taught you that, little minx?"

"Kat, of course," she replied sharply. "And she is quite right. The servants adore her and would do anything for her . . . except Dunstan. He would do anything for me! But you haven't answered me. I would not like to have servants I could not see. One could creep up behind you and . . ."

"Not these servants. They are constructs, not people." He sucked on his lower lip a little, trying to think how to make her understand. "They are made, like the automata you have been shown from time to time. They have no more mind than a clockwork. They can do perfectly what they are designed to do, but they do not really think or feel."

Denoriel was a little surprised to see Elizabeth shiver. He

remembered how amused Harry had been at being cared for by the invisible servants, how totally delighted and thrilled he had been by the beauties of Underhill. How Harry had longed, even after their disastrous arrival, to stay. Plainly Elizabeth did not feel that way.

That was just as well, Denoriel told himself, although he felt a little hurt at her lack of appreciation of the wonders and beauties of his world. She was immune, it seemed, from the danger that mortals who were brought Underhill often fell prey to. Even when their memories of the time spent here were removed, they would retain a sense of something wonderful that had been lost, and would go through their lives searching for they knew not what. He thought, watching Elizabeth's expression as her soup bowl was removed and replaced with a plate of cold meats and fresh vegetables, that she looked more disapproving than enthralled.

Her expression brought an odd little skipped beat to his heart, but under and beyond his disappointment in her lack of appreciation was a deep admiration. She was so much cleverer than Harry, so much more imaginative—not that he loved Harry less; Harry was a still pool of peace, a strong bulwark of solid affection. But Elizabeth challenged him. There was little peace in her presence. One had to be always on guard, and aware of every word.

Teasingly, because of her frown, he asked if she did not like her nuncheon. She looked at him, almost blankly, then smiled and said she liked it very well, but her remark was plainly made with more absent politeness than real attention. However, she ate well enough to show her words were true.

Still, when they were finished, went back into the sitting room, and sat down on the settle before the hearth, she looked at the multicolored flames leaping over and around the crystal logs and shook her head. "Denno, why waste magic on a fire when the temperature is always comfortable?"

Denoriel explained that there was magic enough and more than enough Underhill, that use was a matter of the Talent of the user rather than how much or how strong the ambient magic was. He had a strong Talent, and the fire was for ornament rather than for usefulness. "As one would set a fountain in the garden—one does not need a fountain to bring water to the plants, but it is a pleasant thing to see and hear." Elizabeth nodded understanding but disapproval was again in her face.

"You can make anything you want out of thin air and magic, can you not? If I asked for a garden, doubtless there would be one outside the window in the double-shake of a lamb's tail."

"Outside my window, I could provide the illusion of a garden, yes."

Elizabeth sighed and shook her head again. "Everything is too easy here. You want food, you wave a hand. You want fine clothing . . . I did not even see Lady Alana make a gesture and I was dressed from the skin out in far greater grandeur than I could afford at home. What do you people *do* after you have made two gestures?"

Denoriel laughed heartily. "What do you do? Learn. Read. Hunt and play at games. Sing. Dance. Court a fair lady."

"Gossip. Speak ill of each other." She shook her head impatiently. "Yes, I know all about that!"

Denoriel laughed even harder, but he did not want Elizabeth to think too ill of Underhill and he said, "No, truly. Our lives are not so different from yours. We cannot learn things by magic; magic does not make the words fly from a page into one's memory. An artist still must wield his brushes and chisels to make a painting or a statue. A musician must practice and take instruction from a master in order to play. Real things, real for Underhill, I mean, can be made here also. That takes much more effort than a gesture to call servants or make an illusion. Real things, like the palace of Llachar Lle, are created by the exertion of will in an Unformed land. Only King Oberon could have created Llachar Lle, I think."

"Will I see King Oberon?" she asked with interest.

"I hope not!" Denoriel exclaimed. "He likes little mortal girls. I am afraid you might be too fascinating for him to resist and he might wish to keep you here."

"No," Elizabeth said, and then clamped her lips tight over the reason for her denial.

Even to Denno she would not admit that she dreamed of being queen. It was *treason* for her to dream such a dream; one hint of such a thought and she *would* be executed. Besides that, she loved Edward and wished him ho harm. She wanted him to live long and be crowned. Sometimes she told herself that her dream of being queen was connected with marriage, that she would marry a king or a prince who would come to the throne. But her heart knew she ruled England.

"No, indeed," Denno said. "Did I not promise to bring you home before the evening meal?"

Elizabeth let herself smile, but she had lost her interest in King Oberon. Another idea was more enticing. "You say I have Talent and power," she said. "Could *I* create something in an Unformed place?"

"I hope not." Denno grinned at her. "You are quite willful enough without practicing on a poor Unformed land in Underhill. No, seriously love, creation of real life is so difficult that Sidhe have died trying. However, some have succeeded. I am sure a real garden could be created and if you really want one, I will try."

She shook her head and said correctly, "I would not want you to endanger yourself," but the idea of creating something herself, or even seeing Denno make something that would live and grow made her sigh a little.

To distract her Denoriel said, "There is a place I call Shepherd's Paradise that I would love to show you. As far as I can tell, it was created for no other purpose than to hold a small herd of sheep, which seem to believe that they are in a sheep's version of heaven." Then, thinking of the contented animals—even Miralys and Lady Aeron seemed especially at peace there—Denoriel's tongue slipped and he added, "It's where Harry and I go when we want a quiet place to talk."

There was a sudden tense silence, then Elizabeth said slowly, voice trembling, "Is he coming? Is my Da coming? Is that where we will meet him?"

Furious at himself for having reminded her, Denoriel opened his mouth to say again that he did not know—and was saved. In the air between them appeared a sparkling figure, about the size of one of Elizabeth's hands, sporting iridescent butterfly wings, a tiny, bright purple cap, the sort that fools wore, and shiny black shoes with pointed toes. Other clothing seemed unnecessary as the little creature had skin all over smooth as glass and no sexual organs at all.

"You are summoned," the faery sang in a tinkling voice.

"We are ready," Denoriel said.

Elizabeth's lips parted to object. She wanted her question answered first . . . but she swallowed her words. She had been rigidly trained in court protocol. When the king demanded anyone's presence, that person came at once, even she, regardless of the fact that she was his daughter. Here she did not even have that advantage.

Denno had risen when the messenger spoke, as did Elizabeth, and he went to stand beside her, passing his hand down along his body and ending with as full and elaborate a male version of court dress as Elizabeth wore. A little rod appeared in the faery's hand and was shaken over Denoriel and Elizabeth, releasing a shower of brilliant sparks.

Elizabeth blinked at the brightness and when she opened her eyes she was someplace quite different. Denno was still beside her, but this room was empty of the chairs and settles and tables in his reception room. She was still facing a large window, but beyond it was a completely different scene. Here, rather than a rough meadow, was a smooth-mown lawn graced with large trees.

Beneath one tree, quite close to the window, was a group of children, all apparently human, all perfect, except for one smudged and tattered little boy. The children were playing happily under the eyes of two tall people who had long, pointed ears and eyes with long pupils like Denno and Alana. But had not Denno said that children were rare among his people?

Oh but—weren't those *ordinary* children?

She never thought further than the question. A slight sound drew Elizabeth to turn her head toward the top of the room. Her mouth dropped open. Her breath drew in. On a dais, on a graceful chair seemingly carved out of a single pearl, was a woman so beautiful that Elizabeth's heart seemed to stop.

Beautiful, but not human. Far more than in the case of Denno and Alana, this woman was Other. Denno's ears were a bit pointed and a little longer than a human's, the queen's—for she must be the Queen, Elizabeth thought; power shimmered around her—ears were *quite* pointed, and carefully exposed through her elaborate coils and braids of hair. The hair itself was beyond human; it glistened and glowed like threads of true gold metal. Her eyes . . . Elizabeth stopped thinking.

"This is the child?" the woman asked in so musical a voice that it raised a craving to hear her speak again.

Denoriel swept a deep bow. "Yes, Your Majesty. This is Lady Elizabeth, daughter of King Henry, the eighth of that name, of England in the World Above."

Elizabeth promptly dropped a formal curtsey, right down to

the ground with head bent almost to her knee. Denoriel saw the Queen begin to smile.

"Rise, child," Titania said.

Elizabeth straightened and stood with head demurely lowered, hands folded before her, but Denoriel could see that she was looking up at Titania through her lashes.

"Come closer," the Queen ordered, and held out her hand. And when Elizabeth, urged again by an unmistakable order disguised as an inviting gesture, had stepped up on the dais and taken the Queen's hand, Titania asked, "What do you think of Underhill, Lady Elizabeth?"

"It is very, very beautiful," Elizabeth replied carefully. "And I am quite amazed by what I have seen."

"Amazed? Not enthralled, delighted, not even pleased?" There was laughter in the musical voice.

Elizabeth's hand felt gently warm and the sensation was rising up her arm, but she did not dare think about that. She had to respond to the Queen's question. And she knew she had to answer this queen's questions every bit as carefully as she answered her father's, careful of every word lest she say one that he could misunderstand and be offended. But it was not fair! She knew her father. She knew what might be offensive to him. She did not know this queen at all. Ah, but she knew from the Queen's question that she took great pride in her land.

"All of those, Your Majesty," Elizabeth breathed, "but I am only a little girl. I fear to say too much—or even too little. It is all so wonderful that I . . . I find it hard to believe in it."

"Give me your other hand, child."

Denoriel felt his whole body tighten. Titania's voice, though just as beautiful, to his practiced ear held a sharper note, possibly even a thread of stress. He stirred, drew breath to speak but did not dare when he saw that the Queen's eyes were unnaturally bright, fixed on Elizabeth's face.

"Majesty," Elizabeth said, carefully, as if she were measuring out each word, "This is a wonderful place, better than a dream. But I cannot live in a dream. Although I love to visit there, I could not live here. This place—it is not for such as me. And I think—perhaps—that is a good thing."

Denoriel's breath eased out, silently. All was well. He could not see Elizabeth's expression, because she was too close to Titania and facing her, but her body, although firmly upright, showed no extra stiffness as of resistance to pain, and the side of her cheek that he could see looked as though her mouth might be smiling.

Elizabeth had recovered quickly from the initial impact of Queen Titania's appearance, but she was deeply awed by the Queen's power. Yet she was less afraid. She felt that she had some value she did not understand to the Queen and that Titania did not wish to harm her as long as she did as she was asked.

When the Queen had taken her hand, she felt a little strange, and when Titania held both hands, even stranger, as if a stream of warmth, which she could see as sparkling light—but, somehow *not* with her eyes—was running up from her hands into her shoulders, and from there spreading all through her body.

It was pleasant, but when the sparkling light rose into her head it made her just a trifle dizzy. And for a moment, as she stared into the emerald eyes that bound her, it was as if a tale thousands and thousands of years old rolled out into a dream vision. Suddenly she knew that Olympus had fallen when mortals turned away from the old gods, but the gods themselves, magic intact . . .

Titania dropped her hands and the door to the long corridor of years closed. Elizabeth blinked, about to complain, but remembered where she was in time and stood silent.

"Why did you not say what she was?" Titania was saying to Denno, and her voice was thin and hard.

"Majesty, I do not *know* what she is," Denno replied. "Only that she has Talent and that it must be trained if you desire the FarSeeings to be true."

"Holy Mother, I have not worked so difficult a weaving in a thousand years. She is—" Titania's voice checked and then resumed on a puzzled note "—so strong, so strong, but very different. I hope Tangwystl can reach her."

Elizabeth's lips tightened although she maintained her demure stance and her silence. It was very annoying to be talked about as if she were a pot or a cupboard.

"Strong, yes," Denno agreed. "Yet, Majesty, she was caught in the trap of a spell of dissolution and almost destroyed. And it was nothing exotic, an ordinary Unseleighe spell, so she is vulnerable to the workings of the dark Sidhe. Her strength saved her. She fought the spell for weeks, but she was near the end before I discovered what was wrong. She cannot be left unprotected."

Titania sighed. "That is true. What she carries is too valuable to lose. Her healer was careless, also. I felt the remnants of the spell tangled in her power lines. I cleared them. You will find her unimpaired."

Careless? Mwynwen? Denno swallowed. "I am sorry to hear that. Could those remnants have done her harm?"

Titania shrugged. "No physical harm, certainly. Perhaps some memories might have faded, but I did not think a faulty memory would be a good thing for this child."

"No. Not if the FarSeers are correct. Thank you, Majesty."

Unimpaired? Elizabeth thought. Denno did not tell me there was any danger of being left an idiot. A frisson of cold ran over her, and she began to tell over in her mind some of her recent lessons and even the horrible memories of her terror. While she worried that over, she missed what Denoriel and Titania were saying to each other.

The Queen's silvery laugh drew her attention just in time for Elizabeth to see her flick a sidelong glance at Denno. He shifted uneasily, to Elizabeth's surprise, and even more to her surprise he looked away from the Queen and out of the window. Very faintly, Elizabeth, who had also looked that way, heard the sound of childish laughter.

Denno's face, Elizabeth thought as she looked back at him—the children being of little interest to her—was more flushed than she had ever seen his pale skin. It was interesting, but Elizabeth had no time to think about it. Titania had leaned forward to touch her arm. Elizabeth raised her eyes and was caught once again by the Queen's brilliant emerald gaze.

"I must explain to you, Elizabeth, what I have done so you will not fear that there is anything wrong with you," Titania said. "Ordinarily humans who are brought Underhill or find their own way here are not permitted ever to return to the mortal world."

Elizabeth gasped with fear and involuntarily backed up a step. Titania caught her by the chin. Elizabeth froze.

"You need not be afraid, my dear. You belong in the mortal world and would make great trouble for us if you were not returned. Exceptions are made. You will go back when your lessons are finished." She cast a glance at the window herself, and added, softly, "And those we take to dwell here among us, are those who—sadly—are little missed, and valued even less, in the

World Above. Or—once in a very great, great while, are those who would have died there."

Elizabeth breathed again.

"Usually when we send mortals back, we wipe all memory of Underhill from their minds. However, because you must be taught to protect your mind, I could not do that. You must be able to retain what Tangwystl will show you. Therefore, I have sealed your ability ever in your life, even unto your deathbed, to speak of Underhill while you are in the mortal world. Do you understand?"

"Yes, Majesty."

Elizabeth kept her voice low and respectful. If the Queen could do that to her—and Elizabeth did not doubt Titania could—she could do worse if she were annoyed. But Elizabeth felt resentful. The Queen should have trusted her. In all the years she had known them, never once had she hinted that Denno and Alana were not as others.

"You must not be afraid of this impairment of your speech. No other damage has been done to you. And what we will teach you here will help to save your life, perhaps many times."

There was another burst of childish laughter from the window. The smudged and ragged little boy was now just outside it, his hands on the pane of glass, peering in. The Queen looked that way.

"And now you may go," she said.

Elizabeth sank down to the ground in her deepest curtsey again, murmuring, "Thank you, Majesty."

But before the words were out, she was Elsewhere.

Chapter 14

"Where are we now?" Elizabeth gasped.

Denno looked around, seeming as dazed as she was for a moment. Then he took a deep breath. "Ah, in Avalon. In front of the Academicia." He took another breath. "I didn't know Titania could do that."

Elizabeth gave a slight shiver. "I was afraid for a moment that she could do anything she willed to, anything at all." She reached up and took Denoriel's hand. "What are we supposed to do now?"

"This is where we will find your teacher, the one that Titania has selected for you. There is a door," Denoriel said, a bit uncertainly.

Whenever he had come to the Academicia previously, to consult one of the mages or to study with them, the door in the blank white wall had been open, sometimes with the mage standing in it. He was just about to say that they should both think of the name Tangwystl, when the door did open—as always right in front of him, or, this time, in front of Elizabeth. It occurred to him as the mage stepped out that he was quite a distance from where he usually stood, and the door had found him anyway.

Elizabeth's hand tightened on his own and he returned a reassuring squeeze. Tangwystl was not a sight to raise the spirits of a child who had already been dealt with by Queen Titania. She was darker even than Mwynwen, but without a spark of the other's beauty or warmth. Her hair was black and as straight as if it had been ironed, streaked with gray; her ears barely came to points, but when she wrinkled her nose in distaste at something, one could see that her teeth were as pointed as a cat's. Her eyes were so black that it was impossible to tell whether the pupils were round or long.

Unseleighe, Denoriel thought. Unseleighe, not entirely elven-blooded either, and somehow bound to the Seleighe court, probably by Titania herself. But was it safe to trust a dark Sidhe with Elizabeth's mind?

"I don't believe you can even walk in that stupid dress," Tang-wystl spat, "and I certainly can't teach you anything while you wear it."

The mage made a gesture and snapped the fingers of her hand; Elizabeth cried out in distress. Her dress, her beautiful court dress, was gone! When she looked down she was clothed in . . . in *boy's* clothes—a white shirt, open at the throat with long, full sleeves that were exposed by a sleeveless tunic. The tunic only came down to midthigh over long, footed hose. Elizabeth stared in horror at her shapely but exposed legs. But horror quickly changed to outrage.

"And I won't learn anything from you, even if another bad spell kills me!" Elizabeth shouted. "How dare you make me indecent in boy's clothing! I am a girl! Give me back my dress, I command you!"

Even as she spoke the last sentence, Elizabeth felt a gentle oppression, as if she had been wrapped in a soft, transparent blanket. The mage had gestured at her again, a bare moment after the blanket enclosed her; she felt nothing, but a shower of sparks burst in front of her and the mage gasped and shook her hand as if she had been stung.

Denno's voice was cold and hard. He said, "This is Lady Elizabeth, King Henry's daughter, from the World Above. She is not to be treated as you treat your other students or apprentices. Lady Elizabeth is needful and precious to Queen Titania. She knows only the ways and manners of her mortal realm, and should not be expected to abide by ours."

The dark Sidhe lifted her lip in a sneer. "She must learn attention and respect."

"If you do not deliberately enrage her, you will find her a remarkably attentive student. And abuse will not teach this child respect, only hatred." Denno's voice was just as icy as the mage's. "I must warn you. When she is frightened or angry, she can put out a burst of mortal magic that is very dangerous. It destroyed the Gate of an Unseleighe Sidhe who attacked her and blew him out of the mortal world. Moreover, she is more stubborn than rock. Give her back her dress or we will get no further, and Queen Titania will *not* be pleased."

Tangwystl snarled, showing all her sharp pointed teeth, but Elizabeth was again clothed in her silver and red, wide-fur-sleeved, court dress.

But the dark one was fully as stubborn as Elizabeth, it seemed. "I will not teach her in that dress," the mage said scornfully. "She must have two spells. One does not matter; that is for inside her mind, but for the other she must gesture, and those sleeves will be in the way."

"But, mage," Denno said, his voice now ingratiating, "in the mortal world, she must wear dresses very like the one she is wearing now all the time. She must learn to gesture properly when her arms are so impeded."

The black mage snorted. "I do not care what she does in the mortal world. The Powers will see through her sleeves and recognize the true gesture. But for teaching, I must be able to see her hands and arms."

Elizabeth was stroking the full fur sleeves, very pleased with Denno at the moment. "If you can take us back to your house in Llachar Lle, Denno, Lady Alana said there would be other clothing for me in the closet in my room. I would be willing to change."

Denno turned to her. "Would you, love? But we do not need to go back to Elfhame Logres."

He ran his left hand, palm down, along her body; following his left, his right hand, palm up, traced the same path. Elizabeth gasped. She was now clothed neatly in a pale green dress of embroidered muslin with a neat white lace collar and tight sleeves. In fact, it looked something like the portraits she had seen of her grandfather's queen and her ladies.

"My dress," she cried.

"Safely in the closet, waiting for you," Denno said, grinning. "You will be much more comfortable in this."

"Very good. Very good," Tangwystl said, with grudging approval. "Those sleeves are even better than the ones I devised. Let us go in."

And they were in, standing in the middle of a smallish but very comfortably furnished room. Tangwystl dropped into a large, cushioned chair with its back to a small window that looked out into nothing but the empty, silvery air. There was a low table, on which the mage rested her hands, with two chairs on the other side, both with low backs and arms but no cushioning. One chair was directly opposite Tangwystl's seat, the other to the side.

Elizabeth bit her lips. Remembering the warmth that had flowed from Titania's hands and the sparkling light that had suffused her body, she suspected that the Queen had transmitted whatever spell she used through their linked hands. Elizabeth did not want to take the mage's hands. The fingers were gnarled and twisted and had bulbous, claw-tipped nails, the skin dark and dry, like old ill-treated leather.

Elizabeth repressed a shiver; would the skin of those hands flake off and cling to her own sweat-wet palms? But then she thought of the horror eating her mind, of the somehow evil-looking Denno urging her to be safe forever from all her fears by climbing the tower and leaping off. She paused for a moment, recalling the growing sense of threat that had loomed over her if she did not do away with herself.

And lastly, she realized, for the first time, that if she *had* destroyed herself, she would not only have lost her life, but any chance of Heaven, for suicides lost any chance of God's grace. It could happen again. This time she might not be strong enough, or Denno would not come to her in time. She would die in the blackest of sin, and there would be no hope for her. She drew a deep, steadying breath. She would hold those hands if necessary.

"What is the center of your being?" Tangwystl asked suddenly.

Almost, Elizabeth answered, "My soul—" but she was not sure that these fae creatures understood such a thing even existed. "M-my h-heart," Elizabeth said, eyes wide. She would not speak of the horrors through which she had lived.

"A lumpy, red thing of flesh. Yes. But that is not what I mean . . . or, wait, maybe that will do." Tangwystl narrowed her eyes. "Inside yourself, wrap up your heart in a white cloth."

The words made no sense. "What? How can I do such a thing?"

"Stupid child! Have you no imagination? Does everything need to be done by your hands? Do you never make pictures in your head? See your lump of red flesh wrapped in a white cloth. Or, if you prefer, encase it in a shell of armor."

Elizabeth considered, eyes even wider. "No. No. If I wrap up my heart or encase it in metal, I will not be able to see or hear or feel anything."

"Do not be ridiculous," Tangwystl said impatiently.

Denoriel had at first been so relieved that Tangwystl herself did not intend to invade Elizabeth's mind and make changes in it that he had relaxed and prepared to attend closely in case he might learn something himself. He had his own mental shields—inborn and instinctive; rising of themselves against any invasion. He had never seen the need for more, but now he was interested in anything to do with magic. Thus, watching for Elizabeth's reaction, he saw the little quiver that showed the child's jaw had set hard.

Elizabeth with her jaw set was near immovable. "No, wait," he said. "It is not at all ridiculous. If that is the way Elizabeth feels about it; that may be the way it will be. To learn, Elizabeth must be convinced of the rightness, of the strong probability, that what she wills will be so."

Tangwystl pursed her lips and wrinkled her nose. "She is not yet nine years old. Why can she not simply believe me?"

Without answering Tangwystl, Denoriel said, "Elizabeth, do you remember the large clear window in my house? You know nothing can come in through that window, yet you can see and hear through it. Imagine a piece of glass, but soft so you can bend it into any shape—it can be done, love; when glass is heated it gets soft. Magic can make it soft without heat. Think of using a piece of softened glass to enclose your heart."

Tangwystl's lips tightened with irritation, but she accepted Elizabeth's nod of acquiescence and began to explain what the child must will to make the shield around her thoughts and feelings impermeable. Denoriel could neither see nor feel magic as Elizabeth followed the mage's instructions, but Elizabeth's eyes were sun-bright, fixed on the mage's black orbs. Tangwystl very soon nodded, then nodded again, looking more and more surprised.

After a little while Tangwystl sank back into her chair. She shook her head, looked back at Elizabeth, and told the girl how to dissolve the shield. On the last word of her explanation, she started back, as if lightly struck. A moment later, with a wry twist to her full lips, she said that Elizabeth must be tired and she should rest for a while.

"Such a will," the mage said, turning her attention to Denoriel. "I do not believe I have ever met such a will . . . except . . . His."

Denoriel laughed. "I have reason enough to agree with you. I have been attending upon her . . . oh, except for the years I was voyaging . . . ah . . . I can end that pretense. I was sick for over two mortal years and could not leave Underhill while I was healing."

Tangwystl made a sour moue. "Well, tell her not to release spells so quickly."

"Tell me yourself," Elizabeth snapped. "I am not a porcelain poppet or a block of wood. I am sitting right here in front of you. If I have done something wrong, explain, or show me the right way."

"It is no pleasure to work with you, mistress," the dark mage retorted sourly.

Elizabeth's lips parted on what Denoriel expected to be another smart remark and he cleared his throat. Her eyes did not even flicker toward him but what she said was, "Ah, I am sorry, Mistress Tangwystl, because it *is* a pleasure to work with you. I have never been taught so well or so quickly. I am sorry to have been pert, but I try to be an apt pupil for a clever mistress. If you please, will you tell me or show me how I hurt you?"

The mage smiled, this time softly with closed lips so that her sharpened teeth did not show. "A grateful student, and a sensible one." And she went on to explain how power could be slowly withdrawn rather than simply being cut off so that a spell snapped like a cracked whip. Then she cocked her head at Elizabeth and added, "So you want to be a party to any discussion about you?" She laughed when Elizabeth nodded decisively. "Well then, I must warn you that you will hear some things you will not like. And you must keep any more pert remarks between your teeth; adults do not care for reproofs from babes."

Elizabeth shrugged and sighed. "About myself I rarely hear anything I *do* like. Thank you for your warning."

Denoriel laughed. "Then you should not listen so close. Eaves-droppers are seldom flattered. But I will tell you that despite your curdled disposition, I love you dearly. I find you enchanting. Are those things not good?"

She held out her hand to him and he took it, kissed it, and held it comfortingly in his.

Tangwystl snorted lightly and said, "I must address my remarks to Lord Denoriel, Elizabeth, because he will understand and remember and will be able to explain to you later if necessary. I cannot take the time for that. So, Lord Denoriel, your charge now has a mind shield that should serve her against most mortal assaults. But that is all she has."

"You mean she has not enough power to cast spells?"

"I do not know the answer to that question. Magically, she is the strangest person I have ever come across. I could sense in her what you mentioned, a well of power, but it is confined . . . I would say by her will, except that when I showed her how to breech the confinement, she could not—so is it her *own* will that holds the power? I do not know. It was the only thing I showed her that she could not do at once and repeat perfectly later."

After a moment, Denoriel lifted Elizabeth's hand and kissed it. "It may not be enough," he said to Tangwystl. "Oh, it will protect her if she is again threatened with an amulet carrying a damaging spell, but there is a chance—not a great chance but a real one—that she will need to stand against a dark Sidhe enchanter, at least until I can be summoned from wherever I am."

"She cannot hold, not more than a few . . . ah," Tangwystl's dull eyes brightened. "But a few moments would be all that she would need. I will make her an amulet that she need only invoke. Two words. She will be able to hold her shield firm for the time it will take to say two words—I will teach her that. And once that amulet is invoked, even the Magus Majors would have difficulty breaking through."

"That should be enough," he said to Tangwystl, and then, "Elizabeth, that will give you time to call your guards or Blanche. No dark Sidhe of whom I know can touch you when your cross is exposed and even the strongest dark Sidhe will flee before Blanche's necklace or the guards' steel swords. And if the attacker should try to cast enchantments at the guards, that will divert him from trying to attack you, so you can defend yourself physically. Do you understand?"

Elizabeth nodded cheerfully. "I saw what happened to the bad person that looks like you when Blanche threw one of her crosses at him. It just glanced off him, but he let go of me and staggered back as if something really heavy had hit him. I could stick any attacker with my eating knife or my scissors or hit him with an iron candlestick."

"I have a warning for you, however, mistress," Tangwystl said. "I understand that you can see through illusion, that even when Lord Denoriel pretends to have round ears and round pupils in his eyes that you see him as he is."

She nodded again, but wrinkled her nose. "*Mostly* as he is. I can see a shadow of the round ears but the points go right through it."

"When you invoke the amulet, you will lose that power until the shield is dismissed. The illusion will become real to you. So, before you use the amulet, note carefully who is Sidhe and who is mortal. You would not want to stick a knife into the wrong person or hit a friend with an iron candlestick—especially as you will not be able to explain what you have done or why."

"Oh," Elizabeth said, looking somewhat daunted, but then she perked up again. "Oh, I will find some very good reasons. I am good at finding reasons for things I do."

Denoriel sighed. "Yes, you are. Do not encourage her to make up stories, Mage Tangwystl. She is a past master of the art already. Now tell me what kind of amulet you will need. My sister, Aleneil—"

"No. The amulet will need to be crafted exactly for the purpose," the dark mage said and gestured.

A Gate opened where the window had been behind the mage's chair. It stretched wider and down to the floor. Denoriel rose and took Elizabeth's hand. She looked at the Gate, again with that odd expression. There was no fear now, only a kind of disapproval. At the end of the black tunnel of the Gate, Denoriel could see some dull red lights.

Tangwystl gestured them forward. Denoriel bowed but only signed for her to go first. She shrugged and stepped through the Gate without further hesitation. Denoriel followed, one hand on his sword hilt and the other holding Elizabeth behind him. Tangwystl snorted gently but gave her attention to the creature facing her across a low counter. The light was dim and reddish and the creature clacked a huge claw and hissed at them.

"I need a special amulet, one that will suit this particular child."

"What child? I don't see any child."

The voice was thin and querulous. Two large dark red eyes at the ends of long, flexible feelers peered around. Denoriel drew Elizabeth from behind him to stand at his side.

"I see. That child."

The feelers holding the red eyes drew together and both eyes stared at Elizabeth. Elizabeth stared back, stiff as a rod, thin lips almost disappeared as they closed tight. The claw waved from side to side.

"A mortal child, too. Difficult. Difficult. Very expensive. No warranty." The eyes pulled back almost disappearing under the shadow of the carapace. "And in addition we don't need any magic spells right now. How will you pay?"

"I will pay *when* you need a magic spell. At that time I will give you the spell and you will give me nothing."

There was a long silence during which Elizabeth looked around, since she was not sure it would be polite to stare at the thing to which Tangwystl was speaking. It looked just like a giant crab and the querulous voice was crabby too; it was taking all Elizabeth's strict lessons in polite behavior to keep her from bursting into giggles.

At least the shop was interesting. There was worked stone everywhere, marble polished so highly that it reflected like a mirror, flowers with thin colored petals that Elizabeth longed to touch because they looked so real, a leafless tree in winter or dead, bone white limbs raised in supplication. And in cases on the walls, incredible jewels: a diamond as big as a wren's egg, a ruby that glowed with sullen fire even in the dim light, golden topaz, cool, cloudy, pale green peridot, clear blue sapphire and those more costly, misty with a shining star.

Elizabeth slipped her hand into Denno's, wondering if she could cozen him into buying something for her. To her surprise, his hand closed hard over hers and the background argument to which Elizabeth had paid little attention suddenly stopped. Everyone looked at her, including the extended red eyes on feelers.

There was a silence, and then Denno said, "No. I will give nothing of Elizabeth's. No hair, no fingernail parings, no cloth-ing, no other possession. If I could, I would stop her breathing so no mist from her lungs would float abroad Underhill. Nothing will be left Underhill when she is gone to draw her back or bespell her. No."

"Wait," Tangwystl said. "They use no magic here. For what do you want her hairs, Crustacani?"

The red eyes left off their concentration on Elizabeth, rose and peered at Denoriel. "Each hair is thick and strong, almost like wire. And it is the color of red gold. It shines to my eyes. We will use it to suspend the pans of a balance delicate enough to weigh single grains of sand."

"You see?" Tangwystl said to Denoriel. "There is no harm in that."

"Until someone comes and offers to buy or trade for the hairs. No."

"No one will even know we have them," the crab-being said testily. "Such work is not done in public. Our balances, our workshops, are not open to any but ourselves."

"Will not know unless you tell them. I will not—" Denno's voice checked suddenly; he looked from Elizabeth to the crab, smiled, and went on, "You say you use no magic. Very well. You can have three hairs cut, not pulled, from Elizabeth's head, but I will cast a spell on them. If magic is done to them or even anywhere near enough for those hairs to be affected, they will return to Elizabeth's head."

A crab cannot shrug. The claw made several little circles in the air. "Magic is nothing to us. We do not use it. That is why Tangwystl must come to us to bespell any amulets that are ordered."

"Very well, but she will not be able to bespell anything near the balance supported by Elizabeth's hair. If the hairs feel magic of any kind, they will disappear." Denoriel set his chin, looking just as stubborn as he claimed Elizabeth was.

And the crab clearly could not have cared less. "Agreed. The amulet to be beautiful, of semiprecious stone, and set so it can be worn as an ornament. The payment to be three long hairs cut from the child's head, bespelled against magic."

The creature scuttled out of the shop so rapidly that Elizabeth jumped and jumped again when it reappeared with a rather small, flat box which it set on the counter and from which it lifted the lid. Within were semiprecious stones. Most were already cut into ovals, rounds, or squares. A few were faceted. Elizabeth's eyes were at once caught by a pair of oval-cut, mottled-green stones almost black in the dim reddish light but holding sparks of bright gold.

"Denno, can I have those?"

"No," the Crustacani said before Denno could respond. "A pair. I do not wish to break up a pair. The bargain was for one stone."

"I will give you another three hairs for the second stone," Elizabeth said, eyes gleaming.

"Don't need another three."

There was a silence; Elizabeth drew a sharp breath. Then she smiled. "Do you like fish?" she asked. She was aware of a choking noise from beside and behind her—Denno strangling laughter; she would strangle him if he spoiled her bargain. "Fish from the mortal world? *Real fish?*"

The claw clacked. "Fish. We are talking about stones."

"One cannot eat stones, and I am sure you can find many more of them, but fresh fish—or salt if you prefer salt—from the mortal world are not so easy to come by Underhill."

Silence. From just under where the feelers that held the eyes went into the carapace, a little liquid dripped. Elizabeth heard the choking sound again, but she only looked at the red eyes, which were withdrawn into the carapace and then peeked out again.

"How much fish?"

Coughing now sounded beside her but Elizabeth paid no attention. "A keg," she said, and extracted her hand from Denno's to use both hands to show the size. "So big and well packed. Tell me fresh or salt, and Lord Denno will deliver the cask to Tangwystl, who will bring it to you."

"Done. Both gems for three hairs and a keg of fresh fish. When will the fish come?"

Now Elizabeth had to look up at Denno. His eyes looked suffused and he swallowed hard before he spoke, but he managed to say that he would bring the fish himself within two mortal days—it would be necessary for him to buy in the early morning in the fish market if the fish were to be truly fresh—if the Crustacani would tell him the name of his hold.

"The hold is Carcinus Maenas, but it would be best if you came through Tangwystl's Gate. Since we do no magic, we do not welcome visitors."

"Fish!" Tangwystl said, loathing in her voice. "My rooms will smell of fish for days."

"Do you not like fish?" Elizabeth asked innocently. "Properly cooked it is delicious. And properly *fresh,* it does not smell at all, Master Tangwystl—or no worse than the sea at least."

"It should not be cooked at all," the Crustacani said.

While they were talking Denno had drawn his knife and cut three hairs from Elizabeth's head, which he folded in his hand and whispered over. It seemed to Elizabeth that the hairs actually grew brighter when he held them out to the crab person.

From just above the bottom shell four little bony arms emerged, each tipped with half a dozen jointed, flexible fingers. One arm took the hairs from Denno's hand, another arm uncoiled one. Between them they pulled the hair sharply, recoiled it, and similarly tested the other two. When all were approved, that arm withdrew.

A second and third arm picked up the stones Elizabeth had selected and withdrew with them into the body of the Crustacani. Odd sounds emerged from the creature and the red eyes were closed and withdrawn. Elizabeth went back to examining the stonework and found several little statues that she would like to have, especially if it were to be at no greater cost than kegs of fish. After a time, one of the Crustacani's arms reemerged. The green stones, now set into simple gold bands, each with a loop at the top so the stone could be hung from a chain or a bracelet or hooks for earrings, lay on the table.

Tangwystl picked them up. "We will need to return to my rooms to embed the spells," she said. "Usually I do them here, but I am afraid to be too near the hair."

She turned, and a black spot formed on the outer wall. As it enlarged, Elizabeth said to the Crustacani, "Thank you. You have been very kind to me. If you like the fish, send a message through Master Tangwystl. I will send more for one of the beautiful statues . . . if I am allowed."

The red eyes emerged. Stared. "Thanks taken. Which statues?"

"The elvensteed. The mermaid. The Sidhe."

"If I like the fish . . ."

Elizabeth felt a strong thrust on her back, stumbled, and righted herself by catching at Tangwystl's chair. The mage laid the stones on her table and gestured for Denoriel and Elizabeth to go around the table to their chairs.

"Oh dear," Elizabeth said as she sat down. "Oh! All of that was for nothing. I forgot that Queen Titania said that I could take nothing from Underhill. That it would disappear or turn to dross if I took it with me."

Tangwystl lifted her head but it was Denno who said, "That is quite true, but the stones are not from Underhill, are they? You heard the craftsman, there is no magic there. These are solid and mortal, not of elven-make."

Elizabeth frowned. "And what of the statues I wanted?"

"I . . ." Denoriel hoped he would not soon be so trapped in a maze of lies that he would expose them. "The statues are the same. The statues, you see, are only of common stone, not made by magic but carved by hand—or whatever the Crustacani use. You heard it say it did not use magic. Gold and jewels, as you see about us, they are magic-made. One must go to the Crustacani for real objects, and the more precious they are in your world, the rarer they are in his."

"Too bad." Elizabeth sighed. "I love the necklace that goes with my court dress."

Tangwystl snorted. "Take it then, and see what happens, but do not weep when it becomes a string of acorns." The mage exchanged a glance with Denoriel, who nodded slightly. "Now go. I must work the spells on these amulets and that is no short task, nor an easy one if the amulets must work in an ambiance of cold iron. I will send a messenger to you when I am ready, and Elizabeth must learn when her shields are being attacked and threatening to fail. But she is tired now—" the mage wrinkled her nose and exposed her sharp teeth "—or she should be."

"She must know when to invoke the amulet, yes," Denoriel agreed. "And I can teach her external shields."

"Excellent, for I am not expert in those. Now . . . go."

And they were outside the white building only a few feet from where Miralys was peacefully grazing. Elizabeth stamped her foot in irritation. She was really growing to *hate* the way one was moved here and there like a chess piece at some other person's whim.

Denno looked at her in surprise, but she knew it was useless to tell him, just as it was useless to tell the French ambassador that his overelaborate bows and flowery speech were annoying rather than impressive. Meanwhile, the elvensteed had lifted his

head and come toward them, the double saddle forming on his
back as he took the few steps.

Another ridiculous, impossible thing, but Elizabeth had to admit
to herself that it was much more comfortable than the pillion pads
of what she was coming to think of as the "real" world. Denno
mounted and lifted her onto the saddle behind him. A short ride
over the perfect lawn and down a flower-bordered lane brought
them to the Gate of Avalon where, inured as she had become to
marvels, Elizabeth stared and caught her breath.

The interwoven boughs of eight trees wrought of solid silver
made a gleaming roof, and when Miralys stepped up onto the low
platform his silver hooves rested on a pavement, not of marble,
but a mosaic of an eight-pointed star, formed of thousands of
pearly seashells, each smaller than the nail of a newborn baby's
finger. Four large figures in glowing armor turned as one to
look at them and a voice came—seemingly not from any one
but from all.

"Denoriel Siencyn Macreth Silverhair we know. What mortal
do you carry and by whose permission?"

"The mortal is Lady Elizabeth Tudor, daughter of Henry of
England, by permission of Queen Titania."

A moment passed during which Elizabeth again felt an icy chill
like the one that had passed over her when Denno had brought
her into the palace of Llachar Lle. She could feel Denoriel stiffen,
and then the chill was gone and that disembodied voice said,
"Pass. She is marked in the Guardians' memories." And they were
under the opalescent lace roof of the Gate of Logres.

"Fish," Denno said, as Miralys stepped off the marble platform
on which they had arrived. "How in the world did you think of
asking if the Crustacani liked fish?"

He twisted around so he could see Elizabeth's face. She was
staring at him with a child's scornful surprise at the obtuseness
of grown-ups.

"It was a crab, wasn't it?" she asked. "Crabs eat fish. I don't know
what kind of fish you have here, but if they are made things, like your
servants, perhaps they do not taste as good as real live fish. What
else could I offer in a place where pillars are made of chalcedony
and necklaces of gold and rubies appear out of thin air?" But then
she reached out to clutch at his arm, her face now intense with
eagerness. "Never mind that. Will my Da be waiting for us?"

In that moment Denoriel knew that Elizabeth would have to see Harry in the flesh. Unlike Harry himself, nothing could divert Elizabeth from a purpose truly dear to her heart. The boy had been so distracted by the wonder and strangeness of Underhill that he had almost completely forgotten the horror of being chased and almost taken by the Unseleighe Wild Hunt. Aside from her pleasure in the magnificent court dress Aleneil had created for her, Elizabeth seemed more annoyed than enchanted by the miracles Underhill.

"I don't know," he said. "I hope so. But I can promise nothing. You see how it is here," he added, a little sadly, "there are times when one cannot be sure of anything."

Miralys had been making a leisurely way toward the palace, allowing time to admire it in the distance among the patches of graceful trees and flower-starred fields. But then, having sensed the eagerness of his riders, they were suddenly at the portal. Without another word, they dismounted, hurried through the postern beside the great brass doors, passed the great corridor, and arrived at Denoriel's deceptive doorway. Inside, however, no written message lay on the ivory table in his entrance foyer, no air spirit flitted about impatiently, no invisible servant came to whisper an explanation.

Elizabeth ran past Denoriel into the sitting room and ran out again, tears brimming in her eyes. "He is not here."

"No, I see that."

"Did Lady Alana not give him your message?"

"I am sure she delivered the message, but possibly not to Harry himself. I told you, Elizabeth, that he is a young man who lives a busy life."

"Busy? But he would come to see me! I am sure he would come to see me." The tears overflowed her lower lids and streaked her cheeks; for once, she was all child, and a severely disappointed and disheartened one.

"Yes. I am sure he would—if he had got the message."

Denoriel racked his brain trying to remember just what he had said to Aleneil when she went off to convince Kat Champernowne that Elizabeth was safe in her bed resting. And when he remembered, he felt his heart sink. Fool that he was, afraid of reminding Elizabeth of her demand to see Harry, all he had said was that Aleneil should leave a message that Elizabeth was

Underhill. He had not reminded her of Mwynwen's jealousy of the child. Which probably meant that Aleneil had given his message to Mwynwen and Harry had never heard of it.

"You sent a message," Elizabeth wailed, "why would he not get it?"

"Possibly because Harry was not at home. It is my fault, love." Denoriel tried to think of excuses that would not leave the child hating Mwynwen for her foolish jealousy. "I knew we would be very busy. I had no idea how long Queen Titania would keep us but I suspected she might send us to a mage to teach you to close off your mind. I didn't want poor Harry to be waiting for Dannae knew how long, so I didn't make the message urgent. And constructs—the servants most Sidhe use—sometimes have poor memories."

That last was a flat lie. Because of her work as a healer, Mwynwen's constructs could not only remember word perfect whatever was said but the speed of one's heartbeat, the way one breathed, the heat of one's body, and probably a host of internal signs of which the person him or herself was unaware.

"Can you send another message?" Elizabeth asked, her expression teetering between hope and defeat.

Fury washed through Denoriel. He could not remember ever having been so angry with Mwynwen. At her age, how could she be so childish, so jealous of a mortal child that she would lie to her lover and inflict so much pain on a little girl? And for Mwynwen's own sake, it was stupid. If Harry found out—and he would—he would not only be bitterly angry but become untrusting and suspicious of her.

"I can do better than that, love," Denoriel said. "We can go to the house where Harry lives and catch him when he comes home or find out where he has gone and follow him."

"Oh, Denno!" she caught him around the waist and buried her face in his clothing. "Oh, thank you. Thank you."

It took no time to summon Miralys and ride across Logres to where Mwynwen's house stood just on the edge of a wood of delicate birch and ash trees. The path to the front door between pastel-colored flowers with sweet but not overpowering scents was obviously wide enough for two elvensteeds abreast. Miralys took them to the door which opened welcomingly as they dismounted.

A gentle-faced girl—except that her skin was quite green and her hair looked very much like trailing willow withies—came down the corridor to meet them, asking anxiously whether either were hurt or ill.

"No, I thank you," Denoriel said. "We have come to see Harry FitzRoy. Is he at home?"

"No, nor Lady Mwynwen either," the girl said.

"Too bad," Denoriel said, feeling Elizabeth's hand steal into his. "But I am a long-time friend of Harry's. I will just go back to his apartment and wait there for him."

"But I do not think they are coming back, not anytime soon," the dryad said. "Lady Ceindrych is here to attend to those who were under Lady Mwynwen's care and to treat any new patients."

"I see." Denoriel barely kept himself from cursing the poor dryad, who sensed his anger and shrank into herself (but like her tree, which bent to every blast of wind, stood still firmly rooted). "May I speak to Lady Ceindrych then?"

"Yes, of course. Come, please."

She led them to the end of the corridor and opened the door there, standing aside to let them enter. The room was not very large, only of a comfortable size, and all in soft, slightly glowing colors, one little gathering of chairs around a low table in faded golds and soft reds, warm and caressing; another group in gentle blues and greens touched with silver, cool and refreshing. At the back was a window that seemed to look out on the lovely garden in the front of the house, which was impossible, since this room was at the back. From a pair of chairs rose a woman with large blue eyes and silver hair pulled back from her face with a band of blue sapphires.

"Lady Ceindrych." Denoriel bowed and Elizabeth, taking the cue, made a respectful but not exaggerated curtsey.

"So this is the fearsome Lady Elizabeth," the old healer said, smiling at Elizabeth.

"Fearsome?" Elizabeth repeated, and uttered a sob. "Oh you cannot mean that my Da ran away from me!"

"Oh no, child, no," Ceindrych murmured, going down on her knees and holding out her arms. "It was not Lord Harry who fled." Elizabeth went into those open arms and Ceindrych continued comfortingly, "I do not think he had the faintest idea why that silly Mwynwen suddenly decided she needed a rest and freedom from the demands of patients."

"No, I am quite sure he did not," Denoriel said. "My sister, because of my stupidity, doubtless gave Mwynwen the message really meant for Harry. She simply did not tell him and pretended she needed to go away."

"Yes," Ceindrych agreed, releasing Elizabeth as the child straightened up. "He was totally unaware. When he came to ask me to care for her patients and anyone else who came for help, he also asked me if I thought it was his continuing sickness that was draining her and if there was another healer who could keep him healthy and so spare her."

Denoriel could barely contain his fury when Elizabeth's tearstained and tragic face was lifted from Ceindrych's bosom. "She should be careful what she says," he snarled, "or Harry will refuse treatment from her to save her and kill himself."

"Oh, my poor Da," Elizabeth sobbed. "He was always too good, never caring enough for himself."

"And that is the Mother's pure truth," Denoriel said, pulling Elizabeth against himself and hugging her.

"Well, you are both silly as day-old chicks," Ceindrych said, shaking her head. "He is the light in Mwynwen's life and I assure you she will not allow him to harm himself nor anyone else to harm him." Then she rose from her knees and sighed. "You might as well take Elizabeth home, Denoriel. There is no sense in waiting here or in your home for him to return. I think what Mwynwen is doing is stupid. I told her so, but she would not listen and I am quite sure she will not bring Lord Harry back to Logres until Elizabeth is gone."

"I will go after her and see that Harry learns—"

"Where will you go, silly boy? Do you think she told me or anyone else where she was going so you could pick it out of our heads? To speak the truth, I do not believe she has allowed *herself* to think about a destination."

Denoriel sighed defeat, but Elizabeth took his hand and said to Ceindrych, "But my Da—the one you call Lord Harry—he is alive and well? You saw him with your own eyes?"

The healer put a gentle hand beneath Elizabeth's chin, and tilted her face so that she could look straight into the Sidhe's eyes. "Yes, indeed I did, and I spoke to him also. I promise you he was in the best of health, only worried about his . . . his lady. Now go back to Llachar Lle with Denoriel and don't worry about your Da anymore." Then she smiled. "Mwynwen will not always be able to keep him from you, and the day you and he meet, she *might* realize how foolish she has been."

Elizabeth tightened her grip on Denno's hand, expecting to next see the portal of Llachar Lle or some room in Denno's apartment, but nothing happened. Denno said something she didn't catch to Lady Ceindrych, then turned around and went out the door in the most ordinary way. They went down the corridor and out the front door where Miralys was waiting and then rode, just as if Miralys was her own, ordinary horse, to the palace where Denno helped her down from the saddle and they went inside.

"I'm sorry, love," he said after shepherding her into the dining room and gesturing to the servants to bring food and drink. "I was stupid, and you are being punished for my stupidity."

"But why?" she asked. "Why does this lady hate me so much? What have I done? Can I somehow amend it?"

Denno patted her hand. "She doesn't hate you, love," he said, smiling. "She likes all children, but . . . but you frighten her because Harry loves you so dearly. It is what Lady Ceindrych said about protecting Harry from being hurt. She is afraid that if Harry sees you, he will long for you so much that he will want to go back to the mortal world and he cannot live in the mortal world. His sickness would return and kill him. As long as he is Underhill, he will remain strong and well, but Overhill will kill him."

"Then how could she believe I would try to make him come to me where he would be hurt? I am, it is true, a child, but not so spoiled or silly as that!" She looked at the plate of cheese and cold meats that had settled gently in front of her and the tall glass of milk.

"I know that, and you know that, but Mwynwen—" he shrugged. How to explain to a child of eight that a woman, mortal or Sidhe, is not always sure of the steadfastness of her lover's heart? "Eat something, love. You will feel better when your belly is not so empty."

"At least I know now that you told me the truth when you said my Da was alive and well. I no longer feel that the last person of my own blood that loves me is gone." Then she looked at Denno and tears again streaked her cheeks. "But am I *never* to see my Da again, never touch his hand or have him hug me?"

"Won't my hugs do?" Denno asked, smiling.

Before she thought, Elizabeth shook her head vehemently.

Denno's smile disappeared and he removed his hand from hers. "I'm sorry, Lady Elizabeth. I thought you liked me."

Elizabeth grabbed for his hand and caught it. "Don't be a silly," she said. "Of *course* I like you. But not that way. Not the way I love my Da. You—you're a man not of my blood, a person different from me in all ways. Yes, you're a person I want to be with, I like to talk with you . . . but my Da, to me he's not separate. He's like a part of me but outside of me." She hesitated and her eyes were almost black with fear and sorrow. "He's a place to be when everything else is gone."

Denoriel sat staring at her, grieved at her grief and fear but strangely lighthearted at the difference she drew between her feeling for Harry and for himself. He was not absolutely certain why the fact that she did not include him in the "blood-relation" feeling made him so happy, but he put the problem aside, knowing it was not safe to look too closely at it. He lifted her hand and kissed it, then put it on her fork.

"As long as you enjoy my company, I am content to leave his own special place to Harry. Now eat up, love, and then off to bed with you. Tomorrow will be a hard day. Tangwystl will show you how to defend your shield and know when it is failing so you must invoke the amulet. It will be hard work and more hard work when I teach you physical shielding."

"I am not afraid of hard work," Elizabeth said, smiling. "But when it is done, you will take me home?"

Relief and disappointment warred in Denoriel. Elizabeth would never love and long for Underhill as Harry had. "Yes," he said, "I will take you home to the mortal world."

Chapter 15

Before she was satisfied, Tangwystl had to work with Elizabeth for two full "days," and it took Denoriel another "day" to teach her several different kinds of physical shields. The child, although delighted with her accomplishments, was too exhausted to be taken back to Hatfield at once. Denoriel fed her and then let her sleep herself out before he opened his Gate, set his mind firmly on sunset on the day they had left, and brought Elizabeth through.

Alana had taken back the thick silk-brocade pouch that her cross had stayed in while she was Underhill, and had told her to leave her lovely gowns behind as well. She was wearing the silk nightdress in which she had left Hatfield and in her ears, hanging from gold wires that Denno said were from the mortal world, were the green-gold amulets. Denno had hunted high and low for those earring wires—or seemed to hunt high and low for them. And while he did, Elizabeth had detached a long ribbon from one of the gowns Lady Alana had left in the wardrobe and used it to tie around her waist beneath the nightdress the beautiful necklace that had adorned her court robe.

Elizabeth had a suspicious mind. Young as she was, she understood quite well that the denizens of a place as rich, and as sparsely populated as Underhill, might not want the wealth displayed there to seem ripe for the picking. Thus, she was not taking as true the reiterated statements that the gold and jewels of Underhill would disappear or become worthless when carried into the mortal world until she tested them for herself. Tangwystl had looked surprised, Elizabeth remembered, when she had said that and when Denoriel agreed.

However, the hope Denno and Alana had lied and the wealth of Underhill could be carried home was doomed to disappointment. As she stepped into her bedchamber from the Gate in Logres, Blanche leapt up from her chair and rushed to embrace her mistress. But a moment after the maid dropped to her knees to hug Elizabeth, there was a wet plop and a mess of slimy, black, stinking material fell on Elizabeth's feet. Blanche backed away with a cry, looking at the small pile of withered, fungus-streaked leaves, rotten acorns, disintegrating mushrooms, and crumbling twigs with horror.

Elizabeth regarded it with equal horror, crying, "My necklace. Oh, my pretty necklace."

"Pretty necklace?" Blanche exclaimed. "Child, what is wrong with you? Why do you think *that* is a pretty necklace?"

Elizabeth's lips parted to explain, but nothing came out. It was true, too, that she could not speak of Underhill, not even to a person like Blanche who knew of the Fair Folk and their creatures. She was silent another moment, calling memories, glad she could remember. But she was also aware of Blanche's growing distress.

"It isn't a necklace now," Elizabeth said, tears rising to her eyes. "Never mind. I made a mistake . . . a mistake I will never make again." She smiled through the tears. "I am not losing my mind again, Blanche, but I cannot explain. Just clean it up and forget about it."

Behind her, Denoriel turned away, ostensibly to examine the Gate but actually to hide the grin he couldn't completely suppress. Clever, clever Elizabeth. She had been clever enough to doubt the truth of the tale of faery gold, but not quite clever enough to realize that he and Aleneil knew her very well. They knew she would test the statement she did not want to believe and which was, in truth, a lie, so everything Aleneil had created for her was specially spelled to be dependent on the ambience of magic Underhill. Once that magic was gone, it became forest detritus, pulled from the nearest copse in the World Above.

Now that Elizabeth believed she had proved that constructions of magic could not persist in the mortal world, Denoriel hoped the idea would become fixed, an article of faith she did not need to test again, something she *knew*. When his expression was under control, he came up beside her.

"What a stinking mess," he said. "Too bad. We warned you. But don't cry, love. Lady Alana will try to replace it for you. Now take out your cross again."

"I almost forgot," she said, wiping away her tears with the back of her hand, and then ordered, "Blanche, take that mess out to the midden. It smells too bad to be thrown into the waste pot." And when the maid was gone she said to Denoriel, "How will I know what to do if anyone ever asks me to put the cross away again?"

So for all of her disapproval and seeming indifference, she did hope to make other visits Underhill. For Underhill and its wonders or for the sake of the exquisite garments Aleneil had created for her? Denoriel suppressed a smile at Elizabeth's innocent vanity. She did love elaborate clothing and rich jewels. Which reminded him that the amulets Tangwystl had prepared were now being exposed to the full strength of the iron cross. He "felt" for them and sensed the contained spells bound safe inside the protective armor of the invocation . . . at rest, waiting.

"Good, the cross has not affected your earrings, so that's all right. And you are a clever girl to remind me that I might want to ask you to put the cross away again. Well, that is easy enough. We will have a secret cipher between us, as I had with Harry."

"You had a secret cipher with my Da?" Elizabeth's eyes were bright with interest. "Why?"

Denoriel sighed. "For the same reason I need one with you. The same people wanted to steal him away. If you ever doubt me, you can ask, 'Where were you on . . . whatever day I did not visit you . . . ' And I will reply, 'I was down at the docks, looking for my ship, *The Nereid*.' The key words are 'docks' and the name of the ship. I strongly doubt that anyone else will make that particular reply or know the name of that ship, which no longer exists."

He saw that she was relieved and pleased, too. A child loves secrets and Elizabeth was very good at keeping them—which was fortunate. "Good," she said. "I won't forget."

No, she wouldn't. She didn't seem to forget anything. The thought brought a twinge of worry. Titania said there had been a few tendrils of the dissolution spell left tangled in Elizabeth's Talent. Denoriel didn't believe that Mwynwen could have done that by accident. Titania said the remnants would not have hurt Elizabeth . . . only made some memories fade. Memories of Harry? Maybe Titania should have left those remnants.

But the moment he had the thought, he dismissed it. No, Elizabeth would need her perfect memory. Denoriel smiled at her.

"And you must not forget your lessons either. You must practice both regularly."

She looked suddenly alarmed. "Will you not come to see me to remind me, Denno? There isn't anyone I can practice with, except you."

He took her hand and bent to kiss it. "I will be as frequent a visitor as ever, and it will be very well indeed if you have no one to practice on except me."

Denoriel was not able to keep that promise as fully as he intended because within the month Mistress Champernowne received orders to prepare to join households with Edward again. Kat was not pleased but was not alarmed either. She wrote very firm letters to Sir William Sidney, Edward's chamberlain, and to his steward, Sir John Cornwallis, about the servants they would bring, about separate stabling for Elizabeth's horses, and about how much she was prepared to contribute to the joint household.

Kat knew economy was a real necessity; the royal purse was strained to its limit and beyond, and—as Dunstan put it so bluntly—"Great Harry's by-blows are left sucking hind teat." When money was spent, it was spent in Henry's household first, then that of his son and heir, Edward, and Lady Mary and Lady Elizabeth got what little was left. There was war with Scotland—a lessoning to punish the insult of the Scots' king having failed to keep his agreement to meet Henry in the autumn of 1541. That meant heavy expenses to support and renew the army, which had suffered a defeat at Haddon Rig after Sir Robert Bowes crossed the border at Teviotdale.

Elizabeth's move to join the prince was delayed. Henry had no time to think about his children. Still, news came to Hatfield, via Alana, Denno, and Kat's other visitors, few though they might be given Elizabeth's lessened status.

Putting aside his pique at the duke of Norfolk for his two adulterous nieces, the king had sent his experienced warlord to avenge the losses at Haddon Rig. But Henry was also gathering forces and supplies to join the emperor in a combined attack on France. Thus Norfolk was shorted and could not fulfill the king's order to take Edinburgh. He burnt Roxburg and Kelso, but had to return to England before his soldiers starved.

Nor was that the end of the cost to England, and the cost kept rising. Scotland was building an army for a heavy reprisal. Norfolk did what he could, but without new funds, recruiting more men and the gathering of supplies went slowly. Meanwhile King James's army was ready to avenge Scotland's hurts. The king sent one detachment eastward toward Norfolk while a second, an army of about ten thousand, was sent west under the control of King James's favorite, Oliver Sinclair.

The order to move was delayed again while Henry attended to the war news. The detachment sent east accomplished nothing; Norfolk's force was sufficient to hold off the Scots and send them north again. In the west, Sinclair's force was rent by dissension. The Scottish noblemen were bitterly divided about religion and enraged by being commanded by someone they felt to be unworthy. On 24 November James's unhappy army was confronted by a vastly inferior English force on a marshy ground between the Esk and the Sark called Solway Moss. The Scots utterly disgraced themselves, yielding almost before they fought, and leaving in English hands two earls, five barons, five hundred lairds, and twenty guns—a totally unexpected victory.

In Scotland this was the final blow to King James. Already ill and dispirited, he died on 14 December, leaving the throne to his only living child, a little girl called Mary, who had been born six days earlier on 8 December.

In England the news of the victorious battle was received with considerable enthusiasm; the news of King James's death with doubt because no one could be sure of the character, identity, or intentions of the regency. King Henry, however, was delighted about the baby daughter. He now had a strong hope that he had the means to settle all problems between Scotland and England with the marriage of little Mary to Prince Edward.

Vague rumors of the king's hope filtered from the court to Elizabeth's household, and she was alarmed. She had been looking forward to joining Edward and feared that if the agreement was made, Mary of Scots would be brought to England to live with Edward so they might grow into affection—which would mean that Edward would have someone else there, a baby, in fact, that he could lord it over. Judging by the few boys she knew, she thought that Edward would like that very much, and would lose interest in the older sister who could lord it over *him*. Not that she ever would.

Well, perhaps a little. But mostly she was afraid that Edward would like a little girl who was going to look up to him and who everyone was urging him to love better than he liked a mere half-sister.

Kat Champernowne laughed at her and called her a jealous little cat, pointing out that Mary was only a few months old and would be no rival for Edward's affection for many years.

Denno was no more sympathetic to her anxiety. He was quite certain her fears would not be realized, but to her he said it served her right to worry. Was she not heartless about his loss and loneliness when she went to her brother and he could no longer see her as often? Whereupon she bestowed on him a rare kiss on the cheek and warm assurances that she would ride out *very* often so they could be together.

Despite Elizabeth's fears, the negotiations with the Scots had no effect on domestic arrangements. Because of past experience and clear statement of expectations, the households of Edward and Elizabeth were smoothly combined in the spring of 1443. The children came together with heartfelt delight. Edward had other companions, but none with Elizabeth's combination of motherly affection and a mind as quick as his own.

Elizabeth had the best situation possible. She was truly fond of her little brother and he of her and since, at five, he was still too young to ride out as she did, she was able to meet her Denno three or four times a week. Her grooms and her guards were well accustomed to meeting Lord Denno on the way to wherever they were going.

If any of them wondered how he knew where to meet them no matter which direction they set out, none asked. Elizabeth, of course, had no need to wonder. She saw the pretty little air spirit that was always somewhere near her disappear and knew it had gone to fetch Denno. She never said anything . . . and could not have said anything even if she had wanted to do so.

There was no need for excuses. The men assumed Elizabeth or Mistress Champernowne had managed to send Lord Denno a message, and there was always a handsome pourboire for them when they all parted company again. In that mysterious way servants know their employer's business, they understood that the meetings were not something to be mentioned to anyone but Dunstan. The tips were very welcome indeed because the regular allowance for salaries and living expenses was often not only late but reduced when it did arrive.

When allowances were very late or very reduced, Elizabeth's household did not suffer for long. Gold slipped from Denoriel's hand to Kat's. She protested that she "should not"; that she should manage to live on the allowance made to Elizabeth as Edward was forced to do. Denoriel laughed and told her that he was profiting so much from the business generated by the Scottish war and the proposed war with France that he could well afford to be sure that his dearling Elizabeth lacked for nothing. "And besides," he would add, "it is my duty." And since he did not specify why it was his duty, nor exactly what made it his duty, what could Mistress Champernowne say but to agree?

The lessened demands on the joint household put Sir William and Sir John in total charity with Mistress Champernowne. Elizabeth's visits to Edward were not restricted to formal half hours. The children shared tutors and even some lessons, because the young prince was extremely precocious and of so serious a disposition that study was dearer to him than play. In fact with Elizabeth to share the lessons, they were often much like play, the two children conversing in Latin and giggling together when they translated ordinary things, like "Have another scone" into exotic Greek. Both loved learning and they sparked each other's efforts.

Indeed it was often with laggardly protests that Edward was torn from his books to more active sports. Elizabeth was less reluctant to leave their studies, which surprised some of the older boys a little because she said she would go do her needlework. Ladies liked needlework but most girls moaned and groaned about it. However, when challenged, Elizabeth actually brought forth a beautifully embroidered book cover, which she presented to Edward.

Elizabeth had learned early never to make an excuse she could not support with evidence. In fact she was growing into a competent needlewoman, but not because she practiced it in the afternoons. Once she was in her own apartments, the boys, who were not allowed to intrude into her female privacy, could know nothing of what she did—so she met Denno.

Needlework was for evenings by the fireside, or days when the weather was too foul to ride. And she did love doing it; her heart rejoiced in the rich silks, the vivid wools, the precious metal threads that she couched down upon velvet or satin, the tiny gemstone beads, the minuscule seed-pearls. If her household could not afford the gowns that she wore Underhill, at least she could have some of that same color and sparkle in her hands when she worked her needle, and feel the heavy softness of the fine materials.

In the afternoons, when Edward went with his male companions to play at bowls or tennis or to practice with his little sword, Elizabeth hurried into her riding dress and out through a back exit to the stables. Concealed by the bulk of the palace from the inner court where Edward took his exercise, Elizabeth, her two grooms, and two guardsmen rode out into the wooded park. Around the first sharp curve in the road or a little way into a sheltered side path, Lord Denno would be waiting.

Pasgen had made his peace with Vidal and even gained Aurelia's favor by finding a mortal physician who could deal with Aurelia's headaches. His potions were sometimes ill-tasting, but they worked and did not leave him moaning and complaining or totally unconscious and forever trying to conceal himself from her summons.

Albertus came into her presence eagerly. He was not only a very good physician but a willing immigrant Underhill. An old man who left no close family behind, he had been easily seduced by Pasgen's promise of greatly prolonged life and luxurious living conditions. Because he was not a prisoner unwillingly bound but a willing recruit delighted with his change of status and condition, Aurelia knew she could trust him.

That matter settled to Vidal's and Aurelia's complete satisfaction, Pasgen retreated to his own studies. However, as Vidal's and Aurelia's strength returned, so did Pasgen's caution. Now he set watchers on a number of the lesser creatures of the Unseleighe Court that he knew attended Vidal's convocations regularly.

Thus, even though Vidal did not summon him, Pasgen knew when courts were held and was able to send several of his hulking guards—enhanced to be able to repeat everything they heard—to each meeting. He was still annoyed with himself for telling Vidal to deal with Elizabeth himself. He knew quite well that whatever damage Vidal did would be done disguised as Pasgen.

However, Vidal did nothing. He seemed again to have forgotten Elizabeth's existence. Pasgen was not surprised, for everything was going Vidal's way. The war with the Scots was furnishing misery piled on misery so there was power aplenty for the dark Sidhe. And battlefields were ideal places for witches and boggles and ogres and the other denizens of the Unseleighe Court to amuse themselves. For the Unseleighe, the mortal world was perfect just as it was; none wished to make any changes.

So Pasgen saved a corner of his mind for attending to Vidal's amusements and future plans and gave all the rest to his researches.

Rhoslyn was unable to dismiss the problem of Elizabeth so easily. She was unhappily aware that Pasgen had once tried to kill the child on Vidal's order. And she suspected that to ensure his own peace he would do so again to pacify the prince.

Somehow Rhoslyn had to prevent him, not so much to save the child—although the thought of hurting a child made her sick—but because she knew she could never feel the same about Pasgen if he did. And without Pasgen, Rhoslyn did not think she could go on living surrounded by the ugliness of the beings and spirit of Vidal's domain.

Just now Vidal was letting the matter of Elizabeth slide. Rhoslyn realized that as long as hate and pain and misery were pouring energy into Vidal's pools of power he would not think ahead. He was, thank the Goddess of whom her mother spoke, not a long-sighted person. But as soon as his court began to murmur or he himself was pinched for power, he would be reminded of the reign his FarSeers predicted where misery was in short supply.

Vidal would then begin to prod Pasgen who might easily reach out and destroy Elizabeth with the same absent ferocity with which he would squash a buzzing, stinging insect. Rhoslyn shuddered. She could not let that happen. She must not lose her brother because he did not wish to be annoyed by Vidal. But what could she do? Alone she was not strong enough to confront Vidal and the FarSeers still saw one future where Elizabeth ruled.

For a moment a vision of those golden years—the music, the

art, the poetry—rose up like a promised land. Rhoslyn thrust the images away. It was not promised for her and the only way she knew to save Elizabeth was to eliminate the possibility that she would come to the throne. And that could be done. If Elizabeth was deemed unfit and she was removed from the succession, the FarSeers' images of that brilliant reign would disappear and Vidal would forget the child for good.

Rhoslyn did not for a moment pretend that she could induce Vidal to agree to allow her to deal with Elizabeth. He knew and despised her softness toward mortal children. In fact, to mention Elizabeth to Vidal would almost certainly stimulate him to prod Pasgen to murder or to take action himself. Aurelia, however, was both more afraid to take any action that would bring Oberon's attention to her and more prone to subtle devices that subverted the spirit of the High King's intentions. Aurelia would gladly divert Vidal from attacking Elizabeth if she believed that Rhoslyn would prevent Elizabeth from coming to the throne.

Rhoslyn beckoned to Cannaid of the white ribbon and started toward her mother's apartment, the construct like a shadow behind her. Rhoslyn had found it was necessary to tell Llanelli when she would be away for some days—and to warn the maids to watch her with greater care. Llanelli became irresponsible and forgot all her promises when she felt deserted.

As she approached Llanelli's door, she heard music—the maids were playing for her mother. Rhoslyn again had to suppress the vision of laughing, singing Sidhe and mortals. Llanelli's tales when she and Pasgen were children of a better, brighter place had lingered in Rhoslyn's mind. As she suppressed them again, the vision of joy was overlaid by what passed for dancing and laughter in Vidal's domain—the capering of ogres and boggles and witches around one or more mortals screaming in fear and agony as they were poked and prodded by sharp, envenomed sticks, blazing torches, dull swords, and other instruments. And that was the least subtle of the entertainments. At his most powerful, Vidal had been a past master of the most delicate and prolonged of miseries and despairs.

She shook her head sharply, bade Cannaid to stay outside, and entered Llanelli's apartment.

Llanelli listened to Rhoslyn's statement that she would be away for a while and then asked, "Where are you going? What shall I tell Pasgen, if he asks?"

"That I went to some Unformed land. It is impossible to tell one from another."

"No." Llanelli shook her head. "You are lying, Rhoslyn, and you cannot lie to me. I know how you look when you are going to make things. There is a deep joy in you. Now—"

"Mother," Rhoslyn interrupted, knowing that if she did not cut this conversation short, Llanelli would pester something out of her. Mothers were like that. They knew exactly what strings to pull to make you dance, because they had attached those strings in the first place. "Never mind where I am going. No matter where it is, I will be quite safe. I have Cannaid with me and my lindys and Pasgen has his. If I get into any trouble, he will know it and come to help me."

The fragile *liosalfar* woman shook her head and her gossamer hair floated around her. She caught at Rhoslyn's hands, whispering, "And be caught in the trouble himself. Don't child. Don't. You are going to do something dangerous, I know it."

Rhoslyn sighed. No matter what she said, her mother would act the same. "Yes, but not dangerous to me, Mother. It is a mortal child I fear for, not myself."

"Not worth it. Do not trouble. They are like glow worms, briefly alight and then dead."

"Perhaps, but they live with rare intensity while they live," Rhoslyn said, a little wistfully, "And this one is more alive than most. I *will* save her if I can. Let me go, Mother."

Whereupon Rhoslyn gently detached her hands from her mother's grip, nodded to the servant girls, who closed around Llanelli, and went out. With suitable detours to prevent anyone from finding her domain, she Gated to the empty house, where she collected Talog. Mounted with Cannaid behind her, she Gated to the Goblin Fair and from one of the other Gates in the market to Caer Mordwyn.

On this day when no court had been called, the great doors were closed and at the top of the black marble steps, two slavering ogres were closely chained. The creatures could not attack anyone who stood clear, but their arms were long enough to seize whatever or whoever tried to get through the doors. Cannaid slid down off Talog, but Rhoslyn shook her head and the construct simply stood and waited.

Rhoslyn whistled for the newt-grooms and dismounted. At the foot of the black marble stair she stopped and studied the

ogres. Then she climbed the stair, said a single word, which
froze the ogres into horrific sculptures for a few moments and
another that made the doors swing open. As she and Cannaid
stepped through, a bell clanged insistently. Rhoslyn gestured and
the doors closed.

Beside the closed doors of the throne room, a hunched form
stirred, rose, and came toward her. A dark Sidhe in the black and
silver livery Vidal aped from Oberon's servants but with the loose
lips and blank face of an oleander eater came forward. Rhoslyn
asked whether Princess Aurelia was within. He turned his glazed
eyes on her and nodded.

Rhoslyn waited a moment and then snapped, "Do you wish to
announce me or shall I go myself?"

The dark Sidhe smiled, showing a great many pointed teeth.
"Where then is Pasgen? How does it come that you do not have
your powerful brother along to protect you?"

"Because I don't need him to protect me," Rhoslyn said, as
Cannaid stepped smoothly from behind her.

The spider-leg fingers of one hand circled the Sidhe's neck.
The other hand seized his arm. He screamed as the fingers sliced
through his silk sleeve and blood began to stain it. The grip did
not tighten further.

"Now we will try again," Rhoslyn said. "Will you announce me
to Princess Aurelia? Cannaid can remove your head without the
slightest difficulty. Or your arm. Or both."

Hissing words flowed from the Sidhe's mouth. Rhoslyn blinked.
Cannaid laughed and said, "If you do that again, I will grab you
somewhere infinitely more tender," and released the Sidhe's arm
to make a feint at his crotch.

The dark Sidhe tore himself from the construct's grip—not
realizing that if it had not let him go its fingers would have sliced
through his neck. As it was, he found Cannaid right alongside him,
her pursed lips now spread to show teeth longer and more sharply
pointed than his own. Without more ado, he passed through the red
and gold corridor and mounted a flight of black marble steps.

Rhoslyn followed, glancing once toward the end of the hallway
where Pasgen's room had been when he was managing Vidal's
Unseleighe Court. Rhoslyn sighed briefly. She had enjoyed those
months; they had been, briefly, without fear.

To the left was an oversized door, mercifully closed, that she knew led to Vidal's apartment. She lifted a hand slightly. Cannaid closed in on the dark Sidhe, but he turned right, and Rhoslyn dropped her hand. The Sidhe whispered at a golden mesh set in the door. A moment later, the door swung open. Cannaid stepped in, stepped sideways, and flattened against the wall; Rhoslyn walked straight in. The door closed.

Aurelia reclined on a Roman couch, one hand outstretched toward a small table on which stood a blue glass full of a cloudy liquid. She stared blankly for a moment at Rhoslyn and then said, "Why, Rhoslyn; what a surprise."

As she spoke, her green eyes brightened and she looked around the room, Rhoslyn thought for Pasgen. In general Aurelia looked better than she had for some time. The cream and peaches of her skin owed more to nature and less to art, and the pain lines around her eyes and mouth were less distinct. She now wore her hair down over her forehead in a long fringe to hide the still-visible scars the necklace of crosses had left, but the gold of her hair was more vibrant. Sure that Rhoslyn was alone, except for her construct, Aurelia laughed lightly.

"Your construct doesn't look very sturdy. I've heard you are a great builder and maker, but if that is an example of the best you can do . . . Or is this a case of the shoemaker's children going barefoot?"

"Cannaid serves my purposes very well," Rhoslyn said, "and is capable of much more than is apparent."

"You name them?"

"They are all different. Names make it easier for me to give orders to the one I want."

"I suppose," Aurelia said, obviously losing interest. She lifted the glass from the table and took a sip. "I also suppose that you had a purpose for coming here?"

Rhoslyn took no offense, though offense was intended. Taking affront would not serve her own purposes. "Yes, indeed, Princess. Do you remember when my brother and Prince Vidal argued about Lady Elizabeth?"

"Yes," Aurelia answered, too quickly.

Rhoslyn thought it likely that the princess often did not remember things and hesitated to search her memory only to find nothing. She spoke quickly to divert Aurelia's thought. She needed the princess in a good mood.

"Pasgen told me that Prince Vidal wished to take Elizabeth's fate into his own hands," Rhoslyn continued, watching Aurelia for any signs of recognition. "Is that true?"

Now Aurelia did remember; Rhoslyn saw the slight relaxation that betokened relief. "Vidal had good reason. Pasgen was told that Elizabeth must die and he failed more than once to do his duty."

Although Rhoslyn frowned slightly as though she disapproved of Pasgen's failure, within her, her heart leapt with joy. Pasgen simply did not fail in what he attempted . . . unless he wished to fail.

She shrugged. "Likely because of the need to keep all hint of magic secret. When Oberon hears that the child is dead, he will be furious, and he will winnow the Unseleighe kingdom for any sign, no matter how small or insignificant, that we were involved. His commands were clear. None of the king's family were to be touched by any magic. Ever."

Aurelia bit her lip. Likely she had forgotten Oberon's command. "Oberon does not rule the dark Sidhe," she said pettishly.

Rhoslyn shuddered deliberately. "Oberon rules Underhill. He does not usually interfere with the dark Sidhe, but if it was his will, he could unmake . . . everything. Oberon is not Sidhe. In the days of the ancients, he was more. He was worshiped as a god. It is not safe, it is not sane, to confront Oberon. He might remember what he was—and deal with the Unseleighe accordingly."

Aurelia frowned. "Are you saying you think Vidal is stupid enough to get caught openly attacking Elizabeth?"

"I am saying that even if Vidal, even if *no* Sidhe, had any part in the death of one of Henry's children, that Oberon *would* seek, and seek, and seek, until every creature's mind was naked to him." Rhoslyn stared into Aurelia's eyes, trying to drive the very words into her brain. "The thought freezes me with horror, and I swear *I* have done nothing to which the High King could object. The fate of those who have transgressed—I do not wish to imagine it."

"Then what are we to do?" Aurelia replied, but although she tried to sound angry, there was a note of fear behind her words. "Wait until she rules and we starve?"

"No." Rhoslyn continued to stare. "We make sure she does not come to reign without harming a hair on her head or touching her with a spell."

Aurelia took another sip from the glass of cloudy liquid she had been holding, then put it back on the table. Slowly she shook her head. "You are trying to save the child. Vidal always said you were too fond of mortal children."

"I am fond of mortal children," Rhoslyn admitted, "and I will be glad to see Elizabeth live a long and happy life, so long as she is not queen. But I am *not* doing this for Elizabeth. I am more fond of my brother. I am quite certain that Prince Vidal . . . whatever he does, he will do it disguised as Pasgen."

Aurelia sniffed. "No. Do not be ridiculous."

Rhoslyn disregarded the protest and went on, "But I will not permit that to happen. I will tell you now that I have laid an information . . . more than one, actually . . . with different beings that have easy access to the Seleighe domain. That information will be delivered to King Oberon if blame falls on my brother."

The Unseleighe sat straight up, her eyes blazing with anger. "Stupid bitch!"

Aurelia lifted a hand, but spells did not come as easily to her as they once had and Cannaid had more than enough time to leap away from the wall and place itself before Rhoslyn. Aurelia gestured and spoke and almost instantly shrieked in pain as her spell bounced off the construct and backlashed at her. She seized the glass from the table in both shaking hands and drank until it was empty.

Cannaid stood ready to defend or attack, but Aurelia did not attempt another spell. Her face was briefly distorted, but with pain, not rage, and very soon the expression smoothed. After another moment her eyes studied Cannaid and Rhoslyn behind her with a vague puzzlement that slowly grew into recognition. Rhoslyn touched Cannaid's arm and she stepped aside. Aurelia frowned but real anger was absent.

"Please, Princess," Rhoslyn said in a placatory voice. "I am sure that I can arrange that Elizabeth so besmirch her reputation that her father will strike her out of the succession. That will serve our purpose just as well as her death. No magic at all will be involved, and Oberon will not care a bit."

Aurelia glared at her suspiciously. "How will you do that? And how long will it take?"

"It will not be so quick as killing—it may take even a few mortal years, but what is that to us? King Henry is still alive and like to live a while. Prince Edward seems strong. He will inherit from his father, and his reign will suit the Unseleighe well enough. And if Edward should die . . . well, so much the better. Then Mary will be queen, which is what we want most. And in Mary's reign, even if I have not managed to have Elizabeth removed from the succession . . . the girl will die. At Mary's hand, not ours. So we will have lost nothing."

"How can you be so sure that Mary will wish to be rid of Elizabeth?" Aurelia's voice was no longer vague; she sounded intrigued.

"Because as Rosamund Scot, I am one of Lady Mary's dearest friends. I will make sure that Mary comes to believe Elizabeth is a heretic of the blackest sort, the spawn of Satan, the very anti-Christ—and to Mary, her religion is everything. She is much older than Elizabeth and not in perfect health. For fear that Elizabeth will follow her and bring in the new religion, Mary will find some reason to have her executed."

For a long moment Aurelia looked at her almost without expression. Then she blinked and said, "So what has all this to do with me?"

"You are the only one who has sufficient influence on Prince Vidal to keep him from attacking Elizabeth and bringing Oberon's wrath upon us. If you will divert Prince Vidal and give me time, I will make Lady Mary into Elizabeth's most mortal and deadliest enemy."

"Vidal is not the most patient of beings," Aurelia said, for the first time, with a note of doubt in her voice.

Rhoslyn sighed. "I will do what I can so that he will know an effort is being made. I will place such temptation in Elizabeth's way that she cannot resist. Her father will say she is her mother's daughter, call her whore, and strike her name from those who may inherit the throne." Her lips twisted a little in distaste. "Once she becomes old enough to be a woman, it will take very little to make her blood run hot. The young of the mortal kind see only the glitter of the temptation, and do not think far enough ahead to see the consequences—and this one has inherited hot blood from her dam *and* her sire. Be she never so cautious, when I am done dangling the bait before her, she will take it, and never feel the hook."

Chapter 16

Although Prince Vidal continued indifferent to Lady Elizabeth's existence over the next few weeks and thus no intervention by Aurelia was required, Rhoslyn's visit returned with increasing frequency to Aurelia's mind. Aurelia did not like Rhoslyn. She would have preferred to refuse outright and haughtily anything Rhoslyn asked, but what Rhoslyn had said about Oberon searching through the minds of all Underhill if evil befell the king's daughter terrified her.

Once, while she was healing from whatever had happened to her while Vidal was trying to abduct Elizabeth, Oberon's Thought had passed through the Unseleighe domain. He had not been seeking Aurelia; nonetheless the pain roused by the touch had been excruciating. She had screamed for days, and two healers had died trying to reduce her agony.

Worse yet, Rhoslyn said she had laid an information about attempts made on Elizabeth. Doubtless she had told all sorts of lies, implicating Aurelia and Vidal when it was really Pasgen who had tried to harm the girl. Aurelia frowned. She did not like Rhoslyn, but she did like Pasgen.

Pasgen had brought her Albertus, the mortal physician who had nearly cured her pain. The thought made her reach out and sip from the ever-present glass that Albertus had left for her. She needed the remedy much less frequently now and because she was able to think without feeling as if burning knives were lancing through her head, her mind was much clearer.

No, she did not mind Rhoslyn trying to divert blame from Pasgen. She did not want Pasgen blamed for the harm done to Elizabeth. And what Rhoslyn had said was true. Vidal hated Pasgen and would do his best to make the blame for whatever he did amiss in the mortal world fall upon Pasgen. This was unacceptable.

Aurelia sipped from the glass again, raising her other hand to her temple where a dull knife was pressing, threatening to pierce her skull. Albertus had warned her that shock, irritation, or worry would bring the pain back. Her discomfort meant she did not want Pasgen obliterated by Oberon. Had he not brought her Albertus and asked nothing in return? Aurelia put down the glass and stared speculatively into space. Was that a hint of favor that she had been too pain-ridden, too muddled in her mind, to notice?

She sat up a bit straighter and touched her hair. Thinking about pleasant things diminished her pain and Pasgen was pleasant to think about. Dimly she recalled Vidal raving on about what Pasgen had done while Vidal himself was incapacitated—taking over control of the Unseleighe Court that Vidal had so painstakingly assembled, wiping out troublemakers, bringing the dark Sidhe under control. So . . . now she remembered . . . Pasgen had ruled in Vidal's stead.

Aurelia knew that even when she was completely well she would not be able to rule an Unseleighe Court the size of this one alone. She needed a male to bluster and threaten, to lead the hunts, occasionally to kill with his own hands or sword. Vidal served that purpose very well, but . . . How would it be to replace Vidal with Pasgen?

Nibbling gently on a fingernail, Aurelia considered the idea. She suspected that over the time of Vidal's sickness Pasgen had become stronger in magic, possibly as strong or stronger than Vidal. Thinking it over she became more and more sure that was true, although the young Sidhe did his best to hide it.

Why hide strength? Because he was young and unsure his power could overmatch Vidal? Perhaps. More likely he was hiding his true ability because he was planning to kill Vidal and take over the domain, the court, and all the power that Vidal had amassed.

Then why had Pasgen yielded the rule of the court without a fight when Vidal returned? Of course, because while Vidal was healing, Pasgen could not reach him. Also because Vidal must die in the full sight of the court; otherwise there would always be some who hoped for Vidal's return and who would make trouble in his name. So, that was clever. Pasgen would make Vidal think he was weak and afraid. Vidal, prone to overconfidence and grandiose notions about his own abilities, would be off guard. And one day Pasgen would blast him and seize the court again.

Aurelia realized her heart was pounding, but her head did not hurt at all. She giggled. So the thought of Vidal being blasted dead was not at all shocking or unpleasant. Still, she would need to get her talons firmly fixed into Pasgen before he moved against Vidal.

Consulting her shaky memory produced a surprisingly clear answer. Even Vidal could not discover where Pasgen's domain was. Rhoslyn was the only path to Pasgen. Aurelia sighed. She did not like Rhoslyn. She thought it was Rhoslyn, in her weakness and whimsy, who held Pasgen back from the delights of games of torture and other similar pleasures.

Now she remembered why Vidal had been welcomed back so readily. The dark Sidhe had complained that Pasgen, being overfearful of Oberon, had made the Unseleighe Court dull as ditch-water and sour with rules. No fun and games with mortals or the weaker creatures.

Only because he was so young, Aurelia thought, smiling at the thought—

But the smile faded at the thought that inevitably followed.

—and too much under the hand of his mother and sister. Her eyes narrowed. Maybe that was not all bad; if necessary she could find ways to be rid of the mother and sister, and Pasgen was accustomed to female domination. She could simply substitute herself for them.

As for his lack of appreciation of Unseleighe pastimes, Pasgen would learn under her tutelage . . . if she began to find Vidal tiresome. Even if she did not, it would be wise to gain a hold on Pasgen, and for that she needed Rhoslyn. Aurelia sighed. Always, it came back to Rhoslyn. So, for now, she would support Rhoslyn's plan for dealing with Elizabeth.

Until now she had not needed to say anything to Vidal about Elizabeth because he had been fully absorbed in other matters. The war with the Scots—the pain and death of the soldiers and the misery of the common people overrun by both armies—had brought power in plenty to the Unseleighe. Unfortunately, that period of plenty might be coming to an end.

Had Vidal not begun to complain the last time she saw him that King Henry had called a truce to arrange for the marriage of the infant Scottish princess and his son? If the fighting stopped, their source of power would dry up, and doubtless Vidal would again begin to worry about the possibility of Elizabeth coming to rule.

Yet what Rhoslyn had said about there being plenty of time to deal with Elizabeth was true. The future the FarSeers envisioned for her could not be realized until after her father died, her brother died, and her sister Mary died. It was far more likely that Elizabeth would die than all of those who preceded her in the succession.

Thus it would be foolish to chance Oberon's rage. Let Rhoslyn work at disgracing Elizabeth in her father's eyes. If Henry was sufficiently disgusted with his daughter, it would become safe to deal with her more openly. In fact, if Henry—or Edward or Mary—disowned and disinherited her, then *technically* Elizabeth would no longer be a part of the family, and thus, no longer under Oberon's protection.

Another memory returned to Aurelia. Elizabeth's brilliant mind could have been an asset to the dark Sidhe. Well, it was too late now to raise the child to love the Unseleighe way. However, if she could be taken and the blame laid elsewhere, she could still be useful. Of course, now Elizabeth would have to be broken by fear and pain. Aurelia drew a deep breath and her eyes brightened as she contemplated the pleasure to be had in breaking the girl and the rich harvest of power that would come from her agony and terror.

With a sigh, Aurelia recalled herself from the pleasant dream and considered the problem of abducting Elizabeth. And the moment she did so, sudden pain lanced through the dark Sidhe's head.

The scars on her forehead burned!

The maid!

Aurelia snatched at the glass of potion, gulped half of it down, and closed her eyes.

The worst of the pain receded, but the memory of the maid did not fade. Aurelia ignored the band of pain, like a vise around her head, and ground her teeth. It would be impossible to lay hands on Elizabeth while that maid was with her. The maid could sense Sidhe and the creatures the Sidhe sent into the mortal world . . . and she was close enough to Elizabeth that she could not simply be felled by magic.

But what if the maid's fate came from mortal hands? The band of the vise began to loosen.

Attack by a mortal could be arranged. A slow smile drew Aurelia's lips away from her rather too pointed teeth. Being rid of the maid did not need to wait for Elizabeth's disgrace. The maid could be dealt with at any time and by any mortal means. Oberon was not going to care if grievous injury—even fatal injury—befell a common maid . . . so long as the injury did not appear to be magical.

Moreover, removing the maid would be an ideal device with which to distract Vidal. He would be happy to cooperate in transport and spells and easily believe the maid's death a prelude to Elizabeth's. Aurelia took another sip of the potion although now her headache was gone.

A new idea had occurred to her and she considered it, holding the glass to her lips but not drinking. Why bother Vidal with the preparations for destroying the maid? Far better to present the *fait accompli* to him after the maid was dead.

Pasgen was every bit as skilled with Gates as Vidal. By using Pasgen to arrange her entry into Elizabeth's living place she could achieve a double purpose. She could begin binding him as well as implicate him should there be some backlash from the maid's death.

The trouble was that reaching Pasgen was difficult. No one knew where his personal domain was hidden. She could send a message to the house where only construct servants lived, but Pasgen mostly ignored messages. Aurelia's lips thinned. She would need to ask Rhoslyn to bring him to her.

The tenor of Elizabeth's days had been constant and peaceful in the spring of 1543. The negotiations for the Scottish princess had stalled and were turning nasty. But now, in June, rumors of a new threat . . . or was it a promise . . . had come from the officers of Prince Edward's household to Kat Champernowne and from Kat to Elizabeth.

Kat did not want Elizabeth to be taken by surprise by the news and, because of past sad experience, react improperly, so she told her charge that there appeared to be a strong possibility that her father would marry again very soon. Elizabeth displayed nothing but confusion and Kat told her that she must seem glad and speak a hope that the king would find happiness if such news was brought to her.

To that, Elizabeth replied that she did, most heartily, desire her father to be happy, but she soon fled to her bedchamber—not to weep for Catherine Howard as Kat feared, but to cast her will at the flitting air spirit (which Kat did not know existed) and demand that it tell Denno to meet her in the park. She then went back to Kat and said she must ride out.

Elizabeth was prepared to do battle to get her way, because she had been out riding the previous day and a dancing master was scheduled for that afternoon. But strangely, Kat did not protest, only saying that she understood that Elizabeth needed distraction. Dunstan went himself to order guards and grooms to make ready, and as soon as Elizabeth had changed to riding dress, they were to horse and away.

Denno was waiting on Miralys at the far western end of the park. Elizabeth hallooed at him and touched her little mare with her crop. The guardsmen parted to let her pass. They saw Lord Denno also and knew him to be perfectly competent to protect their lady until they could catch up. They knew, too, that their pourboire was always a little higher when Lord Denno and Lady Elizabeth were given a few moments of complete privacy—well, not complete; they could see the lord and lady, but they could not hear what was said.

It was not any fear of being overheard that induced Denno to add to the small bribe the men received each time he and Elizabeth met, however. What he did not want them to see was the occasional look of pained surprise or the muffled squeak she uttered when she was not quick enough with her shield and the pebble or tiny dart he bespelled to fly at her reached her hand or cheek and nipped and stung.

The first few times Denno had allowed her to emplace the shield before she reached him. Those times, having bespelled the guardsmen and grooms to look elsewhere, he had struck harder and harder blows with fist and sword to make sure the shield was strong enough to withstand a heavy physical attack.

Later he demanded that she only draw the shield around her when she thought he was actually about to strike, because she could not live within a shield; her power was very limited and the shield would soon fail. She needed to be able to invoke it very fast if she perceived a threat.

If she was late in shielding, her punishment was the little prick of pain; if she was early, not only did she need to endure Denno's teasing about her cowardice but the pain would come anyway, when the shield failed and he sent his dart or pebble. That test over, others followed. As they rode through the park and talked idly of this and that, Denno tried to invade her mind and set into it a compulsion to do something silly.

The compulsion was invariably utterly harmless but embarrassing. One day Elizabeth had found herself painting her nose yellow; another day she had insisted on being served stewed apples instead of soup. Elizabeth had a strong sense of dignity. To be embarrassed was almost as bad as living with the terrible sense of fear and despair engendered by the dissolution spell. She worked hard and harder perfecting the shields that Tangwystl had taught her to protect her mind.

By the time of that meeting in June it was very rare indeed for Denno either to score a hit on her person or make any impression on her mind. Today he did not attack her at all, but rode forward with an anxious expression, asking what was wrong.

"I do not know," she said softly. "Kat told me my father is going to marry again." She shuddered very slightly. "Kat says I must be happy for him." Her eyes were dark with memory.

"God's Grace, there's nothing for you to fear, love," Denoriel said soothingly, then glanced quickly at the oncoming guards and Tolliver, but they were all too far off to have heard him call her 'love.' "You are forewarned and forearmed now."

"Yes, but I want to know whether I *need* to be forearmed and forewarned. A faint color rose into her normally pale cheeks. "Perhaps I should have learned better, but I *do* love being at court. I want to know whether Edward and I might be summoned."

Denoriel raised an eyebrow. "You will not have bad memories, my lady?"

The guards had reached them and Denoriel and Elizabeth rode ahead, side by side. The guards and Tolliver followed, but not so close that they would overhear low voices.

Elizabeth smiled faintly. "Oh, no. My memories of the court itself are all very happy." Then she lowered her eyes and Denoriel saw a gleam along the lower lids. "After . . ." Her voice faltered but she swallowed and said, "I will not think of afterward. Denno, will you find out for me what lady is likely to be chosen?"

Denoriel sighed. "Yes, my lady, I will try. But you know, it will be even harder for me to see you if you are called to court."

She glanced up at him, her eyes all golden with laughter. "We will have to devise something. Perhaps you will be able to . . . ah . . . find your way into Blanche's room and we can talk at night. There will be gardens. Surely one will be lonely and neglected enough for us to meet. Or there is Hampton Court, which is my father's favorite palace; it is set within the forest, with access by river also. But you will find out about the lady and let me know?"

Denoriel sighed again. "Yes, my lady."

Elizabeth put out a hand and touched his arm. "And if we are summoned to court, I will find out all I can about the palace in which we will stay. Most like, it *will* be Hampton Court, and it will be easy to meet there. I will send Blanche to you with directions to what part of the palace I will be lodged. And I'm sure that Kat will do her best to get you on the guest list. Do you think it will be a foreign princess?"

"Foreign?" Denoriel frowned. "No. I am almost sure it is not. I would have heard through my merchant connections if any realm was close to such an important treaty. It would affect trade."

"Why?" Elizabeth asked.

Denoriel laughed. Elizabeth had a most unchildlike interest in how he had become so rich—well, perhaps it was not so surprising when she was always being told there was not money enough for this or that. And the more she understood of how politics at court affected England's relations with other nations, the better. The remainder of their ride was spent most blamelessly with Denoriel expounding the intricacies of trade. Even her father would have approved, for Great Harry was always looking for ways to add to his—and England's—wealth.

He had not forgotten, however, the reason Elizabeth had asked him to come was to learn about Henry's new matrimonial enterprise, and he Gated to his London house to consult with his man of business. It was Joseph Clayborne who suggested that the duke of Norfolk, despite being out of favor and still avoiding court, was most likely to have the information Denoriel wanted. Just *because* he was out of favor, Norfolk would urge those of his party to closer observation and himself attend more closely to every rumor and whisper concerning the king. The footman Joseph had hired was sent out to enquire and returned to report that the duke of Norfolk was indeed in residence in his London house.

Although Denoriel breathed a sigh of relief, he was not surprised.

Norfolk might be out of favor as a friend and advisor, but King Henry did not allow his anger to deprive him of a valuable servant. Norfolk had driven back the Scots after the loss at Haddon Rig. Now Henry had a larger prize than Scotland in mind. The king was again negotiating with Emperor Charles to form a league to dismember France.

Hertford had been sent to replace Norfolk in the north, and Norfolk was charged with making preparations for gathering the army to attack France. At this early stage in the arrangements London, with its quick access to ships and roads in all directions, was a most convenient headquarters.

"There is no sense in carrying Turkey carpets or Flemish tapestries to Norfolk," Joseph Clayborne said. "In fact, he might take offense because he knows the courtiers are not now flocking around him and thus—"

"Yes." Denoriel nodded. "To bring such a gift would only remind him of his more favored days. But I need an excuse to visit."

"Not at all," Clayborne declared. "Bring him a dozen bottles of wine, be commiserating without actually saying why, and say you are come to thank him for keeping safe the northern shires—where you have considerable interest in wool."

Denoriel laughed. "Whatever would I do without you, Joseph?"

Clayborne smiled thinly. "The truth is, you would do very well, but I will not urge that truth because I am very happy in my work, in my luxurious lodging and my delicious if sometimes strange meals. Moreover, I am growing rich myself by small trading enterprises, which I arrange aboard your ships. So I will not point out that with just a trifle more attention to your business, you could do without me altogether."

"Grace of God, Joseph, are you going to leave me and set up as a trader yourself?" Denoriel pretended astonishment.

"No, my lord," Clayborne replied. "Did I not just say I was content? I will need to be a great deal richer before I set out on my own—if ever I do. I am wise enough to know that until I can obtain cargoes the way you do, I am best off trading as a gambling venture, while I continue to work as your man."

"You relieve my mind, Joseph." Denoriel grinned; he was sure Joseph suspected he was no ordinary man but that his business manager had long ago decided not to acknowledge his suspicions. As a reward Denoriel continued, "I cannot tell you where and how I find certain cargoes, but I certainly would allow you to take a few shares in them if you wished to venture."

"Yes I would, m'lord, but for now . . ."

He pulled the bell cord that hung behind his chair and when the footman answered told him to fetch half a dozen bottles of the best Bordeaux, wrap them well, and accompany Lord Denno.

Perhaps it was mention of the wine that the footman carried that brought Norfolk's secretary down to invite Denoriel to join Norfolk in his sitting room. Perhaps it was only Norfolk's curiosity, for as soon as Denoriel entered the room, the duke asked somewhat bitterly, "And what brings you here, Lord Denno? Not carpets or tapestries that you want shown off to the king's courtiers. No courtiers come to seek my favor any longer."

Denoriel shrugged. "For the present that may be true, Your Grace, but the future will likely be brighter. In any case the lack of courtiers has no effect on what I hope will be an even more profitable enterprise." He signaled the footman to set down the basket of bottles at the end of long table and leave. "I hope over the years you have come to believe that I am an honest man, with no ulterior motives, no interest in politics other than how it affects business, and that you will be willing to give me a hint about how to arrange to be named one of the suppliers of the army in France."

"Where did you hear about an army in France?" Norfolk snapped.

Denoriel widened his eyes. "I did not know it was meant to be secret. Many of my trading partners in the Low Countries speak openly of the matter. They say that King Henry and Emperor Charles signed a treaty in February, are in agreement about attacking France, and that only details of the attack remain to be settled."

Norfolk's face was an interesting shade of puce as he said, "It seems I should be asking you for news, not you me."

"Well, I am sorry if this secret was meant to be kept, Your Grace, but there are less devoted servants than yourself in the emperor's service as well as in King Henry's." He shrugged. "The news is out, though you deplore the fact, and merchants, with some of whom I am allied, are jockeying for supply contracts. Most are looking to deal with the Empire, but since my contacts and commitments are to England, I thought—"

"I did not know that you dealt in fodder and beans and dried beef," Norfolk remarked with raised brows.

"No more do I." Denoriel laughed. "However, if I have some hope of being included among the suppliers, I could begin to make arrangements to obtain what I would need, and possibly make arrangements to buy at better prices now than later."

Norfolk stared at him for a moment, then stood up and went to the end of the table where he unwrapped the bottles of wine. He looked at the seals stamped into the wax over the corks and sighed.

"Send me a letter of intent," he said. "I will see that it goes to the right person."

"Thank you, Your Grace." Denoriel rose to his feet, started to turn, hesitated, and then said, "Since there is no hint of matrimonial negotiations abroad, I assume that the lady to be honored is English and will cause no ripples in trade?"

Norfolk stared at him again in silence for a long moment and then said, "So you have ears and eyes at court too."

"No, Your Grace," he said, with a knowing look. "Not at *court*."

For a moment Norfolk looked puzzled, then shook his head. "Ah, Mistress Champernowne."

"I did not mean to be mysterious, Your Grace," Denoriel said mendaciously; he *had* wanted to catch Norfolk's interest so he would be kept in conversation. And then went on, lying blithely so he would not need to bring Elizabeth's name into the conversation. "It was from the servants of Prince Edward that I had the news that the king planned to marry again. But they did not know to which lady the honor would be proffered and if she is of a great maritime house or—"

Norfolk's expression darkened. "Not at all. He seems to have chosen Catherine Parr. She is a nobody. Daughter of a simple knight of Northhamptonshire, although a man of good estate. She is no blushing maid either—"

His voice checked suddenly as, Denoriel guessed, he remembered the last "blushing maid" King Henry had chosen, what befell her, and the damage to his influence. Then he continued, hard-voiced, "She has been twice widowed already." But his grim expression eased. "She is a good woman, very devoted to her late husband's children, even after his death."

"Ah, that bodes well for the king's children," Denoriel said brightly. "If she desires young ones around her, likely the king will be happy to bring his family to court."

But the grim expression had returned to Norfolk's face. "She would be a better woman if she were not far too prone to thinking herself wise and a scholar, and offering support to such men as Miles Coverdale and Hugh Latimer."

"A reformer?" Denoriel cocked his head. "The king will not countenance a radical view of religion."

"Well . . . she is not so much a reformer or radical as she is one who questions long proven truths and encourages disputations." Norfolk's expression told clearly what his opinion was of a female who dared to *question* anything. "I prefer the lady who rules the king's children, most especially his heir, to spend more time with her needle than her pen and attend mass for her soul's comfort."

Denoriel murmured agreement and some meaningless phrases of good wishes and farewell and made good his escape. He didn't much care what kind of religion the lady practiced—so long as it didn't get her executed for heresy—but he was very interested indeed in what Norfolk had said about Catherine thinking herself a scholar. That and the fact that she was fond of children, and had taken seriously the care and education of her last batch of stepchildren, made Elizabeth's hopes of coming to court more likely to bear fruit.

He said as much, when next they met out riding. She was delighted with his news, her eyes gleaming gold in the brightening sun of what had begun as a cloudy day. "Shall I write to her?" she asked. "A scholar," she breathed then. "Shall I write to her in Latin and show—"

"You will not write to her at all!" he replied with alarm. "Elizabeth, that too-ready pen of yours will get you into trouble. Remember when you almost wrote to Queen Anne when the king was about to divorce her? You are not supposed to know that your father is about to take another wife. You will get Mistress Champernowne in trouble. Everyone will believe she gave you the news."

"Oh."

She was so crestfallen that he went out of his way to cheer her up. How could he help it? The one treasure she held most dear—regardless of her fondness for bright jewels and beautiful gowns—was her learning and scholarship. He hated to quash one of her rare opportunities to display it to someone who would appreciate it.

But though the bright eyes had dimmed with disappointment, fortunately Elizabeth was not doomed to live with that disappointment for long. On the twelfth of July, Henry did marry Catherine Parr and Elizabeth was able to write to her, wishing her happy and stating her own joy in gaining a stepmother. Unfortunately the letter did not have the effect she desired; Mary was invited to join the king and the new queen on their honeymoon progress, but not the younger children.

Denoriel soothed her by pointing out that Edward, the most important to the king, had not been invited either. Whereupon Elizabeth rather scornfully said that Edward did not ride well enough to go on a progress, and Denoriel riposted by saying that the king could not know how well *she* rode either, since most of her riding had been done in his company and was kept secret.

To his relief, Elizabeth did not say she would expose their clandestine meetings in order to prove how well she rode. That she valued his company more than the chance to join the court on progress made him ridiculously happy. Becoming aware of the unsuitable rush of satisfaction, Denoriel reminded himself that she was only a child, a little girl of ten. But sometimes the way she looked at him sidelong under her thick golden lashes . . .

However, the conversation about her dissatisfaction at not being invited to court was repeated so often through the end of the summer and the autumn, that when the invitation finally came in December Denoriel was almost glad to see her leave Hertford.

His feeling did not last long. He was shaken by the reports from Blanche Parry, transmitted by Ladbroke, of how strongly Elizabeth had responded to the warmth with which Catherine greeted her and Edward.

Denoriel, carefully not thinking about why, promptly wrote to Kat Champernowne and asked when he could hope to be placed on a visitor's list. All he received in return was a harried note saying that she had not yet even discovered to whom she needed to apply for such permission. And then, apologetically, that Elizabeth was so busy and so thrilled by the queen's reorganization of the "nursery" . . .

"Nursery?" Denoriel said, looking up at Ladbroke.

The groom laughed. "Lady Elizabeth wasn't best pleased by the word either and neither was His Highness, but the queen smoothed their feathers by explaining it was just a word to excuse keeping the children separate. The Lady Mary is not with them. She has her own apartment in the palace itself. It made it easier to guard the young ones—well, Her Majesty didn't say who from, but she meant from toadies and favor seekers—and to provide them with freedom, like their own space to play ... and not ruin the formal gardens, which Her Majesty didn't say neither."

Denoriel smiled and shrugged. "The queen does seem to know how to deal with children. I suppose when they are settled—"

"It'll be a while, m'lord. The queen, she set up a school and she's invited a passel of noble lads and one little lady—Lady Jane Grey, which loves her books as much as His Highness and Lady Elizabeth. And you know Lady Elizabeth. She ain't to be bested by anyone, 'specially not in learning. She'll have her nose in the books and not look to anything else until she's the leader 'mongst them all in learning."

Denoriel nodded and sighed. Ladbroke knew his lady, and so did Denoriel. And the queen apparently understood scholars as well as children. Denoriel heard she had named Anthony Cooke, John Cheke, and William Grindal to be the tutors in the nursery. He mentioned them to Norfolk's son, Henry Howard, Earl of Surrey, who scowled and said they were all damned proponents of the reformed religion, but Thomas Wyatt and Francis Bryan sang the scholars' praises.

Then Surrey admitted they were fine scholars but he felt they would lead the children astray into Protestantism. Denoriel thought he could keep Elizabeth on a middle path ... if he could get to her. And of course Elizabeth needed to be well taught if she were to lead her country into the flowering depicted in the FarSeeing lens, but he could not completely put aside his disappointment in not being called on to share her joy.

For Elizabeth it was all joy. For the first time in her life she had the thrill of competing against others—she had always been ahead of Edward despite his almost frightening precocity because of the difference in their ages. Now she showed up very well in competition against the young men the queen had invited to join the royal children's lessons—and none of those young men ever forgot her. Nonetheless, in the midst of her excitement, she remembered her promise to Lord Denno to discover ways for them to meet.

Elizabeth was aware that she did not truly *miss* Denno right now. There were too many new people to study, too many new protocols to fix in her mind, far more demanding lessons. But she was also aware that the excitement of novelty would not last forever. Soon enough life would settle into known patterns, and she would begin to be bored and long for her Denno.

Already she had heard this and that she needed to talk over with him. Most things she could tell her dear Kat, and they would laugh or sigh together at the news and rumors; some things, however, would make Kat look horrified and shush her. Denno never did that. He would always warn her not to talk to anyone else, but then he would explain. As the thought crossed her mind, she smiled. She would send for him soon and show him the maze and the wonderful park.

Hampton Court Palace was ideally suited for clandestine meetings—at least for children. The nursery was quite separate from the palace itself, really an enclosure including a group of buildings rather than a single large structure. To the east, against the wall that extended from the palace, were the royal apartments, luxurious suites of rooms for Edward and herself, smaller but adequate chambers for their upper servants. On the south, nearest the north wall of the palace, were the barracks for the guards and a gatehouse; on the north and west were a variety of buildings, guest houses, kitchens, and storage sheds. Small gardens fronted the royal apartments and the guest houses.

Elizabeth had done no more than glance at those gardens. A medium-sized rabbit could not have concealed itself anywhere in them. She looked up at Kat and sighed.

"There is not even room here to take three quick steps. Where can I go to stretch my legs?"

Instead of replying that she would obtain permission for Elizabeth to walk in the palace gardens, Kat laughed and took her hand. She led her along an inviting graveled path, which passed behind the guesthouses and led northwest into a most entrancing area called the Wilderness. Elizabeth's anxiety about where to meet Denno disappeared. The Wilderness was planted with flowering shrubs, evergreen bushes, and trees and crisscrossed with grassy paths. Only the central area, around a small pond, was open and planted with flowers.

Most wonderful of all, in the northwest corner was a maze. Once in there, no one at more than arms' length would be able to see, and it would be very easy to escape observation by melting from a path into the hedges. So far so good, but Elizabeth put on a disappointed face.

"I cannot ride in here. It is a lovely place to walk but I hope I am not supposed to give up riding."

"Oh, no," Kat Champernowne said. "If you will walk with me past the maze we will come to the Lion Gate and you will be able to see through them to the great park. There is room enough to ride to your heart's content. And past the park is the forest itself, and when you are old enough to join in the king's hunts, you will even be able to find fine sport there."

"Then I could not be happier," Elizabeth sighed.

She meant to send word to her Denno, but she was caught up in the Christmas celebrations. She played a modest but significant role in the singing and set pieces and drew her father's attention. He spoke kindly to her and she replied, but meekly, low-voiced, curtseying to the ground. He asked about her lessons and she told him what she was translating in Latin, a piece by Cato, and that she had done most of the fables by Aesop in Greek. She saw that he was pleased, and yet his blue eyes, sunk so deeply in his fat cheeks, glinted cold, very cold.

Still his favor did not shift. He called her to him several times and teased her gently about her scholarship. Then he spoke to her in French, laughing to the courtiers who surrounded them when she replied easily and fluently in that language. She should keep up her French, he told her—and all the others nearby—because he would soon have French territory. And then the new year came and passed, and in the first days of 1544 the king went on to Greenwich, while the queen stayed at Hampton Court with the children.

Although she could not say why, this made Elizabeth uneasy. There was no sign she or Kat could detect nor was there any rumor about a disagreement between the king and queen. Also the king was much occupied with the preparations for the war against France and it was only reasonable that he not be disturbed by a noisy and exuberant pack of children. It was reasonable that he should go to Greenwich . . . but Elizabeth's belly now and then knotted with anxiety, and she would feel a chill pass across her heart, as if someone had closed a cold, cold hand about it.

Chapter 17

Throughout the late spring and early summer of 1543, Rhoslyn found herself frustrated at every turn in trying to interfere with Elizabeth's life. She could not herself attempt to watch Elizabeth nor could she send her creatures to watch. The child had retained her ability to see through illusion, and the maid could sense a watcher, which then the child could see and point out for the maid to drive away with her accursed cold iron crosses.

Rhoslyn resented her inability to spy on Elizabeth all the more because she was trying to *help* the wretched child. If she could not arrange for her to be disgraced and thus placed outside Oberon's rule, she was very much afraid that Vidal would demand the child's death . . . and Pasgen would arrange it. Cold crept about her heart. She could not live without Pasgen, but she could not live *with* him if he murdered a child. It was a crisis with no solution, unless she found a way to get at the miserable girl.

Fortunately, Aurelia had remained quite determined to take Elizabeth alive, and managed to divert Vidal into other enterprises. That helped, but it did not ease Roslyn's exasperation. Elizabeth's life, under observation of Prince Edward's officers as well as her own governess, was blameless. Rhoslyn suspected that Elizabeth saw Denoriel, but he was an accepted visitor and was never alone with the child. Worse yet, Rhoslyn's conduit to the king, Henry's eldest daughter, Mary, had little to do with Elizabeth these days.

Mary lived on her own estates and did not share households with the younger children.

When the king married again in July of 1543, however, the possibilities for involving Elizabeth in misbehavior became better. Rhoslyn knew at once when Mary received an invitation to accompany the king and his new wife on a progress after they were married. Knowing Mary's constant financial difficulties, Rhoslyn promptly presented herself as Mary's old and dear friend Rosamund Scot, bearing a fat purse of gold coins "to help toward her beloved Lady Mary's expenses in traveling."

It was no great surprise that Mistress Scot should be invited along to accompany Mary on the king's progress, or that Rosamund, always thoughtful and considerate, should mention that it was a pity the king's whole family could not be together. Mary thought that the addition of two young children on a honeymoon trip would be too much to ask of Queen Catherine and that the children's lessons would be too much disturbed.

Much though that was an irritation, it was a minor one, and Lady Rosamund was assiduous in continuing with her gentle hints of familial harmony. It wasn't difficult; Mary longed for a family of any kind, having so long lived without more than a shadow of one. So before the progress was over, and once the king and queen settled into a residence, she told Lady Rosamund that she would speak to the queen about bringing all of Henry's children to court.

Always true to her word—and reminded subtly by Mistress Scot—Mary did so. Catherine was delighted with the idea, particularly as Hampton Court Palace where they were now settled was ideal for children.

Henry adored the palace, built by Cardinal Woolsey, and actually *given* to him by the cardinal as an unsuccessful bribe to avert his own disgrace. It hadn't worked, of course, but Henry could luxuriate in the comforts of an entirely modern palace (unlike some of the other residences he possessed, Hampton Court had been rebuilt from the ground up), and he could look about himself, allow himself a moment of sentimental nostalgia about the builder, secure in the mendacious knowledge that it had been a "gift" and not taken from the unhappy cleric. Then, if he was feeling particularly spiteful, he could gloat over the fact that *he* had won in the battle of wills between himself and the Catholic Church, and Woolsey, the pope's man, had lost.

The king was pleased with Catherine's request that his younger children be added to the family party, had the apartments in the nursery refurbished, and in early December sent for Edward and Elizabeth to celebrate Christmas with the court.

From a safe distance, where Elizabeth was not likely to comment aloud on her pointed ears or cat-pupilled eyes, Rhoslyn watched Elizabeth. Despite the child's prettiness, Rhoslyn was not particularly drawn to her; there was a too-knowing, too-watchful expression on her thin, pale face, and too sharp a tongue when the other children—excepting only Edward—did not dance to her pleasure. However, Rhoslyn could not deny that Elizabeth was superlatively intelligent and inventive.

Christmas Eve was no longer given over entirely to religious practices as it had been in Catherine of Aragon's time as queen. There was a Christmas mass, of course, and a sermon, which carefully avoided both Catholic and Reformist extremes. From the back of the chapel among the high-born attendants of the royal party, Rhoslyn noted the still intensity with which Elizabeth listened to the sermon. After the music—hymns, but only the joyous and triumphant variety—and a masque of Christ's birth with sweet but not particularly holy choruses, the entertainment was ended and Rhoslyn followed Mary to her apartment.

"It all seems a little . . . a little . . . shallow," Rhoslyn sighed. "I miss the depth and beauty of the eve of Christ's birth as it was celebrated in your blessed mother's time."

Mary looked around, but her other ladies were at a distance and seemed well occupied with their duties. Most, she was sure, loved her, but there were some she suspected were spies and would report anything that hinted of criticism on her part of her father's distortion of the true faith.

"I too," she whispered, "but it is better not to speak of such things."

"Of course." Rhoslyn took Mary's hand and kissed it. "The children were very good, were they not?"

Mary smiled. "Well, good enough not to call down a punishment on themselves, but little boys will be little boys and I am so happy to see Edward plump and rosy despite what I hear about him loving his books so well, that a little nudging and whispering during a sermon can be excused."

"Yes. That Edward have good health is the best news for us

all. Elizabeth looks well, too, but she seemed almost fascinated by the sermon, especially the parts about sin. I do not suppose it possible that she could have any reason to be concerned with the redemption of sin . . . unless some lingering memory of her mother—"

"She is only a child," Mary interrupted sharply. "I do not believe she has any memory of that . . . that woman."

"She was almost three. Children of three remember." Well, that hint was not taken well. Time to try a different direction. Rhoslyn sighed heavily and then said brightly, "It is a real delight to see how Edward loves her. Did you see how he ran to her after the sermon? He asked her what she thought of some passage as if she were the authority instead of the priest."

"I think it was only a word he did not understand," Mary said, but a faint frown creased her brow.

"They have both grown very fond of the queen." Rhoslyn's voice was bland, but she fingered the golden cross that hung from a handsome string of pearls. Mary did not seem to notice.

"Yes," Mary said, smiling again. "I, too, am fond of Queen Catherine. She is a delightful woman—kind, intelligent, and very warmhearted."

"That she is," Rhoslyn agreed heartily, lifting the cross and jiggling it so the glittering gold caught Mary's eye. "But you are of an age where affection has no power to lead you away from the truth. For those much younger, what the beloved espouses very often becomes belief."

Mary was silent, staring at the cross which Rhoslyn now allowed to lie quietly on her breast.

"Elizabeth is particularly enamored of the queen, and they tell me she strains to be the foremost student of Cooke and Cheke . . ." Rhoslyn said, meditatively. "Perhaps this is because they have the queen's favor, but perhaps it is because what they say is pleasing to the child." She shrugged. "This will not matter, of course—unless she bends the prince in the same direction."

"I see," Mary breathed. "And the queen would not correct it, as it was she who appointed Cooke and Cheke, and she—"

Mary stopped as Jane Dormer, her long-time and most trusted lady-in-waiting, approached and curtsied. Rhoslyn examined the woman's face anxiously, hoping that Jane had not overheard their conversation, divined danger, and come to put a stop to it. What

Jane heard was not important; she was utterly devoted to Mary and would never repeat a dangerous conversation. But if Jane had heard, others less trustworthy might also have heard.

Rhoslyn knew it was important not to get Mary into trouble with her father. Unfortunately Henry knew quite well that silently, in the depths of her heart, his eldest daughter rejected his claim to be head of the English Church and bitterly repented her submission on rejecting the pope. Thus far, outward conformity kept Henry satisfied, but Rhoslyn did not want him to hear any hint that Mary's conformity and outward obedience was not perfect.

Jane brought no warning, only asked whether Mary wanted anything to drink before retiring. However, Rhoslyn noticed a quick glance in her direction and was forced to stifle a sigh. So, it was a complication that Rhoslyn had not anticipated; Jane was jealous. That was unfortunate, as Mary warmly reciprocated Jane's affection and Jane could turn Mary against Rosamund Scot—well liked and trusted, but not loved as Jane was.

"Here, take my seat, please," Rhoslyn said, getting to her feet and curtseying to Mary. "I was only telling Lady Mary how devoted Prince Edward seems to be to Lady Elizabeth. It is pretty to see them together, he, like a little brother, hanging on her words."

"Yes," Jane agreed, her expression changing from deliberate blandness to thoughtfulness; her glance at Rhoslyn perhaps held even a touch of gratitude. "I remember how much joy the prince took in Lady Mary's visits when he was younger. Now that we are so close and a visit does not mean a whole cavalcade and elaborate arrangements, it would be delightful to see more of the boy."

"Indeed." Rhoslyn curtseyed again. "I agree with you with all my heart, Mistress Dormer. It would be good for Lady Mary to have her family truly about her again, and good for the prince to have Lady Mary to emulate. Lady Elizabeth makes a charming friend for him, but a child should have an adult as a proper model."

Returning to her own chamber—which was small and high under the roof, but private, and thus a mark of great favor (since most of Mary's attendants were bundled together four to a chamber not much larger)—Rhoslyn allowed her maid to undress her and make her ready for bed. Reviewing what she had done, she was well satisfied.

Doubtless Mary would repeat what she had said to Jane, and Mistress Dormer, as passionately and even more cautiously devoted to the old religion than Mary, would understand Rhoslyn's hints more quickly. Queen Catherine obviously had reformist leanings and Elizabeth was absorbing those from the queen and from her teachers . . . and drawing Edward along with her.

Now Mary would try to replace Elizabeth in Edward's affections and counteract the influence of the queen and his teachers on his religious opinions. She would doubtless fail, since it was unlikely that Edward, already showing the headstrong nature of the Tudors, would be moved from the course on which his small feet were set. Edward's stubbornness would make Mary even more resentful of Elizabeth. That would make her quick to accept and believe any ill tales about Elizabeth. And ill tales there would be.

Rhoslyn sipped the tisane her maid had brought her and considered which of the boys being schooled with the king's children she should implant with the need to spy on Elizabeth. There were more than a dozen of them. Of those, three or four were too young, playmates and fellow scholars for the seven-year-old prince. All of the younger ones were overseen very strictly; it was unlikely that they could observe Elizabeth without drawing notice.

Two of the boys were more likely to run to the queen or one of their teachers and complain that they had been asked to spy by one of Mary's ladies. Lord Strange, already imbued with reformist principles and eager to find fault with Mary, and Henry Brandon because of his pride in being close to the king, a nephew, and rather besotted with Elizabeth.

That left the cadre of five older boys, all of whom were intent on gaining Edward's affection—which made a difficulty, as Edward was very fond of his sister and would not thank anyone who made trouble for her. Francis, Lord Russell, was the eldest, but he was so strong a reformist that he would not wish to oblige anyone in Mary's party. The two most likely for her purpose were Lord Stafford and Lord Mountjoy.

Rhoslyn put aside her cup, slid down under the coverlet . . . and sighed. She tried to be comfortable on the lumpy mattress and thought of her cloud-soft bed Underhill. She wondered whether saving Elizabeth was worth all this anxiety and discomfort. Perhaps she should just let Pasgen kill the child.

The breath caught in her throat. Saving Elizabeth was not for Elizabeth's sake. If the girl fell into Aurelia's hands, death would be far kinder. It was about Pasgen. If Pasgen could murder a child without a thought . . . She would not think of that. Nothing could be done until the twelve days of celebration were over, but after that she would choose one of the two boys who would best serve her purpose.

Rhoslyn did not even need to remind Mary about the need to make Edward love her. On the seventh of January 1544 she learned, when she was admitted to Lady Mary's apartment, that Mary had sent a message that she would like to visit the prince. A cordial invitation had been received in reply, and they were to go soon after breaking their fasts.

Rhoslyn was faced with a dilemma. If she went with Mary there was a chance that the little devil Elizabeth would see her and cry out, but if she went, there was also the opportunity to watch both boys. In the end she decided to go, only taking the precaution of raising so heavy a shield that all her magic was trapped within. If her essence as Sidhe did not leak out, there would be nothing to draw Elizabeth's attention.

Elizabeth was said to be very circumspect in her behavior now. Rhoslyn thought that even if she was unlucky and Elizabeth noticed her and saw through the illusions that made her look human, the child might not raise an alarm. No, of course she would not. Surely she would not be willing to point out attributes that no one else could see on one of Mary's ladies-in-waiting.

Both decisions were the right ones. Rhoslyn was reasonably sure that Elizabeth had not noticed her among the gaggle of ladies that accompanied Mary to the nursery schoolroom; certainly the child said and did nothing unusual. And it was immediately apparent that Lord Stafford would serve her purpose best. His expression was calculating, as if he measured every person and situation for the best advantage to himself. A perfectly natural result of the execution of his father, the duke of Buckingham, Rhoslyn thought. The sentence had been for treason and the attainder that followed had cost Stafford all his father's estates. Stafford needed preferment from someone, and he was old enough to know it, but young enough to be reckless about whom he sought it from.

Mountjoy, on the other hand, seemed rather uninterested in those around him, working some strange formulas at a small table near the windows. To make him attend closely to what Elizabeth said and did would be against his natural inclination

Tomorrow she would find Stafford and bespell him. The spell she planned to use would be very small and unobtrusive. It would not twist the boy's mind or nature, only intensify his natural desire to learn all he could about those likely to have power, and it would center that interest on Elizabeth rather than Prince Edward.

Soon Rhoslyn was assured that her spell would draw no attention, because it would have little effect on Stafford's normal behavior. Without any spell she saw that Stafford watched intently when Edward brought something he had written to his sister, who laughed and kissed him and told him he was a wonder. The child glowed with pleasure, and Rhoslyn saw that Stafford noted that also.

Mary saw the same little byplay, and she joined her two half-siblings. But Mary was no scholar, at least not in the class of those two precocious royal creatures. She frowned when Elizabeth, still laughing, challenged Edward to turn the Latin sentence he had brought to her into Greek and gave him three words to start.

Edward was silent, considering, his lips pursed as if he were about to kiss Elizabeth. And Mary made the mistake of saying—as if she thought that Edward would not be able to rise to Elizabeth's challenge—that Edward was indeed a wonder but he should rather play at tennis, for which the other boys were making ready.

Elizabeth laughed again. "Do you think he cannot do both? Dear Edward does not need to study for an hour to make a Greek sentence."

Rhoslyn saw Mary change color when Edward laughed too, and spouted a dozen words, which made Elizabeth clap her hands and kiss his cheek. And seemingly, having her accolade he waited for no more, but ran to join his fellows, who had collected his raquette and balls as well as their own, and were obviously waiting for him to go to the tennis court.

For a long moment Elizabeth and Mary stood confronting each other in the near-empty room. Then Elizabeth curtsied and said in a soft, apologetic voice, "He does so love his books and takes such pleasure in his learning. And you saw that he ran away to take his exercise."

"Yes, of course," Mary replied stiffly. "I am sure you wish your brother no harm."

"No! No, indeed I do not," Elizabeth said with passionate sincerity. "I wish him health and strength and wisdom and all the good that can possibly befall anyone."

"As do I, naturally."

Mary's voice was so cold that Elizabeth stared at her in consternation, and then, recalling that Mary was Edward's heir and might be suspected of *not* wishing him well, compounded her crime by blushing violently.

"No one could doubt it," Jane Dormer said, stepping forward smartly and glaring at Elizabeth.

"Never!" Elizabeth exclaimed, but her glance had for one instant passed over Mary's shoulder when Jane Dormer moved, and she shivered slightly as she brought her gaze back to her sister's face. "So loving a sister you have always been to him, and, indeed, to me for all the years of my life."

Rhoslyn was annoyed with both Mary and Jane Dormer for frightening Elizabeth. The child needed to be confident to act or speak with boldness. If she felt threatened she would commit none of the faux pas that could bring her father's wrath down on her head. With her magic confined, there was nothing Rhoslyn could do, but Mary still retained some of the fondness she had felt when Elizabeth was a babe. Seeing her sister's painful blush, Mary changed the subject to an inquiry about Elizabeth's musical education.

Before Elizabeth could reply, loud shouts and laughter drifted back to the ladies from the open door of the tennis court and Jane, with a single glance at Elizabeth, urged Mary to go and see how well her brother did. Mary hesitated just for a moment and then invited Elizabeth to accompany them.

Elizabeth thanked her with what seemed to be sincerity but, smiling and curtseying deeply, excused herself. She explained that she generally worked with her needle during the time that Edward played games with his male friends.

"I would gladly accompany you to watch Edward play," she said, with evident sincerity, "except that I have started work on Edward's Christmas gift and fear any delay."

Mary seemed to take no umbrage at this excuse and bestowed a pleasant smile on Elizabeth as she and her ladies walked away. Elizabeth stood staring after her sister and her attendants, her eyes following one of the women who seemed to be trying to keep in the center of the group.

"It's all right, love," Blanche Parry whispered in Elizabeth's ear. "She didn't mean any harm to you. Who knows what's in her heart that she regrets and causes her pain? She knows you didn't mean anything more than that you love Edward and wish him well."

"It wasn't Mary. It was that other lady," Elizabeth murmured in reply.

"You mean Jane Dormer? Jane will do you no harm. She only loves Lady Mary and is quick in her defense."

"No, not Jane. I know Jane well. The other one. The dark-haired one who always seemed to be trying to raise her hood to hide herself . . . and I know why." Elizabeth shivered.

"You are cold, m'lady," Blanche said a little too loudly so that anyone possibly watching from concealment would hear. "Come back to your chamber and I will find a warmer gown."

Elizabeth pulled on her cloak and followed Blanche at once, but as soon as they were in her bedchamber with the door closed, she said, "I must speak to Lord Denno. Go down to the stables and bid Ladbroke find some excuse to ride into London so that he can tell Denno to come at once."

"Come? Come where?" Blanche asked softly. "Mistress Champernowne has not yet requested that he be put on a visitor's list because the prince's officers have not yet submitted one. He has to see a place before he can come to it."

"Does he?" Elizabeth uttered a stifled sob. "Tell Ladbroke to describe the maze to him. Perhaps that will do. If not, I will have to . . . oh, I do not know what, but I know we are in danger."

"What danger?" Blanche frowned suddenly, as if recalling an uneasiness that she had not previously thought was of any importance. "Grace of God, then I *did* feel something. But it was so small, so . . ."

"It was one of the others, the bad ones." Elizabeth shook her head. "I only caught one glimpse of her face and I could see—you know what I could see. I must speak to Denno. I must tell him."

"Ladbroke will tell him that you saw one of the Fair Folk in

Lady Mary's entourage. He must know that at once!" She drew a deep breath, wringing her hands. "Oh, my lady, my lady, I fear I am useless to you. I did not feel her presence at all—and I should have. She was not so far from us. Even if I could not see her because she hid herself among the other women, I should have felt her."

Elizabeth's eyes widened. "I did not feel her either," she whispered. "It was only when Jane stepped forward so suddenly that I saw the woman behind her and I saw . . . her ears and her eyes. Oh, heaven, Denno must come."

"Yes, yes. Ladbroke will do his best, you know that." Blanche stared into nothing, thinking for a moment. "But, think, my love, it may not be one of the evil ones. It is not impossible that a watch is being kept on Lady Mary. Lord Denno will know. And for now, you do just as you said. Take up your needle and work on embroidering the book cover. Dunstan will watch over you."

Elizabeth was trembling again, and Dunstan, who had to be in and out on his duties, could not sit with the child. Nor could Kat Champernowne, who—unaware of any unusual circumstance—had gone into London on some private business. After one look at the wide-eyed, pale-faced girl, Dunstan summoned Gerrit into the room. The guardsman's familiar, bulky presence was immediately comforting, especially because Elizabeth knew he was wearing the amulet that protected him from sleep spells. And Dickson, Elizabeth reminded herself, similarly protected, was watching outside the chamber door.

For further comfort she recalled the unsuitable demands she had made of her faithful guardsmen as a baby and teased Gerrit that she needed help in winding embroidery silks. Only once did Gerrit's eyes flick to Blanche, who was pale and fingering the iron crosses under her gown. Then he nodded brusquely, moved his sword so his draw would be unimpeded and held out his thick hands for the skein of delicate silk. Elizabeth blinked back tears and began to wind the bright threads onto small silver spools.

Fortunately, there was no family dinner and Kat was dining with a cousin in town, because Elizabeth could eat nothing. However, her suspense did not last much longer; Ladbroke returned soon after the uneaten meal was taken away with a flat packet wrapped in a clean cloth.

"Your ribbons, m'lady," he said. "Sorry it took so long, but the fool of a merchant didn't understand that they were to be only of three colors to mark the passages in the maze. I hope he chose what would best be visible, but he did suggest that you take them into the maze when you walk there this afternoon to be sure you will be able to see them."

Elizabeth blinked. Ribbons? She had ordered no ribbons. And to mark the passages in the maze would be a sad cheat. But she had known from the age of three how to hold her tongue and she only nodded as he handed over the packet. He proffered it carefully so that Elizabeth's hands were forced to take hold in a certain way, and Elizabeth's breath eased out as she felt something hard, flat, and oval under the cover cloth.

She needed no further explanation. That must be an amulet that would "call" to Denno so he would know where to open a gate. She smiled up at the groom.

"Thank you, Ladbroke. I shall certainly take the ribbons with me when I go for a walk this afternoon."

"And m'lady," Ladbroke said, with emphasis, "If you have *any* trouble seeing the color, he said to *wait a few moments* until your eyes adjust and *look again*."

She nodded as emphatically as he had spoken. "I will surely follow that advice, Ladbroke. Now you may go and have your own dinner. I am sorry it is so late."

The groom glanced at Gerrit, still holding a skein of silk; he did not laugh. He nodded to the guardsman, bowed to Elizabeth. "It is a pleasure to serve you, m'lady."

Elizabeth let the packet lie on her lap while she finished winding up the skein of silk that Gerrit was holding. Then she thanked the guardsman, made a little joke about the odd tasks that came from serving a lady, and dismissed him.

But all the while she had been wondering why Ladbroke was talking about ribbons and marking the maze instead of just telling her that Denno would meet her in the maze during her afternoon walk. And why had Ladbroke not simply handed her the amulet instead of concealing it in the packet of ribbons?

She was certain Ladbroke was acting on Denno's instructions and that those instructions had been given because neither she nor Blanche had been able to sense the Sidhe who had been with Mary. The secrecy raised her fears again. Denno was warning her that if they could not sense the dark Sidhe they would also not be able to sense any watchers.

Elizabeth swallowed. That meant the Sidhe knew she and Blanche could sense magic and that she could see through illusion; the watcher would be well hidden. But if the watcher could feel the amulet . . . or, no. Elizabeth remembered that she had been warned a strong enough shield would prevent her from feeling magic.

So, if the watcher was shielded so strongly that it could not feel the amulet's magic, the watcher would not be able to sense the amulet as being magical. The watcher would be able to see what she did and hear what she said but if the amulet seemed to be an old possession, it would not tell the Sidhe the amulet was a "caller." Elizabeth rose, clutching the packet carefully so the amulet would not slip out.

"You are right, Blanche," Elizabeth said to her maid, who was sitting near her arranging the spools in a workbasket. "I was a little chilled this morning. I will need my warmest cloak and gown, but I still wish to take my walk this afternoon."

"Why do you not change at once, then. You look quite pale with the cold. It is so kind of you, Lady Elizabeth, to make a trail that Prince Edward will be able to follow by tying ribbons to the paths in the maze."

Elizabeth smiled gratefully at Blanche, who had provided a reasonable excuse for marking paths in the maze. She was too old to need such help, but it was reasonable that she would not want her little brother to be lost and frightened.

"Quite right. Let us go and look over my gowns."

In the safety of her bedchamber, with the doors of the wardrobe open to shield any view from either side and her own body blocking the view from the front, Elizabeth knelt to open the packet she had laid on a footstool. There were half a dozen narrow ribbons in each of bright crimson, bright blue, and bright yellow.

"I wonder," she said to Blanche, "whether I should tie these down where Edward could not fail to see them at once or tie them higher up?"

But as she spoke, her hand reached to cover the pretty golden oval on a golden chain showing the lion and the lamb lying together. With it she picked up the ribbons, sat on the stool, and

dropped the ribbons into her lap. Blanche leaned over her, seemingly looking at the ribbons, which she picked up and carried to
a table. She returned with Elizabeth's trinket box. This she set in
Elizabeth's lap while she loosened Elizabeth's necklace. She handed
that to Elizabeth, who dropped it into the box, and then removed
Elizabeth's earrings. Those, too, went into the box.

Elizabeth was quivering with the desire to take the amulet
in hand and run to the maze, but she knew she must not. She
waited patiently to be clothed anew and even contributed to a
brief conversation about which pieces of jewelry would best befit
the new gown; that permitted her to scrabble in her trinket box
and take out the amulet, which Blanche hung around her neck
well away from the cross beneath her clothes. At long last, after
what seemed like hours, Blanche allowed her to pick up the ribbons, leave the apartment, and make her way along the graveled
walk to the wilderness.

They went first to the central pool, around which were low beds
prepared for flowers in the spring. Both searched the surrounding
mostly leafless trees and bushes for any movement. There was no
hint of any unnatural watcher, but just entering the most direct
path into the Wilderness they saw two of the boys from the school.
Elizabeth squeezed Blanche's hand and complained that the wind
was far sharper than she had expected. Blanche, pushing Elizabeth
to the side where they would be less visible from the straight path
to the entrance, said that they should walk by the maze where the
thick yew bushes would shield them from the wind. Trembling with
anxiety, Elizabeth agreed.

They took a side path to the left and then another going right,
pausing as soon as they were around the corner to listen, then to
peer out and watch. Neither saw or heard anything, but Elizabeth
whispered to Blanche that it was not right. She knew the boys from
the school; they should have been talking. Blanche nodded.

Now they hurried, stepping as softly as possible and holding
their skirts close so they would not catch on or touch any bushes.
A last turn to the left brought them to a wider path, across which
were the tall, arched yews that marked the entrance to the maze.
They stopped in the last shelter of the path and listened. Nothing. Cautious glances along the path showed it empty. Elizabeth
shivered.

Perhaps the boys had not stayed in the Wilderness or had taken the most direct path to the Lion Gate, which would take them out to the park. *Wait*, Elizabeth's head said. *You can come back later or tomorrow to use the amulet.* But her heart pounded and her teeth were so tightly clamped that her jaw hurt. Perhaps it was not wise, but Elizabeth wanted her Denno. She *needed* him.

Knowing she should not, Elizabeth pulled Blanche across the path through the entrance to the maze. Inside they waited just out of sight of the entrance but there was still no sight or sound of the boys. They scanned the trees and bushes opposite and the ground around the base of the bushes and paths, but there was no sign of any watcher either.

Elizabeth shivered again and hurried Blanche along toward the center, feeling a little less frightened. She was sure that neither the watcher, if there was one, nor the boys if they had followed, could see any farther through the thick walls of yew than she and Blanche could see themselves.

By choice, Elizabeth would have set the amulet down in one of the dead-end paths, but she had no idea how much space a Gate needed. Those she had seen, at Logres and Avalon, were large enough for several horses. At the center she looked around with great care and examined each of the three pathways. Blanche looked, too. Neither saw anything they thought could be a watcher.

"What if it is a cricket? Or a mouse?" Elizabeth whispered.

"I do not know," Blanche whispered back. "I looked for mice, but I do not believe it could be much smaller and still be able to remember anything. What about those boys?"

For answer, Elizabeth put her fingers to her lips and held her breath as she listened. There was no sound of footsteps or sense of anyone brushing against the tall yews that bordered the paths. Another sweep of the open area and Elizabeth sighed and opened her cloak. Blanche undid the golden chain over her dress and replaced it with another gold chain and locket which she took from her pocket. Elizabeth laid the amulet on the bench and stepped away.

She thought perhaps Ladbroke's warning about looking around if she did not see the "ribbons" at first meant that she should not watch, but she found it impossible not to stare at the amulet. Nor did she have much time to wait with a pounding heart and dry mouth. She had barely retreated far enough to seize Blanche's hand, when a pinpoint formed; a blackness so black that it drew attention like a spot of brightness.

In moments it had enlarged to the size of a window, then to an open door, through which Elizabeth glimpsed a handsome bedchamber. Before she could see more than the edge of a large curtained bed and a sliver of window, Denoriel stepped through . . . and, his arms fettered by his tight-drawn cloak, took another step forward into empty air—

—and fell off the bench into a bed of dead plants.

Chapter 18

"Elizabeth!" Denoriel roared, from his undignified sprawl among the dead foliage. "If you have dragged me here to play games, and to make a fool of me—"

Down on her knees beside him, Elizabeth put an urgent hand over his lips. "I'm sorry, so sorry," she whispered. "No, I was just stupid. I didn't think when I put the amulet on the bench. I forgot you would have to step forward. I didn't realize that the Gate would form above the bench."

Denoriel took a deep breath and rose to his feet, drawing Elizabeth up with him. "Why are we whispering?" he murmured.

She looked about her, furtively, though there was no one there but Blanche. "The watcher, if there is one, can hear."

He shook his head, certain that she was imagining things. "There is no watcher."

"Are you sure?" Elizabeth asked, her eyes wide with fear. "The person I told you about, the reason I called you, was because I could not feel her. Only by accident I saw her eyes and her ears so I knew, I knew what she was. Blanche did not feel her either."

"Shielded," he muttered. "Heavily shielded. But a watcher without senses . . . that makes no sense."

"It can see and hear," Elizabeth insisted. "Can you do nothing to make a silence and darkness around us?"

He shook his head. "No. That—" his head tilted toward the

Gate, which had shrunk to a black pinpoint again "—draws from me. And it was very hard to build at all. I am near empty."

"I do not think there is a watcher, m'lord," Blanche put in; she seemed as certain as Elizabeth was uncertain. "We have both looked very hard and seen nothing."

"Likely there is not," Denoriel agreed. "I cannot see what she could learn from setting a watcher on you."

"That you were coming. That you can build what you built." Elizabeth's anxious voice told him that she was in no way convinced by either of them.

Denoriel pulled Elizabeth into his arms for a brief hug. The cold iron cross she wore stabbed him like a knife, even through their heavy clothing, the pain sharper because of the depletion of his magical energies. He had to release her.

"She knows those things already," he said, soothingly. "Perhaps not that I was coming just now, but what good would that knowledge do her? No, dearling, if this was a Sidhe of the Dark Court, she knows what I can do, and very probably who I am. She can learn nothing from us here except what all of the Dark Court and Bright already know: that you are watched and protected at the High King's orders."

Elizabeth shook her head and Denoriel could see her body relax. "I'faith, I don't know. But what was she doing here?"

The question made Denoriel frown. "The body was a woman's? You are sure?"

"She walked like a woman," Blanche said, with a nod. "And felt like a woman, too. Even from ordinary people, I can usually get a feeling that will tell me if they are male or female."

This was—interesting. "And what did she look like?"

"Black hair, dark eyes, pale skin. She was tall, much taller than my sister, Mary," Elizabeth told him. She sounded very certain of the description. Not Aurelia, then, unless Elizabeth had been deceived. "And that was not illusion? She was not blond and green-eyed beneath the dark color?"

"No." Elizabeth shook her head. "I do not think there was any illusion beyond the eyes and ears."

Denoriel breathed out a long sigh. "Likely that is my half-sister, Rhoslyn."

"Your half-sister? How do you come to have a half-sister as well as a full sister?"

The indignation in Elizabeth's voice made Denoriel smile. His lips parted, then closed, and then he said, "That is a long tale, and I cannot tell it to you here and now. In another place, I will gladly tell you. As for Rhoslyn, I do not believe she will harm you."

"But—" Elizabeth began and then closed her mouth firmly for a moment only to open it to say, "I recall that name. Did you not tell me that she tried to steal away my Da and put something else in his place?"

"Yes, but he was only a little boy then." Denoriel sighed and shook his head. "You must just believe me that it would not be possible to make a changeling like you now, and without the changeling no one would dare try to take you. Not, I think, that there would be any who would dare to try to take you with or without a changeling. There are protections. And if anyone intended abduction, surely the chances would have been better while you were alone at Hatfield or less well guarded at Hertford."

He thought that his reasoning would have convinced her, but she was as stubborn as ever. "But Mary did not come to Hatfield or Hertford so your sister could not conceal herself among the other women. She could not possibly have gotten near me—" her voice betrayed her fear again. He moved to calm it with logic.

"Love, she cannot abduct you from the midst of a crowd of women," he pointed out inexorably. "There is nothing to fear; it is not only that you are surrounded by people now—remember, she did not succeed in abducting Harry because he was wearing the iron cross. You have that cross now and she cannot touch you while you wear it. You have your shields, which Harry did *not* have. If she comes near you, raise them. Then she will not be able to bespell you to go where her mortal servants could seize you. And Blanche also has her necklace, which has already proved a potent weapon! Blanche can drive any Sidhe away with the necklace as soon as you see her."

Finally Elizabeth nodded and sighed. "I will try not to be so easily frightened."

"No, no," he protested. "That was not what I meant at all! You were right to be frightened, until I reminded you what protections you have, and I needed to know of Rhoslyn's presence among Mary's ladies. If you are frightened again, you must send for me at once. In fact, I think I will take the chance of binding an air spirit to watch you again."

"She will know if you do," Blanche put in suddenly.

"Yes," Denoriel agreed. "I think that would be best, for her to know she was seen and know she is being watched."

"Would she harm the air spirit?" Elizabeth asked anxiously, clasping her hands before her so tightly the knuckles were white. "I would not want that. They are so adorable."

"I hope not," he said, reluctant to pledge anything where Rhoslyn was concerned. "I do not think so. But if she does, I will know instantly and come at once."

Elizabeth sighed. "Thank you . . . but I still do not like her being here."

"Ignore her," he advised. "To tell the truth, I do not think she will approach you at all. I think she is with Mary to protect her—although I swear to you that no one among *my* people is trying to do Mary any harm. But there are factions among the Sidhe, Seleighe and Unseleighe, and since Oberon wishes you protected, it is altogether likely that some other faction counters by protecting Mary, and never mind that there is not now and never will be any intent to harm her."

Elizabeth nodded wisely. "I understand. Those who intend harm cannot believe that others do not."

Denoriel sighed. "I am afraid that is too true, but although Rhoslyn herself would not hurt you, Rhoslyn is not her own master. You must be wary. As any subject must bow to your father's will, so Rhoslyn must bow to the will of her prince. And he, the prince, might hurt you—or worse—if he wrested you from her."

Elizabeth stared up at him, eyes wide. "Would you not try to save me?"

He laughed briefly without any humor. "I will come. Never fear for that, or yield to despair. I will come to you no matter what bars the way. Hold your shields and wear your cross. Do not believe their threats, for they are terrible liars. They might threaten to set some dreadful beast on you if you do not take off your cross. But the beast, likely, will fear the cross itself, so do not part with it. If you hold tight your courage and your good sense, I will come and others with me and we will bring you back to England safe and whole."

She put out a trembling hand and Denoriel took it, suppressing the pain that thrummed in his arm. "You have not once called me noxious or a horror or a nasty brat, even though I made you fall off the bench," she said, torn between anguish and an attempt at humor. The anguish won. "Oh, Denno, do you think me in terrible danger?"

Denoriel laughed. "Not at all." He squeezed her hand. "I am just so glad to see you. I thought with all your new friends and the court frivolities you had forgotten me."

Her eyes fixed on his. "I will never forget you . . . never. I am sorry it has been so long, but with the king and queen in residence here, there is constant confusion and coming and going, which makes the guards extra alert."

Denoriel sighed. "We will need to have some arrangement, some place to which I can come. To build what I did . . . it takes too much from me and might leave me helpless to defend you."

"Perhaps one of the dead-end paths here in the maze?" she hazarded, looking around. "I didn't know how much space you would need for a Gate. Or, since I see it can take little room, a screened niche in Blanche's bedchamber?"

"Not in yours?" Denoriel grinned.

"Too many people come into my bedchamber," Elizabeth said perfectly seriously. "Kat comes and Mary used to come when we lived together. If she came now with her ladies . . ."

Denoriel was ashamed of himself. What a suggestion to make to a child not quite eleven. Of course she did not understand his weak attempt at humor.

"Not a real Gate in Blanche's bedchamber, but perhaps I could create a weakness that would facilitate opening a Gate," he ventured, thinking aloud. "I will have to think about it. A place here in the maze, yes, if I must come in a hurry. But I do not think it wise for me to appear too often in a private area of the palace—and we cannot have a horse in the maze."

That made Elizabeth smile. "That will be easily solved. I have not been riding yet, but I know there is a large park beyond the Lion Gate. One reason I did not send Ladbroke to you sooner is that I hoped to find a place in the park where you could come and we could meet and ride together as we did at Hertford with no one but my guards the wiser."

"That makes sense. I should not be too frequent an official visitor, foreign as I am."

"Yes." She sighed, and looked weighted down with cares. "And Kat is afraid to ask for visitor's privilege for you before Edward's officers ask privilege for those who wish to visit the prince. She is afraid it would mark you as special and perhaps—because you are a merchant—permission would be refused. And there are new rules about visitors—you know we have a school here and the boys . . ." She suddenly interrupted her own thoughts, and her eyes widened. "Oh, Grace of God, I almost forgot. There were two boys entering the Wilderness when Blanche and I came into the maze. We listened for them, but did not hear them enter the maze."

Denoriel frowned and held up a hand. Elizabeth, to her amazement, saw the long ears above the round shadows twitch forward and cup slightly. After a while, in a low voice, he said, "They are just walking by on the path outside." Then he frowned and added, even more softly, "I think they have walked back and forth on that path several times." He pointed to Blanche and signed for her to speak.

"I don't know why you don't want to walk with the boys, m'lady," Blanche said promptly, "but I think they are likely gone from the Wilderness by now. If you like I will go and look. Have you yet decided which color of ribbon you will use for the true path and which for a dead end or a loop?"

Elizabeth raised her brows at Denoriel, who looked at the ribbons Blanche was proffering. He pointed to the blue, which would probably best fade into the yew branches as it became soiled.

"This for the dead ends," she said, looking at Denoriel, who nodded his head. "This for the loops and this for the true path."

"We do not have enough ribbon for the whole maze," Blanche pointed out.

"I know. I will only do one path from the Wilderness. After all, Edward will not be allowed to come into the maze on his own." Her laughter sounded artificial to Denoriel, but perhaps the boys would not know the difference. "There will be others to guide him so he will not ever truly be lost. I only want him to be able to show the others that he found the way. The ribbons will be our secret—Edward's and mine."

Denoriel beckoned and they followed him back toward the entrance. Out of sight around the first false path, they stopped and listened.

"I tell you that Lady Elizabeth is talking to her maid, and I would rather not have heard what I did hear. It is perfectly natural for her to want to make the little prince happy, and none of my business either."

Elizabeth recognized the voice of Lord Strange, a very nice boy who often included her in his activities, but her lips tightened when the second boy spoke. Lord Stafford was pleasant enough, but something about him made her uneasy and what he said was terrible.

"But you surely heard a man's voice cry 'Elizabeth' when we first came to the maze."

"I do not know who called the Lady Elizabeth's name. Perhaps it was one of her guards."

"There was no guard with them when we saw them at the pond in the Wilderness. We could search the maze—"

"You know that's hopeless," Lord Strange said, and then, angrily, "Why are you trying to make trouble for Lady Elizabeth, hinting that she goes out to meet a man. She is not even eleven years old. Just because her mother—"

"No!" Stafford exclaimed, sounding appalled. "I meant no such thing, and I have no intention of making trouble for Lady Elizabeth. I am only interested in what she does because she is so great a favorite with Prince Edward."

Denoriel had gripped Elizabeth's arm hard so that she did not attempt to burst out and confront the boys. He shook her slightly, then pointed to himself and back into the heart of the maze. When she nodded, he put her hand into Blanche's and pointed to the exit.

For a long moment Elizabeth stood still, breathing hard. Then she let go of Blanche's hand and shook out her skirts, making sure they caught the lower branches of the yew and caused it to rustle.

"Oh," she cried, "I told you that was a wrong turn. We must go back and turn left at the first cross path to reach the way out."

"Sorry, m'lady," Blanche said immediately, and a little loudly. "I guess I was too sure. You must be right. When we get to the entrance, are you going to go back and tie on the ribbons?"

"No," Elizabeth said, stepping out into the path to the exit. "I'll do it tomorrow after I talk to Edward. I won't do it without his permission."

Denoriel had melted away when Elizabeth first spoke. He would have accompanied her if he had not been afraid to deplete his magical power further with even so small a spell as the Don't-see-me. He still had to return to London, and opening a Gate from the mortal world to another place in the mortal world took far, far more power than to open a Gate from Underhill to the mortal world. Even the double transit, from mortal world to Underhill and Underhill back to the mortal world was easy in comparison.

Back at the center of the maze, Denoriel burst into silent laughter when he saw the amulet on the bench. Now that was a heroic entrance if he'd ever seen one, falling flat on his face into a bed of dead flowers. He took the amulet and went back into the maze to hide it deep among the roots of the hedges in one of the deeper dead ends. Someone would have to be grubbing about in that particular spot with some energy before they had any chance of finding it now.

There, because that false passage went near to the outer wall, he stopped to sense and listen. Elizabeth and Blanche were away from the maze, taking the path on the outer edge of the Wilderness toward the palace. The boys were right across from the entrance to the maze, concealed behind some brush. Denoriel grinned unpleasantly. They would have a long wait.

He then returned to the center of the maze, stepped up on the bench and passed through the Gate to his London house. He closed the Gate, sighing with relief when the draw on his energies ended. Gathering what strength he still had, he Gated, not to Logres but to Avalon.

Before he did something stupid, he would ask Treowth or Gilfaethwy if his notions about setting the Gates was sound. He wanted a Gate in the maze that did not function but could be awakened from Underhill. When that was built, he could use the amulet to create a second Gate of the same kind in Blanche's chamber. Finally he would need a third, ordinary Gate for himself and Miralys, in the park. That one he would have to build from the park to Underhill. How much more difficult it would be, he did not know but Treowth would know, he was sure.

Meanwhile Elizabeth and Blanche had reached the haven of her apartments. Elizabeth was nearly rigid with rage, but she flung off her cloak and kept her jaws tightly clamped together until she and Blanche had again examined every nook and cranny in her bedchamber. Then she turned to Blanche so swiftly that her skirts belled out and nearly touched the maid.

"Did you see them?" she whispered furiously. "Did you see them crouching behind the bushes right across from the entrance to the maze? They are going to wait there and see if the man I was talking to comes out. Oh!"

"But no one will come out," Blanche murmured comfortingly. "No matter how long they wait, no man will come out of the maze. Lord Denno will go back the way he came." She waited, watching the girl's eyes, bright golden and fierce as a lioness's. Elizabeth was listening to her but still panting with fury. "And you must not be too angry with Lord Stafford," Blanche added. "It is because of what happened to his father and the loss of nearly all his estates. You cannot blame him too much if he seeks a way to repair his fortunes."

"By accusing me of meeting with a man!" Elizabeth choked on the words and then, helplessly, began to laugh bitterly. "And it is just what I was doing, is it not? He surely thinks I am conspiring against Edward, or perhaps Mary. What a shame I am not a few years older. Perhaps he could bring the news to my sister and she, to end my influence on Edward—as if I had any—to my father, and they could have my head off, too."

"Nonsense." Blanche's voice was sharp. "No one in the court wanted to harm you. It was all in your own head. And I doubt Stafford will tell anyone. Moreover, I am sure Lord Strange will not support his word if he does. Lord Strange is very fond of you."

"Yes. I like him too, but he's—" she gestured vaguely "—he's so very dull and ordinary. Denno . . . Denno is more worth talking to . . . He wakes up my mind! Denno is well worth any trouble that might come of our meeting."

"Mayhap, m'lady," Blanche replied, with a significant look, "but you must be careful about meeting him, very careful."

But Elizabeth shook her head. "Despite what I said, I am not afraid for myself now that Denno has assured me that that person cannot touch me. At least, I am afraid only in the sense that I am too happy and I know that happiness could be snatched away."

However, Elizabeth's happiness was not snatched away. If Lord Stafford told his suspicions to anyone, no result came of it. Over the next few weeks, Denoriel established Gates in the park, in the maze, and, for dire emergencies, in the chamber where Blanche slept and Elizabeth's gowns were kept. An air spirit appeared—an adorable, nearly transparent little creature that looked like a furry, cuddly and friendly cross between a kitten and a bat—only of course Elizabeth could not cuddle it because it could not bear to be so near her cross.

Soon after the air spirit appeared, the dark Sidhe lady-in-waiting, whose name Blanche had discovered was Rosamund Scot, disappeared. All through January, which turned bitterly cold, Elizabeth's only regret was the weather, which prevented her from riding out and meeting Denno as often as she would have liked. Stafford watched her, but she saw that he watched everyone. And she did understand. She, too, had been stripped of everything and was doing her best to win back her place.

In that, Elizabeth thought she was making progress. King Henry smiled on her—when he noticed her—and she knew she was a great favorite with Queen Catherine. Of course the queen was gentle and kind to everyone, warm and friendly to Mary and very motherly to Edward, but on Elizabeth she lavished not only affection but instruction and long, thoughtful conversations. In Catherine, Elizabeth discovered someone besides Denno who could wake up her mind, and who truly appreciated learning and wit. Catherine was not as much of a challenge as Denno, but she was the closest Elizabeth had ever come to his quick wit.

In February the weather grew milder. Elizabeth was able to ride out with her two guards and her groom. Sometimes she was part of a large group that included her brother, the other boys of the school, and their attendants. She was the only female, and it was a shock to the older boys that she rode as well as they . . . and her horses were better. A few accepted her cheerfully; others would have played nasty tricks on her but for the watchfulness of Ladbroke and the guards.

Other times, when the boys were occupied with instruction in arms or other male pursuits, Elizabeth rode out with only her groom and guards. Whenever she did so, the air spirit disappeared briefly and shortly thereafter, Denno on Miralys rode out of somewhere to meet her. Mostly they had the park to themselves, few taking rides for pleasure in the still-frosty weather. Once in a while another horseman or two would appear in the distance and Denoriel would suddenly be gone from her side.

A distant cloud now appeared on the horizon. In December of the previous year, the Scots had repudiated the treaty they had made with England after the disaster of Solway Moss. Henry had been furious and ordered retaliatory attacks on the lands of those he believed had betrayed him. However, by the time Elizabeth and Edward had been invited to join the court for Christmas, the king had been dissuaded from acting until spring. Promises had been made to Henry by the Earls of Lennox, Angus, and others that they would capture the infant princess Mary and bring Scotland to heel.

By the middle of April Henry was complaining to all and sundry, often within the hearing of the pages being schooled with Edward and Elizabeth, that these promises would not be fulfilled. The boys had much to say about the king's plan to dispatch Lord Hertford with a substantial army to attack Edinburgh and visit such punishment on the Scots that they would bow to his royal will. They were enthusiastic and excited about it, and spoke at length of the great fights to come, and wistfully that they were not old enough to go—and boastfully of what they would do if they were old enough. Only Edward showed no interest in swords and battles, which further kept him by Elizabeth's side.

Since her father was in boisterous good humor while plans were made and Hertford sailed for Scotland, Elizabeth was happy enough. She told Denoriel, when they met at the far end of the park at the beginning of May, that Henry was even jubilant over the messages that came back reporting that Hertford had landed at Leith, blasted the main gate of Edinburgh, and burnt much of the city.

Elizabeth was somewhat disappointed when Denoriel only shrugged and said it would not do. Even when, a week later, she told him that Hertford had successfully carried out all the king's commands, having withdrawn to Leith, sacked that city, and taken his army home, Denoriel shrugged as he had before. All he said was that Henry was keeping the Dark Court happy, but coming no nearer to controlling Scotland.

That Denno had been right soon became apparent. Far from agreeing to Henry's terms, the Scots became more bitter and tenacious, refusing to abide by the treaties with the English and reaffirming their ties to France. Henry snapped at everyone, including his patient and easy-tempered wife and then, quite suddenly, at the beginning of June he departed for Greenwich, leaving Queen Catherine in charge of the children at Hampton Court.

Elizabeth was terrified, black memories forcing their way out of the places where they had been buried—memories of her mother holding her up at a window and weeping as her father rode away, memories of conversations she was not supposed to have heard about Henry riding away from the palace where Catherine Howard was hysterically trying to deny that she was an adulteress.

When she told Kat Champernowne, her governess laughed at her and assured her that her father's mood had nothing to do with the queen. He was upset, Kat explained, because of the recalcitrance of the Scots and because there was little he could do about it. Just now he was committed entirely to another purpose, an agreement he had made with Emperor Charles for a combined assault on France.

That war, Kat pointed out, would take all the king's forces and resources. He had neither men nor money to expend on the Scots, and he was enraged because they would not see the benefit of marrying their infant queen to his heir and thus ending forever the continual wars between the nations.

Elizabeth was still uneasy, despite the fact that everyone she seduced into speaking about the king's retreat to Greenwich agreed it was only so that he could give all his attention to the preparations for the war against France. Ships and men were already on their way to Calais and the king was due to follow them in a few weeks.

Queen Catherine showed no signs of anxiety. She wrote to the king every day and messages, some written and some verbal, came from him several times a day. The queen was as calm and loving and even merry as ever—and all Elizabeth could think of was that she had heard the previous Queen Catherine had been gay and laughing and totally unaware of the dreadful fate about to fall upon her.

She had nightmares about Catherine Howard's death. Her heart pounded and her food was like sawdust in her mouth. Mostly she disguised how little she ate, even from Blanche, but by the end of June there were black half-circles under her eyes, her hands trembled, and her gowns hung loose on her body. To Blanche's anxious questions, Elizabeth said that nothing was wrong, nothing. She was sure she was the only one who saw the doom hanging over her beloved Queen Catherine and also that if she spoke of it, that would somehow make her fears come true.

One night, at her wit's end, Blanche dosed Elizabeth with valerian and tincture of poppy until she slept and sent the air spirit for Denoriel. Aware that Elizabeth had been avoiding him for two weeks, fearful that her shields had failed, and remembering how Mwynwen had left a thread of spell when she Healed Elizabeth the last time, he brought with him a Healer of such authority that Blanche sank down to the ground in a curtsey and could barely explain what was wrong. And when Ceindrych told her to remove Elizabeth's cross, Blanche did so without hesitation.

Although the Healer examined Elizabeth minutely and at great length, she could find no taint of magic and could sense no ill of the body. There was nothing wrong with the girl beyond a violent disturbance of the spirit—and that was so deep-seated, going back to infancy, that even she, Ceindrych said, would not dare meddle. Elizabeth would need to fight that battle with herself by herself. Moreover, Ceindrych added, that turmoil of the spirit was part of what made Elizabeth what she was and what she would be.

Denoriel thanked the old Healer profusely and shepherded her to the Gate, but he paused at the lip to tell Blanche to bring Elizabeth to the maze the next day.

"I will soothe her heart," he promised passionately, "even if I must bring down the moon from the sky to her hand, I will give her peace."

The next day, Blanche nearly dragged Elizabeth to the maze. Elizabeth tried all sorts of excuses—she had been making excuses for two weeks not to meet Denoriel—but this time Blanche stood firm. If Elizabeth did not come, she would make Mistress Champernowne tell Queen Catherine that Elizabeth was sick and was refusing to see a physician. Elizabeth knew a physician could do her no good and to worry Queen Catherine was more than she could bear.

It had to come sooner or later, she told herself. Denno would have one last chance to prove himself. If he did not . . . she shivered as she seated herself on the bench at the center of the maze . . . If he did not, she would need to stand alone . . . forever.

She turned her head to glance at Blanche, who had gone around the bench and settled on the grass out of earshot of soft voices.

Blanche and Kat were loyal and loving, but they were as helpless as she. Denno, she thought, really could save her, but he had lied . . . and swore his lies were true. But if they were true . . .

She sat on the bench in the center of the maze, staring down at the hands folded in her lap. Within minutes Denno came out of the dead-end path. She did not look up, and he dropped to his knees, taking her hands in his.

"What is wrong, Elizabeth?" he begged. "What is wrong? You are not bespelled. Ceindrych says you are making yourself ill."

"I am afraid," she whispered.

"There is nothing to fear," he murmured, bending his head and kissing her hands. "On my life, there is nothing to fear. I have those who are watching the Dark Court and they tell me that—"

"I need to see my Da," she interrupted, as if she had not heard him; her voice was low but its intensity was like a scream. "I need to touch him, to hear his voice, to feel him alive and breathing. Letters are not enough. You could have written those or have had them written—and your swearing to me is useless. I need to be *sure* he is alive and well."

"But he can do nothing for you, Elizabeth." Denoriel protested, puzzled by her insistence. "He cannot live in the mortal world any longer. I swear I will protect you with my sword, with my skill, with my life. God's Grace, child, what do you fear?"

If he had not had elven hearing, he would not have heard her breathe "I fear another Catherine will die under the ax and me with her."

"Elizabeth! It is impossible, I swear it to you." He kept his voice low, but firm. "I have eyes and ears in many places. There is no hint anywhere that the king is displeased with the queen. Unless you know . . ." He drew a breath and hardly louder than Elizabeth had spoken, asked, "Are there men she favors?"

"No!" she replied, sure of that, at least. "There are no men at all, except when my father brought his gentlemen and then the queen was no more than polite. She does not laugh and . . . and flirt like . . . like . . . Now we are all women. Even the gentlemen of her household are not favored to join our amusements and none ever sees her in private, only in the common rooms where all can come."

"But then—"

She drew a sharp breath and spoke more normally. "You need not tell me again that there is nothing to fear. My *head* knows there is nothing to fear, but my heart still leaps and trembles, my belly roils, bile rises in my throat. I cannot eat or sleep. The kinder the queen is to me, the more I cannot help loving her, the greater my terror."

He shook his head doubtfully. "This is madness, Elizabeth."

"Likely." Her voice though low was steady now.

Denoriel took a long breath. "Very well. I will arrange for Harry to come to my house and take you through the Gate in your dressing chamber. You are not likely to be missed for a few hours in the middle of the night."

"No," Elizabeth said, her voice hard and cold. "There I cannot see through illusion. You could bring anyone disguised and I would not know. You must bring my Da here to me in my world. You say he cannot live here. I will not keep him long, I promise. But I must see him, touch him, have him hold me in his arms."

Denoriel stared at her wide-eyed, realizing for the first time that she had never believed his assertions that Harry was alive and well, and thus had never trusted him. He very nearly told her to stew in her own juice, since she would not trust him . . . but then, he thought, who *could* the poor child trust? Her father had murdered her mother, her stepmother had abused her innocence, her father's minister had bespelled her. Denoriel saw her eyes, black with misery, fill with tears and the tears slip down her sunken cheeks.

"I need my Da," she whispered. "If he *is* alive and well, I will know I have somewhere to hide myself if all turns black."

There had been nothing more Denoriel could say. Reason was powerless and there was no doubt that the child would soon be in little better a state than when the spell of dissolution was destroying her. He kissed her hands again and promised her that somehow he would bring Harry to her.

The light that came into her eyes, the deep, easy breath she drew—because the promise that she would see her Da was *proof* that he was alive, proof her friend, her protector was no liar—showed that the promise itself had begun her cure.

Denoriel drew breath to speak, but from around the edge of the yew hedge down the short path to the center came a young man's voice. "See, I told you!"

Instantly Denoriel cast the Don't-see-me spell and slid away to his right toward the dead-end path and his Gate.

"Yes, you did. You were right!" That was a boy's happy exclamation. "There's Elizabeth."

Edward stepped away from his companion and ran the few steps from the end of the yew hedge into the center. The two guards who had followed him stopped where the yew hedge opened into the center path and they could see everything.

"Bess," the prince cried happily, "I am glad to see you here. When Dr. Cheke asked why you were missing lessons, your governess said you were not well."

"How comes it that you are all alone here, Lady Elizabeth?" Lord Stafford asked.

Elizabeth rose to drop a curtsey to Edward and then leaned forward to kiss her brother's cheek. "I felt a little better this morning and thought the air and the quiet here in the maze would do me good, Your Highness." Then she turned to Stafford. "Alone? No, I am not alone."

"I thought not," Stafford said with a tight smile. "Just as we came around the edge into the path, I could swear I saw a man kneeling at your feet."

"A man?" Elizabeth forced herself to take an even breath and then another. "No, I did not bring my guard. Good Lord Stafford, the sun must have dazzled you. You must have seen Blanche. She did kneel down to fasten my shoe, which had come unlaced."

"Oh? And to where did she disappear?" the boy asked, in a know-it-all tone.

"I did not disappear, Lord Stafford," Blanche said, rising from behind the bench. "You startled me when you spoke and I dropped my pocket. I just stepped over the bench and knelt down to gather it up." She held up one of the pockets that she kept tied about her waist beneath her apron.

Stafford stared at Elizabeth but she did not flinch or blush. She looked back at him, her eyes bright gold, shockingly bright, in the sun. There was no particular expression on her face. Stafford wondered if his vision could have dazzled, coming from the shaded path between the hedges into the sunlit center of the maze. Could he have mistaken the kneeling maid for a man?

Elizabeth only smiled, an entirely unreadable smile.

Chapter 19

His presence masked by the Don't-see-me spell, Denoriel stood at the edge of the dead-end path listening to the exchange among Elizabeth, her brother, and the boy Blanche had called Lord Stafford. He did not misunderstand the expression of angry frustration that appeared briefly on Stafford's face. The boy was watching Elizabeth, trying to catch her in wrongdoing. Likely it was Stafford he had caught glimpses of in the distance when he and Elizabeth had been riding. Had Rhoslyn bespelled the boy to spy?

He extended his senses, feeling for magic. Perhaps there was the faintest echo, but if Stafford was bespelled, it was so well done or the spell so small that he could not sense it with any surety. And there could be other reasons for his spying. There was a great deal of pushing and prodding to be close to Edward, and Elizabeth was envied her brother's affection by most of the older boys.

Denoriel sighed. In any case it would be impossible for him to undo such a subtle spell and he did not dare ask Ceindrych or Mwynwen—each for different reasons—to help. He watched as Edward asked Elizabeth if she would walk back with him and she agreed. The boy then asked an eager question about the Latin translation he was working on and took his sister's hand. The older boy fell in behind them, scowling.

As he watched, Denoriel began to reconsider his plans for Harry's visit. He had intended to bring Harry through the dressing room as he had brought Ceindrych, but that now seemed too dangerous. Surely there would be cries of joy and eager conversation between Harry and Elizabeth. The maid's chamber was an inner room, and he could not be sure what other rooms adjoined it—probably servants' rooms, but not impossibly the chambers of some of the less important boys. If one was spying, it was perfectly possible that more were. In any case, the sound of a man's voice in Elizabeth's apartment—whoever heard it—would be utter disaster.

Better they should meet outside. If they were seen it would be far less reprehensible to be walking in the garden than to have a man in her bedchamber. But when and where? He was afraid Stafford would be watching the maze—or having friends or servants watch, which meant that they could not chance meeting Elizabeth there by daylight, *nor* could he and Harry walk out of the maze in daylight to meet her elsewhere. Besides, by daylight there was always the chance that someone who had known Harry would recognize him. Living Underhill, he had changed very little from his appearance at seventeen.

At night then. The moon was nearly full and the weather promised fair for tomorrow. Tomorrow night when the moon was well up. Just before midnight.

Still wearing the Don't-see-me spell, Denoriel followed Elizabeth and Edward as they crossed the very small formal garden in front of the building in which they lodged. He watched Elizabeth say an affectionate farewell to her brother and promise him that she would attend lessons on the morrow. Stafford, Edward, and his guards went toward the prince's apartment and Elizabeth toward her own. Denoriel caught Blanche by the arm.

She gasped with surprise, which drew Elizabeth's attention, but she only nodded very slightly to give permission. Blanche allowed the pressure on her arm to draw her toward a bench shaded by a small tree and several square-clipped bushes. Seated, she immediately opened the housewife attached to her belt and looked diligently at its contents.

"By God's Grace, you have brains," Denoriel murmured from right behind her. "Never mind that you cannot see me. I am here. You heard what I promised Elizabeth. Can you bring her to the maze tomorrow night when the moon is well up? That should be before midnight."

"No, I cannot!" Blanche sounded sharp, although she whispered and looked down at the pins, needles, and thread spread in her lap as if she were telling over the contents of the housewife. "How can I get her that long way through the Wilderness without light? Mostly the moonlight cannot get through the trees there. Do you expect me to carry lighted torches? We cannot see like cats as you can, m'lord."

For a moment Denoriel stood silent, calling himself a fool. As he tried to think of an alternative, his eyes wandered around the small garden. Toward the center there were some flower beds surrounded by a narrow lawn. Beyond the lawn were four benches, each near the middle of one of the square sides of the garden. Each bench was shaded by one or two trees and several well-trimmed bushes.

The benches would be shadowed if the moon were high. Yes, and he could give Harry an amulet carrying the Don't-see-me spell. Harry would only need to touch it and say the words of invocation to disappear. Elizabeth might be scolded for walking in the garden at night, but so close to her chambers and with Blanche in attendance, there should be no real trouble. She could plead a headache, and that she needed the air and the cool.

He said as much, and added, "Very well. Tomorrow night when the moon is high, just before midnight right here. If you slip out of the house wearing dark clothing and sit on the bench in the shadows, no one should see you."

"Can I tell Dunstan?"

That was a good thought. If her twin shadows were in attendance, there would be that much more chaperonage. "Yes, and Ladbroke if necessary, but not the guards."

Blanche uttered a small chuckle. "I doubt anything they see or hear will surprise them, but they are bred to honesty. They might answer questions truthfully—which would never be Dunstan's fault." She sighed. "Oh, I pray that this will settle my lady. She has lived through too much."

"I, too," Denoriel breathed.

When Blanche had gone in, Denoriel made his way back to the maze and Gated from there to Logres. Miralys was waiting and carried him to Llachar Lle, from where he dispatched one of his servants with a message for Harry. If Mwynwen asked for it, the servant was to give it to her but then find Harry and tell him Denoriel had sent a message. Denoriel was taking no more chances on messages going astray.

He need not have worried. The problem of Mwynwen's attitude toward Elizabeth had been dealt with soon after Elizabeth's visit to Underhill. Thoroughly annoyed by Mwynwen's possessiveness, Aleneil had ignored Denoriel's concern for Harry's distress and told him that Elizabeth had been Underhill and had been terribly disappointed over not being able to see him because he had gone away with Mwynwen.

In fact, Harry had noticed that his lover had had something unpleasant on her mind for some time. He had thought it was bad news about his physical condition, and had not questioned her, determined to enjoy himself without worry about the future as long as he felt completely well. He had accepted death before he came Underhill and was not afraid.

After Aleneil's disclosure, it did not take long for Harry to put two and two together, and his reaction had been rather violent. Not that he argued or shouted. Merely at dinner, he repeated to Mwynwen what Aleneil had said and asked—coldly—whether he were a free man or a slave bought by his need for her care.

To his surprise Mwynwen burst into tears and sobbed that she was sorry, so sorry but that wasn't the worst that she had done. Harry just stared in surprise. The Sidhe were not known for saying they were sorry about anything—or, for that matter, for actually *being* sorry. But then Mwynwen confessed that when she had been asked to break the spell of dissolution on Elizabeth and Heal her, she had not removed the spell completely. She had left a piece of the spell—not anything that could harm the child physically, but a twist that might make her memory less perfect.

Harry, whose mind had grown into a man's, even if his body had not altered much, was coming to know his lover and understand her. He realized that it was for herself she wept, for falling short of her Healer's oath, not for any hurt she might have done to Elizabeth. And she had not answered whether he was free to seek another healer or bound to her. He pushed away his untouched food.

"What I was asking was whether I was free to live with Denoriel and find another Healer, or whether my debt to you and the services owed require me to continue to live here," he said, his voice icy.

"What services?" Mwynwen had snapped, lifting her head.

"You mean our play abed? I thought you lived here and loved me because you loved me—and yet you will leave me because of that stupid human child. I did not even try to harm her. I meant the girl only good. I wished to blur her memory of you and ease her pain of loss . . . but what I did was wrong. Not that I meant harm or did harm—and she is only human after all—but I said I would clean the spell from her completely and I could have done so . . . and did not."

"Then I am free to go?" The chill in his voice only deepened.

After a small, tight silence, Mwynwen put her hand over his. "Harry, I said I was sorry. If the girl comes again, I will not keep you from seeing her—but do you not understand that it is very cruel of you to keep her desire for you alive? Let her forget you. Forget her."

"One does not forget one's child," he said. "She may not be the child of my body, but I held her in my arms soon after she was born and she is the child of my heart. She is the daughter I will never have . . . and I cannot forget her nor hope that she will ever forget me."

"Child?" Mwynwen repeated, and her eyes filled. "Richey," she whispered, naming the changeling she had cared for and who had died in Harry's place. "He was truly my child—and yes, you are right, I will never forget him, even though you are his gift to me to fill my heart." She tightened her grip on his hand. "Don't leave me, Harry. For your *child*, I will mend what I did amiss. I promise."

"Then I will stay," he said, leaning forward to kiss her.

Even as passion stirred in him when their lips met, however, he determined to tell Denoriel about the remnant of spell as soon as he could. Perhaps another Healer would be able to remove it. He doubted that Denoriel would trust Mwynwen to do it; he was not sure he trusted her himself. But she was so beautiful and so passionate and she did care for him—and his heart had near broken at the thought of leaving her.

Truthfully, he was not sure he could have fulfilled his threat. He was overjoyed that she wanted him even though he was making it clearer and clearer that he was no longer her child but a man grown; however, he did not forget Elizabeth, and Lady Aeron took him to Denoriel's apartment that very evening. He was lucky and caught Denoriel at home.

It turned out that he had been unnecessarily worried, for

Denoriel was happy to pour out the rest of the story into his ears. When Queen Titania had made it impossible for Elizabeth to speak of Underhill, as Oberon had done to him, the Queen herself had found the bit of spell and removed it.

When Harry returned, he mentioned that to Mwynwen and watched her complexion gray. She said nothing, and he took her in his arms and murmured comfort to her, but he was sure she would not dare to interfere with Elizabeth again—and he was satisfied.

Thus when, many months later, Denoriel's message came for Harry, Mwynwen sent the messenger to him without delay with the message unopened. Harry put aside the delicate and exquisite fly he was tying—he both used them for fishing himself and traded them to a gnome, who had them spelled to attract fish and sold them to a dwarf in a troupe of players.

The gnome took his pay from the dwarf partly in mortal goods and partly in information. The mortal goods, the gnome sold at the Goblin Fair, the information he traded to Harry, who thus had kept up with his father's wives and their fates and to some extent with the political events in England. The flies were more valuable than news, however. The gnome would gladly have paid Harry in gold, but Harry did not need gold, because either Mwynwen or Denoriel would ken for him as much as he wanted. Instead he was building quite a store of favors owed from the gnome.

Lady Aeron was waiting as Harry stepped out of the house and he took time, as he always did, to hug her and kiss her soft muzzle before he mounted. Midway to Llachar Lle, they met Miralys, who paced them as far as the front of the palace.

"I think we'll be right out," Harry said to both of them, which was more true than he had expected because Denoriel was coming out of the palace as he mounted the steps to the portico.

Their eyes met. Harry turned back, went down the stairs he had climbed, and remounted Lady Aeron. Without any words exchanged the elvensteeds brought them to Logres Gate, from there to an Unformed domain, and from there to Shepherd's Paradise. Both dismounted and went to their accustomed seats.

"I'm sorry I've been neglecting you," Denoriel said. "It seems like months since we have been together."

Harry grinned at him. "It has been months."

"I'm sorry," Denoriel repeated. "I hope you are not getting bored and that you haven't been lonely."

"Bored!" Harry's eyes danced. "No, I can assure you I'm not getting bored. And I'm not lonely either. I miss you. I miss hearing about Elizabeth, but I have friends here and I have been doing yeoman work for the Bright Court."

Denoriel looked anxious. "Yeoman work for the Bright Court?" he echoed. "Whatever have you been doing, Harry?"

"Cleaning up some sinkholes that should never have been allowed to form."

"Sinkholes," Denoriel echoed again in a failing voice, then thundered, "Harry! Have you been hunting alone in the chaos lands because I did not take you there as I promised?"

Harry laughed aloud. "Hunting in the chaos lands and other places, yes, but not alone. Did you not know that there were Sidhe tormenting helpless creatures, right on the border of slipping over to the Unseleighe Court, because they could no longer think of how to amuse themselves? And that there were others talking about Dreaming?"

"Of course I knew." Denoriel shrugged helplessly.

Harry stared at him, aghast. "And you did nothing?"

"What could I do? I had nothing to offer them." Denoriel grimaced. "Young as I am, what gave me joy they had seen, done, tasted many, many times, so many that the taste was too well known . . . flat, gone."

"Did you never think to offer them danger?" Harry countered. "A life on the edge of nonbeing tastes sharp and sweet."

"What danger is there in the elfhames?" Denoriel asked.

Harry looked at Denoriel blankly for a moment, then rose from his seat to embrace his friend . . . his father of the heart. Yet like his mortal father, this father too was not perfect. Oh, Denoriel was not selfish and autocratic. Harry was quite sure that Denoriel would fling himself in the path of any harm that threatened his precious boy, but he could only *worry* about Harry being bored; he could not think of a new game, a new challenge to pique his boy's interest.

He settled on the ground beside Denoriel, leaning against his thigh. "Remember when you took me to that Unformed domain and the creature—well, it was like a lion but not fully like—charged at us? Later, I don't remember when, I asked if it would not be wise to hunt down that lion so that no other innocent caught in the domain would be hurt. You remember, I know. Just now you asked if I had gone hunting the lion alone because you could not take me."

"Of course I remember," Denoriel snapped. "I have been busy, not lost my mind."

"Did you know how hard such a beast is to kill?" he asked.

Denoriel laughed. "Yes, I knew, which was one of the reasons I did not wish to take you there before you were fully recovered—and I think that has only been recently."

"Oh, yes," Harry replied, glad that he could give that answer. "I am much stronger. Mwynwen only needs to draw off the poison once a month or so. And for the last year, I have been going hunting whenever a hunt was formed. But it was too easy, Denno. I looked at the poor deer, even a boar, and I thought how unfair, how useless it was to kill them. We did not need the meat. Our weapons . . ."

Denoriel was far from stupid; he saw the way the conversation was going immediately, and he stared at Harry, aghast. "And naturally you immediately thought of the beast in the Unformed domain . . . Harry!"

Harry shrugged insouciantly. "Well, I thought you would not like me to go alone and . . . It was not that I was afraid—"

Denoriel was torn between his horror that Harry had attempted such a thing and his pride in Harry for what had clearly been a successful attempt. "You should have been afraid, you idiot!"

Harry grinned unrepentantly. "But it is not much fun to hunt alone, and a full hunting party is well suited for such tasks. And then I caught Elidir tormenting a gnome—"

"And you told him to stop!" Denoriel threw his hands up in the air. "It is a miracle you are alive, that he did not substitute you for the gnome."

"You forget this." Harry pointed to the blue star on his forehead. "No, to be fair, that wasn't what stopped him. He—he was really ashamed, and he hadn't hurt the gnome, only frightened it, teasing it hard, driving it past being able to think, like a well-fed cat with a mouse. Anyway, I said that if he needed a challenge I knew of something worthwhile that needed killing and told him about the lion. He was the one who told me how hard those creations were to kill while they were in their own place and he knew of other Sidhe who were also getting tired of living. So he asked them, and we formed a party."

"Yes, and I knew about them," Denoriel said slowly, "And I knew about the beasts of the Unformed domains, but I never put the two together." Denoriel shook his head and finally laughed weakly. "Mortal mischief. So what will you do when you have cleaned out that domain?"

"*That* domain is long safe and quiet. We are working in El Dorado now." Harry gave a slight shiver and leaned harder against Denoriel. "I do not know if we will ever cleanse that place. There is something . . . something truly evil that has tainted it."

"Truly evil?" Denoriel raised an eyebrow. "I have never ventured there—"

Harry nodded. "Yes, evil at heart. The beasts in the chaos lands are dangerous, but not truly evil. But what is in El Dorado . . ." He rubbed his face against Denoriel as he had when he was a little boy. "So far we have only found the evil's spawn, not the thing itself. Elidir and Mechain are both working on their magic now that they have a worthy foe." Harry's face lit with a smile of great sweetness. "They are as good and bright as newborn, and many others, too. It only took giving them a purpose again, a noble, fine purpose, and now they are like guardian knights! And who knows, if we can cleanse El Dorado, perhaps it can be a home again for the Seleighe Sidhe. It is a beautiful place."

Denoriel hugged Harry's shoulders. "If we can ever find those that fled it or breed enough Sidhe to need another elfhame. But truly evil? That is dangerous, Harry, far more dangerous than a construct lion."

"You need not worry about me." Harry grinned. "Elidir and Mechain and the others guard me as if I were a precious jewel. They don't want to lose their discoverer of trouble, the one who cured their boredom."

Denoriel laughed and nodded. He was sure that was true. A human who gave freely of his creativity, not constrained or dulled with longing for his lost home and friends, was a precious jewel to the Sidhe. And Harry's eyes were bright, his face alive with interest.

So he asked the question he most needed to know the answer to. "Then you are content to live Underhill, Harry? You do not long for the mortal world?"

"Not at all. I do miss Elizabeth, that I will grant. I long to see her again before she is no longer a child at all, but I always wanted to live Underhill." He sighed, and the sound was full of content. "I am glad to be here. Given the choice of all the worlds and all time, I would still live here."

Denoriel smiled. "Then I will take you to see Elizabeth."

"Now?" Harry shot to his feet.

Denoriel laughed. "No, not this minute, but as soon as I can get an amulet with the Don't-see-me spell and explain a little of the situation to you. I've already sent Aleneil a message about the amulet. I hope it will be in my apartment when we return."

But now Harry was all afire with impatience. "Then let's go now."

"No." Denoriel shook his head. "Sit down again, Harry. I'd like to finish talking about Elizabeth here and I have much to tell you."

He told Harry not only the plan for meeting but tried to prepare him for Elizabeth's lack of trust in everyone and to explain that however young Elizabeth was in years, there was almost nothing childlike about her. Neither her manners nor her speech were other than those of a grown woman. And he explained her precarious situation too, that she was envied and spied on because her brother was fond of her and that many considered her tainted with her mother's promiscuousness and conniving, hoped to use that to make her father reject her.

"Nonsense!" Harry exclaimed. "Anne was a fool, but never promiscuous."

Denoriel shrugged. "I agree, but the fact that Catherine Howard, who was Anne's cousin, really *was* little better than a whore has convinced everyone, even those who at first could not believe the accusations against her, that Anne was also an adulteress."

Harry snorted. "Anne was too clever to commit adultery. She was only a fool in not seeing that even the innocent could be accused, and by the king's will be convicted."

Denoriel nodded. "You and I know that is the truth; however, the fact of Anne's conviction and execution leaves Elizabeth very vulnerable. It would be very bad if Elizabeth were caught with a man, not to mention how you, who are supposed to be long dead, could explain yourself. And do think, Harry! What *else* might be thought of, to see you, who was so nearly the king's heir, talking with Elizabeth, when you have been supposed dead. Would that not stink to high heaven of treason?"

Harry narrowed his eyes. "There have been pretenders e're this," he said slowly, "And heirs who were supposed dead, had men who were in their likeness return."

"And no matter what might come of Elizabeth being seen with

an ordinary man, being seen with one who appears to be the late duke of Richmond . . ." Denoriel prompted.

"Yes, treason. Or a conspiracy to commit treason."

Denoriel nodded. "So you must be prepared to disappear if anyone should appear, no matter how brief your meeting."

"And have my one chance to see Elizabeth cut short!" Harry protested, pain in his voice.

"*One* chance? Oh no, I think not." Denoriel was grinning fit to split his head. "After this, you will be able to see her at many convenient times and without any danger of being overlooked. I can bring her Underhill—she is marked by Titania to come and go. Only this time she insists on you coming to her so she can be sure you are not an illusion." A tinge of bitterness touched Denoriel's voice. "I told you. She does not trust me."

"Poor child," Harry said, grief for her making his voice low. "Poor child. At least I had that. You were my great rock, my safe place. I had you."

They arrived in the maze early, before the moon was fully risen, and made their way carefully through the Wilderness. There were voices near the pond at the center. It was a warm evening, and a few members of the court had sought the greater privacy of that place. Most courtiers went to walk in the great formal gardens that fronted the palace. These voices were young, boy and girl, possibly servants, but they were already saying their farewells. Harry and Denoriel waited.

The moon was barely peeping above the trees when they came out of the wilderness near the wall that surrounded the nursery. Wearing the Don't-see-me spell, Denoriel touched the guard at the gate, leaving him erect but with glazed, unseeing eyes. Harry opened the iron gate with the guard's key, Denoriel slipped past it with a shiver of pain, and they went into the small formal garden where they were to meet Elizabeth. From a shadowed corner, Denoriel pointed out the doorway through which Elizabeth would come.

As the moon rose, it slanted the shadows of the small trees across the benches they shaded. As soon as the shadows were long enough, Harry walked quickly across the exposed lawn and seated himself where he would be able to watch the door for Elizabeth. Denoriel remained in the shadow of the wall. He had dismissed the Don't-see-me spell to save the drain on his power.

He hoped he would not need it, but just in case of discovery he wanted enough power to do magic.

The moon rose higher. Inside her apartment, Elizabeth, who had been trembling with first eagerness and then anxiety, said impatiently, "I can wait no longer. If anyone should see us and ask, I will say that it is so hot that I could not breathe. I had to go out."

She was dressed in black with only a white collar embroidered with silver around her neck. The inner side of the sleeves of her gown were also silver, but they were turned under so the silver side did not show. She and Blanche had discussed removing the collar and then decided that to do so might imply a need for secrecy.

Dunstan held the guard's position at the door. He had sent Nyle on an errand, not because Nyle would have protested Elizabeth's going out but because he would have insisted on following her. When Blanche opened the door, Dunstan signed that all was clear, and the women slipped out and down the stair. Blanche too was wearing black and stepped so quickly out of the door and to the side that Harry did not notice her.

He did hear her low-voiced, "Come, love," and stood, making out a blur of white that was Elizabeth's face as she hurried quickly across the path that separated the garden from the buildings. He started forward at once, eagerness overcoming caution and called softly, "Elizabeth."

In the shadows by the wall, Denoriel bit his lip and cast anxious eyes over the garden. It was barely twilight to him, even in the shadows, and where the moonlight was unimpeded, bright as day. He saw nothing. Even so he extended a thread of perception that should have snagged on anything warm and breathing. It found only Elizabeth and Harry.

Denoriel did not seek in the buildings; there would be many humans there. Thus he did not notice that a young man sat dozing by an open window, seeking a breeze. Harry's voice, Elizabeth's name, snapped his eyes open, but he did not move except to turn his head slowly so he could see.

What he saw was Elizabeth turn toward the voice (a man's strong voice) that called her name, hesitate, and then hurtle toward the man, who had just emerged from the shadows near a bench. Stafford watched without moving long enough to see Elizabeth fling herself into the man's arms. He slipped carefully away from the window then, slowly enough so that any reflection of moonlight on his white shirt would not attract attention, and began hurriedly to dress. He could hear excited voices, one clearly male, but not what was said and he could not wait to listen. He had a long way to go.

Elizabeth had turned her head at the sound of her name, stared for just a moment, and then flung herself forward, careless of being exposed fully in the moonlight, crying, "Da! Da!"

"My baby. My baby." Harry's voice was thick with tears and then laughter as he held her a little away from him to look at her. "Only you are no baby any longer. But you are still Da's girl, are you not?"

To his surprise she began to tremble and weep, pulled a little farther away, fumbled under her skirt for a moment, and then thrust something into his hand. He looked down to see the iron cross that he had worn for nearly all of his life, until he passed it to the infant Elizabeth.

"Sweetheart, dearling," he said, extending the hand with the cross to her, "I am in no danger. You need to keep the cross with you . . ."

And then he realized why she had thrust the cold iron on him without warning. She did not wish to return the cross. She had feared he was a disguised Sidhe or a construct. Neither could have borne the touch of cold iron.

"I am me, love, truly I am," Harry assured her, bending his head and kissing the cross he held. "I am well and whole. Look, I will put the cross on and wear it while I am with you. I swear I was saved. I am alive and well."

Then she embraced him with all the fierce strength of her young arms and burst into a storm of weeping, and clung to him, sobbing. He kissed her hair and hugged her back.

"I never knew what was the truth," she whispered. "Kat only said that you were very far away and would never be allowed to come home because you would be a threat to Edward. But when I asked the guards, the look on their faces told another tale. And once I saw tears run down Gerrit's face when he denied you were dead. I stopped asking because I could see how much it hurt them. They loved you and they knew you were dead."

"Someone else was buried in my place. They did not know that." Harry replied, grief for his friends and protectors thickening his voice. "I knew they loved me. They fought so hard for so many years to keep me safe. It is a miracle that they were not killed more than once. And they fought for you, too, dearling, that night that I was wounded. They are ageing now. Do you need younger men to protect you?"

"No, by God's Grace. I am nearly always lodged with my brother and any palace in which he stays is very well guarded indeed." He heard a firm determination in her voice that was out of keeping with her years. "I will keep them with me as long as they are willing to stay and Denno has promised to help me pension them if they wish to retire. Also, I am not of any importance any longer. Edward is hale and well, God be praised, and he will rule and rule well." At the thought of her brother, she raised her face to look into Harry's, with a tremulous smile. "Oh, it is a shame that you cannot meet Edward. He is so clever—"

"*You* are so clever. Not like me." He shook his head, ruefully. "I always loved my horse and my sword far better than my books. Denno tells me about your progress in languages and your other lessons . . . and about how you skin him alive now and then."

She was silent for a moment, looking into his face in the bright moonlight. "I am sorry," she said in a small voice. "I know I have not always been kind to Denno, but I was so afraid he was lying to me about you. If he lied about one thing, why would he not lie about another? I wanted so much to trust him . . . and I could not."

"But you can, love," he told her firmly. "Really you can. Denno is truer than gold—for gold can be false, as I well know—but Denno cannot. He almost died for you once already, when you were not quite three years old, and he will do anything for you." He lowered his voice to a murmur. "You are his whole purpose in life, Elizabeth, and all he asks in return is love."

"That he has," she admitted. "Which is why I ripped up at him so hard. Because I did not want to love him and could not help it. But I cannot swear I will never say harsh things again, nor refrain from teasing with my claws, like a naughty cat. I—you are sweet, Da. I am not."

Harry laughed heartily. "Oh, do not try to make yourself over for Denno. He loves you just as you are. He has said to me more than once that he could not do without having his blood boiled once or twice a week." As Elizabeth giggled he hugged her tight, then stepped back and took her hand. "Now I cannot tell you anything about where I am and what I do—and you know the reason for that—but you can tell me about how it has gone with you. I am hungry, dearling, to hear everything, every little thing, what time you rise, how and on what you break your fast, and all the doings of your days."

When Stafford was dressed, he took one more quick glance out of the window to make sure it was really Elizabeth and she was really with a man. He was just in time to see her fling her arms around her visitor and squeeze him as tight as she could, to see the man bend his head to kiss her hair and embrace her as fiercely as she embraced him. He then went quickly out of his room and down the stairs, through a servant's passage and out the back door.

A road ran behind the buildings. Stafford turned right on it. He was soon behind the wall of Hampton Court Palace and he walked along quickly until he found a guarded door.

"I am Henry, Lord Stafford," he said to the guard, "and I have important news for the Lady Mary, very important. I know it is late, but could a message be sent to the lady requesting that she see me."

The guard frowned, but behind him in the corridor was a bench on which a page slept. The door he guarded was the closest to the nursery wing and the page was there for the purpose of carrying messages about the children. If the prince should be taken ill, for example, the page would go to the king and he would send for his physicians. Sometimes the servants of one of the younger boys would ask that a message be carried to the mother or father of the child because of some emergency. The guard could not remember ever sending a message to the king's eldest daughter, but there was no rule against doing so.

Stafford waited, barely restraining himself from pacing and wringing his hands. He realized that this was the best opportunity he would ever have to be rid of Lady Elizabeth and have a chance to supplant her in the prince's affection. Beside that, Stafford had been annoyed by the bare-faced lie, told so innocently that he had begun to doubt his own eyes, that it had been her maid and not a man kneeling before her in the maze. The maid's gown was dull gray, the man's doublet a vibrant golden brown—the sun had *not* dazzled his eyes.

He was not held in suspense very long. In a very little time, Jane Dormer returned with the page. "I am very sorry, Lord Stafford," she said coldly, "but my lady does not receive gentlemen in the middle of the night."

Stafford bowed. "Then two words with you in private, Mistress Dormer. My news is not . . . not such as should be spread abroad."

For a moment she stared at him, seemingly unmoved, but then she nodded, stepped out of the door, and walked along the road just far enough that the guard could not hear low voices, although he could still see them.

"Well? What is this news?"

"I do not know what to do, Mistress Dormer. What I saw cannot be allowed to continue and yet . . . yet I dare not . . ."

"Dare not what?"

"Speak of it."

"Are you mad?" Jane said, irritably. "If you dare not speak, what are you doing here requesting an audience with my lady?"

He primed up his face. "She is the only one I could think of to entrust with this horror. Her long affection for Lady Elizabeth assures me she would do her best for her sister—"

Jane's eyes widened. "Lady Elizabeth! Out with it. What horror?"

He tried to make himself look indignant rather than excited. "It is so warm that I was dozing by the open window of my chamber when I heard a man call out 'Elizabeth.' I came awake, thinking I was dreaming, but then I saw Lady Elizabeth come out of the building into the little garden at the front and run to the man. She clipped him and kissed him and he her—"

"Clipped and kissed." It was the lady's turn to look prim. "But Lady Elizabeth is only a child, not yet eleven years old."

"I could hardly believe it myself," he replied, drawing himself up to look as tall as he could, "but when I left my room to come here they were still locked in each others' arms, and I minded several times that I thought I had seen her riding with a man, but when I rode closer she was alone. I did not know what to do. If Lady Mary comes to the nursery and sees them in the garden, surely her authority would banish this man and she could explain to Lady Elizabeth that what she was doing is wrong."

"Wait here," Jane said, and hurried back to the building, nearly running.

Stafford paced the road back and forth, wondering if Elizabeth was still in the garden with her lover. How long would they dare stay together? So young as she was, surely she could not be ruled by passion. How could she be such a fool? But her mother had been fool enough to betray a king because of her passions.

Or was it worse than that? Was it conspiracy? But then, why the embraces? Unless the man he saw was one she had known long and thought of as a father? And in that case, who could the traitor be? For traitor he *must* be, if he could not come to Lady Elizabeth openly by day, and with King Henry's favor.

Stafford bit his lip. There was no one else that Edward favored, except his whipping boy, Fitzpatrick, but Barnaby was no match for the prince's scholarship. Stafford's lips twitched. He was no match for Edward's ability either, but in years more of lessons, however unwillingly, he had learned more than the prince yet knew.

If he were clever, when Elizabeth was gone, he could get Edward to turn to him. He began to plan his campaign, and so soothing did he find those plans that he was surprised to hear Jane Dormer's voice, and when he turned to her to see Lady Mary, two more of her women, and two grooms of her chamber wearing swords.

He was appalled at the size of the party, but all he could do was to beg Lady Mary for quiet. He pointed out that any unusual noise would undoubtedly send Elizabeth's lover—

At which point Mary angrily reminded him that Elizabeth was only eleven years old, and could not have a lover. Stafford bit his lip, knowing there were houses of pleasure that offered children even younger to those who craved such amusement.

"I do not mean that any physical intimacy—aside from the kisses—is involved, only that there is a man who is perhaps trying to win Lady Elizabeth's love so that she will favor him strongly in the future when her father is looking for a husband for her. She is now so far down in the line of succession that the king might—"

Stafford did not realize that he had hit a sore spot in Mary. She had long craved to be married, to have a husband and children of her own, but every negotiation for her marriage had fallen through. That Elizabeth should be courted, even by an unsuitable person, was an outrage.

"That is not to be thought of!" Mary exclaimed. "If she is meeting a man, she should be confined in a convent where she can be properly controlled."

Stafford did not remind Mary that the king had long since closed all the convents in England. He merely said "If she or her ... ah ... visitor hear us ... We are a rather large party and the garden is very small and very quiet. He will disappear out into the Wilderness and ... and I am also afraid that Lady Elizabeth will not admit to her fault."

"I do not believe my sister would lie."

Stafford did not reply to that, and after a significant silence, Mary continued, "And how could anyone get to the Wilderness? There is a guard at the gate, is there not."

"Whoever it is got in," Stafford said, dryly. "Guards can be bribed. And it would be greatly to the guard's advantage if the person escaped without being caught."

They were now approaching the back of the nursery lodgings, and Stafford added desperately, "My lady, if you *wish* to warn Lady Elizabeth, it would still be best if the others of your party would remain inside the building. You could step out of the door and then do what you think best about calling your ladies and grooms."

Mary looked away, wringing her hands and biting her lip. Elizabeth. Always a thorn in her side. Winning Edward's affection, drawing him away from the true faith so that his soul would be lost and the whole realm would be corrupted. A part of her wanted to prove the Boleyn bitch's daughter a loose wanton like her mother. Another part remembered how Elizabeth used to coo at her as an infant, run to greet her with outstretched arms as a babe and wanted to protect the little sister. But she realized that Stafford's advice was sensible; it could be turned either way.

She bade her party remain in the corridor while she herself stepped outside. Stafford touched her arm and pointed to one of the benches. The moon was just overhead and only one corner of the bench was in deep shadow. A dappled silvery light showed the upright figure of a girl near the middle of the bench. Elizabeth.

Hands, large, square hands, certainly a man's hands, reached from the shadowed side of the bench, took Elizabeth's hands, lifted them, presumably to kiss. One hand disappeared, appeared again to press something into the girl's hands. Then the shadow within a shadow stood and stepped backward into the moonlight.

"FitzRoy!" Mary cried, in involuntary recognition.

Chapter 20

Elizabeth shot to her feet and interposed her body in front of Harry's as Mary hurried from the door toward her. She knew she could not hide all of him, but she assumed that he and Denno had a plan for escaping if they were caught. Her Da would, she was sure, have disappeared from sight as soon as he heard the voice.

"Lady Mary," she cried. "Oh, how you surprised me! Did you find it impossible to sleep in this heat as I did? I could not breathe and I begged Blanche to let me sit in the garden before I went to bed."

"I saw . . . I saw . . . *Fitzroy!* But he is dead, dead." Mary shuddered. "Who was the man I saw kissing your hands?"

"Kissing my hands?" Elizabeth repeated, shaking, despite her outward bravado. "Sister . . . Lady Mary . . . There was no man. Who is FitzRoy?"

The last question was perfectly honest. At first Elizabeth did not remember Harry's surname. She had always known him as her Da—or the duke of Richmond—or Harry. Her servants had called him Your Grace or Richmond; Denno had called him Harry.

Mary made an infuriated noise and cried, "Liar. I saw his hands. A man's hands." Her voice was high, near hysterical. "Guard! Guard!"

Her summons did not betray them. From the shadow cast by

the wall, Denoriel had been watching the garden and both exits from the nursery buildings. He had seen Mary and Stafford as movement within the doorway even before they stepped out into the garden. Praying Harry would remember his amulet and disappear, as he was supposed to, Denoriel rushed to the guard at the gate. Quickly, Denoriel turned him around, and whispered to him—as he broke the spell he had laid on him— "See, Lady Elizabeth is in the garden where she has been with her maid for this last half hour." The guard's eyes cleared.

Denoriel stepped away, leaving the guard staring at Lady Elizabeth and Lady Mary, who was just calling out, "Guard! Guard!"

The guardsman rattled the gate behind him to make sure it was closed and hurried forward, bowing. "Yes, m'lady?"

"Who did you let in through that gate?"

The man stared at her, wide-eyed and suddenly fearful. "No one, m'lady. Didn't let in no one. All the young gentlemen were in before I come on duty." He looked around the garden. "And there's no one here, except Lady Elizabeth. Her ladyship didn't come through the gate, she came out of the building, and she's been out in the garden for maybe half an hour. Her maid's here too, though I don't see her."

"Here I am," Blanche said, coming forward from the far side of the small tree near the bench.

Mary ignored her, staring at the guard. "How much did he pay you to let him in?"

"My lady!" The guard went down on his knees. "On my soul, no one gave me nothing and no one passed through that gate since I came on duty. M'lady, your gentlemen are just behind you. This isn't a big place. Ask them to search it. You saw that no one went out, so if there was someone here, he must needs still be here. But I swear there's no one here but us you can see."

Lady Mary's entourage had appeared as soon as she began to cry for the guard. Jane Dormer had been right in the doorway. She had been looking at the bench, but had not been able to see it clearly. Then Mary had cried "FitzRoy" and Jane had looked at her mistress. What she saw next was Elizabeth jump from the bench and turn to face Mary.

When Mary called for the guard, Jane had looked in that direction. She knew that no one had run across the moonlit garden from where Mary stood to the gate; she knew also that no one had gone out of the gate, and that the guard had been standing upright, seemingly awake and alert.

"My lady," Jane said, coming forward and laying a hand on Mary's arm; she spoke very softly, a murmur no one but her lady could hear. "If you accuse the guard of taking bribes, it could be his death, and unless you are very, very sure, you will never forgive yourself."

Sure? How could she be sure when she had seen a dead man, a dead man who disappeared before her eyes. No, that was . . . must be . . . a failure of her eyesight. It was true she did not see clearly at a distance. Surely the resemblance to FitzRoy was an accident. But there *had* been a man.

"But I saw . . ." Mary hesitated, uncertain of just what to say. The hands, she *had* seen a man's hands take Elizabeth's. "I saw a man's hands—"

"Perhaps mine, sister?" Elizabeth asked eagerly. "I was holding my cross; it soothes my heart to do so."

Elizabeth held out her hands, long-fingered, thin hands, star-tlingly white in the moonlight against the black of her gown. From the fingers of one hand a heavy black iron cross dangled from a black iron chain. One could hardly see the cross and chain until Elizabeth swung the cross, caught it in her other hand, released it, swung it again.

"Or perhaps mine?" Blanche said, holding out her hands, which were larger, square and darker colored. "I was sitting on the other end of the bench, Lady Mary. I thought I heard a noise and got up and walked around the tree."

There were murmurs of agreement from Mary's two ladies, and Jane Dormer wondered aloud whether a brief sight of the black-dressed maid disappearing around the bole of the tree as Elizabeth jumped to her feet could have been what her lady had seen.

By the time Jane spoke, Mary's gentlemen had returned from their search. The garden was small. The moon was high and clear. Dutifully, the gentlemen had examined every shadow within the walled area, but it was easy to see that there was no one in the garden but the party standing near the bench.

Even so they had searched carefully, hoping that they would find some page or groom—some boy on whom an eleven-year-old girl might fix her affections. All Mary's ladies and gentlemen loved her. She was gentle and considerate and struggled to support them with limited means—but they all also knew she was a very unhappy lady, a lady who sorely needed a husband. It was not impossible that she had seen the maid moving from the bench to behind the tree and her own desires had made her see a man.

"There is no one, my lady," the elder of the two grooms said, bowing, shaking his head just a little. "And the gate is securely locked."

Mary turned and looked at Stafford.

"There was a man," he said, trying to keep his voice steady. "I woke from a doze by my window and heard a man's voice cry 'Elizabeth.' I saw Lady Elizabeth run to him and embrace him. Then I dressed and came to you. Perhaps he left before we came here."

"No!" the guard cried. "I swear that no one came into the garden while I was on duty, and I didn't let no one out."

"Could not someone have hidden in the garden from before you came on duty?" Stafford asked. "It is true that I did not see anyone come in."

"Don't know," the guard admitted, relieved. "Didn't look. Never been told to clear the garden." He frowned. "But if someone hid in here, where is he now?"

Mary swallowed hard. Witch. Anne Boleyn had been said to be a witch. How else could she have perverted and corrupted so wise and good a man as the king? Could not the daughter have inherited the power from her evil mother? Moreover, Mary had heard of the unnatural love her father's bastard son had shown for the bitch Boleyn's child. Had the witch's daughter conjured up the ghost of the bastard who had loved her?

"I didn't. There was no man," Elizabeth cried and burst into tears.

Blanche moved to her at once, and took Elizabeth in her arms. Looking over her sobbing charge's head, her face set like stone, the maid said, "Beg pardon, Lord Stafford, but could you have been dreaming about my lady running to and embracing a man? It is not her way, you know, to rush up to people and embrace them. She has been taught better manners than that. She knows what is proper; and you know she is no hoyden."

Stafford glanced like a hunted animal, from the sobbing girl, to Lady Mary, who looked frozen. Elizabeth would never forgive him, no matter what he said now. Mary might excuse what she might consider overzealousness. And how had the man disappeared?

Where had he gone? Stafford wished he could believe the guard had been bribed and was lying, but he himself had seen that no one went out the gate after Mary had cried out . . . cried out as if she recognized the man. FitzRoy, she had called him.

"I saw what I saw," Stafford said, but he allowed a sense of doubt to creep into his voice.

Blanche clung to her weeping charge. "Lord Stafford, you said you were dozing by the window. Is it possible that you heard me call out to Lady Elizabeth and that got wound up into your dream? The guard swears, and I do too, that there was no living man in this garden with us tonight. Lady Mary's people have searched and found no one. The gate is locked. Could you have been dreaming?"

"It did not feel like a dream. I got to my feet and got dressed and they were still standing on the lawn—"

"Myself and my lady," Blanche insisted. "It is possible you saw that. I do not remember exactly what we did when we came out of the house. Perhaps we did stroll along the lawn for a while. I am taller and broader than Lady Elizabeth. From above . . ."

By now Mary's two ladies and gentlemen were sighing with relief and nodding agreement with Blanche's explanation. This near attack on a child of eleven, an accusation of her meeting a man was a very ugly thing. To bring this accusation to the king would be a disaster; a worse disaster when there was no proof. All of them felt the truth of the guard's statement. The gate was locked. The guard was already walking toward Lady Mary when they all came into the garden. No one had gone out of the gate. No one had been found in the garden. There had not been any man.

Living man. Mary shivered and took Jane Dormer's arm. Stafford had seen what she had seen, but he was a weak reed. And it was only him and her. The rest of her people had seen nothing. How could she convince them that a little girl of eleven had conjured up a dead man, not a wavering, misty ghost but a dead body solid enough to hug and kiss. Mary's free hand went up to cover her mouth to suppress a retch.

"Man or no man," she said, turning on Blanche. "Take that child to her chamber and see that she does not again go walking in the middle of the night. This is no fit place for a child of eleven to be, near to midnight."

"Yes, my lady." Blanch curtsied as well as she could without releasing her hold on Elizabeth and hurried her shuddering charge into the building and up into her rooms.

"Am I never to be happy?" Elizabeth sobbed quietly as Blanche readied her for bed. "Is there some curse on me that I cannot be happy for more than a moment? It was so wonderful to be with Da. And then Stafford spoiled it all!"

"Do not take a pet against him, my love," Blanche warned, bringing Elizabeth a glass of wine. "Perhaps a sharp word or two about dreaming in the next day, but to hold a grudge too long might imply he was telling the truth."

"I don't care about him, only that he spoiled my joy. I was so afraid that Da would be different, that I would not feel for him what I used to feel. But it was not true. It was just as it had been, as I had remembered . . . and I was happy, truly happy . . . and . . . it was all spoiled."

"No, m'lady, not really." Blanche nodded encouragingly as Elizabeth sipped the sweet, strong wine. "You know now that His Grace *is* alive and well. You know that Lord Denno has been speaking the truth and that you can trust him. Moreover, you know that when the time is right, you may be able to visit His Grace. Now drink up your wine and go to sleep."

Elizabeth's expression had lightened as Blanche named the two great goods that had come out of that evening's adventure. And when the glass of wine was empty, she stretched out on the bed and closed her eyes. A small smile curved her lips. It would be better to see Da Underhill—Elizabeth could think the name, although she could not speak it. He would tell her what he had been doing rather than her telling him what she had for breakfast and dinner. They could walk and talk, ride and tease each other, without any fear of watchers.

Then her eyes snapped open and she half sat up, catching her breath. "Mary," she whispered to Blanche. "Mary does not love me anymore. She does not like it that Edward is fond of me. She . . . she recognized Da . . . but she called him FitzRoy. Why did she call him FitzRoy?"

"That was his name before the king raised him up to be Duke of Richmond, Duke of Somerset, and Earl of Nottingham." Blanche bit her lip. "I am sure she will not tell anyone she saw a man eight years dead in the garden." Blanche tried to sound reassuring, but her voice was too hearty.

"But she will not keep it secret," Elizabeth whispered, her voice shaking. "Even though no one saw anything. Her own ladies and gentlemen agreed that the garden was empty except for us. And you were so clever about hinting it was you she saw. She is very shortsighted . . . But you think she will speak of it."

Blanche did not answer that; all she said was, "Lie down again, m'lady and sleep. Remember that your Da is alive and Lord Denno will help as he can whatever happens."

Comforted, Elizabeth did sleep, but she woke apprehensive and while she dressed and broke her fast, she and Blanche talked about what Stafford could have seen and, half asleep, mistaken for Elizabeth greeting a man in the garden.

The ax did not fall that morning, however. Elizabeth, as she had promised her brother, attended the lessons given by Dr. Cheke. The younger boys greeted her with their usual clamor, the older boys with calm nods. Lord Stafford was not present. That was a relief.

Later Elizabeth realized that she should have been worried by his absence. She should have guessed that he had been summoned by Mary to support her story, but she did not think of it. So she had a very pleasant morning and left her brother with a fond kiss to have her nuncheon in her own chambers in good enough spirits to eat bread and jam and slices of fruit.

She was just wondering aloud to Blanche where Kat could be, when that lady stepped into the room. Elizabeth saw at once that Kat was very pale and she exclaimed and asked what was wrong.

"Where were—" Kat began and then said hurriedly, "No. Do not answer that. You are summoned to the queen, Elizabeth."

Elizabeth rose at once, her eyes filling with tears. "There was no man," she said to her governess.

Kat came to her and gave her a hug and a kiss. "You need not assure me of that."

In the queen's small private closet, Elizabeth sank down into a deep curtsey. Catherine Parr gestured for her to rise and then held out a hand. With tears running down her cheeks Elizabeth kissed the hand, which then patted her fondly.

"Whatever were you doing, love? Mary obviously had not slept at all last night and she was nearly hysterical when she came to me this morning."

"I only went out into the garden because I was so hot," Elizabeth sobbed. "My head ached so, and I felt as if I could not breathe. I was afraid to lie down. I would have choked . . . Oh, madam, I swear I will never do so again, but I could not see that it was so wrong a thing to do. I had my maid with me, and we were only in the little garden right in front of my rooms."

"But Lord Stafford said he saw you run to and embrace a man—"

Elizabeth wiped the tears from her cheeks with the back of her hand. "My maid and I have been talking about that. Neither of us remembers exactly what we did. It was not important. We thought we were just going out until I felt cooler, but what we think now is that the maid must have stepped out first to make sure the garden was empty."

Catherine frowned, just a little. "Why did you need to be sure of that?"

Elizabeth made her voice small and meek-sounding. "My maid was afraid that it was not proper for me to be out so late at night. And I did not want to do what was wrong, but I have been so unwell lately, and oh! I wanted air so badly."

Tears welled over her eyelids again as Elizabeth tried to swallow her fears for this woman who had become, in a few short weeks, more of a mother than she had ever had. Oh, Kat loved her and so did Blanche, but they were both servants. Queen Catherine's care was freely offered when nothing in the world obliged her to give it.

"But why did Lord Stafford believe you met a man in the garden?" Catherine asked, now clearly puzzled by the absolute contradiction between the two stories.

Now she was on surer ground. "He told us he was dozing by the window. My maid and I both think he was half asleep and dreaming. Blanche must have walked out into the center, near the flowers, and called out to me. He said he heard a voice cry 'Elizabeth.' And I must have come from the building when she called. Perhaps I ran or skipped—it was such a pleasure to feel the cool air. Perhaps I hugged the maid out of pure high sprits or perhaps I caught my foot and tripped and she caught me. Neither of us remember this. It is just something we thought might have explained what Lord Stafford thought he saw."

Queen Catherine sighed, both with relief and exasperation. "It sounds very likely. I cannot imagine why he rushed out to involve Lady Mary in this nonsense. But she said she saw someone seated on the other end of the bench."

"I think that would have been the maid. Likely when I fell against her she told me to mind my manners and sit down quietly. Just as likely, without thinking, I told her to sit down too, as I would have said to Mistress Champernowne. But of course the maid would not have been accustomed or comfortable sitting. I am afraid I didn't think about her. I just closed my eyes and sat enjoying the cool breeze. Perhaps I was playing with my cross. The maid must have got up, and then I heard someone call out 'FitzRoy' and I jumped to my feet."

Catherine frowned, but this time her look was troubled. "But how could Mary have mistaken your maid for . . . for a man eight years dead?"

There was a little silence and then Elizabeth said, reluctantly, "I do not mean to say any wrong about Lady Mary, who has always been very kind and loving to me, but . . . but her long vision is not very good. She must hold her needlework almost to her nose to see it well. Unless she knows the color of a lady's gown or man's doublet, she must even wait to hear a voice before she knows who is beside her." Elizabeth grimaced a little. "She sees—what she has been told to see, I think, or what she *thinks* she should see. Lord Stafford told her there was a man, so any thing, my maid, a tree, or a shadow, must be a man."

"God's Grace, I had forgotten that!" Catherine exclaimed, and laughed ruefully. "Of course, all she saw was a blur but she would hate to admit that."

"Lady Mary cannot be wrong," Elizabeth replied, in tones that implied that Lady Mary all too often *was* wrong, and stubbornly would not admit the fact.

Catherine sighed. "Well, I will write to the king and explain to him what really happened. I tried to convince Mary not to write to him about this, but I had not heard what you had to say and she was not . . . completely rational. She will not write that you were with a man, but she insisted that the king must know his daughter was wandering abroad in the middle of the night."

"If she will write, I am sorry. I cannot think of a way to stop her. But you must not try to excuse me. Please!" Elizabeth caught at the queen's hand. "Oh, madam, the king is so overwrought with this coming war and all the plans to be made. Please do not trouble him with this nonsense about me. I should not have gone out so late at night. If His Majesty wishes to punish me, I deserve it. Please, please do not interpose yourself to take the blow meant for me."

The queen patted Elizabeth's wet cheek with her free hand, her expression full of sympathy. "But it was only a little foolishness, not a great sin, to wish to be cool. If I explain and remind him of the Lady Mary's short sight—"

"Not now." Elizabeth barely prevented herself from screaming in her terror. She saw the queen accused of complicity in allowing the king's daughter to meet a man at midnight; she saw them both executed. "Not when His Majesty is so very busy," she gasped. "If you think the punishment too . . . too severe, perhaps you could beg him for mercy for me, but do not associate yourself with my mistake."

Catherine sighed. "It is true that the king is very busy and not overly happy with Emperor Charles's plans, which makes him irritable now. You may be right, that to try to excuse you would only make matters worse. Let us just be quiet and see what happens."

They did not need to hang in suspense very long. Before the end of the week, an irritated but not furious note came from King Henry through Secretary Wriothesley commanding the queen to have Elizabeth and her household removed to St. James's Palace in London. "She is too lively, too clever, and too much an attraction to the young gentlemen, who at the same time envy that she holds her brother's strong affection. If she is separated from them, fewer tales will be told of her."

Although Elizabeth wept bitterly over the news of her exile from the lively schoolroom and the gay activities of the queen's court, she also wept with relief. Queen Catherine had not needed to oppose her husband's will over so light a correction. Moreover, Catherine pointed out that the king's indulgent words coming through Wriothesley's formal letter spoke of Henry's affection. The queen also was able, without mentioning Elizabeth to the king, to appoint William Grindal as her tutor so she would not miss the lessons she loved so well.

Sensing the queen's strong sympathy for Elizabeth, Kat Champernowne took her courage in both hands and asked for permission for Lord Denno to visit while Elizabeth was at St. James's. Under a strict and careful interrogation, Kat explained about Lord Denno's long association, first with His Grace of Richmond and then with Lady Elizabeth, who, Kat said, he seemed to regard as a legacy from Richmond.

"And most certainly he speaks of both of them as God's own replacements for his lost small brothers and sisters, Majesty," she added fondly. "No father could be more careful with her, nor more generous."

Before she agreed, Queen Catherine interviewed Denoriel herself. He took great care with his dress, which was sober in hue but extravagantly rich in ornament. He also took considerable care with his appearance, making sure his eyes were round-pupilled, that his ears showed no sign of points, and that there were lines that bespoke age in the skin around his eyes and his mouth. Together with his snow-white hair, he looked near three-score years—not of an age to interest a girl of eleven, except as a gift-bearing "uncle." And certainly he looked nothing like the sort of young fellow that *might* have been mistaken for Henry Fitzroy—if such a young fellow existed outside of Lady Mary's imagination.

Permission for limited visits was granted. Queen Catherine was eager to do anything she could to comfort Elizabeth, whom she was coming to love most dearly. Catherine did not quite understand why Elizabeth should blame herself so bitterly, but she promised that as soon as the king asked about his children, she would tell him that Elizabeth was much chastened and begged to be restored to her brother's and sister's company.

That aroused Elizabeth's anxiety again, but Catherine laughed at her and promised to do nothing that could irritate the king. Much less anxious, Elizabeth kissed the queen's hand in farewell and set out for St. James's Palace.

When Rhoslyn heard that Elizabeth was gone and with her any chance of encountering Denoriel, Rosamund Scot returned to Mary's household. She found Lady Mary much distressed over her half-sister and the fact that she had not told her father of the depth of Elizabeth's depravity.

"She is a witch," Mary whispered to her cleverest and most sympathetic maid of honor.

She had hinted of witchcraft to Jane Dormer, who was her most faithful attendant, whose devotion she never doubted. But Jane tried not to indulge her mistress's emotional moods and often tactfully corrected her for her own good. Mary had seen Jane recoil from the word "witch," had seen the disbelief in Jane's eyes, and heard Jane beg her never to make such an accusation against Elizabeth without hard proof. Mary knew Jane was right.

No one would believe her if she said an eleven-year-old child had done a conjuration capable of bringing back the dead. And Mary knew she had no proof at all, only her own certainty of her brief glimpse of FitzRoy. And who would believe that? Even Jane had murmured about her shortness of sight. But she remembered well the conformation of his body, the way he held his head.

Also, Mary had heard Elizabeth say "Da." There was nothing wrong with her ears, and Elizabeth had never called anyone but FitzRoy "Da." Mary, sick with loathing, had heard one bastard call the other "Da" many times before the whore-witch got her just reward. Stafford might confirm that he had seen a man in Elizabeth's arms, but he had never known FitzRoy and could not identify him.

But Rosamund had no doubts and no reservations about what Mary told her. "And her mother was a witch before her," Rosamund whispered in Mary's ear, nodding, but then, still leaning close, the maid of honor asked, "But why do you say so now? She is only a child."

Mary needed someone to believe her and she knew Rosamund believed fervently in the old religion and the miracles of the Church. The Bible said "Thou shalt not suffer a witch to live," so Rosamund would believe witches existed—and knew what should be done with them. Although Mary was uneasy about confiding what Jane distrusted to another lady, she could not resist.

"I saw her conjure up a person I know to be eight years dead," Mary whispered.

Rhoslyn stared, open-mouthed. Before she had presented herself to Mary, she had made her way, using the Don't-see-me spell, to Stafford's chamber. He was abed, and Rhoslyn had not wakened him; she had thrust him deeper into sleep and then ruthlessly plundered his mind of the memories of the last few days. He would wake with a violent headache but no memory of her visit. Thus she was already aware of every move of the confrontation in the garden—but only from Stafford's point of view.

Widening her eyes into an expression of horror and deep interest, she said, "You saw this?"

Mary nodded, and there was even a welcome hint of fear in her expression. "I saw the man and I recognized him."

"Only *you* saw him?" Rhoslyn persisted.

Mary nodded and sighed in defeat, describing what she had seen and heard to Rhoslyn. Rhoslyn listened in silence, only nodding and uttering murmurs to encourage Mary to recount all the details. This adventure held the seeds of a more satisfactory and more permanent solution of the problem Elizabeth presented to the Unseleighe.

Rhoslyn had originally been furious over the way so promising a scandal had been hushed over—more furious because she knew the mild reprimand of separating Elizabeth from the other children for a few weeks or months was her own fault. If she had been present, Mary's letter would have had a far more serious effect. And Rhoslyn knew why she had not been present to "help" Mary write her letter. She simply did not want a child dead or in Unseleighe hands.

But this—an accusation of witchcraft . . . No! They would burn her. Not a child, even one she liked as little as she liked Elizabeth.

"It is dreadful," she said softly to Mary. "But I think you cannot do anything more now. It would be too hard to convince anyone. And—my lady, perhaps it was no conjuration, but a revenant. I have never heard anyone say of FitzRoy that he was evil; only that he loved little Elizabeth, and she him. Perhaps that alone was enough to call him to her side? And Elizabeth herself likely thought she was dreaming." As doubt flickered over Mary's features, Rhoslyn continued. "Anyway, she is away from the court and the children and cannot corrupt Prince Edward any more. That is an accomplishment. Elizabeth is not important. Edward is."

That assurance brightened Mary's expression and she talked for a little while about her young brother, speaking of a book of prayers she hoped to give him.

Rhoslyn remembered Pasgen saying that Vidal's desire to be rid of Elizabeth now was ridiculous. It would be many years before she was a real threat to Unseleighe power. And in a few years, Elizabeth would no longer be a child. Mortals got old so quickly, and Rhoslyn suspected she would like the adult Elizabeth even less than she liked the child. There would be plenty of time to bring forward the accusation of witchcraft. Mary would not forget.

Uncanny things were known to happen around girls just rising into womanhood and surely further incidents could be arranged. For now, Rhoslyn did not need to worry about Vidal. The situation between England and Scotland was worse than ever, with constant raiding bringing death and misery. There was power enough for Vidal's court.

As she half listened to Mary and agreed that for a child who loved his books as well as Edward, an illustrated Book of Hours would be a welcome gift, Rhoslyn considered her real problem. Aurelia. Aurelia had been determined to have the breaking of Elizabeth and would now be disappointed. It might be possible to convince her to wait, but it might not. Rhoslyn thought of Aurelia's arrogance and her moments of confusion, and shuddered.

"Oh, my dear Mistress Scot," Mary said, "you are still tired and cold from the journey from your brother's house, and I have kept you talking about my pleasures. I will let you go and rest."

"Thank you," Rhoslyn said, rising and accepting the hand Mary held out to kiss. "You have done what was right, my lady, and secured considerable good. To have done more might not have been wise."

Mary nodded. "Jane said so too."

"Mistress Dormer is very wise and loves you very much." Rhoslyn sighed and shook her head. "And I know I have just arrived, but may I ask one day's leave to do an errand for my brother in London? As you know he is not well and traveling to the city is very hard for him."

"I give you leave, and gladly!" Mary was always pleased with an opportunity to be gracious, especially when it cost her little. "And you must forgive me for not asking sooner about your brother's health. That was unkind, but I was so overset by the events we spoke of, that I quite forgot."

Rhoslyn smiled. "You are never unkind, my lady. You have been so understanding about my absences. But he is such a good, kind brother and has no one except the servants. I feel I must be with him when he has these bad spells."

"Of course you must." Mary patted Rhoslyn's hand. "I am very well attended and also have the queen's company. She is a fine woman, except . . . I could wish for different clerics around her. No, no. Do not be troubled over your absences. I enjoy your company, Mistress Scot, and always look forward to your attendance, but it is no great hardship if you must be away."

Rhoslyn thanked her again, curtsied, and backed away, pleased that Mary had not this time asked a dozen questions about Rosamund's wholly imaginary brother. When Rhoslyn had been appointed one of Mary's maids of honor, she fabricated this brother to explain Rosamund's frequent absences from her duties. The brother, Patric Scot, Rhoslyn told Mary, was confined by a mysterious illness, which physicians could not identify or cure, to a rural but wealthy estate.

Always having been frail, Rhoslyn added, Patric had never married and clung to his sister Rosamund, who was his heir and to whom he was very generous. That was why Rosamund had no need for a stipend from Lady Mary and could even, from time to time, make Mary little gifts to relieve financial embarrassment. Mary, grateful to Rosamund and of an affectionate nature, readily accepted Rosamund's absences to attend her brother when he had particularly bad spells.

The next day Roslyn did indeed travel to London where she went to Pasgen's house. From there she Gated directly to the empty house in which she and Pasgen pretended to live Underhill. On arriving she sent a servant for Talog, riding the not-horse to an outer Gate, and Gated to Caer Mordwyn.

The Gate had changed. What had been the jaws of an enormous serpent, which threatened to snap shut a thousand glittering teeth on any arrival—and occasionally did—was now an elaborate temple of glittering black glass over a clear floor. Below the floor was a pit of seemingly boiling lava from which thin, sharp spires of rock reached upward. The clear floor showed suspicious cracks. Rhoslyn stared in astonishment. What had been going on in her absence?

Chapter 21

When she saw the deep cracks in the transparent floor above boiling lava, and the stalagmites that threatened to pierce anyone who fell, instinct bade Rhoslyn spur Talog to leap forward. Instead she tightened her hands on Talog's reins. Rhoslyn knew stalagmites could not exist in boiling lava; nonetheless she did not desire to fall on one. Still, since Vidal had doubtless created the lava and the stalagmites to drive arrivals out of the Gate, caution bade Rhoslyn hold the reins steady while she looked ahead.

The path from the Gate had changed also. Where there had been one broad way, lined by writhing carnivorous plants that threatened to reach out and catch anyone going past them, but safe enough if traveled carefully, there were now three paths, all very innocent-looking gravel.

Rhoslyn promptly thrust a spear of force at the central way, which looked as if it went directly to the palace. Black ooze bubbled up through the gravel. A second thrust of force at the right-hand path went right through; there was no path, only illusion over nothing. The thrust at the left-hand path resulted in a burst of counterforce that could have torn Talog and herself apart.

There was no safe path.

Rhoslyn drew a breath, preparing to command the Gate to take her back to the vale of the empty house. It was too late. Talog hissed horribly and leapt forward as the floor of the Gate began to open along one of the cracks.

The not-horse landed with a loud squelch in the center path. Stinking black liquid fountained up as the creature's clawed feet struck the path, liberally spattering mount and rider. To Rhoslyn's surprise, aside from the fetid odor, it did no harm.

Rhoslyn muttered a few choice expletives over Vidal's sense of humor. Few of the Dark Court would believe the most direct path was essentially the safest; most would fall afoul of the traps to left and right. Rhoslyn now assumed the traps were not fatal, because presumably Vidal would not wish to deplete his court by killing too many of his followers . . . but with Vidal, one could never tell. However, the not-horse seemed quite satisfied with the footing and was already trotting forward. A dozen strides took them past the black ooze.

A spell to clean herself and Talog was Rhoslyn's immediate concern. For a moment she curbed that impulse, realizing that use of magic could alert Vidal to her arrival. She did not wish to see Vidal and possibly remind him about Elizabeth. After all, she had come to see Aurelia, not Vidal. Then she shrugged. The lances of force she had used to test the path had doubtless already betrayed her, and she liked being stained with the fetid sludge even less than she liked finding some excuse for her presence to Vidal. A firm thought and a gesture removed all evidence of the filth, and she rode on toward Vidal's palace, resigned to the idea that Vidal would be waiting for her when she arrived—or, at the least, would send someone to meet her to deliver orders to attend upon him.

Even so, the newt-servants who came to take Talog had no message for her, nor did any Sidhe come hurrying from the palace to intercept her. Rhoslyn breathed a sigh of relief. Either Vidal was not in Caer Mordwyn, or he did not wish to see her. Either possibility was equally satisfactory to Rhoslyn, who hurried up the black marble stairs toward the doors.

Preoccupied with what she intended to say to Aurelia, Rhoslyn slipped through the magically opened door and negotiated the minor traps in the corridors and stairway without really noticing them. At the head of the stair the same half-drugged Sidhe as always was on guard; this time he did not argue when Rhoslyn sent him to inform Aurelia of her arrival. Rhoslyn wondered whether he was so drug-addicted that he no longer possessed a will of his own, but he carried the message correctly. The Sidhe brought Aurelia's invitation to enter as he came out.

"Well? Is Elizabeth free for our taking?" Aurelia asked with a show of impatience, before Rhoslyn had properly shut the door.

Rhoslyn turned and bowed slightly. The Roman couch on which Aurelia had reclined the last time Rhoslyn had seen her was gone. Now she sat in a cushioned chair drawn up to an elegant gilded desk on which lay an open book. From the way the pages writhed and flickered when Rhoslyn glanced at them, she was sure the book was a grimoire sealed to Aurelia. Beside the book was the ubiquitous glass of cloudy bluish liquid, but it was full.

Aurelia's direct question left no room for prevarication. Rhoslyn sighed. "Unfortunately Elizabeth is still beyond our touch, even though the boy I set to watch her did catch her in a serious indiscretion. She went out near midnight and apparently flung herself into the arms of a man."

Aurelia's lips thinned. "And the king tolerated such behavior?"

"He never learned of it." Rhoslyn sighed again and told Aurelia what had taken place in the garden from the time Stafford had seen Elizabeth run into a man's arms to the glimpse Mary had had of a man she knew to be long dead.

"Only Stafford saw the man Elizabeth ran to meet, and only Mary caught one glimpse of the man she believes Elizabeth conjured from the dead and who disappeared before her eyes," Rhoslyn admitted, with a grimace. "The guard at the gate—and all agree that he was standing right there, upright and alert—swore that no one had entered the garden or left it. Mary's gentlemen searched the whole place most thoroughly and could find no one but Elizabeth and her maid, and the maid explained everything Stafford and Mary thought they saw, insisting they had mistaken her for the man."

"The maid," Aurelia repeated darkly, as she turned fully to face Rhoslyn and raised a hand to rub her forehead. "I would know more about this mortal. Is this the same maid who has been with Elizabeth since her birth? The maid who wears a necklace of black iron crosses?"

"Yes, I believe it is the same maid," Rhoslyn said, rather

surprised at how easily Aurelia had been distracted from the target of Elizabeth.

Aurelia reached out and took a sip from the glass on the desk, stared into it for a moment, then set it aside.

The gaze she now turned on Rhoslyn was penetrating—and fierce. "The maid is a commoner with no important connections except Elizabeth herself—true?"

"Yes." Rhoslyn was still puzzled.

Aurelia smiled smugly. "And it is by the maid's word and by her clever explanations that the mistake Elizabeth made was kept from her father?"

"Ah." It appeared that Aurelia's mind was not wandering from the subject of Elizabeth, after all. Rhoslyn nodded, also smiling, pleased to have found something that was a lawful target for Aurelia's obsession. And the maid was an adult. Neither Oberon, nor Rhoslyn's conscience, would be troubled over being rid of the woman. "Then, madam, I see your thought; we must get rid of the maid."

"Agreed," Aurelia said. "We must get rid of the maid, by purely mortal means—one of the other servants must attack her. And I would like to see to that myself."

"That will not be so easy." Roslyn swallowed, thinking of Aurelia's arrogance and her moments of confusion; bringing her to the mortal world might well be a disaster. "I am known as Mary's lady, so I have a place at court and a reason for being there. But Elizabeth did not escape intact from her escapade. She has been banished to St. James's palace in London, and I have no reason for being *there*."

"I did not plan to walk up to the gate and demand entry," Aurelia snapped. "I am sure there are many places in so large a building or on the grounds where so skilled a Gate builder as your brother could open a Gate for me. He has not been of much use in any other way."

"No matter how skilled the Gate builder," Rhoslyn replied swallowing down her irritation and anxiety, "he needs to know the terminus, or the Gate might go awry."

"So?" Aurelia waved a careless hand. "You have been no more successful than your brother in removing Elizabeth from the line of successors of Henry VIII. The least you can do is find a way for *me* to begin to solve the problem myself. The maid must be removed; you agreed with me on that score. Without her we should have far less trouble in arranging Elizabeth's death or removal. And for what she did to me, I must in my own person make sure that she suffers."

Rhoslyn argued for a while, trying this excuse and that for dealing with the maid herself. In a very short time, however, she realized that all she was accomplishing was to annoy Aurelia. Before Vidal's consort dismissed her and said she would take the matter to him, Rhoslyn agreed to arrange for a Gate to transport her.

"In no long time," Aurelia said grimly, as she gestured Rhoslyn to leave. "I have waited long enough. I will not wait much longer for my revenge."

Furious but helpless, Rhoslyn left. Mounting Talog, she rode around the palace, and then to the opposite end of the domain, entering the first Gate to which she came. Although it took three extra stops, Rhoslyn eventually arrived at the Bazaar of the Bizarre. Following the winding path Pasgen had laid out for her, three more Gatings took her to her brother's domain. By the time she arrived at his door, his burly guards were waiting to take Talog, and Pasgen himself was at the door gesturing her inside into his living room.

"I heard you coming two Gates away," he said, grinning, when she had seated herself. "My, my, Rhoslyn. I didn't know you knew such language."

She laughed, albeit reluctantly. "It must have been more pungent than I realized to drag you out of your workshop."

He shrugged, evidently in good humor. "Ah, no. I was only sitting here reading—or trying to read—some old texts about the djinn from Alhambra."

"Alhambra!" She looked at him with surprise. "I thought that elfhame was dead and cursed."

"Yes. Dead *and* cursed. I did not stay long." He shook himself, like a dog ridding its coat of something noxious. "But what brings you here in such a mood?" He frowned, showing a touch of anxiety. "Not Mother?"

"No, Mother is fine and she seems to be taking a real interest in healing since she helped soothe your bruises," Rhoslyn replied, glad enough of the chance to ease into the subject that had brought her here. "I am encouraging her. No, it's not Mother. Did you remember that Aurelia had set her mind on having

Elizabeth disgraced and stricken from the succession so she could be abducted?"

Pasgen made a disgusted noise. "Idiots. There are three lives between her and the throne. If Edward lives a full life, he will marry and have sons and *they* will stand between her and the throne also. She could catch some childish ailment and die. She could grow to womanhood, and plague could carry her off. She could, all by herself, fall into some conspiracy and be imprisoned or executed. Or she could succumb to her own hot blood and fall into disgrace. Why chance raising Oberon's ire, when natural events in the mortal world are likely to remove Elizabeth?"

Rhoslyn shook her head. "I think Aurelia's desire to seize her is . . . is personal. Even though Elizabeth was only a baby at the time of that battle, Aurelia blames her for what happened. But she hasn't lost sight of the fact that it was the maid who actually damaged her. Right now she wants to get into St. James's Palace so she can personally see that the maid is attacked, hurt, and killed."

For a moment Pasgen stared past his sister. Then he said, "Did you know that Aurelia is far less of a fool than Vidal?"

Rhoslyn laughed weakly. "She is a woman, after all. To be cleverer than a man is natural." Then she said more soberly, "I suspected she had more brains than Vidal when she first came, but she was far more damaged than Vidal in the battle."

Pasgen nodded. "And she knows it—and admits it, which is more than Vidal does. He is recovering, but I think he may never recall all that he lost, whereas Aurelia is seizing grimoires from every mage she can dominate and is relearning what she lost. She may come out well ahead of Vidal in control of magic, in fact."

Rhoslyn nodded wisely. "Ah, I thought that was a grimoire on her desk, but it shimmered and coiled away from my sight as if it had been sealed to her."

"That was the bargain she made with several mages." Pasgen laughed, but his expression was full of admiration. "They write one for her and seal it to her and she will leave the original grimoire with its master. But if I were one of those mages, I would never perform a spell that is not already written in the book I gave her—or at least, I would never perform it where or when she could learn about it. She is very vindictive."

Rhoslyn gave him a sharp look. "Did you give her any spells-for Gates?"

"I gave her nothing," Pasgen said coldly.

Rhoslyn lifted one brow. "I thought you found her . . . attractive."

"What has that to do with anything?" Pasgen asked, and then added, with a wry twist to his lips, "She is not so beautiful any longer. Most of her looks are illusion."

"You can see through illusion now?" That was a surprise. She didn't think any Sidhe could do that—or at least, not without dispelling the illusion itself.

"No one can see through illusion Underhill," he replied dismissively. "Underhill *is* illusion. No, I can feel the spells humming around her. Never mind that. You said Aurelia wanted to get into St. James's Palace to arrange the death of the maid. So take her through the Gate to the London house, bespell the guards—"

"No!" Rhoslyn countered emphatically. "Aurelia wants to go now, and she wants *you* to make it possible. I have tried to convince her to wait a few weeks until Elizabeth's household is settled, but she will not. I think she believes I am delaying for some secret purpose—although what secret purpose she thinks I could have, I do not know. And to bespell the guards now would be disastrous."

"Hmmm, yes," he agreed, rubbing the side of his nose thoughtfully. "With supplies and messengers coming every other moment, to find the guards frozen at the gate would scream of magic."

"Yes, and though getting in would be easy enough, after the maid is killed there will certainly be a hue and cry, so getting out will not be so easy," she reminded him sharply. "What I would like is for you to build a Gate from Caer Mordwyn to wherever I am in the mortal world and hold it until we return."

It was not what Aurelia had demanded, but Rhoslyn was in no mood to give Vidal's consort a Gate into the palace where Elizabeth dwelled at least part of the time. Given such a tempting tool, Aurelia was bound to use it.

"Rhoslyn!" Pasgen protested. "Do you know how much power that will take?"

She sighed. "Yes, but I have a bad feeling about this business. Aurelia wants to prolong the maid's suffering to punish her, but she wants to arrange the punishment to come from another mortal . . . well, that is very sensible. Still, the maid is unlikely to suffer in silence. She will scream and struggle and attract attention, and Aurelia wants to be there to enjoy it all."

Pasgen snorted. "Surely in a great palace with wide grounds there would be private places?"

"Yes?" Rhoslyn was exasperated with him. *He* had spent enough time in the World Above to know how it was there! "And how am I to draw the maid there? I cannot go near her because of that accursed necklace she wears, so I cannot bespell her. Even assuming that my spell would not go awry because of the iron in the necklace. She hardly ever leaves Elizabeth—and Elizabeth can see through whatever illusions we use so I cannot tempt the maid away by, say, appearing like Champernowne." She sighed. "It will have to be a time and place where she customarily goes alone or remains alone after Elizabeth has been taken elsewhere."

"Hmmm, yes." Pasgen did not seem upset by Rhoslyn's display of temper. "That child's Talent is a cursed nuisance. And the maid would not leave her alone in a secret place. Likely the best place to deal with the maid will be the stable. Elizabeth rides and the maid does not, but the maid will certainly escort her charge *to* the stable."

Rhoslyn brightened, not the least because the stable was one of the safer places for an intruder to lie in wait. "Now that is an excellent thought, brother. I will go myself and discover how often Elizabeth rides, who accompanies her, and what the maid does when Elizabeth leaves." Rhoslyn nodded briskly. "That is my part and I will take care it is well done. If it would make your part easier, I could leave a token where I wanted the Gate to be."

Pasgen nodded. "That *would* make it easier. I could build the Gate at leisure and only activate it at your need. Then the power for building and sustaining would be separated. But I still do not see the need for the Gate to be held open. Surely you would be able to send an imp to me to tell me when to reopen it?"

Rhoslyn shook her head, her lips compressed to a thin line. "Aurelia is much recovered, but she still has moments when she cannot fix her mind. There is too much chance that she will freeze if something goes wrong. If the maid should throw one of the crosses in our direction, for example. I cannot bear cold iron, but

Aurelia is violently sensitive to it now. I need to be able to push her through a Gate if we are likely to be discovered."

Pasgen looked thoughtful and then nodded. Satisfied and much less anxious, Rhoslyn agreed to have a meal with him, and they talked of pleasanter things. Rhoslyn was attempting to make a pattern around which she could force the mists of the chaos lands to form; that would save her from needing to create a creature from the basic mist each time she wanted one.

Pasgen still had not discovered a way to inactivate the red mist, but the self-motivated bit Rhoslyn had discovered was becoming very cooperative. It seemed to be responding well to learning mental commands, which Pasgen rewarded by feeding it portions of the substance of the chaos lands.

"Just don't feed it any of that red mist or vice versa," Rhoslyn said as she sat sipping her wine at the end of the meal. "Just think of a self-willed devourer."

"Hmmm." Pasgen's lip's pursed.

Rhoslyn sat upright. "Pasgen!" she exclaimed. "No. Promise me you will not."

"Well . . . not without considerable thought and study. But . . ." He saw how distressed she was and laughed. "Very well, sister. I promise."

Rhoslyn stood up. "I had better get back to London and stop in at St. James's Palace. Perhaps I can find a suitable groom to explain the arrangements for riding. With Aurelia so set on revenge, I want to be done with this as soon as possible."

Although the return path to the Bazaar of the Bizarre was extremely tortuous, Rhoslyn arrived there safely, and in only three more transits was back in Pasgen's house in the World Above. As Pasgen's house, off the Strand, was no great distance from St. James's, Rhoslyn simply wrapped herself in a nondescript cloak and walked.

Passing Whitehall, she entered the broad avenue where Henry VIII had once played at *paille-maille*. Young courtiers, squires, and pages still played when the king was in residence, but that was very rare these days; usually Henry stayed in Whitehall. Thus the broad, carefully mown lane was empty. Still, Rhoslyn kept well to the side, almost invisible as she passed along the avenue of trees and bushes that bordered the playing field. As she neared the end of that avenue and approached the gate that provided entrance to the palace grounds, she whispered the Don't-see-me spell.

As she had expected, by Queen Catherine's order there was considerable traffic of supplies and even furnishings still coming into St. James's. Rhoslyn did not need to wait very long before the guards opened the gate to a cart carrying hangings for Elizabeth's bedchamber. She followed it in, but did not turn left along the lane that led to a side door. Rhoslyn went the other way, skirted the side of the palace and came to the gate that opened into the deer park and riding paths.

A bored guard, half asleep, stood at the Gate. Rhoslyn took shelter behind an ornamental bush—sometimes when one meddled with a person's mind, that would cause the Don't-see-me spell to fail—and pushed the thought of opening the gate and looking around into the guard's mind. When he did step into the park, Rhoslyn stepped in almost on his heels and was safe inside before, shaking his head and wondering why he had decided to do something so gormless, he stepped out again.

From there it was a short walk to the stables in their separate enclosure near the palace. Rhoslyn slipped in the unguarded gate and made her way softly—taking care that her shadow should not draw attention to a person who was not there—into the stable itself.

Here there was activity. Rhoslyn immediately recognized Elizabeth's servants, a strong, dark-haired older man and a broad-shouldered but still boyishly spare younger one. In a few moments she had their names: the younger called the elder Kip, another groom called him Ladbroke. The same groom called the younger man Tolliver, while Ladbroke called him Reeve. More important, in the next few minutes she had the information for which she had come.

"'S th'lady ridin' agin t'arternoon?" the groom asked. "Be so, th'guard's 'orses need readyin.'"

"Those were my instructions from Mistress Champernowne," Ladbroke said. "Until further notice, Lady Elizabeth will be at her books in the morning and then will ride out every day the weather is fine in the afternoon for her health and to exercise."

"Nice bits o' 'orseflesh she rides. Know a nag what could pass as t'is 'un's sister," the groom observed. "Make a puckle coin in th'change."

Tolliver, who had been brushing one of the horses' fetlocks, stood up suddenly, the brush in one hand clenched as a weapon, the other in a fist.

"I chose Lady Elizabeth's horses myself," Ladbroke said. "I know every hair on their bodies—"

"Nah!" the groom replied in alarm. "Wasn't tryin' t' chouse *you*. Would I'a said 't if'n I were? Bet m'lady wouldn' know."

Tolliver laughed, and to Rhoslyn, the laughter had the overtones of anger in it. "I should take that bet. You deserve to be done out of your money. My lady would certainly know if her mount did not recognize her, who had been riding her for four years, or if her horse was suddenly less spirited than before. Young as she is, my lady knows more than you would think."

Hidden in a shadowed corner and by the spell, Rhoslyn smiled mirthlessly. Out of loyalty and admiration her own servants were building a foundation for a charge of witchcraft. How convenient.

"A babe?" The groom snorted. "Royal babe 't that?"

"Willful she can be," Ladbroke said, grinning, "but the boy is quite right. Lady Elizabeth would know before she mounted that it was not her horse." The grin was replaced by a scowl. "And that is quite enough, Stover. There will be no meddling with any of the mounts of our party. I should like to know why the guards' horses are not already ready to go out. If you have left them foul to ease an exchange, I will have your place!"

The groom swelled belligerently. "You 'nd who else?"

"Me, for one," Tolliver snapped, stepping forward.

How convenient, Rhoslyn thought again. If Aurelia used Stover to attack the maid, Ladbroke and Tolliver would not be in the least surprised by his bad behavior and would doubtless testify against the man instead of being stubbornly silent. Pleased at how easily a plan had worked itself out, she sidled out of the stable.

Originally Rhoslyn had been planning to suggest that Aurelia bespell Tolliver, thinking it would serve that pest Elizabeth right to have one of her servants kill another. It was believable that Tolliver could have come to desire the maid, who was still young and comely. But then Rhoslyn remembered that Ladbroke had once lived Underhill. And he was one of those who had not forgotten. It was in his eyes. He might sense the spell on Tolliver. Stover was a better choice.

Now she had to find a place for Pasgen to set his Gate. Because Aurelia would be Gating into this place in broad daylight, the place would need to be concealed. Rhoslyn had first thought of choosing a spot in the stable itself, but the horses would most likely react poorly to a Gate appearing in their midst. Any whinnying or stamping unrest by those tenderly nurtured beasts would certainly bring their attentive grooms.

One side of the stable was used as the wall of a small paddock, the back of the stable faced the start of one of the bridle paths. Rhoslyn looked out into the deer park, wondering if she would have to choose some patch of brush, but that would mean she and Aurelia would have to cross some distance to reach the stable, likely in sight of Elizabeth, who would be riding out at the same time as they appeared. Elizabeth could see through illusion, and she might see them despite any spells they used to conceal themselves.

Fortunately the side of the stable that faced the palace was shielded by a tall yew hedge. Rhoslyn worked her way between the hedge and the stable wall. In some places she could barely squeeze past, encumbered with farthingaled skirts as she was, but she found a place where several branches had died out and had been broken to form a sort of hollow. There she laid her token from Pasgen on the ground. She and Aurelia would step out of nowhere into a place of privacy where they could not possibly be seen. Then all they needed was to take care not to shake the branches of the yews too much as they moved toward the entrance to the stable.

The rest of the day was very busy. She Gated to the empty house Underhill, and from there sent a message to Pasgen through the mind speakers who lived there. Then she sent an imp to Aurelia and was immediately called to Caer Mordwyn where she explained what had been arranged. Aurelia was pleased and with behavior unlike her past, autocratic performances, was perfectly willing to fall in with Rhoslyn's plans.

Elizabeth's entire staff focused on distracting her mind from what she had lost by going out into the garden in the middle of the night. Master Grindal gave Elizabeth only the day on which they arrived before he set her a heavy task of translation. He had heard the queen say, he told her, that she would like very much to read Margaret of Navarre's long poem *The Mirror of the*

Sinful Soul, but that her French was weak and spoiled the sense of the work.

He was sure he said to Elizabeth that the queen would truly value *The Mirror* turned from French into English. With Elizabeth's elegant handwriting, it would be, Grindal said, a perfect gift for Queen Catherine for Christmas. And to make it even more personal, Elizabeth could also embroider a cover for the work.

Since Master Grindal also expected Elizabeth to keep up with her Latin and Greek—so she should not be shamed when they rejoined the group at Hampton Court, he told her sternly—she had enough to keep her mornings full. And when she came to eat her nuncheon, Kat Champernowne told her that a messenger had come from Lord Denno to ask if Elizabeth could ride with him in the deer park that very afternoon. And when Elizabeth pettishly said she was too tired and sad to ride out, Kat shook her head.

"Oh, you must, my dear. He has missed being with you so much all this time you were at court. Do not be so unkind. Lord Denno has been such a good friend to us."

"But he—" Elizabeth began and then bit her lip. "Oh, very well. I should look at the park, I suppose, and I might as well do it in his company."

Kat did not know, of course, how often Denno had met her in the maze or how often they had ridden together in the park beyond the Wilderness. And he was worried about what had happened after he and her Da had returned Underhill. And it was *not* poor Denno's fault that she had been caught in the garden with Da. It was all her own fault, all her own.

That was the bitterest part, that Elizabeth could blame no one except herself for her exile. If she had not been so suspicious, if she had trusted Denno, she could have met Da Underhill in perfect safety.

But now she *knew* he was real, *knew* he was alive . . . and knew Denno had never lied to her. If she had not taken the chance—yes, and suffered the consequences—she would never be entirely sure that Da was really, truly alive.

"There, that's my gracious, smiling lady," Kat said approvingly. "I knew you weren't going to meet poor Lord Denno with such a scowl on your face as you have been wearing since that trouble in the garden. And it is such a lovely palace, Lady Elizabeth, and right *in* London. When we are settled, we can go and look at the markets and the shops."

Elizabeth's eyes brightened. "Yes. And Denno will give me money so I can buy."

"Oh, my love, my lady, I will find something for you," Kat said in distress. "You must not ask Lord Denno."

Elizabeth shook her head. "Kat, you have not two pennies to clink together in your purse, and it is just fortunate that Dunstan has the trust of our old servants and they are willing to wait for their wages until the start of the new quarter or we would be rattling around in this palace without anyone to make the beds or cook or serve. Anyway, why should I not ask Denno?"

Kat rubbed her hands together uneasily. "It is unwise for a lady situated like yourself, so close to the king and the king's heir, to be in debt to a . . . a foreign merchant."

"That is ridiculous," Elizabeth said. "You know Denno does not need any favors from me, and I would never *dare* approach my father on such a subject even if Denno asked."

"I'faith, you are only a little girl now," Kat warned darkly, "but such debts can have a long life. I would like you to promise me that you will not ask Denno for money."

Elizabeth looked at her governess from under her lashes. Her eyes were bright with amusement. She knew she had only to show a preference for any item and Denno would buy it. She would not need to ask.

"Very well, I promise not to ask him for money."

She was surprised when a manservant reached around her arm and removed her plate—surprised because she had not realized that she had eaten the entire portion Kat had placed on it. She had expected the food to stick in her throat as it had been doing for the past few days while they readied themselves for the move and the litany "all my fault, all mine" repeated in her head

Now, although she did miss the stimulation of trying to outdo the young gentlemen who had years more of study under their caps, she knew she had enjoyed Master Grindal's pointed remarks on her successes and failures. Most of the young dolts only thought about translating the words; Master Grindal wanted her to think about what each word meant in the context of the entire work. He stimulated in another way.

Replying absently to Kat's continued remarks about the advantages of being in St. James's Palace, Elizabeth finished the remainder of her meal, drank her wine, and went to change her dress for riding. Blanche, as usual, accompanied her to the stable, where Denno came forward to greet her. Her horse was brought out, Denno lifted her to the saddle, Dickson and Gerrit also mounted, and they all rode out with Tolliver trailing two horse-lengths behind.

Blanche stood talking to Ladbroke, wondering whether it was worthwhile to walk back to the palace. She did not think, she told him, that Elizabeth would ride long today. Ladbroke shrugged and offered her a stool to sit on if she intended to wait. She accepted with thanks. He went to get the stool and Blanche took her spindle from the basket she had carried on her arm. She pinched up some carded wool from the basket and began to spin.

"'Eard 'bout some princess prickin' 'er finger on t'at toy 'nd fallin' asleep a hundret years," a coarse voice said. "Nice 't see pretty 'oman spin."

Blanche smiled, although she drew back a little from the smell of the man. Still, it never hurt to be polite. "Thank you for the compliment," she said. "And who are you?"

"Stover's m'name. Re-si-dent groom," he added carefully as if the proper pronunciation did not come easily to him. "Ran whole stable afore tey'uns come. Who needs 'um?"

"Ladbroke and Tolliver have been my lady's grooms since she was about three years old," Blanche said, a little stiffly. "They are very devoted to her, and she to them. They are very honest and knowing."

Stover snorted. "So sharp tey'd cut theirselfs if'n tey ain't careful."

Ostentatiously Blanche looked away from him toward the inside of the stable.

"So, wach'y do when young'uns t'bed?" Stover asked, coming closer.

Taking a step back, Blanche said sharply, "I have duties enough to keep me busy, I assure you."

"Dull sleepin' alone."

"But safe and comfortable," Blanche snapped. "And I am sure you, too, have duties you should be attending. I recommend that you get to them."

"And I recommend the same." Ladbroke's voice was hard and cold. "There's plenty of harness that needs cleaning." He set one of the stools he carried in the open doorway, dusting it off carefully. "Sorry to be so long, Mistress Parry. I was looking for this lazy lout to remind him about the harness, and to tell him to muck out the stalls of Dickson's and Gerrit's horses while they're out."

"Horses don' care," Stover said.

Both Ladbroke and Blanche stared at him for a moment. Blanche turned her back, muttering—but loud enough to hear—"Disgusting." Ladbroke pointed in silence to the interior of the stable. Apparently Stover saw something in Ladbroke's face that induced him not to push his luck any further.

"That was the outside of enough," Ladbroke said, anger in his voice. "I wanted to give him a week to get used to us and working, but I will have to tell the steward to get rid of him at once."

"It is my fault," Blanche said apologetically. "He began by talking about that fairy tale in which the princess pricks her finger on a spindle, and then sleeps for a hundred years. It made me think he was better than his station."

"He's got tastes above his station—or below it. I'll agree to that much," Ladbroke replied. "He proposed to me to sell Lady Elizabeth's horses and substitute God-knows-what that look a bit alike to replace them."

Blanche shook her head. "What a fool. Maybe he believes in fairy tales where the so-called clever lad always tricks his betters!"

Ladbroke looked past her. Blanche did not think he was seeing either the stable wall or the courtyard beyond. He said no more, but Blanche thought he might be seeing the fairy place where he had once lived. To her surprise, she could detect no regret in his face. Whatever he remembered was pleasant, but not longed for.

Blanche continued to spin in silence, but not for very much longer. Less than a full hour had passed when Ladbroke stopped polishing the harness on which he had been working and lifted his head. A moment later, Blanche heard hooves on the hard driveway and Ladbroke went to open the gate of the outer courtyard for the riding party.

When they arrived at the stable, Denoriel did not dismount, allowing Ladbroke to lift Elizabeth from her horse. Denoriel just leaned down from Miralys to touch the girl's face. "I will be away for a few days," he said, "but you know the messenger that can reach me in an emergency. Only I do hope there will be none."

Elizabeth laughed. "What sort of emergency can happen in a virtually empty palace?" she asked. "Unless I am so foolish as to fall down the stairs!"

"God's kind Grace forefend!" Denoriel exclaimed, making an odd sign in the air. "Remember, if you remain cheerful and all else goes well . . ."

"We will go . . . adventuring," Elizabeth finished, after her lips had formed another word, one she could not say.

Denoriel understood and nodded, and Miralys started down the road to the main gate. Elizabeth sighed, but she was not really sad, and was grateful to Kat for making her ride out. Denno had brought all kinds of joyous messages from Da and such tales of his delight at being with her that her exile seemed worthwhile. She smiled at Tolliver, who was leading her mount away, waved at Ladbroke, and followed Blanche, who had packed away her yarn and spindle, toward the palace.

As she passed the yew hedge, Elizabeth hesitated. Something inside her echoed faintly the feeling of Underhill—

But it was not enough to stir either recognition or warning. So, although she sensed the amulet Rhoslyn had left, she did not recognize it and passed on.

Later in the day—actually while Pasgen was setting and testing his Gate—Ladbroke grew uneasy. He had no Talent and could not feel magic, but he had lived so long with it that a familiar sense of prickling and heaviness in the air teased him. He went all over the barn checking each stall and each animal. There was nothing either amiss or too familiar.

All he found was that Elizabeth's two mounts were unusually alert for the time of day, eyes wide open and ears cocked. Ladbroke examined them and the whole stall carefully and found nothing; the horses were not nervous, merely expectant. That was odd, but he felt odd himself—as he had when Elizabeth used to ride out to meet Lord Denno. Ladbroke suspected that Denno made her cast and ward against spells. Ladbroke had that same feeling now, so perhaps the mare and gelding associated the feeling of magic with their rider and were waiting for her to appear.

What magic, though? Ladbroke continued his investigation with great thoroughness, but he could not find anything inside or outside the stable. By the time he got to making his way past the yew hedge, Pasgen was finished with his work and had retrieved the amulet. The feeling of magic being done was gone, and Ladbroke found nothing.

But he could not know that was only because there was no longer anything to find.

Chapter 22

Pasgen came to Rhoslyn's domain to tell her that the Gate was ready and tested. Somewhat to his surprise, Llanelli came down and greeted him with real pleasure and none of her past hysterical pleas and warnings. She was so calm, even amusing, that Pasgen agreed to have a meal with her and Rhoslyn, and actually enjoyed himself. His mother was interested in what he had to say about the chaos lands without being prying, so much so that he engaged in a real, pleasurable conversation with her long past the time when he would usually have departed.

Afterward he took Rhoslyn to see where he had set the Caer Mordwyn terminus of the Gate to the stable. It was concealed not far from Vidal's own Gate, which now looked as if it was disintegrating. The black glass seemed dull and scratched, the cracks in the floor were wider, the lava no longer bubbled and roiled, and some of the stalagmites had fallen over. Gaps of emptiness showed in the path to the right, and some of the foul black slime had oozed up through the gravel in the middle path. Rhoslyn was not interested enough to test the left-hand path. She wondered, though, what could have caused Vidal to so neglect one of the main ways into his domain.

The noisy overflow of magic from Vidal's Gate completely concealed Pasgen's neat working. Rhoslyn would never have found the place if Pasgen had not taken her there and showed her the odd formation of dead trees and brush that marked it.

He regarded it with resignation. "I suppose I can sit behind the brush and wait for you and Aurelia to return, but I hope you will not keep me waiting long. I doubt anyone will notice the Gate in that magical mess that Vidal left over there, but a person's aura is different. A number of unpleasant things, including Vidal himself, will be able to sense me."

"I don't know," Rhoslyn said, her brow creased with worry. "I don't know how long we will have to wait for the girl to come. I know she rides out in the afternoon every day that is fine, but I don't think the time is set."

Pasgen grimaced. "Why can't I just leave the Gate for Aurelia to use when she wants? I haven't tied it into any of the power in this domain. In a few days it will just die."

"Perhaps leaving Aurelia stranded." Rhoslyn shuddered. "The Great Evil only knows what she would do then. She's not to be trusted on her own. And to speak the truth, Pasgen, I don't want her roaming around a royal palace at her own will, for even the shortest time. If she sees an attractive servant, she would almost certainly abduct him or her. If she did that a few times in a few days . . . the whole palace would be in an uproar and Elizabeth would know and tell Denoriel."

Pasgen frowned. "I thought you said Aurelia was more reasonable than she used to be. You could warn her. Couldn't you?"

Rhoslyn shook her head. "I doubt my warning would have any effect. She is better, but *will not* remember that mortals are not quite dumb animals; she thinks she can do whatever she wishes, and they won't notice, or will soon forget. And who knows what else might blunder through an open Gate to the mortal world? Any Unseleighe creatures that found themselves there would *certainly* cause an uproar."

"Yes." Pasgen sighed. "There's that. But I really don't fancy being bound to this spot for Dannae knows how long." He stared contemplatively at Rhoslyn and then, suddenly, laughed. "What an idiot I am sometimes. I will bind the Gate to you."

"Me?" Rhoslyn actually squeaked with surprise. "The only thing I know about Gates is how to use them."

Pasgen laughed, his good humor restored. "That's all you need to know about this one. It's even simpler than the usual Gate because it has only one terminus. When you—and it will be only you and what you touch—step into the Gate, it will take you to the yew hedge near the stable, nowhere else. Remember that. You will not be able to will it to take you anywhere else. And when you step back into it at the stable, it will take you to this terminus in Caer Mordwyn, nowhere else."

"All right," she agreed reluctantly, "but I don't have the kind of power you now have, brother. If you bind the Gate to me, will it leach from me?"

The statement surprised Pasgen. Before that terrible night when they had tried to abduct Elizabeth and he, as well as Vidal and Aurelia, had been so severely wounded, Rhoslyn had been fiercely competitive. She would never have admitted that he was more powerful. She would have struggled to find a way to match or overmatch him.

However, Rhoslyn had changed during the time she cared for him while he recovered. And she had cared not only for his body; she had supported his spirit too. She had changed the rooms in which he lived so the furnishings suited his ascetic taste, removing carving and gold leaf, providing bed and chairs in the stark black and white that he preferred. Odd that he had not thanked her or appreciated what she had done at the time, and only remembered it now. He touched her hand.

"No," he said reassuringly, "the Gate is self-powered. It will not draw on you, but that is why it will last only a few days, a week at most. If you need it longer, you will have to tell me. But it will be simple enough to recharge it." He paused, and added, "I would prefer if Aurelia and Vidal did not know that it is so easy for me to ingather energy, or they will have me charging up bottomless pits for them to draw on."

Rhoslyn laughed, then suddenly kissed him on the cheek. "Thank you for being so kind to Mother. I think she is really getting over the drug. It means a lot to her when you are willing to be in her company. It makes her struggle worthwhile."

He shook his head. "Then she is still a fool. It is your approval she should seek."

That made Rhoslyn laugh again. "Oh no. It is always sons a mother favors; a daughter can be a friend, but the son is her shining knight who is all-in-all to her. Now if our father had lived—"

A brief expression of regret shadowed Rhoslyn's expression, but she smiled again almost at once and told Pasgen to go ahead with his binding. It was soon done and Pasgen moved away to where Vidal's confusion of magic would block his influence on his own Gate.

Rhoslyn willed the Gate active, stepped through into a black night in which only the prickly needles and the odor identified the yew hedge, and stepped back. Another thought closed the gate to a small, blacker-than-black hole. Satisfied, she said farewell to her brother and made her way to the palace, where she informed Aurelia that all was in readiness for the removal of Elizabeth's maid.

Aurelia was delighted with Rhoslyn's promptness. Her spell was ready and only required her to touch the man on any bare skin. She rose, sipped from the glass of blue liquid, and placed a flask from beside it in her pouch. They walked from Aurelia's apartment down the grand staircase and then toward the outer door, and talked about the spell while Aurelia summoned transportation for them.

This took the form of a small but elaborate open carriage that would seat two. Shafts protruded from the front, but no animal was harnessed. A clap of Aurelia's hands brought four dull-eyed human slaves, who picked up the shafts. At Aurelia's gesture, Rhoslyn climbed into the carriage, wondering why the woman used mortal slaves when constructs were stronger. But when Aurelia was seated beside her, she gestured and black spots appeared on the slaves' backs. They all gasped, the carriage jerked forward.

"Smoothly," Aurelia called.

The blackened areas on the slaves' backs broadened. They moaned but hesitated and then moved again with matched strides. Aurelia breathed in deeply.

Rhoslyn now understood why Aurelia preferred human slaves. A miasma of acrid power flooded out of the pain and fear of the slaves and flowed back toward the carriage. Rhoslyn breathed in also, out of habit, out of need, because it was not wise to refuse extra power when it was available. But the pain was like acid along her power channels.

Why, she wondered, was there so much power awash in the Bright Court? Why were the Unseleighe domains so thin of power that they needed to draw on the misery of humans? She wished there was some other way. Pasgen had found another way, she was sure. Would he teach her? Could she learn?

When they reached Vidal's Gate, Aurelia looked at it with a total lack of expression. "From here?" she asked.

Rhoslyn shook her head and pointed in the right direction. "No. We need to go where that dead tree is tangled in the brush. We can pass behind this Gate to reach Pasgen's."

Aurelia's gaze sharpened as she looked in the indicated direction. "Where is he?"

"Elsewhere," Rhoslyn said quickly. "He did not think it wise to, perhaps, draw Vidal's attention, which his presence might do. Instead he sealed the Gate to me."

"Why not to me?" Aurelia asked, and there was no mistaking the sour tone of the question.

Rhoslyn shrugged. "Pasgen is impatient. I was here. You would have to be summoned, which, again, might draw Vidal's attention."

"Ah, yes." Aurelia's tone evened again. "Pasgen is—wise—to avoid Vidal's attention."

There was something in Aurelia's voice that disturbed Rhoslyn, something that hinted Aurelia knew Pasgen was only pretending fear. Or was it that Aurelia thought Pasgen did not understand yet that he had no need to fear Vidal? The slaves meanwhile had somehow been directed to Pasgen's Gate. They stopped before the tangle of brush and dead tree. Rhoslyn stepped out of the carriage and took Aurelia's hand.

The Gate opened before them, and they stepped through, right into the midst of dripping yew branches. In moments they were well soaked. Rhoslyn stifled an exclamation of disgust, and was all for simply stepping back through the Gate, but Aurelia held her firmly.

"I want to see the man who will be my tool."

Rhoslyn was not convinced of the wisdom of this idea. "It will be safest to bespell him just before he must act. You would not want him to attack some other female who just happened to pass this way."

Aurelia glanced at Rhoslyn with unspoken contempt. "Not because of *my* spell. It will work on him over the extra time so that it becomes part of the way he thinks, but he will not act, no matter whom he sees or speaks to or touches, until I say the word of release. I *will* be there to savor my revenge."

Rhoslyn shrugged. Aurelia had always been good with the spells that manipulated the mind, and Pasgen had told Rhoslyn that she was relearning everything she had lost and more. Rhoslyn gestured and stepped forward, then hesitated and turned back. Aurelia was not following her but had shrunk back into the wet embrace of the yew.

"Iron," Aurelia breathed.

Rhoslyn carefully kept her face expressionless, but she felt a wash of relief. Aurelia was still too sensitized to iron to find the mortal world easy to use—or even abide. She said, "Mortals use iron for everything. The building has iron braces and iron nails, and there are a lot of iron objects in the barn—tools and parts of the harness and horseshoes. I can feel it, but if you want, I will—"

"No." Aurelia felt in the pouch fastened to her belt and withdrew the flask from which she took a long swallow.

"We need the Don't-see-me spell," Rhoslyn warned, watching Aurelia straighten up and the frown smooth from her brow. What was in that potion? "Can you cast your own?"

Aurelia took a step forward. Her voice was cold and hard. "Do not irritate me, Rhoslyn. Just be quick about finding this mortal."

But Stover was not apparent when they first entered the barn and Aurelia started toward Ladbroke, who was standing stock still in the wide aisle between the horse stalls, slowly turning his head from side to side. Not wishing to risk even a whisper, Rhoslyn seized Aurelia by the arm and pulled her away toward the back of the barn.

"Not him!" she muttered in Aurelia's ear. "He lived long Underhill before he returned to the mortal world. If you touched him, he would see you, spell or no spell."

As if to affirm her words, Ladbroke's moving head turned toward them and his gaze fixed. Rhoslyn stiffened, but it was plain enough that he could not really see them. He squinted, trying to force himself to look at them. Then his lips thinned and he picked up a pitchfork and began to swing it back and forth, advancing slowly in their direction.

Instead of sidling away, Aurelia stood staring at the threatening mortal as if she could not believe her eyes. She began to lift a hand, but Rhoslyn seized it and pulled her away. She turned then toward Rhoslyn, her face scarlet with rage, but Rhoslyn spun her around forcefully, pointing over her shoulder.

At the entry to an empty stall stood the man Rhoslyn had heard Ladbroke call Stover. Where Ladbroke was hard and square, Stover was soft and fat, his gut hanging over the dirty cord that held up his breeches, which were smeared with manure. He was staring too, but not at her and Aurelia; he was watching Ladbroke swing at nothing with the pitchfork, a very ugly expression on his face.

As Ladbroke came slowly forward, Stover slipped out of the stall and slid sideways toward the front of the barn until he was behind Ladbroke. Then he started forward, gripping the handle of the shovel with which he had been mucking out the stall. He was intent on Ladbroke, who was intent on the place where Rhoslyn and Aurelia had been standing. Stover lifted the shovel slowly.

"He is the one," Rhoslyn murmured, pushing Aurelia forward. "Set the spell quickly, while he is stalking the other man."

Soft as she had spoken, Rhoslyn saw Ladbroke shift his attention to the place they now stood. He seemed to have extraordinarily keen hearing. Aurelia, however, had darted across the aisle and was gesturing and whispering as she approached Stover. Rhoslyn backed away a few steps before Ladbroke's advance, even making a small hissing sound to hold Ladbroke's attention. His movement had put him just out of reach of Stover's shovel.

Aurelia, teeth set over the pain that the proximity of iron was causing her, stepped forward again and pressed her index finger to Stover's neck, just below and a trifle behind his ear. He felt her touch or, perhaps, felt the spell flow into him, because he made a sound of surprise and irritation. Ladbroke whirled around toward him instantly, the pitchfork raised.

"Naw, then," Stover said. "Drunk ar'y?"

Ladbroke did not lower the pitchfork. "I thought I told you to muck out Pleasaunce's stall."

"Was doin' 'till y'started t' wave t' fork 'round. Who're y' arter wiv't?" the man asked, slyly. "Seein' t'ings?"

While the men spoke, Aurelia hurried past them to the stable door. Rhoslyn followed close behind. Aurelia was almost running by the time she squeezed past the meeting of the barn side with the yew hedge, but she stopped in the shelter of the hedge, hissing with impatience because she could not find the Gate. Rhoslyn, catching up, laid a hand on her shoulder. The Gate opened. They darted through, Aurelia moving as if she could not rid her feet of mortal soil quickly enough.

Safe Underhill, Aurelia turned her back on Vidal's decaying Gate and snapped at Rhoslyn, "Why did you stop me from blasting that arrogant mortal? How dare he threaten me?"

"I stopped you because that particular mortal has frequent meetings with Lady Elizabeth and possibly with Denoriel," Rhoslyn snapped back. "He already suspected our presence. Do you think he would not cry aloud of being bespelled? Denoriel would believe him and set some kind of watch. Believe me, the chances of killing the maid will be much less if anyone suspects an enchantment has been used."

Aurelia glared at Rhoslyn, but obviously could not think of an adequate riposte, because she tossed her head and said, "See to it that we do not need to spend more than a few moments waiting for the maid. All that cold iron does me no good. Could you not have found a better place?"

"Not a place where we could be sure the maid would come." Rhoslyn sighed at Aurelia's stupidity. "Where would you suggest? In the palace there is double, treble the amount of cold iron. The maid does not go to the woods or the fields and the groom does not go into the garden. Elsewhere there is little chance for concealment and a great deal of opportunity for rescue."

"Very well," Aurelia spat. "The stable it must be."

Rhoslyn nodded. "I can set an imp where it can see the entrance to the stable, but where it will itself be concealed—you remember that Elizabeth can see the creatures and can see through any illusion. The imp will come to me when Elizabeth and the maid arrive at the stable. I will send the imp to you, and you can meet me here."

"By which time the maid will be on her way back to the palace where a groom would not dare follow her." Aurelia's lips turned down in a discontented grimace.

"That is possible," Rhoslyn admitted, "but I think not. It always takes some time to get all the horses out and everyone mounted. And sometimes, like yesterday, the woman does not return to the palace at all, but waits for Lady Elizabeth in the stable. In any case, she usually has a few words with Ladbroke. And do not forget, I can adjust the time to arrive a moment after the imp departed."

Aurelia nodded. "And the bespelled one will be close. He will not attack until I say the word, but he will be drawn to the woman. Very well, I will await the imp."

Whereupon, she turned away and gestured. From behind the tangled, half-formed brush, the four slaves drew the elegant little carriage. Aurelia stepped into it and sat; a new gesture woke burns on a different part of the slaves' backs and they hurried forward. Rhoslyn stood watching with thinned lips, furious at being abandoned. Not that she wanted to ride with Aurelia, but now she had the choice of using Vidal's deteriorating Gate, walking to the other end of the domain, or summoning Pasgen. Selfish, vicious, and cruel; that was Aurelia.

She settled for the last, stroking the little furry snake nestled under her collar and saying, "Come and get me, Pasgen. I'm stranded near the stable Gate. Bring Torgen."

In a shorter time than Rhoslyn expected, the Gate she had been told led only to and from the stable at St. James's Palace opened wider than Rhoslyn thought it could. Pasgen rode Torgen out.

"What do you mean you are stranded?" he asked irritably.

"Did you want me to use that?" Rhoslyn asked, gesturing toward Vidal's Gate.

There were now more cracks than floor and, though the lava was no more than cold red rock now, anyone who slipped through would have a nasty fall and might still be impaled on the few stalagmites that were upright.

Pasgen frowned, in the way of someone confronted with a terrible, even criminal waste. "Why does he let that happen? It is a disgrace."

"Either he gets some amusement out of seeing those who come here cope or fall victim, or he has forgotten it even exists." Rhoslyn shrugged. "Take me up on Torgen. I left Talog in the stable of Caer Mordwyn."

"Then how did you get here?" Pasgen asked, hauling her up to sit pillion on Torgen's hindquarters.

The not-horse snorted and Rhoslyn could feel the muscles of his rump tighten as he prepared to buck her off. "Don't you dare, Torgen!" she snapped.

Pasgen laughed as the not-horse quieted. "They still obey you. I suspect that even my guards would obey you."

Rhoslyn blinked. "I never thought of it. I suppose they would. Would you like me to—"

"No." Pasgen shook his head, an amused expression on his face. "Actually, it is a kind of safeguard. If I should be struck down or some accident make me helpless, it is well that the guards would obey you."

Rhoslyn tightened her grip on Pasgen slightly, warm with pleasure at his trust, but all she said was, "As to how I was stranded here, Aurelia took me with her from the palace but she was displeased because I would not let her strike down Elizabeth's chief groom—he who was once a servant Underhill—and out of pique, she would not take me back. It is rather too long to walk, especially in a gown."

"She needs a lesson in manners," Pasgen said, as Torgen's long strides brought them to the gates of Caer Mordwyn. His voice was cold, and he gestured at the gates, which immediately opened inward with such force that they slammed the walls to either side.

"Gently, dear heart," Rhoslyn said. "You are too careful of my pride. It is true that she holds herself too high and mighty, but often that makes her useful because she tells me what Vidal is doing in order to make herself seem important."

Pasgen did not reply to that, and Rhoslyn slid down from Torgen's back when Pasgen stopped it by the stable. A newt-servant hurried out and Rhoslyn asked that Talog be brought to her. Ichor oozed from the shoulder of the groom who brought the creature and Rhoslyn saw wheals on Talog's hide.

"Who did that?" she snarled.

The groom collapsed on the ground, releasing Talog's rein, and the not-horse promptly rose and brought its clawed feet down. In moments the groom was a bloody ruin. Rhoslyn said, "Enough," to the not-horse, who snapped at her irritably. She struck its muzzle so that blood flowed from the lip, cut on the predator's teeth, but she also turned and ran her hand over the wheals and they disappeared.

Together she and Pasgen rode to a little-used Gate at the back of the palace, made two transfers from different Gates, and arrived at the empty house. Only this time when the not-horses were sent off to the stable they settled down in the seldom-used parlor.

Rhoslyn called up an imp and dispatched it with clear mental commands as to where it was to wait and what should trigger its return—a return to her presence, not to the place it started from. When it was gone, she told Pasgen everything that had happened. He was not much interested, except in the fact that Ladbroke seemed sensitized to the use of magic. And he shook his head over the drink to which Aurelia seemed addicted.

"It soothes her and relieves her pain and it is prepared for her by a mortal healer?" he asked. "It seems unlikely. When have mortals ever been able to do anything to heal the Sidhe?"

"I have not asked, but that is what observation tells me," Rhoslyn replied.

Pasgen shrugged. "Does it muddle her mind too?"

Rhoslyn took pains to recall everything she could. "Of that, I am not sure. Once when the pain struck her hard and she emptied the glass, she seemed to forget who I was for a moment. But the memory returned. And when she takes less of it, it does not seem to affect her mind or abilities. The spell she set on the groom was faultless."

"Ah, well, it is something to keep in mind," Pasgen said as he rose to his feet. And as he left, he looked over his shoulder to say, "Be careful, sister. Call if you need me."

Rhoslyn allowed the servants to bring her a meal. It was not very good—mostly the servants were used to transfer messages—but it was wise once in a while to act as if she and Pasgen did live in the house. While she ate, Rhoslyn thought of Pasgen's trust in her and smiled slightly.

It was a rare thing in the Unseleighe Court . . . trust. But then she thought of his reason for allowing his guards to obey her—that he might be struck down or be made helpless. Struck down by whom? Had Pasgen enemies of whom he had not told her? Made helpless? By that accursed mist? She did not like the questions that were occurring to her, but there was little she could do about them. Pasgen would do what he was going to do, and she could not stop him.

Eventually Rhoslyn left the empty house and made the multiple Gate transfers that would take her from there to her own domain. To her surprise, her mother came down to meet her, somewhat flushed with pride and pleasure. One of the male constructs had torn its hand badly while gardening. It had been waiting, moaning softly, for Rhoslyn to return and Llanelli had found it, and had used a healing spell on it.

"I did not know whether a spell designed for us would work on a construct," she said, with pleasure and pride, "but since it was a spell of construction I thought it could do no harm. And it worked!"

"Well, now, Mother, I am very glad to know that," Rhoslyn said, leading her mother into the living room where they both sat down. "Of course when I make them out of the mists in the chaos lands, I suppose I draw on my knowledge of what a Sidhe looks like and likely how my own muscles work, so I suppose it is reasonable that what would heal me would also heal the constructs. Still, it is of worth to have that proven. You have done all of us a valuable turn today!"

"Yes, and I was glad to do it, very glad to know that the spells I have been learning work," Llanelli said, flushing. "But . . . but I am coming to a point in my studies when I really need to . . . to practice what I have learned."

"But I can't let you advertise for patients and have them come here," Rhoslyn protested. "You know why Pasgen and I keep our true dwellings secret. Vidal Dhu and, even more, Aurelia cannot be trusted. They might destroy everything just for spite or lay some trap to catch us unaware so that we might be bound to their wills."

"And you think I want to be free so I can get oleander." Llanelli sighed. "It isn't so. I hardly ever think of it now that I have something else to think of. But if all the study is just sterile make-work to keep my hands and mind busy . . ."

Rhoslyn shook her head. "Actually, I wasn't thinking about the oleander. I thought at first that perhaps you could set up as a healer in one of the markets, but it would make you too vulnerable—not so much to the drug as to Vidal. No, I would *like* for you to set up as a healer. There are few enough among the Unseleighe; you could earn many favors, and make allies for us as well."

Llanelli said nothing, only clasped her hands and watched her intertwined fingers.

After a long moment, Rhoslyn said slowly, "There is the empty house. Perhaps it could be safeguarded. With your maids, a couple of my girls, who are very clever, and perhaps Pasgen's guards or a few special constructs . . ."

Llanelli's face transformed with enthusiasm, and she seemed

to light up from within. Her eyes became more green, less like transparent marbles. "Oh, yes. There are Gates from all three markets to the empty house. It would be easy for patients to come to me."

"Easy for anyone," Rhoslyn said rather flatly, but when she saw the life fading from Llanelli, she smiled and added, "On the other hand, the servants there are all keyed to my mind and Pasgen's so we could be summoned from wherever we were... Let me talk to Pasgen about this, Mother."

Llanelli wilted. "Pasgen will say no."

Rhoslyn laughed. "Yes he will, but only at first. I will explain, and once he thinks about it, I believe he will agree. Meanwhile I will tell the girls and the servants here that if they are hurt they should not wait for me, but go to you for help."

"You won't tell the girls to hurt the other servants just so I can have patients," Llanelli said doubtfully, knowing the ways of the Unseleighe.

"No, I won't do that," Rhoslyn said, laughing again. "There are accidents enough among them to keep you from being entirely bored—they are like children, you know, who try things with little judgment and no care for consequences. But how will you let those who come to the market know that you are a healer and keep your real identity secret?"

They talked about that for a while, seriously at first and then suggesting ridiculous ploys to each other so that they giggled like children. And after a while, Llanelli, still smiling, leaned forward and kissed Rhoslyn.

"Thank you, my love, thank you," she said. "I'll go now and look at the gardener's hand to see if my spell is holding and the construct flesh is binding together as Sidhe flesh would heal. You have things to do, I'm sure."

In fact, Rhoslyn did have a few projects waiting, the creation of constructs for several of the dark Sidhe, but she had time yet and was not in the mood for building sex objects that looked mortal but were more durable than the poor mayfly humans, or guards that could rival an ogre in strength. And suddenly, thinking of the horrible death coming to the maid, she felt unutterably weary. Sidhe did not sleep as such, but that was exactly what Rhoslyn wanted to do... sleep.

Too much Aurelia, she told herself, as she climbed the stairs and let herself into her suite of rooms. There was a bed, of course, usually used for purposes other than sleep—but there had been no one for a long time that Rhoslyn could tolerate as a bedmate. She did not even think of that as she waved her clothing away and lay down.

Sidhe did not usually sleep, but Rhoslyn achieved that state, or something close to it before she was jarred out of her peaceful meditations on nothingness by a lance of pain—

The pain of having her hair pulled. She nearly blasted the imp that was laughing as it tugged, but it began to chitter, "On the path. Near. Near." And she remembered setting the imp to watch for Elizabeth and her maid.

She sent it off to Aurelia and sprang from the bed. A thought clothed her in full mortal dress and she rushed out, mentally calling to her servants to bring Talog. It was there in moments. Rhoslyn mounted and rode to her private Gate, cursing the need for the circuitous route to protect her privacy. In no long time, however, she rode Talog out of the little-used Gate in the rear of Caer Mordwyn. This time she did not dismount in the courtyard, only sent a servant to inform Aurelia that she had arrived.

Vidal's consort emerged promptly but made a grimace of dissatisfaction on seeing Roslyn mounted. "I thought to supply you with a little extra power," she said. "My slaves do not get enough exercise these days."

"The less I need to adjust the time the better," Rhoslyn replied, and added mendaciously, "The Gate is temporary—Pasgen had not the strength nor the audacity to build a new permanent Gate in our lord's domain—and it might fail if it is tweaked too much. I hope that you will settle for swiftness and ride."

Aurelia did not look happy, but she called for a mortal servant to bring her horse, and when he did and had helped her to mount, she broke his arm and seared his naked chest, sucking in the outflow of pain and terror. Rhoslyn did not crowd close to take in whatever Aurelia missed.

Rhoslyn found she had less and less taste for the sour burning power of mortal misery, and as they cantered away, she thought again of Pasgen's ability to take into himself some of the power intrinsic to the roiling mists of the chaos lands. They were twins, almost the same blood and bone; surely if Pasgen could do it, she could too. The next time she molded mists into a living construct, she would—

"Here is Vidal's Gate," Aurelia said, breaking into Rhoslyn's thoughts. "Has Pasgen's died already? I do not see any sign of it."

"No," Rhoslyn affirmed. "I can feel it, and it is in better condition than Vidal's."

"Vidal is careless sometimes," Aurelia replied, not looking toward the disintegrating Gate; the roof of the black glass temple had fallen in places and the left-hand path had disappeared completely.

Rhoslyn directed Talog around Vidal's Gate and stopped the not-horse by the bent tree rising out of the unfinished mess that was probably meant to be brush. She dismounted and led the not-horse behind the ill-defined bushes. Aurelia followed, dismounted, and looked at the ground, frowning. A glowing copper rod with loops at the end of a crossbar appeared. Aurelia fastened her horse to one loop and invited Rhoslyn to use the other. Rhoslyn laughed.

"Talog could have that out of the ground in one pull." She turned to the not-horse, put a finger on its forehead and said, "You will stay here and wait for me. You will *not* eat the horse that is tied here. You may eat anything else that comes along, but do not go far from this place."

For answer, the not-horse snapped at her and she clouted it, but it did not attempt to savage her when she turned her back on it. Vicious as its temper was, it obeyed her, and that vicious temper was useful at times like this. Around in front of the bent tree, Rhoslyn took Aurelia's hand. The Gate opened to her will.

They stepped through into a perfect summer day. The sun was bright, there was a cool but very gentle breeze, everything smelled fresh—if rather strongly of yew—and the sound of voices, a girl's and a woman's, came to them through the hedge. They hurried forward toward the open area near the stable door, Aurelia pulling her flask from her pouch.

Rhoslyn glanced at Aurelia and quickly covered her elaborate, diamond-studded gown with the illusion of an upper servant's sober dress. Aurelia drank from her flask, closed her eyes, sipped again, then capped it and put it away. Rhoslyn breathed a small sigh of relief, having been afraid that Aurelia would take too much.

Both whispered the Don't-see-me spell, but Rhoslyn pulled

Aurelia close and reminded her that Elizabeth could see through it and that they must remain hidden until the girl was gone. They did not need to wait long. Apparently a message had gone down to the stable that Elizabeth would ride and all the horses were ready. It was only necessary to lead them out. Nyle and Shaylor mounted. Ladbroke lifted Elizabeth to the saddle.

"I hope you don't mind, my lady," he said as she settled herself, "if Tolliver rides with you today. There was some funny business in the stable yesterday."

Elizabeth replied sharply, "Funny business?"

Rhoslyn pulled Aurelia farther back, away from the opening in the hedge. They could no longer see what was happening, but they could hear.

"Don't know, my lady. I just felt . . . something was in the air, like many years ago in the place I worked before I came into His Grace of Richmond's service."

There was a pause. Rhoslyn could imagine glances meeting over words that could not be spoken. Then Elizabeth said, "Very well, Ladbroke. Do you think I should send a message to Lord Denno?"

Another pause, then Ladbroke said, "Don't want to take up his lordship's time. I couldn't find nothing wrong in the stable and nothing strange happened. Maybe the feeling was just in my head."

"Very well," Elizabeth repeated, and then, "stay here."

Rhoslyn cocked her head. That had sounded like an order rather than permission. Rhoslyn hoped it was for the maid so this unpleasant experience need not be repeated. Through breaks in the hedge she could see that one guardsman had already ridden out of the stable yard. Elizabeth followed, and the other guardsman and the groom called Tolliver rode out after her. Rhoslyn watched them and then nodded at Aurelia, who was just capping her flask after taking another drink from it. Before Rhoslyn could caution her about using too much of the potion, Aurelia started forward.

Fortunately Aurelia seemed alert and aware as she slipped around the side of the stable. The maid, who was talking to Ladbroke, suddenly stiffened and looked around.

"Something's here," she said. "You weren't imagining it yesterday."

Rhoslyn stopped where she was, not wanting to increase the feeling of magic caused by the Don't-see-me spells and set Ladbroke to feeling around with a pitchfork again. She frowned, now sensing a different kind of magic than that created by Aurelia and herself, but before she could seek it out her attention was distracted by Aurelia, who slipped past the two standing in the doorway.

The maid's head followed the Sidhe, but Aurelia disappeared into the stable. Rhoslyn did not dare call out to warn her to wait, that Elizabeth's party was still too close. As quickly as she could, Rhoslyn now followed Aurelia. She kept as close to the wall as she could, but the maid's head snapped around toward her.

If she intended a warning to Ladbroke, it was too late. Aurelia had already found Stover lurking nearby in the stall vacated by Elizabeth's horse. She crossed right in front of him, stepped aside, and touched him—again on the neck, below and behind the ear, muttering, *"Dyna ben!"*

Stover, who had been staring at Blanche with red-rimmed, burning eyes, roared like a beast freed from confinement and leapt forward. His mad rush knocked Ladbroke to the ground, and he seized on Blanche with a grip that drew a scream from her. He could have killed her in that moment, but killing was not enough to sate the pain and hatred that had been churning and building in him all day and all night.

Aurelia had followed Stover. Almost salivating with eagerness to absorb Blanche's agony and terror, to sate her need for vengeance and drink in power, she drew close to watch Stover beat, mutilate, and kill the maid.

Ladbroke began struggling to his feet. His movement distracted Aurelia; then she took on an expression more like a rictus than a smile, and she raised a hand to stop his heart.

Chapter 23

Not so far distant in the park, Elizabeth tensed in her saddle and drew rein. She was not certain what was bothering her. She thought she had heard a faint cry, but it was not repeated. A glance around told her that the air spirit had not followed her and had obeyed her command to stay at the stable, but yet . . . She could not feel it!

Well, but they were much farther apart now than she usually was when she felt for the creature.

No. No, that was not right; it didn't *feel* right. There was something wrong.

Shaylor, becoming aware of the absence of the sound of hooves behind him, turned his horse and came back. Nyle and Tolliver closed in from behind.

"My lady?" Shaylor asked.

"I don't know," she said fretfully. "I don't know—"

But before the last word was clear of her lips, she felt a terrible wrenching and a tremendous pressure on her throat and breast. Crying aloud, she pulled her mare's head around, kicked her, and struck her with her little whip, starting the horse in a leap back to the stable. Blanche! Something was terribly wrong with Blanche!

Blanche was in trouble. *Blanche was in danger!*

✧   ✧   ✧

The thrust that had sent Ladbroke sprawling struck the maid with such force that she staggered back before Stover could grab her. Instinctively she reached for the necklace of crosses and gripped one, trying to pull it loose. She had it in her hand, but Stover was on her before she could try to sense the Sidhe who was directing him. He struck her a backhanded blow with his fist and she staggered back with the force of it, out into the stable yard where she tripped on her skirt and went down on her back.

Aurelia followed, giggling and licking her lips. Her hand was raised to fling a death spell at Ladbroke if he interfered again, but she was so entranced by Blanche's growing fear that she found it harder and harder to pay heed to anything else. The maid was not yet frightened enough to exude much life force, but the energy that came from her pain was so sweet, so intoxicating, that Aurelia was drawn closer and closer, her attention riveted.

Stover blundered after Blanche, red-faced and growling like a beast. This time when he caught her, he seized her by the arm and hauled her up, wrenching the limb as if he intended to tear it off. Blanche screamed with the pain, struck at him with her other fist, and tried to kick him. She was hampered by her long, full skirt, but the toe of her shoe did catch him on the shin, which hurt enough to make him roar again and batter her with his free fist.

Ladbroke scrambled to his feet, and rushed at Stover, unconsciously swerving slightly to detour around Aurelia. He barreled into Stover with his shoulder, but the man was heavier, and already braced against Blanche's struggles. Ladbroke literally bounced off him, then came around swinging and hit him hard on the side of the head. When that had no effect, Ladbroke seized Stover's arm and tried to pull Blanche free.

He might as well have tried to pull the castle wall apart with his bare hands.

When he could not break the groom's grip, Ladbroke battered at his thick body with both fists, but Stover ignored it all. He gave Blanche another backhanded blow that she managed to fend off with her free arm and then pulled her close, baring his teeth as if he intended to tear at her with them.

Aurelia's eyes had been glazing with pleasure, but she snarled at Ladbroke's interference and again raised her hand to cast a spell at him.

The pounding of hooves in the distance told Rhoslyn that the plan had miscarried. If it wasn't to turn into a disaster, she would have to get Aurelia away—now!

Rhoslyn seized her arm and shook the Unseleighe sorceress, hissing urgently at her, "Elizabeth is coming back! We are undone! Give over, curse you! She will see us—come away *now*."

Stover now seemed to notice Ladbroke's attack. He flung Blanche to the ground so hard that the maid gasped as all breath was knocked from her. Drawing his big knife from his belt, he slashed at Ladbroke.

Ladbroke saw the danger in time to jump aside.

But the moment Ladbroke was out of range, Stover lost interest in him. He whirled on the half-stunned Blanche, and lunged at her, his knife stabbing down at her.

Though winded, she managed to roll aside so that he just missed her.

Ladbroke again launched himself at the bespelled groom and knocked him sideways so that his next thrust at Blanche also missed. The two men rolled on the ground, grappling, Ladbroke struggling to hold off the larger and heavier man's knife hand, Stover fixated on getting back to Blanche. All that was saving Ladbroke was that he was only something in the way.

Aurelia had wrenched herself free of Rhoslyn and again hovered on the edge of the battle between the two mortals, hissing and moaning with satisfaction. She was like one drugged now, and nothing mattered but the intoxication. She was far too entranced with the power of hate and fear and pain pouring out of the three to hear the sound of the thudding hooves, too involved with her own voluptuous pleasure to hear Elizabeth's voice, high and childish with terror, shriek, "There, Blanche, there! In front of the yew hedge beside you!"

Battered and bruised though she was, Blanche forced herself upright and threw the cross in her hand at what she hoped was man-height toward the opening of the yew hedge. It would never have hit anything, if Aurelia had not been so very close to her, bending forward the better to suck in what flowed out of Blanche and the nearby men locked in combat.

There was a loud scream and Aurelia became visible to all, her hands to her head where the broken link that had held the cross to the necklace had caught in her hair so that the cross dangled over her forehead. She shrieked and gibbered, batting at the cross, making abortive attempts to tear the torment off her head.

But every time her hand touched the metal it burned like a white-hot poker. The pain was so intense she could not grip the iron. She was losing herself in the agony. Aurelia began to sink down on the ground, howling, angry red blotches and blisters appearing on her forehead.

Although no one else noticed, Elizabeth perceived a woman (who was hard to see clearly) rush forward and catch the one who was falling. An expression of horror crossed the face of the one coming to help, and she swatted at the cross tangled in the fainting woman's hair. She pulled her hand back as if it had been hurt, but then she tried again, and this time she slapped the iron cross out of the other's hair to the ground, crying out involuntarily with pain when she touched it.

Even as the cross hit the ground, Stover threw Ladbroke over and was atop him, banging his head against the ground. As Ladbroke's grip on Stover's knife hand loosened, Stover wrenched free and raised the knife. However, his head was still turned toward Blanche and before he struck, he saw her trying to get to her feet. Slamming a last blow into Ladbroke, Stover raised himself into a crouch and prepared to launch himself at Blanche.

The guardsmen and Tolliver were just entering the stable yard. All of them shouted aloud when they saw the blood, Ladbroke and Stover struggling, Blanche sprawled on the ground, trying to get up amid a tangle of skirts, and the upraised knife in Stover's hand.

They scrambled off their horses, but Elizabeth could see they would never reach Blanche in time to stop Stover from plunging his knife into her. Even if he missed a vital spot, that was death—a more horrible death than a clean blow that stopped the heart. A wound from a groom's knife nearly always ended in a terrible death—screaming through locked jaws from the pain of arching one's back to breaking, a death that could take hours, even days to finally come.

In desperation, praying that the magic could do *something,* Elizabeth cast the spell for a shield over her beloved nursemaid. The knife in Stover's hand came down with all the force he could muster as the shield snapped into place.

He let out a howl of mingled rage, frustration, and pain as the knife bounced off Blanche's belly and flew out of his hand. Blanche had cried out too, as she saw the knife descending. Now she screamed again, as if she had been stabbed, and rolled away.

Stover lurched forward on his knees and scrabbled for the knife. He caught it up in his hand and jumped to his feet, but it was too late. Nyle and Shaylor had dismounted and run toward him. Nyle blocked his path to Blanche, who Tolliver was trying to assist, exclaiming as his hands would not touch her. Shaylor attempted to seize Stover, trying to grab his arms from behind. Stover struggled, wrenching the hand in which he held the knife free, and slashing wildly with it.

From the opening in the yew hedge to which she had supported Aurelia, Rhoslyn muttered and gestured.

Stover seemed to try to stab at Shaylor, who was behind him, but he was screaming now—and not with rage—as the knife turned in his hand and slashed into his own throat.

Blood fountained out, spraying over Nyle who was coming to aid his fellow guardsman, spotting Shaylor's arm and hand, gushing down Stover and dying his dirty clothing crimson—

—pooling on the ground as Stover fell forward.

In the moment of stunned silence that followed, Elizabeth looked toward the opening in the yew hedge, but no one was there now. She felt a swell of magic, almost urged her mare forward to look at the hedge more closely, but at that moment Miralys came thundering along the path and burst into the stable yard. On Denoriel's shoulder, the air spirit cried, "Help! Help!" in a thin, shrill voice.

Denoriel's glance skipped over the dead groom, who was no longer a threat, saw Tolliver trying to take hold of Blanche, who was wavering on her feet. But Tolliver's hand would not close on Blanche, and his face showed an expression of growing fear.

Elizabeth was just sliding down from her saddle on her own, but before her foot was free of the stirrup, Denoriel was there, catching her and setting her gently on her feet. However, his face was not gentle.

He looked like a thundercloud, and hissed in her ear, "Cursed fool! Remove that shield at once! What madness is this?"

Responding to the urgency of his tone, Elizabeth gestured and the shield was gone. Tolliver's hand caught Blanche's arm, and she sagged against him.

But now Elizabeth turned on Denoriel, quick as a snake, hissing back, "I cast that shield to save Blanche's life!"

He looked around, but Nyle and Shaylor were staring at the dead man, Tolliver was talking to Blanche, who was leaning heavily on him, and Ladbroke was shakily getting to his feet, rubbing the back of his head.

Though they were paying no attention to him, Denoriel did not think they were careless in their protection of Elizabeth. He had no doubt that all of them had ascertained who he was immediately and were content to leave Elizabeth in his hands.

So he kept his voice low, but he took advantage of the moment to say, "And put your own life in danger, you little fool. Do you want to be accused of being a witch?"

"By whom?" Elizabeth snapped back. "Do you think Tolliver will accuse me? Or Nyle? Or Shaylor? Ladbroke perhaps? Blanche?"

"Of course not! But what of the women who were here?" he demanded fiercely.

"How do you know anyone was here?" Elizabeth asked. "They were gone by the time you arrived. You said you would not come for several days. Are you spying on me?"

"Spying? Is that what you call my care for your safety?" he snapped back, livid. "But this time I was not attending to you. The air spirit came for me, crying for help. As to how I knew about the women, I felt them just as Miralys brought me into the stable yard. Then they were gone."

Her face was as stormy as his. "If they were gone, they were . . . of your kind, and I do *not* think they are likely to complain to a priest or the sheriff!"

Denoriel grabbed her shoulders and shook her. "Will you stop acting the fool, which I know you are not? One of those women, I am sure, was my half-sister, Rhoslyn. She has several personas that she uses when she is . . . here. And I am sure she has access to Lady Mary. I would not be surprised if it was by her connivance that Mary came upon you when you were in the garden with Harry!"

"Then I hope you will be able to stop her from accusing me or save me if she does," Elizabeth spat, "because I will not permit Blanche to be killed to save me from accusations! What good are the shields if I cannot use them?" she demanded passionately.

"You were not supposed to use the physical shields! They were to be invoked only as a last resort to protect *yourself*," he said angrily. "It was the mental shields that are important. And no one can see those, so you may use them freely."

Denoriel's rebuke was automatic, but his brow was creased by a frown. It had not previously occurred to him that the next Unseleighe ploy might be to remove Elizabeth's trusted servants. The servants were not under protection, and it was quite clear that Rhoslyn had intended Blanche's death to be brought about by an attack from a mortal man. No one would cry magic or believe it if anyone did complain.

The loss of Blanche would be a disaster, the loss of Kat Champernowne less so but still dangerous. Particularly now when Elizabeth was on a thin edge of self-blame. If anything should happen to her close companions, those few that she trusted and believed she could depend upon to protect her, it could push her over into behavior that would end in disaster. At the least, she might find herself banished from the succession. At the worst—

He did not want to think about the worst. Better such a thing should be prevented. But there must be simple spells she could use. She could have pushed the mad groom away from Blanche, perhaps made him run headfirst into a wall.

"Perhaps—you were right—" he began.

"Oh, thank you," Elizabeth said, sarcasm dripping from every word as she wrenched herself free.

She ran to her maid, clutching Blanche's arms as the young woman did her best not to wince away. "Oh, my poor Blanche! Your face!" she cried, and burst into tears.

Denoriel's teeth set, and he suppressed a desire to turn her over his knee. Still, what she said made good sense. She could not, being Elizabeth, stand by idly while her own people were in danger. And she should not have to. It was up to him to find something she could use as a weapon that would not betray her Talent. As soon as he could arrange it, he would take her back Underhill and have Tangwystl teach her a few spells for active defense. But he wished she would not try to flay him every time he offered her advice.

Then he sighed. Every one of them was badly shaken, even Nyle. The youngest guard, who had come close and was waiting to speak to him, was shuddering slightly. It was unfair to expect Elizabeth not to snap at whoever approached her. He held up a hand toward Nyle, asking him to wait, and turned to beckon to Tolliver, who was not bloodied.

"It's only bruises," Blanche was saying to Elizabeth, half embracing the child and half leaning on her. Tolliver stepped back respectfully, and Blanche tried to smile at the groom over Elizabeth's head. "Thank you," she said. "I will do now and I think Lord Denno wants you."

"If you need him, Blanche—" Elizabeth began.

But Blanche shook her head and waved Tolliver away. Denno promptly told him to take a horse and ride for the sheriff.

Nyle looked uneasy. "Pardon, m'lord," he said, "but how do we explain this? I mean, there's a man dead with his throat cut and I'm all over blood and Shaylor is nearly as bad. And Mistress Blanche is all beaten and so is Ladbroke."

"No problem. You tell the sheriff the truth."

"Yes, m'lord," the young man stammered, "but I don't know any truth that explains what happened. When me and Shaylor arrived, Ladbroke was out on the ground and Stover was crouched down just about to jump at Mistress Blanche. And her face was all bruised and bloody so we knew he had hit her before. We went for him, Stover, I mean. I ran to keep Stover off Mistress Blanche and Shaylor went to try to grab him. Stover was swinging that knife, maybe to keep me off and to threaten Shaylor, and suddenly he began to scream, like 'No. No,' and then he stuck the knife in his own neck. The sheriff will never believe me."

"I can make some sense of it," Ladbroke said, a hand to his head. "Two days ago when Lady Elizabeth rode out, Mistress Blanche decided to wait for her in the stable. I went to get her a stool, and Stover made an indecent proposal to her. Mistress Blanche naturally turned him away cold. After Lady Elizabeth was back in the palace, I told Stover that I was going to speak to the steward and get him turned away if he even looked Mistress Blanche's way. But yesterday I heard him muttering and mumbling all day long."

"Well, that explains most of it," Denoriel said, thanking all the Powers That Be for so logical a reason for Stover to make an attack. "As for the rest—well, the man went mad, is all, and there is no explaining what the mad will do. He's simply managed to cheat Jack Ketch of his hangman's fee, and there's an end to it."

"Yes m'lord," Ladbroke said.

Denoriel patted him on the shoulder. "There's no reason why Nyle and Shaylor shouldn't change their clothing and wash, if

you feel well enough to wait for the sheriff, Ladbroke. I will take
Lady Elizabeth and Mistress Parry back to the palace. If you need
Mistress Parry to give evidence or even require Lady Elizabeth
to explain what she saw, since she was the first to arrive, ask
the sheriff to go up to the palace or send Tolliver to summon
whoever is needed."

Rhoslyn saw the knife go home in Stover's throat and used
every obscenity in her adequate store as she backed away into the
yew hedge and toward the Gate. They had failed again. The maid
was unhurt . . . But possibly they had not failed completely. Possibly the incident had opened another path, a path to Elizabeth's
final doom.

The young groom had encountered the shield Elizabeth had
cast over her maid and was clearly frightened. He would talk
about it. The older groom, who Rhoslyn knew had once lived
Underhill, might even know what it was. Possibly he would talk
too, but would he believe that Elizabeth, a mere child, could cast
such a spell, or would he think it was the maid?

Aurelia moaned when the Gate opened, and despite Rhoslyn's
support, began to slide to the ground. Rhoslyn gripped her more
firmly, but was barely able to pull her through the Gate, and she
slipped out of Rhoslyn's grasp and fell heavily to the earth when
they passed through. Rhoslyn stepped over her and hurriedly
pulled her clear of the Gate. If it had closed before Aurelia had
gotten clear . . . Rhoslyn shuddered and then paused, her brows
furrowed in speculation.

Just what would have happened, if Aurelia had not gotten clear?
Well, in any case, it was too late to worry about it now. She went
in search of their mounts.

The not-horse was near where Rhoslyn had left it, but its breast
and muzzle were stained with blood. Apparently it had taken to
heart Rhoslyn's permission to eat anything but the tethered horse.
"Wait," Rhoslyn said to it and returned to see if she could rouse
Aurelia.

A few minutes of slapping and prodding, even an attempt to
get the flask from Aurelia's pouch—which Rhoslyn was unable to
open—failed to produce any sign of consciousness. Aurelia simply
lay there, uttering a soft moan with every outgoing breath.

Rhoslyn was sorely tempted to take Talog and leave Aurelia

lying there, but it was too dangerous to abandon her, no matter how tempting. Aurelia might not survive. There were inimical creatures roaming about Caer Mordwyn and she might be hurt or killed.

Furious as she was at Aurelia, her injury or death did not matter much to Rhoslyn at the moment—except that the blame for it would fall squarely on her. It was likely that Aurelia had told others where she was going, why, and with whom. Also, there were the servants who had seen her ride off with Aurelia not long ago, and if Aurelia died, or was hurt, Vidal would soon come to know of it and of Rhoslyn's involvement.

Rhoslyn sighed. Not to mention that if Aurelia woke and found herself abandoned, her life might be as dedicated to revenge on Pasgen and herself as it now was directed against Elizabeth's maid.

Rhoslyn tried, but could not get Aurelia up on either her horse or the not-horse and eventually she had to appeal to Pasgen to come and help her. He was as swift in arriving as when she had first called him, but she knew he was not going to be pleased at what he found.

She was right. He came riding through the Gate with fair brows drawn together in a ferocious frown and spells on his lips and fingertips because all she had been able to tell him through the lindys was that she was in trouble. When he saw Aurelia sprawled ungracefully on the ground, he looked as if he were about to spit down on her from Torgen's back.

"I'm sorry," Rhoslyn said, meekly. "I just didn't have the strength to lift her onto the horse, and I knew if I left her here—well, nothing but ill would come of it."

"Waste of time. She'd only fall off," Pasgen replied, dismounting.

He lifted Aurelia to the front of Torgen's saddle where Rhoslyn held her steady while Pasgen remounted—once letting go with one hand to smack Torgen, who was snaking his head back, trying to take a piece out of Aurelia's thigh. Then she unfastened the reins of Aurelia's horse and took them in hand, mounted Talog, and followed Pasgen, who had already set out for the palace.

To Rhoslyn's surprise, Pasgen did not ride into the courtyard, but skirted the palace to a place on the rear wall that was roughly opposite the old Gate Rhoslyn had been using. There he dismounted, dragged Aurelia from Torgen's back onto his shoulder, and walked a few steps along the wall where a sharp command caused a click. A well-concealed door opened.

Rhoslyn, who had dismounted from Talog, swallowed her surprise to ask, "Horses in or out?"

"In," he said shortly. "There's a small back garden where Torgen and Talog can wait. I hope we won't be long. Holy Mother Dannae, this bitch weighs like a full tun of ale!"

There was a small open area between the outer wall and the palace. Rhoslyn would not have called it a garden, but she thought that Talog and Torgen couldn't do it much harm. Pasgen, rather breathlessly, said he would dump Aurelia in her apartment and asked Rhoslyn to take her horse to the stable in the front.

"Right willingly," Rhoslyn murmured, then turned to bid Talog and Torgen stay.

When she looked back, Pasgen was gone. She was startled at his sudden vanishment, but then realized there must be another hidden back door, and reminded herself that Pasgen had ruled Caer Mordwyn for several years. He would certainly have set himself to discover everything there was to know about the palace. It would have been very necessary because Vidal Dhu was just the kind to have put traps all over the place for anyone wandering about without his company or his instructions.

By the time she had led Aurelia's horse around the side of the palace, handed it over to the newt-servants, and made her way back to where Torgen and Talog were waiting, Pasgen was also there waiting for her.

"What happened?" he asked, his voice ice-cold and not at all hushed. "Aurelia looks very much as you described her appearing after the battle in Elizabeth's room." Rhoslyn waved a hand for quiet, but Pasgen shook his head impatiently. "Vidal is not here. He is having a real holiday up in Scotland."

"Let's be gone from here anyway," Rhoslyn said, still feeling uneasy. Vidal might not be here himself, but who could tell what was listening? "Come to my house. I am delighted that Vidal is busy in Scotland. Long may he make trouble there. And if Aurelia was hurt as badly as I hope, with luck, neither of us will be troubled with the affairs of the World Above for some time."

Pasgen looked at her with raised brows and, seemingly taking in the expression on her face, simply nodded.

They went through the back gate, which Pasgen sealed again so that it was totally invisible, and then made their way to Rhoslyn's domain. The girls opened the door for them. Lliwglas, she of the blue ribbon, gestured toward the stair with her head. Rhoslyn saw one of her mother's maids peeping down at her and she shook her head infinitesimally. She did intend to speak to Pasgen about Llanelli, and her mother's hopes to practice as a healer, but she had some things to explain first.

Pasgen sank into a deep, soft armchair and sighed. "Well, what has put your nose so out of joint, sister?"

"That mortal brat Elizabeth was surely begot of the Great Evil," Rhoslyn snarled, sinking into the corner of the sofa at right angles to Pasgen's chair. "Anything to do with her is a disaster." She blew out an exasperated breath and added, "Although there is no doubt that Aurelia contributed to the catastrophe."

"How was she hurt?" he asked.

"By cold iron, in the craziest accident you could imagine." She shook her head. "It should never have happened."

"Accident?" Pasgen repeated.

Rhoslyn shrugged. "The plan Aurelia made should have worked. It was simple and sensible. She bespelled a mortal to attack and kill Elizabeth's maid. The maid is Talented, there can be no doubt of that. Aurelia thought, and I agreed with her, that if we could be rid of the maid, Elizabeth would be much more vulnerable."

Her brother nodded. "That does sound reasonable, and Oberon would not be much interested in the death of a maid. I agree too that it was a good idea. So what went wrong?"

Furious at the catastrophe that had unfolded, and fully as angry at Aurelia as at the miserable mortal child, Rhoslyn gave Pasgen a blow-by-blow description of what had taken place in the stable yard of St. James's Palace.

She ended with, "We would have been safe away if Aurelia had not virtually bent over the woman to suck up the power that leaked from her fear and pain. That was when the maid threw the cross and it stuck in Aurelia's hair and touched her forehead. She screamed and lost the Don't-see-me spell, and we were utterly undone. The idiot! If she had not gone to the struggle like a moth to a flame, naught would have come of this and she and I would be safely back by now!"

Pasgen sighed. "The fresh pulses of power from agony and

terror are irresistible to some." He cocked his head inquisitively, watching Rhoslyn. "But not to you, sister?"

"Not to me." Rhoslyn's voice was flat, and she shivered slightly. "I must find another source of power to feed on."

Pasgen smiled and his eyes gleamed with mischief. "You can try my way," he said, "but if it does not suit you ... we can steal from the Seleighe. I will go with you. With Vidal totally immersed in making trouble in Scotland and Aurelia incapacitated, we will be free to do what we like."

That distracted her from her anger for a moment. "What *is* going forth in Scotland?"

"I do not know the details—those who watch for me are not much larger, or cleverer, than the lindys—but Vidal has set strong hooks into Cardinal Beaton. Beaton is one of the rulers of Scotland now that King James is dead—as much as anyone can be said to rule so brawling and contentious a people—and he is opposed to the government set up by King Henry, which agreed, albeit most reluctantly, to a treaty with England in which the Scottish queen, little Mary, would marry Prince Edward."

"I can see why Vidal would be opposed to that." Rhoslyn raised her brows and nibbled on her lower lip, intrigued by all the possibilities of meddling with such a tangled situation. "It would mean peace between England and Scotland, not only now but in the future. No war, no death, no misery—and no sour power for the Unseleighe."

Pasgen shrugged, but one corner of his mouth quirked. "Well, the Scots would be unlikely to give over border raiding and such, but there would be no major invasions with total destruction. And with Henry's grip on England so firm, there is quiet in England and little chance of the kind of chaos Vidal needs. Thus, Vidal must be sure that Scotland resists and that the war continues."

"And he must actually be there most of the time?" she asked, wondering why, but glad that it was true.

Pasgen nodded. "If he wishes to keep the pot boiling, I think so. You see there are three strong parties and Vidal's grip is only on Beaton. There is also the government that Henry placed in power and then there is the greater part of the Scottish nobles, who are of no party but their own and shift back and forth, making alliances and breaking them, seeing only the needs and wants of their clans and nothing beyond the benefit of the moment." His voice was full of scorn for such shortsightedness.

Rhoslyn nodded. "I see. If Henry's agents should offer enough, it might even be possible for that middle party to seize the queen and deliver her to England."

But over that, he shook his head. "Not likely. More likely that the middle party—or enough of it to seize a preponderance of power—will make alliance with one side or another and the fighting among the Scots themselves will die down. Then when England sends an army, there might be a sharp defeat of the English, which will certainly mean the end of war until the king returns from France. The only way to keep things unsettled is to keep those nobles from bringing a majority to one side or the other. And for that, Beaton must be most carefully directed."

"Then Vidal's attention *will* remain in Scotland. Very good. And Aurelia may well have no attention to give—" Rhoslyn's voice checked and she bit her lip, thinking back on how terrible the Unseleighe sorceress had looked. "Could you tell how badly she was hurt?" she asked, feeling guilty. "I did try to help. I struck the cross out of her hair." She held out her hand where red burn wheals and blisters marred her fingers. "But not soon enough to save her, I fear."

"I don't know whether she was seriously damaged or just stunned by shock and pain," Pasgen said. "When I brought her in, her servants called her mortal physician, but he seemed totally confused. I suppose sooner or later one of the servants will find sense enough to summon a true healer."

"That may not help," she pointed out. "It is the mortal physician who has been most successful. He provided the potion that she uses. Likely he was puzzled by what caused her collapse."

Guilt dulled the last of Rhoslyn's anger at Aurelia and warred with her desire to avoid Vidal's consort. But on the other hand, although Rhoslyn did not *like* Elizabeth, she still hated being driven to cause the misery, perhaps even the death, of a child who had never personally hurt her—and all for the sake of an outpouring of power that sickened her. Pasgen watched her silently.

Rhoslyn shrugged. "At least I can stay away from the World Above until Aurelia demands my help. I will tell Mary that my brother needs me again." She hesitated, then sighed. "I wish we could leave Elizabeth alone for good."

There was another brief silence during which Pasgen stared past his sister at nothing. "She has escaped harm so often," he said softly. "Sometimes I think there is *something* that does not want Elizabeth to die or be ruined. And—" he hesitated, then added, slowly "—I am not altogether certain that her most powerful guardian is High King Oberon."

Chapter 24

The sheriff of London came himself to respond to the call from St. James's Palace, because it involved the Lady Elizabeth. It took several hours to find him but once he had been informed of the circumstances, he arrived promptly. And it took every bit of that time to bring Elizabeth to the point where she would promise not to use her ability to shield any person except herself.

In the end, it was only Denoriel's assurance that he would take her Underhill again and have her taught other methods of defense that convinced her. Truthfully, Denoriel was greatly alarmed by the gleam in her golden eyes when she finally offered her promise that as soon as she was *sure* she could save her people by other means she would never use her shield. He had a strong impulse to demand that she also promise not to push those she did not like down a flight of stairs or strike them with flying objects, but he clamped his teeth over the words. It was possible she had not yet thought of that mischief; to put it into her head was lunacy.

The sheriff made no problems. His clerk took Nyle and Shaylor's evidence and made note of Ladbroke's explanation of Stover's behavior. He did come to the palace to question Blanche to make sure her tale agreed with what Ladbroke had told him. Since both were telling the truth, Blanche only added confirming detail. Elizabeth, whom he did not ask any questions, offered voluntarily what she had seen when she arrived at the stable yard.

"I thought he was a madman," she said, in a little-girl voice, blinking back tears. "Blanche has been with me since I was born and I thought he was going to kill her. I was too frightened to give the men any order, but I assure you I would have bid them do everything to save her, so you may say I ordered my men to defend Blanche."

"And so I would do, if it were necessary," the sheriff agreed. "But it seems, Lady Elizabeth, that this will not be necessary. He *was* a madman, for all agree that your armsmen did not kill him. When he realized he could not harm Mistress Parry any further, he turned the knife on himself. Your man Ladbroke seems to think he knew he would face the hangman, and preferred to take his own life."

Having pleased everyone and satisfied himself that no one was to blame and that there never had been any threat to the king's daughter, the sheriff made ready to depart. Mistress Champernowne, following him to the outer door, asked nervously whether there was any need to report the matter to the king since no threat had been directed at Lady Elizabeth, and that, indeed, it was purely by accident that Lady Elizabeth had returned to the stable and been present.

The sheriff hemmed and hawed a bit, but since he had not the slightest desire to bring Henry's irritable attention on himself, since so few people knew of the incident and all of them would be silent, and since Mistress Champernowne explained how very anxious Lady Elizabeth was not to trouble her father when he was so busy planning the war against France, the sheriff had his clerk tear up the pages.

Stover, who had no family, was buried quietly on the waste-ground used for paupers' graves, and Ladbroke found a new groom, solidly honest and respectable, to take his place. In the palace, life returned to normal. Elizabeth studied with Master Grindal in the morning and, depending on the weather, rode or did needlework in the afternoon—except that Denoriel now always met her in the stable rather than in the park.

Normal, however, had little to do with peaceful. Elizabeth wanted the weapons Denoriel had promised her, and she prodded him constantly to arrange for her visit Underhill. The matter was not totally within Denoriel's control; he needed to arrange for lessons with Tangwystl—and he could not find her. She was gone from the Academicia on some business for Queen Titania.

Had it been anyone else, Denoriel would have pursued Tangwystl, since his meetings with Elizabeth were degenerating into sparring matches of "You promised" and "Have patience." However, Denoriel did not want to draw Titania's attention to the situation, and he bemoaned Elizabeth's intransigence and impatience to Harry one day when they were dining together at his house. Harry laughed heartily and reminded him that they had both bewailed the color of Elizabeth's hair even when she was a baby.

"That," Denoriel said, grimacing, "is the horrible truth, but of no help at all."

"Yes, but I think I *can* be of help," Harry said, between chuckles. "I don't suppose you want her taught any of the great magics—"

"Grace of God, no!" Denoriel exclaimed, looking horrified. "I shudder to imagine what she would do with them. Probably turn *me* into a toad. And, anyway, I do not think she has the power to use them—except if she were badly frightened or furiously angry."

"Ah . . ." Harry raised his brows and then shook his head. "I do not think that would be a good time to invoke the greater magics. No, what you would want is some small, simple spells that could delay any threat until Dunstan or her guardsmen arrived."

"Exactly," Denoriel agreed, the corners of his mouth twitching. "Tanglefoot, for instance. Or the ability to push a person without touching him or even coming near."

Harry nodded and grinned. "And let us hope she will not take to pushing those who annoy her down the stairs." He nodded again, looking satisfied. "Elidir or Mechain could teach her such simple spells. Even fire-lighting."

"No!" Denoriel exclaimed, thinking of all too many ways Elizabeth could cause mischief with that spell. "She will surely lose her temper and set someone's hair afire—likely mine! Let us leave out fire-lighting."

Chuckling, Harry agreed to tell his friends not to teach Elizabeth to light fires. Then he frowned. "My only doubts are that they are old, Denno, old. They may not wish to teach a mortal."

Only it seemed that Harry had not realized quite how old Elidir and Mechain were. They had been young in a time when Sidhe and mortal were far closer and they were quite enthusiastic about teaching a mortal child. Add in that Harry was ecstatic at the chance to see Elizabeth again, and they were all in Denoriel's house before he and Elizabeth arrived.

For the purpose of Elizabeth getting her own way, nothing could have been better. She arrived in her nightdress—because Denoriel had decided to take her Underhill while she was supposed to be asleep, thus saving any need for excuses for her absence—looking very small and frail. Harry enveloped her in his arms, and she clung to him, weeping a little with joy. That was more than enough to win her the elder Sidhes' favor; such sweet expressions of emotion were as nectar to their senses. Then he presented her to the two Sidhe. She curtsied prettily to each of them and asked what she should call them.

Denoriel almost groaned aloud as he saw delighted expressions begin to steal over their faces. It was plain in minutes that both were already enslaved and soon would be as besotted as Harry. Denoriel hurried Elizabeth upstairs to change her clothes, but it was already too late.

"Such a sweet child," he heard Elidir say.

"And clever too," Mechain added with a little sigh. "Did you see how bright were her eyes?"

Perhaps if Elizabeth had been slow to learn, they would have grown bored with her. But all her initial awkwardness with doing magic had been rubbed away by Tangwystl, and she responded with eager willingness to their gentler instruction. She learned Tanglefoot quickly, picking up the liquid syllables and repeating them together faultlessly—just as Denoriel was crossing the dining room. He tripped and would have fallen hard if he had not caught himself on the table.

Elizabeth jumped to her feet, her eyes wide, her hands across her mouth. Elidir laughed. Harry choked. Mechain apologized for not having noticed him.

She shook her head, her white hair flowing about her shoulders like a mist. "I should have warned Elizabeth that she must not look at anyone before starting the spell or it would take hold on that person. I am so sorry."

Denoriel gave Elizabeth an "I'll talk to you about this later" look but to Mechain he said, smiling, "She is full of mischief, this mortal, but I am very glad your teaching is bearing fruit."

"Her power is mostly locked within," Elidir said, frowning. "And I cannot see any way to reach it, but she is quick and clever at using what she can touch. With small spells—"

"Will not the one be enough?" Mechain asked. "The child is tired."

That was true. Elizabeth's eyes were heavy-lidded and her shoulders slumped.

"Bessie, why didn't you say you were tired?" Harry cried, going to stand beside her. "Here, love, I'll carry you up to your room and you can sleep. I forgot that Denno brought you here after a full day in the Upper World."

"But I want to learn the other spells," Elizabeth protested, tears coming to her eyes.

"And we want to teach them to you," Mechain said, reassuringly, also coming to her and stroking her hair. "Go up to bed now, sweet child, and we will decide whether to come again or to make this a longer visit. Fear not, Denoriel can return you to your bed an hour or so before dawn, no matter how many days you spend here."

Courteously, Denoriel asked whether waiting now for Elizabeth to wake and eat or returning at some other time would be better for Mechain and Elidir. Both laughed.

"We have little enough to do just now," Elidir said. "We have set traps in Alhambra and must wait some time to ease the suspicions of our enemies before we can spring them. El Dorado . . . that is another problem."

Mechain nodded. "None of us can think of a plan for dealing with the Great Evil. Sawel even brought a priest from the Upper World with his books and candles and holy water. I could swear it laughed . . ."

"Laughed?" Elidir repeated. "I could swear it and what the priest believed were of the same kind, only it was perverted into a kind of madness."

"So Sawel and others are studying what has been done to deal with the Great Evil in the past," Mechain said. "And we, who are not scholars but merely the hands that do the work, are free to teach that enchanting child how to protect herself. The question is what is best for her, and, of course, for you, Denoriel."

"My sole business of late is to guard Elizabeth." Not knowing how much Harry had told them, Denoriel explained the danger that threatened Elizabeth from the Unseleighe-driven forces, and from simple human envy. By that time, Harry had come down and reported that Elizabeth was sound asleep.

Some discussion followed on who must not learn of Elizabeth's absences, what the consequences of such a discovery would be, and how a discovery of the absences might occur. At last Elidir said, "How good is your control of time through the Gates, Denoriel? *Could* you bring her back before morning of the night you took her if we kept her here for some time?"

"I kept Harry for several sleeps—which were probably equivalent to that many days—and brought him back safely perhaps twelve mortal hours after I had taken him Underhill. I am better at magic now, but I would not want the mortal time to be more than ten hours, nine would be better. One more sleep would be safe. If time is compressed too much there can be ill effects on mortals."

Elidir looked at Mechain. "Will that be time enough?"

"It depends." Mechain turned her eyes on Denoriel and he saw how pale and grayed the green had become over the eons; nonetheless, the eyes were bright. "How much magic and how complex you want the child to have."

"As simple as possible and not dangerous. No fire-lighting," he said, just a little sternly. "You call her sweet, but that child has a temper to match the color of her hair and she *is* only a child. If she were a few years older, I would say to teach her anything her limited power could accomplish." He closed his eyes for a moment in thought. "Perhaps when she is older I *will* bring her back for more lessons, but for now I cannot trust her to moderate what she does. It would be best if she had only spells to delay or confound an attack on herself or her maid until she can scream for help. Remember, help is never far from the king's daughter. Her guardsmen are usually right outside her door."

"Then what would be best, I think, is to keep her here this time," Elidir said. "Coming and going is always more dangerous even in the World Above. Gates are not perfect, especially temporary ones, which you said you have set into her maid's chamber, so you want to use them as seldom as possible. Also if you were to be caught in the maid's room, that would be bad. Yes, we will also teach her *gwthio-cilgwthio* and what you call stickfoot, for now."

"She will confuse them," Mechain protested. "Several elements of both spells are similar." Then she nodded. "But, no, *I* know how we can do it in a short time. We can teach her the first spell as soon as she rises and has eaten. Then we will take her to look about Underhill a little. When she is rested and the *gwthio-cilgwthio* spell is cleared from her mind, we can teach her stickfoot."

Since Denoriel agreed that there was no sense in stressing his temporary Gate and that repeated coming and going would more likely be detected than a single absence, he accepted the plan. They ate a meal; Denoriel was able to explain more fully the FarSeers' predictions about the three future rulers. Eventually Harry went up to sleep in Denoriel's bed and the three Sidhe sat together talking.

When Elizabeth woke, she asked at once about the new spells, which made Elidir and Mechain marvel at her eagerness and application. She said she was accustomed to learning and that she took great pleasure in it, and there was no mistaking her pride—nor her certainty that she could master anything she put her mind to.

Mechain carefully explained that magic was different than anything she had learned until now. "A small mistake in a Latin translation only requires scraping out and correction; a small mistake in a spell can have disastrous results."

Elidir then told her their plan for making sure she had the spells well separated. She was delighted with the idea of seeing more of Underhill in between lessons, but what she really wanted to see, she told her doting Da and teachers, was one of the chaos lands. She wanted to see something created from the magical mists.

Elidir and Mechain were enchanted by the idea. Of course a mortal would be interested in creation, they said to each other and, she was Talented. She might even feel the power in the mists. They consulted seriously about which of the Unformed places they knew would be best. Denoriel urged an old one, thinned of most of its power. Elizabeth protested. Her besotted Da and his friends suggested a compromise.

There was a particular place that Elidir and Mechain had been using to create creatures that assisted them in their hunts in Alhambra and El Dorado. They knew the place to be particularly sensitive to creation, and although the beasts they had made were dangerous, they were quite certain that they had not allowed any of them to escape. In addition, the creatures were keyed not to attack *them* and, of course, Harry would stand by with his gun in case all else failed.

"And when you have created something for me, we can go to one of the markets, can we not?" Elizabeth asked, bright-eyed . . . and boldly biting off the whole hand since a finger had been offered. "And will you buy me something that I *can* bring back with me so I can remember you all better?" she begged pathetically.

"Of course I will—"

Denoriel sighed. That had been a chorus of three voices. But there were also expressions of surprise at what the child had said, and Denoriel murmured quickly, "*Nic yn awr.*"

Later, while Elidir was teaching Elizabeth not only the spell but how to create it and store it, all except the invoking word, so it was ready for use in a moment, Denoriel drew Mechain aside and explained to her why Elizabeth had been convinced that nothing the Sidhe had was real in the World Above unless it was specially bespelled.

"If she is queen and hard pressed for funds, might she not come here to take home gold for her needs . . . if she believed the gold would save her realm?" he pointed out. "Even Queen Titania had that fear, and I think it is a wise one. I do not say she would wish to do it, but necessity is a hard master, and we cannot answer for what the adult will do that the child would never even consider."

"Mortals were not thus in the past," Mechain sighed. "Yet I know what you say is true, for it was mortals, driven by this perverted spirit, that destroyed Alhambra and El Dorado. It is sad to lie to a child, but a wise precaution."

Elidir, having completed his lesson, called Mechain to test Elizabeth's comprehension and accomplishment. They went out into the palace and found a few human servants upon whom Elizabeth could use *gwthio-cilgwthio.* First she sharply shoved an innocent boy, fortunately only carrying linens, down a long corridor so that the tablecloths flew every which way out of his arms. Mechain applauded the correct use of *gwthio.*

Next Elizabeth caused one of the mortal grooms in the stable to be unable to reach the manger he was going to clear, pushing him back every time he tried to step forward. That was an adequate demonstration of her understanding and use of *cilgwthio.* It was also, Mechain pointed out, a good example of the difference in result produced by one half syllable and a slightly higher tone of voice. Elizabeth took serious note of what Mechain said . . . and then pushed another groom so that he sat down suddenly in a pile of manure.

Mechain was laughing too much to reprove her charge adequately and she brought a happily giggling Elizabeth back, singing praises to how well the child had learned and how competently she had used the spells.

"I never doubted that she would learn," Denoriel said sourly. "Elizabeth learns everything well and easily, but did you tell her that she is only to use the spells when they are necessary for protection?"

Elizabeth sniffed.

Elidir chuckled and said, "She is only a child, Denoriel. A little playfulness . . ."

"A little playfulness in the mortal world could get her called 'witch' and send her to the gallows or the stake," Denoriel said sharply, then turned to her and added, "Did you hear me, Elizabeth? If people continually trip on their own feet, fall down stairs, or cannot reach a goal in your presence, the accidents will soon be connected with you. Think how quickly Stafford ran to report that you were meeting a man in the garden. Think what he would say if you were always present about so many 'accidents.' Nothing would protect you then. Think how many people would be pleased to call you 'witch'! And while you are at it, think about who would or could be accused of teaching you witchcraft, and what would happen to them!"

He did not remind her that her mother had been (and often was still) called a witch. That it was not on the charge of witchcraft, but adultery, that she had been executed was perhaps only because Henry had found "evidence" enough for the latter charge.

And Blanche *was* a witch. She would certainly go to the stake. Kat Champernowne might. Her faithful menservants might come in for accusation. And certainly her beloved tutors would. The stain might even spread upward, to the queen.

Elizabeth hung her head; Harry came close and put an arm around her. "Love, Denno's right. You need to be careful."

"I *always* need to be careful," Elizabeth said tearfully.

Harry dropped a kiss on her head. "I know—and I really *do* know. It was like that for me, too. It isn't much fun to be always watched and need to be careful. I wish there were something I could do, but even if I could live in the World Above I would be more harm than help. We could hardly ever be together and never alone—your enemies and mine would say we were conspiring against Prince Edward."

"Oh, I never would," Elizabeth cried. "Edward is my brother and a very good, sweet, little boy. I love him."

"You know that and I know that," Harry said sadly. "*I* never wanted to be king. It made my skin crawl to think of bearing that burden. But no one ever believed me."

"You never wanted to be king, Da?" she asked, sounding surprised.

"No, love." Harry kissed her again, this time on the forehead. "I would have been a very bad king. I would never have been able to do anything to curb or reprove a friend, and soon, I think, the nobles would have been having their own way of it, quarreling among themselves, tearing England apart, and leaving us open to our enemies. You are different, I think. I believe you would not wish harm to Edward, but there is something in you . . ." He shook his head. "I think others see it too. I think you would make a good king—yes, I say *king*, because you have the stomach of a king, and would need no man beside you to rule. Because of that, you must be even more careful than I was. Listen to Denno and Alana."

Elizabeth sighed, and a single tear ran down her cheek. "I do. I do. But it isn't any fun."

Elidir and Mechain, who had been watching and listening, now came close. Mechain wiped the tear from Elizabeth's cheek and Elidir said, "I am sure Denoriel and Harry have given you advice it would be wise to follow in the World Above, but now you are Underhill with us, and there is no reason at all why you should not have all the play and pleasure you want."

Elizabeth stared at Elidir for a moment with a look of surprise, but then she smiled and took the hand he held out to her. "That is true!" she exclaimed. "Here in Underhill it does not matter that I am King Henry's daughter. Here I can just be Elizabeth."

Denoriel's lips parted to warn her that Underhill could be as dangerous to her as the World Above, but she looked so young and full of joy, her mouth soft and smiling instead of drawn into a tense line, her eyes wide with anticipation. He could not spoil the little while she had to be a carefree child. He would be doubly wary, he told himself, as they all left his apartment.

When they stepped out onto the portico of Llachar Lle, there were four elvensteeds waiting at the foot of the steps. Lady Aeron's delicate blue and Miralys's ebon black contrasted with the pale dappled silver and pearly white of the other two steeds. They were as perfect of form as Harry's and Denoriel's mounts, but something about them, like the faded eyes of their riders, hinted of long millennia of living.

Harry took Elizabeth up on Lady Aeron before Denoriel reached them, the elvensteed providing a comfortable pillion before she was even asked.

"I need to get my gun," Harry called back.

So they all rode to Mwynwen's house. She did not come out to greet them but Harry explained when he emerged, loading several of the flat, top-seated cartridges with iron bolts, that she was gone to help Ceindrych with a difficult patient. Before he mounted, he slid the gun and cartridges into a spelled holder which he fastened to his belt. Once inside, the weapon and its iron bolts caused no discomfort, but the holder would allow Harry to draw the gun and its cartridges at a word.

Harry offered drink or food, but had no takers. They had all eaten when Elizabeth had broken her fast. So then they were off again, Elidir and Mechain leading this time.

An old Gate not far from the Healers' houses took them to a quiet, pleasant hold. The ground was gently rolling, covered with the ubiquitous soft green moss and small white flowers. Graceful trees leaned gently this way and that, some standing alone, some in elegant groups, their trailing leaves rustling gently. A narrow brook followed the gentle valleys; wildflowers grew on the banks. Here and there was a glimpse of a tiled roof, a white wall.

"Old Elves Hame," Elidir said with a wry twist of the lips. "Perfect in every way. The ideal place to be bored into Dreaming, but—"

At which moment a loud explosion rent the air. Everyone jumped. Even the elvensteeds looked startled.

"Oh, my," Mechain said. "Sawel must have done something thoroughly unacceptable to the holy water."

"Shall I go and see if he's all right?" Denoriel asked.

"It can't hurt *him*," Elidir said, "but he might have to rebuild his house."

Elizabeth giggled. "It seems lively enough here to me. Can we go see the exploded house?"

"Better not," Mechain said. "Sawel will be in a temper. Besides, there really isn't anything to see. When the spells holding the house together are broken, it just disappears. And the last time, all Sawel's clothes disappeared too." She smiled, looking ridiculously youthful despite the faded eyes and thin, mist-white hair. "You're a little too young for that, sweetling."

"And it doesn't do much good for Sawel's disposition either," Elidir remarked. "Doubtless there are going to be a lot of toads and worms around until his curses wear off. We'd better just go on and show Elizabeth how to make something nice out of mist. All ready? I'll spell us through. The terminus Gate is smaller, but the area around it is safe so anyone can step off."

Again there was that brief sensation of falling and utter blackness, but this time Elizabeth was not in the least afraid. She could feel Lady Aeron's silky side against her ankle where her skirt had hiked up and her arms were firmly around her Da's waist. And, of course, she had hardly enough time to think of it when they were out into a real pea-soup of a fog. Lady Aeron stepped delicately down from the Gate. Miralys, who had been behind her, stepped down to her right, and Elidir and Mechain on their steeds came down to the left immediately after.

"So, this, my dear, is an Unformed land. Now we dismount and walk a little way into mist," Elidir said, suiting his action to his words.

Harry set Elizabeth on her feet but kept a grip on her hand. "Don't wander away without holding on to me or to Denno," he said. "The mist is very thick and can thicken even more. And it makes sound very deceptive, so if you get lost it will take us a long time to find you."

"I won't get lost," Elizabeth said. "If we do get separated, don't worry. I'll just come back to the Gate and wait right here for you."

"You won't be able to see the Gate," Denoriel warned, coming up from the side. "A few steps away and it will seem to disappear."

Elizabeth did not argue, partly because she wasn't sure how to explain why she was certain she could find the Gate again. Besides, she was very happy holding Harry's hand and feeling like any little girl with a doting relative. She skipped after Elidir and Mechain, who could just be made out through the swirling mists.

"Let her come between us," Mechain said, "so she can see what we do. And you, Harry, just step off to the side where you will have a clear shot at anything coming at us. Denoriel, if you will go to the left and stand ready with your sword, we will be grateful."

"I thought you said you had cleaned out the inimical creatures," Denoriel said, drawing his sword.

"We are reasonably sure we did, but a really creative mist like this one . . . I have sometimes felt we took away more than we had designed."

"You mean the mist created more by *itself*?"

"I don't know." Elidir sounded troubled. "Possibly it just echoed what I was doing. Possibly . . . No." He shook his head at Denoriel and turned toward Elizabeth. "Now what would you like us to make, love?"

"A bird," Elizabeth said promptly.

Just as promptly the mist roiled differently. A patch just before Elidir pinched off from the main mass and began to curl around and around. Wide-eyed, Elizabeth watched. She could feel a kind of pressure, not unlike the pressure she felt when creating a shield, but yet different.

There was something behind the pressure, a *willing*. As soon as she identified what she felt, Elizabeth almost called up her shield. She had felt that *willing* before, when the bad Sidhe that looked so much like Denoriel had tried to kill her in the garden. But now the *willing* was not directed at her; it was causing the pinched off bit of mist to grow more solid and, as it solidified, to change.

Indistinct at first but becoming clearer and more defined, wide wings spread. An indefinite blob soon had huge glowing eyes, a cruel hooked beak. Feathers fluffed, feathered legs under an oval body now showed long, sharp talons that opened and closed spasmodically.

An owl. A very *large* owl, bigger than any such beast that Elizabeth had ever seen before. She was used to the comical, monkey-faced barn owls that lived in every stable in the country, but this was four, five times the size of one of those. This one had enormous yellow eyes, not dark eyes, and two hornlike tufts of feathers on the top of its head. Elizabeth took an involuntary step backward.

"Whhooo," the bird cried.

The wings flapped, very silently. The bird rose into the air, circled, uttered its questioning cry again, and flew off. Elizabeth watched, lips parted with wonder, eyes wide.

"Ah!" Elidir shook his head. "I had meant to make a smaller bird, but it has become such a habit to make hunting beasts—"

"It was beautiful," Elizabeth breathed, then looked concerned. "But will it find anything to eat here? The place looks so barren."

"While it is here, it will not need food," Mechain said. "It will draw in power and sustenance from the mist."

Still Elizabeth frowned. "I know it is said that owls are very wise. Will the poor bird not be bored to death being all alone and having nothing to do?"

"We will not leave it here long," Elidir assured her. "We will transport it to a place where it will find enough to hunt. Now, what else would you like to have made?"

Elizabeth giggled. "A rabbit? I do not think you will be able to make that into anything fierce—but if you can, I would surely like to see a fierce rabbit."

There was a stirring in the mist off to the left that went against the general drift and curl. Denoriel lifted his sword and stepped forward toward the denser spot. Elizabeth felt a sharp prod of *will*, again not directed at her, and the mist flowed smoothly again.

"I do not think a rabbit would last long in this mist-land," Mechain said. "Perhaps you would like a bouquet of flowers?"

"Then I would have to carry them." Elizabeth giggled again. "How about a little patch of garden, right here where we stand. That would be a great surprise to anyone who came to this Gate."

"Hmmm. And a pleasant place for us to sit while we work, but not easy to do. Let me talk to Elidir about this."

Elizabeth obligingly moved toward Harry so the two Sidhe could be closer together. He was well off to the side, just visible in the mist. She started to speak to him, but he was watching the mist intently, his gun in his hand. Elizabeth looked out at the mist too. There, not far from her a patch seemed somehow a little separate. She looked at it, imagining upright pointed ears, large bright eyes, a rounded furry body, four legs, a long fluffy tail . . . and wings.

She saw an adorable kitten. Elizabeth liked kittens. She wished the kitten was real, wished hard . . . And there was a flapping noise and a kitten plopped into her arms.

Simultaneously she heard Elidir and Mechain call her name and the next moment they came running out of the mist with Denoriel on their heels.

"What happened?" Mechain cried. "We felt the mists wrenched, as if in birthing, but we had *willed* nothing. Has something threatened you?"

Elizabeth laughed and held out the kitten. "I think I made this."

There was a moment of stunned silence and then Elidir whispered, "You *think* you created a . . . a living thing?"

Bright-eyed and grinning, Elizabeth explained how Harry was too intent on his guard duty to talk to her and how she thought she saw two pointed ears. When she got to the kitten popping into her arms, she shook her head.

"Poor thing," she said, "it's the color of the mist. I never got around to thinking of colors for it."

"It doesn't need color," Mechain said, tickling the kitten's head. "That silvery beige is very pretty."

Elizabeth had settled the kitten comfortably in the crook of her arm and now looked at Denoriel. "Can I keep it, Denno? Could your servants take care of it, or maybe Lady Alana? I know I can't take it home, but it wouldn't be safe to leave it here. The owl would get it, or one of the things Da is watching out for. It isn't mean. It likes people."

"So I see," Denoriel said. "Did you really create that, Elizabeth? Or is this something you and your new friends cooked up to tease me?"

"No, Lord Denoriel," Elidir said. "I swear on the Great Mother that Mechain and I were surprised half out of our wits when we felt a making taking place. "And we felt it from the direction in which we had sent Elizabeth to be with Harry. We both called her name and ran to where we thought she must be. It had to have been her making."

"Indeed it is her making," Mechain added. "There is no other Sidhe in this place, only you and we two." She looked around in a worried way, met and held Elidir's eyes, and then said, "We will not make that garden here. Perhaps this mist has been used too often."

"And I think Elizabeth has seen quite enough of the chaos lands," Elidir said, eyeing the kitten. "Perhaps we should move on to the Goblin Fair now."

Mechain cleared her throat. "I've lost the Gate," she said, reluctantly. "I'll need a little while to orient myself—"

"It's that way," Elizabeth interrupted, pointing.

"That way," Elidir repeated, his gaze fixed on Elizabeth, his voice flat.

"Likely it is," Harry said, grinning. "Elizabeth has odd Talents. She can see through illusion—"

"Not here," Elizabeth remarked. "I see the meadow and the trees and the manor out of Denno's windows just like everyone else, and he says that's an illusion. And I don't see the Gate. There's just a place where I feel the mist isn't and a humming. I think that's the Gate. That's what it felt like when we stepped out of it."

Mechain, Elidir, and Denoriel all stared at her as if she had grown an extra head. Elizabeth looked from one to the other anxiously, wondering for the first time if she had done something wrong. Then Harry came up behind her, put his arm around her waist and swept her forward in the direction she had pointed.

"Never mind, love," he said laughing. "They are only wondering why they never thought of feeling for the Gate."

Mechain cleared her throat again. "That's true, young mortal. We can see an open Gate, and that is what we look for. Once you pointed out the effect of the power of the Gate, we too could feel it. Just, we never connected the concentration of power with the Gate."

By the time Mechain finished speaking, the Gate was in sight with the four elvensteeds grouped around it, grazing.

"Grazing?" Mechain said. "From whence came the grass? Elidir, does it seem to you that we should look for a different Unformed place?"

"Yes. Yes indeed." Elidir agreed. "Grazing. But there was no grass when we came." He sighed, looked at Elizabeth accusingly.

"It wasn't me," she protested. "God's Grace, I was nowhere near. It wasn't me."

They all looked suspiciously at the elvensteeds, who ignored them and continued to crop grass. Then they all looked out at the mist, but it was behaving in a perfectly normal way.

After a few moments, Elizabeth sighed heavily and then asked plaintively, "Can we go to the market now?"

Chapter 25

Pasgen stepped out of the fourth Gate he had transited on his way home from Rhoslyn's domain, frowning. It was a nuisance, he thought, looking around the Goblin Fair, to waste so much time in devising devious routes so that no one could identify his home or Rhoslyn's. Then he smiled. They both had been extra careful since he had found and retrieved the token of Rhoslyn's skin and flesh their mother had given Vidal.

The retrieval had not been very difficult, using the lindys. *That was a nice piece of mutual work*, Pasgen thought as he walked into the body of the market. Rhoslyn had created the little creatures, but he had modified the spells on them so that they were much more useful.

His eyes lingered for a moment on a memory book displayed open on a counter. Words began to form on the clear blank pages. He sought the key. It was a simple one; he found it and erased the words. He chuckled softly as he turned away. Vidal could use one of those. Likely he did not even know the token was lost . . . if he remembered ever having it.

Pasgen glanced around and oriented himself. He knew the market very well because of passing through so often. Now, which Gate should he use this time? He had sensed no interest in him since he left Rhoslyn's domain and Vidal was not even at Caer Mordwyn. Still, he would take the Gate to that Unformed land that was so peculiarly alive. The echoes that resonated in that mist would totally confuse anything that clung to him.

On his way, he noticed a narrow booth that had no real occupant. A lifeless simulation smiled and beckoned to anyone who approached the booth and proffered a sheet of paper. Doubtless it had a name and address and an explanation of what the owner of the booth offered.

Pasgen hesitated, walked up to the booth and examined it carefully. He did not take the sheet the simulation offered. He was not the least bit interested in torture and murder no matter how lifelike the simulacra were. It was the booth and the idea of advertising for clients that interested him.

Rhoslyn had told him about his mother's desire to set up as a healer—and not confine her work to those of the Unseleighe domains. Pasgen's immediate reaction had been to forbid such a harebrained scheme, but Rhoslyn's suggestion of using the empty house and the change in his mother had both worked on him. He continued to walk toward his goal, now examining the people who patronized the Goblin Fair.

There were every kind. A party of mortals laughing and joking among themselves passed him—possibly changelings stolen from the World Above, but also possibly mortal mages, who had keys to come here. Two Sidhe, definitely Bright Court, came from a side aisle. They glanced at him. One started to raise a hand in greeting and then dropped it. Pasgen lifted the side of his lip. Faery-folk flitted here and there. A group of dark Sidhe came from an aisle opposite the Bright Court Sidhe. They stopped abruptly and stared. Pasgen heard the heavy tramp of an ogre behind him.

Certainly Llanelli was right about there being a wide enough range of folk to be clients. And with a simulacrum—Pasgen had found the lifeless simulation rather unpleasant and Rhoslyn could provide a much better booth-tender—to hand out the sheets and even answer simple questions, Llanelli might well draw some clients.

Whether any Bright Sidhe would be willing to be attended by a Dark Court healer was a different problem entirely. Pasgen hoped not. It would be safer for Llanelli if her clientele was principally Unseleighe or those, like the gnomes and fauns and nymphs, who had allegiance to neither court. But when she explained what she wanted to do, Llanelli was so much more *alive*, almost what he remembered her to have been like when he and Rhoslyn were children, before Vidal had bent so much of her spirit in trying to break it, and before she had sought oblivion in drugs and Dreaming.

Pasgen swung left and saw ahead of him the area in which those who came to the Fair left their transportation. The Gate he wanted was at the far end of that field. The ogre's steps were getting too close. Pasgen stepped aside between two booths just as four elvensteeds came up to the end of the transport area. He heard the ogre grunt with anger and sheer off in the opposite direction.

Two ancient Bright Court Sidhe slid down from equally ancient elvensteeds. The male hurried over to another elvensteed which was, inexplicably, carrying a young mortal man and held up his arms to . . .

Elizabeth! Pasgen could hardly believe his eyes. That fool Denoriel, just dismounting from his own elvensteed, had brought the girl Underhill! Pasgen's eyes glowed. Now he would have her! The mortals who had passed him a few moments ago would make perfect tools. And had he not seen fauns and nymphs . . . and goblins, too?

The fauns and nymphs could be set to dancing and playing a silly game, then the goblins could try to join in. No matter if the goblins had no evil intent, the nymphs and fauns would panic. Pasgen drew a deep breath of satisfaction. Utter confusion would result—not enough for *Removal* but enough for his purpose. Pasgen watched for one more moment to be sure that the party was coming in to the Fair and then slipped away in the direction he had seen the mortals going when they passed him.

Denoriel was somewhat anxious about taking Elizabeth to one of the great markets, but Elidir and Mechain and Harry, who had proposed the Goblin Fair because it had more of the kind of toys that might amuse a child, had no doubts. Three Sidhe and a mortal should surely be enough to protect one girl-child at the Goblin Fair which, like the other great markets, did not allow the use of weapons or violence. And, again, he could not bear to disappoint Elizabeth, who was dancing about on her toes—with the winged kitten she had created in her arms—flushed and eager.

The Gate they had almost lost in the mists of the chaos land took them safely back to Old Elves Hame Gate where Elidir called up a subsidiary control plaque. That there could be such a device caused Denoriel to raise his eyebrows. His surprise made the old Sidhe chuckle.

"We could not pattern and repattern," Elidir admitted, "but we could have as many controls as we wanted. True, you have to touch it, not think at it. This one only has the three markets as termini."

"Most of us had nowhere else to go and nothing to do so we used to go to the markets a lot." Mechain laughed. "But since the advent of this busybody—" she smiled at Harry "—we have plenty to keep us occupied. For today though, the Goblin Fair it is."

And darkness and falling were replaced by a enormous open space in which were set, tied, chained, and otherwise fastened every kind of beast and vehicle Elizabeth had ever seen—and a great many that she was sure no one on earth had ever seen. She would have begged to get down and walk, although the distance was considerable, just to look at the weird beasts and even weirder conveyances, but the elvensteeds were already cantering down a wide central aisle to what was apparently an entry to the Fair itself.

A high arch over the aisle said GOBLIN FAIR and below that ALL WELCOME. But directly in front of the arch, so that one had to walk to one side or the other to pass, was a large notice board that said NO SPELLS, NO DRAWN WEAPONS, NO VIOLENCE and below those words another line: ON PAIN OF PERMANENT REMOVAL.

"How strange," Elizabeth said.

"What's strange, love?" Harry asked, and then began to laugh. "Now that was a stupid question. I'm sure everything is pretty strange to you."

"Yes." Elizabeth laughed too, but she pointed to the signs. "It's strange that the words should be in English . . . isn't it?"

"Oh no, they're much stranger than that," Denoriel said, coming up on her other side. "The signs are in any language whoever is looking at them can read. And, I suspect, if the being can't read—like an ogre or an imp—what the sign says makes speech or . . . or just *is* inside their heads."

"And they mean what they say," Harry said, accepting a silver wire from Denoriel and fastening it across the place where the holder opened to let him seize his gun.

"They do indeed mean what they say," Denoriel warned, wiring the hilt of his sword to the scabbard. "The *Removal* is permanent. No one I know of has ever found out to where the being is *Removed*, and I've never heard of anyone coming back either. While you're here, Elizabeth, no spells, no mischief, no fighting."

She shook her head. "Really, Denno, when have you ever known me to strike anyone?"

He laughed. "That tongue of yours can draw blood."

About to riposte as they passed under the arch, instead Elizabeth stopped to stare at still another huge sign blocking the aisle. This one said CAVEAT EMPTOR.

"What language is that sign in, Denno?" she asked.

"Elven for me. What is it for you, Harry?"

"Same as it's always been. Latin. 'Buyer beware.' I wonder why it's in Latin rather than English?"

"To fix your mind on it better," Elizabeth said. "When I *have* to remember something, I usually write it down in French. Then it sticks in my head."

Denoriel smiled and then sobered. "That's another sign that means what it says. It's said of the Goblin Fair that if you find your heart's desire here and can purchase it, to have it will make your heart break."

But Elizabeth wasn't listening. They had passed around the sign and she was staring from side to side at the brilliantly colored booths with their counters full of an endless variety of goods. She hurried to the right to pick up an exquisite comb carved of horn and set with sparkling jewels. The vendor began to tell her of the wonderful things the comb would do for her hair. He was a tall, very thin being, apparently unclothed except for the flashing scales on his skin. From the way his body bent and his arm curved, he seemed boneless. And when he lifted another comb, seemingly of ivory, Elizabeth could see that his fingers—of which there were too many to count—were webbed almost to their tips.

"Do you want that, dear heart?" Harry asked, a hand on his purse.

"Perhaps," Elizabeth replied, smiling at him, "but not now. We have barely come in." She looked around. "I can see that it is not possible to visit the entire Fair, but I need to look a little farther before I decide." She looked up at the vendor. "Thank you for telling me about the combs. I will remember. We must pass this way to leave the Fair so I will have a second chance to look at your combs."

They went forward a few feet before Elizabeth darted left to examine some ribbons. Those did not hold her long, although they were of colors no person from the World Above would ever see. However, they twisted and writhed in a way that made her think of worms on a hook and she put them down and backed away.

The momentary disgust passed in wonder over a kaleidoscope that showed not patterns of crystals but moving pictures of people at a dinner and then dancing and then climbing a stair and then . . . "Oh!" Elizabeth said; Harry took the tube and put it to his eye, also said, "Oh!" and put the instrument back on the counter.

"My fault," Denoriel said, beginning to laugh. "Look there. It says 'Cycle of Life.' But I didn't know it would show everything."

They wandered on. Mechain bought Elizabeth a frozen treat on a stick. It was lusciously sweet and rich but so cold it made her teeth ache so she could not bite it and it started to melt. That was easily attended. The kitten quickly licked all the drips off her hand and cleaned up the bottom of the stick too.

The vendor there looked mortal, except that his eyes were strange, almost without pupils behind large spectacles. It was safe to eat, Mechain assured Denoriel. But Elizabeth had already gone ahead with Elidir who was showing her a small but beautifully engraved silver mirror. Elizabeth held it up to her face, and gasped.

"What is it, child?" the old Sidhe asked, putting his arm around her as she shuddered and handed him the mirror. He looked, shook his head. "I only see my face, sweetling. What do you see?"

"Also my face," Elizabeth replied, but in a breathless, shaking voice, and tilted the mirror so that it showed both of them.

Elidir looked like Elidir, the skin perhaps a trifle more transparent, the hair whiter, thinner. And Elizabeth looked like Elizabeth, but her face was different, taut with tension, hard with ambition, and the eyes . . . the eyes were almost as old as those of Elidir.

The Sidhe put the mirror down. Elizabeth reached toward it as if she would pick it up, and a squat, wide-mouthed goblin popped up behind the counter.

"The mirror is priceless," the goblin began. "With it you can see inside those you must deal with. You can see—" Its voice checked and its eyes fastened on the kitten, which was suddenly squirming in Elizabeth's grip. "What is that?"

"A kitten," Elizabeth replied, using the hand that had been reaching toward the mirror to stroke the little creature to quiet it.

"With wings?"

She tilted her head to one side. "Ah, I am not quite sure how that came about."

"Can it fly?" the goblin asked, and suddenly stretched a very small, stubby pair of wings on its own back.

"A little," Elizabeth said, recalling that it had got from where it was created to her in the Unformed land, but not very gracefully and it had virtually fallen into her arms. The kitten was now squirming more violently. "Poor thing, I think it wants to get down, but I can't let it go. It will get lost and stepped on."

"Give it to me," the goblin said. "I will put it down in the booth."

"You will give it back?" Harry said, coming up from behind.

"If the little mistress wants it back, yes."

Elizabeth, who was in the act of handing the kitten across the counter, almost snatched it back, but it leapt from her hands to the goblin's naked shoulder where it stood, its claws unsheathed and digging into the goblin's skin. The goblin seemed totally unaware that the claws should hurt. It raised a hand to tickle the kitten under the chin, and the kitten responded with a rasping purr. A beatific smile widened the goblin's mouth until it seemed the creature's head would split in two.

"You want the mirror?" the goblin asked. "Look again. Look at your friends, at those who say they love you. Know the truth. I will trade you the mirror for the kitten."

Elizabeth's hand went out toward the mirror. She pulled it back. "That would not be fair," she said. "The kitten is a construct. I do not know how long it will . . . exist."

The kitten rubbed its furry head against the goblin's cheek. It closed its eyes and stroked the kitten with one finger, careful of the wings.

"For an hour or a day or however long it can live," the goblin said.

Elizabeth reached for the mirror again, but paused before she touched it. She examined the goblin's rather horrendous appearance, the green-gray leatherlike skin, the round, flat yellow eyes, the wide mouth where bottom teeth peeped over the upper lip and fangs hung down from the upper jaw, the cruel, curved claws on the hands. Her eyes slid to the mirror but she did not pick it up.

"I don't want the kitten to be frightened or hurt," she said. "Not the mirror nor anything else is worth that."

"Does it look frightened?" the goblin asked. "And I will swear to you that I will do nothing to hurt it and I will not let anyone else hurt it."

"Elizabeth," Denoriel said. "Take back the kitten. I will care for it. I told you so. That mirror is an evil thing. It will break your heart."

"It is *not* evil," the goblin said. "It is mindless justice without mercy, but not evil."

Denoriel snatched up the mirror, pulled Elizabeth to his side, and held the mirror so she could see his face. He expected it to be deformed into a mask of greed, lechery, and hate, but it was not. The mirror showed his face, but lined with pain and worry, the large eyes full of fear. Elizabeth uttered a sob and pulled the mirror down. Harry snatched it away and looked into it. His glance traveled from Denoriel to Elizabeth.

"What?" he asked. "What is wrong? It shows my face, that's all."

Elizabeth came around beside him to look and the shock drained out of her expression. Her Da looked younger, the lines of pain graved around his mouth and between his brows during his illness were gone. Love shone in his eyes and sweetness and goodness dwelt in the curve of the lips.

"Oh, Da," Elizabeth said and flung her arms around his neck. "Oh, Da. As long as you are here and I know you are safe and well, I will never be afraid." Then suddenly she sighed and uttered a frustrated laugh. To the goblin, she said, "I've been a fool. I would take the mirror, but I must return to the World Above and I cannot bring anything made with magic there."

The creature stroked the kitten gently. "The mirror was not made in this world. There are things here that come from—" he shrugged "—elsewhere. Metals not known Underhill or in the World Above, tools that do things on their own if a being activates them. The mirror is not Underhill magic. Whether it will work in the World Above, I do not know." It shrugged again. "As you do not know how long the kitten will exist."

"Don't, Elizabeth!" Denoriel pleaded. "It is better not to know some things."

"Mayhap," she said softly, picking the mirror up and tucking it into the pouch tied to her belt. But then she took Denoriel's hand, which she held very tight. "It showed me the truth about you, Denno, and about my Da. It might break my heart . . . but it might save my life, too."

"What's the matter?" Harry asked again.

"The mirror shows what's inside a person, Harry," Denoriel said, his voice reflecting his inner tension.

Harry shook his head, completely bewildered. "No, it doesn't. It just showed my face."

Denoriel began to laugh. "Yes, Harry. It just showed what you are—better than gold, better than anything in this world or the World Above."

"Does the mirror—"

Elizabeth had turned toward the inside of the booth, intending to ask if the mirror needed any special care, but the goblin was gone as was the kitten, and the counter in front of the booth was empty. Elizabeth's hand flew to her pouch, but the mirror was there, and when she looked into it, it showed the same hard face that she had seen before.

"I'm not sure I like that," Denoriel said. "It's as if he and the booth were set here just to attract Elizabeth. Let me see that mirror again and make sure there is no spell in it that will slowly affect her."

Somewhat reluctantly Elizabeth took the mirror from her pouch. Denoriel looked at it, felt it, touched it with his tongue, finally shook his head. Mechain took it from his hand and stared at it, obviously extending her senses. After a moment she also shook her head and handed the mirror to Elidir.

"It has no magic at all," Elidir said, sounding shocked. "No magic I can sense." He shuddered slightly. "How can it do what it does without magic?"

"There is power in it," Denoriel said with knitted brows, "I could feel it, but I cannot touch it. It is a different kind of power than what we use."

Elidir was also frowning. "And Elizabeth did not choose the mirror. She was looking at a strange thing with a black panel. The goblin pushed a button and pictures that moved formed on the panel. I did not like the pictures for a young girl so I showed her the mirror." He cocked his head. "Does it not seem to you, Denoriel, that the goblin was strange?"

"Its tenderness to the kitten was certainly unlike any goblin I know," Mechain said.

"That was not pretense?" Harry asked.

The three Sidhe all shook their heads. "One can feel the anger and evil in them," Denoriel said, then smiled. "You always react to them with loathing, Harry. How comes it that you did not pull Elizabeth away from the booth?"

"I don't know." Harry frowned. "I didn't feel the disgust I usually do."

"What does it matter?" Elizabeth asked. "The mirror is still here and it still works." She tucked her prize away again.

Mechain said, "No harm. But I will say this, that I have never felt from a goblin what I felt when it stroked that construct. If I dared to think that a goblin could love anything, I would say that it loved that kitten. Long may it live."

Denoriel still seemed uneasy, but there was no sense in standing by the empty booth. They continued on, looking at this and that. Elizabeth was transfixed by a huge roasted drumstick. She kept shaking her head and saying she could not imagine what kind of chicken could grow such a leg and that she surely did not want to meet it. Elidir laughed and bought the leg and when she bit into it her eyes widened with pleasure.

"It isn't chicken," she said, handing the leg to Harry.

He took a bite and agreed with her strongly enough to walk back and purchase a leg for each member of the party. They walked along, eating, stopping at still another booth to buy cloth to wipe their greasy hands and chins. Then they stopped in a tent where drinks were served. Elizabeth asked for ale, which she said would go best with the taste of the leg she was eating. Elidir and Mechain obtained mead. Harry and Denoriel drank wine.

As time passed, the worried frown smoothed from Denoriel's brow. They talked of the strange wares offered for sale. Elizabeth was particularly interested in the books, Harry in the weapons, most especially in those that used cold iron in some form, Mechain and Elidir in spells, some on single sheets, some in grimoires. Eventually, rested and drinks finished, they rose and walked on, but this time they did not get far.

Just ahead, the aisle they had been walking down debouched into an open area. It was not very large, perhaps as large as two great halls, but five other aisles also opened into it, and around the sides were not more booths of merchandise but platforms upon which various acts and entertainments were being displayed.

Elizabeth cried out with delight and darted ahead. The rest of her party followed, but not urgently. The acts had plenty of watchers, but the open space was not crowded and Elizabeth could be seen plainly. Harry caught up with her as she watched a set of tumblers, who were performing really phenomenal acts of levitation. He was surprised to see that she looked faintly disapproving.

"They cheat," Elizabeth said, when he asked what fault she could find with the act. "They are using magic to add to their balance and the height they can leap. I think without that help they would not be as good as some tumblers I have seen in the World Above."

Harry raised an eyebrow at her. "You object to magic?"

Elizabeth laughed and tugged Harry toward the next stage. It held a magician who was creating waterfalls of sparkling color, which then ran away onto the audience's shoes, dying them.

"Ugh," Harry said, as his modest brown boots turned bright yellow and twinkled. "I wonder how long it will last?"

Farther along an ogre was displaying feats of strength, and Harry stopped suddenly to watch him. "Hmmm," he said, gesturing Mechain and Elidir closer. "You two should think about ways to bind a few such creatures to our service. Their strength might be useful in uncovering some of the hidden ways."

"Having an ogre take service with us would be easy." Elidir remarked. "Keeping it from falling into the power of that which whispers to us in those accursed lost hames and domains would be far more difficult. I would think twice—Harry, where is Elizabeth?"

Harry caught his breath and whirled around, but Elizabeth was in sight, about halfway across the open area, and Denoriel was not far behind her. All three breathed sighs of relief. Elidir opened his mouth to continue what he had been saying, and a sudden rush of laughing nymphs and fauns almost knocked him down and whirled Harry and Mechain around. They all pelted off toward the center of the area where they began to dance in little groups, laughing and singing.

"I don't like that!" Mechain said.

"Oh, they don't mean any harm." Harry laughed.

"No, Mechain's right," replied Elidir, frowning. "They are all sucking sweets."

"Is that harmful?" Harry asked.

"No, but it makes them very wild and excited. No one in a market will sell fauns and nymphs sweets because, meaning no harm, they can be destructive in their wildness."

"Elizabeth!" Harry exclaimed.

He could not see her among the whirling figures and Denoriel seemed to have disappeared too. Harry and the two older Sidhe started forward, but were buffeted aside—Harry actually being knocked to the ground—by a troop of goblins all crying, "Dance too! Dance too!" and capering around so wildly that the three companions were driven apart.

When she was first surrounded by the laughing, singing nymphs and fauns, Elizabeth laughed heartily. They tugged at her and pushed her slightly, but there was nothing at all threatening about the touches. None of the creatures was much larger than she, and they were all obviously being playful. Only there were so many of them, and they were just tall enough to block her view of her companions.

Elizabeth tried to turn around so that she could find Denoriel, who had been a few steps behind her, but suddenly the gay laughter of the nymphs and fauns changed to little shrieks. All of them stopped dancing and gathered closer together, then began rushing past her, dragging her along with them.

When the crowd had nearly passed her, Elizabeth again attempted to turn around, but her arms were seized. She cried out and pulled hard to get loose. The grip on her only tightened and she realized that it was not any nymph or faun that had seized her. She looked up and from side to side and cried out again.

Two mortal men—from the round ears and round-pupiled eyes—had her by her arms and were dragging her along in the midst of the rout of nymphs and fauns. They were both short but very strong. When Elizabeth tried to set her feet and not move, they simply lifted her up by the arms so that her feet did not touch the ground and carried her.

She shrieked for Denno and for her Da, but her voice was lost in the noise the nymphs and fauns and goblins were making. Then one of the men said, "Shut your mouth," and slapped her lightly. Terror and rage strangled the cries in Elizabeth's throat, and she saw with a shock that they had worked their way out of the group of nymphs and fauns and were rushing down one of the aisles.

"I need my hands free," one man said.

The other grunted agreement and lifted her up. Elizabeth tried to roll out of his grasp and cried out, but the man only tightened his grip on her thighs and pushed his arm under her neck so he could clamp one hand over her mouth.

Elizabeth was so frightened now that she felt weak and dizzy. There was no one to cry to for help. The aisle was not lined with booths but with shops where business was done within doors. A few beings looked at Elizabeth being carried along, but they did not seem to care. Beside that, the men were moving so swiftly that there was really no time for anyone (or anything) to interfere.

By the time Elizabeth's paralysis of fear was reduced enough for her to kick and squirm, the man who was not carrying her had turned into a narrow alley. Her captor followed, grunting as she almost wriggled out of his arms. Elizabeth worked her lips back from her teeth and bit hard. The man carrying her shrieked, and the one in front turned.

Elizabeth saw that the man who had led had an amulet in his hand. She screamed as loud as she could for Denno, for Da. The man advanced threateningly, hand raised either to strike or cast a spell, and Elizabeth suddenly remembered her protections and cast a shield around herself.

The man who was carrying her cried aloud in shock as his arms lost contact with her body and another desperate twist pulled her out of his grip. She fell free, but so heavily that she was stunned and could not spring to her feet and run. She stood at bay, panting with rage and fear, but she saw she could not have escaped anyway. One man was ahead and one behind. They closed in on her. Elizabeth screamed and screamed, but the shield muffled her voice and no one was in the alley. The few back doors to shops were closed.

The men tried to seize her, but their hands would not grip. The one with the amulet tried to strike her; she felt the pressure of the blow, which pushed her back into the man behind her. The blow did not hurt, but the man behind pushed her forward so fiercely that to save herself from falling she ran a few steps on the way they wanted her to go. He laughed and pushed her again.

Elizabeth tried to strike back, and she did hit the man who had been ahead of her but he only laughed and stepped aside and shoved her when he was behind to make her run forward again. The next push was so hard that she fell. Both men laughed. They scooped her up—-they had already worked out that they could not grip her but they could lift her shield and all—set her on her feet and pushed her again.

Now Elizabeth began to run ahead as fast as she could. Being shielded, knowing her abductors could not touch her reduced her panic so she could think. She realized she was going where they wanted her to go, but she hoped she would get there far enough ahead of them that she could see some way to escape.

The move took the men by surprise and she forged ahead. Both men shouted; she could hear them pounding close behind her, but even renewed fear could not lend her more speed.

And suddenly, ahead, there was a black wall.

She was trapped.

Elizabeth could only shriek with terror.

Chapter 26

Denoriel had been whirled round and round by the playful
nymphs and fauns. At first he laughed and let them have
their way with him, but then, when he realized that he was being
separated from Elizabeth, he began to push them away. The fauns
pushed back, butting him with their blunt-horned heads; the
nymphs draped themselves around him, hanging on his neck,
kissing him all over his face. Denoriel strained upward, looking
wildly around for Elizabeth's red hair. A nymph slid down his
body and embraced his knees. A faun slammed into him from
behind. Denoriel fell forward and a dozen frolicsome creatures
piled on top of him, laughing and singing snatches of song.

Heaving and rolling, Denoriel struggled to get rid of his playful tormentors, but he was not having much success until the
laughter changed to little shrieks of fear and they all leapt off
him and began to rush away. Denoriel climbed to his feet and
bellowed for Elizabeth.

She was nowhere to be seen.

And in the next moment, Harry, Mechain, and Elidir rushed
toward him shouting that they had lost sight of her when the
fauns and nymphs had raced into the area. He felt his throat
close with fear.

First they spread out to look for her, afraid she too had been
knocked down and hurt. The search did not take long because

all except Harry could sense Elizabeth's aura—which was strong for a mortal. She was nowhere near. Harry sprinted off to ask the performers if they had seen anything. The magician, who spent a lot more time looking out at his audience than performers like tumblers, remembered the red-haired mortal who had enjoyed his display and left a coin in his box.

"She was caught up in the riot of nymphs and fauns." He shook his head. "Curse whoever gave them those sweets; they have cost me half my performance time."

"The girl," Harry urged. "What happened to the girl?"

"Oh, yes. The redhead. She went off arm in arm with two males—maybe mortals. They were not tall enough to be Sidhe."

"Where did she go, in God's name?" Harry took a gold coin from his purse and held it up. "I will pay you well to tell me where she went."

The magician grimaced. "Down one of the aisles—sorry I can't say which one. Believe me, I would if I could."

"Which side? You should be able to guess that. Farthest from you or nearest?"

"This side, I think." He gestured. Harry threw the coin and he caught it. "But I must tell you the truth; I was not really watching her. I was watching the goblins chasing the fauns. I cannot be sure where the girl went."

It was something. There were only three aisles on the side to which the magician gestured. They could discount the one that opened almost behind him; he would have remembered that. Only two to examine. Elidir and Mechain down one; he and Denno down another.

"Oh, I will get her back." Harry heard Denoriel say as he reached them. Denoriel's face was utterly colorless, his eyes blind with guilt and horror. "I will go at once to King Oberon. He will order that Elizabeth be brought to him or he will send out a Thought seeking her—"

"No!" Harry, Elidir, and Mechain cried in chorus. "Even Mother Dannae could not guess what Oberon would do to you."

"What does that matter?" Denoriel said harshly. "I have failed in my trust. Elizabeth is lost!"

"No, she's not!" Harry cried, catching at his arm. "Denno, don't be a fool. I almost know where she was taken."

"What?" The green eyes cleared.

"It has to be down one of those two aisles. The magician saw it. He said she went off arm in arm with two males, not tall enough to be Sidhe. I suppose they were holding her by the arms. She wouldn't have gone off arm in arm with strangers."

"Seized in the rout. Oh, those accursed, brainless—"

"Someone gave them sweets," Mechain said, darkly.

"Then it was all planned." Denno hesitated, then shook his head. "Why waste the time? We don't know how far down any aisle they took her. We don't know whether they turned off. No, I'd better go to Oberon at once."

"Why?" Elidir asked, laying a hand on Denoriel's arm. "No one will hurt her. Oh, in days or weeks, if she has been taken by the Unseleighe, they will try—"

"The Unseleighe want her dead!" Denoriel cried, suddenly beginning to shake.

Mechain patted his shoulder. "If the purpose was to kill her, it is already too late to go to Oberon. They only needed to take her outside the market, which they must have reached already, and do it. But then why go to the trouble of such an elaborate scheme? It would have been easy enough to wait in the place where transport is kept and shoot her with elfshot when we left the market."

Denoriel was as white as snow. "If she is dead—"

"Not dead."

All three spun around toward the harsh voice. Behind them was a goblin, a goblin clutching a very satisfied-looking kitten that was licking a paw and applying that to its whiskers.

"Not hurt," the goblin continued. "Not intended and not by those who took her. She is a valuable prize. They went out by the Orbis Gate."

"Where?" Harry cried, emptying his purse so he could hold out a handful of gold. "Where did they go?"

But the goblin did not reach for the gold. He raised a peculiar-looking rod. Denoriel shouted and threw himself physically in front of Harry. There was a faint buzz, a faint blue light . . . and the goblin was gone.

Denoriel spun around and grasped Harry to him. "Are you all right? Did that set off your wound?"

Harry hugged Denoriel and shook his head. "You've got to stop trying to protect me," he muttered, rubbing his face against Denoriel's neck. "I'm fine. I don't think that was a weapon."

"No, indeed," Mechain said. "It was something like a Gate, a portable Gate. It took him somewhere. And that's what happened to all the things in his booth. I saw him wave his hand over the counter while we were all looking at the mirror, and then he and everything else was gone."

"Hmmm," Elidir remarked, frowning. "I thought that all movement inside the market was supposed to be on one's own. I will have to speak to the management—after we have recovered Elizabeth. The Orbis Gate."

"I do not remember an Orbis Gate when I was coming to the market," Mechain said.

"Nor I," Elidir agreed.

"Doesn't matter," Harry said, impatiently. "It has to be down one of those aisles. You go down the left one. Feel for Elizabeth and ask as you go along if anyone saw a red-haired girl escorted by two men, and ask for the Orbis Gate."

Accustomed to acting on Harry's ideas, the two Sidhe started for the aisle to the left. Harry turned to Denoriel who was still white-faced, and put his arm around his friend's shoulders.

"Come on," he said. "If we find the Orbis Gate, you can read the termini. If we have to we can go to each one in turn, but maybe you'll even be able to feel which one has been most recently used."

"But if she is taken—"

"What if she is?" Harry said, his lips pulling back from his teeth in what was not a smile. "Once we know where, we can get up a nice little hunting party. All the Sidhe in my hunt would be thrilled to be asked along. And we might not even get into trouble for hunting in an Unseleighe domain. Likely we'll even be able to get permission from Oberon to retrieve Elizabeth."

Denoriel blinked and nodded and he smiled, too—but his teeth suddenly looked very long and very sharp. "Hunting. Yes. We will go hunting."

Suddenly Harry chuckled. "And we won't even need to tell Oberon. We can ask Titania's permission."

Denoriel took a deep breath and struck Harry lightly on the shoulder. "You are getting too full of mischief, my lord. If you plunge Underhill into a new conflict between our rulers you are not likely to be thanked." He sighed. "Better to go hunting in Unseleighe territory without any permission. Very well. Let us see what we can find."

They struck—if not quite gold—silver almost immediately. Only a few yards down the aisle, a tall Sidhe just coming out of a shop nodded when they asked about the red-haired girl with two men.

"Yes. I did see them although only for a moment. I was inside the shop and could not get out in time, but I thought that the girl-child was being taken unwilling." The Sidhe looked faintly troubled. "Of course she was mortal, and the men pulling her along were mortal. I did wonder from whom she had tried to escape. A Seleighe Sidhe I am sure, since she was unhurt and spirited." He shrugged. "I thought I might try to discover whose slave she was and offer a price for her since she seemed unwilling to stay with her present master."

Harry flushed slightly. "She was not a slave at all but given special permission to visit Underhill by Queen Titania. She was reft unwilling from our company."

"So?" The Sidhe sucked on his lower lip. "I am sorry I have no more to tell. It was but a passing thought and I was not interested enough to follow."

"I thank you nonetheless," Denoriel put in. "We know we are on the right track now. Did you come by the Orbis Gate?"

"No. I never heard of that, but I suppose it is one of the Gates within the market. My elvensteed awaits me at the main Gate."

"Again our thanks," Harry said, and bowed.

The Sidhe inclined his head and continued on his way. They went on down the aisle asking on both sides. Twice more they got nods of recognition, but both beings—another Sidhe and a being with a scaled head, a ruff of feathers around its neck, and folded wings—claimed that the red-haired girl was now being carried.

"She began to fight them, I suppose," Denoriel said, his voice catching. "Pray Dannae that they do not hurt her."

Harry looked white to the lips, but he shook his head. "They won't. Mortals down here are under some Sidhe's orders and that Sidhe went to a lot of trouble to snatch Elizabeth. Whoever has her wouldn't dare hurt her."

But they could not meet each other's eyes. Both now believed they knew which of the Sidhe would think it worth so much expense and trouble to abduct Elizabeth. To everyone but Vidal Dhu Elizabeth was no more than a red-haired mortal child, a child too old to be of interest to Titania and too young to be of interest to Oberon—not worth snatching. And only Denoriel's half-sister and brother could recognize her or give a description of her to abductors.

They went on down the aisle, asking . . . and now no one had seen the man carrying Elizabeth or Elizabeth being towed along between two men.

"Did the Sidhe meet them and spell them invisible?" Harry asked in a shaking voice.

"That isn't possible," Denoriel replied. "Remember, NO SPELLS." His hands were still shaking, but his eyes were intent. "Wait. They must have turned off. That thing that looked like a walking stick waved to the side when I asked about the Orbis Gate. 'Not in the aisle' he said."

They turned to retrace their steps, still pausing to ask anyone they saw and entering shops to ask the shopkeepers about Elizabeth and the Orbis Gate. At first they got no useful answers at all. None of the shopkeepers had seen a struggling red-haired child and none knew of the Orbis Gate. Denoriel stopped Harry, who was about to cross the road, and shook his head.

"We are only wasting time, Harry. Let me go to seek Oberon."

"Not yet." Harry clutched Denoriel's arm. "See, there are only five shops before we come to the place where that feathered being saw Elizabeth. If we can get no answers when we reach that place . . . I will give up."

Denoriel did not believe the young man for a moment. He was sure Harry would find some new excuse to keep him when they came to the last shop, but he said nothing. He put his arm around Harry's shoulder and they went into another shop. But this time when they asked for the Orbis Gate, the shopkeeper looked disgusted.

"It's right down the alleyway," he said. "But there's no sense in your going there. You'll never find it because it's closed. Been closed as long as I can remember. Most beings hereabout don't even know it exists anymore."

Elizabeth was running so fast that she had no hope of stopping. She was sure the lane had been clear just a moment before, so the wall was surely the doing of the men behind her. All she could do was throw up her arms. Between one stride and the next she felt a strong pulse of magic. "No Spells?" But the men were still behind her. Gate! It must be a Gate.

Escape. All the Gates she had been through took her to places of open land where there was no place to hide. Her captors—she had felt a pressure on her shoulder, but if it was one of her abductors, his hand had slipped off her shield—would catch her within steps. No. There *was* a place to hide. The mists of the Unformed land would hide her. Elizabeth plunged into the black wall, her mind fixed on the swirling mists.

Blackness. Falling. But she wasn't falling, she was running.

"Catch her. Quick."

"How?"

"She'll get lost in the mist!"

"Where the hell are we?

"Not where we're supposed to be. That's sure."

Elizabeth had stopped as soon as she could no longer see the men. She was not far away from them, she knew, because she could hear their voices clearly, but the mists were hiding her completely. They seemed to be even thicker and more restless than when she and Denno and Da had been there earlier with Elidir and Mechain.

Free and in a place she knew, Elizabeth's fear diminished, but she was beginning to feel a little weak and dizzy. Because she had been so afraid, she wondered? And then she remembered the warnings Tangwystl had given her about using the shields for too long. The power had to come from her and it was draining her. She would have to dismiss the shield.

"Do you think the amulet didn't work right?"

The voice was closer. Elizabeth jumped.

"It opened the Gate, like the damned Sidhe said it would. It must be working. And it's glowing, see? Maybe this was only a stop on the way and if we get back in the Gate it will take us where we're supposed to go."

"Then we've got to find the girl. Do you want to tell that Sidhe we lost her?"

Elizabeth stepped away cautiously, deeper into the mist. She could feel the Gate behind her and she knew she had to get back to the Fair to find her friends. They would all be frantic, thinking her stolen away. But she didn't dare try to get past her abductors and get up on the Gate while the men were so close and could grab her. She would have to lead them deeper into the mist.

If it were only a little thinner they could get a glimpse of her.

"There she is!" one bellowed and plunged toward her.

Elizabeth ran away as fast as she could, thinking, *Hide me. Hide me.* And the mists closed in again. She stopped running and drew a deep breath. That had been very convenient, almost as if the mist obeyed her. Well, it had obeyed Mechain and Elidir. And it had let her make a kitten . . . The man's voice broke her thought.

"Gone again—oh God, where's the Gate?"

"It's okay. I'm still near it. Just come to my voice."

Elizabeth bit her lip. That had not worked out well. Now the men knew they could be lost in the mist and one of them would stay near the Gate even if she could draw the other away. She could wait, but not forever. Da and Denno must be half out of their wits. And poor Elidir and Mechain would feel so guilty. They would blame themselves for her being taken when they had only meant well by her, wanting to clear her mind so she would learn the spells right.

Spells. What a fool she had been. She could have used tangle-foot . . . no, she could not. Spells were forbidden in the markets although shields weren't, it seemed. And anyway, while the men held her, having them fall down wouldn't have helped much.

Only they weren't holding her now. And she wasn't in the market. Could she use *gwthio* or *cilgwthio* to push them away from the Gate?

Elizabeth bit her lip again. She didn't know how strong a push she could give, and tanglefoot wouldn't work very well unless they were running. If she thinned the mist so they would run after her . . . No, that was too dangerous. She needed them to run away from her. If only she could change herself to look like a monster . . .

Ah! Perhaps she could *make* a monster. Elizabeth drew in a deep breath. She was very angry and frightened and there was a hot feeling inside her. She had made a kitten. Why not a . . . a lion. She knew what a lion looked like; there was one in the Royal Menagerie in the Tower. Yes. If the mist would be so good? She looked around at it, thinking how kind a mist it was and how beautiful. Would it be kind to her, and protect her from these horrible men? It had already hidden her from them. Would it let her make a lion out of it?

The mist swirled around in shining coils. Elizabeth's eyes were as bright as the sun as she built an image of a fierce and terrible lion in her mind.

"It's thicker 'n ever out there. What're we goin' to do?"

"Don't worry. She's only a mite of a brat. She'll get scared about being lost pretty soon and start bawling for help. Hey, feels like there's grass here. We can sit down."

Lion, Elizabeth thought, feeling even hotter. She didn't like being called a brat who would bawl for help. Then shame built even more heat in her. She *had* been bawling for help from Denno and Da—but that was different, like calling one's guardsmen. She was *supposed* to get help from Denno and Da.

But she was still angry and thought more intensely—*lion*.

Somewhere there was a faint roar. Elizabeth's eyes shone still brighter.

Thank you, mist.

Lion.

The roar came closer. Hastily Elizabeth said the spells for *gwthio* and *cilgwthio* and then cast the shield spell. She felt a little weak-kneed again, but wasn't sure whether it was the draining of her power or just that she was frightened.

She shrieked and spun around when the next roar sounded almost in her ears. And the mist parted. And it was there! Huge, with the thick mane she had imagined, round yellow eyes and teeth . . .

At the same moment, both men yelled, "There she is!" and started forward. Elizabeth leapt sideways, away from the lion and the lion himself leapt forward, ignoring her, his terrible eyes fixed on the men.

Both men screamed. Both turned to run.

The lion was on them in a moment, enormous paws swatting at them. One man went down shrieking. Elizabeth did not wait to see what happened after that.

She ran blindly toward the feeling of "no mist" that meant Gate to her. The second man was also running toward the Gate.

"*Minnau ymbil gwthio*," Elizabeth screamed.

Pushed violently, the man fell backward, screeching. The lion sprang from its first victim toward its second. Elizabeth thought, *Goblin Fair*, but the picture that formed in her mind was Denno and Da. The place where the Gate had been began to darken, but there was no wall of black, no sense of falling. And the lion looked up from what it was crouching on. Elizabeth could see its haunches tighten and rise.

Maybe the mist was kind to her, but the lion was no longer part of it.

"Denno!" she cried. "Da!"

Harry and Denoriel were making their way slowly along the alley. There was no sign of a Gate. They reached the alley's end and Denoriel shook his head, his mouth in a hard, thin line.

"I'll go to Oberon now. That shopkeeper said the Gate was closed and lost. I couldn't feel a thing."

"Denno," Harry cried, "they went into the alley. They didn't come out. The Gate must have worked for them."

"Pasgen has a way with Gates. He may have done a one-time activation—"

"If he did it, you can too," Harry insisted.

Denoriel shook his head, frantic now. "It would take me too long, not even knowing where the Gate is. Get Elidir and Mechain. Maybe they can find it. I can't wait any longer, Harry. I don't know what's happening to her." He bent forward and kissed Harry on the forehead. "You'll be all right. You have Mwynwen and your work. I . . . I can't bear it. I had rather be ended . . ."

"Denno, wait!" Harry grasped his friend's arm. "At least let us search backward as far as the aisle." He put his arms around the Sidhe's neck as he used to do when he was a little boy. "Please, Denno. I love Mwynwen but . . . Don't leave me all alone."

Denoriel drew a shaking, agonized breath. He could not. Not even for Harry could he leave Elizabeth in the hands of the Unseleighe. They would try to break her by torture. But not immediately. Not in the next few hours. He had time enough to walk back to the aisle they had come from. *Elizabeth*, he thought, *Elizabeth*, imaging her look and even more the bright, indomitable spirit, feeling for her more than for a Gate.

A black tunnel opened showing silvery mists at the other end, an untidy heap on the ground streaked with bright red... and Elizabeth popped out shrieking, "Close the Gate! Close the Gate! There's a lion..."

Harry caught Elizabeth in his arms and dragged her back. Denoriel felt for the power of the Gate. A lion's head came half-way through. Elizabeth shouted, *"Minnau ymbil gwthio."* The lion's head disappeared and showed tiny, infinitely far away, above the heap that had once been a man.

"Lileu dyddymu!"

Elidir's voice came from beyond the black tunnel and Mechain added, *"Difelio! Dyna ben!"*

The Gate collapsed and disappeared.

Denoriel braced himself on the wall feeling about to collapse himself. "Thank you," he whispered, voice shaking. "I hadn't the vaguest idea of how to close it."

Mechain laughed shakily. "Oh, we're experts on closing things and shutting things down." Then she smiled like a sun rising. "I see you got her back. Are you all right, Elizabeth?"

"She got herself back," Denoriel said, blinking back tears. "I couldn't even find the Orbis Gate. We'd walked all the way up the alley, and there wasn't a hint of power." He took Elizabeth from Harry's arms and hugged her, tears running down his face. "Sweetling, are you all right? Were you hurt in any way?"

"Not by those stupid men, but the lion almost caught me," Elizabeth told him in a voice that trembled with the aftermath of fear and exhaustion.

"What lion? Where did they take you?" Harry asked, staring at her in consternation.

Elizabeth blinked and sagged a little in Denoriel's embrace. "Can we go sit down somewhere?" she asked. "I feel as if I had run from Hampton Court to London."

Denoriel immediately swept her up into his arms. They all hurried out of the alley and down the aisle. In the open area was an eating place. Mechain went to look inside and came out to gesture them in. Elizabeth lifted her head from Denoriel's shoulder and breathed a sigh of relief. The single large room was very much like any inn in the World Above, even to the smell of spilled ale and wine and the tired bar woman going about and wiping the tables with a none-too-clean rag.

At least the place was reasonably light. Glowing mage lights hung in cages from the ceiling. That was not all a benefit, Elizabeth thought. The clear light showed a most unusual clientele. As Denoriel wound around occupied tables Elizabeth counted four lizards, all with different-colored scales, one with a Sidhe face and another with long, curling hair. A badger (man-sized), a man with a fox head, and a girl with the boneless arms of a snake and scaled skin sat together talking pleasantly. Elizabeth only pressed closer to Denoriel when she saw a table full of humans. Here Underhill the strangest creatures were not at all terrifying; it was humans who were dangerous.

A deep growling voice drew her attention, and she winced when she saw the maned head of a lion lifted toward her. Her grip on Denoriel's neck tightened, and then she saw that the lion's mane was braided with jewels and it had human hands instead of clawed paws. It called out, "Do you want to be free of that Sidhe, pretty child?"

"No," Elizabeth replied, but smiling. "He is my Denno. He cares for me."

The lion may have said something more, but they were past him and Harry was standing by a table near the wall. Denoriel set Elizabeth down on the most sheltered bench. Harry knelt down by her side and kissed her hands. Elidir and Mechain also came and kissed her. Denoriel stood behind her with a hand on her shoulder as if he wished to be able to grab her if someone threatened to pull her away.

In a few moments plates were on the table. A basket of warm bread, a bowl of mixed roasted vegetables, and a huge platter of steaming meat stood ready to slake appetite.

"My," Elizabeth said, somewhat indistinctly because of a large mouthful of food, "I wouldn't have believed I would be so hungry after eating that great big drumstick, but I'm starving."

"Been doing a lot of magic, love?" Mechain asked with a smile. "That would account for it."

"Can you tell us what happened, dearling?" Denoriel asked as he sat down beside her, then hastened to add, "Not if speaking of it makes you frightened or uncomfortable."

"No, why should it?" Elizabeth said, smiling brilliantly. "I know one is not supposed to boast of one's own deeds or cleverness, but . . . by the Grace of God, I was both brave and clever."

"And you saved yourself while we were running about like

ninnies," Harry said with a broad grin. "Boast all you like, Bessie, you deserve it."

"So where did they take you?" Denoriel urged, thinking he would visit that domain and make it clear that the pursuit of little girls by lions was not an acceptable amusement in his opinion.

But Elizabeth dumbfounded him by saying, "I don't think they took me. I think I took them. *I* wanted to go to the Unformed land, and that's where the Gate took us. And one of the men asked the other where they hell they were, so I must guess *they* didn't know."

Mechain muttered that Gates did not respond to mortals, and Elidir shrugged and said Elizabeth was Talented and had a deep reserve of power. Perhaps it was that to which the Gate responded.

Elizabeth paid no attention to them, going on to tell the whole story, beginning with the two men pulling her out of the small riot of fauns, nymphs, and goblins, remembering her shield, and being pushed into the Gate ahead of them, thinking of the roiling mists of the Unformed land and ending with her decision to create something that could frighten them away from the Gate.

"But I forgot . . . well, I didn't forget; I didn't know how to arrange that the lion shouldn't attack me. And it did come after me because I didn't know how to open the Gate, but Denno and Da must have done it from the other side." She turned to look at Elidir and Mechain. "And the mist was just *wonderful*. It was so friendly and helpful. When I needed to be hidden, it got thick as thick, and when I wanted it to show me, I just thought it would be nice if it got a little thinner."

"The mist . . . you felt the mist to be friendly and . . . er . . . helpful?" Elidir had lifted a bite of meat on his knife but he just let it sit there.

"Yes. When I was first running away I needed to hide so badly, and the mist got thicker and coiled around and it glistened. I thought how beautiful it was and how kind, and I thanked it. And then later when I realized I would have to draw the men away from the Gate to use it myself and the best way to do that was for them to catch a glimpse of me . . . the mist got thinner."

"And you thanked it again?" Mechain said.

"Yes, and I asked it if I could make the lion . . . and it let me.

At least, I soon heard a lion roar and the mist got thinner and the lion popped out."

Harry laid his head on her lap and sighed, "Bessie. Bessie. That was very dangerous."

"Don't ever do that again, Elizabeth," Denno said.

"I had to do *something!*" Elizabeth snapped. "I didn't think it would be a good idea to let those men take me where they intended to take me."

Denoriel took a deep, sighing breath, leaned over and kissed her hair. "You are perfectly right, dearling. And you did right, and I was wrong. You did what you had to do, and you did it well. *We* must simply teach you more than we had thought we must."

Elizabeth turned her head to look at him. "You're going to take me back to Llachar Lle, aren't you?"

"You must be exhausted, Bess," Harry said, finally standing up.

"Oh, no," Elizabeth replied, feeling specially cheerful in the wake of hearing Denno actually agreeing that she had been in the right to use magic the way she had. "It is true that I felt dizzy when I got out of the Gate, but now that I've eaten I feel fine."

Elidir started to laugh. "Ah, the joys of youth. You may be completely refreshed by a meal and a short rest, Lady Elizabeth, but the rest of us, I dare say, are badly shaken by nearly losing you."

"You may say it for me," Harry sighed.

"And for me," Denoriel said. "I know the Sidhe do not sleep, but that is just what I wish to do, lie down in a bed and become unconscious."

"And there is still the last spell to teach you, my lady," Mechain pointed out. "I think we have seen quite enough of the Goblin Fair. Now we are all ready to return to Llachar Lle."

Sighing, Elizabeth allowed herself to be convinced. At any time she loved learning new things, and after the demonstration of how useful the spells she learned could be, she was soon reconciled to returning to Denoriel's apartment. She could come back, she thought, and Da and Denno would take her to see the other great markets. Her hand went down to touch the outline of the mirror in her purse. She would not even mind going back to St. James's Palace. There were a few faces she wanted to watch in the new mirror.

Elizabeth did not intend to include Blanche's among those faces, but because she was wearing only her nightdress, she had the mirror in her hand when Denoriel returned her to St. James's

Palace. The maid, who looked tired and drawn after a night of watching and worrying, took Elizabeth in her arms and got bruised by the mirror.

"What's this?" she cried, taking it from Elizabeth's hand. "What a beautiful mirror." She peered into it. "And so clear and bright."

"You like the image?" Elizabeth asked, not turning her head to look at it herself.

Blanche laughed. "Well, I think I look younger and rather worried. But I *was* worried, Lady Elizabeth. I always worry when you go . . . ah . . . away with Lord Denno."

Elizabeth's mouth opened, but the only thing she could get out was an assurance that Denno took good care of her. And when she took the mirror from Blanche's hand, she dared to look and again saw only the face she knew and loved, a face darkened only by worry. She restrained a shiver. What would she have done if Blanche's face were changed?

The mirror might be a good thing, but for now it was better not to use it. It had shown her only what she knew about those she loved. As for strangers—what if she did see something she did not understand in someone's face? She might make a dreadful mistake. But she would need it, she thought. Someday she would need it.

For now Elizabeth put the mirror away at bottom of the little chest in which she kept her few jewels. Then she dressed, ate a hearty breakfast, and sat down to make a fair copy of a passage she had translated into Italian. It felt very odd to be completing work that the calendar said she had done the night before and her memory told her, according to the number of times she had eaten and slept in Denoriel's rooms, was three days past.

However, by the time she completed the copy and checked it against the original she was feeling much more settled. And when Master William Grindal arrived and began to explain the history lesson they had begun the previous morning—in his reckoning of time—Elizabeth listened to him with only a fleeting thought of tanglefoot, stickfoot, and gwthio-cilgwthio.

Since the history lesson soon branched out into her tutor's explanation of the balance of power among Spain, France, and England and therefore why it was necessary to make war on France, all thought of Underhill faded from Elizabeth's mind. She gave her tutor her full attention.

There she could ask a mist to make a lion to destroy her enemies; here it was not so easy. Even a man so powerful as her father needed to plan most carefully and negotiate most skillfully to accomplish a purpose. And this was her world; this was where she must live. The dangers in it were not so obvious as lions, but she understood instinctively that they were just as real, and that knowing these things was more important than any magic spell.

Chapter 27

When Pasgen was assured that the rout of half-crazed fauns and nymphs had separated Elizabeth and Denoriel and the mortal slaves he had hired had caught her and started toward the reawakened Orbis Gate, he began the transits that would take him home. After all, what could possibly go wrong at this stage? Confidently, on arriving, he passed through the interior Gates into the escape-proof holding chamber he maintained.

It was empty.

For one long moment he just stared at the place where Elizabeth *should* have been, as if by staring, he would make her appear out of nothing.

Then he got hold of himself. Quickly Pasgen estimated the time it had taken him to arrive at home and compared it to the time his amulet should have opened the Orbis Gate and flicked Elizabeth and the two men into his holding chamber. Then he shook his head and laughed at himself. The imp had told him when they turned into the alley. Likely by then the girl had recovered her wits and at that moment, she began to give the men trouble.

Trouble—

Suddenly he remembered the burst of power that had destroyed his Gate and could have flung him into the void the last time he had tried to abduct the girl. Fury should have burned in him; instead he felt a reluctant admiration.

And after all, he had planned for this. The men he had hired were mortals. They would not be affected if she unleashed some wild mortal magic, and if she loosed that kind of power, Goblin Fair would react. If she were Removed, in the sense that the Fair *Removed* things, that would end the problem and no shadow would fall on him or on the Unseleighe.

In a way, that would be even better than abduction. No one would know but Vidal and Rhoslyn that he had been the reason the child loosed her magic. He would not even have to justify his actions to Rhoslyn. He could say with truth that *Removal* was not what he intended; that he had only wanted to bring her into Unseleighe hands. And he could not possibly have known that she would lash out with magic within the confines of the Fair. For that matter, the signs were there for all to see, and surely if Denoriel had given her the ability to use her magic, and had not driven the warning home, well, that was not his fault. It was Denoriel who had taken her Underhill in the first place, and Denoriel who should bear the blame for whatever happened.

Pasgen should have felt relieved and satisfied, but a flicker of regret touched him. That child was so strong, so vital—and she would make untold trouble for the Unseleighe if she did come to rule.

Did he *care* about trouble for the Unseleighe? Pasgen looked around the empty holding chamber. Even if Elizabeth resisted, they should have arrived by now.

He was uneasy, and he grew more and more uneasy as the moments passed. Moments into minutes, minutes into a quarter and then a half hour. Pasgen stood staring into nothing. *Removed?* Or had something else entirely gone wrong?

For some reason Pasgen felt cold. Finally he set an alarm to tell him if something arrived in his holding chamber and Gated into the main body of his house. He ate a meal, but the alarm did not summon him. With a very strange light in his eyes, Pasgen left his house and made his way back to the Goblin Fair.

From the mouth of the alley, he followed Elizabeth's aura—it was very strong for a human—to the Gate. Around the Gate he sensed Denoriel and two other Sidhe; their auras flickered with violent emotion. The Gate was dead. Deader than it had been when he first sensed it and decided to use it. Delicately Pasgen probed.

The Gate had been shut down a-purpose, but by a purely Sidhe negation of its working. The Fair itself had had no part in killing the Gate. He raised his brows. It still retained some power.

And it had been shut down from *this* side.

Pasgen had a way with Gates. He worked around the cancellation spells that had shut it down and even discovered where it had carried Elizabeth and her abductors.

Which was not where it had been supposed to go. Now, this was more than interesting, it was fascinating.

His eyes alight with interest and curiosity, Pasgen made the same transit. The corpse of one of the men he had hired lay right beside the Gate. Pasgen repelled the roiling mist and saw the corpse of the second not far away.

As he stood there, frowning, puzzled by what could have happened—how could one little mortal girl have done *this* to two grown men—a furious roar echoed, from nearby.

Much too close, in fact. Pasgen's head shot up, and his eyes widened as a second roar came from much nearer at hand. Then he stifled a gasp as a lion's forequarters and head seemingly materialized out of the mist. He did not wait to see more of the beast, and when he closed the Gate down, he made sure it was not going to be reopened by accident. Then he stood still for a moment, waiting until his racing heart slowed, willing himself to look and seem calm when he walked back into the tenanted parts of the Fair.

When he strode back into the main aisles of the Goblin Fair, Pasgen went to the players' area and stopped at several eating houses. The expenditure of power to do magic made one hungry; and surely one small child would not have anywhere near the physical resources of an adult mage. It was not at all difficult to discover the place where Elizabeth and her companions had eaten. He sat down at the same table and extended his senses—all of them.

Happy. They had all been so happy.

He ordered wine. It was good wine, but sour in his mouth. He put down the goblet, but before he could rise to leave the place, a goblin was standing before him. He had a bright-eyed kitten perched on his shoulder—a kitten with wings. The goblin laid several amulets on the table.

"She made the kitten, but was willing to trade it to me," the

goblin said. "When it came to me I became changed. I am learning to duplicate and preserve it. It will be of great value to my
people."

Pasgen shrugged and pushed the amulets back toward the goblin.
"I am glad you benefited. There is no rule against that."

The goblin shook its head. "I told her protector that the men
had taken her to the Orbis Gate, so I am giving back your payment for delaying her so that she would be caught in the rout
of fauns and nymphs and could be abducted." The creature's face
wrinkled with thought, and it said slowly, "However, it was not
the protector who saved her. She and the men went through the
Gate. Only she returned. Perhaps I will keep two of the amulets.
Is that fair?"

"Fair?" Pasgen looked at the kitten, which had folded its wings
and draped itself around the goblin's neck, then returned his gaze
to the goblin's face, now feeling sorely puzzled. "When did your
kind worry about fair?"

Stroking the kitten, the goblin said, "You evidently mistook
me for something else." And he took out his little rod and disappeared.

Pasgen pocketed the remaining amulet, wondering why the
goblin was allowed to use the rod for transport within the
Fair. Everyone else used his own two or four or any number
of feet. Then he remembered that he had never seen the goblin
move ... well, change place; it had moved its arms to lay down
the amulets and to stroke the kitten. Perhaps it could not move
except by the power of that rod, and if the Fair permitted that,
the power, Pasgen thought, was not magic—at least not any
magic he knew. And why in Dannae's name was he thinking
about that meaningless goblin?

Because he did not want to think about Elizabeth. Pasgen
sighed. He was going to have to order his thoughts and sort
through his emotions. Being puzzled by the child was interesting,
but the happenings of this day were going beyond puzzlement to
irritation. That mortal child ...

Pasgen got a grip on his jangled emotions, sorted them, and
finally was able to look at the situation with some objectivity.

Elizabeth was gone.

A serving girl had overheard the group with the child say they
were returning to Llachar Lle. She was safe from him there, and

safe in the mortal world too. He did not know for certain, but he could not imagine his half-brother being so careless as to leave her unprotected after this incident. She would be shielded now against any attempt to invade her mind, and probably able to shield her body too.

Pasgen lifted his wine and sipped. He would have to go to Rhoslyn and tell her that Elizabeth had escaped once more.

Oddly, now that he was calm again, he found that he did not mind at all—and he did not think that Rhoslyn would mind either. He thought of the lion and the two dead men and smiled. England would be an interesting place when Elizabeth came to rule.

And she would, he thought. In fact, she should. The FarSeers had seen it, and perhaps the Vision was more than a possibility. Could it be that events were taking on their own momentum, impelling the present toward all three specific futures shown? If so, Vidal would not be able to stop her . . . and he, Pasgen lifted his head and took a deep breath—he was through trying.

He sipped the wine again. It was good wine, he thought.

For Elizabeth life slipped back into a comfortable pattern. Lord Denno came almost every day. Most days he came openly and rode out with her. Other times he met her in the park in secret. On those days, they stayed hidden in what cover they could find and Elizabeth practiced tanglefoot and stickfoot on innocent passersby. Once or twice she did *gwthio* or *cilgwthio* but that was dangerous. Anyone could trip or find a foot caught in something and think nothing of it. To be pushed violently or held in place against an attempt to move forward was too unnatural.

Her more ordinary, mortal lessons were pleasant too, her knowledge of Italian improving apace. William Grindal was a good tutor. Elizabeth missed Cheke's brilliance and Ascham's appreciation of her increasingly lovely penmanship, but Grindal's interest in history also included current events. Thus, Elizabeth knew that her father had sailed for France on the fourteenth of July and had arrived safely to supervise the siege of Boulogne.

Grindal was kept abreast of the doings of the court by Ascham, who had been Grindal's teacher and had got him the position as Elizabeth's tutor. Grindal told Elizabeth that Queen

Catherine had been made regent in Henry's absence. Elizabeth was thrilled. No queen consort had been so honored since the days of Catherine of Aragon; it betokened Henry's trust in his wife and salved much of Elizabeth's fear that her father would rid himself of this wife too. With that dark shadow lightened, Elizabeth began to feel impatient of peace and crave the excitement of court life.

On the last day of July, Elizabeth wrote to the queen in Italian, both to show off her new skill and so that no casual glance would expose what she was really requesting:

" . . . I have not dared write to him [the King's Majesty]. Wherefore I humbly pray your most Excellent Highness, that, when you write to His Majesty, you will condescend to recommend me to him, praying ever for his sweet benediction, and similarly entreating our Lord God to send him best success, and the obtaining of victory over his enemies, so that Your Highness and I may, as soon as possible, rejoice together with him on his happy return."

It was the nearest she dared come to a plea to be allowed to return. She did not utter that plea in vain. The queen, with no children of her own, and especially no daughter, was starved for childish affection—Mary was hardly a substitute for Elizabeth, who shared Catherine's intellectual curiosity and love of learning, and who was still young enough to want a guide.

Catherine Parr's recommendations were apparently of such good effect, that by August Elizabeth rejoined the rest of the children—there were now a flock of young maidens to give her countenance, too—and by the eighth of September Henry wrote to his wife, that he sent his hearty blessings to *all* his children. Elizabeth was no longer in disgrace.

Although she did not know it at the time, Elizabeth had never been in serious disgrace. She had been punished for indiscretion, the simple folly of wandering in a dark garden when she should have been abed, but no more than that. However, to her distress, Mary had hardly greeted her. Nonetheless, it was through Mary that she learned, quite by accident, that her father had never intended to do more than slap her wrist.

In the heat of the afternoon, Elizabeth with Lady Alana, Kat

Champernowne, Lady Jane Grey, Ann Parr (the queen's younger sister), and two of the four daughters of Anthony Cooke had walked out into the palace gardens. Elizabeth carried with her the book cover that she was embroidering to enclose her New Year's gift for the queen. She sat down to work on it on a bench in the shade of a hedge. Lady Alana kept her company while Kat went with the other girls to look at the little pond in the center of the garden.

Elizabeth had hardly set ten stitches in the hearts-ease flowers when she stiffened and looked over her shoulder at the dense hedge behind her. "Someone . . . someone like *you* is coming," she whispered to Lady Alana, and then more faintly, "With my sister, Mary. Should we join the others?"

But Aleneil had also sensed Rhoslyn and heard the soft murmur of Mary's voice, and she laid a hand over Elizabeth's and murmured, "Shield."

A sigh eased out of Elizabeth as she cast her shield. She was always forgetting she had that protection. Relieved of fear, she listened. Her ears were very keen—sometimes to her sorrow—because she heard Mary say that she did not know what to do. She had tried to protest to the queen about Elizabeth's recall to court, to explain that the king would be angry.

"And she told me," Mary's voice rose just a little so that it was very clear, "that my father did not really believe any ill of Elizabeth. And to assure me of that, she told me of the bequeathing of the crown as delineated in the will he had written just before he sailed for France."

"He named Elizabeth?"

Elizabeth stiffened again, this time with surprise. The woman with Mary, who Elizabeth was sure was Sidhe, sounded not only surprised but pleased. Elizabeth's breath eased out. Then this Sidhe—it must be Mistress Rosamund Scot; Elizabeth had never seen another Sidhe in Mary's company—was no enemy to her. It was odd that neither Denno nor Alana talked much about her except for a mild warning, but the Sidhe was attached to Mary and possibly Elizabeth was not supposed to know her.

"By name!" Mary said bitterly, her voice louder as the two women came closer. "After my brother Edward and his issue, to any issue begotten on his dearly beloved wife, and for lack of such issue it was to descend first to me and my heirs—and what heirs will I have, no husband ever having been chosen for me?—then to her, by name, Lady Elizabeth."

Elizabeth's mouth opened, but Lady Alana shook her head very hard, and Elizabeth swallowed her joy. Her eyes were blazing, as yellow as those of the lion she had created to destroy her abductors.

Now Lady Alana gestured and Elizabeth put away her embroidery and rose from the bench. If Mary and her companion came to the edge of the hedge and turned, they would see her sitting where she could hear them speak. Elizabeth dropped her shield and Alana pulled her silently away in the opposite direction toward the other maidens near the pond.

Lady Alana squeezed her hand. "Not a word," she warned. "Not a word until you have heard this from another source that you can acknowledge to the queen. Catherine is not the kind to approve of those who listen in secret. And do try not to look so . . . so unreasonably happy."

"But my father loves me!"

"Yes, and knows what will be good for his realm too."

Elizabeth's eyes opened wide but, fortunately, before she could ask what Alana meant and just as they arrived at the pond, Ann Cooke slipped and one foot plunged into the water. Everyone cried out. Lady Alana with her unexpected swiftness of movement caught the girl before she could topple into the pond, and everyone's attention was fixed on her so that Elizabeth's excitement passed unnoticed.

Behind the hedge, Rhoslyn had said, "I see."

"But you do not see enough," Mary nearly wailed. "She is a bastard!"

"She has been declared illegitimate, my lady," Rhoslyn said carefully, trying to remind Mary that she, too, had been declared illegitimate.

"No! I don't mean that. I mean that Elizabeth is not my father's child. Anne was an adulteress and she was with child before she ever married my father. I even warned the queen, but she will not hear it."

For a moment Rhoslyn was speechless. If prejudice was set aside, it was impossible to doubt that Elizabeth was Henry's daughter. She resembled him so closely, from her red head to her agile mind; she resembled Henry much more than did Mary.

"Oh, my lady," Jane Dormer said from behind, "I have begged you not to speak of that to the queen. The king would be angry if she raised the question with him. You do not want to make trouble for Queen Catherine, who is so kind."

Jane Dormer had stopped to look at a specially lush bush of roses and now hurried forward and insinuated herself between Rhoslyn and Mary. Rhoslyn dropped back very willingly. She was in a quandary as to what to say. Rosamund Scot had won special favor with Mary because she had always subtly agreed with Mary when she denigrated Elizabeth or tried to make trouble for her sister.

Now . . . Rhoslyn's mind went back to a most significant meeting with Pasgen two months earlier.

He had come to Iach Hafan, her domain, to tell her that his latest attempt to seize Elizabeth had been a failure. True, he admitted, it had been a spur-of-the-moment arrangement because he had seen her arrive at the Goblin Fair purely by accident. Still, everything had worked, until Elizabeth's shock at being seized had worn off. Then, somehow, she had diverted a Gate to take her to her own destination rather than respond to the amulet he had given her mortal abductors.

"But Gates do not respond to mortals," Rhoslyn remembered protesting.

"It seems they do to Elizabeth," Pasgen had said, and she had *not* imagined the reluctant admiration in his voice. "She has Talent and, more to the point, she can use it. She took the men to an Unformed land and created a lion that killed them. And not half an hour later, she was sitting with Denoriel and others exuding happiness."

"What?"

Pasgen had not bothered repeating himself. He knew that Rhoslyn had heard him and was merely expressing her shock, shock because a mortal child had been able to overpower one of her brother's amulets, had seen two men killed . . . and had not been shaken and distraught.

"I will meddle no more with Elizabeth," Pasgen had said, with the firm nod that she knew meant his mind was made up, and there would be no shifting him. "I think we have misunderstood the Visions we have shared with the FarSeers. We believed that those were three different possibilities, because that is usually the way FarSeeing works. I no longer think that is so. I think we have been Seeing what *will* be. The boy will rule, then Mary, and then Elizabeth."

Rhoslyn stared at her brother for a moment, absorbing what he had said. She did not *like* Elizabeth but she could not help but admire her—even more now; a child of eleven who could create in an Unformed land and fight back against adult male abductors with such ferocity. And a small feeling of contentment moved her. From the first time she had Seen the glory of Elizabeth's reign she had desired it to come to pass.

"But what will you do?" she asked. "Is it now that we must confront Vidal? He surely will not accept the fact of Elizabeth coming to the throne."

Rhoslyn's moment of contentment had been drowned by fear. She knew that Pasgen could defeat Vidal one-on-one, but it would not be that way if Pasgen openly defied the Dark Prince. Vidal would bring the whole herd of dark Sidhe down on them. Pasgen was strong and she had her strengths too, but they could not prevail against the whole Unseleighe host.

Usually that threat was negligible. It was very hard to get the dark Sidhe and the other creatures of the Dark to unite about anything. Ordinarily Vidal could manage to control only a few, but all the Unseleighe would unite to prevent Elizabeth from coming to the throne. Beside that aim, they would be glad to bring her and Pasgen down together if he defied Vidal.

"I think I will disappear," Pasgen said, looking suddenly very happy. "I will make a study of chaos lands and Unformed places. I know that they move around, but perhaps I can find a way to fix them or, better, to mark them so I can return to chosen places. In any case, I do not think Vidal's minions will be able to track me down too easily in those environs."

Rhoslyn remembered taking her brother's hand. "Chaos lands and Unformed places can be dangerous, Pasgen. Be sure to carry the lindys with you."

Pasgen smiled at her. "I will. And it will not be as dangerous as being attacked en masse by the dark Sidhe . . . which I think would happen soon even if I did not defy Vidal. It would have happened already, if Vidal were not so busy in Scotland."

Rhoslyn nodded. At court she had heard a great deal about how the Scots refused to abide by the Treaty of Greenwich and give the infant Queen Mary of Scotland into Henry's hands.

"May the Powers bless King Henry for being such a stubborn idiot and demanding just what the Scots will not give," Pasgen continued, with the first wholly cheerful smile she had seen on his face in an age. "If he did not think he already ruled them so that he can issue demands and have them instantly bow, they might be won over. However, Henry's stubbornness is encouraging Vidal to stir the pot. Long may the Scottish wars rage." Then he bit his lip. "What about you, Rhoslyn? Will you disappear too?"

"I cannot. Mother—"

Pasgen snapped his fingers. "Idiot that I am. I meant to tell you sooner that I agree to her moving to the empty house—" he laughed "—we will have to learn to call it something else. And I have thought of a good way to get clients for her. If you will make three simulacra . . ."

Rhoslyn's mind skipped over his ideas for a booth at each of the great markets with broadcast sheets describing Llanelli's services and instructions for Gating to the empty house. At the time she had seized on the ideas and they had spent a long time discussing how to protect Llanelli. Now, however, that work was done and Llanelli established, and what shone in Rhoslyn's mind like a beacon was the end of the conversation she had had with Pasgen.

"And perhaps I will look specially at empty domains closer to Seleighe places . . ." he had said, leaving the suggestion hanging.

But Rhoslyn remembered how her heart had leapt—with hope, not fear. "Yes!" she remembered exclaiming. "Yes. Oh, Pasgen, do you think we could—"

The joy had drained away from his expression and he had shaken his head. "If they did not kill us out of hand, we would be pariah dogs, never accepted, never trusted . . ."

"And how is that different from what we have now?" Rhoslyn asked bitterly. "Except that among the Seleighe we would not need to fear hate spells and enchanted weapons!"

He had not answered that, only put out a hand to stroke her cheek. "Will you be safe if I go?"

Rhoslyn had tried to shake off the dream of moving out of the Dark and smiled. "Oh, yes. I will go to the mortal world and take up residence as Mary's lady. If Aurelia asks what I am doing, I can say that Mary is the best path to Elizabeth's destruction but, since I may not use any spell on her, it takes time and skill to influence her by mortal persuasion."

Mary's voice speaking her mortal name cut through Rhoslyn's memories and she came back to the present with a feeling of mingled amusement and frustration. "But Rosamund thinks there is danger that Elizabeth will further influence the prince into ways that will damn him," Mary said. "Do you not, Rosamund?"

Rhoslyn swallowed a sigh. She herself had strongly aided in building the wall of doubt and fear over which Mary regarded her sister. Now, stone by stone and inch by inch of mortar, she would have to take down that wall. Not only take it down but set in its place another—a wall that would protect Elizabeth from real harm during Mary's reign. But to go too fast would destroy Mary's trust and her influence with Mary.

Rhoslyn tried to keep her voice flat and neutral when she said, "It is indeed true that Elizabeth leans toward the reformed religion and that Edward is very fond of her, but since she was sent away, Elizabeth is more careful. I notice she does not stray beyond King Henry's dogma."

"But that is still dangerous," Mary insisted. "Edward is a sweet boy. To teach him to acknowledge the king as—"

"But it is only natural," Jane Dormer said, "for a little boy to believe his father is all powerful."

"Yes." Rhoslyn smiled. "And you need not fear that Christ or his merciful mother would condemn a little boy for believing what his father told him. You will have many years to teach him better ways."

The smile felt stiff on her face and she suggested that it was still too warm to find walking in the garden entirely pleasurable. Perhaps a bower in the shade and a game . . . Rhoslyn was not really too warm but she wanted to get out of the area where Elizabeth's voice rose above that of the other girls as they exclaimed over a mishap to one of their number. Mary could be quite an interesting companion when she could be diverted from the subject of religion.

As the whole group of girls fussed over Ann Cooke's wet shoe and stocking, Elizabeth brought from the small basket that contained the book cover she was embroidering, the piece of cloth usually used to protect the embroidery. For now it could serve to dry Ann's foot and stocking. Her older sister, Mildred, was using dry grass to wipe out the shoe as well as she could. Amid laughter and thanks, Elizabeth and Lady Alana were absorbed into the group.

Although she now had her delight under control so it would not burst out and make the other girls wonder, Elizabeth was very happy in her return to court.

Admittedly, there was a dark side to this restoration in that Denoriel was no longer free to visit as he had been in St. James's. Nor did he and Elizabeth dare meet in the Wilderness as they used to do.

Whether Stafford was still watching, they did not know but Elizabeth had determined to be a model of propriety. Now when she went out to walk or ride, she made sure to be accompanied not only by her own servants, who were known to be devoted and all too ready to lie for her, but by some of the young ladies being schooled in the queen's enlarged nursery.

Because of Denoriel's enforced absence, Aleneil had taken up her place in Elizabeth's small entourage as Lady Alana. The war in France was eating money, far in excess of what had been planned, so that allowances were being cut to the bone or discontinued entirely. Kat Champernowne had been forced to dismiss some of Elizabeth's ladies and gentlemen; thus Lady Alana's offer to return to service was welcomed warmly. Lady Alana did not require any stipend and would be a helpful support. Kat introduced Alana to Queen Catherine, who soon found Lady Alana better company than many of her own ladies. Lady Alana was approved.

In the weeks that followed Aleneil had detected no threat to Elizabeth, and Aleneil was actually in a better position to watch for threats than Denoriel, because she was very often present in Elizabeth's chambers. The only thing that troubled her was that she had sensed Sidhe—almost certainly Rhoslyn—in Mary's company and she associated that with the growing coldness between Mary and Elizabeth.

At least, Aleneil told Denoriel when she Gated to Llachar Lle after everyone else at Hampton Court was asleep, Rhoslyn, if it was Rhoslyn, never came near Elizabeth and there was no sense of magic in or around Mary. However, Aleneil could not tell whether the Sidhe was causing Mary to be cold and eye Elizabeth with fear and suspicion. Worse, she did not know what to tell Elizabeth. She did not want to frighten her nor worsen the situation between her and Mary.

"You think Rhoslyn may be encouraging Mary to believe Elizabeth is a witch?" Denoriel asked anxiously. "Aleneil, warn Elizabeth not to use stickfoot or tanglefoot. Rhoslyn will sense those spells immediately."

"I will remind her, although I know she has not used any spell at all at court. I do not know whether Mary still has some doubts about Elizabeth or is now accounting what she saw in the garden that night as owing to her near sight. More likely it is because Edward is so warm to Elizabeth that Mary is so cold."

Denoriel frowned. "It must be Rhoslyn influencing Mary to hate Elizabeth. I remember Mary as being sweet and gentle and fond of Elizabeth, too, when Elizabeth was only a baby."

"Mary is jealous," Aleneil sighed. "I think she desires Edward's love for herself. But, even more important, because religion in the form of the old faith is the wellspring of her life, she fears Elizabeth's influence will encourage Edward toward the reformed religion. He is taking great interest in Elizabeth's New Year's gift for the queen."

That made Denoriel gape at her in mild surprise. "Edward is interested in women's clothing?"

Aleneil laughed. "No more than any boy of his age. What has taken his fancy is Elizabeth's translation from French into English of a long—" she sighed "—and incredibly boring poem by Margaret of Navarre, called—at least the translation is called—*The Mirror of the Sinful Soul*."

He shook his head. "But if Elizabeth thinks the poem is boring—"

"I did not say that *Elizabeth* thought the poem was boring, and neither does Edward. It puts forth the idea that since all people are sinful only God's mercy can save a person from hell and only faith can gain God's mercy. Good works, as in the old religion—which resulted in the extreme wealth of the Church—are no longer necessary."

Denoriel groaned; it was clear he found all the convolutions and flourishes of mortal religions incomprehensible as well as absurd. "The things these mortals can dream up to worry about.

Who cares? I surely hope that Elizabeth will grow out of this fancy."

"I am sure she will." Aleneil laughed. "It is not a heart preoccupied with guilt and sin that brought about such a flowering as we ForeSee."

"True enough." Denoriel smiled. "And she certainly does not seem preoccupied with sin when she goes Underhill. Nor is she worried about doing 'witchcraft' when we teach her spells. She loves them." He sighed. "I miss her."

"You would see more of her, although under formal circumstances, if you found yourself a good friend at court that you could visit."

"No, not yet." Denoriel sighed. "The men I need are with the king in France." He sighed again. "This war cannot come to a good end. Henry and the emperor Charles have entirely different purposes and plans. Charles desires to attack and take Paris and Henry wants to extend his influence in France by taking the towns near the Pale of Calais. Do you know that when Norfolk and Suffolk first brought the army across the narrow sea they had no idea what the king intended them to do there?"

Aleneil nodded. "One of the privy councilors had a letter from Norfolk saying very tartly that he had expected to know, when he set out with the vanguard from Calais, where he was supposed to be going!"

Denoriel laughed at the absurdity of it. "Yes, and then Henry decided that they should attack Montreuil or Ardres, which is just outside the Pale. Naturally this did not please Charles, because if the English only hang about Calais, they will never help him take Paris."

Aleneil frowned. "Can the result of the war have any influence on Elizabeth?"

Denoriel shook his head. "Not unless Henry so infuriates the emperor Charles that he breaks his agreement with England and makes truce and treaty with France. Then Henry would be odd man out. If France and the Empire combine against him he might become desperate enough to offer Elizabeth as a bride to gain an ally."

Aleneil looked startled and anxious. "She is nearly old enough and such a marriage might take her out of the line of succession. Denoriel, you had better make some connections in court so we can be warned of any such plans and arrange to counter them."

"There is no hurry," Denoriel assured her. "First we must see what the end of this war will be. It may not fall out the way I now see it." He stared unseeingly at the wall for a moment, then added, slowly, "What we must guard against right now is Mary's animosity. She has the queen's ear and might influence her against Elizabeth. And that would be beyond either of us to counteract."

Chapter 28

Elizabeth had been feeling the effects of Mary's coldness for some considerable time now, and it troubled her even more than it troubled Aleneil. Of course, Elizabeth knew Mary had been the one to accuse her of meeting a man in the garden, which resulted in her exile to St. James's Palace. However, her opportunity to visit Underhill and spend so much time with her Da made Elizabeth very forgiving of her exile.

Even so, at times she had longed to be at court, to be with her little brother, and to avail herself of all of the opportunities for learning that she enjoyed there. In fact, she and Da had talked about Mary, about the many times, soon after her mother was lost, that Mary had produced a toy or a garment for her little sister despite her own straightened circumstances. In her heart, Elizabeth wished she could recall that "old" Mary again.

Just now Elizabeth was in charity with the whole world and she wanted to mend matters with her sister—especially since Mary had unwittingly passed to her such precious information. The trouble was that Elizabeth was afraid she would have to reject Edward to be reconciled with Mary, and that she was not willing to do.

At first Elizabeth had only been warmed and delighted by her brother's enthusiastic welcome. He had run to her and embraced her and told her how much he had missed her and how glad he was that she had returned. Elizabeth had not given Mary's reaction a thought; she always thought of Edward as being an ordinary little boy—except for becoming king one day.

To Elizabeth that seemed infinitely distant; her father still was, and to her would always be, the one and only Great Harry, the King of All England, now and forever. Perhaps, in some dim and far-off future, Edward would take the throne—but not now. Now he was just a little boy, and little boys, Elizabeth thought, often were glad to see sisters who shared their lessons.

Elizabeth did not even think Edward particularly clever because she was herself so clever—she didn't praise him unless he deserved it, and she didn't flatter him as some of the other boys did to gain his favor. But as time passed, because they had been apart for months, she realized that Edward was *especially* fond of her. She could now see that he was growing into a strange child, far too serious and formal—even more so than herself, and Edward did not have the terrible fears that had made her so careful.

Edward still played with the young friends that Queen Catherine had chosen for him, but the only one (besides herself) to whom he showed any real warmth was Barnaby Fitzpatrick. And he always had a smile and even occasionally a kiss for her, whereas he treated Mary with great courtesy, but formally, and not as if she was his sister at all.

On and off, Elizabeth worried about how to regain Mary's affection without losing Edward's. She could not be formal with Edward. For one thing, she loved him and would not hurt him for the world; for another thing, Edward *would* someday be king—even if Elizabeth could not really envision how it would happen—but if it did, he would be more important to her future than Mary. Elizabeth thought and thought and finally came up with an idea that really pleased her.

She knew that although Mary had publicly accepted King Henry as the head of the Church of England, where and when Mary could, she clung to the strict theology of the old religion. Edward's tutors leaned the other way. Although they conformed to the king's interpretation of theology, they went much further in denying the need for good works and ardently supporting a Bible and Prayer Book in English.

If she asked Mary to explain to her why such wise men supported those ideas, Elizabeth hoped Mary would believe that she could direct her sister into a safer theology. And Mary might be right, Elizabeth thought. Sometimes the things Master Cheke said were startling, and altogether unsettling.

Feeling very righteous, Elizabeth set forth with only Blanche to accompany her to visit her sister. She really did not want to involve any of the other girls in a discussion of religion. The distance was not great and they met no one along the way. There was a guard outside Mary's door, but he recognized Elizabeth and simply opened the door for her.

Elizabeth stopped near the doorway, somewhat at a loss. Mary was not in her reception room. No one was there but a maid, wiping away dust and plumping cushions.

"Oh," Elizabeth said. "Is my sister not in her rooms?"

"I do not believe she has yet come from her bedchamber," the maid whispered, large-eyed, dropping a deep curtsey.

"I see I have come too early," Elizabeth said, but she was surprised; Mary was an early riser. "I am sorry. Can you tell Lady Mary that I was here and will return later in the day?"

The maid looked frightened and Elizabeth had to assume that she was not accustomed to speaking to Mary or any of the upper servants. Elizabeth was about to say "Never mind," that she would send Mary a note, when a Sidhe came out of the door to an inner chamber.

The air spirit that always hung somewhere about Elizabeth fled. Blanche caught at Elizabeth's arm and reached for the necklace of black iron crosses. The Sidhe abruptly stopped where she was, but she pretended not to see Blanche's defensive gesture.

"I am very sorry," the Sidhe said, "but Lady Mary is unwell today and will not be able to receive you."

"Oh, I am so sorry to hear that my sister is not well, Mistress—" Elizabeth's eyes flicked to the long, pointed ears, the slit-pupiled eyes, but she did not allow the expression on her face to change.

"Rosamund Scot is my name, Lady Elizabeth." If there were ever prizes given for maintaining a bland, even blank expression, Mistress Scot would surely take them all.

"Thank you, Mistress Scot." Elizabeth decided to err on the side of exceptionally good manners, and since the woman was her superior in age, if not in rank, she bobbed in the token curtsey she would have given someone her equal in rank. "I did not mean to disturb my sister. Would you be so good as to tell Lady Mary that I was sorry to hear of her indisposition and that when she is better and has a little time to spare for me, I have some questions about points Master Cheke has raised on the subject of good works."

"Certainly," Rhoslyn said, already reaching back for the door handle.

"Wait, Mistress Scot," Elizabeth said, suddenly deciding that it was more than time to make another set of amends. "It seems to me that when I was a little girl and did not know any better I was very rude to you about your appearance when you came with my sister to visit me."

The Sidhe's eyelids dropped a little, veiling whatever lurked in the back of her mind. "I am sure you were not, Lady Elizabeth."

Elizabeth smiled slightly and ignored the disclaimer required by etiquette. "I said something about your ears and your eyes, I believe. Please forgive me and be assured that I will never again make such an unwarranted personal remark."

The Sidhe might be good at concealing her feelings, but this did take her by surprise; she blinked. "That is very kind, Lady Elizabeth, I thank you but assure you it is not necessary. I do not remember any such incident."

"Well," Elizabeth replied, "I remember, even if you do not." Once again the Sidhe moved to leave—and Elizabeth braced herself. If *this* particular fence could be mended—"But wait, don't go yet, Mistress Scot. There is something else I must tell you. I know you think my Denno did a terrible thing before I was even born, but he didn't."

Rosamund Scot froze.

Elizabeth continued on, determined to correct what she was sure was a terrible mistake. "He didn't hurt the—" the word *changeling* was in her mind but would not come out of her mouth, and Elizabeth finished "—the little boy."

Rhoslyn let go of the door handle and came forward. Before she could reach out, however, the baleful influence of the iron crosses sent a mind-fogging miasma of pain washing over her body.

She stopped in her tracks. She wanted to back away. Blanche had now taken out the necklace of crosses. But Rhoslyn couldn't move. All the pain, all the grief she had carried over the years held her fast.

"What do you mean?" She could control the words, but the voice she uttered them in quivered and pleaded.

Elizabeth's mouth opened, but nothing came out until she said, desperately. "I can't tell you *here*. I know the whole story, but I am forbidden . . . constrained. I can't speak about it here."

"What story?" Now Rhoslyn's voice was harsh. "There is no story. He died."

"No. No." Elizabeth wrung her hands. "At least, he did die, but many years later. Not until I was almost three years old. Denno had nothing to do with that. If I were . . . elsewhere . . . I could tell you."

"I can take you to a safe place—"

"No!" Blanche cried. "You mustn't go, my lady. Only with Lord Denno. She'll make you put your cross away and then she could take you anywhere, do anything to you."

"Where could you take her, Rhoslyn?"

Elizabeth turned to find Lady Alana just behind her, but the voice was not Lady Alana's soft, insinuating coo; it was Aleneil's, only hard and cold rather than teasing and laughing.

But Rosamund—Rhoslyn—was a changed person. Where her face had worn no expression at all before, now she was clearly desperate and pleading. "Nowhere harmful, Aleneil, I swear. I swear by . . . by my brother's life and safety that I mean Elizabeth no harm. I only want to hear . . . I *have* to know what happened to the child."

Lady Alana looked startled, even shocked. And when she spoke, her voice was softer, and tinged with reluctant sympathy. "Have you grieved for him all these years? I am so sorry. I did not know." Her voice was softer still. "Where did you want Elizabeth to go?"

"Only to the Elves' Market. You know the rules," Rhoslyn said, her hands outstretched a little. "I could not hurt her there. All the Bright Sidhe would be watching too. And from what Pasgen tells me, she has her own defenses." She hesitated, bit her lip. "Please Aleneil, let her come with me. Come yourself if that seems safer. Or you tell me."

"I only know the beginning," Aleneil said slowly. "It is Elizabeth who knows the end, having heard it from the other . . . child . . . who, of course, is a child no longer."

"Please, Aleneil." Tears shone in the dark eyes. "I *must* know!"

"Do you have a Gate?" Aleneil asked. "I dare not show you mine or use it. Denoriel would murder me."

"Yes!" Rhoslyn said so eagerly that Blanche pulled Elizabeth backward. When she saw the movement, Rhoslyn uttered a single sob. "It has only one terminus, only one. At the Elves' Market. That is for my own safety. You can go alone and then return, Aleneil. If anything happens to you, Elizabeth will not go, so I will have lost everything."

"My lady, don't go!" Blanche exclaimed. She remembered Rhoslyn with fangs and claws fighting Aleneil on the floor of Elizabeth's bedchamber. "Wait until Lord Denno comes. To go you'll have to cover your cross. That's dangerous."

"I know," Elizabeth said and looked doubtfully at Rhoslyn. The Sidhe said nothing, but tears streaked the elegant face . . . and Elizabeth could see they were real tears visible on the cheeks under the illusion. "But I don't think Denno would let me go because he doesn't understand how sad this lady is. I really want to tell her what Da told me. My Denno *didn't* do anything wrong." She turned her gaze toward Aleneil. "Please—don't *you* see?"

"Is the Gate far?" Aleneil asked.

"In the garden," Rhoslyn replied. "I will bring us back within a few minutes of when we left. If Lady Elizabeth walks with both of us, no one will think ill of a short stroll in the garden."

"Lady Alana!" Blanche protested.

"I know you are worried, Blanche," Aleneil said, "but I think Rhoslyn is being honest with us. Still, if we are not back before it is time for Elizabeth's lessons, send the little one to bring Lord Denno and tell him where we were supposed to go and with whom. There will be such a harrowing of the Dark lands . . ."

Aleneil's eyes were very bright and Rhoslyn shook her head, whispering, "No. No. I mean no harm."

Blanche returned to Elizabeth's apartment to make excuses if they were necessary and Elizabeth walked with Lady Alana and Mistress Scot out into the formal garden of Hampton Court. At the end of the Privy Garden, not far from where the stair went down to the river was a small clump of trees. There was no brush, but the grass was rough among them, not as welcoming to those who strolled as the graveled path.

There were a few small groups of ladies on the path, and Elizabeth and her companions had to go and look down the steps toward the river. After a while their end of the garden was empty, and they hurried to a bench, which stood in the shelter of the trees.

Rhoslyn looked around once to make sure they were the only ones near, and said, "Gate." Aleneil stepped into the black maw that appeared. It was gone and almost instantly Aleneil was standing where she had disappeared.

"Very well," she said. "The Gate did, indeed, take me to the Elves' Market and let me open it to return here. Still," she turned to Elizabeth, "are you sure you want to do this, my love?"

"I want Mistress Scot—" Elizabeth now knew the Sidhe's name was Rhoslyn, but she always called the Sidhe in her world by their mortal-world names "—to know that my Denno is not an evil creature and did no harm. I want—" she hesitated "—I want as much accord among us as there can be."

Elizabeth had stood up while she was speaking. She too looked around to be sure that no one was watching and walked in under the trees. Then she slipped her cross into its spelled cover; Aleneil took a good grip on her and glared at Rhoslyn who had held out her hand. Rhoslyn retracted her hand and said, "Gate."

The Gate appeared. Aleneil immediately stepped into it, pulling Elizabeth with her. Dark. Falling. Elizabeth was no longer in the least afraid and was ready to step out into a cul-de-sac barricaded with empty crates the moment she saw light. Rhoslyn was not with them. Aleneil drew in her breath, looking very disappointed. To Elizabeth she said, "Shield."

Obediently Elizabeth raised her shields, both mental and physical, and in that moment, Rhoslyn appeared. She made no comment on Aleneil's obvious distrust, but her mouth turned down a little at the corners and her voice was not completely steady when she asked if Aleneil wished to walk around to the front and choose a drinking house or would enter through the back of the one where the Gate terminated.

They went around to one of the main aisles of the Elves' Market and a full cross lane away from the place they had entered before Aleneil saw a place she liked. Elizabeth saw that Rhoslyn was uncomfortable and asked her what was wrong.

"The landlord and other patrons of this place will not like it that I am here," she said.

Elizabeth looked around. "No one seems to mind. Why should they?"

Rhoslyn looked resigned. "Because I am of the Dark Court and they of the Bright."

Now Aleneil laughed. "How are they supposed to know that if you do or say nothing to tell them? I doubt that many even know that Elizabeth is mortal."

"Do they not know?" Rhoslyn asked doubtfully, then sighed. "Another lie." She shook her head. "Never mind that. Tell me about my poor little changeling. You claim Denoriel did not kill him?"

"Of course not! What kind of a monster do you think my brother . . . your own half-brother . . . is?"

"All I know is that my Making, my child, was gone and there was no trace of him. If Denoriel had not sucked out the power that held him together, why could I not feel him?"

"Because Miralys, the elvensteed, had covered him with his aura," Aleneil said. "We are going about this wrong. You need one whole tale from beginning to end. I do not know how you got into Windsor or convinced FitzRoy's guardian to give him into your care."

"I didn't attempt that," Rhoslyn asserted, head high. "I didn't need to. I came dressed as a nun bringing a gift from Mary to her half-brother. Norfolk . . . is a self-centered, self-important man. It did not take much of a spell to convince him. It was harder to break the watchfulness of the boy's men-at-arms."

"Da told me that part," Elizabeth put in. "Da didn't suspect anything but he was annoyed because he was sure the nun was going to give him a long lecture about something. He was a little surprised about being led to the carriage house, but then he saw Denno, who told him to go back up the path. It was then that he saw his men-at-arms sort of frozen and staring into space."

"And when I went to the carriage, where I had left my poor little copy of Richmond . . . he was gone." Her voice almost broke on a sob, then hardened. "And Denno was right behind me, gloating."

"He wasn't gloating," Aleneil said, then stopped as a dryad with beflowered, trailing willow-withies for hair asked what they would have.

Elizabeth wanted lemonade—to which she had been introduced on her last trip Underhill. Rhoslyn asked for wine. Aleneil chose ale.

"Not gloating?" Rhoslyn repeated when the server was gone. "Perhaps. But he was very well pleased with himself."

"Likely he *was* pleased with himself," Aleneil agreed without much sympathy. "Certainly he wanted to frighten you enough that you would not again try to replace Harry with a changeling."

Rhoslyn closed her eyes, remembering the months during which she had built her substitute Richmond and the weeks of joy and pain when she patiently created a mind that could answer questions and hold ideas. Elizabeth put her hand over Rhoslyn's and patted it.

"Denno did want to frighten you, Mistress Scot, but that was fair. He was charged with the protection of my Da. However, he had nothing against the little boy you had made. He wouldn't do anything to hurt *him*. He might have been a made-thing, but he didn't *ask* to be made."

"That's true, Rhoslyn," Aleneil said, her voice softer again. "In fact Denoriel was terribly worried about the false Richmond. The enchanted sleep you had put on him was draining his power, and in the mortal world there was no way to supply more. As soon as he was sure you were gone, Denoriel took the changeling to the best healer he knew. Richey—that was what Mwynwen called him—lived with her for seventeen years."

"Seventeen years!" Rhoslyn exclaimed, eyes wide. "That's impossible. The child . . . he was a child to me, but he was only a construct, and a construct in the mortal world, with no way to replenish its power . . ."

"Yes, well, he wasn't in the mortal world," Aleneil pointed out. "The healer to whom Denoriel took him was Underhill, of course. And the healer had long desired a child. She kept Richey and raised him as her own. He had everything a child could desire . . . everything. She doted on him, and he on her. He had a very happy childhood."

"How long?" Rhoslyn breathed.

"He was fourteen or fifteen before the power-gathering spell that Mwynwen had put on him failed and power had to be forced on him. By then he was old enough to understand when Mwynwen explained. It wasn't like torturing a little boy who didn't know why he was being hurt. But I . . ." Aleneil hesitated, then went on hurriedly, "I told Mwynwen she was doing wrong." She shook her head. "Foolish of me, that was. All that did was deprive Richey of my company." Suddenly she smiled softly. "He was a darling child, Rhoslyn. It was a marvelous creation."

Rhoslyn was now weeping openly. "It was wrong," she sobbed, "wrong. It was very wrong to make a construct that could think and feel." She looked pleadingly at Aleneil. "But I thought he would just fade away in a week or two in the mortal world. I did not think he would suffer. Poor Richmond. Poor Richmond. What happened to him in the end?"

"I know about that because Da told me," Elizabeth said. "There was a fight over seizing me and Da was barely touched by a nearly spent elf-shot. For a Sidhe that would not have been very serious, but for a mortal . . . It was bad. In only a few weeks, Da was coughing and soon, he couldn't breathe."

Remembering that night, Rhoslyn shuddered. Vidal and Pasgen both unconscious; Aurelia with the crosses burned into her forehead being dragged across the floor by Blanche.

Elizabeth saw her shiver but went on with her story. "Meanwhile, my Denno had hurt himself—I'm not sure I understand exactly how; it was something about the kind of power in the mortal world that burned him—and he was in the same healer's house as Richey."

"Denoriel kept asking for Harry," Aleneil put in. "And Mwynwen said he was so sick that she didn't dare tell him Harry was dying. Richey was sitting with us. It was one of his good days, when he could get out of bed. He was always interested in hearing about Harry. Then we began to talk about a way to get Harry Underhill where he could be cured without causing a dreadful row when he disappeared—and there was no hope he wouldn't be missed or that we could get him back soon after he was taken away. He would have to stay Underhill for so long that there would be no reconciling mortal time with Underhill."

Elizabeth nodded. "But by then, Da says, Richey wanted to die. He was in awful pain because somehow putting the power into him hurt him and even when he didn't have to take the power, he was so tired all the time. And . . . and Da told me his . . . his flesh was beginning to fall apart."

Rhoslyn covered her face with her hands. "I loved him. I never meant for him to suffer."

"But he didn't," Elizabeth said quickly. "Well, he did hurt, but at first he didn't mind because he loved Mwynwen and was happy with her. Only at the very end . . . and that didn't last long because he made Mwynwen see that his time had come, and they changed him for my Da. Then nothing hurt him anymore, and he finally got to see the World Above, which he'd always wanted to see, and sit in real sunlight. And my Da's people, they all loved him, and so Richey slipped away peacefully in a few days, never alone, never afraid, always with those who cared for him near. Da's people *loved* Da, and they loved Richey just as much, because they thought he was Da, and I think—" her brow wrinkled as she tried to put what she felt into words "—I *think* that must have made him very, very happy, because now that I'm old enough, when they talk to me about him, they always say how happy and peaceful he was in his last days."

"Is it true?" Rhoslyn had dropped her hands and lifted her head, and now she looked from Elizabeth to Aleneil. "Can I believe you? Can I? Or is this some cruel joke?"

Both Aleneil and Elizabeth looked horrified. "No," Elizabeth said. "My Da told me because I wanted to know why everyone in the mortal world thought he was dead. And Denno told me to beware of you because you hated him and might hurt me to revenge yourself. But I didn't think you wanted to hurt me. The bad Sidhe who looks like my Denno, he tried to kill me, but you never did."

"In the Bright Court we are sometimes careless and thoughtless in a way that is cruel," Aleneil said, "but it is not our way to be cruel a-purpose, just to hurt another."

"Not even to punish me for such a creation?" Rhoslyn asked.

Aleneil looked startled. "No. I have had no order from Oberon or Titania. I doubt that they even know what you did. Although it is true that Oberon does not like constructs from Underhill to go into the World Above, sometimes even *he* has made such things, to substitute for a child we mean to take from a life of pain and sorrow. But it is absurd to imagine that we would make up such a tale. How could it punish you to know that your poor creation had a happy life and a peaceful death? Truly Rhoslyn, Elizabeth and I want to give you a little comfort, not hurt you."

Rhoslyn took a deep breath, and blinked hard, as if her eyes were stinging her. "If what you say is true, you will have patched a broken heart. I cannot help but grieve over what I made and loved, but at least I do not need to hate as well. If my poor Richmond was happy . . . He is still gone, but I do not need to feel that I made him only to die for a cruel purpose."

"It is true that he died at peace," Elizabeth said. "And you do not need to take it on my word alone. Ask Dunstan, my major-domo, when you can catch him alone. The guardsmen, too. Gerrit, Nyle, Shaylor, and Dickson. They were with Richey when he died. Of course, they thought he was my Da and they'll call him His Grace of Richmond, but now you know the truth. And if you are still doubting, well, Da is alive and Denno will take you to see him if you want; you know that Da cannot possibly be Richey, so the Richmond that died is your little made-boy."

Rhoslyn again looked from one to the other. "I do not think I will push Denoriel's good nature so far," she said, after a long pause. "But I do not think you would have told me such things if they were not true, for you have given me the means to verify the truth on my own. You have told me the name of the healer—and even a Sidhe of the Dark Court has leave to seek out any healer of the Bright. So I have but to visit—and soon or late, I shall see your Richmond alive."

Aleneil smiled a little. "And of course, there is no reason for Mwynwen *not* to verify what we have said." She held out her hand to Rhoslyn. "So, if we cannot be friends, at least *you and I* need not be enemies?"

"Nor I and Lady Elizabeth, I pledge it by all I hold dear," Rhoslyn replied, with a light in her eyes that made Elizabeth very glad that she had gone to all this trouble. "But you need not be afraid of Pasgen any longer either, Lady Elizabeth. He is very sorry for trying to hurt you in the past, and will not do so again." She smiled a little, and it was a wry smile. "In no small part because *you* have taught him a sharp lesson on the danger of meddling with mortals!"

Chapter 29

After Elizabeth, Aleneil, and Rhoslyn had returned safely to Hampton Court and taken up their usual pursuits, Aleneil warned Elizabeth not to trust Rhoslyn despite her appearance of sincerity, and certainly not to trust Pasgen.

"They are all terrible liars in the Dark Court. They can look so sincere and still be lying." She uttered Lady Alana's soft contagious laugh. "Of course the Bright Court is not overly dedicated to truthfulness either, but we do not lie when it is a matter of life and death."

"I will be careful," Elizabeth promised.

However, as it happened, there was nothing to be careful about. She rarely saw Rhoslyn, and then only from a distance, when in the train of her sister Mary. Pasgen she did not see at all. And in any event, she was not long at court.

The king returned from France safely in October, but the war, as Denno had predicted, had not gone well. King Henry did take Boulogne, but the emperor Charles did not take Paris. Indeed, Charles's war went so ill that the emperor made peace with King Francis of France without consulting Henry, leaving Henry open to the full weight of the French army—and added to that a treaty that committed the Empire to support France against any attack.

Mired in political recriminations with Charles, and nearly

461

bankrupt, Henry pared his court down to what was by previous standards a mere skeleton—and he only kept on necessary officials. However, one of the acts passed by Parliament in 1544 was a new Act of Succession. The act essentially duplicated the provisions in the king's will—the throne to go first to Edward, second to any lawful issue of the king's marriage to Catherine Parr, third to his eldest daughter, Mary, but after that to Elizabeth, equal to Mary in all but the date of her birth. Named in an act of Parliament, Elizabeth's place in the succession was assured more certainly than by a clause in a will, which could be eliminated by a single pen-drawn line.

Warned to caution by both Denoriel and Aleneil, Elizabeth gave no sign of her feeling of triumph, but she was more at peace than she had ever been. And Denoriel did not choose to break that peace; he never told her that England was facing serious threats, as France and the Empire sealed their new alliance with plans to invade. For security as well as to get them out of the way, the two younger children were sent to Ashridge together. Mary, older and sometimes useful as a diplomatic pawn, remained with the court or retired to her own estates, as Henry or her own health dictated.

Elizabeth and Edward were delighted to be together again. In the private setting, the prince was less formal and rigid, and their tutors were even more flexible and amusing; there was no need for strictness with two such eager students. The children were well guarded but more to save them from annoyance than from any fear that anyone wished them ill.

In this climate, Denoriel had easily enough ingratiated himself with Sir Anthony Denny, chief gentleman of King Henry's Privy Chamber, by bringing secret information from France. He said the news came to him from his ship captains who traded in French ports, but he actually got the information from friends in Elfhame Melusine. When Sir Anthony asked him why he brought such news, ensconced as they were in the privacy of his study, Denoriel laughed.

"Because in these times any foreigner is suspect, and a foreigner like myself, who has a large trading empire, could be in danger of having his property confiscated and being cast out. I am not much worried about confiscation; most of my worth is in ships spread all over the eastern seas, and I have credit in many cities of the Hanse," he added, "but I consider this land my home, and I am loathe to find myself barred from it."

"No threat is being directed against our merchants," Sir Anthony said quickly, though his eyes were not on Denoriel when he said it, but rather, looking just past Denoriel's shoulder.

Denoriel smiled and shook his head. He knew and Sir Anthony knew that if the choice came between paying the king's mercenaries and stripping the merchants bare, the merchants would be stripped. But assurances were offered, however mendacious, because no one wanted the merchants to flee.

"As I said, I am not much troubled about confiscation, but I do not wish to be cast out," Denoriel repeated. "I have lived in England for over twenty years now. I have deep roots in this country and eagerly desire its well-being. And I have known and loved Pr—I beg pardon, the *Lady* Elizabeth, since she was a babe."

"Ah, yes. I remember. It was you Norfolk was obtaining a pass for." Sir Anthony laughed, his hands toying idly with a goose-quill. "He is much puzzled by you, Lord Denno. He cannot understand your attachment to the royal children since you never ask them . . . or him, for that matter . . . for favors."

Denoriel drew himself up. "I do not need any favors. I can and will always make myself useful and valuable to England because it has provided for me a haven, a true home."

A small spell accompanied the words; it did not need to do much because Sir Anthony was half convinced already. But when it took hold Sir Anthony would always like and admire Lord Denno and trust him completely.

"You mean that, I see, Lord Denno," Sir Anthony said. "Well, I am grateful for the news you brought and hope you will bring more. And I will see that, whatever happens, you remain welcome in this realm and have free access to Lady Elizabeth."

"That is the only favor I desire," Denoriel said, seriously, and with a little bow. "As for the children, Harry—I mean His Grace of Richmond—was such a child and growing into such a man as was reward enough just to know him. 'Tis said the good die young," he added with a sigh.

Sir Anthony nodded sympathetically. "His Grace of Richmond was a fine, open-hearted lad," he agreed.

"The Lady Elizabeth—" Denoriel uttered a warm chuckle "—now she is another kettle of fish entirely . . . a very spicy kettle of fish.

She is a refreshment to the mind and the heart and I thank you sincerely for the permission to visit her."

Sir Anthony did feel a small qualm of suspicion that permission to visit Elizabeth would bring the foreign merchant into contact with Prince Edward, but Norfolk had accorded the man the same permission with Henry FitzRoy. Despite the spell—it was a little, gentle thing not designed to override clear thought—when Denoriel was gone again, Sir Anthony wrote to the prince's tutors to ask if Denno seemed to be influencing Edward in any way. He was promptly reassured that Denno did not spend much time with the prince and seemed to have no purpose with either child but amusement.

It was true that such amusements might lead to friendship and influence when the prince was a man, but that was many years away, and right now Sir Anthony was profiting by bringing the king information no one else had. Denno was always welcome at court, and aside from the information, Sir Anthony found him a most comfortable friend.

By the New Year of 1546 the threat of invasion had passed. As New Year gifts Denoriel brought Edward a fine astrolabe and a remarkable kaleidoscope. He brought Elizabeth, who was now edging toward her thirteenth year and womanhood, a set of gold pens, some intricate earrings into which her spell-bearing stones could be fastened, and a magnificent necklace—very like that which had turned to dross when she first returned from Underhill.

She kissed him when she saw the necklace and then said, "I cannot keep it, Denno. It will make all kinds of trouble if anyone sees it. Even Edward would not believe it was a free gift, not shackled to me with promises."

"You do not have to wear it," he said, flushing as he returned the kiss with perhaps a touch more enthusiasm than was fitting. "Put it in your box and only try it on for me. You have such a beautiful long throat."

She laughed and shook her head. "I could not resist showing it off. Keep it for me."

Denoriel did not continue to protest. He guessed he might not need to keep the necklace for very long, and it might win him another kiss when he brought it back. Henry was desperately seeking allies who would help him drive Emperor Charles into a new alliance that would force the French into peace and permit Henry to keep Boulogne. One way was through marriage, and Henry began offering his younger daughter to any nation he hoped to secure as an ally.

Most rulers, or their advisors at least, wary of being involved in Henry's difficulties, offered many speeches about how much they were honored, leading to polite refusals. One or two wished to keep negotiations open for their own reasons and sent flashy but—by royal or imperial standards—inexpensive pieces of jewelry to the proposed bride.

Elizabeth was frightened at first; she did not want to be anyone's bride. She knew, deep in her heart, though she could not have said *how* she knew it, nor why, that a foreign marriage was wrong for her, that she must never leave England. But Denno soon put her mind at rest. Through sources in the Hanse, he himself had brought Sir Anthony the information that one party was angling for trade concessions, not to support Henry's war.

As for the other offer, news did not travel only one way; Sir Anthony told Denoriel that the other party was actually too insignificant for Henry to give his daughter, even if he himself had proposed the idea in a fit of temper. Although nothing came of the marriage negotiations, Elizabeth was allowed to keep the relatively valueless trinkets—and to them was added Denoriel's necklace.

Both Edward and Elizabeth had been invited by Queen Catherine to celebrate Christmas 1545 and the New Year 1546 with the court. They had received lavish gifts of cloth for clothing and other marks of favor, but no one seemed to be interested in marrying any of the children at this point, and King Henry, suffering now for his lifelong pursuit of pleasure, found the continual full court something of an irritant. Since for the present time the children were useless as diplomatic pawns, there was no purpose in keeping them with the king, and soon after the New Year they returned to the country.

Edward probably actually preferred living in the country, as he did not seem much to enjoy the entertainments of court. Elizabeth loved being at court, but she was frankly terrified of being a treaty bride and hoped the retreat to Hatfield, which her father had ordered, meant the end of that danger. Also, she loved Edward and was glad to see him happy, and he was never happier than when he was alone with his tutors. She loved her books, too, and Denno was a frequent visitor, so she did not repine.

In fact Denoriel was so frequent a visitor at Hatfield, where he had long-established Gates and could come and go with great ease, that soon a slip of the tongue here and there revealed to him Elizabeth's adventure with Rhoslyn. Denoriel was horrified, and warned Elizabeth even more forcefully than Aleneil had to avoid Rhoslyn and never to trust Pasgen.

"Mistress Scot does not come near me," Elizabeth assured him, "and I have never seen Pasgen after that time he attacked me in the garden. But I am sorry for the dark lady. She really loved that little boy, and she is very sad. And I do not think she hates you anymore."

Denoriel felt a little sorry for Rhoslyn himself. He remembered her expression, and the tears that had poured down her face when she thought he had killed the changeling. He knew, too, what he would have suffered if Harry had actually died, and he could not help but think that she must have felt something similar for the changeling. After all, not only was Rhoslyn female, and equipped by nature with maternal instincts, she had actually created poor Richey and could presumably regard herself as something of his mother. Nonetheless, one of the times that Mary was at court, he waylaid her maid of honor, Rosamund Scot.

"Stay away from Elizabeth," he said, in tones as cold as a blast of icy wind. "If any attempt is made on her—"

Rhoslyn turned flashing black eyes on him. Bull-headed and bull-mannered; he always had been, and likely would never learn better.

Aleneil had told him, she thought. Stupid chit, could she keep nothing to herself? She should have been able to hold her tongue on that score, even if he was her brother. But that petulant thought made Rhoslyn smile slightly because she herself could keep very little from Pasgen.

So instead of sneering and turning her back on him, she said pacifically, "I mean her no harm. I am even doing my best to undo the evil notions I have given Mary."

Unfortunately the hint of a smile made Denoriel quite sure she was planning something evil. "I am not saying that you would, of yourself, intend to do Elizabeth harm," he said, his lifted brows implying disbelief, "but Pasgen might have other notions."

Pasgen would have troubles enough when Vidal realized that he was nowhere to be found. Rhoslyn did not want the Bright Court mobilized against him too. "No," she said trying to make Denoriel feel her sincerity. "Pasgen no longer wishes any harm to come to Elizabeth. He told me he will not act against her because he has reinterpreted the FarSeeings. He has come to think that Elizabeth is meant to come to the throne no matter what we do or do not do, and that future is as set and immutable as the past." She put a hand on Denoriel's arm. "I swear to you, he has withdrawn from the Unseleighe Court."

Denoriel stared for a moment, wondering if he could believe her. He could detect no levels beneath her overt words—but he did not dare rely on her swearing.

Finally, he shrugged. "Whatever you and Pasgen would prefer, you might not be able to disobey Vidal Dhu. So heed me: I do not want you or your brother near Elizabeth."

For a moment Rhoslyn was tempted to spit in his face. "We will do as we please, Pasgen and I," she hissed, but keeping her voice low. "Certainly we are not subject to *your* orders." Then she swallowed and shook her head; she owed it to that bright-haired princess, who had gone out of her way to give her an end to her grief, to at least bring the situation to a point of neutrality. "Believe me or do not believe me, but I really do wish Elizabeth well now, so I will give you a piece of advice. Do not watch me and Pasgen so closely that you miss the real threat to her."

"Real threat?" His voice was hardly a murmur. It would not be heard except by Rhoslyn herself, and the way he leaned toward her hinted at amorous dalliance.

"Watch for Vidal Dhu himself," she murmured back. "Now he is still amusing himself in Scotland. There is more than sufficient power from pain and misery pouring out of Scotland to keep the Dark Court fed full. Do what you can to make King Henry adamant about the Scottish treaty and pursuing the war with the Scots, for the more it is prolonged, the longer Vidal will tarry, and forget about Elizabeth entirely."

"The king is adamant enough without any help from me," Denoriel admitted.

"Good." Rhoslyn nodded. "That is Elizabeth's best warranty of safety. As long as Vidal is busy keeping the Scots from considering any compromise with Henry, he will not remember Elizabeth.

But if the war stops and Henry dies, Vidal will act. *He* is very determined that Elizabeth not come to the throne."

Denoriel held up a hand, looking angry and horrified. Even to speak in the negative those two words, Elizabeth and throne, were treason. Rhoslyn pressed her lips together in angry frustration, knowing she should not have said that last sentence, that Denoriel would think she said it to make trouble.

Just then Mary turned from her conversation with Wriothesley. Rhoslyn's angry expression made her smile. Mary did not like Lord Denno. She gestured and Rhoslyn walked away from Denoriel.

He stood looking after her, very much troubled in his mind. There was something different about Rhoslyn, about the way she had spoken, even the way she had held herself while she talked. What she said could be a blind, of course, to fix his attention on Vidal so they could . . . what? They were too cautious to attack Elizabeth directly. Vidal, if he could see a way to direct the blame elsewhere, was not. So was the warning genuine?

And if it was—where was the new danger lurking?

Although Rhoslyn had been perfectly honest with Denoriel, she had inadvertently misled him. He did not believe her enough to relax his guard about Elizabeth, but her conviction that Vidal Dhu was in Scotland and single-mindedly devoted to Scottish affairs made him less alert to the prince's meddling with others.

In fact Vidal *was* devoted to Scottish affairs. He would have preferred to be in Scotland to keep a closer watch on Cardinal Beaton, the Earl of Angus, and several others. The men could be pointed in a particular direction easily, but they were so inconstant of purpose—except in the purpose of forwarding their own interests—that they could not be trusted without close supervision. Thus Vidal had tried to seek out Pasgen to work on Scottish affairs from the English end.

Vidal found no sign of Pasgen Underhill or in the World Above. He found Rhoslyn easily enough attending on Lady Mary in the mortal world, and she replied to his questions with sincerity—and by Vidal's own reading with perfect truth—that she did not know where Pasgen was. The last he had told her was that he wished to do some research in the Unformed lands. Vidal cursed her for a simple-minded and incurious fool, and left her to her own business. Control of Lady Mary without overt spells was important.

A visit to the servant in Fagildo Otstargi's house in London had already made clear that Pasgen had not been there in a long time. Vidal left and returned as Otstargi a few days later. He had spoken to his FarSeers and was clear headed and well informed. He did not send out any general notice of Otstargi's return but arranged for private messages to be delivered to several men on the council.

His note to the Earl of Hertford was returned unopened. Sir Anthony Denny sent a polite rejection of Otstargi's invitation. Paget made an appointment for the next week. Wriothesley appeared at Otstargi's front door only a few hours after the message was received.

Vidal received him in Pasgen's study, a place thick with ominously heavy volumes bound in curious leathers, and sporting upon the shelves a number of curiosities among the books. These were objects guaranteed to give a visitor pause—skulls that few in England would be able to identify, the requisite stuffed owl and crocodile that every self-respecting sorcerer was required to own, crystal globes and mineral specimens, and brass instruments of uncertain use.

As he had several years in the past, Wriothesley asked angrily where Otstargi had been and was told coldly that he had been away on his own business, which was no business of any other man. Since Wriothesley was not at all eager to hear about Otstargi's magical practices—which were illegal by act of Parliament—he did not enquire further. What he did ask was how to stem the king's spending on war. There simply was no money to be wrested from the realm.

"You cannot stop him altogether," Vidal said, leaning across the desk to emphasize his point. "King Henry must conquer something. Now that the Church is in his hand he wants to wrest away parts of France. Guide him into making peace with France—"

"The French will not accept his terms," Sir Thomas said, all but grinding his teeth. "Francis is determined to have Boulogne back and Henry is equally determined to hold it."

"So agree to give it back—" Vidal persisted.

"I just told you Henry would not hear of it. Ask the moon to agree to come down out of the sky and adorn the clock tower at Hampton Court; you will get as much cooperation," Sir Thomas retorted, temper barely held in check.

"Nor will you hear how to accomplish it if you keep interrupting me," Vidal said, barely holding in his own temper. "All Henry—or, thank God the agents he will send to do the negotiating—needs to do is to make the return of Boulogne contingent on something that the French will not want to do but that is possible of being done. Set a high price on the ransom of the city."

That gave Sir Thomas pause for a moment, and he sat back in his chair. "Hmmm. The king might not reject such a proposal out of hand. I will certainly suggest it to the council."

"Yes, but do not cut off all plans for war," Vidal added. "If you make peace on all sides, Henry will become restless, and his restlessness will burst out in a new and more expensive place—like supporting the Germans against the empire."

"God's sweet Grace forefend!" Wriothesley breathed.

"So . . . do not make peace with the Scots," Vidal continued, urging the project he truly wanted.

In a perverted way, Vidal was enjoying this. On the one hand, the mortals were so easily led—but on the other, the machinations he had to go through to lead them, the convoluted plotting and planning, made him feel challenged, and more like his old, clever self than he had in many a mortal year.

"Let Henry bend his warlike intentions on the Scots," Vidal continued. "You know that war with the Scots is cheap. It does not require large mercenary armies because the English of the northern shires are always willing to fight the Scots. And by God's grace, the Scots are always willing to fight anyone. Let there be peace for six months, and they will fight each other."

"Ah," Wriothesley said, smiling. "Yes. I see the wisdom of your advice, Master Otstargi." He laid a well-filled purse on the table between them. "And have you any advice for me, personally?"

"Yes." Vidal now sat back in his chair, resting his elbows on the carved arms, steepling his fingers in front of his chin. "Be more circumspect in your support of those who lean toward the old religion—except for Lady Mary. Aid *her* in any way you can, except for a direct confrontation with the king. A time is coming when adherents of the old religion will have shorter shrift than this king allows."

Wriothesley's face paled visibly. "This king . . ." He shuddered, glanced anxiously around the room, which was empty and bare of anything a listener could hide behind, then whispered. "Are you saying that . . . that Henry . . . will die?"

Vidal shrugged. "All men die. Sooner or later is the question . . . and this, my glass says, may be sooner. But certainly not tomorrow or next week. Let him make peace with France while offering conquest of Scotland and the union of the kingdoms by the marriage of Mary and Edward as the prize."

Wriothesley was still pursuing the earlier hare. "But you are not telling me the king will make even greater changes in . . ." He flushed. "God's Grace upon us all, he was speaking about the mass just the other day. But—no." Sir Thomas shook his head vehemently. "He will not order that mass not be said. Why . . . why he even spoke to the pope's emissary . . ."

Otstargi shook his head. "My glass does not say what the king will do. It shows many, many events, none clear. I only advise you to be cautious so you can move either way."

"You are telling me to give up my faith?" Sir Thomas stared hard at him.

Vidal waved a hand. "I never meddle with any man's faith. Caution and a closed mouth are not a change of faith. But if you do not keep the king's mind on the Scottish war, he will have too much time to consider religious problems. The Scottish war will not prolong the king's life, but also will not shorten it, as his sojourn in France may have done. And a peace with France will reduce the strain on the king's purse. Keep to these matters, and mind what company you keep. That is all."

Although Denoriel was making it his purpose to be in court even more often as the king's health wavered, he got no hint of Vidal's presence. Vidal never came near the court, and what Wriothesley advised was so much a matter of plain common sense that Denoriel never thought of outside influences. Paget and the council were soon advising the same political expedients.

At first the king seemed to ignore the council's advice. Soon after the children were settled in Hatfield, the king sent Edward Seymour, the Earl of Hertford, to Boulogne as if to begin a major enterprise. Denoriel talked to Sir Anthony and even to Sir Thomas Wriothesley but Sir Thomas simply shook his head, admitting that he had hoped Henry would make peace. They assumed the king intended to attack Etaples, which he had long wished to destroy.

Then, however, before Denoriel could consider how to interfere to turn Henry's attention to Scotland again, he discovered his work had been done for him. The king did a right-about-face and appointed commissioners to begin new peace talks with France.

Henry's first demands were impossible. He wanted the French to cease supporting the Scots against the English, asked for eight million crowns to reimburse English war expenses, and insisted that Boulogne and its surrounding area be ceded to England.

Later, when it was clear that the French were about to abandon the negotiations, he permitted his envoys to make concessions, agreeing that the Scots should be comprehended in the treaty if the infant queen were delivered to England, and then, the further concession that he would accept hostages in Mary of Scotland's stead. He even agreed that Boulogne would be returned to France in eight years if two million crowns were paid.

Although Henry signed the agreement in July and Francis ratified it on August sixth, no one was very serious about the terms. Nonetheless the treaty permitted Henry to dismiss the expensive mercenaries and reduce his own forces in Boulogne . . . which was still in English hands. The imperial ambassador remarked that if Henry was going to wait to return Boulogne for the payment of two million crowns, he would hold the city forever. To which Henry, who never intended to return Boulogne, made no reply beyond a satisfied smile.

By November, despite the fact that Henry's agreement with the French included the Scots, the king was castigating the Scottish ambassadors so violently, complaining that the Scots had broken the peace, that they became sure the English would attack them again and appealed to France for help. Henry did not seem to care what answer Francis would make; he went on ordering the assembly of more forces in preparation for another assault on Scotland.

To Denoriel's questions, Sir Anthony shrugged. The behavior was typical of the king. Thus Denoriel felt free to spend most of his time with Elizabeth, and it was just as well because at the end of November she and Edward were separated. Edward was sent to Hertford and Elizabeth to Enfield. Both felt the parting keenly, but Edward (who had no Lord Denno to keep his spirits up) wrote sadly in Latin to Elizabeth:

> *The change of place, in fact, did not vex me so much, dearest sister, as your going from me. Now, however, nothing can happen more agreeable to me than a letter from you ... But this is some comfort to my grief, that I hope to visit you shortly ...*

The king's planning action against the Scots was all to the good as far as Elizabeth's safety, but very privately in his own home Sir Anthony confessed to Denoriel that the entire council was very worried about the king. He was clearly failing—and did not himself seem aware of it ... unless the feverish orders to prepare to fight to protect Boulogne, the buildup of troops on the Scottish border, the negotiations with everyone about everything, possible and impossible, were because he feared he would not have time enough to complete what he intended to do.

The elven siblings discussed the situation in the one place where they need not fear being overheard—in Denoriel's own suite in Llachar Lle. "So do we warn Elizabeth?" Denoriel asked Aleneil after he had told her what Sir Anthony believed.

"He has seemed to fail before and rallied," Aleneil said. "Nothing in the FarSeers' lens is different."

"No, because Edward will come to the throne." Denoriel sighed, and leaned back into the cushions on his settle. "I hope you do not think those who support the old religion will put Mary forward?"

"They may try, but Mary will have none of it," Aleneil said certainly. "For one thing, she is not yet sure that Edward cannot be enticed back to Rome..."

"To Rome?" Denoriel laughed. "But Edward is a hotter little reformist than Elizabeth, who abides strictly by her father's middle way and says—taking Henry's words from his last speech to Parliament—that she will be neither 'mumpsimus' nor 'sumpsimus' but worship God without argument."

Aleneil shrugged. "But Mary has not really spoken to Edward for nearly a year, and some months ago she was given hope that Henry could be drawn back to Rome."

Denoriel stared at her for a moment, then said disbelievingly, "Henry? Surely that must be a fantasy."

"In a way, yes, but also a mystery." Aleneil shrugged. "A man called Guron Bertano arrived in England to discuss with Henry a reconciliation with the pope. That Henry would accept, I do not believe, but why was Bertano allowed to come? Why did he remain in England for two whole months? Why did he have a meeting with the king and two with Paget?"

"It seems quite mad," Denoriel said. "And Sir Anthony never even mentioned this Bertano."

Aleneil nodded. "It is possible that Bertano's mission has been kept secret from Denny or he was so sure it would come to nothing that it was not worth mentioning." She toyed with the beaded tassel of the jeweled belt around her loose gown, so unlike the corseted clothing she wore as Lady Alana. "Also, he leans slightly toward the reformed persuasion so I would imagine that Paget and Wriothesley were the men sent to deal with the pope's emissary—if he was the pope's emissary." She shrugged. "Likely also no one wanted word passed that Mary had some part in urging Paget to meet with Bertano."

Denoriel's brow wrinkled. "What this Bertano offered was thought to be tempting?"

Aleneil pursed her lips. "Mary believes that the pope offered to accept everything Henry has done, the divorce, the dissolution of the monasteries . . . everything . . . so long as Henry would acknowledge the pope's primacy."

Denoriel shook his head. "But that, although it was several times wrapped up in white linen, and perhaps Henry did not himself see it at first, was what the king really wanted from the beginning—to rule absolute in his own realm with no interference from the Church. Wasn't it?"

"I am not sure Mary ever understood that or could understand it." Aleneil sighed at Mary's thick-headedness.

"Elizabeth could." Denoriel laughed. "But how did *you* become familiar with this? I thought Lady Mary would have nothing to do with you."

Aleneil smiled. "From Rhoslyn." She shook her head at Denoriel's scowl. "I tell her nothing about Elizabeth and she does not ask. I think you are wrong about her. She *is* trying to change Mary's mind about Elizabeth. When Mary asked if Elizabeth would turn back to Rome if Henry agreed to Bertano's terms, Rhoslyn replied very cleverly that Elizabeth always bowed to the authority of the king, and would obey him in everything. And thus she has also covered Elizabeth's acceptance of the reformed religion in Edward's reign."

"Which brings us back to whether we should or should not warn Elizabeth that her father may soon die," Denoriel pointed out.

"She is so happy now," Aleneil said in a small voice. "There have been so few times in her life when she could be happy. I cannot bear to take it away from her."

"But the shock..." Denoriel's voice faltered. He, too, could not bear the thought of spoiling even a few days of this halcyon time.

So they said nothing, and Elizabeth, usually so quick to perceive anxiety in her guardians, did not seem to notice. Later they both thought she had been deliberately blind, but the blindness had given her two more months of peace.

It was not so peaceful for others. In December Henry Howard, Earl of Surrey and Harry Fitzroy's childhood friend, was accused first of heresy and then, worse, of treason. Denoriel had lost touch with the young man whose faults of quick temper and intemperate pride had worsened as he grew.

More shocking to Denoriel was that the duke of Norfolk, who had survived with no more than a brief period of eclipse the adultery of two nieces married to the king, was also seized, stripped of his staff of office and his garter, and thrown into the Tower. Judicious bribery bought Denoriel a secret visit with Norfolk, to whom he offered what help he could give, but the old man only laughed bitterly.

"I have done this and that evil in my life," he admitted without a sign of regret, "but I can truly rejoice in my absolute and unfailing loyalty to my master. And if it is his will to take my life without cause, in this I will be obedient, too. No, Lord Denno, there is nothing you can do for me—but I must say that I see I was mistaken about you. You, too, have never failed in friendship."

Denoriel left the Tower feeling both troubled, and strangely, honored.

However, Norfolk did not lose his life. His son was found guilty of treason—on no evidence beyond rumor and hearsay and the fact that he had dared quarter his arms with those of Edward the

Confessor—and was executed on January 21. The duke, however, confessed various crimes, although not treason, and threw himself on the king's mercy.

This time it seemed obedience would not save him. A bill of attainder was passed in Parliament and orders were given on January 27 for Norfolk's execution on January 28 . . . only in the dark hours before dawn of the same day, it was the king who died.

Chapter 30

A month earlier, when the king was first so ill that his ministers despaired of his life, Wriothesley sat across the handsome table from the man he believed to be his tame magician. He wrung his hands.

"What will become of this nation?" he moaned. Thin veils of smoke wafted in and out of the light coming from the lone mullioned window.

Vidal was worried himself, because he was not at all sure he would be able to keep the conflict between Scotland and England alive, especially not if King Henry died. Cardinal Beaton had been murdered in May, and without his fanatical resolve to resist any rapprochement with the English, and without Henry's equally fanatical resolve to subdue the Scots, Vidal was afraid that peace would be made. For the present, the hunt for Beaton's killers and the violent resistance of the Calvinists (who had brought about Beaton's death) against the Catholic government was causing sufficient trouble to keep the Unseleighe well satisfied. But that could not last forever.

"Its government will change," Vidal said impatiently; he needed to be alone to think out how to keep strife alive, if not against the Scots—why then, a civil war in England would do as well. He wanted to be rid of this importunate mortal so that he could lay other plans. "You, however, are fortunate in being where you can know what is happening and perhaps in some small measure direct it."

"It will be very difficult . . . and dangerous, too," Wriothesley said, looking pale and drawn. "Paget and I have almost no support in the council. We tried—we even induced Denny to present our case because he is not of our persuasion but is far less extreme than Hertford—to have Bishop Gardiner restored to the Regency Council. The king would not hear of it."

Vidal curbed his impatience. "Cannot the principal secretary add a line to the will?"

"God's Grace, no!" Wriothesley exploded. "The whole council was present when the will was read. And Hertford, Paget, and Sir William Herbert were with the king when the fair copy was signed at the top and the bottom. It was witnessed by the officers of the household, sealed with the king's signet, and handed to Hertford." Wriothesley snorted. "Add a line indeed!"

"Then I suggest you pray hard for the king's recovery, which will give you more time to assemble supporters," Vidal replied shortly, already weary of this fool who could not arrange matters properly.

"Does your glass say nothing of this, of an event of such monumental importance?" Wriothesley said, despairingly.

Vidal frowned. The man had a point. If he was what he was pretending to be, how could he *not* be able to ForeSee the king's end? He shook his head slowly. "It shows nothing of the king's death or of a ruling council. Hmmm. Perhaps, deceived by how ill the king seemed, I was looking too closely in time. I will try to see further into the future."

"Please," Wriothesley said, "do so. With all speed."

Vidal stood up, frowning—which allowed him to look down on Wriothesley. "Speed is not a word compatible with the workings of the ancient secrets, my lord," he replied portentously. "Nevertheless, I will attempt to pierce the veils of time on your behalf. But I do require privacy—"

That was enough (at last!) to make Sir Thomas take his leave.

Having rid himself of his client, Vidal Gated right from Otstargi's house to Caer Mordwyn. However, his efforts to force his Far-Seers to a more certain prediction about the king's life resulted only in their exhaustion and collapse. All Vidal learned was that

Henry would not die in the next two weeks but would be dead before spring.

Vidal left the FarSeers, some weeping, some unconscious, cursing everything and everyone as he made his way to his private quarters for allowing Pasgen and Rhoslyn to slip out of his absolute control. They could have made sense of the FarSeers' mouthings, he told himself, but Pasgen was gone and Rhoslyn was nothing without him.

Vidal knew he needed new plans, more options. The king was not yet dead, but by the time that happened, he must have decided what to do.

If all else failed, could he goad Rhoslyn into bespelling Mary into a try for the throne? But in the next moment, he discarded the plan. It was one that risked much—too much. If that ploy failed, Mary would be lost and Elizabeth would be the next heir to the boy. Elizabeth . . . Vidal licked his lips. He had forgotten all about Elizabeth.

Now Vidal cast himself into the most favored, deeply cushioned chair in his apartment. With one hand idly caressing the black leather, he pondered the situation. One thing he was sure of without any prediction was that there would be a desperate scrambling for place and power when the king did die. A second thing he was sure of was that Wriothesley was a frail reed to lean on for information or influence.

He needed several things: a way to reach Elizabeth so he could decide whether to try again to take her or just arrange for her to die; he needed also a tool of strength and daring who would have some influence on the regency government; and finally he needed the information that would make the first two needs possible of fulfillment.

First, and above all else, he needed information. With King Henry at death's door, there was no one with power enough to launch or even cry for an assault on Underhill, even if absolute evidence that all would believe was held before the foolish mortal noses.

Vidal smiled. He could do quite as he pleased . . . so long as no strong trail of magic led back to him for the High King to follow.

The smile turned into a grimace. That accursed Oberon would hunt down anyone who bespelled the king's council or household just for his pride's sake, because he had ordered it not be done.

But servants . . .

Servants! Vidal ground his teeth. That idiot Aurelia and her need for revenge! She had cost him dearly; he needed her competence now, and her quick wits, and he had neither. Now she was almost back to forgetting her own name and was useless to him.

However, there was a crumb to be salvaged out of her idiocy. Her attempt had proved that Oberon was not going to avenge attacks on the servants of royalty. *Yes.* That would permit him to put a Sidhe right into the royal household—

In fact, he decided, he would replace a body servant to the king. Whoever looked at a servant? So long as the service was satisfactory—oh, perhaps the servant's immediate supervisor might, but that minor point was easily taken care of with a befuddlement spell.

Now that was a plan with no drawbacks. A few commands, a spell or two, and he would have news as soon as Henry died.

Then there was Elizabeth to consider.

Vidal tensed in his comfortable chair. The satisfaction he had felt when he decided he would be able to place a Sidhe in Henry's very bedroom disappeared. No Sidhe could infiltrate Elizabeth's household. The girl could see through illusion, as Aurelia's misadventure proved, and her maid could sense Sidhe.

Very well, then, to get to Elizabeth he must have a minion in the household of someone who would visit her.

Ah. Vidal relaxed again against his cushions. Her brother, the little king-to-be. Until very recently they had lived together and it had been impossible to place a Sidhe in his household either—but of late, they had been separated. The separation was likely to hold, at least until Henry died, so Elizabeth would not be in the way when Edward was pronounced king.

However, the boy was said to be very much attached to her. It was possible he would be allowed to visit her to assuage his grief when he heard of his father's death. And a servant, a long-familiar and faithful body servant, could suggest a visit if the boy did not think of it himself. Yes, that would be ideal; Elizabeth would not look for a Sidhe planted among her brother's men.

As to the tool who could influence the council, Vidal had an idea, although he was not yet ready to move on it. He remembered Wriothesley complaining about Hertford's brother, Thomas

Seymour. A wild young man and dangerously ambitious, Wriothesley said, but he acknowledged that Seymour was extraordinarily handsome and appealing to women and well liked among many of the courtiers too.

Yes. Seymour must fall into the toils of Fagildo Otstargi . . . but that was for after Henry died and the council was ruling England.

Meanwhile, Vidal thought over the dark Sidhe who were the least likely to betray him, and the most able to withstand the cold iron in the mortal world. When he had fixed on those two best suited to his purpose, he sent imps to summon them.

They came with commendable alacrity, and he was so pleased by this that he did not even keep them waiting. Instead, he had them brought before him immediately. As the two of them, garbed quite soberly in black velvet and scarlet satin, stood before him in attitudes of servility, he lounged on his dais and explained what they would need to do.

They were agreeable, even eager, and suggested at once that they kill the servants whose places they would take. Knowing how his minions would react once the reality of their situation hit home, Vidal had to point out that then they would need actually to perform the servants' duties, and remain in the mortal world all the time lest the servant be missed.

The underlings were not pleased to hear that, but Vidal suggested another expedient.

"You will merely take the place of these servants temporarily. In that way the servants themselves can perform the actual labor. You would not know, after all, just what all those duties are—some might include a great deal of handling of cold iron, for instance."

After some objection, and a little growling over the loss of the exhalation of pain and life force they would have gained by killing, the dark Sidhe agreed.

"It will be simple enough to control them," Vidal said. "You have magic enough for that, I suppose. There will be no difficulty in replacing their memories. No new memories need be grafted into their minds; all they would remember was that they had gone about their usual tasks in their usual way."

Agreement was reached. The servants would be accosted in their own rooms and their memories tapped; then they would be rendered unconscious and concealed, unless they were needed to perform some task that the Sidhe could not or would not undertake themselves. The Sidhe wearing the servant's features and clothes would attend on the king or the prince just long enough to be sure of what was happening. As soon as the king died, an imp must be dispatched to tell Vidal. Then the mortal who had served the king could be put back in place, and that Sidhe return.

The Sidhe attached to the prince need do nothing until a visit to Lady Elizabeth was arranged. Then he must prepare the slow-acting poison that so closely mimicked consumption and form it into a thorn. When they visited Elizabeth, he must be in the group that accompanied the prince, even if he needed to kill and replace another gentleman on the road.

Vidal considered for a moment and then added the fact that the Sidhe should throw a bolt to numb the girl's mind as soon as he could focus on her. Otherwise she would recognize him as Other and might cry out—although she was accustomed to having Sidhe about her and might not react with fear.

As soon as she was subdued, he must find an excuse to pass by her and stab the thorn into her. As reward if he were successful, Vidal would not only give him a domain of his own but he was free to take anything of value that he wanted from the prince or anyone else.

And the Sidhe in the king's household was also free to help himself as he wished as soon as the king died.

Only the king did not die. He hung on the brink the entire first week of January then slowly began to mend. Vidal sighed with exasperation. By the sixteenth of January, Henry was again well enough to receive ambassadors.

Vidal had had enough. In Scotland the first furious reactions to Beaton's death were fading and the government was gaining control. Vidal had to find a new tool who would resist England and arouse the animosity of the reformists if he wanted the misery of that nation to continue. He made sure that the Sidhe he had left to watch the king and encompass Elizabeth's death still understood their duties and were bound to them, then he left for Scotland.

Coincidentally Denoriel was also away from London. When the king had first fallen ill in the beginning of January, he had hurried to Elizabeth at Enfield, which was conveniently only ten miles east of London. This permitted him to ride Miralys, who could cover the distance in a few minutes if necessary, and saved him from the effort of creating Gates.

Enfield was convenient in other ways. There was a huge chase for hunting and gardens with formal beds, archways, trellises and arbors for climbing vines—although they were not of much use in winter weather—and there was also a chapel that had dark corners, where a frightened girl could be cuddled and reassured: corners dark enough, that if any footstep was heard, or Blanche coughed a warning, there was no possibility of the sort of mischance that had befallen them over Harry's first visit.

That first week of January, Denoriel simply found an empty room in the palace and made himself as comfortable as he could when he was not actually with Elizabeth. He expected to be summoned by the air spirit any moment after she had news of Henry's death and he was forced to use the Don't-see-me spell more than he liked.

By the eleventh or twelfth of January, Denoriel was feeling dangerously empty, and Henry still would not die. When it seemed as if the king had recovered as much as he was likely to—which meant he might die in two days or live another six months—Aleneil insisted Denoriel go Underhill to restore himself.

Since Lady Alana would remain with Elizabeth and could send for him if he were needed, Denoriel left word at his house in London and sent special messages to particular friends to say he would be away until the end of the month. He would actually have returned sooner because he now found the affairs of the mortal world much more interesting than balls and celebrations Underhill, but Harry came to visit him to relate a most curious circumstance.

Elidir and Mechain had found their wandering Unformed land. It was now, as they suspected, nearer to Unseleighe domains than those of the Seleighe; still they had not been able to resist slipping quietly in and examining the mists. Could the mists be sentient enough to help those who praised them and resist manipulation by others?

While they were composing themselves to think kindly of the mists rather than setting their minds to commanding, they noticed that instead of an aimless shifting and flowing, thin tentacles were approaching them as if they were curious. That was odd, but they never discovered whether the behavior had meaning, because a tall Sidhe, who looked something like Denoriel had before his hair had turned to white, stepped out of the mist and asked them what they were doing there.

"Pasgen," Denoriel said, identifying the mysterious Sidhe without difficulty. "Odd. I never knew him to be a creator, except of Gates. It was always Rhoslyn who made things. I wonder what he was doing there. I hope he was not building a simulacrum to replace Elizabeth!"

"I don't think so," Harry said, looking worried nonetheless. "I think Elidir or Mechain would have felt efforts at creation in the mists. I will ask them more specifically; I'm sorry now it didn't occur to me, but at the time I didn't think of Pasgen's interest in Elizabeth."

Denoriel frowned. "Rhoslyn swears he has none. That he is engaged in his own researches—but I am not at all sure that we can take her word. Did he say anything else to your friends?"

"I don't think they gave him the chance. Elidir says that they could feel his power, and Mechain said that she saw the mist sort of lining up behind him as if it were making ready to rush forward and engulf them. Anyway, they said they were sorry to intrude and just stepped back through the Gate. But here's another funny thing. Both said they didn't sense any threat from the Sidhe. It was only that they were near an Unseleighe domain that made them cautious."

Denoriel heaved out a sigh. "I think I liked it better when I knew Pasgen and Rhoslyn to be dedicated enemies. Now I hardly know whether to greet them as potential allies, to ignore them, or to attack them." He sighed again. "If you think Elidir and Mechain would be willing to take me, I would like to go to that Unformed land myself and confront Pasgen."

Mechain and Elidir were perfectly willing, but they had some trouble focusing the Gate. In the end, they found the way, but no one was there, and the mists were not at all friendly. They did not produce anything dangerous or attack, but they resisted blandishment and actively fought command. After some effort to leave a message for Pasgen, Denoriel threw up his hands. He was full charged with power and becoming anxious about what had happened in the World Above in his absence.

❖   ❖   ❖

In the late morning of 30 January at Enfield Palace, Elizabeth was complaining to Kat Champernowne that the place was like a tomb. It was too cold and nasty to go riding and even her Lord Denno had not been next or nigh her for over a week. She was just about to ask Kat whether it would be thought ill of if she wrote to Denno, when a message came from the gate that Lord Hereford had brought Prince Edward to see his sister.

Elizabeth jumped to her feet, her face glowing with pleasure, crying, "Edward! How wonderful. Oh, Kat, am I fine enough? Is my hair neat? Will he be able to stay, do you think? Does this mean we are to be together again?"

"It cannot do harm if you spend a moment tidying your hair and washing your hands, which have ink on two fingers," Kat said, without any of the enthusiasm she generally displayed when the prince paid a call.

Elizabeth was so excited that she did not notice that Kat's voice sounded strained and she rose uneasily to her feet. Her eyes met Blanche's over Elizabeth's head, but the nurse's expression was no help. And when Elizabeth returned a few minutes later, Kat was standing and watching the door. Elizabeth did not see her wringing her hands.

What Elizabeth did see as soon as the door opened, was four men in the prince's livery enter the room, look around to make sure there was no threat in it to the prince, and step aside, two right and two left of the door.

Only—one of the men was not mortal; at the distance Elizabeth could not see the pupils of his eyes, but she could see plainly that the round human ears were a shadowy superposition over long, elven points.

The Sidhe turned to look at her . . . and Elizabeth went cold with fear, touched her ear and muttered, *"Minnau ymbil!"*

Even as she felt what she imagined as a clear, flexible sheet close around the vague, glowing *presence* she imagined to be her heart and soul, a blow struck it. Elizabeth blinked, and saw the mortal near the Sidhe look at him with a slight frown as he staggered and gasped. Then she saw no more because Edward was through the door and running toward her with his hands outstretched.

"Elizabeth!" he cried. "I am going to London, but my uncle Hertford was so kind as to say we could stop and visit you."

Elizabeth embraced her brother fondly and kissed his cheek. "I am so glad to see you Edward," she said, but she had seen that Hertford, who was following his nephew, was not smiling.

Anxiously, she kissed Edward again, this time on the forehead, afraid the child was fevered. But his skin was cool and dry and his eyes were bright—and that was a stupid idea anyway. If Edward was ill, the physicians would come to him; his uncle would not make him ride to London on such a nasty January day. And why should Edward go to London?

Elizabeth knew that her father had been very ill in the beginning of January, but she had been quite satisfied with the reports of his recovery. Henry had been ill many times in the past three years, especially after he had returned from the war in France, but each time he had recovered. Now her grip on Edward tightened convulsively and she looked up at Lord Hertford, who was staring down at them with his lips in a tight, thin line.

"Father?" she whispered. "Is he ill again?"

"No," Edward said cheerfully. "I am going to London to be created Prince of Wales . . ."

"No, Your Majesty," Hertford said, in a voice heavy with portent, and tones that made Edward look up, eyes wide. "You are going to London to be crowned king. I deeply grieve to have to tell you, but your father, King Henry, the eighth of that name, died two days ago. The king is dead," he added, gravely, "And may God protect and save Your Majesty, Edward, my king."

The arm with which Elizabeth was holding Edward slipped away, and the boy turned to look at his uncle. "No," he whispered. "Not Papa. No."

There was no comfort to be had from Hertford's unhappy face and he turned to Elizabeth who was white, with staring eyes, and burst into tears. She did so too, clutching him in her arms. But even as she bent her head over her brother, she saw the men who had been at the door coming toward them.

The Sidhe was shaking his head and staggering slightly. Elizabeth began to tremble with fear. He *had* cast a spell at her that had been cast back at him when it touched her mental shield. But God only knew what he would do when he reached her. Elizabeth cast the spell for her physical shield. She felt it fold around her, covering her head and shoulders and her back, but where she gripped Edward to her, it felt thin and light.

As all the adults in the room moved toward the weeping children, Elizabeth felt a light blow on her shoulder. A long-fingered hand slid over her shield and sank down through the weaker part of the shield onto Edward's shoulder. The hand patted Edward consolingly and then withdrew. Amid her sobs, Elizabeth sighed with relief. The Sidhe must be a guard for Edward, as Rosamund Scot was a guard for Lady Mary. And then she heard Kat Champernowne sobbing aloud and the full impact of her loss, which had been delayed by her fear and confusion, hit her.

Her father was dead! Whatever she had ever feared or doubted about King Henry, Elizabeth had known surely and with perfect confidence that so long as she was in his favor, he would never permit anyone else to harm her. Or Edward. Now they were naked to the world. Elizabeth wailed aloud.

On arrival at his house in London, Denoriel found that two full weeks had passed and he had, indeed, arrived toward the end of the month. It was the twenty-ninth of January. Joseph Clayborne had attended to all the business correspondence and made excuses for any invitations while he was away, but there were several notes with future invitations.

Denoriel looked through them quickly, saying, "No. No. Yes. Yes, very gladly, thank you. No. No, but very sorry, please try again. Yes. No. Ah!"

"Ah?" Joseph Clayborne was amused.

"This is very interesting," Denoriel said. "Very interesting, indeed. It is an invitation to attend church with Sir Anthony Denny and his family tomorrow. You do not need to answer this. I will simply go and present myself with an apology to say I was away until late today."

Denoriel was pleased. This invitation was a step up in Denoriel's relationship with Sir Anthony. They had been friendly for over two years in the casual way of men and Denoriel had met Sir Anthony's wife on several formal occasions, but to be invited to a family party was a higher degree of intimacy than Sir Anthony had hitherto offered.

Thus Denoriel was very puzzled when he was turned away from Sir Anthony Denny's door on Sunday morning, January 30. The footman offered no excuse, only said that no one was at home. Somewhat nonplused, Denoriel left a note saying how sorry he was to be deprived of the family's company and asking if he had somehow offended. He did not at first associate the empty house with public affairs.

Since he was out, dressed in clothing suitable for church, and he had nothing else to do, he went to church. He did not mind; he always found attending the service a rather amusing experience. The music, although primitive compared to elven music, was very interesting and had the attraction of being full of spirit and very original, and the sermon was so ridiculous that he had to grit his teeth to prevent himself from laughing aloud.

In church he was hailed by a fellow merchant, who asked heartily where Denoriel had been and when he admitted, most mendaciously, that he had been in France, invited Denoriel to come home with him to dinner. Having nothing better to do, Denoriel closed with this offer. It was a good meal and the merchant's wife saved him from needing to prevaricate about doing business with France by asking him question after question about Lady Elizabeth.

Nothing delighted Denoriel more than talking about Elizabeth and the merchant was hardly less interested than his wife, so it was nearly dusk when he returned to his house. The footman, who Joseph had hired, told him as he entered that there was a message waiting for him from Sir Anthony Denny.

The note said no more than that Denny was sorry he had forgotten to inform Lord Denno that Lady Denny and the children had needed to go to the country. If Lord Denno would forgive him and stop at his house for a glass of wine, Denny would explain more fully.

Needless to say Denoriel hurried to Sir Anthony's house where a servant led him to the smaller withdrawing room. Sir Anthony rose from his chair by the fire and came forward with a hand outstretched. Denoriel was shocked by his pallor, dark-ringed eyes, and unshaven cheeks.

"My dear Sir Anthony," he said softly, coming forward and taking the hand extended to him, "I can see that something is very wrong. If I can be of any help, please tell me at once how."

"You are a good friend, Lord Denno. I have heard it from a number of people . . . including Norfolk . . . and it is true."

"Norfolk," Denoriel repeated unhappily. "He would not accept any help. He said he had been an obedient servant all his life and if the king wanted his life also, he would still be obedient."

"Norfolk is alive," Denny said, flatly. "It is the king who is dead."

Denoriel just stood and stared and then finally managed to blurt out, "When? Just today? There are no bells. The city is quiet."

Denny sighed. "No, His Majesty died two days ago, in the dawn of the twenty-seventh. I suppose it is safe to tell you now. It will be announced tomorrow morning. I hope I have done no wrong in agreeing . . . in supporting the Earl of Hertford . . ."

"I am sure you did what you believed to be right and best," Denoriel said. "But if it can do no harm for me to know—and I will swear on the souls of my murdered family that I will never speak a word of what passes between us here unless you give me leave to speak—I would wish to understand what happened."

Denny did not answer at first, just gestured for Denoriel to take the chair opposite the one he had been using. When Denoriel had seated himself, Denny, still silent, rang for a servant and asked for wine and cakes. While he waited, he paced the room.

Denoriel set a little spell of calm and confidence and trust in his path. He stopped when he had walked into it and nodded, just as the servant came in. When the bottles and glasses and tray of sweetmeats had been set on a small table and the door closed behind the servant, Denny poured two glasses of wine, brought one to Denoriel, and seated himself.

"You know that I am—was—the First Gentleman of the Privy Chamber," he began, "and thus I have—had been with the king as he grew weaker and weaker. About midday on the 27th I saw that he could not survive but that he did not yet understand his danger. I—I have—had been with His Majesty for many years. I loved him; I loved him, though many feared him, and I think I understood him better than many a man of greater rank. I could not bear to think that he could die without confession and absolution . . . so I told him he was dying and asked if he desired spiritual consolation."

Denoriel could do nothing more than say, "That was a brave and generous act, Sir Anthony."

A very faint smile touched Denny's lips and he sighed and sipped his wine. "I was aware," he said. "I knew that men had died for mentioning the possibility of the king's death. But . . . but he knew that I would never betray him and never tell him what was not true, and he asked for Archbishop Cranmer. I sent to Croyden as soon as the king had fallen asleep, but by the time Cranmer came, His Majesty could no longer speak. Still, he nodded to Cranmer's questions and the archbishop gave him absolution."

"There is nothing in this for which to blame yourself, Sir Anthony," Denoriel said, finishing the wine in his glass and rising to refill it. "That you are sorry to lose a master you loved, I understand, but you seem troubled beyond that."

"I am, indeed. When I left the room to send for Cranmer I also spoke to the Earl of Hertford and William Paget and told them that . . . that the king could not live out the next day." He hesitated, put his wineglass aside, and put one hand to the side of his face, torn with conflicting emotions. "The realm was about to lose its head!" he exclaimed. "Someone had to seize the rudder and steer the ship."

"I agree," Denoriel said, soothingly. "King Henry had been a very strong king. The council had mostly followed his orders. The shock of His Majesty's death could well have unbalanced the councilors so that they could not agree on how to act and chaos could have erupted."

Sir Anthony gave a long sigh. "So you see it the same way? Yes, but somehow . . . when I saw those two, Paget and Hertford, pacing the dimly lit corridor outside of the king's apartment and making plans . . . It seemed so cold-blooded."

Now Denoriel refilled Sir Anthony's glass and put it in his hand. He took a long swallow.

"And I was just as cold-blooded, I fear," Denny continued. "I sent away the physicians and everyone else beside Cranmer." His voice failed and was hoarse and clogged when he spoke again. "And when at last the king no longer breathed, I went out and summoned Hertford and Paget and I agreed when they decided that the king's death should not be announced immediately."

But Denoriel nodded. Cold-blooded? Hardly. Cold-blooded actions would have entailed moving to enrich himself while Henry's body was still cooling. There was a whole kingdom to think of—and within that kingdom, one small boy who needed to be protected before anyone else learned what had come to pass. One small boy—and perhaps, one not-so-small girl?

"You fear to have done wrong, but I do not think you did. It was only because I presented myself at the offices of our family's business with plans for what cargoes to take and a schedule for trading that the business survived. Do you think my heart did not weep tears of blood? That I did not wake in the night with tears on my cheeks? I still grieve. To grieve ... one cannot help that. But grief is for the dead—and for those who are not dead, there must be action."

Denny nodded. "But it was ... is ... very hard. Still, there was much to be done if chaos was to be avoided. The first thing was to protect the new king. It was decided that Hertford would go to Edward—now King Edward—and bring the child back to Whitehall Palace. Only when the new king was safe in his uncle's hands, would the late king's death be announced."

"Hertford is best," Denoriel said firmly. "I know somewhat of the man; he is strong, certain of will, and there is nothing that anyone can say touching his honor. Once Edward is secured, no one would dare a rising against Hertford's military ability. The army is accustomed to his command. He is the boy's uncle and I have seen that he is fond of Edward when he visited and I happened to be visiting Lady Elizabeth."

Suddenly Denoriel swallowed and his heart leapt into his throat. When would Edward be told that Henry was dead? And would they tell Elizabeth? He barely prevented himself from leaping to his feet and rushing out to go to Enfield. For a few more minutes he continued to listen while Sir Anthony explained how and why the Earl of Hertford would be named Lord Protector and rule in Edward's name. It seemed reasonable enough to Denoriel, but he didn't care. He needed to go to Elizabeth.

A whispered spell as he lifted his glass to drain it and Sir Anthony slumped over, sound asleep. Denoriel leapt up in time to catch his glass and place it safely on the table, and a second spell ensured that when he woke, he would recall Lord Denno listening, agreeing with all he had said and done, offering him commiseration, and then leaving after several assurances and expressions of condolence. Then he slipped out of the house. Miralys was at the door waiting for him.

Chapter 31

Denoriel did not remember the ride from London to Enfield. He must have stopped at the gates and been passed by the guards, but all he could recall was that Dunstan had muttered, "Thank God you are here, my lord," as he led him to the door of Elizabeth's private withdrawing room and Gerrit sighed with relief when he opened the door. It was a small room and with the heavy curtains drawn against the dark and a bright fire burning in the hearth, quite warm.

Elizabeth was sitting by the fire with Kat Champernowne and two other ladies seated behind her, Aleneil crouched on the rug at her feet, and Blanche stood behind her chair. Nonetheless, Elizabeth's face, when she turned it toward him, was white as a bone, and he could see she was shivering.

"Where have you been?" she cried when he entered.

Instead of saying he had been about his own business and he was not a slave to be always at her beck and call, he sank down on the carpet in front of her chair, in the place Aleneil had vacated, and took her icy hands.

"I did not know," he said. "I only came back to London this morning and . . . and they had not yet announced . . ."

"My father is dead," Elizabeth said, her voice trembling, her eyes staring into his. "It cannot be true. It *cannot*. He was the *king*. He cannot be dead. He ruled us all. He protected us. What will happen to us? What will happen to the nation?" And at the last, in a thin little whisper, "What will happen to me?"

He raised her cold hands to his lips and kissed them. "Nothing bad will happen to you, I swear it."

She blinked slowly and repeated, "To me." And after a moment added, as her eyes slowly lost some of that shocked look, "Yes. I believe you can protect *me*. But Denno," she swallowed, and then continued, "Denno, for once I am not the most important person in the world. What will happen to *England*?"

He hesitated, shocked, realizing that the girl-child was almost a woman now. "It will be different," he said. "There is no one like your father, that is true, but there are good and clever men who love this country and served your father. And these same men will swear to and serve your brother. Elizabeth, there is still a king."

"Poor Edward." She bent her head and began to weep. "I have lost him too."

"Lost Edward?" Denoriel echoed, horror in his voice. "What do you mean? He was hale and hearty when I saw him only a few days since."

"He is the king," Elizabeth said, simply and sadly, raising her head and releasing one of his hands to wipe her eyes. "I will never again take him in my arms and kiss him when he cries or laugh at him when he makes a mistake. I will curtsey to the ground and he will tell me to rise and call me 'dear sister' but there will be a wall between us."

For a long moment Denoriel was silenced by this sad truth. Edward simply did not have the kind of spirit that would brush away the rules so he could expose his heart.

"It is true that you will no longer be able to run to him and hug him," Denoriel said, "but he will remember that you once did. And it is likely true that you will not be able to laugh when he makes a mistake, but even a king has times when he is at ease. He will call you to him then. You *are* his dear sister."

"Am I?" There was just a hint of color in her cheeks. "Am I really?" Then she sighed. "But it will not be the same. We will never again live together just as brother and sister." She sighed again. "Where *will* I live?"

"I am not sure which estates will have been assigned to you in your father's will, but I know that you will have several manors and an income to support them ... and if you need help," he smiled past her at Kat, "you will have that too."

She looked at him, almost smiled, and then said almost in her old, petulant tone, "Will I? Lady Alana sent a messenger after Lord Hertford left with Edward and when you did not come ... I was afraid that now that Edward is king I would no longer be of any use to you and ... and your great lady."

He bent his head and kissed the hand he still held. "That is one of the silliest things I have ever heard you say. Why should you think such a thing when I have cared for you since you were a babe?"

"Because there was a—" she struggled to say a word for a moment, could not, and went on "—a guard with Edward, like the lady that guards my sister Mary—"

"What?"

That was not only Denoriel's voice, loud with shock and protest, but Aleneil's also. Both started to speak again and stopped. Aleneil rose from the chair she had been sitting on. Elizabeth was beginning to look frightened and she swallowed hard, but she did not speak, only began to weep again. Denoriel rose from the rug.

"Guard?" Kat Champernowne sounded surprised and puzzled. "But only Sir Robert Tyrwhitt and Sir William Paulet came in with Lord Hertford and the prin ... oh! the king."

Elizabeth began to shiver again, and Denoriel leaned forward and hugged her briefly. "My dear, you are exhausted," he said. "Why do you not go to bed now? Blanche will make you a tisane that will help you to sleep and sit with you so that you are not disturbed by anyone. Will this not be best Mistress Champernowne?"

"Indeed it will," Kat replied. "I have been trying to get her to go to bed since Lord Hertford left, but she wanted to wait for you to come."

"I am sorry I was so slow to arrive, but I never got the message because I have not been home all day. But you will go to bed now, Lady Elizabeth, will you not? I promise you, your dreams will be sweet."

"Not with my father dead," Elizabeth said, but she rose from her chair. "Still, I am exhausted and everyone else is, too. I will try Blanche's tisane and try to sleep. And Kat, it is late and dark and cold, do you think it would be possible to find a bedchamber for Lord Denno?"

"He may have my chamber," Aleneil said, smiling. "He has been host to me often enough. I will go in with Blanche, if she will have me."

"Of course, my lady," Blanche said, dropping a curtsey. "There is a trundle bed in Lady Elizabeth's chamber, and I intended to use that tonight anyway."

The only thing that was not easy was building a Gate to Logres from behind the rack that held Elizabeth's clothes. Denoriel and Aleneil were both nearly drained when Elizabeth at last covered her cross and they were able to bring her between them to the opalescent Gate on its pillars of chalcedony in Logres. Miralys and Ystwyth were waiting for them and in moments they were in Denoriel's apartment.

Aleneil, staggering slightly, collapsed onto the sofa. Denoriel, already much restored because of his spell for drawing power, took one look at Elizabeth's face and sent an air spirit with a message for Harry. Then he sat her in one of the cushioned chairs near the fireplace and knelt down before her.

"Now, my sweet, first things first," he said, "And this is not because you are not still the most important creature in all your mortal realm to me, it is because you might have uncovered a danger none of us anticipated. You saw a Sidhe in the party with Prin—I mean King Edward?"

"Yes, oh, I thought he was sent to comfort Edward as you have comforted and cared for me." Her face was white. "Now—you tell me this means he was a danger? What will he do to my brother?" Her face crumpled. "Oh, why did I not protect him? It is my fault! All my fault."

Denno shook his head and tightened his grip on her hands. "Elizabeth, it is not your fault at all! How can it be your fault?"

"When I first saw him by the door, looking about the room as if for any threat . . . I do not know why, but I was very frightened, and I invoked Tangwystl's spell from my earring." She blinked back tears. "And I thought I felt a blow upon it and that the Sidhe staggered and shook his head."

"Backlash," Aleneil said faintly. She had propped herself in a corner of the sofa and looked a little less as if she would faint.

"When he tried to attack me, I should have known!" Elizabeth cried. "I should have done more to protect Edward!"

"More? What did you do?" Denoriel asked.

"After the man with the Sidhe steadied him, Edward came rushing into the room and I was busy greeting him. But when Lord Hertford told us of my father ... my father's ... death—" Elizabeth took a long trembling breath, and then continued, "Edward cried out that it could not be true and he burst into tears. I took him in my arms and I was crying too. Then all the people in the room came toward us, and I was frightened, and I cast my shield."

"Clever girl," Aleneil said, sitting up straighter.

"But that was why I thought he was a guard for Edward," Elizabeth said on a sob. "He was one of the first to reach us, but he only pat-ted my shoulder and then patted Edward's, and then he drew back with the other men. I thought he meant no harm and I dropped the shield." She swallowed nervously. "Will he harm Edward?"

"I doubt it very much, sweeting," Aleneil said. "If he wanted to do Edward any harm, he had time in plenty while the party was riding from Hertford to Enfield. What easier than to make Edward's horse bolt or otherwise cause him to fall and see that he died of it?" Then she turned toward Denoriel and smiled. "I say, Elizabeth may have the right of it. The Sidhe may be a guard for Edward. You know that the Unseleighe Court has been look-ing forward to Edward's reign. They wouldn't hurt him, but it is possible they feared we would interfere."

"God's Grace, I never thought of that," Denoriel said and hugged Elizabeth again. "But just to be on the safe side I think I will go and complain to Oberon about Elizabeth seeing a Sidhe among the new king's gentlemen. Oberon will be livid. He knows that the barest smell of magic around Edward will set Hertford off on a 'thou shalt not suffer a witch to live' campaign."

"Do you not think I should be the one to complain?" Elizabeth asked, looking from Denoriel to his sister and back again.

Denoriel and Aleneil consulted each other in glances. Her evi-dence would be more convincing than hearsay, but there was the danger that Oberon would be attracted to such a pretty mortal girl. Before they could come to any conclusion the door opened and Harry ran into the room.

Elizabeth leapt to her feet, crying, "Da, oh, Da, such a terrible thing has happened."

"As long as you are alive and well," Harry said, hurrying to her and taking her in his arms, "I don't care."

"Father is dead," Elizabeth wailed, sounding for the first time like the child she truly was.

Harry's arms tightened and then slackened. "F-father?" he repeated. "The king? King Henry is dead?"

A kaleidoscope of memories rushed past him, memories of Henry's warmth and humor, memories of Henry's selfishness and cruelty, memories of Henry's cleverness and stupid stubbornness. All the memories, however were endowed with the huge vitality of the king, a king who seemed more than any mere mortal. Elizabeth was crying again.

"Dead?" Harry repeated, hugging her closer with one arm as he turned his head to Denoriel. "How is that possible?" And then with real ferocity, "Does he need to be avenged?"

"He was not strong as you remember him, Harry," Denoriel said. "He has been failing for years now. He could not take as much exercise as in the past but ate as well or better because he had so few other pleasures. He had grown immense, so large he had to be wheeled about in a chair; he suffered from putrefying sores that would not heal. His heart could not sustain him, I think."

The tenor of the conversation had communicated itself to Elizabeth and she realized that her Da was all ready to go to the mortal world to take revenge on anyone who had harmed his father. But Da could not live in the mortal world, and besides that, Elizabeth herself knew how close her father had been to death several times recently. His body had simply failed to rally at last.

She hastily wiped her eyes and said, "He has been very ill for months, Da. No one did anything bad to him." She smiled tremulously.

Harry led Elizabeth back to her chair and drew another close to it. He kissed her and hugged her, then patted her shoulder and began to talk to Denoriel about what would be likely to happen in England. At first Elizabeth sat quietly, staring into the colored flames leaping over the crystal logs. Once she held out her hands to them as if to warm them, because even the magic of Underhill could not warm the cold within her. But no heat came from the flames and she bit her lip.

"I can make them give off warmth," Denoriel said.

The soft words showed that though her Denno was talking to her Da he was still very much aware of her. And Da looked at her again and touched her cheek. The feeling of total emptiness, that with her father dead she was lost and alone, began to ease. She shook her head to Denno's offer and folded her hands together in her lap.

"Sweeting," Harry urged, "will you not have something to eat, or a glass of wine heated with spices? You are so pale. Are you not tired, love? You could sleep for a while."

"No," she said. "It is terrible to think that King Henry is dead, but when you and Denno talk about who will manage the affairs of England, then I know that life will not end. It will go on and I with it. And I still have you, Da, and Denno, and . . . and Blanche and Lady Alana and Kat. No, I am not all alone." She lifted her chin a little. "Indeed—I am not alone."

"Then do you think you can eat something at last?" Denoriel asked. "You have had nothing since you broke your fast this morning."

Some of the cold inside her ebbed. She managed a real smile—albeit a sad one. And a thread of hunger replaced the cold nothingness that had been in her stomach. "Something warm?" she asked.

So they adjourned into the dining room and were served by the invisible servants, who made Harry grin and Elizabeth frown, and the talk soon drifted away from English affairs to problems Underhill.

And it was as if all of her life in the real world became, for a little while, something like a dream—while her life here took on the solidity of reality. Usually, she fought that feeling, but not now. Not today. Today—she wanted to forget that on the other side of that Gate was an England in which the name of the king was not Henry, but Edward. When she returned, it would still all be there, after all. Just because she was forgetting it for a little while didn't mean she was shirking her duty—no more than if she had drunk some hairy old doctor's potion and was sleeping away some of her grief.

So for once, she let this place take hold of her, and for once, she *lived* in it, as her dear Da lived in it.

Harry told Elizabeth that the Unformed land which Elidir and Mechain used to use had drifted near an Unseleighe domain and that the mists were behaving even more strangely.

"Oh, my," Elizabeth said. "Oh. I hope I did no wrong there. Did Mechain or Elidir ever dissipate that lion?"

"What lion?" Aleneil asked.

So she heard the story of Elizabeth's abduction and how she rescued herself by creating an eternally hungry lion.

"It almost ate me!" Elizabeth exclaimed. "Only the Gate opened and Elidir or Mechain or both got it closed just as the lion was poking its head through."

"It didn't attack us when I went with Elidir and Mechain or when you came with us, Denno," Harry said. "Likely it fell apart. After all, Elizabeth didn't have much practice as a maker."

"But I didn't really make it," Elizabeth pointed out. "I asked the mists to make it and I thought of how it should look and should be hungry. The mists made it."

Now Harry began to look troubled. "And the mists could keep it alive. I don't know. They really acted very strange when we saw Pasgen—if it was Pasgen—and if Pasgen has reformed and is staying there to avoid Vidal, don't you think we ought to warn him?"

"Or get rid of the lion," Elizabeth said. "I want to go too. Maybe it will be easier for me to do it because I made it. I mean, I could explain to the mist that it was dangerous to have that lion running loose."

Elizabeth sounded almost cheerful and Denoriel and Harry exchanged glances. Both had been wondering how to find an excuse to keep her Underhill for several days, until the first shock and grief of her father's death wore off. She would have refused to go to one of the markets, they were sure. It would seem frivolous to run around a market when one's father was lying dead. Ridding an Unformed land of a dangerous lion, however, seemed quite justifiable.

"I'll have to get word to Elidir and Mechain," Harry said. "We had a terrible time finding the place the last time and I'm sure I couldn't find it alone. And I'll have to go home to get my gun."

Harry was back before Aleneil, Denoriel, and Elizabeth had finished their meal and they settled down to discuss how to accomplish their purpose without exposing Elizabeth to too much danger.

"But you will all be with me," Elizabeth pointed out impatiently. "Da has his sword and gun, Denno has his sword, and I'm sure Lady Alana is not defenseless, not to mention Elidir and Mechain. And I have my shields for my head and my body. And I know stickfoot and tanglefoot and *cilgwthio* and *gwthio* which will probably be stronger Underhill. What could hurt me?"

✧   ✧   ✧

The imp bearing the news that Henry would not live out the twenty-seventh of January arrived at a terrible time for Vidal. He was not free to act on the information. The leaders of Scotland were in almost as great uncertainty as those of England. Angus and Albany and Mary of Guise all knew that Henry was dying and they could not decide whether to continue with their internecine strife, attack England, or just be quiet and hope that when the intransigent king was dead his ministers would be more reasonable and make peace.

Vidal could have arranged for spells to be cast on all of them, but he did not know *what* spell to cast. In this delicate situation a blanket spell for hatred or rage or spite would not be sufficient. He really needed to be in Scotland, watching each move and countering it or furthering it to suit his purpose. No matter the dying king in England, Vidal had to delay two days more in Scotland to set everyone along the right path . . . he hoped.

But he could delay no longer. He also needed to be in England where the confusion and panic that would follow the king's death would open all sorts of possibilities for him. If the confusion was sufficient, could he engineer a civil war between Edward's supporters and Mary's? He would prefer Mary on the throne; the FarSeers showed that her reign would be a rich feast for the Unseleighe.

No, there had better be no civil war. There was too good a chance that Edward's supporters would win. Reasonably enough, the English preferred a male ruler. In that case, Mary would have committed treason and would be executed. No, she was too valuable to lose. Let the boy come to the throne unopposed; his reign would be almost as good for the Unseleighe as Mary's.

The only danger was Elizabeth. Vidal thought fleetingly of the chance of snatching her and dismissed it. If she disappeared, the whole kingdom would be roused to search for her he feared, and using a simulacrum was out of the question. Edward's reformists liked witchcraft no better than the Inquisition. His decision to use a slow poison on her seemed still to be the best choice. It did not really matter when she died, so long as it was before Edward and Mary.

Only, when he arrived in London on January 30, he learned that his plans had again gone awry. Prysor, the Sidhe who had taken on Sir William Paulet's appearance, came to Otstargi's house, fearful of punishment but afraid worse would befall him if he did not confess, to inform his master that he had not, after all, poisoned Elizabeth.

"Idiot! Why not?" Vidal roared.

Prysor was wearing every protection he had and he was angry, too. "Her mind was shielded so strongly that the backlash of the spell of confusion and incomprehension struck *me*," he hissed. "*You* told me to render her helpless! And you did not warn me that her mind was closed and protected. I have never felt such a wall!"

"She is only a mortal child," Vidal snarled. "How can she have such protection?"

"I would suspect from the Seleighe Court," Prysor snapped; he was not nearly as strong as Vidal magically, but sometimes he thought his master's mind was muddled. "Where else? Anyhow, the rest is short to tell. When the backlash of my spell hit me, my reason deserted me. If I could have thought, I would have left and tried again later under some pretense, but as I was, nearly mindless, I could only do what you had commanded. When the children were in each other's arms, weeping, the whole court moved toward them to comfort them. I was in the forefront, and I plunged your poison thorn right into the girl's shoulder in the pretense of patting it to give her comfort."

Vidal's brows drew together. "Then why do you say you failed to poison her? If the thorn even scratched her lightly, she will die. It will take longer than a real stab into her flesh where the whole thing could dissolve, but . . ."

"But her body was shielded, too!" Prysor exclaimed, his voice breaking with frustration. "The thorn slipped right off her shoulder and I lost it! It slid out of my fingers and shot between her and the prince. They were close embraced. I sought for it in the guise of patting him, too, but I could not find it. I think it was caught in his gown, but I dared not feel around for it. *She* was watching. She was weeping, but she saw what I was."

"Useless! You are worse than useless!" Vidal lifted his hand. The Sidhe saw torture, even death, in his eyes.

"No, I am not!" Prysor cried. "I learned something you would like to know."

Vidal's hand dropped. "Well?"

"They are taking her Underhill. When my mind cleared, I knew I had failed and that you would be angry so I went back alone to Enfield, pretending I came to ask after Lady Elizabeth's well-doing. Once I was admitted, it was easy enough to put on the Don't-see-me spell and to listen at the door."

"Listen at the door? At the *door*? You fool! You were already beyond their sight."

"Not beyond *hers*. She saw through the disguise I was wearing and could easily see through Don't-see-me. It is not a very strong spell—" He hesitated for a moment, then continued. "Ah, it matters not whether she could see me, I could not go in no matter if she could or no; they were *all* there. The two Bright Court devils who are always somewhere about her and that accursed maid with her necklace of cold iron—it nearly killed me to be in the same room with her. But I heard enough, that they were going to build a Gate to Logres."

"Logres," Vidal sneered, lifting his hand again. "Do you think I needed your stupid spying to tell me they would take the girl to Logres? Denoriel lives there, idiot!"

"But I went through the Gate after them!"

Vidal paused. Prysor was nothing in magic—and in a way that was good; think of the danger Pasgen presented—but Prysor liked pain, even his own, and he was very daring.

"They did not notice you?"

The Sidhe smiled. "Not with them, after them. Just before the Gate closed, I leapt in. They were still in the Gate when I arrived, but the two Sidhe were drained out and did not notice me. It is no light task to force a Gate from the mortal world to Underhill. And the girl . . . I do not understand why, but before I could leap off the Gate and hide, she looked right at me and did not see me."

"That is very interesting," Vidal said, staring at the Sidhe. "Are you sure?" Prysor nodded. "I remit you half your pains," Vidal murmured.

Now Prysor laughed aloud. "You will remit the rest in a moment. I could not get into Denoriel's apartment, but that fool has these huge windows in the palace wall and I was able to listen near them without showing myself."

Vidal watched his minion; the Sidhe's eyes were bright and a mottled color rose in his cheeks. It was true the fool had failed to kill Elizabeth, Vidal thought, but he was foolishly daring. To be caught spying in Seleighe territory . . . One would be thrust into Dreaming, to suffer the horrors of one's own fears for eternity. Vidal shuddered.

Nor was Prysor such a fool, really. When he failed in his assigned mission, he had not simply fled. He had come about and tried to do *something*.

"Oh, yes," Vidal said. "Your punishment is remitted. Now tell me something that is worth a reward."

"A reward . . . something to cut apart very slowly?" Prysor asked, his mouth suddenly so wet that bubbles showed at the corners of his lips. "A mortal?"

"By all means." Vidal smiled. Here was a Sidhe with inclinations very like his own.

"They are taking the girl to an Unformed land to kill a lion that she created there," Prysor said triumphantly. "And the Unformed land is an Unseleighe domain, or near enough to it to make them cautious."

Vidal's expectations, which had flown high on Prysor's jubilant expression, came crashing down. "An Unformed land," he mocked. "You idiot! Unformed lands are myriad."

"Lord, I am *not* an idiot," Prysor snapped back, his voice suddenly hard and his eyes almost glowing. "I am not strong in magic, but I can do small things very well once I am shown how. I will know *which* Unformed land the party enters because I made another thorn, not with poison but with a silent alarm, a tiny little watchdog to bark its alert to lead us to where they are."

"Ah!" Vidal leaned forward across Otstargi's table, then frowned. "They will feel it and discard it.

"Lord, there is nothing to feel. The tag is dead, until they step out of the Gate at their destination. Then it will signal me . . . but in the ambience of the Gate such a small flicker of magic will not be noticed."

Oh, that was clever, clever— "You have earned your reward . . . *if* we follow your signal and find those we seek." Vidal stood up. "We will Gate to Goblin Fair and wait by that Gate for your signal. I can redirect a market Gate to harken to that signal and take us there. And if our party is there, do not leave the Gate. Go back to the market and at once to Caer Mordwyn. Gather up any creatures that are there and the two mages resident and bring them back with you. And if we succeed in ridding ourselves of Elizabeth and her Bright Court companions . . . I will not only give you a domain but build what you like upon it."

Chapter 32

Eventually the air spirit Harry had sent after Elidir and Mechain found them, and brought them to Denoriel's apartment. The two elder elves were a bit puzzled at Elizabeth's presence Underhill, and some time was spent explaining where they wanted to go and why . . . and when Harry could get one of them alone informing them more completely . . . about Henry's death and the need to divert Elizabeth until the worst of her grief had passed.

"And you?" Mechain asked him.

Harry paused for a moment, considering his own reaction now that the shock was over. "I am sorry my father is dead," he said. "I loved him when I was a child, but when I grew older, I saw other things. And he was no longer the center point of my life. Denoriel has been more of a father to me . . . or brother, now that I am a man. I do grieve, but it does not wrench my soul as it does Elizabeth's." He sighed. "Perhaps—well, I should not speculate. It is enough that she came to us in tears and in fear."

"Then we surely must divert her," said Mechain with a decisive nod, "and not with games and pleasantries. You are quite right about that, Harry, as you so often are. To deal with the Unformed land is a kind of good work, and will surely occupy all of her mind."

All in all, it was some time before they left. When they came out of Llachar Lle, however, both Mechain and Elidir turned suddenly to look left. Both frowning, each went in a different direction and

505

looked around the portico. They came back shrugging, admitting they had found no one—but that just for a moment, both of them had felt an inimical presence. They looked at Elizabeth, who shook her head.

"In the mortal world I can feel magic and see through illusion, but here . . . I am so flooded with magic . . ." she gestured helplessly. "The very air is full of magic. I didn't notice anything."

Still, all of them anxiously examined Elizabeth, checking her clothing, her hair, everything. They found nothing, and after again looking around the portico and cursorily through the ornamental gardens around the palace, they mounted their elvensteeds and set out for the Gate.

Ignoring the pattern plaque of the Logres Gate, even though there were always two termini kept blank for temporary patterning, Mechain called up an antique plaque of her own and activated it.

"We had so much trouble finding this place and it was so strange," she said as they arrived at the Gate in the Unformed land, "that I made a plaque just tuned to this Gate."

"Hmmm." Elidir looked around and then stepped off the slight rise of the Gate platform. "It looks much better," he said.

The mists did seem to be back to normal, not so dense or dark or angry looking as at their last visit and twisting and flowing without any sign of particular purpose. Mechain followed Elidir. There was no change in the behavior of the mist. Harry stepped down, then Elizabeth, then Denoriel.

Mechain and Elidir turned to look back at the Gate. "Did you feel that?" they asked each other almost simultaneously and then shook their heads.

"Nothing now," Elidir said after standing and listening with his head cocked.

"I agree," Mechain said, "but I could swear that I felt something, like an echo of the Gate closing." She too listened intently and then shook her head. "Whatever it was is gone now and I cannot sense anything wrong with the Gate. Come down, Aleneil, and let me see if it happens again."

However, nothing happened that Elidir or Mechain could detect, which was reasonable enough because Prysor's tag had struck Denoriel rather than Elizabeth and fallen into a fold of his sleeve.

"Elizabeth?" Denoriel asked.

She shook her head. "I didn't feel anything. Just the usual Gate feeling of blackness and falling and then being here. But the mists don't feel funny. Not angry."

She stepped forward and the mists seemed to bow back away from her, not as if they were avoiding her but almost in invitation. Denoriel, to her right, put a hand on her shoulder as if to hold her back and Harry paced forward with her to the left. The rest of the party followed, spreading out

"Be careful, Elizabeth," Denoriel said. "The mist could close in on you if you go much farther forward into it."

"It doesn't matter," Elizabeth said. "I can feel the Gate behind me. And the mist is so pretty. See how it sparkles? Though—" her brow wrinkled "—that is rather strange because there's nothing to make it sparkle . . . no sun, no moon."

She had been walking forward as she spoke, but the mists did not curve around as if to engulf her. They kept their distance and she smiled at them and thanked them as she would have thanked any mortal servant. Then she turned to see where the rest of the party was. Aleneil was not immediately apparent, and she turned farther—and froze.

"Who is that?" she asked, her eyes fixed on the Gate.

Denoriel and Harry whirled around both with hands on their swords. This was tentatively Unseleighe territory, since Pasgen had claimed it for his own, and their presence might well be considered an invasion that called for instant attack.

And the figure who appeared in the Gate was the last person Underhill that they wanted to see.

"What are you doing on Unseleighe land?" Vidal roared, his hands glowing with dark power, his face black with rage.

"It is my fault, sir," Elizabeth said, before either Denoriel or Harry could answer.

Denoriel put his hand out to draw Elizabeth back, but he could not touch her and knew her shield was up. He added another layer but said nothing. Vidal had not drawn a weapon or raised his hand to cast any bolts.

Nonetheless, Elizabeth's warning had come too late. On the flanks of the party, Elidir and Mechain had been angling toward the Dark Prince. Elidir had drawn his sword, but there was a flash of light, and suddenly Mechain's hands were at her throat where one of Vidal's pretty glowing ribbons had fixed itself. Her breathing was not yet impeded, but Vidal could strangle her at will.

"And who are you, worthless mortal?" Vidal said, lip curled in disdain.

"Mortals are not worthless," Elizabeth snapped back, touching her left ear and murmuring, "*Minnau ymbil.*" Then louder, "But it *is* my fault that we are all here. Some time ago, this place was Seleighe and at that time I—I somehow caused a lion to form, a very hungry lion. Now that the place has moved, I felt a creature so dangerous should be removed, not allowed to prey on . . . on those who did not know of the lion's existence."

Vidal smirked down at her, a superior and exceedingly haughty gaze of one who is certain he is not to be gainsaid. "Lion or no lion, you had no right—"

"Enough, Elizabeth," Denoriel said, interrupting Vidal and stepping in front of her. "You cannot reason with this one. It is Vidal Dhu, and he has been behind all the attacks on you. He does not really care about our being on Unseleighe territory. He only wants to be rid of all of us. Let Mechain go, Vidal. If you harm her, you will not be able to escape us all."

"If you harm Mechain or try that ribbon trick on me, you will die quite horribly," Harry said, drawing his gun. "I assure you I can shoot you before you can strangle her or me."

Vidal laughed, but he was really *very* annoyed with Elizabeth. The girl had a penchant for fouling his luck. He could hardly believe in his good fortune when no one noticed his arrival. They were all intent on the mists ahead of them and had not seen him. To Vidal every minute they looked away brought closer the time when his servants would flood through the Gate to support him. Then Elizabeth had turned.

Now all he could do was pretend it did not matter and play for more time. He stepped out of the Gate, sneering, "O brave and honorable denizens of the Seleighe Court, you are five to my one. Why should I not try to even the odds? I have done your companion no harm, and will do her no harm if you do me none. It is Denoriel Siencyn Macreth Silverhair whom I owe a grudge. Denoriel, who once unfairly used mortal magic to defeat me. What do you say, Denoriel, will you meet me here, where there is no mortal magic? Will you vie with me in duel arcane and bid your companions to swear not to interfere?"

"Don't, Denno," Harry said, immediately. "He'll cheat. You know he will."

Denoriel gripped Harry's arm fondly and looked back at Elizabeth. She was wide-eyed and a little pale but showed no sign of panic. He swung around to Vidal and smiled slowly. Vidal had been the better magician when they met in Elizabeth's bedchamber over ten years ago, but Denoriel had studied magic quite earnestly for some years now. And furthermore, Vidal had been far more gravely injured in that duel than Denoriel. The odds were good that his mind was still not altogether sound.

He stared back at Vidal, coolly. "I will meet you gladly, Vidal, and ask oath of my companions not to interfere with our battle . . . so long as they are free to defend themselves from any of your servants or companions."

"You see I am alone here, you puppy!" Vidal roared. "Make them swear as I command!"

Mechain made a choking sound. Harry raised his gun, and took a step forward, taking clear aim at Vidal's body where he could hardly miss.

It was enough. Vidal winced as the cold iron directed at him sent a slicing of pain across his chest, even at that distance. The pain eroded the last of his self-restraint, and his temper escaped its bonds, which had been tenuous to begin with.

Vidal jumped off the Gate platform and charged toward Denoriel who backed hurriedly away, thrusting Elizabeth toward Harry, who lowered his gun to put a protective arm around her shoulders. The signal was clear. As long as Vidal concentrated on Denoriel, Harry was bound not to help, and his mortal weapon was out of play.

Denoriel was backing up less because he wished to avoid Vidal than because he wanted to draw Vidal to where he would not readily be able to see the others. That this took Denoriel farther from the Gate, he cared not at all.

Denoriel's and Vidal's rush would have carried them into the mists, but those pulled away also, and neither hid Denoriel nor proved any barrier to the triple stream of arcane darts that flashed toward him. He paid no mind to them and they all struck his shield, flared, and disappeared. Instead, he stared fixedly at Vidal; Vidal took that for fear, and readied his next attack, exaltation surging through his veins.

While Vidal watched the course of his knives, a swift, glinting array of near-invisible ribbons of light flashed toward him, not toward his neck and head, which would have drawn his attention, but toward his feet. The harmless-seeming ribbons slithered past his shield and up to his ankles where they suddenly tightened, entangling his feet, and pulling at him with a sudden jerk, so that he nearly fell. The monstrous creature he was in the midst of evoking howled with pain as it began to dissolve before it had entirely formed. In obedience to the last command Vidal had given it, it thrashed at Denoriel.

The violent slash of magical claws that would have pierced Denoriel's shield, merely slid across it.

Vidal kicked loose the ribbons of force with a curse, bringing his shields down across them to sever them. By the time he had refocused his concentration so that the monster was reforming, a thousand tiny creatures had swarmed over it and were feeding voraciously.

They first attacked its eyes, so that it could not see and then its claws, which blunted, softened, then, as the monster howled in pain and confusion, every possible appendage was blanketed in the swarm, and all it could do was thrash and wail, helplessly. Vidal roared with anger, cursing impotently. Denoriel danced aside and the thing blundered ahead blindly into the mist.

Vidal had rid himself of the ribbons at last, and he readied a volley of levin bolts, but before he could launch them, the earth humped up suddenly under his feet and he staggered again, destroying his aim. A volley of energy, formed into bolts of lightning, flashed by Denoriel and off into the mist.

Before Vidal could correct the flight of the bolts, the humps collapsed into shallow holes, and water filled them, creating a glutinous mud. Vidal slipped, fighting to keep to his feet, as once again he was thrown off balance. The magic he gathered sputtered uselessly in a shower of sparks. He screamed curses with his will behind them instead; he who knew only too well how to set a curse in motion, and Denoriel, who had not thought to guard against something he himself would never use, gasped as a grinding pain caught his gut and nearly doubled him over.

A curse of illness, flung at one of the Sidhe, who were never ill—it caught Denoriel completely off his guard. A straightforward attack, he was prepared for, but not this! Fighting the pain, he sent a cloud of butterflies toward Vidal. Although equally beautiful, they were not as innocent as the butterflies of the World

Above. These could bite and sting, and like the little beasts that had swarmed Vidal's monster, they blanketed Vidal.

But their abilities proved useless against Vidal's personal shield. All the butterflies could do was effectively blind Vidal by cocooning his head in their lovely wings. He brushed them away and crushed them, but they swarmed in again and again, giving Denoriel time to use what counterspells he could against Vidal's attack.

But he was no healer, and he had no idea how to successfully counter the curse. His efforts were only minimally successful at easing his pain and the bolts of fire and ice he threw splashed harmlessly into nothing on Vidal's shield. Worse, because Denoriel could not bear to draw on Unseleighe power, his ability to send manifestations against Vidal was weakening. Worse yet, he was facing the Gate and saw that Vidal's trap had been sprung. Three ogres, five boggles, and a clutch of pixies, hags, and phookas leapt off the Gate platform, leaving room for three dark Sidhe. His heart cramped, then went cold as ice.

Denoriel immediately shouted a warning, but the boggles gave their own game away. Instead of quietly sneaking up on Harry and Elizabeth, who were watching the battle between Vidal and Denoriel, one of the boggles leapt off the platform right onto Elidir's back. Elidir had been on his knees working over the ribbon that encircled Mechain's neck and the boggle caught him totally unaware.

Elidir fell flat atop Mechain, who grunted under his weight. But she was an old Sidhe, and had not grown old by being inattentive. She did not permit the fact that Elidir had flattened her to distract her. As the boggle tried to bite through the back of Elidir's neck, she swiftly drew the knife from Elidir's belt and thrust upward, stabbing the creature in the throat. The blow was more furious than aimed, but the knife was broad and well honed and the boggle was dead before it could cry out.

The others paid the first boggle no mind; perhaps they thought that their companion was feeding on the bodies it was lying on. They ran toward Harry and Elizabeth on whom the three ogres were also advancing. But now both Harry and Elizabeth were aware of their presence and their intentions, and neither of them were going to be easy prey.

Harry shot one ogre in the eye, the second in the throat and the third in the chest.

All three continued to advance, though staggering; Harry backed away, unable to decide whether to expend his two final bolts on the four boggles or hope to hold all four off with his sword. Meanwhile, he pushed Elizabeth aside, telling her to run into the mist.

She resisted, moving with him, then pointed and waved her finger. All four boggles tripped over their own feet and fell to the ground. And the ogre Harry had shot in the eye also toppled over. Too stupid, Harry thought a little hysterically, to realize for a while that it was dead. Soon Harry saw that the hysterical thought might be near true; blood was pouring down the chest of the one he had shot in the throat and although it was wavering on its feet, it was not seeking him. Instead, it was circling blindly in place, in a sickly-comic parody of a dancer—

The one he had shot in the chest, however, was picking up speed and still charging toward him with purpose—until its feet stuck firmly to the ground. The momentum of the advance carried the upper body of the creature forward and it fell, driving Harry's bolt right through the body. The ogre did not attempt to rise.

Harry ducked around the fallen ogre, trying to push Elizabeth behind him, and drew his sword as the boggles climbed to their feet. Elizabeth peered around Harry's shoulder and two went down again. The third leapt straight at Harry, screaming, hands extended to grip and claw, teeth bared to bite; all Harry had to do was raise his sword and it spitted itself. The fourth was waving a club, and it took Harry a few minutes to work around the vicious slashes and thrusts to kill the creature.

The two who had twice been tripped were up again, howling with rage. Elizabeth drew breath to invoke *gwthio*. She was beginning to feel sort of hollow and shaky, but suddenly the tenor of the boggles' cries changed from fury to terror. They began to beat at their bodies as if they were being stung all over. At the edge of the mist, Pasgen appeared, his face white with anger over the invasion of his private experimental domain. He gestured. The boggles broke and fled to the Gate.

Then Pasgen fixed his eyes on the Sidhe who was still standing on the Gate platform, apparently holding the Gate open and gesturing to a gang of goblins. Those suddenly stopped, as if they had run into a wall. Pasgen blinked; he had not done that.

The Sidhe on the platform, who was raising a hand to throw a spell at Elizabeth, drew Pasgen's attention away from the furious goblins. Pasgen gestured; the Sidhe's hand fell limply to his side and then he fell too, crumpling bonelessly to the ground near the platform. Pasgen spoke one sharp word, and the Gate closed.

Elidir and Mechain had regained their feet and their weapons and went back to back. Just in time. In a moment, they were holding off three phookas. At the other side of the gate, Aleneil, a sword of light in her hand, was facing a hissing hag. Another hag lay twitching at her feet. The pixies, shrieking that this was no game and they did not wish to play, had fled back through the Gate just before Pasgen closed it, falling afoul of the goblins and pushing them back.

The phookas attacking Mechain and Elidir were laughing insanely, changing form, and charging the two Sidhe. But Elidir and Mechain were old hands at dealing with malignant magical creatures and were throwing spells, slashing at them with whips of power, lashing them with branches of fiery thorns, so they cried and retreated. If Vidal began to strangle Mechain again, they would be in trouble, but Vidal himself was too busy to remember Mechain.

While Denoriel's butterflies bedeviled Vidal, barely giving the Dark Prince a moment's sighting of his enemy to cast spells, levin bolts, and curses at him, Denoriel had draped his enemy in a sparkling mesh that tightened around him erratically, interfering with his gestures and aborting half his spells. Denoriel had also been working desperately to deepen and widen the mud pit in which Vidal was standing. He had not added any water to the pit, so Vidal was not completely aware that he was almost hip deep in the ground.

The two dark mages who had come with Prysor were aware of Vidal's increasing danger. For some moments they hesitated, glancing at each other. If they did nothing, there was a chance that the Bright Court Sidhe he was battling would best him and they would be rid of him. And then both sighed, almost simultaneously. They would not be rid of him. There was little chance that the Bright Court mage would kill Vidal. And Vidal knew they were there. And he would know that they had done nothing to help him . . . and what he would do to them when he was finally victorious would be unspeakable.

Denoriel's butterflies were almost gone. Three or four still fluttered around Vidal's head but they no longer obscured Vidal's vision enough to protect Denoriel. The bright mesh was melting away. In his own territory Vidal could draw power to replace all that he expended in his attacks on Denoriel. Denoriel had no such resource and his shield was growing very thin. Twice Vidal's knives almost came through and only a desperate effort at blocking the exact place they would have pierced saved him. But the last of the shield was dissolving, and he had no power to restore it.

When the boggles ran for the Gate, Elizabeth had watched them to be sure they would not return. It was then she saw the two mages standing just before it pointing at her Denno. A swift glance showed her that Denno was down on his knees, showed her that the knives Vidal was throwing had nearly touched her Denno. Terror welled up in Elizabeth. Her Denno was already hurt. He would be killed. Rage mingled with the terror and a terrible heat began to build in her body.

There was no spell she could use on Vidal—and she knew she must not interfere in Denno's battle directly. Anyway, Vidal's feet were already useless. *Cilgwthio* could not affect a man in a hole. But those mages pointing at Denno must be doing something to harm him. She would fix them!

"*Cilgwthio, myfi ymbil*" she screamed, pointing at the mage to the right.

The push was so violent that the Sidhe's chest caved in and he disappeared completely.

The other mage, seeing what had happened, began to run toward Elizabeth, raising a hand, mouthing some spell.

"*Stickfoot, myfi ymbil*" she shrieked. "*Myfi ymbil! Myfi ymbil!*"

The mage stopped dead and began to scream, not spells or curses but plain shrieks of pain and terror. His feet had not merely stuck to the ground momentarily, they had become part of the ground.

But Vidal—Vidal was about to—he was going to—

Stop

Everything stopped. Profound silence. Total stillness.

Elizabeth's mental shield rang like a bell inside her skull. By the Gate, atop an elvensteed black as night, there was a being, male but not a man, so beautiful that despite her fear and anger, despite the desperation of their situation, Elizabeth's still-nascent sexuality yearned toward him.

Who has loosed mortal magic in my realm?

If not for the shield, Elizabeth thought, she would have been knocked unconscious. She shook her head slightly, looked around for help, but Denno and Da were frozen into statues, and so was everyone else.

"Oh, that was me," Elizabeth said in a very small voice, and the dark eyes of the being turned to look quite *through* her, to pin her in place like an errant bit of lace. "But I *am* mortal. I don't have any other kind of magic." Then her body straightened, her lips firmed, her jaw jutted forward, her voice strengthened. "And those people . . . well, there's only one of them left . . . they were hurting my Denno! And it wasn't allowed. We all took oath not to interfere with the duel."

King Oberon's expression had slowly been transmuting from enraged and implacable to astonished and uncomprehending, and he was by now looking almost as stunned as those he had rendered immobile.

"Who are you?" he asked in a much more normal tone of voice, without all of those—*forces* behind it.

Elizabeth had not been bred to court life to no purpose. She recognized authority, even if she could not put a name to it, and she sank into a curtsey right down to the ground.

"I am the Lady Elizabeth, youngest daughter of King Henry . . . oh," her voice caught on a sob. "He . . . he is dead. My father is dead." The eyes raised to Oberon were now swimming with tears."

"I am sorry to hear that," Oberon said.

He *was* sorry to hear it. Henry's rule had suited him very well and he knew Edward's reign and Mary's would be far more perilous for the magical world. Now he dismounted. The elvensteed nodded gravely, and disappeared off into the mist. He made an idle, absentminded gesture, and a black throne on a dais appeared beneath and behind him. When he was seated, he beckoned Elizabeth closer. She rose and came forward, curtsying again—but then stood straight up, bringing up her chin, determined to face him as one of royal blood.

"I am King Oberon," he said. "What is a mortal princess doing Underhill?"

"It is a very long story, Your Majesty," Elizabeth said, slowly, to gain her time for thought. "I am more than willing to explain, but I am afraid I would bore you or waste your time."

"There are quicker ways to get information than listening to long stories," Oberon said, and reached carelessly into her mind . . . only to bruise himself on the shield. "Tangwystl," Oberon muttered, recognizing her touch at once and thus understanding that Titania was involved.

For a moment red gleamed within the black of his eyes, and

Elizabeth sank down into a curtsey again, head bent against her knee, recognizing royal anger when she saw it. Oberon stared down at her. He could, of course, have broken through the shield—it had only stopped him because he did not expect it to be there—but to break the shield might damage the raped mind.

For a moment, irritation with his willful queen almost sealed Elizabeth's fate. Titania deserved to have her pet destroyed . . . but the visions of Elizabeth's reign were more potent. That would be a time for the Sidhe! They would be almost as free of the mortal world as they were of Underhill. And the music, and the poetry, the art and the plays . . . Marlowe, Webster . . . Shakespeare . . .

"Stand up, child," he said with impatience. "You mentioned a duel. Why?"

"Because we—at least my friends of the Bright Court and I—we were in Unseleighe territory. At least, they said it might be Unseleighe territory. But, Your Majesty, we didn't mean any harm. It was the lion. I was afraid it would hurt someone. And Denno and Lady Alana and Elidir and Mechain they all came to help me."

"The lion," Oberon repeated, his lips twitching. "And why was the lion your responsibility?"

Elizabeth looked down and her voice was small again as she said, "Because I asked the mists to make it." She looked up. "But, sire, I had to do *something*. There were two men who had abducted me. I wanted the lion to frighten them but . . ." Her voice faded again. "But I think it ate them."

Oberon was staring at her this time with intense curiosity. "You *asked* the mists to make a lion?"

"I didn't know how. Not really. But I had seen Elidir and Mechain create—" Once again, her knowledge of the ways of kings and their courts saved her. She caught the small gesture that indicated King Oberon had heard enough. Elizabeth stopped speaking and waited.

Oberon turned his head slightly. "Elidir and Mechain," he said.

They stood where they had STOPPED. A phooka was shying away from Mechain's sword, and a spell still sparkled on Elidir's fingertips. Oberon pointed—once, twice, thrice; the phookas were gone.

"You are grossly recovered from the last time I had news of you, slipping away into Dreaming," Oberon said, gesturing for Mechain and Elidir to approach.

"We have had work to do, Majesty. Useful work. *Intriguing* work. Harry," Mechain said, bowing, knowing that the whole story was doubtless unreeling into Oberon's mind, "decided that what now lived in El Dorado and Alhambra was unhealthy. We have cleared much of the surface evil away, but we have no way as yet to reach the Great Evil."

Oberon leaned forward, suddenly intent. "But you intend to do that? You are not afraid it will touch *you*? You cannot destroy it, you know."

"Yes, we know, Lord Oberon," Elidir said. "But Harry . . . we think the Great Evil is afraid of Harry; there is something in him—his goodness, perhaps?—that it fears. And Harry thinks we can trap it somewhere . . . perhaps the Void. Then—"

"Harry thinks." Oberon stared at Harry, who straightened from the lunge into which he had STOPPED and came forward.

"The little FitzRoy," Oberon said. "You are with us for good now, I see. So you think you can cleanse Alhambra and El Dorado. How quickly you are grown into a man."

"Mortals do age quickly, Great Majesty," Harry said, bowing deeply, and seeming not at all perturbed by Oberon's overwhelming *presence*. The fighting had disarranged his hair and the blue star burned bright on his forehead. "And yes, if it does not displease you, Lord Oberon, I do wish to make the forbidden cities open again. It seems a small repayment for the shelter that the Bright Court has offered me. As they stand, they are an invitation to the Inquisition to find a foothold Underhill and threaten us."

Oberon laughed. "Mortals! Always thinking ahead."

The laugh emboldened Elizabeth, who had been anxiously waiting for Denoriel to be freed. His face was frozen into an expression of anguish and his body twisted in an effort to avoid a levin bolt.

"Your Majesty," she said, pleading in every inch of her, "please free my Denno."

The black eyes turned to her; the eyes did not smile. "He is *my* Lord Denoriel, not *your* Denno."

Elizabeth met Oberon's gaze with more courage than sense but in the golden eyes Oberon saw the delights of an age of furious creation, even new worlds to be discovered. What a queen she would be! But she was very tender of those she loved. Could she be hard enough to her enemies?

So he asked, "And what of the other, Prince Vidal?"

The golden eyes glowed even brighter. "Well, *I* do not rule here, and I do not know your ways or laws. But if I were in your place, Your Majesty," she said coldly as Denoriel straightened, rose to his feet, and came toward them, a hand pressed to his belly. "I would, I'faith, just make that hole as deep as his sins and as dark as his cold heart, and drop him down it. But I confess to you that I am prejudiced against him. He keeps trying to kill me, you see, and I think it only fair to return the gift."

Now, at a gesture of Oberon's index finger, Vidal rose out of the hole Denoriel had dug for him. The levin bolt hissed in his fingers. He twisted and tried to throw it at Denoriel. It popped in his hand, and he howled. Oberon sighed and set him down a little apart from the others.

Aleneil, who happened to be nearest to him, hurried away to stand near her brother. Her hands followed Denoriel's to his pain, and her lips began to move. Denoriel gritted his teeth. Oberon's index finger twitched, and Denoriel sighed with relief. Oberon wanted neither spells nor a perception of pain to annoy him.

"Hear my words and heed them, for they are final! To kill Lady Elizabeth is forbidden," Oberon said flatly. "Find some other way to gain your ends, Prince Vidal. And do not say that I am unfair. It is equally forbidden to the Bright Court to harm in any way the new little king or the Lady Mary. Two are protected from them while only one is forbidden to you. That, I think is fair enough. I will also overlook the broken oath—"

But Vidal pounced upon that statement with the glee of a lawyer finding a gap in the law. "My followers took no oath. It is Denoriel's friends who did not abide by our agreement. And they came onto my ground. I have every right to defend my territory."

"Unformed land is no one's ground," Oberon said, with a glare that should have warned Vidal that he was venturing into treacherous territory. "Until it is formed it is free to all." He looked away from them, into the depths of the mist, hesitated for a moment, and then nodded. "Still, this place is nearer domains held by Unseleighe than by Seleighe. I cede you the right not to welcome Bright Court Sidhe here, but you called assistance when you had agreed to a duel."

"They were five to my one! Why should I trust them?"

Oberon's eye swept the Bright Court Sidhe. Harry stepped forward. "Sire, we defended ourselves but none of us interfered with the duel."

Oberon lifted an eyebrow. "Well, Prince Vidal? Who beside Denoriel contested with you?"

"No one," Vidal snarled; Oberon would know the truth, it was useless to lie. "But that was only because they were all engaged with my people."

Oberon's eyes rested briefly on Elizabeth, but she was looking at Denoriel; the Sidhe smiled back at her to give comfort, although he was pallid and drained. Insensibly they drew closer together. Oberon was reasonably sure that he had arrived just in time to prevent Elizabeth from killing Vidal, as she had killed the mage whose body was floating in the void when she loosed the magic that drew him to this place. Now *that* would have been an unpardonable breech of the law. But it had not happened, and he was inclined to let things lie as they were.

"There is no proof either way," Oberon said to Vidal. "Thus, you may go about your business, Vidal Dhu, but do not transgress against the Lady Elizabeth again."

If hate could have killed, Oberon would have dissolved under Vidal's glare, but the King did not even deign to notice, although Vidal did not leave. Oberon looked at Denoriel and crooked a finger. Denoriel came forward and bowed.

"You know the rules about bringing a mortal Underhill." Denoriel winced as Oberon extracted from his already bruised mind the whole tale of how and why Elizabeth was first brought Underhill, and then that of her grief for her father and his desire to let her heal more quickly.

"This is no playground for sad mortals," Oberon snapped. "I think you are far too much engaged with Lady Elizabeth. I think it is time for a new guardian—"

"No." Elizabeth's voice as she interrupted him was firm and hard. "I do not desire any other guardian. I do not *need* any other guardian. My Denno—"

"He is *not* your Denno," Oberon growled. "He is *mine!*"

Elizabeth swallowed hard, but she did not lower her head. Her eyes were yellow flames that still met Oberon's challengingly. "*Mine,*" she said, "or no Sidhe at all in the mortal world ever again!"

Oberon was so outraged that he stood up. Denoriel leapt in

front of Elizabeth to take whatever blow might be launched. Oberon's lips parted . . .

And a bolt of white lightning struck between the king and those he was about to punish.

Out of it came Queen Titania, a creature of white flame and white-hot anger, fully a match for Oberon's black fury. So much power burned in and around her that she did not need any weapon. She was not an avenger—she was something more powerful than that.

She was a *protector*. And woe betide whatever threatened what she protected.

"And she is *mine!*" Titania said, her voice like the trumpets on a battlefield. "She will not be bent or broken. She will have what will feed her spirit and let her nurture an entire nation into life and light and joy, whether you will or no!"

Oberon's face turned livid with fury. "I will—"

But Titania was quicker. *"Begone!"* she commanded, making a sweeping gesture so that the trailing sleeves of her gown flared like the wings of an angel, and again her voice rang out with power and glory that could not be withstood. ***"All here begone to their home places."***

Utter blackness, and falling, and this time pain as contending forces seemed to be trying to tear Elizabeth apart. But before she could even try to scream, she was lying on the hearthrug in her own bedchamber.

"Denno," she breathed, as Blanche cried out with surprise and rushed to lift Elizabeth up. She hugged herself with pain and terror, and tears started up in her eyes. "I am going to lose my Denno," she wailed. "What will I do? What will I do? My father is dead and my protector is reft from me."

"My lady, my lady, how did you come to be lying on the rug?" Blanche cried, clutching her shivering mistress in her arms, as she wept and would not be comforted. "I thought . . . I thought Lord Denno and Lady Alana—"

Then she breathed a sigh of relief as Denoriel rushed out of the dressing room. The relief did not last long when she saw the bruises and burns on his face and hands and that his clothing was very nearly in rags. Blanche had no chance to say anything, however, because Elizabeth wrenched herself out of Blanche's arms and flung herself into Denno's, and now she wept as if all the comfort she had lost had suddenly been restored to her, unlooked for.

Whatever had just happened—well, it was beyond the understanding of a simple mortal witch. But one thing a simple mortal witch *did* understand, and that was that food was generally, if not the answer to all needs, certainly a great comfort in itself.

Blanche shook herself and went to get wine and cakes; both looked as if they could use refreshment.

"Are you all right?" Elizabeth gasped, dashing the tears out of her eyes. "Oh, Denno, I *am* so sorry. I shouldn't have gone on saying you were mine. But you aren't his. You belong to yourself."

"Yes, but no more than any king's subject. I owe him service and loyalty." He smiled broadly. "But the look on his face ... There aren't many who dare claim what is my lord's."

"It was so foolish," she said, burying her face in his breast. "If I had had the sense to plead with him, we would not all be in such trouble. If ..." *the Queen* was what Elizabeth wanted to say but could not, so she compromised with "If *she* had not arrived ..." And then her eyes grew rounder. "Oh, Grace of God, when his face turned that color ... What will happen? Will they destroy each other?"

Denoriel held her tight; she could feel him chuckling. "Wanting to be with you was not the only reason I arrived here so quickly I did not even wash or change my clothes. There may be some titanic explosions in my home place and I wanted to be well out of the way."

"Will he hurt her?" Elizabeth breathed, not inclined to laugh.

"No, love, he will not. He will rant and rage and doubtless blast some innocent landscape, but he will never harm *her*."

"Or she him?" Elizabeth asked anxiously. It was very rare in these times for a man not to dominate his wife, but when it happened, sometimes the wife took gross advantage. And she could not bear the thought of two beings so beautiful, and so matchless, ever harming one another. She could not bear the thought of them even being angry with one another—

"No, nor she him," Denoriel said, still smiling. "They love one another, you see, so there will be a great deal of shouting and screaming, but in the end they will come to agreement."

"To take you away from me?" Elizabeth barely whispered.

"Oh, no. I do not think *he* was ever in earnest about that." He chuckled again. "At least not until you stood there looking him in the eye and saying 'he is *mine.*'"

"But I thought I would lose you," she whispered, feeling sick at how nearly she *had.*

"You cannot lose me," Denoriel murmured bending his head so that he spoke into her bright hair. "You cannot ever lose me."

"Even though you are ... Other? I have always been afraid that you would grow tired of me."

"Whatever I am—" He pulled away enough to look deep into her golden eyes. "I am yours, utterly and completely yours, for now and for every day of your living. It is my duty and my joy. You are the light in my life. And you will be that, now and forever, no matter who would say us nay."